D0560530

THE
Master=Christian

BY
Marie Corelli

Author of

"A Romance of Two Worlds," "Barabbas,"
"The Sorrows of Satan."

*"Why call ye Me 'Lord, Lord' and
do not the things which I say?"*

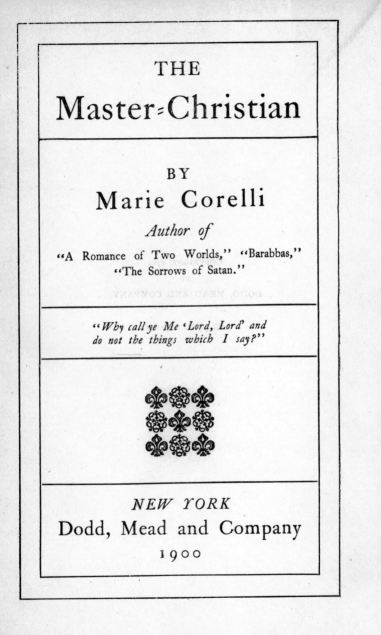

NEW YORK
Dodd, Mead and Company
1900

COPYRIGHT, 1900,

BY

DODD, MEAD AND COMPANY.

TO

ALL THOSE CHURCHES

WHO QUARREL

IN THE NAME OF CHRIST.

The Master-Christian.

I.

ALL the bells were ringing the Angelus.

The sun was sinking;—and from the many quaint and beautiful grey towers which crown the ancient city of Rouen, the sacred chime pealed forth melodiously, floating with sweet and variable tone far up into the warm autumnal air. Market women returning to their cottage homes after a long day's chaffering disposal of their fruit, vegetable, and flower-wares in the town, paused in their slow trudge along the dusty road and crossed themselves devoutly,—a bargeman, lazily gliding down the river on his flat unwieldly craft, took his pipe from his mouth, lifted his cap mechanically, and muttered more from habit than reflection—" Sainte Marie, Mère de Dieu, priez pour nous!"—and some children running out of school, came to a sudden standstill, listening and glancing at each other, as though silently questioning whether they should say the old church-formula among themselves or no? Whether, for example, it might not be more foolish than wise to repeat it? Yes;—even though there was a rumour that the Cardinal-Archbishop of a certain small, half-forgotten, but once historically-famed Cathedral town of France had come to visit Rouen that day,—a Cardinal-Archbishop reputed to be so pure of heart and simple in nature, that the people of his far-off and limited diocese regarded him almost as a saint,—would it be right or reasonable for them, as the secularly-educated children of modern Progress, to murmur an "Angelus Domini," while the bells rang? It was a doubtful point;—for the school they attended was a Government one, and prayers were neither taught nor encouraged there, France having for a time put God out of her national institutions. Nevertheless, the glory of that banished Creator shone in the deepening glow of the splendid heavens,—and—from the silver windings of the Seine which, turning crimson in the light, looped and garlanded the time-honoured old city as with festal knots of rosy ribbon, up to the trembling tops of the tall poplar trees fringing the river banks, —the warm radiance palpitated with a thousand ethereal hues of soft and changeful colour, transfusing all visible things into the misty semblance of some divine dwelling of dreams.   Ding-dong—ding dong!   The last echo of the last bell died away upon the air—the last words enunciated by devout priests in their cloistered seclusion were said—"*In hora mortis nostræ!   Amen!*"—the market women went on their slow way homeward,—the children scampered off in different directions, easily forgetful of the Old-World petition they had thought of, yet left unuttered,—the bargeman and his barge slipped quietly away together down the windings of the river out of sight;—the silence following the clangour of the chimes was deep and impressive—and the great Sun had all the heaven to himself as he went down.   Through the beautiful rose-window of the Cathedral of Notre Dame, he flashed his parting rays, weaving bright patterns of ruby, gold and amethyst on the worn pavement of the ancient pile which enshrines the tomb of Richard the Lion-Hearted, as also that of Henry the Second, husband to Catherine de Medicis and lover of the brilliant Diane de Poitiers,—and one broad beam fell purpling aslant into the curved and fretted choir-chapel especially dedicated to the Virgin, there lighting up with a warm glow the famous alabaster tomb known as "Le Mourant" or "The Dying One."   A strange and awesome piece of sculpture truly, is this same "Mourant"!—showing, as it does with deft and almost appalling exactitude, the last convulsion of a strong man's body gripped in the death-agony.   No delicate delineator of shams and conventions was the artist of olden days whose ruthless chisel shaped these stretched sinews, starting veins, and swollen eyelids half-closed over the tired eyes!—he must have been a sculptor of truth,—truth downright and relentless,— truth divested of all graceful coverings, and nude as the "Dying One" thus realistically portrayed.   Ugly truth too,—unpleasant to the sight of the worldly and pleasure-loving tribe who do not care to be reminded of the common fact that they all, and we all, must die.   Yet the late sunshine flowed very softly on and over the ghastly white, semi-transparent form, outlining it with as much tender glory as the gracious figure of Mary Virgin herself, bending with outstretched hands from a grey niche, fine as a cobweb of old lace on which a few dim jewels are sewn. Very beautiful, calm and restful at this hour was "Our Lady's Chapel," with its high, dark intertwisting arches, mutilated statues, and ancient tattered battle-banners hanging from the black roof and swaying gently with every little breath of wind. The air, perfumed with incense-odours, seemed weighted with the memory of prayers and devotional silences,—and in the midst of it all, surrounded by the defaced and crumbling emblems of life and death, and the equally decaying symbols of immortality, with the splendours of the sinking sun shedding roseate haloes about him, walked one for whom eternal truths outweighed all temporal seemings,—Cardinal Felix Bonpré, known favourably, and sometimes alluded to jestingly at the Vatican, as "Our good Saint Felix." Tall and severely thin, with fine worn features of ascetic and spiritual delicacy, he had the indefinably removed air of a scholar and thinker, whose life was not, and never could be in accordance with the latter-day customs of the world; the mild blue eyes, clear and steadfast, most eloquently suggested "the peace of God that passeth all understanding" ;—and the sensitive intellectual lines of the mouth and chin, which indicated strength and determined will, at the same time declared that both strength and will were constantly employed in the doing of good and the avoidance of evil. No dark furrows of hesitation, cowardice, cunning, meanness or weakness marred the expressive dignity and openness of the Cardinal's countenance,—the very poise of his straight spare figure and the manner in which he moved, silently asserted that inward grace of spirit without which there is no true grace of body,—and as he paused in his slow pacing to and fro to gaze half-wistfully, half-mournfully upon the almost ghastly artistic achievement of "Le Mourant" he sighed, and his lips moved as if in prayer. For the brief, pitiful history of human life is told in that antique and richly-wrought alabaster,—its beginning, its ambition, and its end. At the summit of the shrine, an exquisite bas-relief shows first of all the infant clinging to its mother's breast,—a stage lower down is seen the boy in the eager flush of youth, speeding an arrow to its mark from the bent bow,—then, on a still larger, bolder scale of design is depicted the proud man in the zenith of his career, a noble knight riding forth to battle and to victory, armed cap-à-piè, his war-steed richly caparisoned, his lance in rest,— and finally, on the sarcophagus itself is stretched his nude and helpless form, with hands clenched in the last gasping struggle for breath, and every muscle strained and fighting against the pangs of dissolution.

" But," said the Cardinal half aloud, with the gentle dawning of a tender smile brightening the fine firm curve of his lips,—" it is not the end! The end here, no doubt; —but the beginning—*there!*"

He raised his eyes devoutly, and instinctively touched the silver crucifix hanging by its purple ribbon at his breast. The orange-red glow of the sun encompassed him with fiery rings, as though it would fain consume his thin, black-garmented form after the fashion in which flames consumed the martyrs of old,—the worn figures of mediæval saints in their half-broken niches stared down upon him stonily, as though they would have said,—" So we thought,—even we!—and for our thoughts and for our creed we suffered willingly,—yet lo, we have come upon an age of the world in which the people know us not,—or knowing, laugh us all to scorn."

But Cardinal Bonpré being only conscious of a perfect faith, discovered no hints of injustice or despair in the mutilated shapes of the Evangelists surrounding him,— they were the followers of Christ,—and being such, they were bound to rejoice in the tortures which made their glory. It was only the unhappy souls who suffered not for Christ at all, whom he considered were truly to be compassionated.

" And if," he murmured as he moved on—" this knight of former days, who is now known to us chiefly, alas! as ' Le Mourant ', was a faithful servant of our Blessed Lord, why then it is as well with him as with any of the holy martyrs. May his soul rest in peace!"

Stopping an instant at the next sculptural wonder in his way—the elaborately designed tomb of Cardinal Amboise, concerning the eternal fate of which "brother in Christ" the good Felix had no scruples or fears whatever, he stepped softly down from the choir-chapel where he had been wandering to and fro for some time in solitary musings, and went towards the great central nave. It was quite empty;—not even a weary silk-weaver, escaped from one of the ever-working looms of the city, had crept in to tell her beads. Broad, vacant, vast, and suggestive of a sublime desolation, the grand length and width of the Latin Cross which shapes the holy precincts, stretched into vague distance; one or two lamps were burning dimly at little shrines set in misty dark recesses,—a few votive candles, some lit, some smouldered out, leaned against each other crookedly in their ricketty brass stand, fronting a battered statue of the Virgin. The Angelus had ceased ringing some ten minutes since,— and now one solemn bell, swinging high up in the Cathedral towers, tolled forth the hour of six, slowly and with a strong pulsating sound which seemed to shake the building down to its very vaults and deep foundations. As the last stroke shivered and thundered through the air, a strain of music, commencing softly, then swelling into fuller melody, came floating from aloft, following the great bell's vibration. Half way down the nave, just as he was advancing slowly towards the door of egress, this music overtook the Cardinal like an arresting angel, bringing him to a sudden pause.

"The organist practises late," he said aloud, as though speaking to some invisible companion; and then was silent, listening. Round him and above him surged the flood of rich and dulcet harmony,—the sunset light through the blue and red stained-glass windows grew paler and paler—the towering arches which sprang, as it were, from slender stem-like side-columns up to full-flowering boughs of Gothic ornamentation, crossing and re-crossing above the great High Altar, melted into a black dimness,—and then—all at once, without any apparent cause, a strange, vague suggestion of something supernatural and unseen began suddenly to oppress the mind of the venerable prelate with a curious sense of mingled awe and fear. Trembling a little, he knew not why, he softly drew a chair from one of the shadowy corners, where all such seats were piled away out of sight

so that they might not disfigure the broad and open
beauty of the nave, and, sitting down, he covered his
eyes with one hand and strove to rouse himself from the
odd, half-fainting sensation which possessed him. How
glorious now was the music that poured like a torrent from
the hidden organ-loft! How full of searching and poten-
tial proclamation!—the proclamation of an eternal, un-
guessed mystery, for which no merely human speech
might ever find fit utterance! Some divine declaration of
God's absolute omnipresence,—or of Heaven's sure near-
ness,—touched the heart of Felix Bonpré, as he sat like
an enchanted dreamer among the tender interweavings of
solemn and soothing sound;—carried out of himself and
beyond his own existence, he could neither pray nor
think, till, all at once, upon the peaceful and devout silence
of his soul, some very old, very familiar words struck
sharply as though they were quite new,—as though they
were invested suddenly with strange and startling significance—

" When the son of Man cometh, think ye He shall find
faith on earth? "

Slowly he withdrew his hand from his eyes and gazed
about him, half-startled, half-appalled. Had anyone
spoken these words?—or had they risen of themselves as
it were in letters of fire out of the sea of music that was
heaving and breaking tumultuously about him?

*" When the Son of Man cometh, think ye He shall find
faith on earth?"*

The question seemed to be whispered in his ears with
a thrilling intensity of meaning; and moved by a sudden
introspective and retrospective repentance, the gentle old
man began mentally to grope his way back over the past
years of his life, and to ask himself whether in very truth
that life had been well or ill spent? Viewed by his own
inner contemplative vision, Cardinal Felix Bonpré saw
in himself nothing but wilful sin and total unworthiness;
—but in the eyes of those he had served and assisted, he
was a blameless priest,—a man beloved of God, and almost visibly encompassed by the guardianship of angels.
He had been singularly happy in his election to a diocese
which, though it had always had an Archbishop for its
spiritual head, boasted scarce as many inhabitants as a
prosperous English village,—and the result of this was

that he had lived altogether away from the modern world, passing most of his time in reading and study,—while for relaxation, he permitted himself only the innocent delight of growing the finest roses in his neighbourhood. But he had pious scruples even about this rose-growing fancy of his,—he had a lurking distrust of himself in it, as to whether it was not a purely selfish pleasure,—and therefore, to somewhat smooth the circumstance, he never kept any of the choice blooms for his own gratification, but gave the best of them with a trust, as simple as it was beautiful, to the altar of the Virgin, sending all the rest to the bedsides of the sick and sorrowful, or to the coffins of the dead. It never once occurred to him that the "Cardinal's roses," as they were called, were looked upon by the poor people who received them as miraculous flowers long after they had withered,—that special virtues were assigned to them—and that dying lips kissed their fragrant petals with almost as much devotion as the holy crucifix, because it was instinctively believed that they contained a mystic blessing. He knew nothing of all this;—he was too painfully conscious of his own shortcomings,—and of late years, feeling himself growing old, and realising that every day brought him nearer to that verge which all must cross in passing from Time into Eternity, he had been sorely troubled in mind. He was wise with the wisdom which comes of deep reading, lonely meditation, and fervent study,—he had instructed himself in the modern schools of thought as well as the ancient,—and though his own soul was steadfastly set upon the faith he followed, he was compassionately aware of a strange and growing confusion in the world,—a combination of the elements of evil, which threatened, or seemed to threaten, some terrible and imminent disaster. This sorrowful foreboding had for a long time preyed upon him, physically as well as mentally; always thin, he had grown thinner and more careworn, till at the beginning of the year his health had threatened to break down altogether. Whereupon those who loved him, growing alarmed, summoned a physician, who, (with that sage experience of doctors to whom thought-trouble is an inexplicable and incurable complication) at once pronounced change of air to be absolutely necessary. Cardinal Bonpré must travel, he said, and seek rest and mind-distraction in the contemplation of new and varying scenes. With smiling and resigned patience the Cardinal obeyed not so much the command of his medical attendant, as the anxious desire of his people,—and thereupon departed from his own Cathedral-town on a tour of several months, during which time he inwardly resolved to try and probe for himself the truth of how the world was going,—whether on the downward road to destruction and death, or up the high ascents of progress and life. He went alone and unattended,—he had arranged to meet his niece in Paris and accompany her to her father's house in Rome,—and he was on his way to Paris now. But he had purposely made a long and round-about journey through France with the intention of studying the religious condition of the people; and by the time he reached Rouen, the old sickness at his heart had rather increased than diminished. The confusion and the trouble of the world were not mere hearsay,—they in very truth existed. And what seemed to the Cardinal to be the chief cause of the general bewilderment of things, was the growing lack of faith in God and a Hereafter. How came this lack of faith into the Christian world? Sorrowfully he considered the question,—and persistently the same answer always asserted itself—that the blame rested principally with the Church itself, and its teachers and preachers, and not only in one, but in all forms of Creed.

" We have erred in some vital manner," mused the Cardinal, with a feeling of strange personal contrition, as though he were more to blame than any of his compeers —" We have failed to follow the Master's teaching in its true perfection. We have planted in ourselves a seed of corruption, and we have permitted—nay, some of us have encouraged—its poisonous growth, till it now threatens to contaminate the whole field of labour."

And he thought of the words of St. John the Divine to the Church of Sardis—

" *I know thy works,—that thou hast a name that thou livest and art dead.*

" *Be watchful, and strengthen the things that remain, that are ready to die,—for I have not found thy works perfect before God. Remember therefore how thou hast received and heard, and hold fast and repent.*

" *If, therefore, thou shalt not watch, I will come on*

*thee as a thief, and thou shalt not know what hour I will
come upon thee.*

*"Thou hast a few names even in Sardis, which have
not defiled their garments, and they shall walk with me
in white, for they are worthy.*

*"He that overcometh, the same shall be clothed in
white raiment; and I will not blot his name out of the
Book of Life, but I will confess his name before my
Father and before his angels."*

Dimmer and duskier grew the long shadows now gathering in the Cathedral,—two of the twinkling candles near
the Virgin's statue suddenly sank in their sockets with
a spluttering noise and guttered out,—the solemn music
of the organ continued, growing softer and softer as it
sounded, till it crept through the vastness of the building like a light breeze wafted from the sea, bringing with
it suggestions of far flower-islands in the tropics, golden
shores kissed by languid foam, and sweet-throated birds
singing; and still the Cardinal sat thinking of griefs and
cares and inexplicable human perplexities, which were not
his own, but which seemed to burden the greater portion
of the world. He drew no comparisons,—he never considered that, as absolutely as day is day and night is
night, his own beautiful and placid life, lived in the faith
of God and Christ, was tortured by no such storm-tossed
tribulation as that which affected the lives of many others,
—and that the old trite saying, almost despised because
so commonplace, namely that "goodness makes happiness," is as eternally true as that the sun shines in heaven,
and that it is only evil which creates misery. To think
of himself in the matter never occurred to him; had he
for a moment entertained the merest glimmering of an
idea that he was better, and therefore happier than most
men, he would, in his own opinion, have been guilty of
unpardonable arrogance and presumption. What he saw,
and what sincerely and unselfishly grieved him, was that
the people of this present age were unhappy—discontented
—restless,—that something of the simple joy of existence
had gone out of the world,—that even the brilliant discoveries of science and the so-called "progress" of men
only served apparently to increase their discontent,—
that when they were overcome by sorrow, sickness, or
death, they had little philosophy and less faith to support

them,—and that except in the few cases where Christ was still believed in, they gave way altogether and broke down like frightened children in a storm.

"*Thou hast a few names, even in Sardis!*" A few names! But how few! Universal weariness of life seemed a disease of the time,—there was nothing that seemed to satisfy—even the newest and most miraculous results of scientific research and knowledge ceased to be interesting after the first week of their triumphant public demonstration and acceptance.

"The world must be growing old," said the Cardinal sadly,—"It must be losing its vigour,—it is too tired to lift itself to the light; too weary and worn out to pray. Perhaps the end of all present things is at hand,—perhaps it is the beginning of the promised 'new heavens and new earth.'"

Just then the organ-music ceased abruptly, and the Cardinal, waking from his thoughts as from a trance, rose up slowly and stood for a moment facing the great High Altar, which at that distance could only just be discerned among its darkening surroundings by the little flickering flame of the suspended lamp burning dimly before the holy Tabernacle, wherein was locked with golden key behind snowy doors of spotless marble, the sacred and mysterious Host.

"*When the Son of Man cometh, think ye He shall find faith on earth?*"

Again that searching question repeated itself in his mind so distinctly as to be echoed in his ears,—the deep silence around him seemed waiting expectantly for some reply, and moved by a strange spirit of exaltation within him, he answered half aloud—

"Yes! Surely He will find faith,—if only in the few! There are 'a few names, even in Sardis!' In the sorrowful and meek,—in the poor and patient and downtrodden martyrs of humanity, He will find faith;—in the very people He died to save He will discover that most precious and inspiring of all virtues! But in the so-called wise and brilliant favourites of the world He will not find it,—in the teachers of the people He will search for it in vain. By the writers of many books He shall find Himself scorned and rejected,—in the cheap and spurious philosophy of modern egotists He will see His doctrines mocked at and denounced as futile. Few men there are in these days who would deny themselves for His sake, or sacrifice a personal passion for the purer honouring of His name. Inasmuch as the pride of great learning breeds arrogance, so the more the wonder of God's work is displayed to us, the more are we dazzled and confounded; and so in our blindness we turn from the worship of the Creator to that of His creation, forgetting that all the visible universe is but the outcome or expression of the hidden Divine Intelligence behind it. What of the marvels of the age!—the results of science!—the strange psychic prescience and knowledge of things more miraculous yet to be!—these are but hints and warnings of the approach of God himself—'coming in a cloud with power and great glory'!"

As he thus spoke, he raised his hand out of old habit acquired in preaching, and a ray from the after-glow of the sunken sun lit up the jewel in the apostolic ring he wore, warming its pale green lustre to a dim violet spark as of living fire. His fine features were for a moment warm with fervour and feeling,—then,—suddenly, he thought of the great world outside all creeds,—of the millions and millions of human beings who neither know nor accept Christ,—of the Oriental races with their intricate and beautiful systems of philosophy,—of savage tribes, conquered and unconquered,—of fierce yet brave Turkish warriors who are, with all their faults, at any rate true to the faith they profess—and lastly—more than all —of the thousands upon thousands of Christians in Christian lands, who no more believe in Him whose holy name they take in vain, than in any Mumbo-Jumbo fetish of untaught barbarians. Were these to perish utterly? Had *they* no immortal souls to save? Had the churches been at work for eighteen hundred years and more, to bring about no better results than this,—namely that there were only "*a few names in Sardis*"? If so, were not the churches criminally to blame? Yea, even holy Mother-Church, whose foundation rested on the memory of the Lying Apostle? Rapidly, and as if suggested by some tormenting devil, these thoughts possessed the Cardinal's brain, burning into it and teasing and agonising the tender fibres of his conscience and his soul. Could God, the great loving Creator of countless universes, be so cruel as to wantonly destroy millions of helpless creatures in one small planet, because through ignorance or want of proper teaching they had failed to find Christ?—was it possible that he could only extend his mercy and forgiveness to the " few names in Sardis " ?

" Yet our world is but a pin's point in the eternal immensities," argued the Cardinal almost wistfully—" Only a few can expect to be saved."

Nevertheless, this reasoning did not satisfy him. Again, what of these millions? Were they to be forever lost? Then why so much waste of life? Waste of life! There is no such thing as waste of life—this much modern science the venerable Felix knew. Nothing can be wasted,—not a breath, not a scene, not a sound. All is treasured up in Nature's store-house and can be eternally reproduced at Nature's will. Then what was to become of the myriads of human beings and immortal souls whom the Church had failed to rescue? *The Church had failed!* Why had it failed? Whose the fault?—whose the weakness?—for fault and weakness were existent somewhere.

" When the Son of Man cometh, think ye He shall find faith on earth?"

" No!" whispered the Cardinal, suddenly forced, as it were in his own despite, to contradict his former assertion—" No!" He paused, and mechanically making his way towards the door of the Cathedral, he dipped his fingers into the holy water that glistened dimly in its marble basin near the black oak portal, and made the sign of the cross on brow and breast;—" He will not find faith where faith should be pre-eminent. It must be openly confessed—repentingly admitted,—He will *not* find faith even in the Church He founded,—I say it to our shame!"

His head drooped, as though his own words had wounded him, and with an air of deep dejection he slowly passed out. The huge iron-bound door swung noiselessly to and fro behind him,—the grave-toned bell in the tower struck seven. Outside, a tender twilight mellowed the atmosphere and gave brightness to approaching evening; inside, the long shadows, gathering heavily in the aisles and richly sculptured hollows of the side-chapels, brought night before its time. The last votive candle at the Virgin's shrine flickered down and disappeared like a firefly in dense blackness,—the last echo of the bell died in a tremulous vibration up among the high-springing roof-arches, and away into the solemn corners where the name-less dead reposed,—the last impression of life and feeling vanished with the retreating figure of the Cardinal—and the great Cathedral, the Sanctuary and House of God, took upon itself the semblance of a funeral vault,—a dark, Void, wherein but one red star, the lamp before the Altar, burned.

II.

LOVELY to a poet or an artist's eye is the unevenly-built
and picturesque square of Rouen in which the Cathedral
stands,—lovely, and suggestive of historical romance in
all its remote corners, its oddly-shaped houses, its byways and crooked little flights of steps leading to nowhere, its gables and slanting roofs, and its utter absence of all structural proportion. A shrine here, a broken
statue there,—a half-obliterated coat-of-arms over an old
gateway,—a rusty sconce fitted fast into the wall to support a lantern no longer needed in these days of gas and
electricity,—an ancient fountain overgrown with weed,
or a projecting vessel of stone for holy water, in which
small birds bathe and disport themselves after a shower
of rain,—those are but a few of the curious fragments of
a past time which make the old place interesting to the
student, and more than fascinating to the thinker and
dreamer. The wonderful "Hotel Bourgthéroulde," dating from the time of Francis the First, and bearing on its
sculptured walls the story of the Field of the Cloth of
Gold, in company with the strangely-contrasting "Allegories", from Petrarch's "Triumphs", is enough in itself
to keep the mind engrossed with fanciful musings for an
hour. How did Petrarch and the Field of the Cloth of
Gold come together in the brain of the sculptor who long
ago worked at these ancient bas-reliefs? One wonders,
but the wonder is in vain,—there is no explanation :—and
the "Bourgthéroulde" remains a pleasing and fantastic
architectural mystery. Close by, through the quaint old
streets of the Epicérie and "Gross Horloge", walked no
doubt in their young days the brothers Corneille, before
they evolved from their meditative souls the sombre and
heavy genius of French tragedy,—and not very far away,
up one of those little shadowy winding streets and out at
the corner, stands the restored house of Diane de Poitiers,
so sentient and alive in its very look that one almost expects to see at the quaint windows the beautiful wicked

face of the woman who swayed the humours of a king by her smile or her frown.

Cardinal Bonpré, walking past the stately fourteenth-century Gothic pile of the Palais de Justice, thought half-vaguely of some of these things,—but they affected him less than they might have done had his mind not been full of the grand music he had just heard in the Cathedral, and of the darkness that had slowly gathered there, as though in solemn commingling with the darkness which had at the same time settled over his soul. A great oppression weighed upon him;—almost he judged himself guilty of mortal sin, for had he not said aloud and boldly, while facing the High Altar of the Lord, that even in the Church itself faith was lacking? Yes, he, a Cardinal-Archbishop, had said this thing; he had as it were proclaimed it on the silence of the sacred precincts,—and had he not in this, acted unworthily of his calling? Had he not almost uttered blasphemy? Grieved and puzzled, the good Felix went on his way, almost unseeingly, towards the humble inn where he had elected to remain for the brief period of his visit to Rouen,—an inn where no one stayed save the very poorest of travellers, this fact being its chief recommendation in the eyes of the Cardinal. For it must be conceded, that viewed by our latter-day ideas of personal comfort and convenience, the worthy prelate had some very old-world and fantastic notions. One of these notions was a devout feeling that he should, so far as it was humanly possible, endeavour to obey the Master whose doctrine he professed to follow. This, it will be admitted, was a curious idea. Considering the bold and blasphemous laxity of modern Christian customs, it was surely quite a fanatical idea. Yet he had his own Church-warrant for such a rule of conduct; and chief among the Evangelic Counsels writ down for his example was Voluntary Poverty. Yes!—Voluntary Poverty,—notwithstanding the countless treasures lying idle and wasted in the Vatican, and the fat sinecures enjoyed by bishops and archbishops; which things exist in direct contradiction and disobedience to the command of Christ. Christ Himself lived on the earth in poverty,—He visited only the poorest and simplest habitations,—and never did He set His sacred foot within a palace, save the palace of the High Priest where He was con-

demned to die. Much symbolic meaning did Cardinal
Felix discover in this incident,—and often would he muse
upon it gravely.

"The Divine is condemned to die in all palaces," he
would say,—" It is only in the glorious world of Nature,
under the sunlit or starlit expanse of heaven, that the god
in us can live; and it was not without some subtle cause
of intended instruction to mankind that the Saviour always taught His followers in the open air."

There was what might be called a palace hard by, to
which Bonpré had been invited, and where he would have
been welcome to stay as long as he chose,—the house of
the Archbishop of Rouen—a veritable abode of luxury as
compared with the Hotel Poitiers, which was a dingy
little tumble-down building, very old, and wearing a conscious air of feebleness and decrepitude which was almost apologetic. Its small windows, set well back in
deeply hollowed carved arches had a lack-lustre gleam,
as of very aged eyes under shelving brows,—its narrow
door, without either bolts or bars, hung half-aslant upon
creaking rusty hinges, and was never quite shut either
by day or night,—yet from the porch a trailing mass of
"creeping jenny" fell in a gold-dotted emerald fringe
over the head of any way-worn traveller passing in,—
making a brightness in a darkness, and suggesting something not altogether uncheery in the welcome provided.
They were very humble folk who kept the Hotel Poitiers,
—the host, Jean Patoux, was a small market-gardener
who owned a plot of land outside Rouen, which he chiefly
devoted to the easy growing of potatoes and celery—his
wife had her hands full with the domestic business of the
hotel and the cares of her two children, Henri and Babette,
the most incorrigible imps of mischief that ever lived in
Rouen or out of it. Madame Patoux, large of body, unwieldy in movement, but clean as a new pin, and with a
fat smile of perpetual contentment on her round visage,
professed to be utterly worn to death by the antics of
these children of hers,—but nevertheless she managed to
grow stouter every day with a persistency and fortitude
which denoted the reserved forces of her nature,—and
her cooking, always excellent, never went wrong because
Babette had managed to put her doll in one of the sauce-
pans, or Henri had essayed to swim a paper boat in the

soup. Things went on somehow; Patoux himself was perfectly satisfied with his small earnings and position in life—Madame Patoux felt that " le bon Dieu " was specially engaged in looking after her,—and as long as the wicked Babette and the wickeder Henri threw themselves wildly into her arms and clung round her fat neck imploring pardon after any and every misdeed, and sat for a while *" en penitence "* in separate corners reading the " Hours of Mary ", they might be as naughty as they chose over and over again so far as the good-natured mother was concerned. Just now, however, unusual calm appeared to have settled on the Patoux household;—an atmosphere of general placidity and peace prevailed, which had the effect of imparting almost a stately air to the tumble-down house, and a suggestion of luxury to the poorly-furnished rooms. Madame Patoux herself was conscious of a mysterious dignity in her surroundings, and moved about on her various household duties with less bounce and fuss than was her ordinary custom,— and Henri and Babette sat quiet without being told to do so, moved apparently by a sudden and inexplicable desire to study their lessons. All this had been brought about by the advent of Cardinal Bonpré, who with his kind face, gentle voice and beneficent manner, had sought and found lodging at the Hotel Poitiers, notwithstanding Madame Patoux's profuse apologies for the narrowness and inconvenience of her best rooms.

" For look you, Monseigneur," she murmured, deferentially, " How should we have ever expected such an honour as the visit of a holy Cardinal-Archbishop to our poor little place! There are many new houses on the Boulevards which could have accommodated Monseigneur with every comfort,—and that he should condescend to bestow the blessing of his presence upon us,—ah! it was a special dispensation of Our Lady which was too amazing and wonderful to be at once comprehended! "

Thus Madame Patoux, with breathless pauses between her sentences, and many profound curtseyings; but the good Cardinal waived aside her excuses and protestations, and calling her " My daughter ", signed the cross on her brow with paternal gentleness, assuring her that he would give her as little trouble as any other casual visitor.

" Trouble!—Ah, heaven!—could anything be a trouble

for Monseigneur!" and Madame Patoux, moved to tears
by the quiet contentment with which the Cardinal took
possession of the two bare, common rooms which were
the best she could place at his disposal, hurried away,
and hustling Henri and Babette like two little roly-poly
balls before her into the kitchen, she told them with much
emphasis that there was a saint in the house,—a saint fit
to be the holy companion of any of those who had their
niches up in the Cathedral near the great rose-window,—
and that if they were good children they would very likely
see an angel coming down from heaven to visit him.
Babette put her finger in her mouth and looked incredulous. She had a vague belief in angels,—but Henri, with
the cheap cynicism of the modern French lad was anything
but sure about them.

"Mother," said he, "There's a boy in our school who
says there is no God at all, and that it's no use having
priests or Cardinals or Cathedrals,—it's all rubbish and
humbug!"

"Poor little miserable monster!" exclaimed Madame
Patoux, as she peered into the pot where the soup for the
Cardinal's supper was simmering—"He is arranging
himself to become a thief or a murderer, be sure of that,
Henri!—and thou, who art trained in all thy holy duties
by the good Père Laurent, who teaches thee everything
which the school is not wise enough to teach, ought never
to listen to such wickedness. If there were no God, we
should not be alive at all, thou foolish child!—for it is
only our blessed Saviour and the saints that keep the
world going."

Henri was silent,—Babette looked at him and made a
little grimace of scorn.

"If the Cardinal is a saint," she said—"he should be
able to perform a miracle. The little Fabien Doucet has
been lame for seven years; we shall bring him to Monseigneur, and he will mend his leg and make him well.
Then we shall believe in saints afterwards."

Madame Patoux turned her warm red face round from
the fire over which she was bending, and stared at her
precocious offspring aghast.

"What! You will dare to address yourself to the Cardinal!" she cried vociferously—"You will dare to trouble him with such foolishness? Mon Dieu!—is it pos-

sible to be so wicked! But listen to me well!—If you presume to say one saucy word to Monseigneur, you shall be punished! What have you to do with the little Fabien Doucet?—the poor child is sickly and diseased by the will of God."

"I don't see why it should be God's will to make a boy sickly and diseased——" began the irrepressible Henri, when his mother cut him short with a stamp of her foot and a cry of—

"Tais-toi! Silence! Wicked boy!—thou wilt kill me with thy naughty speeches! All this evil comes of the school,—I would thy father had never been compelled to send thee there!"

As she said this with a vast amount of heat and energy, Henri, seized by some occult and inexplicable emotion, burst without warning into loud and fitful weeping, the sound whereof resembled the yelling of a tortured savage,—and Babette, petrified at first by the appalling noise, presently gave way likewise, and shrieked a wild accompaniment.

"What ails my children?" said a gentle voice, distinct and clear in its calm intonation even in the midst of the uproar, and Cardinal Bonpré, tall and stately, suddenly appeared upon the threshold—"What little sorrows are these?"

Henri's roar ceased abruptly,—Babette's shrill wailing dropped into awed silence. Both youngsters stared amazed at the venerable Felix, whose face and figure expressed such composed dignity and sweetness; and Madame Patoux, hastily and with frequent gasps for breath, related the history of the skirmish.

"And what will become of such little devils when they grow older, the Blessed Virgin only knows!" she groaned —"For even now they are so suspicious in nature, that they will not believe in their dinner till they see it!"

Something like a faint grin widened the mouths of Henri and Babette at this statement made with so much distressed fervour by their angry mother,—but the Cardinal did not smile. His face had grown very pale and grave, almost stern.

"The children are quite right, my daughter," he said gently,—"I am no saint! I have performed no miracles. I am a poor sinner,—striving to do well, but alas!—for

'ever striving in vain. The days of noble living are past,
—and we are all too much fallen in the ways of error to
deserve that our Lord should bless the too often half-
hearted and grudging labour of his so-called servants.
Come here, ma mignonne!'' he continued, calling Babette,
who approached him with a curious air of half-timid boldness—'' Thou art but a very little girl,'' he said, laying
his thin white hand softly on her tumbled brown curls—
'' Nevertheless, I should be a very foolish old man if I
despised thee, or thy thoughts, or thy desire to know the
truth for truth's sake. Therefore to-morrow thou shalt
bring me this afflicted friend of thine, and though I have
no divine gifts, I will do even as the Master commanded,
—I will lay my hands on him in blessing and pray that
he may be healed. More than this is not in my power, my
child!—if a miracle is to be worked, it is our dear Lord
only who can work it.''

Gently he murmured his formal benediction,—then,
turning away, he entered his own room and shut the
door. Babette, grown strangely serious, turned to her
brother and held out her hand, moved by one of those er-
ratic impulses which often take sudden possession of
self-willed children.

'' Come into the Cathedral!'' she whispered impera-
tively—'' Come and say an *Ave*.''

Not a word did the usually glib Henri vouchsafe in
answer,—but clutching his sister's fingers in his own
dirty, horny palm, he trotted meekly beside her out of the
house and across the Square into the silence and darkness of Notre Dame. Their mother watched their little
plump figures disappear with a feeling of mingled amazement and gratitude,—miracles were surely beginning, she
thought, if a few words from the Cardinal could impress Babette and Henri with an idea of the necessity of
prayer!

They were not long gone, however;—they came walking back together, still demurely hand in hand, and settled themselves quietly in a corner to study their tasks
for the next day. Babette's doll, once attired as a fashionable Parisienne, and now degenerated into a one-eyed
laundress with a rather soiled cap and apron, stuck out
its composite arms in vain from the bench where it sat
all askew, drooping its head forlornly over a dustpan,—

and Henri's drum, wherewith he was wont to wake alarming echoes out of the dreamy and historical streets of Rouen, lay on its side neglected and ingloriously silent. And, as before said, peace reigned in the Patoux household,—even the entrance of Papa Patoux himself, fresh from his celery beds, and smelling of the earth earthy, created no particular diversion. He was a very little, very cheery, round man, was Papa Patoux; he had no ideas at all in his bullet head save that he judged everything to be very well managed in the Universe, and that he, considered simply as Patoux, was lucky in his life and labours,—also that it was an easy thing to grow celery, provided God's blessing was on the soil. For the rest, he took small care; he knew that the world wagged in different ways in different climates,—he read his halfpenny journal daily, and professed to be interested in the political situation just for the fun of the thing, but in reality he thought the French Senate a pack of fools, and wondered what they meant by always talking so much about nothing. He believed in "La Patrie" to a certain extent,—but he would have very much objected if "La Patrie" had interfered with his celery. Roughly speaking, he understood that France was a nation, and that he was a Frenchman; and that if any enemies should presume to come into the country, it would be necessary to take up a musket and fight them out again, and defend wife, children, and celery-beds till the last breath was out of his body. Further than this simple and primitive idea of patriotism he did not go. He never bothered himself about dissentient shades of opinion, or quarrels among opposing parties. When he had to send his children to the Government school, the first thing he asked was whether they would be taught their religion there. He was told no,—that the Government objected to religious teaching, as it merely created discussion and was of no assistance whatever in the material business of life. Patoux scratched his head over this for a considerable time and ruminated deeply,—finally he smiled, a dull fat smile.

"Good!" said he—"I understand now why the Government makes such an ass of itself now and then! You cannot expect mere men to do their duty wisely without God on their side. But Père Laurent will teach my children their prayers and catechism,—and I dare say Heaven will arrange the rest."

And he forthwith dismissed the matter from his mind. His children attended the Government school daily,—and every Wednesday, Saturday, and Sunday afternoons Père Laurent, a kindly, simple-hearted old priest, took them, with several other little creatures " educated by the State", and taught them all he knew about the great France-exiled Creator of the Universe, and of His ceaseless love to sinful and blasphemous mankind.

So things went on ;—and though Henri and Babette were being crammed by the national system of instruction, with learning which was destined to be of very slight use to them in their after careers, and which made them little cynics before their time, they were still sustained within bounds by the saving sense of something better than themselves,—that Something Better which silently declares itself in the beauty of the skies, the blossoming of the flowers, and the loveliness of all things wherein man has no part,—and neither of them was yet transformed into that most fearsome product of modern days, the child-Atheist, for whom there is no greater God than Self.

On this particular night when Papa Patoux returned to the bosom of his family, he, though a dull-witted man generally, did not fail to note the dove-like spirit of calm that reigned over his entire household. His wife's fat face was agreeably placid,—the children were in an orderly mood, and as he sat down to the neatly spread supper-table, he felt more convinced than ever that things were exceedingly well managed for him in this best of all possible worlds. Pausing in the act of conveying a large spoonful of steaming soup to his mouth he enquired—

" And Monseigneur, the Cardinal Bonpré,—has he also been served ? "

Madame Patoux opened her round eyes wide at him.

" But certainly ! Dost thou think, my little cabbage, thou wouldst get thy food before Monseigneur ? That would be strange indeed ! "

Papa Patoux swallowed his ladleful of soup in abashed silence.

" It was a beautiful day in the fields," he presently

observed—" There was a good smell in the earth, as if
voilets were growing,—and late in the autumn though it
is, there was a skylark yet singing. It was a very blue
heaven, too, as blue as the robe of the Virgin, with clouds
as white as little angels clinging to it."

Madame nodded. Some people might have thought
Papa Patoux inclined to be poetical,—she did not. Henri
and Babette listened.

" The robe of Our Lady is always blue," said Babette.

" And the angels' clothes are always white," added
Henri.

Madame Patoux said nothing, but passed a second
helping of soup all round. Papa Patoux smiled blandly
on his offspring.

" Just so," he averred—" Blue and white are the colours of the sky, my little ones,—and Our Lady and the
angels live in the sky ! "

" I wonder where ? " muttered Henri with his mouth
half full. " The sky is nothing but miles and miles of
air, and in the air there are millions and millions of planets
turning round and round, larger than our world,—ever so
much larger,—and nobody knows which is the largest of
them all ! "

" It is as thou sayest, my son," said Patoux confidently—" Nobody knows which is the largest of them
all, but whichever it may be, that largest of them all belongs to Our Lady and the angels."

Henri looked at Babette, but Babette was munching
watercress busily, and did not return his enquiring
glances. Papa Patoux, quite satisfied with his own reasoning, continued his supper in an amiable state of mind.

" What didst thou serve to Monseigneur, my little
one ? " he asked his wife with a coaxing and caressing
air, as though she were some delicate and dainty sylph of
the woodlands, instead of being the lady of massive proportions which she undoubtedly was,—" Something of
delicacy and fine flavour, doubtless ? "

Madame Patoux shook her head despondingly.

" He would have nothing of that kind," she replied—
" Soup *maigre,* and afterwards nothing but bread, dried
figs, and apples to finish. Ah, Heaven ! What a supper
for a Cardinal-Archbishop ! It is enough to make one
weep ! "

Patoux considered the matter solemnly.

"He is perhaps very poor?" he half queried.

"Poor, he may be," responded Madame,—"But if he is, it is surely his own fault,—whoever heard of a poor Cardinal-Archbishop! Such men can all be rich if they choose."

"Can they?" asked Henri with sudden vivacious eagerness. "How?"

But his question was not answered, for just at that moment a loud knock came at the door of the inn, and a tall broadly built personage in close canonical attire appeared in the narrow little passage of entry, attended by another smaller and very much more insignificant-looking individual.

Patoux hastily scrambled out of his chair.

"The Archbishop!" he whispered to his wife—"He himself! Our own Archbishop!"

Madame Patoux jumped up, and seizing her children, held one in each hand as she curtsied up and down.

"*Benedicite!*" said the new-comer, lightly signing the cross in air with a sociable smile—"Do not disturb yourselves, my children! You have with you in this house the eminent Cardinal Bonpré?"

"Ah, yes, Monseigneur!" replied Madame Patoux—"Only just now he has finished his little supper. Shall I show Monseigneur to his room?"

"If you please," returned the Archbishop, still smiling benevolently—"And permit my secretary to wait with you here till I return."

With this, and an introductory wave of his hand in the direction of the attenuated and sallow-faced personage who had accompanied him, he graciously permitted Madame Patoux to humbly precede him by a few steps, and then followed her with a soft, even tread, and a sound as of rustling silk in his garments, from which a faint odour of some delicate perfume seemed wafted as he moved.

Left to entertain the Archbishop's secretary, Jean Patoux was for a minute or two somewhat embarrassed. Henri and Babette stared at the stranger with undisguised curiosity, and were apparently not favourably impressed by his appearance.

"He has white eyelashes!" whispered Henri.

"And yellow teeth," responded Babette.

Meanwhile Patoux, having scratched his bullet-head sufficiently over the matter, offered his visitor a chair.

"Sit down, sir," he said curtly.

The secretary smiled pallidly and took the proffered accommodation. Patoux again meditated. He was not skilled in the art of polite conversation, and he found himself singularly at a loss.

"It would be an objection no doubt, and an irreverance perhaps to smoke a pipe before you, Monsieur—Monsieur——"

"Cazeau," finished the secretary with another pallid smile—"Claude Cazeau, a poor scribe,—at your service! And I beg of you, Monsieur Jean Patoux, to smoke at your distinguished convenience!"

There was a faint tone of satire in his voice which struck Papa Patoux as exceedingly disagreeable, though he could not quite imagine why he found it so. He slowly reached for his pipe from the projecting shelf above the chimney, and as slowly proceeded to fill it with tobacco from a tin cannister close by.

"I do not think I have ever seen you in the town, Monsieur Cazeau," he said—"Nor at Mass in the Cathedral either?"

"No?" responded Cazeau easily, in a half-querying tone—"I do not much frequent the streets; and I only attend the first early mass on Sundays. My work for Monseigneur occupies my whole time."

"Ah!" and Patoux, having stuffed his pipe sufficiently, lit it, and proceeded to smoke peaceably—"There must be much to do. Many poor and sick who need money, and clothes, and help in every way,—and to try and do good, and give comfort to all the unhappy souls in Rouen is a hard task, even for an Archbishop."

Cazeau linked his thin hands together with an action of pious fervour and assented.

"There is a broken-hearted creature near us," pursued Patoux leisurely—"We call her Marguerite La Folle;—I have often thought I would ask Père Laurent to speak to Monseigneur for her, that she might be released from the devils that are tearing her. She was a good girl till a year or two ago,—then some villain got the ruin of her, and she lost her wits over it. Ah, 'tis a sad sight to see her now—poor Marguerite Valmond!"

"Ha!" cried Henri suddenly, pointing a grimy finger at Cazeau—"Why did you jump? Did something hurt you?"

Cazeau had indeed "jumped," as Henri put it,—that is, he had sprung up from his chair suddenly and as suddenly sat down again with an air of impatience and discomfort. He rapidly overcame whatever emotion moved him, however, and stretched his thin mouth in a would-be amiable grin at the observant Henri.

"You are a sharp boy!" he observed condescendingly —"and tall for your age, no doubt. How old are you?"

"Eleven," replied Henri—"But that has nothing to do with your jumping."

"True," and the secretary wriggled in his chair, pretending to be much amused—"But my jumping had nothing to do with you either, my small friend! I had a thought,—a sudden thought,—of a duty forgotten."

"Oh, it was a thought, was it?" and Henri looked incredulous. "Do thoughts always make you jump?"

"Tais-toi! Tais-toi!" murmured Patoux gently, between two whiffs of his pipe—"Excuse him, Monsieur Cazeau,—he is but a child."

Cazeau writhed amicably.

"A delightful child," he murmured—"And the little girl—his sister—is also charming—Ah, what fine dark eyes!—what hair! Will she not come and speak to me?"

He held out a hand invitingly towards Babette, but she merely made a grimace at him and retired backwards. Patoux smiled benevolently.

"She does not like strangers," he explained.

"Good—very good! That is right! Little girls should always run away from strangers, especially strangers of my sex," observed Cazeau with a sniggering laugh —"And do these dear children go to school?"

Patoux took his pipe out of his mouth altogether, and stared solemnly at the ceiling.

"Without doubt!—they are compelled to go to school," he answered slowly; "but if I could have had my way, they should never have gone. They learn mischief there in plenty, but no good that I can see. They know much about geography, and the stars, and anatomy, and what they call physical sciences;—but whether they have got it into their heads that the good God wants them to live straight, clean, honest, wholesome lives, is more than I am certain of. However, I trust Père Laurent will do what he can."

"Père Laurent?" echoed Cazeau, with a wide smile —"You have a high opinion of Père Laurent? Ah, yes, a good man!—but ignorant—alas! very ignorant!"

Papa Patoux brought his eyes down from the ceiling and fixed them enquiringly on Cazeau.

"Ignorant?" he began, when at this juncture Madame Patoux entered, and taking possession of Henri and Babette, informed Monsieur Cazeau that the Archbishop would be for some time engaged in conversation with Cardinal Bonpré, and that therefore he, Monsieur Cazeau, need not wait,—Monseigneur would return to his house alone. Whereupon the secretary rose, evidently glad to be set at liberty, and took his leave of the Patoux family. On the threshold, however, he paused, looking back somewhat frowningly at Jean Patoux himself.

"I should not, if I were you, trouble Monseigneur concerning the case you told me of—that of—of Marguerite Valmond,"—he observed—"He has a horror of evil women."

With that he departed, walking across the Square towards the Archbishop's house in a stealthy sort of fashion, as though he were a burglar meditating some particularly daring robbery.

"He is a rat—a rat!" exclaimed Henri, suddenly executing a sort of reasonless war-dance round the kitchen —"One wants a cat to catch him!"

"Rats are nice," declared Babette, for she remembered having once had a tame white rat which sat on her knee and took food from her hand,—"Monsieur Cazeau is a man; and men are not nice."

Patoux burst into a loud laugh.

"Men are not nice!" he echoed—"What dost thou know about it, thou little droll one?"

"What I see," responded Babette severely, with an elderly air, as of a person who has suffered by bitter experience; and, undeterred by her parents' continued laughter she went on—

"Men are ugly. They are dirty. They say 'Come here my little girl, and I will give you something,'—then when I go to them they try and kiss me. And I will not kiss them, because their mouths smell bad. They stroke my hair and pull it all the wrong way. And it hurts. And when I don't like my hair pulled the wrong way, they tell me I will be a great coquette. A coquette is to be like Diane de Poitiers. Shall I be like Diane de Poitiers?"

"The saints forbid!" cried Madame Patoux,—"And talk no more nonsense, child,—it's bed-time. Come,—say good-night to thy father, Henri;—give them thy blessing, Jean—and let me get them into their beds before the Archbishop leaves the house, or they will be asking him as many questions as there are in the catechism."

Thus enjoined, Papa Patoux kissed his children affectionately, signing the cross on their brows as they came up to him in turn, after the fashion of his own father, who had continued this custom up to his dying day. What they thought of the benediction in itself might be somewhat difficult to define, but it can be safely asserted that a passion of tears on the part of Babette, and a fit of demoniacal howling from Henri, would have been the inevitable result if Papa Patoux had refused to bestow it on them. Whether there were virtue in it or not, their father's mute blessing sent them to bed peaceably and in good humour with each other, and they trotted off very contentedly beside their mother, hushing their footsteps and lowering their voices as they passed the door of the room occupied by Cardinal Bonpré.

"The Archbishop is not an angel, is he?" asked Babette whisperingly.

Her mother smiled broadly.

"Not exactly, my little one. Why such a foolish question?"

"You said that Cardinal Bonpré was a saint, and that perhaps we should see an angel come down from heaven to visit him," replied Babette.

"Well, you could not have thought the Archbishop came from heaven," interpolated Henri, scornfully,—"He came from his own house over the way with his own secretary behind him. Do angels keep secretaries?"

Babette laughed aloud,—the idea was grotesque. The

two children were just then ascending the wooden stairs
to their bedroom, the mother carrying a lighted candle
behind them, and at that moment the rich sonorous voice
of the Archbishop, raised to a high and somewhat indignant tone, reached them with these words—" I consider that you altogether mistake your calling and position."

Then the voice died away into inaudible murmurings.

" They are quarrelling! The Archbishop is angry!"
said Henri with a grin.

" Perhaps Archbishops do not like saints," suggested
Babette.

" Tais-toi! Cardinal Bonpré is an archbishop himself,
little silly," said Madame Patoux—" Therefore those
great and distinguished Monseigneurs are like brothers."

" That is why they are quarrelling!" declared Henri
glibly,—"A boy told me in school that Cain and Abel were
the first pair of brothers, and they quarrelled,—and all
brothers have quarrelled ever since. It's in the blood,
so that boy says,—and it is his excuse always for fighting *his* little brother. His little brother is six, and he is
twelve;—and of course he always knocks his little brother
down. He cannot help it, he says. And he gets books
on physiology and heredity, and he learns in them that
whatever is *in* the blood has got to come out somehow.
He says that it's because Cain killed Abel that there are
wars between nations ;—if Cain and Abel had never quarrelled, there would never have been any fighting in the
world,—and now that it's in the blood of every
body——"

But further sapient discourse on the part of Henri was
summarily put an end to by his mother's ordering him to
kneel down and say his prayers, and afterwards bun-
dling him into bed,—where, being sleepy, he speedily forgot all that he had been trying to talk about. Babette
took more time in retiring to rest. She had very pretty,
curly, brown hair, and Madame Patoux took a pride in
brushing and plaiting it neatly.

" I may be like Diane de Poitiers after all," she remarked, peering at herself in the small mirror when her
thick locks were smoothed and tied back for the night—
" Why should I not be?"

" Because Diane de Poitiers was a wicked woman," said

Madame Patoux energetically,—" and thou must learn to be a good girl."

" But if Diane de Poitiers was bad, why do they talk so much about her even now, and put her in all the histories, and show her house, and say she was beautiful?" went on Babette.

" Because people are foolish," said Madame, getting impatient—" Foolish people run after bad women, and bad women run after foolish people. Now say thy prayers."

Obediently Babette knelt down, shut her eyes close, clasped her hands hard, and murmured the usual evening formula, heaving a small sigh after her " act of contrition," and looking almost saintly as she commended herself to her " angel guardian." Then her mother kissed her, saying—

" Good-night, little daughter! Think of Our Lady and the saints, and then ask them to keep us safe from evil. Good-night!"

" Good-night," responded Babette sleepily,—but all the same she did not think of Our Lady and the saints half as much as of Diane de Poitiers. There are few daughters of Eve to whom conquest does not seem a finer thing than humility; and the sovereignty of Diane de Poitiers over a king, seems to many a girl just conscious of her own charm, a more emphatic testimony to the supremacy of her sex, than the Angel's greeting of " Blessed art thou!" to the elected Virgin of the world.

III

MEANWHILE a somewhat embarrassing interview had taken place between the Archbishop of Rouen and Cardinal Bonpré. The archbishop, seen by the light of the one small lamp which illumined the "best room" of the Hotel Poitiers was certainly a handsome and imposing personage, broad-chested and muscular, with a massive head, well set on strong square shoulders, admirably adapted for the wearing of the dark violet soutane which fitted them as gracefully as a royal vesture draping the figure of a king. One disproportionate point, however, about his attire was, that the heavy gold crucifix which depended by a chain from his neck, did not, with him, look so much a sacred symbol as a trivial ornament,—whereas the simple silver one that gleamed against the rusty black scarlet-edged cassock of Cardinal Bonpré, presented itself as the plain and significant sign of holiness without the aid of jewellers' workmanship to emphasize its meaning. This was a trifle, no doubt;—still it was one of those slight things which often betray character. As the most brilliant diamond will look like common glass on the rough red hand of a cook, while common glass will simulate the richness of the real gem on the delicate white finger of a daintily-bred woman, so the emblem of salvation seemed a mere bauble and toy on the breast of the Archbishop, while it assumed its most reverent and sacred aspect as worn by Felix Bonpré. Yet judged by mere outward appearance, there could be no doubt as to which was the finer-looking man of the two. The Cardinal, thin and pale, with shadows of thought and pain in his eyes, and the many delicate wrinkles of advancing age marking his features, would never possess so much attractiveness for worldly and superficial persons as the handsome Archbishop, who carried his fifty-five years as though they were but thirty, and whose fresh, plump face, unmarred by any serious consideration, bespoke a thorough enjoyment of life, and the things which

life,—if encouraged to demand them,—most strenuously
seeks, such as good food, soft beds, rich clothing, and
other countless luxuries which are not necessities by any
means, but which make the hours move smoothly and
softly, undisturbed by the clash of outside events among
those who are busy with thoughts and actions, and who,
—being absorbed in the thick of a soul-contest,—care little
whether their bodies fare ill or well. The Archbishop
certainly did not belong to this latter class,—indeed he
considered too much thought as mischievous in itself, and
when thought appeared likely to break forth into action,
he denounced it as pernicious and well-nigh criminal.

"Thinkers," he said once to a young and ardent novice, studying for the priesthood, "are generally socialists and revolutionists. They are an offence to the
Church and a danger to the community."

"Surely," murmured the novice timidly,—"Our Lord
Himself was a thinker? And a Socialist likewise?"

But at this the Archbishop rose up in wrath and flashed
forth menace;—

"If you are a follower of Renan, sir, you had better admit it before proceeding further in your studies," he said
irately,—"The Church is too much troubled in these days
by the members of a useless and degenerate apostasy!"

Whereupon the young man had left his presence
abashed, puzzled, and humiliated; but scarcely penitent,
inasmuch as his New Testament taught him that he was
right and that the Archbishop was wrong.

Truth to tell, the Archbishop was very often wrong.
Wrapped up in himself and his own fixed notions as to
how life should be lived, he seldom looked out upon the
larger world, and obstinately refused to take any thoughtful notice of the general tendency of public opinion in all
countries concerning religion and morality. All that he
was unable to explain, he flatly denied,—and his preju-
dices were as violent as his hatred of contradiction was
keen. The saintly life and noble deeds of Felix Bonpré
had reached him from time to time through various rumours repeated by different priests and dignitaries of the
Church, who had travelled as far as the distant little
Cathedral-town embowered among towering pines and
elm trees, where the Cardinal had his abiding seat of
duty;—and he had been anxious to meet the man who

in these days of fastidious feeding and luxurious living, had managed to gain such a holy reputation as to be almost canonized in some folks' estimation before he was dead. Hearing that Bonpré intended to stay a couple of nights in Rouen, he cordially invited him to spend that time at his house,—but the invitation had been gratefully yet firmly refused, much to the Archbishop's amazement. This amazement increased considerably when he learned that the dingy, comfortless, little Hotel Poitiers had been selected by the Cardinal as his temporary lodging,—and it was not without a pious murmur concerning " the pride which apes humility " that he betook himself to that ancient and despised hostelry, which had nothing whatever in the way of a modern advantage to recommend it,— neither electric light, nor electric bell, nor telephone. But he felt it incumbent upon him to pay a fraternal visit to the Cardinal, who had become in a manner famous without being at all aware of his fame,—and when finally in his presence, he was conscious not only of a singular disappointment, but an equally singular perplexity. Felix Bonpré was not at all the sort of personage he had expected to see. He had imagined that a Churchman who was able to obtain a character for saintliness in days like these, must needs be worldly-wise and crafty, with a keen perception and comprehension of the follies of mankind, and an ability to use these follies advantageously to further his own ends. Something of the cunning and foresight of an ancient Egyptian sorcerer was in the composition of the Archbishop himself, for he judged mankind alone by its general stupidity and credulity;—stupidity and credulity which formed excellent ground for the working of miracles, whether such miracles were wrought in the name of Osiris or Christ. Mokanna, the " Veiled Prophet," while corrupt to the core with unnameable vices, had managed in his time to delude the people into thinking him a holy man; and,—without any adequate reason for his assumption,—the Archbishop had certainly prepared himself to meet in Felix Bonpré, a shrewd, calculating, clever priest, absorbed in acting the part of an excessive holiness in order to secure such honour in his diocese as should attract the particular notice of the Vatican. " Playing for Pope," in fact, had been the idea with which the archbishop had invested the Cardinal's reputed sanctity, and he was astonished and in a manner irritated to find himself completely mistaken. He had opened the conversation by the usual cordial trivialities of ordinary greeting, to which Bonpré had responded with the suave courtesy and refined gentleness which always dignified his manner,—and then the Archbishop had ventured to offer a remonstrance on the unconventional— "Shall we call it eccentric?" he suggested, smiling amicably,—conduct of the Cardinal in choosing to abide in such a comfortless lodging as the Hotel Poitiers.

"It would have been a pleasure and an honour to me to welcome you at my house"—he said—"Really, it is quite a violation of custom and usage that you should be in this wretched place; the accommodation is not at all fitted for a prince of the Church."

Cardinal Felix raised one hand in gentle yet pained protest.

"Pardon me!" he said, "I do not like that term, 'prince of the Church.' There are no princes in the Church—or if there are, there should be none."

The archbishop opened his eyes widely.

"That is a strange remark!" he ejaculated—"Princes of the Church there have always been since Cardinals were created; and you, being a Cardinal and an Archbishop as well, cannot be otherwise than one of them."

Felix Bonpré sighed.

"Still, I maintain that the term is a wrong one," he answered, "and used in the wrong place. The Church has nothing, or should have nothing to do with differing titles or places. The ordinary priest who toils among his congregation day and night, scarcely resting himself, working and praying for the spiritual welfare of others, should to my thinking be as greatly held in honour as the bishop who commands him and who often—so it chances —is able to do less for our Lord than he. In things temporal, owing to the constant injustice of man practised against his brother-man, we can seldom attain to strict impartiality of judgment,—but in things spiritual, there surely should be perfect equality."

"Seriously speaking, are those your views?" enquired the Archbishop, his features expressing more and more astonishment.

"Assuredly!" responded the Cardinal gently,—"Are

they not yours? Did not the Master Himself say 'Whosoever will be chief among you, let him be your servant'?
And 'Whosoever shall exalt himself shall be abased'?
These statements are plain and true,—there is no mistaking them."

The Archbishop was silent for a minute or so.

"Unfortunately we cannot apply our Lord's words
literally to every-day exigencies," he murmured suavely
—"If we could do so——"

"We *should* do so," said the Cardinal with emphasis—
"The outside world may be disinclined to do so,—but we
—we who are the representatives of a God-given faith,
are solemnly bound to do so. And I fear—I very much
fear—that it is because in many cases we have not shown
the example expected of us, that heresy and atheism are
so common among the people of the present day."

"Are you a would-be reformer?" asked the Archbishop good-humouredly, yet not without a touch of satire
in his tone,—"If so, you are not alone—there have already been many!"

"Nay, I desire no reforms," responded the Cardinal, a
faint flush warming the habitual pallor of his cheeks—"I
simply wish to maintain—not alter—the doctrine of our
Lord. No reform is necessary in that,—it is clear, concise, and simple enough for a child to understand. His
command to His disciples was,—'Feed my sheep'—and
I have of late been troubled and perplexed, because it
seems to me that the sheep are not fed;—that despite
churches and teachers and preachers, whole flocks are
starving."

The Archbishop moved uneasily in his chair. His
habitual violent spirit of contradiction rose up rebelliously
in him, and he longed to give a sharp answer in confutation of the Cardinal's words, but there was a touch of
the sycophant in his nature despite his personal pride,
and he could not but reflect that Cardinals ranked above
Archbishops, and that Felix Bonpré was in very truth a
"prince of the Church" however much he himself
elected to disclaim the title. And as in secular affairs
lesser men will always bow the knee to royalty, so the
Archbishop felt the necessity of temporising with one
who was spiritually royal. Therefore he considered a
moment before replying.

"I think," he said at last, in soft persuasive tones, "that your conscience may perhaps be a little tender on this subject. But I cannot agree with you in your supposition that whole flocks are starving;—for Christianity dominates the better and more intellectual part of the civilized world, and through its doctrines, men are gradually learning to be more tolerant and less unjust. When we recollect the barbarous condition of humanity before the coming of Christ——"

"Barbarous?" interrupted the Cardinal with half a smile,—"You would hardly apply that term to the luxury-loving peoples of Tyre and Babylon?—or to the ancient splendours of Athens and Rome?"

"They were heathens," said the Archbishop sententiously.

"But they were men and women," replied Bonpré, "And they too had immortal souls. They were all more or less struggling towards the fundamental Idea of good. Of course then, as now that Idea was overgrown by superstitious myths and observances—but the working tendency of the whole universe being ever towards Good, not Evil, an impulse to press on in the right direction was always in the brain of man, no matter how dimly felt. Primitive notions of honour were strange indeed; nevertheless honour existed in the minds of the early barbarians in a vague sense, though distorted out of shape and noblest meaning. No,—we dare not take upon ourselves to assert that men were altogether barbarous before the coming of Christ. They were cruel and unjust certainly,—and alas! they are cruel and unjust still! Eighteen hundred years of Christian teaching have not eradicated these ingrained sins from any one unit of the entire mass."

"You are a severe judge!" said the Archbishop.

Cardinal Bonpré lifted his mild blue eyes protestingly.

"Severe? I? God forbid that I should be severe, or presume to sit in judgment on any poor soul that sought my sympathy! I do not judge,—I simply feel. And my feelings have for a long time, I confess, been poignantly sorrowful."

"Sorrowful! And why?"

"Because the impression has steadily gained upon me that if our Church were all it was originally intended to be by its Divine Founder, we should at this time have neither heresies or apostasies, and all the world would be gathered into the 'one fold under one Shepherd.' But if we, who are its ministers, persist in occupying ourselves more with 'things temporal' than 'things spiritual,' we fail to perform our mission, or to show the example required of us, and we do not attract, so much as we repel. The very children of the present day are beginning to doubt our calling and election."

" Oh, of course there are, and always have been heretics and atheists," said the Archbishop,—" And apparently there always will be."

" And I venture to maintain that it is our fault that heretics and atheists continue to exist," replied the Cardinal; " If our Divine faith were lived divinely, there would be no room for heresy or atheism. The Church itself supplies the loophole for apostasy."

The Archbishop's handsome face crimsoned.

" You amaze me by such an expression ! " he said, raising his voice a little in the indignation he could scarcely conceal—" you talk—pardon me—as if you yourself were uncertain of the Church's ability to withstand unbelief."

" I speak but as I think," answered the Cardinal gently. " And I admit I *am* uncertain. In the leading points of Creed I am very steadfastly convinced ;—namely, that Christ was divine, and that the following of His Gospel is the saving of the immortal soul. But if you ask me whether I think we do truly follow that Gospel, I must own that I have doubts upon the matter."

" An elected favourite son of the Church should surely have no doubts ! " said the Archbishop.

" Ah, there you come back to the beginning from which we started, when I ventured to object to your term ' prince of the Church.' According to our Master, all men should be equal before Him ; therefore we err in marking differences of rank or favoritism in questions of religion. The very idea of rank is anti-Christian."

At this the Archbishop began to look seriously annoyed.

" I am afraid you are indulging in very unorthodox ideas," he said with impatience—" In fact I consider you altogether mistake your calling and position."

These were the words which had reached the attentive ears of the Patoux children on their way up to bed, and had caused Henri to declare that the Archbishop and the Cardinal were quarrelling. Felix Bonpré took the somewhat violent remark, however, with perfect equanimity.

"Possibly I may do so," he responded peaceably. "We are all subject to error. My calling, as I take it, is that of a servant of Christ, whose instructions for work are plainly set down in His own words. It is for me to follow these instructions as literally and exactly as I can. With regard to my position, I am placed as the spiritual head of a very small diocese, where the people for the most part lead very innocent and harmless lives. But I should be selfish and narrow in spirit if I allowed myself to limit my views to my own circle of influence. My flock are mere rustics in intellectual capacity, and have no conception of the manner in which the larger tide of human events is flowing. Now and then one or two of the people grow weary of their quiet pastures and woodlands,—and being young, hopeful, and ardent, start forth into the great world, there to seek fairer fortunes. Sometimes they come back to their old homes. Far more frequently they never return. But those who do come back are changed utterly. I recognise no more the young men and maidens whom I confirmed in their faith, and laid my hands on in blessing ere they fared forth to other lives and scenes. The men are grown callous and worldly; without a heart, —without a thought,—save for the gain or loss of gold. The women are—ruined!"

He paused a moment. The Archbishop said nothing.

"I love my people," went on the Cardinal pathetically —"No child is baptised in our old Cathedral without my praying for its future good,—without my hope that it may grow into that exquisite mingling of the Divine and Human which our Lord taught us was the perfection of life, and His desire to see fulfilled in those He called His own. Yes,—I love my people!—and when any of them go away from me, and then return to the scenes of their childhood broken-hearted, I cannot meet them with reproach. My own heart is half broken to see them thus cast down. And their sorrows have compelled me naturally to meditate on the sorrows of others,—to consider what it is in the world which thus corrodes the pure gold of innocence and robs life of its greatest charm. For if

Christ's spirit ruled us all, then innocence should be held more sacred. Life should engender happiness. I have studied, read, and thought long, upon these matters, so that I not only feel, but know the truth of what I say. Brother!—" and the Cardinal, strongly moved, rose suddenly and confronted the Archbishop with a passionate gesture—"My great grief is that the spirit of Christ does *not* rule the world! Christ is being re-crucified by this generation! And the Church is looking on, and silently permitting His second murder!"

Startled by the force of this expression, the Archbishop sprang up in his turn, his lips parted as if to speak—then—his angry glance met the clear, calm, steadfast look of Felix Bonpré, and he faltered. His eyes drooped—and his massive figure seemed for a moment to shrink with a sort of abasement. Like an inspired apostle the Cardinal stood, one hand outstretched,—his whole frame sentient with the strong emotion which possessed him.

"You know that what I say is true," he continued in quieter but no less intensely passionate accents—"You know that every day sees our Master crowned with new thorns and exposed to fresh torture! You know that we do nothing!—We stand beside Him in His second agony as dumb as though we were unconscious of it! You know that we *might* speak and will not! You know that we fear the ephemera of temporary governments, policies, and social conventionalities, more than the great, real, and terrible judgment of the world to come!"

"But all these things have been said before," began the Archbishop, recovering a little from the confusion that had momentarily seized him,—"And as I just now observed, you should remember that there have always been heretics from the very beginning."

"Oh, I remember!" and the Cardinal sighed, "How is it possible that any of us should forget! Heretics, whom we have tortured with unheard-of agonies and burned in the flames, as a proof of our love and sympathy with the tenderness of Christ Jesus!"

"You are going too far back in time!" said the Archbishop quickly. "We erred in the beginning through excess of zeal, but now—now——"

"Now we do exactly the same thing," returned Bonpré—"Only we do not burn physically our heretics, but

morally. We condemn all who oppose us. Good men
and brave thinkers, whom in our arrogance we consign to
eternal damnation, instead of endeavouring to draw out
the heart of their mystery, and gather up the gems of their
learning as fresh proofs of the active presence of God's
working in, and through all things! Think of the
Church's invincible and overpowering obstinacy in the
case of Galileo! He declared the existence of God to us
by the utterance of a Truth,—inasmuch as every truth is
a new message from God. Had he pronounced his theories before our divine Master, that Master would have
confirmed, not denied them! Have we one single example of Christ putting to the torture any poor soul that
did not believe in Him? Nay—He Himself submitted
to be tortured; but for those who wronged Him, His
prayer was only—' Father, forgive them, for they know
not what they do.' *They know not what they do!* The
ministers of truth should rather suffer themselves than
let others suffer. The horrors of the Inquisition are
a blot on religious history; our Master never meant us
to burn and torture men into faith. He desired us to love
and lead them into the way of life as the shepherd leads
a flock into the fold. I repeat again, there would have
been no room for atheism if we—we—the servants of
Christ, had been strictly true to our vocation."

By this time the Archbishop had recovered his equanimity. He sat down and surveyed the up-standing figure of the Cardinal with curiosity and a touch of pity.

"You think too much of these things," he said soothingly—" You are evidently overwrought with study and
excessive zeal. Much that you say may be true; nevertheless the Church—*our* Church—stands firm among
overwhelming contradictions,—and we, its ministers, do
what we can. I myself am disposed to think that the
multitude of the saved is greater than the multitude of
the lost."

"I envy you the consolation such a thought must give,"
responded the Cardinal, as he resumed his seat opposite
his visitor—" I, on the contrary, have the pained and bitter sense that we are to blame for all this ' multitude of
the lost,' or at any rate that we could have done more in
the way of rescue than we have done." He paused a moment, passing one hand across his forehead wearily. " In

truth this is what has for a long time weighed upon my mind, and depressed my spirits even to the detriment of bodily health. I am nearing the grave, and must soon give an account of my stewardship;—and the knowledge of the increasing growth of evil in the world is almost more than I can bear."

"But you are not to blame," said the Archbishop wonderingly,—"In your own diocese you have fulfilled your duty; more than this is not expected of you. You have done your best for the people you serve,—and reports of your charities and good works are not lacking——"

"Do not credit such reports," interrupted the Cardinal, almost sternly,—"I have done nothing—absolutely nothing! My life has been too peaceful,—too many undeserved blessings have been bestowed upon me. I much fear that the calm and quiet of my days have rendered me selfish. I think I should long ago have sought some means of engaging in more active duties. I feel as if I should have gone into the thick of the religious contest, and spoken and fought, and helped the sick and wounded of the mental battle,—but now—now it is too late!"

"Nothing is too late for one in your position," said the Archbishop—"You may yet sit in St. Peter's chair!"

"God forbid!" ejaculated Bonpré fervently—"I would rather die! I have never wished to rule,—I have only sought to help and to comfort. But sixty-eight years of life weigh heavily on the faculties,—I cannot wear the sword and buckler of energetic manhood. I am old—old!—and to a certain extent, incapacitated for useful labour. Hence I almost grudge my halcyon time spent among simple folk,—time made sweet by all the surroundings of Nature's pastoral loveliness;—the sorrow of the wider world knocks at my heart and makes it ache! I feel that I am one of those who stand by, idly watching the Master's second death without one word of protest!"

The archbishop listened in silence. There was a curious shamed look upon his face, as if some secret sin within himself had suddenly been laid bare in all its vileness to the light of day. The golden crucifix he wore moved restlessly with a certain agitated quickness in his breathing, and he did not raise his eyes, when, after a little pause, he said—

"I tell you, as I told you before, that you think too much; you are altogether too sensitive. I admit that at the present day the world is full of terrible heresies and open blasphemy, but this is part of what we are always bound to expect,—we are told that we must 'suffer for righteousness' sake——'"

"We!" said the Cardinal—"Yes, we! that is, ourselves;—the Church—we think, when we hear of heresies and blasphemies that it is we who are 'suffering for righteousness' sake,' but in our egotism we forget that we are not suffering at all if we are able to retain our faith! It is the very heretics and blasphemers whom we condemn that are suffering—suffering absolute tortures—perchance 'for righteousness' sake'!"

"Dare we call a heretic 'righteous'?" enquired the Archbishop—"Is he not, in his very heresy, accursed?"

"According to our Lord, no one is accursed save traitors,—that is to say those who are not true. If a man doubts, it is better he should admit his doubt than make a pretence of belief. The persons whom we call heretics may have their conception of the truth,—they may say that they cannot accept a creed which is so ignorant of its own tenets as to condemn all those who do not follow it,—inasmuch as the very Founder of it distinctly says—'If any man hear my words and believe not, I judge him not; for I came not to judge the world, but to save the world.' Now we, His followers, judge, but do not save. The atheist is judged by us, but not rescued from his unbelief; the thinker is condemned,—the scientist who reveals the beauty and wisdom of God as made manifest in the composition of the lightning, or the germinating of a flower, is accused of destroying religion. And we continue to pass our opinion, and thunder our vetoes and bans of excommunication against our fellowmen, in the full front of the plain command 'Judge not, that ye be not judged'!"

"I see it is no use arguing with you," said the Archbishop, forcing a smile, with a vexation the smile could not altogether conceal,—"You are determined to take these sayings absolutely,—and to fret your spirit over the non-performance of imaginary duties which do not exist. This Church is a system,—founded on our Lord's teaching, but applied to the needs of modern civilization. It is not humanly possible to literally obey all Christ's commands."

" For the outside world I grant it may be difficult,—but for the ministers of religion, however difficult it may be, it should be done," replied the Cardinal firmly. " I said this before, and I deliberately maintain it. The Church *is* a system,—but whether it is as much founded on the teaching of our Lord, who was divine, as on the teaching of St. Paul, who was *not* divine, is a question to me of much perplexity."

" St. Paul was directly inspired by our Lord," said the Archbishop—" I am amazed that you should even hint a doubt of his apostleship! "

" I do not decry St. Paul," answered Bonpré quietly— " He was a gifted and clever man, but he was a Man— he was not God-in-Man. Christ's doctrine leaves no place for differing sects; St. Paul's method of applying that doctrine serves as authority for the establishment of any and every quarrelsome sect ever known! "

" I cannot agree with you," said the Archbishop coldly.

" I do not expect to be agreed with "—and Bonpré smiled a little—" An opinion which excites no opposition at all is not worth having! I am quite honest in my scruples, such as they are;—I do not think we fit, as you say, the Church system to the needs of modern civiliza- tion. On the contrary, we must fail in many ways to do this, else there would not be such a crying out for help and comfort as there is at present among all Christian peoples. We no longer speak with a grand certainty as we ought to do. We only offer vague hopes and dubious promises to those who thirst for the living waters of sal- vation and immortality,—it is as if we did not feel sure enough of God ourselves to make others sure. All this is wrong—wrong! It forebodes heavy punishment and disaster. If I were younger, I could express perhaps my meaning more clearly,—but as it is, my soul is weighted with unutterable thoughts,—I would almost call them warnings,—of some threatening evil; . . . and to- day—only this afternoon—when I sat for an hour in the Cathedral yonder and listened to the music of the great organ——"

The Archbishop started.

"What did you say?"

The Cardinal repeated his words gently,—

"I said that I sat in the Cathedral and listened to the music of the great organ——"

"The great organ!" interrupted the Archbishop,— "You must have been dreaming! You could not possibly have heard the great organ,—it is old and all out of gear;—it is never used. The only one we have for service just now is a much smaller instrument in the left-hand choir-chapel,—but no person could have played even on that without the key. And the key was unobtainable, as the organist is absent from the town to-day."

The Cardinal looked completely bewildered.

"Are you quite sure of this?" he asked falteringly.

"Sure—absolutely sure!" declared the Archbishop with a smile—"No doubt you thought you heard music; overwrought nerves often play these tricks upon us. And it is owing to this same cause that you are weary and dispirited, and that you take such a gloomy view of the social and religious outlook. You are evidently out of health and unstrung;—but after you have had sufficient rest and change, you will see things in quite a different aspect. I will not for a moment believe that you could possibly be as unorthodox as your conversation would imply,— it would be a total misconception of your true character," and the Archbishop laughed softly. "A total misconception," he repeated,—"Why, yes, of course it would be! No Cardinal-Archbishop of Holy Mother Church could bring such accusations against its ministry as you would have suggested, unless he were afflicted by nervous depression, which, as we all know, has the uncomfortable effect of creating darkness even where all is light. Do you stay long in Rouen?"

"No," replied the Cardinal abstractedly, answering the question mechanically though his thoughts were far away —"I leave for Paris to-morrow."

"For Paris? And then?"

"I go to Rome with my niece, Angela Sovrani,—she is in Paris awaiting my arrival now."

"Ah! You must be very proud of your niece!" murmured the Archbishop softly—"She is famous everywhere,—a great artist!—a wonderful genius!"

"Angela paints well—yes," said the Cardinal quietly,—
"But she has still a great deal to learn. And she is unfortunately much more alone now than she used to be,—
her mother's death last year was a terrible blow to her."

"Her mother was your sister?"

"My only sister," answered the Cardinal—"A good,
sweet woman!—may her soul rest in peace! Her character was never spoilt by the social life she was compelled
to lead. My brother-in-law, Prince Sovrani, kept open
house,—and all the gay world of Rome was accustomed
to flock thither; but now—since he has lost his wife,
things have changed very much,—sadness has taken the
place of mirth,—and Angela is very solitary."

"Is she not affianced to the celebrated Florian
Varillo?"

A fleeting shadow of pain darkened the Cardinal's
clear eyes.

"Yes. But she sees very little of him,—you know the
strictness of Roman etiquette in such matters. She sees
little—and sometimes—so I think—knows less. However, I hope all will be well. But my niece is over sensitive, brilliantly endowed, and ambitious,—at times I have
fears for her future."

"Depression again!" declared the Archbishop, rising
and preparing to take his leave—"Believe me, the world
is full of excellence when we look upon it with clear
eyes;—things are never as bad as they seem. To my
thinking, you are the last man alive who should indulge in
melancholy forebodings. You have led a peaceful and
happy life, graced with the reputation of many good
deeds, and you are generally beloved by the people of
whom you have charge. Then, though celibacy is your
appointed lot, heaven has given you a niece as dear to
you as any child of your own could be, who has won a
pre-eminent place among the world's great artists, and is
moreover endowed with beauty and distinction. What
more can you desire?"

He smiled expansively as he spoke; the Cardinal looked
at him steadfastly.

"I desire nothing!" he answered—"I never have desired anything! I told you before that I consider I have
received many more blessings than I deserve. It is not
any personal grief which at present troubles me,—it is

something beyond myself. It is a sense of wrong,—an appeal for truth,—a cry from those who are lost in the world,—the lost whom the Church might have saved!"

"Merely fancy!" said the Archbishop cheerily—"Like the music in the Cathedral! Do not permit your imagination to get the better of you in such matters! When you return from Rome, I shall be glad to see you if you happen to come through Normandy on your way back to your own people. I trust you will so far honour me?"

"I know nothing of my future movements," answered the Cardinal gently,—"But if I should again visit Rouen, I will certainly let you know, and will, if you desire it, accept your friendly hospitality."

With this, the two dignitaries shook hands and the Archbishop took his leave. As he picked his way carefully down the rough stairs and along the dingy little passage of the Hotel Poitiers, he was met by Jean Patoux holding a lighted candle above his head to show him the way.

"It is dark, Monseigneur," said Patoux apologetically.

"It is very dark," agreed Monseigneur, stumbling as he spoke, and feeling rather inclined to indulge in very uncanonical language. "It is altogether a miserable hole, mon Patoux!"

"It is for poor people only," returned Jean calmly—"And poverty is not a crime, Monseigneur."

"No, it is not a crime," said the stately Churchman as he reached the door at last, and paused for a moment on the threshold,—a broad smile wrinkling up his fat cheeks and making comfortable creases round his small eyes—"But it is an inconvenience!"

"Cardinal Bonpré does not say so," observed Patoux.

"Cardinal Bonpré is one of two things—a saint or a fool! Remember that, mon Patoux! *Bon soir! Benedicite!*"

And the Archbishop, still smiling to himself, walked leisurely across the square in the direction of his own house, where his supper awaited him. The moon had risen, and was clambering slowly up between the two tall towers of Notre Dame, her pure silver radiance streaming mockingly against the candle Jean Patoux still held in the doorway of his inn, and almost extinguishing its flame.

"One of two things—a saint or a fool," murmured Jean with a chuckle—"Well!—it is very certain that the Archbishop is neither!"

He turned in, and shut his door as far as it would allow him to do so, and went comfortably to bed, where Madame had gone before him. And throughout the Hotel Poitiers deep peace and silence reigned. Every one in the house slept, save Cardinal Bonpré, who with the Testament before him, sat reading and meditating deeply for an hour before retiring to rest. A fresh cause of anxiety had come upon him in the idea that perhaps his slight indisposition was more serious than he had deemed. If, as the Archbishop had said, there could have been no music possible in the Cathedral that afternoon, how came it that he had heard such solemn and entrancing harmonies? Was his mind affected? Was he in truth imagining what did not exist? Were the griefs of the world his own distorted view of things? Did the Church faithfully follow the beautiful and perfect teachings of Christ after all? He tried to reason the question out from a different and more hopeful standpoint, but vainly;—the conviction that Christianity was by no means the supreme regenerating force, or the vivifying Principle of Human Life which it was originally meant to be, was borne in upon him with increasing certainty, and the more he read the Gospels, the more he became aware that the Church-system as it existed was utterly opposed to Christ's own command, and moreover was drifting further and further away from Him with every passing year.

"The music in the Cathedral may have been my fancy," he said,—"But the discord in the world sounds clear and is *not* imagination. A casuist in religion may say 'It was to be';—that heresies and dissensions were prophesied by Christ, when He said 'Because iniquity shall abound, the love of many shall grow cold';—but this does not excuse the Church from the sin of neglect, if any neglects exists. One thing we have never seemed to thoroughly understand, and this is that Christ's teaching is God's teaching, and that it has not stopped with the enunciation of the Gospel. It is going on even now

—in every fresh discovery of science,—in every new national experience,—in everything we can do, or think, or plan, the Divine instruction steadily continues through the Divine influence imparted to us when the Godhead became man, to show men how they might in turn become gods. This is what we forget and what we are always forgetting; so that instead of accepting every truth, we quarrel with it and reject it, even as Judæa rejected Christ Himself. It is very strange and cruel;—and the world's religious perplexities are neither to be wondered at nor blamed,—there is just and grave cause for their continuance and increase."

He closed the Testament, and being thoroughly fatigued in body as well as mind, he at last retired. Lying down contentedly upon the hard and narrow bed which was the best the inn provided, he murmured his usual prayer,— " If this should be the sleep of death, Jesus receive my soul!"—and remained for a little while with his eyes open, looking at the white glory of the moonlight as it poured through his lattice window and formed delicate traceries of silver luminance on the bare wooden floor. He could just see the dark towers of Notre Dame from where he lay,—a black mass in the moonbeams—a monument of half-forgotten history—a dream of centuries, hallowed or blasphemed by the prayers and aspirations of dead and gone multitudes who had appealed to the incarnate God-in-Man before its altars. God-in-Man had been made manifest!—how long would the world have to wait before Man-in-God was equally created and declared? For that was evidently intended to be the final triumph of the Christian creed.

" We should have gained such a victory long ago," mused Cardinal Bonpré—" only that we ourselves have set up stumbling-blocks, and rejected God at every step of the way."

Closing his eyes he soon slept; the rays of the moon fell upon his pale face and silvery hair like a visible radiant benediction,—and the bells of the city chimed the hours loudly and softly, clanging in every direction, without waking him from his rest. But slumbering as he was, he had no peace,—for in his sleep he was troubled by a strange vision.

IV.

As the terrors of imagined suffering are always worse
than actual pain, so dreams are frequently more vivid
than the reality of life,—that is we are sure that life is
indeed reality, and not itself a dream within a dream.
Cardinal Bonpré's sleep was not often disturbed by af-
frighting visions,—his methods of daily living were too
healthy and simple, and his conscience too clear;—but
on this particular night he was visited by an impression
rather than a dream,—the impression of a lonely, and
terrifying dreariness, as though the whole world were
suddenly emptied of life and left like a hollow shell on
the shores of time. Gradually this first sense of utter
and unspeakable loss changed into a startled consciousness of fear;—some awful transformation of things familiar was about to be consummated;—and he felt the
distinct approach of some unnameable Horror which was
about to convulse and overwhelm all mankind. Then in
his dream, a great mist rose up before his eyes,—a mingling as of sea-fog and sun-flame,—and as this in turn
slowly cleared,—dispersing itself in serpentine coils of
golden-grey vapour,—he found himself standing on the
edge of a vast sea, glittering in a light that was neither
of earth nor of heaven, but that seemed to be the inward
reflection of millions of flashing sword blades. And as
he stood gazing across the width of the waters, the sky
above him grew black, and a huge ring of fire rose out
of the east, instead of the beloved and familiar sun,—
fire that spread itself in belching torrents of flame upward and downward, and began to absorb in its devouring heat the very sea. Then came a sound of many
thunders, mingled with the roar of rising waters and
the turbulence of a great whirlwind,—and out of the
whirlwind came a Voice saying—"Now is the end of all
things on the earth,—and the whole world shall be burnt
up as a dead leaf in a sudden flame! And we will create
from out its ashes new heavens and a new earth, and we

49

will call forth new beings wherewith to people the fairness of our fresh creation,—for the present generation of mankind hath rejected God,—and God henceforth rejecteth His faithless and unworthy creatures! Wherefore let now this one dim light amid the thousand million brighter lights be quenched,—let the planet known to all angels as the Sorrowful Star fall from its sphere forever, —let the Sun that hath given it warmth and nourishment be now its chief Destroyer, and let everything that hath life within it, perish utterly and revive no more!"

And Cardinal Felix heard these words of doom. Powerless to move or speak, he stood watching the terrible circle of fire, extend and expand, till all the visible universe seemed melting in one red furnace of flame;—and in himself he felt no hope,—no chance of rescue;—in himself he knew that the appalling work of destruction was being accomplished with a deadly swiftness that left no time for lamentation,—that the nations of the world were as flying straws swept into the burning, without space or moment for a parting prayer or groan. Tortured by an excruciating agony too great for tears, he suddenly found voice, and lifting his face towards the lurid sky he cried aloud—

"God of Eternity, stay Thy hand! For one remaining Cause be merciful! Doom not Thy creature Man to utter destruction!—but still remember that Thou wast born even as he! As helpless, as wronged, as tempted, as betrayed, as suffering, as prone to pain and death! Thou hast lived his life and endured his sorrows, though in the perfect glory of Thy Godhead Thou hast not sinned! Have patience yet, oh Thou great Splendour of all worlds! Have patience yet, Thou outraged and blasphemed Creator! Break once again Thy silence as of old and speak to us!—pity us once again ere Thou slay us utterly, —come to us even as Thou camest in Judæa, and surely we will receive Thee and obey Thee, and reject Thy love no more!"

As he thus prayed he was seized with a paralysing fear, —for suddenly the red and glowing chaos of fire above him changed into soft skies tinged with the exquisite pearl-grey hues of twilight, and he became conscious of the approach of a great invisible Presence, whose awful unseen beauty overwhelmed him with its sublimity and

majesty, causing him to forget altogether that he himself existed. And Someone spoke,—in grave sweet accents, so soft and close to him that the words seemed
almost whispered in his ears,—

"Thy prayer is heard,—and once again the silence
shall be broken. Nevertheless remember that 'the light
shineth in darkness and the darkness comprehendeth it
not'."

Deep silence followed. The mysterious Presence
melted as it were into space,—and the Cardinal awoke,
trembling violently and bathed in a cold perspiration. He
gazed bewilderedly around him, his mind still confused
and dazzled by the strong visionary impression of the
burning heavens and sea,—and he could not for a moment realize where he was. Then, after a while, he recognised the humble furniture of the room he occupied,
and through the diamond-shaped panes of the little lattice
window, perceived the towers of Notre Dame, now
gleaming with a kind of rusty silver in the broader radiance of the fully uplifted moon.

"It was a dream," he murmured,—"A dream of the
end of the world!" He shuddered a little as he thought
of the doom pronounced upon the earth,—the planet
"known to all angels as the Sorrowful Star"—"Let the
Sun that hath given it warmth and nourishment be now
its chief Destroyer."

According to modern scientists, such was indeed the
precise way in which the world was destined to come to
an end. And could anything be more terrifying than
the thought that the glorious Orb, the maker of day and
generator of all beauty, should be destined to hurl from
its shining centre death and destruction upon the planet
it had from creation vivified and warmed! The Vision
had shown the devastating ring of fire rising from that
very quarter of the heavens where the sun should have
been radiantly beaming,—and as Felix Bonpré dwelt upon
the picture in his mind, and remembered his own wild
prayer to the Eternal, a great uneasiness and dread overwhelmed him.

"God's laws can never be altered;" he said aloud—
"Every evil deed brings its own punishment; and if the
world's wickedness becomes too great an offence in the
eyes of the Almighty, it follows that the world must be

destroyed. What am I that I should pray against Divine Justice! For truly we have had our chance of rescue and salvation;—the Way,—the Truth,—and the Life have been given to us through Christ our Redeemer; and if we reject Him, we reject all, and we have but ourselves to blame."

At that moment a plaintive wailing, as of some human creature in distress broke on his ears through the deep silence of the night. He listened attentively, and the sorrowful sound was repeated,—a desolate yet gentle cry as of some sick and suffering child. Moved by a sudden impulse the Cardinal rose, and going to the window looked anxiously out, and down into the street below. Not a living creature was to be seen. The moonlight spread itself in a vast silver glory over the whole width of the square, and the delicate sculpture of the great rose-window of the Cathedral, centrally suspended between the two tall towers, looked in the fine pale radiance like a giant spider's web sparkling with fairy dew. Again —again!—that weary sobbing cry! It went to the Cardinal's heart, and stirred him to singular pain and pity. " Surely it is some lost or starving creature," he said— " Some poor soul seeking comfort in a comfortless world."

Hastily throwing on his garments he left his room, treading cautiously in order not to disturb the sleeping household,—and feeling his way down the short, dark staircase, he easily reached the door and passed noiselessly out into the square. Walking a few steps hurriedly he paused, once more listening. The night was intensely calm;—not a cloud crossed the star-spangled violet dome of air wherein the moon soared serenely, bathing all visible things in a crystalline brilliancy so pure and penetrative, that the finest cuttings on the gigantic grey façade of Notre Dame could be discerned and outlined as distinctly as though every little portion were seen through a magnifying glass. The Cardinal's tall attenuated figure, standing alone and almost in the centre of the square, cast a long thin black shadow on the glistening grey stones,—and his dream-impression of an empty world came back forcibly upon him,—a world as empty as a hollow shell! Houses there were around him, and streets, and a noble edifice consecrated to the worship of God,—nevertheless there was a sense of absolute deser-

tion in and through all. Was not the Cathedral itself
the mere husk of a religion? The seed had dropped out
and sunk into the soil,—" among thorns " and " stony
places " indeed,—and some " by the wayside " to be devoured by birds of prey. Darker and heavier grew the
cloud of depression on the Cardinal's soul,—and more
and more passionate became the protest which had for a
long time been clamouring in him for utterance,—the
protest of a Churchman against the Church he served!
It was terrible,—and to a " prince of the Roman Church "
hideous and unnatural; nevertheless the protest existed,
and it had in some unaccountable way grown to be more
a part of him than he himself realized.

"The world is empty because God is leaving it," he
said, sorrowfully raising his eyes to the tranquil heavens,
—" and the joy of existence is departing because the Divine and Holy Spirit of things is being withdrawn! "

He moved on a few paces,—and once more through
the deep stillness the little sobbing cry of sorrow was
wafted tremulously to his ears. It came or seemed to
come from the Cathedral, and quickening his steps he
went thither. The deeply hollowed portal, full of black
shadows, at first showed nothing but its own massively
sculptured outlines——then——all at once the Cardinal
perceived standing within the embrasured darkness,
the slight shrinking figure of a child. A boy's desolate
little figure,—with uplifted hands clasped appealingly and
laid against the shut Cathedral door, and face hidden and
pressed hard upon those hands, as though in mute and inconsolable despair. As the Cardinal softly drew nearer,
a long shuddering sigh from the solitary little creature
moved his heart anew to pity, and speaking in accents
of the utmost gentleness he said—

"My poor child, what troubles you? Why are you
here all alone, and weeping at this late hour? Have you
no home?—no parents? "

Slowly the boy turned round, still resting his small
delicate hands against the oaken door of the Cathedral,
and with the tears yet wet upon his cheeks, smiled. What
a sad face he had!—worn and weary, yet beautiful!—what
eyes, heavy with the dews of sorrow, yet tender even in
pain! Startled by the mingled purity and grief of so
young a countenance, the Cardinal retreated for a mo-

ment in amaze,—then approaching more closely he repeated his former question with increased interest and tenderness—

"Why are you weeping here alone?"

"Because I am left alone to weep," said the boy, answering in a soft voice of vibrating and musical melancholy—"For me, the world is empty."

An empty world! His dream-impression of universal desolation and desertion came suddenly back upon the prelate's mind, and a sudden trembling seized him, though he could discover in himself no cause for fear. Anxiously he surveyed the strange and solitary little wayfarer on the threshold of the Cathedral, and while he thus looked, the boy said wistfully—

"I should have rested here within, but it is closed against me."

"The doors are always locked at night, my child," returned the Cardinal, recovering from his momentary stupor and bewilderment, "But I can give you shelter. Will you come with me?"

With a half-questioning, half-smiling look of grateful wonder, the boy withdrew his hands from their uplifted, supplicating and almost protesting attitude against the locked Cathedral-door, and moving out of the porch shadows into the wide glory of the moonlight, he confronted his interlocutor—

"Will I come with you?" he said—"Nay, but I see you are a Cardinal of the Church, and it is I should ask 'will you receive me?' You do not know who I am—nor where I came from, and I, alas! may not tell you! I am alone; all—all alone,—for no one knows me in the world, —I am quite poor and friendless, and have nothing wherewith to pay you for your kindly shelter——I can only bless you!"

Very simply, very gravely the young boy spoke these words, his delicate head uplifted, his face shining in the moon-rays, and his slight, childish form erect with a grace which was not born of pride so much as of endurance, and again the Cardinal trembled, though he knew not why. Yet in his very agitation, the desire he had to persuade the tired child to go with him grew stronger and overmastered every other feeling.

"Come then," he said, smiling and extending his hand,

" Come, and you shall sleep in my room for the remainder
of the night, and to-morrow we will talk of the future.
At present you need repose."

The boy smiled gratefully but said nothing, and the
Cardinal, satisfied with the mere look of assent walked
with his foundling across the square and into the Hotel
Poitiers. Arrived at his own bed-room, he smoothed his
couch and settled the pillows carefully with active zeal
and tenderness. The boy stood silently, looking on.

" Sleep now, my child," said the Cardinal,—" and forget all your troubles. Lie down here; no one will disturb you till the morning."

" But you, my lord Cardinal," said the boy—" Are you
depriving yourself of comfort in order to give it to me?
This is not the way of the world!"

" It is *my* way," said the Cardinal cheerfully,—" And
if the world has been unkind to you, my boy, still take
courage,—it will not always be unjust! Do not trouble
yourself concerning me; I shall sleep well on the sofa
in the next room—indeed, I shall sleep all the better for
knowing that your tears have ceased, and that for the
present at least you are safely sheltered."

With a sudden quick movement the boy advanced and
caught the Cardinal's hands caressingly in his own.

" Oh, are you sure you understand? " he said, his voice
growing singularly sweet and almost tender as he spoke
—" Are you sure that it is well for you to shelter me?—
I—a stranger,—poor, and with no one to speak for me?
How do you know what I may be? Shall I not perhaps
prove ungrateful and wrong your kindness? "

His worn little face upturned, shone in the dingy little
room with a sudden brightness such as one might imagine
would illumine the features of an angel, and Felix Bonpré looked down upon him half fascinated, in mingled
pity and wonder.

" Such results are with God, my child," he said gently
—" I do not seek your gratitude. It is certainly well for
me that I should shelter you,—it would be ill indeed if
I permitted any living creature to suffer for lack of what
I could give. Rest here in peace, and remember it is for
my own pleasure as well as for your good that I desire
you to sleep well."

" And you do not even ask my name? " said the boy,

half smiling and still raising his sorrowful deep blue eyes to the Cardinal's face.

" You will tell me that when you please," said Felix, laying one hand upon the soft curls that clustered over his foundling's forehead—" I am in no wise curious. It is enough for me to know that you are a child and alone in the world,—such sorrow makes me your servant."

Gently the boy loosened his clasp of the Cardinal's hands.

" Then I have found a friend!" he said,—" That is very strange!" He paused, and the smile that had once before brightened his countenance shone again like a veritable flash of sunlight—" You have the right to know my name, and if you choose, to call me by it,—it is Manuel."

" Manuel!" echoed the Cardinal—" No more than that?"

" No more than that," replied the boy gravely—" I am one of the world's waifs and strays,—one name suffices me."

There followed a brief pause, in which the old man and the child looked at each other full and steadfastly, and once again an inexplicable nervous trembling seized the Cardinal. Overcoming this with an effort, he said softly,—

" Then—Manuel!—good night! Sleep—and Our Lady's blessing be upon you!"

Signing the cross in air he retired, carefully shutting the door and leaving his new-found charge to rest. When he was once by himself in the next room, however, he made no attempt to sleep,—he merely drew a chair to the window and sat down, full of thoughts which utterly absorbed him. There was nothing unusual, surely, in his finding a small lost boy and giving him a night's lodging? —then why was he so affected by it? He could not tell. He fully realized that the plaintive beauty of the child had its share in the powerful attraction he felt,—but there was something else in the nature of his emotion which he found it impossible to define. It was as though some great blankness in his life had been suddenly filled;—as if the boy whom he had found solitary and weeping within the porch of the Cathedral of Notre Dame, belonged to him in some mysterious way and was linked to his life

so closely and completely as to make parting impossible.
But what a fantastic notion! Viewed by the light of
calm reason, there was nothing in the occurrence to give
rise to any such sentiment. Here was a poor little wayfarer, evidently without parents, home, or friends,—and
the Cardinal had given him a night's lodging, and to-
morrow——yes, to-morrow, he would give him food and
warm clothing and money,—and perhaps a recommendation to the Archbishop in order that he might get a
chance of free education and employment in Rouen, while
proper enquiries were being made about him. That was
the soberly prosaic and commonplace view to take of the
matter. The personality of the little fellow was intensely winning,—but after all, that had nothing to do
with the facts of the case. He was a waif and stray, as he
himself had said; his name, so far as he seemed to know
it, was Manuel,—an ordinary name enough in France,—
and his age might be about twelve,—not more. Something could be done for him,—something *should* be done
for him before the Cardinal parted with him. But this
idea of " parting " was just what seemed so difficult to
contemplate! Puzzled beyond measure at the strange
state of mind in which he found himself, Felix Bonpré
went over and over again all the events of the day in
order,—his arrival in Rouen,—his visit to the Cathedral,
and the grand music he had heard or fancied he heard
there,—his experience with the sceptical little Patoux
children and their mother,—his conversation with the
Archbishop, in which he had felt much more excitement
than he was willing to admit,—his dream wherein he had
been so painfully impressed with a sense of the desertion, emptiness, and end of the world, and finally his discovery of the little lonely and apparently forsaken boy,
thrown despairingly as it were against the closed Cathedral, like a frail human wreck cast up from the gulf of
the devouring sea. Each incident, trivial in itself, yet
seemed of particular importance, though he could not
explain or analyse why it should be so. Meditatively he
sat and watched the moon sink like a silver bubble falling
downward in the dark,—the stars vanished one by one,
—and a faint brown-gold line of suggestive light in the
east began the slow creation of a yet invisible dawn.
Presently, yielding to a vague impulse of inexplicable

tenderness, he rose softly and went to the threshold of the room where his foundling slept. Holding his breath, he listened—but there was no sound. Very cautiously and noiselessly he opened the door, and looked in,—a delicate half-light came through the latticed window and seemed to concentrate itself on the bed where the tired wanderer lay. His fine youthful profile was distinctly outlined,—the soft bright hair clustered like a halo round his broad brows,—and the two small hands were crossed upon his breast, while in his sleep he smiled. Always touched by the beauty, innocence and helplessness of childhood, something in the aspect of this little lad moved the venerable prelate's heart to an unwonted emotion,— and looking upon him, he prayed for guidance as to what he should best do to rescue so gentle and young a creature from the cruelties of the world.

" He has trusted me," said the Cardinal,—" I have found him, and I cannot—dare not—forsake him. For the Master says ' Whosoever shall receive one such little child in My name receiveth Me'."

V.

THE next morning broke fair and calm, and as soon as the Patoux household were astir, Cardinal Bonpré sought Madame Patoux in her kitchen, and related to her the story of his night's adventure. She listened deferentially, but could not refrain from occasional exclamations of surprise, mingled with suggestions of warning.

"It is like your good heart, Monseigneur," she said, "to give your own bed to a stray child out of the street,—one, too, of whom you know nothing,—but alas! how often such goodness is repaid by ingratitude! The more charity you show the less thanks you receive,—yes, indeed, it is often so!—and it seems as if the Evil One were in it! For look you, I myself have never done a kindness yet without getting a cruelty in exchange for it."

"That is a sad experience, my daughter," returned the Cardinal smiling,—"Nevertheless, it is our duty to go on doing kindnesses, no matter what the results to ourselves may be. It is understood—is it not? that we are to be misjudged in this world. If we had nothing to suffer, what would be the use of exercising such virtues as patience and endurance?"

"Ah, Monseigneur, for you it is different," said Madame Patoux shaking her head and sighing—"You are like the blessed saints—safe in a niche of Holy Church, with Our Lady for ever looking after you. But for poor people such as we are—we see the rough side of life, Monseigneur—and we know that there is very little goodness about in the world,—and as for patience and endurance!—why, no one in these days has the patience to endure even the least contradiction! Two men,—aye even brothers,—will fight for a word like mongrels quarrelling over a bone;—and two women will scream themselves hoarse if one should have a lover more than the other—asking your pardon, Monseigneur, for such wicked talk! Still, wicked as it may be, it is true—and not all the powers of Heaven seem to care about making things better. And for this boy,—believe me,—you had better leave him to his own way—for there will be no chance of getting such a poor little waif into the school unless his father and mother are known, or unless someone will adopt him, which is not likely . . . for Rouen is full of misery, and there are enough mouths to feed in most families——and . . . mon Dieu!—is that the child?"

Thus abruptly she broke off her speech, utterly taken aback as she suddenly perceived the little Manuel standing before her. Poorly clad in the roughest garments as he was, his grace and plaintive beauty moved her heart to quick compassion for his loneliness as he came towards the Cardinal, who, extending one hand, drew him gently to his side and asked if he had slept well?

"Thanks to your goodness, my lord Cardinal," the boy replied, "I slept so well that I thought I was in Heaven! I heard the angels singing in my dreams;—yes!—I heard all the music of a happy world, in which there never had been known a sin or sorrow!"

He rested his fair head lightly against the Cardinal's arm and smiled. Madame Patoux gazed at him in fascinated silence,—gazed and gazed,—till she found her eyes suddenly full of tears. Then she turned away to hide them,—but not before Cardinal Bonpré had observed her emotion.

"Well, good *mother*" he said with gentle emphasis on the word—"Would you have me forsake this child that I have found?"

"No, Monseigneur,—no," said Madame Patoux very softly and tremulously—"It is almost as if he were a little lost Angel sent to comfort you."

A curious thrill went through the Cardinal. An angel to comfort him! He looked down at Manuel who still clung caressingly to his arm, and who met his earnest scrutiny with a sweet candid smile.

"Where did you come from, Manuel?" asked Bonpré suddenly.

"I cannot tell you," the boy answered, straightly, yet simply.

The Cardinal paused a moment, his keen penetrating eyes dwelling kindly on the noble young face beside him.

"You do not wish to tell me,—is that so?" he pursued.

"Yes," said Manuel quietly—"I do not wish to tell

you. And if, because of this, you regret your kindness to me, my lord Cardinal, I will go away at once and trouble you no more."

But at these words the Cardinal felt such a sharp consciousness of pain and loss that his nerves ached with positive fear.

"Nay, nay, my child," he said anxiously—"I cannot let you go. It shall be as you please,—I will not think that you could do yourself or me a wrong by concealing what would be right for you to tell. It is true that you are alone in the world?"

"Quite, quite alone!" answered Manuel, a faint shadow darkening the serenity of his eyes—"No one was ever more alone than I!"

Madame Patoux drew nearer and listened.

"And there is no person living who has the right to claim you?"

"None!"

"And is it not strange, Monseigneur," murmured Madame Patoux at this juncture—"The little lad does not speak as if he were ignorant! It is as though he had been well taught and carefully nurtured."

Manuel's deep eyes dwelt upon her with a meditative sweetness.

"I have taught myself;" he said simply—"Not out of books, perhaps, but out of nature. The trees and rivers, the flowers and birds have talked to me and explained many things;—I have learned all I know from what God has told me."

His voice was so gentle and tender that Madame Patoux was infinitely touched by its soft plaintiveness.

"Poor child!" she murmured,—"He has no doubt been wandering through the country, without a soul to help him. Alas, that troubles should begin for one so young! Perhaps he does not even know a prayer!"

"Oh yes!" said Manuel quickly—"Prayer is like thought,—God is so good that it is only natural to thank and praise Him. Is it not so?"

"It should be natural, my boy," answered the Cardinal slowly and with a slight accent of melancholy,—"But for many of us in these days I fear it is more natural still to forget than to remember. Too often we take gifts and ignore the giver. But come now and breakfast in my room;—for the present you shall remain with me, and I will see what can best be done for your future welfare."

And turning to Madame Patoux he added smilingly—" You, my daughter, with children of your own to care for, will no longer blame me for my interest in this child, who is without protection in a somewhat rough world. We of the Church dare not ' offend one of these little ones'."

" Ah, Monseigneur ! " murmured Madame,—" If all in the Church were like you, some poor folks would believe in God more willingly. But when people are starving and miserable, it is easy to understand that often they will curse the priests and even religion itself, for making such a mock of them as to keep on telling them about the joys of heaven, when they are tormented to the very day of their death on earth, and are left without hope or rescue of any kind——"

But the Cardinal had disappeared with his young charge and Madame's speech was lost upon him. She had therefore to content herself with relating the story of " Monseigneur's foundling " to her husband, who just then came into the kitchen to take his breakfast before starting off to work in his market-garden. He listened with interest and attention.

" A boy is always a trouble," he said sententiously— " And it is likely that so Monseigneur will find it. How old would the child be ? "

" About twelve, I should say," answered Madame— " But beautiful as a little angel, Jean ! "

" That's a pity ! " and Patoux shook his head ominously —" 'Tis bad enough when a girl is beautiful,—but a boy ! ——Well, well ! Monseigneur is a wise man, and a saint they say,—he knows best,—but I fear he has taken a burden upon himself which he will very soon regret ! What dost thou think of it, *petite?* "

Madame hesitated a moment before replying.

" Truly, I do not know what to think," she answered —" For myself, I have not spoken to the child. I have seen him,—yes !—and at the sight of him a something in my throat rose up and choked me as it were,—and stopped me from saying a rough word. Such a lonely gentle lad !—one could not be harsh with him, and yet——"

"Yet! Oh, yes, I know!" said Patoux, finishing his coffee at a gulp and smiling,—"Women will always be women,—and a handsome face in girl or boy is enough to make fools of them all. Where are the children? Are they gone to school?"

"Yes—they went before the Cardinal was up. 'Tis a Saturday, and they will be back early,—they are going to bring little Fabien Doucet to Monseigneur."

"What for?" enquired Patoux, his round eyes opening widely in amazement.

"Oh, for a strange fancy! That he may bless the child and pray Our Lady to cure him of his lameness. It was Babette's whim. I told her the Cardinal was a saint, —and she said,—well! she said she would never believe it unless he worked a miracle! The wicked mischief that girl is!—as bad as Henri, who puts a doubt on everything!"

"'Tis the school," said Jean gloomily—"I must speak to Père Laurent."

"Truly that would be well," said Madame—"He may explain what we cannot. All the same, you may be sure the children *will* bring Fabien Doucet to Monseigneur; —they have made up their minds about it,—and if the little miserable's lameness gets no better, we shall have work enough in future to make the saints respected!"

Patoux muttered something inaudible, and went his way. Life was in his opinion, a very excellent thing,— nevertheless there were a few details about it which occasionally troubled him, and one of these details was decidedly the "national education" question. It struck him as altogether remarkable that the State should force him to send his children to school whether he liked it or no; and moreover that the system of instruction at the said school should be totally opposed to his own ideas. He would have certainly wished his son to learn to read and write, and then to have been trained as a thorough florist and gardener;—while for his daughter he also desired reading and writing as a matter of course, and then a complete education in cooking and domestic economy, so that she might be a useful and efficient wife and mother when the proper time for such duties came. Astronomy he felt they could both do without, and most of the "physical sciences." Religion he considered an absolute necessity, and this was the very thing that was totally omitted from the national course of education. He was well aware that there are countless numbers of unhappy people nowadays who despise religion and mock at the very idea of a God. Every day he saw certain works exposed for sale on the out-of-door bookstalls which in their very titles proclaimed the hideous tone of blasphemy which in France is gradually becoming universal,—but this did not affect his own sense of what was right and just. He was a very plain common man, but he held holy things in reverence, and instinctively felt that, if the world were in truth a bad place, it was likely to become much worse if all faith in God were taken out of it. And when he reached his plot of ground that morning, and set to work as usual, he was, for a non-reflective man, very much absorbed in thought. His heavy tramping feet over the soil startled some little brown birds from their hidden nests, and sent them flying to and fro through the clear air uttering sharp chirrups of terror,—and, leaning on his spade, he paused and looked at them meditatively.

"Everything is afraid," he said,—" Birds, beasts, and men,—all are afraid of something and cannot tell what it is that frightens them. It seems hard sometimes that there should be so much trouble and struggle just to live —however, the good God knows best,—and if we could not think and hope and believe He knew best, we might just as well light up a charcoal fire, shut all the doors and windows, and say ' Bon jour! Bon jour, Monsieur le bon Dieu!—for if *you* do not know *your* business, it is evident we do not know ours, and therefore 'tis best for both our sakes to make an end of sheer Stupidity!'"

He chuckled at his own reasoning, and moistening his hands vigorously, seized his spade and began to bank up a ridge of celery, singing " Bon jour, Monsieur le bon Dieu!" under his breath without the slightest idea of irreverence. And looking up at the bright sky occasionally, he wished he had seen the stray boy rescued from the streets by Cardinal Bonpré.

"That he will be a trouble, there is no doubt," he said as he turned and patted the rich dark earth—" Never was there a boy born yet into the world that was not a

trouble except our Lord, and even in His case His own
people did not know what to make of Him!"

Meantime, while Jean Patoux dug in his garden, and
sang and soliloquized, his two children, Henri and Babette, their school hours being ended, had run off to the
market, and were talking vivaciously with a big brown
sturdy woman, who was selling poultry at a stall, under
a very large patched red umbrella. She was Martine
Doucet, reported to have the worst temper and most vix-
enish tongue in all the town, though there were some who
said her sourness of humour only arose from the hardships of her life, and the many troubles she had been
fated to endure. Her husband, a fine handsome man,
earning good weekly wages as a stone-mason, had been
killed by a fall from a ladder, while engaged in helping
to build one of the new houses on the Boulevards, and
her only child Fabien, a boy of ten had, when a baby,
tumbled from the cart in which his mother was taking her
poultry to market, and though no injury was apparent at
the time, had, from the effects of the fall, grown into a
poor little twisted mite of humanity with a bent spine,
and one useless leg which hung limply from his body,
while he could scarcely hobble about on the other, even
with the aid of a crutch. He had a soft, pretty, plaintive
face of his own, the little Fabien, and very gentle ways,
—but he was sensitively conscious of his misfortune, and
in his own small secret soul he was always praying that
he might die while he was yet a child, and not grow up
to be a burden to his mother. Martine, however, adored
him; and it was through her intense love for this child of
hers that she had, in a strange vengeful sort of mood
abandoned God, and flung an open and atheistical defiance in the face of her confessor, who, missing her at
mass, had ventured to call upon her and seriously reproach
her for neglecting the duties of her religion. Martine
had whirled round upon him,—a veritable storm in pet-
ticoats.

"Religion!" she cried—"Oh—hè! What good has it
done for *me,* if you please! When I said my prayers night
and morning, went to mass and confession, and told my
rosary every Mary-Feast, what happened? Was not my
man killed and my child crippled? And then,—(not to
lose faith—) did I not give the saints every chance of

behaving themselves? For my child's sake did I not earn good money and pay it to the Church in special masses that he might be cured of his lameness? And Novenas in plenty, and candles in plenty to the Virgin, and fastings of my own and penitences? And is the child not as lame as ever? Look at him!—the dear angel!—with never an evil thought or a wicked way,—and will you try to make me believe there is a good God, when He will not help a poor little creature like that, to be happy, though He is prayed to night and morning for it! No— no! Churches are kept up for priests to make a fat living out of,—but there is never a God in them that I can see; —and as for the Christ, who had only to be asked in order to heal the sick, there is not so much as a ghost of Him anywhere! If what you priests tell us were true, poor souls such as I am, would get comfort and help in our sorrows, but it is all a lie!—the whole thing!—and when we are in trouble, we have got to bear it as best we can, without so much as a kind word from our neighbours, let alone any pity from the saints. Go to mass again? Not I!—nor to confession either!—and no more of my earnings will click into your great brass collection plate, *mon révérend!* Ah no!—I have been a foolish woman indeed, to trust so long in a God who for all my tears and prayers never gives me a sign or a hope of an answer,— and though I suppose this wretched world of ours was made by somebody, whoever it is that has done it is a cruel creature at best, so *I* say,—without as much good feeling as there is in the heart of an ordinary man, and without the sense of the man either! For who that thinks twice about it would make a world where everything is only born to die?—and for no other use at all! Bah! It is sheer folly and wickedness to talk to me of a God!—a God, if there were one, would surely be far above torturing the creatures He has made, all for nothing!"

And the priest who heard this blasphemous and savage tirade on the part of Martine Doucet, retreated from her in amazement and horror, and presently gave out that she was possessed of a devil, and was unfit to be admitted to the Holy Sacrament. Whereat, when she heard of it, Martine laughed loudly and ferociously.

"Look you!—what a charitable creature a priest is!" she cried—" If you don't do the things he considers ex-

actly right and fitting, he tells your neighbours that the
devil has got you!—and so little does he care to pick you
out of the clutches of this same devil, that he refuses you
the Sacrament, though *that* is said to drive away Satan
by the mere touch of it! But wait till I *ask* to have the
Sacrament given to me!—it will be time enough then to
refuse it! Many a fat chicken of my stock has the reverend father had as a free gift to boil in his soup *maigre!*"
and again she laughed angrily—" But no more of them
does he get to comfort his stomach while doing penance
for his soul!—the hypocrite! He must find another silly
woman to cheat with his stories of a good God who never
does anything but kill and curse us every one!—he has
had all that he will ever get out of Martine Doucet!"

It was to this redoubtable virago that Henri and Babette had betaken themselves in the market place directly
school was over. She always held the same stall in the
same position on market days,—and she sat under her
red umbrella on a rough wooden bench, knitting rapidly,
now keeping an eye on her little lame son, coiled up in a
piece of matting beside her, and anon surveying her
stock-in-trade of ducks and geese and fowls, which were
heaped on her counter, their wrung necks drooping limply
from the board, and their yellow feet tied helplessly together and shining like bits of dull gold in the warm
light of the September sun. She listened with an impas-
sive countenance while Babette poured out her story of the
great Cardinal,—the Cardinal Felix Bonpré, whom people said was a saint,—how he had come unexpectedly to
stay two nights at the Hotel Poitiers,—how " petite
maman " had declared he was so good that even angels
might visit him,—how kind and gentle and grand he
seemed,—" Yes," said Babette somewhat eagerly, " there
was no doubt that he *looked* good,—and we have told
him all about Fabien and he has promised to bless him
and ask Our Lord to cure his lameness."

" Well, and of what use is that, *mignonne?* " demanded
Martine, clicking her knitting-needles violently and stooping over her work to wink away the sudden tears that
had risen in her bold brown eyes at Babette's enthusiastic
desire to benefit her afflicted child,—" Asking our Lord
is poor business,—you may ask and ask, but you never
get answered!"

Babette hung her curly brown head despondingly, and looked appealingly at her brother. Now Henri was a decided cynic;—but his sister exercised a weird fascination over him,—a sort of power to command which he always felt more or less constrained to obey. He stared solemnly at Martine, and then at the little Fabien, who, half rising from his mat, had listened with a visibly painful interest to Babette's story.

" I think you might let us take Fabien and see if a Cardinal *can* do anything," he said with a kind of judicial air, as of one who, though considering the case hopeless, had no objection to try a last desperate remedy. " This one is a very old man, and he must know a good deal. He could not do any harm. And I am sure Babette would like to find out if there is any use at all in a Cardinal. I should like it too. You see we went into Notre Dame last night,—Babette and I,—and everything was dark,— all the candles were out at Our Lady's statue—and we had only ten centimes between us. And the candles are ten centimes each. So we could only light one. But we lit that one, and said an Ave for Fabien. And the candle was all by itself in the Cathedral. And now I think we ought to take him to the Cardinal."

Martine shook her head, pursed up her lips, and knitted more violently than ever.

" It is all no use—no use! " she muttered—" There is no God,—or if there is, He must be deaf as well as blind! "

But here suddenly the weak plaintive voice of Fabien himself piped out—

" Oh, mother, let me go! "

Martine looked down at him.

" Let thee go? To see the Cardinal? Why he is nought but an old man, child, as helpless as any of us. What dost thou think he can do for thee? "

" Nothing! " and the boy clambered up on his crutch, and stood appealingly before his mother, his fair curls blowing back in the breeze,—" But I *should* like to see him. Oh, do let me go! "

Babette caught him by the hand.

" Yes, oh yes, Martine! " she exclaimed—" Let him come with us! "

Martine hesitated a moment longer, but she could never altogether resist an imploring look in her boy's eyes, or refuse any request he made of her,—and gradually the hard lines of her mouth relaxed into a half smile. Babette at once perceived this, and eagerly accepted it as a sign that she had gained her point.

"Come, Fabien!" she exclaimed delightedly—"Thy mother says yes! We will not be long gone, Martine! And perhaps we will bring him home quite well!"

Martine shook her head sorrowfully, and paused for a while in her knitting to watch the three children crossing the market-place together, Henri supporting her little son on one side, Babette on the other, both carefully aiding his slow and halting movements over the rough cobbles of the uneven pavement. Then as they all turned a corner and disappeared, she sighed, and a couple of bright tears splashed down on her knitting. But the next moment her eyes were as bold and keen and defiant as ever while she stood up to attend to two or three customers who just then approached her stall, and her voice was as shrill and sharp as any woman's voice could be in the noisy business of driving a bargain. Having disposed of three or four fat geese and fowls at a good profit, she chinked and counted the money in her apron pockets, hummed a tune, and looked up at the genial sky with an expression of disfavour.

"Oh, yes, 'tis a fine day!" she muttered,—"And the heavens look as if the saints lived in them;—but by and by the clouds will come, and the cold!—the sleet, the snow, the frost and the bitterness of winter!—and honest folk will starve while thieves make a good living!—that is the way the wise God arranges things in this world."

She gave a short laugh of scorn, and resumed the clicking of her needles, not raising her eyes from her work even when her neighbour, the old woman who sold vegetables at the next stall, ventured to address her.

"Where is thy unfortunate boy gone to, Martine?" she enquired,—"Is it wise to let him be with the Patoux children? They are strong and quick and full of mischief, —they might do him fresh injury in play without meaning it."

"I will trust them," answered Martine curtly,—"They have taken him to see a Cardinal."

"A Cardinal!" and the old woman craned her withered neck forward in amazement and began to laugh feebly,—

"*Nom de Jésus!* That is strange! What does the Cardinal want with him?"

"Nothing," said Martine gruffly—"It seems that he is an old man who is kind to children, and the girl Babette has a fancy to get his blessing for my Fabien,—that is all."

"And that is little enough," responded the old vegetable-vendor, still laughing, or rather chuckling hoarsely—"A blessing is not worth much nowadays, is it Martine? It never puts an extra ounce of meat in the *pot-au-feu*,—and yet it is all one gets out of the priests for all the prayers and the praise. Last time I went to confession I accused myself of the sin of envy. I said 'Look here, my father, I am a widow and very old; and I have rheumatism in all my bones, and I have only a bit of matting to sleep on at home, and if I have a bad day with the market I can buy no food. And there is a woman living near me who has a warm house, with a stove in it,—and blankets to cover her, and a bit of money put by, and I envy her her blankets and her stove and her house and her money. Is that a sin?' And he said it was a sin; but that he would absolve me from it if I said ten Paters and ten Aves before Our Lady of Bon-Secours. And then he gave me his blessing,—but no blankets and no stove and no money. And I have not said ten Paters and Aves yet, because my bones have ached too much all the week for me to walk up the hill to Bon-Secours. And the blessing has been no use to me at all."

"Nor is it likely to be!" scoffed Martine—"I thought you had given up all that Church-nonsense long ago."

"Nay—nay—not altogether,"—murmured the old woman timidly—"I am very old,—and one never knows—there may be truth in some of it. It is the burning and the roasting in hell that I think of,—you know that is very likely to happen, Martine!—because you see, in this life we have nothing but trouble,—so whoever made us must like to see us suffering;—it must be a pleasure to God, and so it is sure to go on and on always. And I am afraid!—and if a candle now and then to St. Joseph would help matters, I am not the one to grudge it,—it is better to burn a candle than burn one's self!"

Martine laughed loudly, but made no answer. She could not waste her time arguing against the ridiculous superstitions of an old creature who was so steeped in ignorance as to think that a votive candle could rescue her soul from a possible hell. She went on knitting in silence till a sudden shadow came between her and the sunlight, and a girl's voice, harsh, yet with a certain broken sweetness in it, said—

" A fine morning's killing, aye! All their necks wrung, —all dead birds! Once they could fly—fly and swim! Fly and swim! All dead now—and sold cheap in the open market!"

A shrill laugh finished this outburst, but Martine knew who it was that spoke, and maintained her equanimity.

" Is that you again, Marguerite?" she said, not unkindly—" You will tire yourself to death wandering about the streets all day."

Marguerite Valmond, " la folle " as she was called by the townsfolk, shook her head and smiled cunningly. She was a tall girl, with black hair disordered and falling loosely about her pale face,—her eyes were dark and lustrous, but wild, and with a hunted expression in them, —and her dress was composed of the strangest remnants of oddly assorted materials and colours pinned about her without any order or symmetry, the very idea of decent clothing being hardly considered, as her bosom was half exposed and her legs were bare. She wore no head-covering, and her whole aspect was that of one who had suddenly awakened from a hideous dream and was striving to forget its horrors.

" I shall never be tired!" she said—" If I could be tired I should sleep,—but I never sleep! I am looking for *him,* you know!—it was at the fair I lost him—you remember the great fair? And when I find him I shall kill him! It is quite easy to kill—you take a sharp glittering thing, so!" and she snatched up a knife that lay on Martine's counter—" And you plunge it—so!" and she struck it down with singular fury through the breast of one of the " dead birds " which were Martine's stock-in-trade. Then she threw the knife on the ground—rubbed her hands together, tossed her head, and laughed again— " That is how I shall do it when I meet him!"

Martine said nothing. She simply removed the one stabbed bird from among the others, and setting it aside, picked up the knife from the ground and went on knitting as calmly as ever.

"I am going to see the Archbishop," proceeded Marguerite, tossing back her dishevelled locks and making one or two fantastic dance-steps as she spoke—"The great Archbishop of this wonderful city of Rouen! I want to ask him how it happened that God made men. It was a mistake which He must be sorry for! The Archbishop knows everything;—he will tell me about it. Ah!—what a beautiful mistake is the Archbishop himself!—and how soon women find it out! Bon jour, Martine!"

"Bon jour, Marguerite!" responded Martine quietly.

Singing to herself, the crazed girl sauntered off. Several of the market women looked after her.

"She killed her child, they say," muttered the old vegetable-seller—"But no one knows——"

"Sh—sh—sh!" hissed Martine angrily—"What one does not know one should not say. Mayhap there never was a child at all. Whatever the wrong was, she has suffered for it;—and if the man who led her astray ever comes nigh her, his life is not worth a centime."

"Rough justice!" said one of the market porters, who had just paused close by to light his pipe.

"Aye, rough justice!" echoed Martine—"When justice is not given to the people, the people take it for themselves! And if a man deals ill by a woman, he has murdered her as surely as if he had put a knife through her;—and 'tis but even payment when he gets the knife into himself. Things in this life are too easy for men and too hard for women; men make the laws for their own convenience, and never a thought of us at all in the making. They are a selfish lot!"

The porter laughed carelessly, and having lit his pipe to his satisfaction went his way.

A great many more customers now came to Martine's stall, and for upwards of an hour there was shrill argument and driving of bargains till she had pretty well cleared her counter of all its stock. Then she sat down again and looked to right and left of the market-place for any sign of the Patoux children returning with her little son, but there was not a glimpse of them anywhere.

"I wonder what they are doing!" she thought—"And I wonder what sort of a Cardinal it is they have taken the child to see! These great princes of the Church care nothing for the poor,—the very Pope allows half Italy to starve while he shuts himself up with his treasures in the Vatican;—what should a great Cardinal care for my poor little Fabien! If the stories of the Christ were true, and one could only take the child to Him, then indeed there might be a chance of cure!—but it is all a lie, —and the worst of the lie is that it would give us all so much comfort and happiness if it were only true! It is like holding out a rope to a drowning man and snatching it away again. And when the rope goes, the sooner one sinks under the waves the better!"

VI.

THE Cardinal was still in his room alone with the boy Manuel, when Madame Patoux, standing at her door under the waving tendrils of the " creeping jenny " and shading her eyes from the radiance of the sun, saw her children approaching with Fabien Doucet between them.

" Little wretches that they are! " she murmured— " Once let them get an idea into their heads and nothing will knock it out! Now I shall have to tell Monseigneur that they are here,—what an impertinence it seems!—and yet he is so gentle, and has such a good heart that perhaps he will not mind . . . "

Here she broke off her soliloquy as the children came up, Babette eagerly demanding to know where the Cardinal was. Madame Patoux set her arms akimbo and surveyed the little group of three half-pityingly, half-derisively.

" The Cardinal has not left his room since breakfast," she answered—" He is playing Providence already to a poor lad lost in the streets, and for that matter lost in the world, without father or mother to look after him,—he was found in Notre Dame last night,—"

" Why, mother," interrupted Henri—" how could a boy get into Notre Dame last night? When Babette and I went there, nobody was in the church at all,—and we left one candle burning all alone in the darkness,—and when we came out the Suisse swore at us for having gone in, and then locked the door."

" Well, if one must be so exact, the boy was not found actually *in* Notre Dame, obstinate child," returned his mother impatiently—" It happened at midnight,—the good Cardinal heard someone crying and went to see who it was. And he found a poor boy outside the Cathedral weeping as if his heart were breaking, and leaning his head against the hard door for a pillow. And he brought him back and gave him his own bed to sleep in;—and the lad is with him now."

Little Fabien Doucet, leaning on his crutch, looked up with interest.

" Is he lame like me? " he asked.

" No, child," replied Madame compassionately—" He is straight and strong. In truth a very pretty boy."

Fabien sighed. Babette made a dash forward.

" I will go and see him! " she said—" And I will call Monseigneur."

" Babette! How dare you! Babette! "

But Babette had scurried defiantly past her mother, and breathless with a sense of excitement and disobedience intermingled, had burst into the Cardinal's room without knocking. There on the threshold she paused,—somewhat afraid at her own boldness,—and startled too at the sight of Manuel, who was seated near the window opposite the Cardinal, and who turned his deep blue eyes upon her with a look of enquiry. The Cardinal himself rose and turned to greet her, and as the wilful little maid met his encouraging glance and noted the benign sweetness of his expression she trembled,—and losing nerve, began to cry.

" Monseigneur . . . Monseigneur . . . " she stammered.

" Yes, my child,—what is it? " said the Cardinal kindly —" Do not be afraid,—I am at your service. You have brought the little friend you spoke to me of yesterday? "

Babette peeped shyly at him through her tears, and drooping her head, answered with a somewhat smothered " Yes."

" That is well,—I will go to him at once."—and the Cardinal paused a moment looking at Manuel, who as if responding to his unuttered wish, rose and approached him—" And you, Manuel—you will also come. You see, my child," went on the good prelate addressing Babette, the while he laid a gently caressing hand on her hair— " Another little friend has come to me who is also very sad,—and though he is not crippled or ill, he is all alone in the world, which is, for one so young, a great hardship. You must be sorry for him too, as well as for your own poor playmate."

But Babette was seized with an extraordinary timidity, and had much ado to keep back the tears that rose in her throat and threatened to break out in a burst of convulsive sobbing. She did not know in the least what was the matter with her,—she was only conscious of an immense confusion and shyness which were quite new to her ordinarily bold and careless nature. Manuel's face frightened yet fascinated her; he looked, she thought, like the beautiful angel of the famous stained glass "Annunciation" window in the crumbling old church of St. Maclou. She dared not speak to him,—she could only steal furtive glances at him from under the curling length of her dark tear-wet lashes,—and when the Cardinal took her by the hand and descended the staircase with her to the passage where the crippled Fabien waited, she could not forbear glancing back every now and then over her shoulder at the slight, supple, almost aerial figure of the boy, who, noiselessly, and with a light gliding step, followed. And now Madame Patoux came forward;—a bulky, anxious figure of gesticulation and apology.

"Alas, Monseigneur!" she began plaintively—"It is too shameful that your quiet should be disturbed in this way, but if you could only know the obstinacy of these children! Ah yes!—if you knew all, you would pity their parents!—you would indeed! And this is the unhappy little creature they have brought to you, Monseigneur,—a sad sight truly!—and afflicted sorely by the will of God,—though one could hardly say that God was anywhere about when he fell, poor baby, from his mother's cart and twisted his body awry,—one would rather think the devil was in the business, asking your pardon, Monseigneur; for surely the turning of a human creature into a useless lump has little of good, or divine kindness in it! Now make thy best bow to the Cardinal," went on Madame with a gasp for breath in her voluble speech, addressing the little cripple—"And it is a pity thou hast no time to confess thy sins and take the Sacrament before so holy a man lay hands on thee!"

But at these words Cardinal Bonpré turned to her with a reproving gesture.

"I pray you do not call me holy, my daughter," he said earnestly, the old shadows of pain and protest gathering in his eyes, "Nothing can make me more sorrowful than to hear such an epithet applied to one who is so full of errors and sins as myself. Try to look upon me just as I am,—merely an old man, nearing the grave, with nothing of merit in me beyond the desire to serve our Lord and obey His commands,—a desire which is far stronger than the practical force to obey it. Much that I would do I cannot; and in much that I attempt I fail. Come to me, my child."

Here, interrupting himself, he bent down, and putting his arms tenderly round Fabien, lifted him bodily, crutch and all, and carried him into the next room, and as he did so, the young Manuel glided in before him, and stood beside his chair, his blue eyes shining with a soft and eager light of interest, and a little smile lifting the delicate upper curve of his lips as he looked on. Fabien meanwhile, perched on the Cardinal's knee, and held close in the Cardinal's arms, was not at all frightened,— he simply sat, contented, gazing up confidingly at the pale venerable face above him. Henri and Babette, having as they considered, got their way, stayed at the door half afraid to enter, and their mother peered over their heads at the little scene in mingled awe and curiosity.

"My poor child," then said the Cardinal gently—" I want you to understand quite clearly how sorry I am for you, and how willingly I would do anything in the world to make you a strong, well, and happy boy. But you must not fancy that I can cure you. I told your little friends yesterday that I was not a saint, such as you read about in story-books,—and that I could not work miracles, because I am not worthy to be so filled with the Divine Spirit as to heal with a touch like the better servants of our Blessed Lord. Nevertheless I firmly believe that if God saw that it was good for you to be strong and well, He would find ways to make you so. Sometimes sickness and sorrow are sent to us for our advantage,— sometimes even death comes to us for our larger benefit, though we may not understand how it is so till afterwards. But in Heaven everything will be made clear; and even our griefs will be turned into joys,—do you understand?"

"Yes," murmured Fabien gravely, but two large tears welled up in his plaintive eyes as the faint glimmer of hope he had encouraged as to the possibility of his being miraculously cured by the touch of a saintly Cardinal, expired in the lonely darkness of his little afflicted soul.

"That is well," continued the Cardinal kindly—" And

now, since it is so difficult for you to kneel, you shall stay where you are in my arms,—so!"—and he set him on his knee in a position of even greater comfort than before. "You shall simply shut your eyes, and clasp your little hands together as I put them here,"—and as he spoke he crossed the child's hands on his silver crucifix—"And I will ask our Lord to come and make you well,—for of myself I can do nothing."

At these words Henri and Babette glanced at each other questioningly, and then as if simultaneously moved by some inexplicable emotion, dropped on their knees,—their mother, too stout and unwieldy to do this with either noiselessness or satisfaction to herself, was contented to bend her head as low as she could get it. Manuel remained standing. Leaning against the Cardinal's chair, his eyes fixed on the crippled Fabien, he had the aspect of a young Angel of compassion, whose sole immortal desire was to lift the burden of sorrow and pain from the lives of suffering humanity. And after a minute or two passed in silent meditation, the Cardinal laid his hands tenderly on Fabien's fair curly head and prayed aloud.

"Oh merciful Christ! Most pitying and gentle Redeemer!—to Whom in the days of Thy sacred life on earth, the sick and suffering and lame and blind were brought, and never sent away unhealed or uncomforted; consider, we beseech Thee, the sufferings of this Thy little child, deprived of all the joys which Thou hast made so sweet for those who are strong and straight in their youth, and who have no ailment to depress their courage or to quench the ardour of their aspiring souls. Look compassionately upon him, oh gentle King and Master of all such children!—and even as Thou wert a child Thyself, be pleased to heal him of his sad infirmity. For, if Thou wilt, Thou canst make this bent body straight and these withered muscles strong,—from death itself Thou canst ordain life, and nothing is impossible to Thee! But above all things, gracious Saviour, we do pray Thee so to lift and strengthen this child's soul, that if it is destined he should still be called upon to bear his present pain and trouble, grant to him such perfection in his inward spirit that he may prove worthy to be counted among Thy angels in the bright Hereafter. To Thy care, and to Thy comfort, and to Thy healing, great Master, we

commend him, trusting him entirely to Thy mercy, with
perfect resignation to Thy Divine Will. For the sake and
memory of Thy most holy childhood mercifully help and
bless this child! Amen!"

A deep silence ensued. Only the slow ticking of the
big old-fashioned clock in Madame Patoux's kitchen,
which was next door to the room they were all in, could
be distinctly heard. Henri and Babette were the first to
stir. They got up from their knees, brushed the dust of
the floor from their clothes, and stared curiously at Fabien. Was a miracle going to happen? Fabien, however—still resting against the Cardinal's breast, with his
meagre little hands clasped tight on the Cardinal's crucifix, kept his eyes solemnly shut and gave no sign, till the
Cardinal himself gently moved him and set him down.
Then he glanced around him bewilderingly, tottered, and
would have fallen had he not been given his little crutch
for support. Very pathetic was the smile which then
quivered on his pale lips,—very doleful was the shake of
his head as he prepared to hobble away.

"Thank you very much, Monseigneur," he murmured
gently—" I felt almost cured while you were praying,—
but I am afraid it is no use! You see there are so many
miserable people in the world,—many cripples, too,—I am
not the only one. Our Lord must have enough to do if
He is asked to heal them all! But I am sure you have
done everything you can for me, and I am grateful to you,
Monseigneur. Good-bye!"

"Good-bye, my child!" and the Cardinal, strongly
moved by the sight of the little helpless twisted figure,
and painfully impressed too by the sense of his own entire powerlessness to remove the cause of the trouble,
bent down and kissed him—" Believe me, if the giving of
my own life could make you strong, you should have that
life willingly. May God bless and heal you!"

At that moment Manuel moved from the place he had
kept near the Cardinal's chair. With a light, eager step
forward, he went up to the little cripple, and putting his
arms round him kissed him on the forehead.

"Good-bye, dear little brother!" he said smiling—
"Do not be sad! Have patience! In all the universe,
among all the millions and millions of worlds, there is
never a pure and unselfish prayer that the great good

God does not answer! Be sure of that! Take courage, dear little brother! You will soon be well!"

Fabien stared, half amazed, at the gentle young face that shone upon him with such an expression of hope and tenderness.

"You are very kind," he said—"And you are just a boy yourself,—so you can perhaps guess how it must feel not to be like other boys who can run and leap and walk for miles and miles through the fields and the green shady forests where the birds sing,—and where there is so much to see and think about,—when one is lame one cannot go far you know—and then there is my mother—she is very sad about me,—and it will be hard for her if I live to be a man and still can do nothing to help her . . ."

His weak voice broke, and two large tears filled his eyes and brimmed over, trickling slowly down his pale cheeks. Manuel took his hand and pressed it encouragingly.

"Do not cry!" he said gently—"Believe in what I say —that you will soon be quite well. The Cardinal has prayed for you as only good men *can* pray,—without one selfish thought, in faith and deep humility,—such prayers draw angels down! Be patient—be brave! Believe in the best and the best will come!"

His words rang out with a sweet convincing clearness, and even Cardinal Bonpré felt a sense of comfort as he listened. The little cripple smiled through his tears.

"Oh, yes," he murmured—"I *will* hope and I *will* believe! I am always sure God is near us, though my mother thinks He must be very far away. Yes,—I will be as brave as I can. You are very good to me,—I know you understand just how I feel, and I thank you very much. I hope you will be happy yourself some day. Good-bye!" Then, turning to Henri and Babette he asked, "Shall we go now?"

Henri's brows were drawn together in a dark frown.

"I suppose so," he replied—"I suppose there's nothing more to be done?" This, with a somewhat sarcastic air of inquiry directed at the Cardinal, who met his bold bright glance, mildly and half compassionately.

"Nothing more my child"—he answered—"Did you expect a miracle? I told you from the first that I was no saint,—I can do no good unless our Lord wills it."

" The Pope believes in miracles "—said Henri, flushing as he spoke with the heat of a sudden angry emotion— " But only those that are performed on his own behalf! *He* thinks that God's chief business is to look after *him!* "

A silence ensued,—whether of horror or embarrassment could hardly be determined. The Cardinal said nothing,—Babette trembled a little,—what a dreadful boy Henri really was, she thought!—Madame Patoux shut up her eyes in horror, crossed herself devoutly as against some evil spirit, and was about to speak, when Henri, nothing daunted, threw himself into the breach again, and turned with a fiery vehemence of appeal towards the young and thoughtful-looking Manuel.

" It's just as I say! " he declared hotly—" The Pope is taken as much care of as if he were a peach wrapped in wadding! Was Christ taken care of? No,—He suffered all sorts of hardships and at last was crucified! The Pope shuts himself up in the Vatican with millions and millions of money's worth, while thousands of people around him in Italy alone, are starving and miserable. Christ would not allow such a thing. Christ said ' Sell half that thou hast and give to the poor '—now the Pope doesn't sell half, nor a quarter, nor a bit of a quarter! He takes all he can get and keeps it! And yet God is supposed to work miracles for an old man like that!—Oh I know all about it! Boys read the newspapers as well as grown men! "

" Henri! " gasped Madame Patoux, extending her fat arm and hand with a solemn gesture of reproach— " Henri, thou art mad . . . wicked . . . "

But Henri went on unheedingly, still addressing Manuel.

" Now you are a boy, and I daresay you can read and think,—you are about my age I suppose. And you are left all alone in the world, with nobody to care for you, —well, do you think that is well-arranged?—And do you think there is any sense in believing in a God who does such a lot of cruel things? And when He won't help us ever so little? How can people be good if they keep on praying and praying, and hoping and hoping, and working and working—and yet nothing comes of it all but trouble and pain and loss . . . " He stopped for sheer lack of breath to go on.

Manuel looked at him quietly, full in the eyes.

"Yes, it is hard!" he said—"Very hard! But it is not God who does any cruel thing. God is Love,—and the Spirit of Love cannot be cruel. It is the people of the world themselves,—the people who injure each other in thought, word and deed,—and who have no spirit of love in them,—these invite sorrow and pain, and rush upon misfortune. Then they blame God for it! Ah, it is easy to blame God!—so much easier than to blame one's self! And if you ask me if it is well for those who suffer cruel things to still believe in God, I say yes, I do think it well,—for it is the only chance they have of finding the right way of life after much wandering in the wrong."

His sweet voice fell on the silence like a soft chime, and Henri, for no particular reason that he could give, felt suddenly abashed. Cardinal Bonpré listened to the words of this strange foundling with a singular emotion, —an emotion too deep to find any outlet in speech. Babette raised her brown trustful eyes, and timidly ventured to put in her opinion—

"Yes"—she said—"I am sure that is true. You see, Henri"—with a wise glance at her brother—"you see it is always the same,—when anyone suffers something unfortunate, there is certain to be some cause for it. Now everybody says that if poor Martine had not put Fabien in the cart to save herself the trouble of holding him on her knee, he would not have tumbled out and been hurt. That was the beginning of it. And that was not God's fault. Come Fabien!—we'll take you back now."

At this, Madame Patoux started from her stricken condition of horrified dumbness into speech and action.

"Ah yes, it is indeed time!" she exclaimed— "Enough trouble has been given, I am sure, to Monseigneur, and if such a prayer as his does not reach Heaven, why then there is no Heaven at all, and it is no good bothering ourselves about it. And what things have been said by my son!—_my_ son!—against the Holy Father! Ah, mon Dieu! The wickedness of it!—The horror! And if thou learnest such blasphemy from newspapers, Henri, thou shalt not read them——"

"Who is to prevent me?" demanded Henri, his eyes sparkling defiantly.

"Hush—hush my child!" interposed the Cardinal

quietly " Nothing indeed can prevent thee,—no one can
hinder thee from walking the world according to thine
own will and direction. Thou must take good and evil
as they come, and strive thy best to discern between them
—and if the love of God cannot help thee—well!—perchance the love of thy mother may!"

There was a pause. Henri's head drooped, and quick
tears filled his eyes. He said nothing further, but turned
to assist Babette in guiding the little Fabien's hesitating
steps as he hobbled from the room. The emotional
Madame Patoux choked back a rising sob.

" God bless you Monseigneur!" she murmured—
" Henri will not forget those words—the lad has a hasty
temper, but a good heart—yes, believe me—a good
heart——"

" That I am sure of "—responded the Cardinal—" He
is quick and intelligent—and seeks to know the truth. If
he could feel an asserted ' truth ' to be really true, I am
confident he would frame his life upon it, and be a good,
brave man. Yes—he is a clever lad,—and our modern
system of education pushes the brain to a precocity exceeding bodily years,—his impatience and anger only
come from puzzling over what he finds it difficult to understand. It is all a puzzle to him—all a puzzle!—as it is
to most of us!" He sighed—then added in a lighter
tone—" I shall want nothing more at your kindly hands,
my daughter. I have decided to leave Rouen for Paris
to-day and will take an early afternoon train. Manuel "
—and he hesitated a moment—" Manuel will go with
me."

Madame was scarcely surprised at this announcement.
She had indeed expected it. She glanced at Manuel himself to see how he accepted this sudden change in his
fortunes, but he was entirely absorbed in watching Henri
and Babette lead their little crippled friend away. After
all, there was nothing to be said. The Cardinal was a free
agent,—he had a perfect right to befriend a home-
less boy and give him sustenance and protection if he
chose. He would make, thought Madame, a perfect
acolyte, and would look like a young angel in his little
white surplice. And so the good woman, deciding in
her own mind that such was the simple destiny for which
the Cardinal intended him, smiled, murmured something

deferential and approving, and hastened from the room, to prepare for Monseigneur, whether he asked for it or not, a dish of her most excellent soup, to strengthen and support him before starting on his journey. And ere four o'clock had chimed from all the towers of the city, the Hôtel Poitiers was deprived of its honoured guest,— the Cardinal, accompanied by his foundling, had departed, and the black, smoky, snake-like train had rushed with them through the smiling peace of the Normandy pasture-lands on towards the brilliant " city enthroned in wickedness," which sparkles like a jewel on the borders of the Seine as gloriously as ever Babylon sparkled on the shores of Euphrates. As godless, as hollow to the very core of rottenness, as her sister of ancient days, wanton " Lutetia " shines,—with the ghastly and unnatural lustre of phosphorescent luminance arising from old graves—and as divinely determined as the destruction of the old-time city splendid, is the approaching downfall of the modern capital. To the inhabitants of Rouen, the very name of Paris carries with it a kind of awe,—it excites various emotions of wonder, admiration, longing, curiosity and even fear,—for Paris is a witches' cauldron in which Republicanism, Imperialism, Royalism, Communism and Socialism, are all thrown by the Fates to seethe together in a hellish broth of conflicting elements—and the smoke of it ascends in reeking blasphemy to Heaven. Not from its church-altars does the cry of " How long, O Lord, how long ! " ascend nowadays,—for its priests are more skilled in the use of the witty *bon-mot* or the polished sneer than in the power of the prophet's appeal,—it is from the Courts of Science that the warning note of terror sounds, —the cold vast courts where reasoning thinkers wander, and learn, and deeply meditate, knowing that all their researches but go to prove the fact that apart from all creed and all forms of creed, Crime carries Punishment as surely as the seed is born with the flower,—thinkers who are fully aware that not all the forces of all mankind, working with herculean insistence to support a Lie, can drive back the storm-cloud of the wrath of that " Unknown Quantity " called God, whose thunders do most terribly declare the truth " with power and great glory." " How long O Lord, how long ! " Not long, we think, O friends!—not long now shall we wait for the Divine Pronouncement of the End. Hints of it are in the air,—signs and portents of it are about us in our almost terrific discoveries of the invisible forces of Light and Sound,—we are not given such tremendous powers to play with in our puny fashion for the convenience of making our brief lives easier to live and more interesting,—no, there is some deeper reason,—one, which in our heedless way of dancing over our own Earth-grave, we never dream of. And we go on making our little plans, building our ships and making loud brags of our armies, and our skill, and our prowess both by land and sea, and our amazing importance to ourselves and to others,—which importance has reached such a height at the present day as to make of us a veritable spectacle for Olympian laughter,—and we draw out our little sums of life from the Eternal exchequer, and add them up and try to obtain the highest interest for them, always forgetting to calculate that in making up the sum total, that mysterious " Unknown Quantity " will have to come in, and (unless it has been taken into due counting from the first) will be a figure likely to swamp the whole banking business. And in this particular phase of speculation and exchange, Paris has long been playing a losing game. So steadily has she lost, in honour, in prestige, in faith, in morals, in justice, in honesty and in cleanly living, that it does not seem possible she can ever retrieve herself. Her men are dissolute,—her women shameless—her youth of both sexes depraved,—her laws are corrupt—her arts decadent—her religion dead. What next can be expected of her?—or rather to what extent will Destiny permit her to go before the bolt of destruction falls ? " Thus far, and no farther " has ever been the Principle of Nature—and Paris has almost touched the " Thus far."

Sitting quietly in her tidy kitchen near the open window, after the Cardinal's departure, Madame Patoux knitted busily, her thoughts flying faster than her glittering needles. A certain vague impression of solemnity had been left on her mind by the events of the morning, —she could not quite reason out the why or the wherefore of it—and yet—it was a fact that after Monseigneur had gone, she had, when entering the rooms he had vacated, felt a singular sense of awe.

"Almost as if one were in the Cathedral at the ringing of the 'Sanctus'" she murmured under her breath, glancing about timidly at the plain furniture and bare walls. And after putting everything in order, she closed and locked the doors jealously, with a determination that she would not let those rooms to the first chance-comer for a long time,—no, though she might have to lose money by her refusal. And now, as she sat actively employed in knitting socks for Henri, whom she could see sitting with his sister outside on the bench under the house porch, reading or pretending to read, she began to wonder what opinion those two young miscreants had formed in their minds respecting the Cardinal, and also what they thought of the boy who had been taken so suddenly under his protection. She was almost tempted to call Henri and ask him a few questions on the subject,—but she had learnt to value peace and quietness when she could secure those rare blessings at the hands of her children, and when they were employed with a book and visibly out of mischief she thought it wisest to leave them alone. And so she left them in the present instance, pushing her window open as she sat and knitted, for the air was warm and balmy, and the long rays of sunshine streaming across the square were of the hue of a ripe nectarine just gathered, and the delicate mouldings and traceries and statues on the porch of the Cathedral appeared like so many twinings of grey gossamer web glistening in a haze of gold. Now and then neighbours passed, and nodded or called a greeting which Madame Patoux answered cheerily, still knitting vivaciously; and the long shafts of sunshine grew longer, casting deeper shadows as the quarters chimed. All at once there was a cry,—a woman's figure came rushing precipitately across the square,—Madame Patoux sprang up, and her children ran out of the porch as they recognised Martine Doucet.

"Martine! Martine! What is it!" they all cried simultaneously.

Martine, breathless, dishevelled, laughing and sobbing alternately, tried to speak, but could only gesticulate and throw up her hands in a kind of ecstasy, but whether of despair or joy could not be guessed. Madame Patoux shook her by the arm.

" Martine!—speak—what is it!"

Martine made a violent effort.

" Fabien!—Fabien——" she gasped, flinging herself to and fro and still sobbing and laughing.

" Mon Dieu!" cried Madame in horror. " Is the child dead?"

" No, no!——" and Martine again tossed her arms aloft in a kind of frenzy. " No—but look you!—there *is* a God! Yes!—we thought He was an invention of the priests—but no—He is a real God after all!—Oh *mes enfants!*" and she tried to grasp the amazed Henri and Babette in her arms, " You are two of His angels!—you took my boy to the Cardinal——"

The children glanced at each other.

" Yes—yes!" they murmured breathlessly.

" Well! and see what has happened!—See!—Here comes Fabien——!"

And as she spoke exultantly with an excitement that seemed to inspire every nerve of her body, a little figure came running lightly towards them,—the light strong figure of a boy with fair curls flying in the wind, and a face in which the large, grey, astonished eyes flashed with an almost divine joy.

" Mother!—Mother!" he cried.

Madame Patoux felt as though the heavens had suddenly opened to let the angels down. Was this Fabien? Fabien, who had hobbled painfully upon crutches all his life, and had left her house in his usual condition an hour or so ago?—This straight-limbed child, running with the graceful and easy movement of a creature who had never known a day's pain?

" Fabien, is it thou?" almost screamed Henri, " Speak, is it thou?"

" It is I" said Fabien, and he stopped, panting for breath,——then threw his arms round his mother's neck and faced them,—" It is I—strong and well!—thanks to God and the prayers of the Cardinal!"

For a moment there was a dead silence,—a silence of stupefied amazement unbroken save by the joyful weeping of Martine. Then suddenly a deep-toned bell rang from the topmost tower of Notre Dame—and in the flame-red of the falling sun the doves that make their homes among the pinnacles of the great Cathedral, rose floating in cloudy circles towards the sky. One bell— and then another—yet another!—

"The Angelus!" cried Babette dropping on her knees and folding her hands, "The Angelus!—Mother—Martine—Henri!—Fabien!—the Angelus!"——

Down they all knelt, a devotional group, in the porch through which the good Cardinal had so lately passed, and the bells chimed sweetly and melodiously as Fabien reverently repeated the Angelic Salutation amid responses made with tears and thanksgiving, and neighbours and townfolk hearing of the miracle came hastening to the Hotel Poitiers to enquire into its truth, and pausing as they saw the cluster of kneeling figures in the porch instinctively and without question knelt also,— then as the news spread, group after group came running and gathering together, and dropping on their knees amazed and awe-struck, till the broad Square showed but one black mass of a worshipping congregation under the roseate sky, their voices joining in unison with the clear accents of one little happy child; while behind them rose the towers of Notre Dame, and over their heads the white doves flew and the bells of the Angelus rang. And the sun dropped slowly into the west, crimson and glorious like the shining rim of a Sacramental Cup held out and then drawn slowly back again by angel hands within the Veil of Heaven.

VII.

MEANWHILE, unconscious of the miracle his prayer had wrought, Cardinal Bonpré and his young charge Manuel, arrived in Paris, and drove from the station direct to a house situated near the Bois du Boulogne, where the Cardinal's niece, Angela Sovrani, only daughter of Prince Sovrani, and herself famous throughout Europe as a painter of the highest promise, had a suite of rooms and studio, reserved for her occasional visits to the French capital. Angela Sovrani was a rare type of her sex,— unlike any other woman in the world, so those who knew her best were wont to declare. Without being actually beautiful, according to the accepted lines and canons of physical perfection, she created around her an effect of beauty, which was dazzling and exciting to a singular degree,—people who came once within the charmed circle of her influence could never forget her, and always spoke of her afterwards as a creature apart ;—a " woman of genius,—yes ! "—they said, " But something more even than that." And this " something more," was just the inexplicable part of her which governed her whole being, and rendered her so indescribably attractive. And she was not without beauty—or perhaps it should be termed loveliness rather,—of an exquisitely suggestive kind, which provoked the beholder into questioning where and how the glamour of it fell. In her eyes, perhaps, the secret lay,—they were violet-grey in hue, and drowsy-lidded, with long lashes that swept the delicate pale cheeks in a dark golden fringe of shadow, through which the sparkle of vision gleamed,—now warningly, now tenderly,—and anon, these same half-shut and deep fringed lids would open wide, letting the full brilliance of the soul behind the eyes pour forth its luminance, in flashes of such lightning-like clearness and compelling force, that it was impossible not to recognise something higher than mere woman in the dazzle of that spiritual glory. In figure she was wonderfully slight,—so slight indeed that she suggested a delicate willow-withe such as can be bent and curved with one hand—yet this slightness stood her in good stead, for being united with extreme suppleness, it gave her a grace of movement resembling that of some skimming mountain bird or sea-swallow, which flies with amazing swiftness yet seeming slowness. Angela never moved quickly,—no one had ever seen her in what is termed a " rush," or a vulgar hurry. She did everything she had to do without haste, without noise, without announcement or assertion of any kind ;—and all that she did was done as perfectly as her ability could warrant. And that ability was very great indeed, and displayed itself in small details as well as large attempts. Whether she merely twisted her golden-brown hair into a knot, or tied a few flowers together and fastened them on her dress with a pearl pin, either thing was perfectly done—without a false line or a discordant hue. Her face, form, voice and colouring were like a chord of music, harmonious,—and hence the impression of satisfaction and composure her presence always gave. In herself she was a creature of remarkable temperament and character ;—true womanly in every delicate sentiment, fancy and feeling, but with something of the man-hero in her scorn of petty aims, her delight in noble deeds, her courage, her ambition, her devotion to duty and her unflinching sense of honour. Full of rare perceptions and instinctive knowledge of persons and motives, she could only be deceived and blinded where her deepest affections were concerned, and there she could certainly be fooled and duped as completely as the wisest of us all. Looking at her now as she stood awaiting her uncle's arrival in the drawing-room of her " suite," the windows of which faced the Bois, she expressed to the air and surroundings the personality of a thoughtful, charming young woman,—no more. Her black silk gown, cut simply in the prevailing mode of definitely outlining the figure from throat to hips, and then springing out in pliant folds of trailing drapery, had nothing remarkable about it save its Parisian perfection of fit,—the pale " Gloire de France " rose that rested lightly amongst the old lace at her neck, pinned, yet looking as though it had dropped there merely out of a languid desire to escape from further growing, was her only ornament. Her hair, full of curious lights and shades run-

ning from brown to gold and gold to brown again, in a
rippling uncertain fashion, clustered thickly over her brow
and was caught back at the sides in a loose twist after the
style of the Greek vestals,—and her fine, small white
hands and taper fingers, so skilled in the use of the artist's
brush, looked too tiny and delicate to be of any service
save to receive the kisses of a lover's lips,—or to be
raised, folded pure and calm, in a child-like appeal to
Heaven. Certainly in her fragile appearance she expressed nothing save indefinable charm—no one, studying
her physiognomy, would have accredited her with genius,
power, and the large conceptions of a Murillo or a
Raphael;—yet within the small head lay a marvellous
brain—and the delicate body was possessed by a spirit
of amazing potency to conjure with. While she watched
for the first glimpse of the carriage which was to bring her
uncle the Cardinal, whom she loved with a rare and tender
devotion, her thoughts were occupied with a letter she
had received that morning from Rome,—a letter " writ in
choice Italian," which though brief, contained for her
some drops of the essence of all the world's sweetness, and
was worded thus—

" MY OWN LOVE!—A century seems to have passed
away since you left Rome. The hours move slowly without you—they are days,—even years!—but I feel your
spirit is always with me! Absence for those who love,
is not absence after all! To the soul, time is nothing,
—space is nothing,—and my true and passionate love for
you makes an invisible bridge, over which my thoughts
run and fly to your sweet presence, carrying their delicious burden of a thousand kisses!—a thousand embraces and blessings to the Angela and angel of my life!
                    From her devoted lover,
                              " FLORIAN."

Her devoted lover, Florian! Yes; Florian Varillo—
her comrade in art, was her lover,—a genius himself,
who had recognised *her* genius and who bowed before it,
conquered and subdued! Florian, the creator of exquisitely delicate landscapes and seascapes, with nymphs
and cupids and nereids and sirens all daintily portrayed
therein,—pictures so ethereal and warm and bright in

colour that they were called by some of the best Italian
critics, the "amoretti" of painting,—he, this wonderful man, had caught her soul and heart by storm, in a few
sudden, quickly-whispered words one night when the
moon was at the full, hanging high over the gardens of
the Pincio,—and, proud of her security in the love she
had won, Angela had risen by leaps and bounds to a magnificence of creative effort and attainment so far beyond
him, that old and wise persons, skilled in the wicked ways
of the world, would sometimes discourse among themselves in dubious fashion thus: "Is it possible that he is
not jealous? He must surely see that her work is superior to his own!" And others would answer, "Oh no!
No man was ever known to admit, even in thought, that
a woman can do better things in art than himself! If a
masculine creature draws a picture on a paving-stone he
will assure himself in his own Ego, that it is really much
more meritorious simply as 'man's work' than the last
triumph of a Rosa Bonheur. Besides, you have to remember that in this case the man is the woman's lover—
he could soon kill her genius if he chose. He has simply
to desert her,—such an easy thing!—so often done!—and
she will paint no more. Women are all alike,—they rest
on love,—when that fails, then everything fails, and they
drop into old age without a groan." And then perhaps a stray cynic would say, "But Angela Sovrani
need not depend on one lover surely?—" and he would
get for answer, "No, she need not—but it so happens
that she does,"—which to everybody seemed extraordinary, more particularly in Italy, where morals are so
lax, that a woman has only to be seen walking alone
in the public gardens or streets with one of the opposite sex, and her reputation is gone for ever. It is no
use to explain that the man in question is her father,
her brother or her uncle,—he simply could not be. He
is THE man, the one inevitable. Few Italians (in Italy)
believe in the chastity of English women,—their reasons
for doubt being simply because they see the fair and free
ones going to parties, theatres and other places of amusement with their friends of the other sex in perfect ease
and confidence. And in the case of Angela Sovrani,
though she was affianced to Florian Varillo with her
father's consent, (reluctantly obtained,) and the knowl-

edge of all the Roman world of society, she saw very little of him,—and that little, never alone. Thus it was very sweet to receive such consoling words as those she had had from him that day—" Time is nothing,—space is nothing,—and my true and passionate love for you makes an invisible bridge over which my thoughts run and fly to your sweet presence!" The letter lay warm in her bosom just under the " Gloire de France" rose; she pressed it tenderly with her little hand now simply for the childish pleasure of hearing the paper rustle, and she smiled dreamily.

" Florian," she murmured half aloud!—" *My* Florian!" And she recalled certain lines of verse he had written to her,—for most Italians write verse as easily as they eat maccaroni;—and there are countless rhymes to " amor" in the dulcet Dante-tongue, whereas our rough English can only supply for the word " love" some three or four similar sounds,—which is perhaps a fortunate thing. Angela spoke English and French as easily and fluently as her native Tuscan, and had read the most notable books in all three languages, so she was well aware that of all kinds of human speech in the world there is none so adapted for making love and generally telling lies in, as the " *lingua Toscana in bocca Romana.*" And this particular " *lingua*" Florian possessed in fullest perfection of sweetness, so far as making love was concerned; —of the telling of lies he was, according to Angela's estimate of him, most nobly ignorant. She had not many idle moments, however, for meditation on her love matters, or for dreamy study of the delicate beginnings of the autumnal tints on the trees of the Bois, for the carriage she had been awaiting soon made its appearance, and bowling rapidly down the road drew up sharply at the door. She had just time to perceive that her uncle had not arrived alone, when he entered,—and with a pretty grace and reverence for his holy calling, she dropped on one knee before him to receive his benediction, which he gave by laying a hand on her soft hair and signing the cross on her brow. After which he raised her and looked at her fondly.

" My dear child!"—he said, tenderly,—and again " My dear child!"

Then he turned towards Manuel, who had followed

him and was now standing quietly on the threshold of the apartment.

"Angela, this is one of our Lord's 'little ones,'" he said,—" He is alone in the world, and I have made myself his guardian and protector for the present. You will be kind to him—yes—as kind as if you were his sister, will you not?—for we are all one family in the sight of Heaven, and sorrow and loneliness and want can but strengthen the love which should knit us all together."

Raising her candid eyes, and fixing them on Manuel, Angela smiled. The thoughtful face and pathetic expression of the boy greatly attracted her, and in her heart she secretly wondered where her uncle had found so intelligent and inspired-looking a creature. But one of her *un*feminine attributes was a certain lack of curiosity concerning other people's affairs, and an almost fastidious dislike of asking questions on matters which did not closely concern her. So she contented herself with giving him that smile of hers which in itself expressed all sweetness, and saying gently,—

"You are very welcome! You must try to feel that wherever my uncle is,—that is 'home'."

"I have felt that from the first,"—replied Manuel in his soft musical voice, "I was all alone when my lord the Cardinal found me,—but with him the world seems full of friends."

Angela looked at him still more attentively; and the fascination of his presence became intensified. She would have liked to continue the conversation, but her uncle was fatigued by his journey, and expressed the desire for an hour's rest. She therefore summoned a servant to show him to the rooms prepared for his reception, whither he went, Manuel attending him,—and when, after a little while, Angela followed to see that all was arranged suitably for his comfort, she found that he had retired to his bed-chamber, and that just outside his door in a little ante-room adjoining, his "waif and stray" was seated, reading. There was something indescribable about the boy even in this reposeful attitude of study,—and Angela observed him for a minute or two, herself unseen. His face reminded her of one of Fra Angelico's seraphs, —the same broad brow, deep eyes and sensitive lips, which seemed to suggest the utterance of wondrous speech or melodious song,—the same golden hair swept back in rich clusters,—the same eager, inspired, yet controlled expression. A curious fluttering of her heart disturbed the girl as she looked—an indefinable dread—a kind of wonder, that almost touched on superstitious awe. Manuel himself, apparently unconscious of her observation, went on reading,—his whole attitude expressing that he was guarding the door to deter anyone from breaking in upon the Cardinal's rest, and Angela at last turned away reluctantly, questioning herself as to the cause of the strange uneasiness which thrilled her mind.

"It is foolish, of course,"—she murmured, "but I feel just as if there were a supernatural presence in the house, . . . however,—I always do have that impression with Uncle Felix, for he is so good and noble-minded,—almost a saint, as everyone says—but to-day there is something else——something quite unusual——"

She re-entered the drawing-room, moving slowly with an abstracted air, and did not at once perceive a visitor in the room;—a portly person in clerical dress, with a somewhat large head and strongly marked features,—a notable character of the time in Paris, known as the Abbé Vergniaud. He had seated himself in a low fauteuil, and was turning over the pages of the month's "Revue de Deux Mondes", humming a little tune under his breath as he did so,—but he rose when he saw Angela, and advanced smilingly to greet her as she stopped short, with a little startled exclamation of surprise at the sight of him.

"Forgive me!" he said, with an expressively apologetic gesture,—"Have I come at an inopportune moment? I saw your uncle arrive, and I was extremely anxious to see him on a little confidential matter—I ventured to persuade your servant to let me enter—"

"No apologies are necessary, Monsieur l'Abbé" said Angela, quickly, "My uncle Felix is indeed here, but he is tired with his journey and is resting——"

"Yes, I understand!" And Monsieur l'Abbé, showing no intention to take his leave on account of the Cardinal's non-presence, bowed low over the extended hand of "the Sovrani" as she was sometimes called in the world of art, where her name was a bone for envious dogs-in-the-manger to fight over—" But if I might wait a little while—"

" Your business with my uncle is important?" questioned Angela with slightly knitted brows.

" My dear child, all business is important,"—declared the Abbé, with a smile which spread the light of a certain satirical benevolence all over his plump clean-shaven face, " or so we think—we who consider that we have any business,—which is of course a foolish idea,—but one that is universal to human nature. We all imagine we are busy—which is so curious of us! Will you sit here?— Permit me!" And he dexterously arranged a couple of cushions in an arm-chair and placed it near the window. Angela half-reluctantly seated herself, watching the Abbé under the shadow of her long lashes as he sat down opposite to her. " Yes,—the emmets, the flies, the worms and the men, are all of one equality in the absurd belief that they can do things—things that will last. Their persistent self-credulity is astonishing,—considering the advance the world has made in science, and the overwhelming proofs we are always getting of the fact that we are only One of an eternal procession of many mighty civilizations, all of which have been swept away with everything they have ever learnt, into silence,—so that really all we do, or try to do, amounts to doing nothing in the end!"

" That is your creed, I know," said Angela Sovrani with a faint sigh, " But it is a depressing and a wretched one."

" I do not find it so," responded the Abbé, complacently looking at a fine diamond ring that glittered on the little finger of his plump white hand, " It is a creed which impresses upon us the virtue of being happy during the present moment, no matter what the next may bring. Let each man enjoy himself according to his temperament and capabilities. Do not impose bounds upon him—give him his liberty. Let him alone. Do not try to bamboozle him with the idea that there is a God looking after him. So will he be spared much disappointment and useless blasphemy. If he makes his own affairs unpleasant in this world, he will not be able to lift up his hands to the innocent skies, which are only composed of pure ether, and blame an impossible Large Person sitting up there who

can have no part in circumstances which are entirely unknown outside the earth's ridiculously small orbit."

He smiled kindly as he spoke, and looked paternally
at "the Sovrani," who flushed with a sudden warmth
that sent a wave of pale rose over her face, and made her
cheeks the colour of the flower she wore.

"How cruel you are!" she said,—"How cold—how
didactic! You would give each man his freedom according to habit and temperament,—no matter whether
such habit and temperament led to crime or otherwise,—
you would impose upon him no creed,—no belief in anything higher than himself,—and yet—you remain in the
Church!"

The Abbé laughed softly.

"Chère Sovrani! You are angry—deliciously angry!
Impulsively, enthusiastically, beautifully vexed with me!
I like to see you so,—you are a woman of remarkable
genius, and yet you are quite a little child in heart,—a
positive child, with beliefs and hopes! I should not wonder if you even believed that love itself is eternal!—that
most passing of phantoms!——yes—and you exclaim
against me because I venture to think for myself? It is
appalling that I should think for myself and yet remain
in the Church? My dear lady, you might just as well,
after unravelling the dirty entanglement of the Dreyfus
case, have turned upon our late friend Faure and exclaimed 'And yet you remained President!'"

Angela's violet eyes glowed.

"He was not allowed to remain President," she said.

"No, he was not. He died. Certainly! And I know
you think he would not have died if he had done his best
to clear the character of an innocent man. To women
of your type, it always seems as if God—the Large Person up above—stepped in exactly at the right moment. It
would really appear as if it were so at times. But such
things are mere coincidences."

"I do not believe in coincidences," said Angela deci-
sively, "I do not believe in 'chance' or 'luck', or what
you call 'fortuitous' haphazard arrangements of any sort.
I think everything is planned by law from the beginning;
even to the particular direction in which a grain of dust
floats through space. It is all mathematical and exact.
And the moving Spirit—the Divine Centre of things,

whom I call God,—cannot dislodge or alter one particle of the majestic system without involving the whole in complete catastrophe. It is our mistake to 'chance' things—at least, so I think. And if I exclaim against you and say,—"Why do you remain in the Church?' it is because I cannot understand a man of conscience and intellect outwardly professing one thing while inwardly he means another. Because God will take him in the end at his own interior valuation, not at his outward seeming."

"Uncomfortable, if true," said the Abbè, still smiling. "When one has been at infinite pains all one's life to present a charmingly virtuous and noble aspect to the world, it would be indeed distressing if at the last moment one were obliged to lift the mask . . . "

"Sometimes one is not given the chance to lift it," interposed Angela, "It is torn off ruthlessly by a force greater than one's own. 'Call no man happy till his death,' you know."

"Yes, I know," and the Abbè settled himself in his chair more comfortably;—he loved an argument with "the Sovrani", and was wont to declare that she was the only woman in the world who had ever made him wish to be a good man,—"But that maxim can be taken in two ways. It may mean that no man *is* happy till his death,— which I most potently believe,—or it may mean that a man is only *judged* after his death, in which case it cannot be said to affect his happiness, as he is past caring whether people think ill or well of him. Besides, after death it must needs be all right, as every man is so particularly fortunate in his epitaph!"

Angela smiled a little.

"That is witty of you," she said, "but the fact of every man having a kindly-worded epitaph only proves goodness of heart and feeling in his relatives and friends——"

"Or gratitude for a fortune left to them in his will," declared the Abbè gaily, "or a sense of relief that the dear creature has gone and will never come back. Either motive, would, I know, inspire me to write most pathetic verses! Now you bend your charming brows at me,— *mea culpa!* I have said something outrageous?"

"Not from the point of view at which *you* take life," said Angela quietly, "but I was just then thinking of a cousin of mine,—a very beautiful woman; her husband treated her with every possible sort of what I should term civil cruelty,—polite torture—refined agony. If he had struck her or shot her dead it would have been far kinder. But his conduct was worse than murder. He finally deserted her, and left her penniless to fight her own way through the world. Then he died suddenly, and she forgot all his faults, spoke of him as though he had been a model of goodness, and lives now for his memory, ever mourning his loss. In her case the feeling of regret had nothing to do with money, for he spent all her fortune and left her nothing even of her own. She has to work hard for her living now,—but she loves him and is as true to him as if he were still alive. What do you say to that?"

"I say that the lady in question must be a charming person!" replied the Abbè, "Perfectly charming! But of course she is deceiving herself; and she takes pleasure in the self-deception. She knows that the man had deserted her and was quite unworthy of her devotion;—but she pretends to herself that she does *not* know. And it it is charming, of course! But women will do that kind of thing. It is extraordinary,—but they will. They all deceive themselves in matters of love. Even *you* deceive yourself."

Angela started.

"I?" she exclaimed.

"Yes—you—why not?" And the Abbè treated her to one of his particularly paternal smiles. "You are betrothed to Florian Varillo,—but no man ever had or ever could have all the virtues with which you endow this excellent Florian. He is a delightful creature,—a good artist—unique in his own particular line,—but you think him something much greater than even artist or man— a sort of god, (though the gods themselves were not impeccable) only fit to be idealised. Now, I am not a believer in the gods,—but of course it is delightful to me to meet those who are."

"Signor Varillo needs neither praise nor defence," said Angela with a slight touch of hauteur, "All the world knows what he is."

"Yes, precisely! That is just it,—all the world knows what he is,—" and the Abbé rubbed his forehead with an air of irritation, "And I am vexing you by my talk,

I can see! Well, well!—You must forgive my garrulity; —I admit my faults—I am old—I am a cynic—I talk too much—I have a bad opinion of man, and an equally bad opinion of the Forces that evolved him. By the way, I met that terrible reformer and socialist Aubrey Leigh at the Embassy the other day—the man who is making such a sensation in England with his 'Addresses to the People.' He is quite an optimist, do you know? He believes in everything and everybody,—even in me!"

Angela laughed, and her laughter sweet and low, thrilled the air with a sense of music.

"That is wonderful!" she said gaily,—"Even in you! And how does he manage to believe in you, Monsieur l'Abbé? Do tell me!"

A little frown wrinkled the Abbé's brow.

"Well! in a strange way," he responded. "You know he is a very strange man and believes in very strange things. When I treat humanity as a jest—which is really how it should be treated—he looks at me with a grand air of tolerance, 'Oh, you will progress;' he says, 'You are passing through a phase.' 'My dear sir,' I assure him, 'I have lived in this "phase", as you call it, for forty years. I used to pray to the angels and saints and to all the different little Madonnas that live in different places, till I was twenty. Then I dropped all the pretty heaven-toys at once;—and since then I have believed in nothing —myself, least of all. Now I am sixty—and yet you tell me I am only passing through a phase.' 'Quite so,' he answered me with the utmost coolness, 'Your forty years —or your sixty years, are a Moment merely;—the Moment will pass—and you will find another Moment coming which will explain the one which has just gone. Nothing is simpler.' And when I ask him which will be the best Moment,—the one that goes, or the one that comes—he says that I am making the coming Moment for myself—'which is so satisfactory' he adds with that bright smile of his, 'because of course you will make it pleasant!' '*Il faut que tout homme trouve pour lui même une possibilité particulière de vie supérieure dans l'humble et inévitable realité quotidienne.*' I do not find the '*possibilité particulière*'—but this man assures me it is because I do not trouble to look for it. What do you think about it?"

Angela's eyes were full of dreamy musing.

"I think Mr. Leigh's ideas are beautiful," she said, slowly, "I have often heard him talk on the subject of religion—and of art, and of work,—and all he says seems to be the expression of a noble and sincere mind. He is extraordinarily gifted."

"Yes,—and he is becoming rather an alarming personage in England, so I hear,—" returned the Abbé— "He writes books that are distinctly dangerous, because true. He wants to upset shams like our Socialist writer Gys Grandit. Gys Grandit, you know, will never be satisfied till, like Rousseau, he has brought about another French Revolution. He is only a peasant, they say, but he writes with the pen of a prophet. And this Englishman is of the same calibre,—only his work is directed against religious hypocrisies more than social ones. I daresay that is why I always feel so uneasy in his presence!" And Vergniaud laughed lightly. "For the rest, he is a brilliant creature enough, and thoroughly manly. The other evening at the Club that little Vicomte de Lorgne was chattering in his usual offensive manner about women, and Leigh astonished everyone by the way in which he pulled him up. There was almost a very pretty quarrel,—but a stray man happened to mention casually, —that Leigh was considered one of the finest shots in England. After that the dear Vicomte vanished, and did not return."

Angela laughed.

"Poor de Lorgne! Yes—I have heard that Mr. Leigh excels in everything that is distinctly English—riding, shooting, and all that kind of thing. He is not effeminate."

"Few Englishmen are," said the Abbé,—"And yet to my mind there is something not altogether English in this man. He has none of the heavy British mental and physical stolidity. He is strong and muscular certainly,— but also light and supple,—and with that keen, intellectual delicate face of his, he is more of the antique Greek type than like a son of Les Isles Sans-Soleil."

"Sans-Soleil," echoed Angela, "But there is plenty of sunshine in England!"

"Is there? Well, I have been unfortunate,—I have never seen any,—" and the Abbé gave a shrug of half regret, half indifference. "It is very curious the effect that this so brave England has upon me! In crossing to its shores I suffer of course from the *mal de mer* —then when I arrive exhausted to the white cliffs, it is generally raining—then I take train to London, where it is what is called black fog; and I find all the persons that I meet either with a cold, or going to have a cold, or just recovering from a cold! It is not lively—the very funerals are dull. And you—this is not your experience?"

"No—frankly I cannot say it is," replied Angela, "I have seen rain and fog in Rome that cannot be surpassed for wretchedness anywhere. Italy is far more miserable in cold weather than England. I passed a summer once in England, and it was to me like a glimpse of Paradise. I never saw so many flowers—I never heard so many birds —(you know in Italy we kill all the singing birds and eat them), and I never met so many kind and gentle people."

"Well!—perhaps the religious sects in England are responsible for the general feeling of depression in the English atmosphere," said the Abbé with a light laugh, "They are certainly foggy! The one round Sun of one Creed is unknown to them. I assure you it is best to have one light of faith, even though it be only a magic lantern, —a toy to amuse the children of this brief life before their everlasting bedtime comes——" He broke off abruptly as a slow step was heard approaching along the passage, and in another moment Cardinal Bonpré entered the room.

"Ah, le bien aimé Felix!" cried Vergniaud, hastening to meet him and clasp his outstretched hand, bowing slightly over it as he did so, "I have taken the liberty to wait for you, cher Monseigneur, being anxious to see you—and I understand your stay in Paris will not be long?"

"A few days at most, my dear Abbé",—replied the Cardinal, gently pressing the hand of Vergniaud and smiling kindly. "You are well? But surely I need not ask—you seem to be in the best of health and spirits."

"Ah, my seeming is always excellent," returned the Abbé, "However, I do not fare badly. I have thrown away all hard thinking!"

"And you are happier so?"

"Well, I am not quite sure! There is undoubtedly a pleasure in analysing the perplexities of one's own mind.

Still, on the whole, it is perhaps better to enjoy the present hour without any thought at all."

" Like the butterflies ! " laughed Angela.

" Yes,—if butterflies *do* enjoy their hour,—which I am not at all prepared to admit. In my opinion they are very dissatisfied creatures,—no sooner on one flower than off they go to another. Very like human beings after all ! But I imagine they never worry themselves with philosophical or religious questions."

" And do you? " enquired Bonpré, smiling, as he sat down in the easy chair his niece placed for him.

" Not as a rule !—" answered Vergniaud frankly, with a light laugh—" But I confess I have done a little in that way lately. Some of the new sciences puzzle me,—I am surprised to find how closely they approach to the fulfil-ment of old prophecies. One is almost inclined to believe that there must be a next world and a future life."

" I think such belief is now placed beyond mere in-clination," said the Cardinal—" There is surely no doubt of it."

Vergniaud gave him a quick side-glance of earnest scrutiny.

" With you, perhaps not—" he replied—" But with me,— well !—it is a different matter. However, it is really no use worrying one's self with the question of ' To be, or not to be.' It drove Hamlet mad, just as the knotty point as to whether Hamlet himself was fat or lean nearly killed our hysterical little boy, Catullus Mendès. It's best to leave eternal subjects like God and Shakespeare alone."

He laughed again, but the Cardinal did not smile.

" I do not agree with you, Vergniaud," he said—" I fear it is because we do not think sufficiently for our-selves on the One eternal subject that so much mischief threatens us at the present time. To take gifts and ignore the Giver is surely the blackest ingratitude, yet that is what the greater part of humanity is guilty of in these days. Never was there so much beholding and yet ignor-ing of the Divine as now. Science is searching for God, and is getting closer to Him every day;—the Church remains stationary and refuses to look out beyond her own pale of thought and conventional discipline. I know,—" and the Cardinal hesitated a moment, " I know

I can speak quite plainly to you, for you are what is called a freethinker—yet I doubt whether you are really as free as you imagine!"

The Abbé shrugged his shoulders.

"I imagine nothing!" he declared airily, "Everything is imagined for me nowadays,—and imagination itself is like a flying Geni which overtakes and catches the hair of some elusive Reality and turns its face round, full-shining on an amazed world!"

"A pretty simile!" said Angela Sovrani, smiling.

"Is it not? Almost worthy of Paul Verlaine who was too 'inspired' to keep either his body or his soul clean. Why was I not a poet! *Hélas!*—Fact so much outweighs fancy that it is no longer any use penning a sonnet to one's mistress's eyebrow. One needs to write with thunderbolts in characters of lightning, to express the wonders and discoveries of this age. When I find I can send a message from here to London across space, without wires or any visible means of communication,—and when I am told that probably one of these days I shall be able at will to *see* the person to whom I send the message, reflected in space while the message is being delivered,—I declare myself so perfectly satisfied with the fairy prodigies revealed to me, that I have really no time, and perhaps no inclination to think of any other world than this one."

"You are wrong, then," said the Cardinal, "Very wrong, Vergniaud. To me these discoveries of science, this apparent yielding of invisible forces into human hands, are signs and portents of terror. You remember the line 'the powers of heaven shall be shaken'? Those powers are being shaken now! We cannot hold them back;—they are here, with us;—but they mean much more than mere common utility to our finite selves. They are the material declarations of what is spiritual. They are the scientific proofs that Christ's words to '*this* generation,' namely, this particular phase of creation,—are true. 'Blessed are they which have not seen and yet believed,' He said;—and many there are who have passed away from us in rapt faith and hope, believing not seeing, and with whom we may rejoice in spirit, knowing that all must be well with them. But now—now we are come upon an age of doubt in the world—doubt which

corrodes and kills the divine spirit in man, and therefore we are being forced to *see* that we may believe,—but
the seeing is terrible!"

"Why?"

"Because in the very beholding of things we remain
blind!" answered the Cardinal, "Our intense selfishness
obscures the true light of every fresh advance. We accept new marvels of knowledge, as so much practical use
to us, and to the little planet we live on,—but we do not
see that they are merely reflections of the Truth from
which they emanate. The toy called the biograph, which
reflects pictures for us in a dazzling and moving con-
tinuity, so that we can see scenes of human life in action,
is merely a hint to us that every scene of every life is reflected in a ceaseless moving panorama *Somewhere* in the
Universe, for the beholding of *Someone*,—yes!—there
must be Someone who so elects to look upon everything,
or such possibilities of reflected scenes would not be,—
inasmuch as nothing exists without a Cause for existence. The wireless telegraphy is a stupendous warning of
the truth that 'from God no secrets are hid', and also
of the prophecy of Christ 'there is nothing covered that
shall not be revealed'—and, 'whatsoever ye have spoken
in darkness shall be revealed in light.' The latter words
are almost appalling in their absolute accord with the
latest triumphant discoveries of science."

Abbé Vergniaud looked at the Cardinal, and slightly
raised his eyebrows in a kind of wondering protest.

"*Tres-saint* Felix!" he murmured, "Are you turning
into a mystic? One of those doubtful personages who
are seeking to reconcile science with the Church?——"

"Stop!" interposed the Cardinal, raising his hand with
an eloquent gesture, "Science is, or should be, the
Church!—science is Truth, and Truth is God! God cannot be found anywhere in a lie; and the Church in many
ways would make our Divine Redeemer Himself a lie
were it not that His words are every day taking fresh
meaning, and bringing new and solemn conviction to
those who have eyes to see and ears to hear!"

He spoke as if carried beyond himself,—his pale cheeks
glowed,—his eyes flashed fire,—and the combined effect
of his words and manner was startling to the Abbé, and
in a way stupefying to his niece Angela. She had never

heard him give utterance to such strong sentiments before, and she shrank a little within herself, wondering whether as a Cardinal of the Roman Church he had not been too free of speech. She glanced apprehensively at Vergniaud, who however only smiled a little.

"If you should be disposed to express yourself in such terms at the Vatican,—" he began.

The Cardinal relapsed into his usual calm, and met the Abbé's questioning, half cynical glance composedly. "I have many things to speak of at the Vatican," he answered,—"This matter will probably be one of them."

"Then——" But whatever Vergniaud was about to say was interrupted by the entrance of the boy Manuel, who at that moment came into the room and stood beside the Cardinal's chair. The Abbé gave him an upward glance of surprise and admiration.

"Whom have we here?" he exclaimed, "One of your acolytes, Monseigneur?"

"No," replied the Cardinal, his eyes resting on the fair face of the lad with a wistful affection, "A little stray disciple of our Lord,—to whom I have ventured to offer protection. There is none to question my right to do so, for he is quite alone in the world."

And in a few words he related how he had discovered the boy on the previous night, weeping outside the Cathedral in Rouen. Angela Sovrani listened attentively, her violet eyes darkening and deepening as she heard,—now and then she raised them to look at the youthful waif who stood so quietly while the story of his troubles was told in the gentle and sympathetic way which was the Cardinal's usual manner of speech, and which endeared him so much to all. "And for the present," finished Bonpré, smiling—"he stays with me, and already I have found him skilled in the knowledge of many things,—he can read Scripture with a most musical and clear emphasis,— and he is a quick scribe, so that he will be valuable to me in more ways than one."

"Ah!" and the Abbé turned himself round in his chair to survey the boy more attentively, "You can read Scripture? But can you understand it? If you can, you are wiser than I am!"

Manuel regarded him straightly.

" Was it not once said in Judæa that *it is the Spirit that quickeneth'?*" he asked.

" True!—And from that you would infer . . . ?"

" That when one cannot understand Scripture, it is perhaps for the reason that *'the letter killeth, because lacking the Spirit that giveth life.'*"

The boy spoke gently and with grace and modesty,— but something in the tone of his voice had a strange effect on the cynical temperament of Abbé Vergniaud.

" Here," he mused, " is a lad in whom the principle of faith is strong and pure,—shall I drop the poison of doubt into the open flower of his mind, or leave it uncontaminated?" Aloud he said, kindly,

" You speak well,—you have evidently thought for yourself. Who taught you to recognise 'the Spirit that giveth life'?"

Manuel smiled.

" Does that need teaching?" he asked.

Radiance shone in his eyes,—the look of purity and candour on his young face was infinitely touching to the two men who beheld it,—the one worn with age and physical languors, the other equally worn in mind, if not in body. In the brief silence which followed,—a silence of unexpressed feeling,—a soft strain of organ-music came floating deliciously towards them,—a delicate thread of grave melody which wove itself in and out the air-spaces, murmuring suggestions of tenderness and appeal. Angela smiled, and held up one finger, listening.

" That is Mr. Leigh!" she said, " He is in my studio improvising."

" Happy Mr. Leigh!" said the Abbé with a little malicious twinkle in his eyes, " To be allowed to improvise at all in the studio of the Sovrani!"

Angela flushed, and lifted her fair head with a touch of pride.

" Mr. Leigh is a friend," she said, " He is welcome in the studio always. His criticism of a picture is valuable, —besides—he is a celebrated Englishman!" She laughed, and her eyes flashed.

" Ah! To a celebrated Englishman all things are conceded!" said the Abbé satirically, " Even the right to enter the sanctum of the most exclusive lady in Europe! Is it not a curious thing that the good Britannia appears to stick her helmet on the head, and put her sceptre in the hand of every one of her sons who condescends to soil his boots by walking on foreign soil? With the helmet he defies the *gendarme,*—with the sceptre he breaks open every door,—we prostrate ourselves before his face and curse him behind his back,—*c'est drôle!*—yet we are all alike, French, Germans, Austrians, and Italians;—we hate the Englishman, but we black his boots all the same,—which is contemptible of us,—*mais, que faire!* He is so overwhelming in sheer impudence! With culture and politeness we might cross swords in courtly duel,—but in the presence of absolute bluff, or what is called ' cheek ', we fall flat in sheer dismay! What delicious music! I see that it charms our young friend,—he is fond of music."

"Yes," said Manuel speaking for himself before any question could be put to him, " I love it! It is like the fresh air,—full of breath and life."

"Come then with me," said Angela, " Come into the studio and we will hear it more closely. Dearest uncle," and she knelt for a moment by the Cardinal's chair, " Will you come there also when Monsieur l'Abbé has finished talking with you? "

Cardinal Bonpré's hand rested lovingly on her soft hair.

"Yes, my child, I will come." And in a lower tone he added,—" Do not speak much to Manuel,—he is a strange lad; more fond of silence and prayer than other things, —and if such is his temperament I would rather keep him so."

Angela bowed her head in acquiescence to this bidding, —then rising, left the room with a gentle gesture of invitation to the boy, who at once followed her. As the two disappeared a chill and a darkness seemed to fall upon the air, and the Cardinal sank back among the cushions of his fauteuil with a deep sigh of utter exhaustion. Abbé Vergniaud glanced at him inquisitively.

"You are very tired, I fear? " he said.

"Physically, no,—mentally, yes. Spiritually, I am certainly fatigued to the death."

The Abbé shrugged his shoulders.

"*Hélas!* There is truly much in spiritual matters to engender weariness! " he said.

With a sudden access of energy the Cardinal gripped both arms of his chair and sat upright.

"For God's sake, do not jest," he said earnestly, "Do not jest! We have all been jesting too long, and the time is near when we shall find out the bitter cost of it! Levity—carelessness—doubt and final heresy—I do not mean heresy against the Church, for that is nothing——"

"Nothing!" exclaimed the Abbé, "*You* say this?"

"I say it!" And Bonpré's thin worn features grew transfigured with the fervour of his thought. "I am a priest of the Church—but I am also a man!—with reason, with brain, and with a love of truth;—and I can faithfully say I have an almost jealous honour for my Master —but I repeat, heresy against the Church is nothing,— it is heresy against Christ which is the crime of the age, —and in that, the very Church is heretic! Heresy against Christ!——Heresy against Christ! A whole system of heresy! 'I never knew you,—depart from me, ye workers of iniquity,' will be our Lord's words at the Last Judgment!"

The Abbé's wonderment increased. He looked down a moment, then looked up, and a quizzical, half-melancholy expression filled his eyes.

"Well, I am very much concerned in all this," he said, "I wanted to have a private talk with you on my own account, principally because I know you to be a good man, while I am a bad one. I have a trouble here,—" and he touched the region of his heart, "which the wise doctors say may end my days at any moment; two years at the utmost is the ultimatum of my life, so I want to know from you, whom I know to be intelligent and honest, whether you believe I am going to another existence,— and if so, what sort of a one you think is in prospect for such a man as I am? Now don't pity me, my dear Bonpré,—don't pity me!—" and he laughed a little huskily as the Cardinal took his hand and pressed it with a silent sympathy more eloquent than words, "We must all die, —and if I am to go somewhat sooner than I expected, that is nothing to compassionate me for. But there is just a little uncertainty in my mind,—I am not at all sure that death is the end—I wish I could be quite positive of the fact. I was once—quite positive. But science, instead of giving me this absolute comfort, has in its later progress upset all my former calculations, and I am afraid I must own that there is indubitably Something Else,—which to my mind seems distinctly disagreeable!"

Though the Abbé spoke lightly, the troubled look remained in his eyes and the Cardinal saw it.

"My dear Vergniaud," he began gently, "I am grieved at what you tell me—"

"No, don't be grieved," interrupted Vergniaud, "because that is not it. Talk to me! Tell me what you truly think. That this life is only a schoolroom where we do our lessons more or less badly?—That death is but the name for another life? Now do not *force* your faith for me. Tell me your own honest conviction. Do we end?—or do we begin again? Be frank and fair and true; according to the very latest science, remember!—not according to the latest hocus-pocus of twelfth-century mandate issued from Rome. You see how frank I am, and how entirely I go with you. But I am going further than you,—I am bound for the last voyage—so you must not offer me the wrong pass-word to the shore!"

"No, I will give you the right pass-word," said the Cardinal, a fervid glow of enthusiasm lighting up his features. "It is *Christ* in all, and through all! Christ only;—Christ, the friend and brother of man;—the only Divine Teacher this world has ever had, or ever will have!"

"You believe in Him really,—truly,—then?" exclaimed the Abbé wonderingly.

"Really—truly, and with all my heart and soul!" responded the Cardinal firmly,—"Surely, you too, believe?"

"No," said the Abbé firmly, "I do not! I would as soon believe that the lad you have just rescued from the streets of Rouen is divine, as that there is any divinity in the Man of Nazareth!"

He rose up as he spoke in a kind of petulance,—then started slightly as he found himself face to face with Manuel. The boy had entered noiselessly and stood for a moment glancing from one priest of the Church to the other. A faint smile was on his face,—his blue eyes were full of light.

"Did you call me, my lord Cardinal?" he asked.

The Cardinal looked up.

" No, my child! "

" I thought I heard you. If you should need me, I am close at hand."

He went away as quietly as he had entered; and the same silence followed his departure as before,—a silence which was only disturbed by the occasional solemn and sweet vibrations of the distant music from the studio.

VIII.

" A STRANGE lad!" said Abbé Vergniaud, abruptly.

" Strange? In what way do you find him so?" asked the Cardinal with a touch of anxiety.

The Abbé knitted his brows perplexedly, and took a short turn up and down the room. Then he laughed.

" Upon my word, I cannot tell you!" he declared, with one of those inimitable gestures common to Frenchmen, a gesture which may mean anything or nothing,—" But he speaks too well, and, surely, thinks too much for his years. Is there nothing further to tell of him save what you have already said? Nothing that you know of him, beyond the plain bare fact of having found him weeping alone outside the doors of the Cathedral?"

" Nothing indeed!" replied the Cardinal bewildered. " What else should there be?"

The Abbé hesitated a moment, and when he spoke again it was in a softer and graver tone.

" Forgive me! Of course there could be nothing else with you. You are so different to all other Churchmen I have ever known. Still, the story of your foundling is exceptional;—you will own that it is somewhat out of the common course of things, for a Cardinal to suddenly constitute himself the protector and guardian of a small tramp—for this boy is nothing else. Now, if it were any other Cardinal-Archbishop than yourself, I should at once say that His Eminence knew exactly where to find the mother of his protégé!"

" Vergniaud!" exclaimed the Cardinal.

" Forgive me! I said ' forgive me ' as a prelude to my remarks," resumed Vergniaud, " I am talking profanely, sceptically, and cynically,—I am talking precisely as the world talks, and as it always will talk."

" The world may talk itself out of existence, before it can hinder me from doing what I conceive to be my duty," said Felix Bonpré, calmly, " The lad is alone and

absolutely friendless,—it is but fitting and right that I
should do what I can for him."

Abbé Vergniaud sat down, and for a moment appeared
absorbed in thought.

"You are a curious man;" he at length observed,
"And a more than curious priest! Here you are, assum-
ing the guardianship of a boy concerning whom you
know nothing,—when you might as well have handed
him over to one of the orphanages for the poor, or have
paid for his care and education with some of the monastic brethren established near Rouen,—but no!—you
being eccentric, feel as if you were personally responsible to God for the child, simply because you found him
lost and alone, and therefore you have him with you.
It is very good of you,—we will call it great of you—but
it is not usual. People will say you have a private motive;
—you must remember that the world never gives you
credit for doing a good action simply for the pure sake
of doing it,—'There must be something behind it all,'
they say. When the worst *cocotte* of the age begins to
lose her beauty, the prospect is so alarming that she
thinks there may be a possible hell, after all, and she
straightway becomes charitable and renowned for good
works;—precisely in the same way as our famous stage
'stars', knowing their lives to be less clean than the
lives of their horses and their dogs, give subscriptions and
altar-cloths and organs to the clergy. It is all very
amusing!—I assure you I have often laughed at it. It is
as if they took Heaven by its private ear in confidence,
and said, 'See now, I want to put things straight with
you if I can!—and if a few church-ornaments, and can-
dlesticks will pacify you, why, take them and hold your
tongue!'"

He paused, but the Cardinal was silent.

"I know," went on the Abbé, "that you think I am
indulging in the worst kind of levity to talk in this way.
It sounds horrible to you. And you perhaps think I cannot be serious. My dear Saint Felix, there never was a
more serious man than I. I would give worlds—universes—to believe as you do! I have written books of
religious discussion,—not because I wanted the notice of
the world for them,—for that I do not care about,—but
for the sake of wrestling out the subject for myself, and

making my pen my confidant. I tell you I envy the woman who can say her rosary with the simple belief that
the Virgin Mary hears and takes delight in all those repetitions. Nothing would have given me greater pleasure
than to have composed a volume of prayers,—a 'Garland
of Flowers'—such as an innocent girl could hold in her
hands, and bend her sweet eyes over. It would have
been a taste of the sensual-spiritual, or the spiritual-
sensual,—which is the most exquisite of all human sensations."

"There is no taint of sensuality in the purely spiritual,"
said the Cardinal reprovingly.

"Not for your nature,—no! You have made your
body like a transparent scabbard through which the glitter of the soul-sword is almost visible. But I am different. I am so much of a materialist that I like to pull
down Heaven to the warm bosom of Earth and make
them mingle. You would lift up Earth to Heaven! Ah,
that is difficult! Even Christ came down! It is the chief
thing I admire in Him, that He 'descended from Heaven
and was made Man'. *Très cher* Felix, I shall bewilder
you to death with my specious and frivolous reasoning,—
and after all, I had much better come to the main fact of
what I intended to tell you,—a sort of confession out of
church. You know I have already told you I am going
to die soon, and that I am a bad man confessedly and
hopelessly,—but among other things is this, (and if you
can give me any advice upon it I will take it,) that for
the last four or five years I have been dodging about to
escape being murdered,—not because I particularly mind
being murdered, because I probably deserve it,—and one
way of exit is as good as another,—but because I want
to save the would-be murderer from committing his crime.
Is not that a good motive?"

Cardinal Bonpré gazed at him in astonishment. Vergniaud appeared to him in an entirely new light. He had
always known him as a careless, cynical-tempered man;—
a close thinker,—a clever writer, and a brilliant talker,—
and he had been inclined to consider him as a "society"
priest,—one of those amiable yet hypocritical personages,
who, by the most jesuitical flatteries and studied delica-
cies of manner, succeed in influencing weak-minded persons of wealth, (especially women) to the end of secur-

ing vast sums of money to the Church,—obtaining by these means such rank and favour for themselves as would otherwise never have been granted to them. But now the Abbé's frank admission of his own sins and failings seemed a proof of his inherent sincerity,—and sincerity, whether found in orthodoxy or heterodoxy, always commanded the Cardinal's respect.

"Are you speaking in parables or in grave earnest?" he asked. "Do you really mean that you are shadowed by some would-be assassin? An assassin, too, whom you actually wish to protect?"

"Exactly!" And Vergniaud smiled with the air of one who admits the position to be curious but by no means alarming. "I want to save him from the guillotine; and if he murders me I cannot! It is a question of natural instinct merely. The would-be assassin is my son!"

Cardinal Bonpré raised his clear blue eyes and fixed them full on the Abbé.

"This is a very serious matter," he said gently, "Surely it is best to treat it seriously?"

"Oh, I am serious enough, God knows!" returned Vergniaud, with a heavy but impatient sigh, "I suppose there is, there must be, some terribly exact Mathematician concerned in the working of things, else a man's past sins and failings being done with and over, would not turn up any more. But they *do* turn up,—the unseen Mathematician counts every figure;—and of course trouble ensues. My story is simply this;—Some twenty-five years ago I was in Touraine;—I was a priest as I am now—Oh, yes!—the sin is as black as the Church can make it!—and one mid-summer evening I strolled into a certain quaint old church of a certain quaint old town,— I need not name it—and saw there a girl, as sweet as an apple blossom, kneeling in front of the altar. I watched her,—I see her now!—the late sunlight through the stained glass window fell like a glory on her pretty hair, and on the little white kerchief folded so daintily across her bosom, and on her small hands and the brown rosary that was twisted round her fingers. She was praying, so she told me afterwards, to her guardian angel,—I wonder what that personage was about just then, Bonpré! Anyhow, to her petition came no answer but a devil,—a

devil personified in me,—I made her love me,—I tempted
her by every subtle and hellish persuasion I could think
of,—I can never even now think of that time without
wondering where all the eloquent evil of my tongue came
from——and—well!—she never was able to ask the
guardian angel any more favours! And I?——I think I
loved her for a while,—but no, I am not sure;—I believe
there is no such good thing as absolute love in my composition. Anyway, I soon left Touraine, and had almost
forgotten her when she wrote to tell me of the birth of
her child—a son. I gave her no reply, and then she
wrote again,—such a letter!—such words! At the moment they burnt me,—stabbed me—positively hurt me,—
and I was not then easily hurt. She swore she would
bring the boy up to curse his father,—and, to put it quite
briefly,—she did. She died when he was twenty, and it
now appears the lad took an oath by her death-bed that
he would never rest till he had killed the man who had
dishonoured his mother, and broken her heart, and
brought him into the world with a stigma on his name.
No filial respect, you see!" And Vergniaud tried to force
a smile. "To do the boy justice, he apparently means to
keep his oath,—he has not rested; he has been at infinite
pains to discover me; he has even been at the trouble to
write me a warning letter, and is now in Paris watching
me. I, in my turn, take care to protect myself;—I am
followed by detectives, and am at enormous pains to guard
my life; not for my own sake but for his. An odd complication of circumstances, is it not? I cannot have him
arrested because he would at once relate his history, and
my name would be ruined. And that would be quite as
good a vengeance for him as the other thing. You will
admit that it is a very dramatic situation!"

"It is a retribution!" said the Cardinal in a low voice,
"And a terrible one!"

"Yes, I suppose it is. I imagined you would consider
it in that light," and Vergniaud half closed his eyes,
leaning back in his chair languidly, "But here I am,
willing to set things as straight as I can, and it really
seems impossible to arrange matters. I am to die soon,
according to the doctors;—and so I have made my will,
leaving everything I possess to this ridiculous boy who
wishes to kill me; and it is more than probable that he,—

considering how he has been brought up and educated—will cast all the money into the dirt, and kick at my grave. But what can I do?"

"Nothing," said the Cardinal, "You can do nothing, Vergniaud! That is the worst of having inflicted a wrong upon the innocent,—you can never by any means retrieve it. You can repent,—and it is probable that your very repentance ensures your forgiveness at a higher tribunal than that of earth's judgment,—but the results of wrong cannot be wiped out or done away with in this life;—they continue to exist, and alas!—often multiply. Even the harsh or unjust word cannot be recalled, and however much we may regret having uttered it, somehow it is never forgotten. But—" here leaning forward, he laid one hand gently on Vergniaud's arm, "My dear friend—my dear brother—you have told me of your sin; —it is a great sin,—but God forbid that I should presume to judge you harshly when our Lord Himself declared that 'He came not to call the righteous but sinners to repentance'. It may be that I can find a way to help you. Arrange for me to see this misguided son of yours,—and I will endeavour to find a means of restitution to him and to the memory of his mother before you pass away from us,—if indeed you are to pass away so soon. Under the levity you assume I perceive you have deep feeling on this matter;—you shall not die with a wrong on your soul, Vergniaud!—you shall not if I can prevent it! For there undoubtedly *is* another life; you must go into it as purely as prayer and penitence can make you."

"I thought," said the Abbé, speaking somewhat unsteadily, "that you might when you heard all, hurl some of Rome's thunderous denunciations upon me . . . "

"What am I, and what is Rome, compared with the Master's own word?" said the Cardinal gently. "If our brothers sin against us seventy times seven we are still to forgive, and they are still our brothers! Denunciations, judgments and condemnations of one another are not any part of our Lord's commands."

Vergniaud rose up and held out his hand.

"Will you take it," he said, "as a pledge that I will faithfully do whatever you may see fitting and right to retrieve the past?—and to clear my son's soul from the thirst of vengeance which is consuming it?"

Cardinal Bonpré clasped the extended hand warmly. "There is your answer!" he said, with a smile which irradiated his fine countenance with an almost supernatural beauty and tenderness, "You have sinned against Heaven, and you have sinned against the Church and your own calling,—but the greatest sinner can do no more than repent and strive to make amends. For I see you fully know and comprehend the extent of your sin."

"Yes, I know it," and Vergniaud's eyes were clouded and his brows knitted, "I know it only too well! Greater than any fault of Church-discipline is a wrong to human life,—and I wronged and betrayed an innocent woman who loved me! Her soul was as sweet as the honey-cup of a flower,—I poisoned it. That was as bad as poisoning the Sacrament! I should have kept it sweet and pure; I should have let the Church go, and been honest! I should have seen to it that the child of my love grew up to honour his father,—not to merely live for the murder of him! Yes!—I know what I should have done—— I know what I have not done——and I am afraid I shall always know! Unless I can do something to atone I have a strange feeling that I shall pass from this world to the next—and that the first thing I shall see will be her face! Her face as I saw it when the sunshine made a halo round her hair, and she prayed to her guardian angel."

He shuddered slightly, and his voice died away in a half whisper. The Cardinal pressed his hand again warmly and tenderly.

"Courage, courage!" he said. "It is true we cannot do away with our memories,—but we can try and make them sweet. And who knows how much God may help us in the task? Never forget the words that tell us how 'the angels rejoice more over one sinner that repenteth than over ninety and nine just persons.'"

"Ah!" and the Abbé smiled, recovering somewhat of his usual manner, "And that is so faithfully enforced upon us, is it not? The Churches are all so lenient? And Society is so kind?—so gentle in its estimate of its friends? Our Church, for example, has never persecuted a sinner?—has never tortured an unbeliever? It has been so patient, and so unwearying in searching for stray sheep and bringing them back with love and tenderness and pity to the fold? And Churchmen never say anything which is slanderous or cruel? And we all follow Christ's teaching so accurately? Yes!—Ah well —I wonder! I wonder what will be the end! I wonder why we came into life at all—I wonder why we go! Fortunately for me, by and by, there will be an end of all wondering, and you can write above my tomb, ' Implora pace '! The idea of commencing a new life is to me, horrible,—I prefer ' Nirvana ' or nothingness. Never have I read truer words than those of Byron,

> ' Count o'er the joys thine hours have seen,
>   Count o'er thy days from anguish free,
>   And know whatever thou hast been,
>   'Tis something better not to be.' "

" I cannot think that is either true or good philosophy," said the Cardinal, " It is merely the utterance of a disappointed man in a misanthropic mood. There is no ' not to be ' in creation. Each morning that lights the world is an expression of ' to be '! And however much we may regret the fact, my dear Vergniaud, we find ourselves in a state of *being* and we must make the best of it,—not the worst. Is that not so? "

His look was gentle and commanding,—his voice soft yet firm,—and the worldly Abbé felt somewhat like a chidden child as he met the gaze of those clear true eyes that were undarkened by any furtive hypocrisies or specious meanings.

" I suppose it is, but unfortunately I have made the worst of it," he answered, " and having made the worst I see no best. Who is that singing? "

He lifted his hand with a gesture of attention as a rich mezzo-soprano rang out towards them,—

> " Per carità
>   Mostrami il cielo ;
>   Tulto è un velo,
>   E non si sa
>   Dove è il cielo.
>   Se si sta
>   Cosi colà,
>   Non si sa
>   Se non si va.
>   Ahi me lontano !
>   Tulto è in vano !
>   Prendimi in mano
>   Per carità!"

"It is Angela," said the Cardinal, "She has a wonderfully sweet voice."

> "Prendimi in mano,
> Per carità !"

murmured Abbé Vergniaud, still listening, "It is like the cry of a lost soul!"

"Or a strayed one," interposed the Cardinal gently, and rising, he took Vergniaud's arm, and leaned upon it with a kindly and familiar grace, an action which implied much more than the mere outward expression of confidence,—"Nothing is utterly lost, my dear friend. 'The very hairs of our head are numbered,'—not a drop of dew escapes to waste,—how much more precious than a drop of dew is the spirit of a man!"

"It is not so unsullied," declared Vergniaud, who loved controversy,—"Personally, I think the dew is more valuable than the soul, because so absolutely clean!"

"You must not bring every line of discussion to a pin's point," said Bonpré smiling, as he walked slowly across the room still leaning on the Abbé's arm. "We can reduce our very selves to the bodiless condition of a dream if we take sufficient pains first to advance a theory, and then to wear it threadbare. Nothing is so deceptive as human reasoning,—nothing so slippery and reversible as what we have decided to call 'logic.' The truest compass of life is spiritual instinct."

"And what of those who have no spiritual instinct?" demanded Vergniaud.

"I do not think there are any such. To us it certainly often seems as if there were masses of human beings whose sole idea of living is to gratify their bodily needs,—but I fancy it is only because we do not know them sufficiently that we judge them thus. Few, if any, are so utterly materialistic as never to have had some fleeting intuition of the Higher existence. They may lack the force to comprehend it, or to follow its teaching, —but in my opinion, the Divine is revealed to all men once at least in their lives."

They had by this time passed out of the drawing-room, and now, ascending three steps, they went through a curtained recess into Angela Sovrani's studio,—a large and lofty apartment made beautiful by the picturesque disorder and charm common to a great artist's surroundings. Here, at a grand piano sat Angela herself, her song finished, her white hands straying idly over the keys,—and near her stood the gentleman whom the Abbé Vergniaud had called " a terrible reformer and Socialist " and who was generally admitted to be something of a remarkable character in Europe. Tall and fair, with very bright flashing eyes, and a wonderfully high bred air of concentrated pride and resolution, united to a grace and courtesy which exhaled from him, so to speak, with his every movement and gesture, he was not a man to pass by without comment, even in a crowd. A peculiar distinctiveness marked him,—out of a marching regiment one would have naturally selected him as the commanding officer, and in any crisis of particular social importance or interest his very appearance would have distinguished him as the leading spirit of the whole. On perceiving the Cardinal he advanced at once to be presented, and as Angela performed the ceremony of introduction he slightly bent one knee, and bowed over the venerable prelate's extended hand with a reverence which had in it something of tenderness. His greeting of Abbé Vergniaud was, while perfectly courteous, not quite so marked by the grace of a strong man's submission.

"Ah, Mr. Leigh! So you have not left Paris as soon as you determined?" queried the Abbé with a smile, " I thought you were bound for Florence in haste?"

"I go to Florence to-morrow," answered Leigh briefly.

"So soon! I am indeed glad not to have missed you," said Cardinal Bonpré cordially. "Angela, my child, let me see what you have been doing. All your canvases are covered, or turned with their faces to the wall;—are we not permitted to look at any of them?"

Angela immediately rose from the piano, and wheeled a large oaken chair with a carved and gilded canopy, into the centre of the studio.

"Well, if you want to see my sketches—and they are only sketches," she said,—" you must come and sit here. Now," as her uncle obeyed her, " you look enthroned in state,—that canopy is just fitted for you, and you are a picture in yourself!—Yes, you are, dearest uncle! And not all the artists in the world could ever do you justice!

Monsieur l'Abbé, will you sit just where you please?—
And Mr. Leigh, you have seen everything, so it does not
matter."

"It matters very much," said Leigh with a smile, "For
I want to see everything again. If I may, I will stand
here."

And he took up his position close to the Cardinal's
chair.

"But where is the boy?" asked Vergniaud, "Where is
the foundling of the Cathedral?"

"He left us some minutes ago," said Angela, "He
went to your room, uncle."

"Was he pleased with the music?" asked the Cardinal.

"I think he enjoyed every note of it," said Leigh, "A
thoughtful lad! He was very silent while I played,—but
silence is often the most eloquent appreciation."

"Are we to be silent then over the work of Donna
Sovrani?" enquired the Abbé gaily. "Must we not express our admiration?"

"If you have any admiration to express," said Angela
carelessly, setting, as she spoke, an easel facing the Cardinal; "but I am afraid you will greatly disapprove of
me and condemn all my work this year. I should explain to you first that I am composing a very large picture,—I began it in Rome some three years ago, and it is
in my studio there,—but I require a few French types of
countenance in order to quite complete it. The sketches
I have made here are French types only. They will all
be reproduced in the larger canvas—but they are roughly
done just now. This is the first of them. I call it 'A
Servant of Christ, at the Madeleine, Paris.'"

And she placed the canvas she held on the easel and
stood aside, while all three men looked at it with very
different eyes,—one with poignant regret and pain,—the
other with a sense of shame,—and the third with a thrill
of strong delight in the power of the work, and of triumph
in the lesson it gave.

IX.

Low beetling brows,—a sensual, cruel mouth with a loosely projecting under-lip,—eyes that appeared to be furtively watching each other across the thin bridge of nose,—a receding chin and a narrow cranium, combined with an expression which was hypocritically humble, yet sly,—this was the type Angela Sovrani had chosen to delineate, sparing nothing, softening no line, and introducing no redeeming point,—a type mercilessly true to the life; the face of a priest,—" A servant of Christ," as she called him. The title, united with that wicked and repulsive countenance, was a terribly significant suggestion. For some minutes no one spoke,—and the Cardinal was the first to break the silence.

" Angela,—my dear child "—he said, in low, strained tones, " I am sorry you have done this! It is powerful —so powerful that it is painful as well. It cuts me to the heart that you should find it necessary to select such an example of the priesthood, though of course I am not in the secret of your aims—I do not understand your purpose . . ."

He broke off,—and Angela, who had stood silent, looking as though she were lost in a dream, took up his unfinished sentence.

" You do not understand my purpose?—Dearest uncle, I hardly understand it myself! Some force stronger than I am, is urging me to paint the picture I have begun,— some influence more ardent and eager than my own, burns like a fever in me, persuading me to complete the design. You blame me for choosing such an evil type of priest? But there is no question of choice! These faces are ordinary among our priests. At all the churches, Sunday after Sunday I have looked for a good, a noble face; —in vain! For an even commonly-honest face,—in vain! And my useless search has ended by impressing me with profound sorrow and disgust that so many low specimens of human intellect are selected as servants of our Lord. Do not judge me too severely! I feel that I have a work to do,—and a lesson to give in the work, when done. I may fail;—I may be told that as a woman I have no force, and no ability to make any powerful or lasting impression on this generation;—but at any rate I feel that I must try! If priests of the Church were like you, how different it would all be! But you always forget that you are an exception to the rule,—you do not realise how very exceptional you are! I told you before I showed you this sketch that you would probably disapprove of it and condemn me,—but I really cannot help it. In this matter nothing—not even the ban of the Church itself, can deter me from fulfilling what I have designed to do in my own soul!"

She spoke passionately and with ardour,—and the Cardinal looked at her with something of surprise and trouble. The fire of genius is, as he knew, a consuming one, —and he had never entirely realized how completely it filled and dominated this slight feminine creature for whom he felt an almost paternal tenderness. Before he could answer her the Abbé Vergniaud spoke.

"Donna Sovrani is faithful to the truth in her sketch," he said, "therefore, as a lover of truth I do not see, my dear Bonpré, why you should object! If she has,—as she says,—some great aim in view, she must fulfil it in her own way. I quite agree with her in her estimate of the French priests,—they are for the most part despicable-looking persons,—only just a grade higher than their brothers of Italy and Spain. But what would you have? The iron hand of Rome holds them back from progress, —they are speaking and acting lies; and like the stage-mimes, have to put on paint and powder to make the lies go down. But when the paint and powder come off, the religious mime is often as ill-looking as the stage one! Donna Sovrani has caught this particular example, before he has had time to put on holy airs and turn up the footlights. What do you think about it, Mr. Leigh?"

"I think, as I have always thought," said Leigh quietly, "that Donna Sovrani is an inspired artist,—and that being inspired it follows that she must carry out her own convictions whether they suit the taste of others or not. 'A Servant of Christ' is a painful truth, boldly declared."

Angela was unmoved by the compliment implied. She only glanced wistfully at the Cardinal, who still sat silent. Then without a word she withdrew the offending sketch from the easel and set another in its place.

"This," she said gently, " is the portrait of an Arch-bishop. I need not name his diocese. He is very wealthy, and excessively selfish. I call this, ' *Lord, I thank thee that I am not as other men* '."

Vergniaud laughed as he looked,—he knew the pic-tured dignitary well. The smooth countenance, the little eyes comfortably sunken in small rolls of fat, the smug smiling lips, the gross neck and heavy jaw,—marks of high feeding and prosperous living,—and above all the perfectly self-satisfied and mock-pious air of the man,— these points were given with the firm touch of a master's brush, and the Abbé, after studying the picture closely, turned to Angela with a light yet deferential bow.

"Chère Sovrani, you are stronger than ever! Surely you have improved much since you were last in Paris? Your strokes are firmer, your grasp is bolder. Have your French confrères seen your work this year?"

"No," replied Angela, " I am resolved they shall see nothing till my picture is finished."

" May one ask why? "

A flash of disdain passed over the girl's face.

"For a very simple reason! They take my ideas and use them,—and then, when my work is produced they say it is *I* who have copied from *them,* and that women have no imagination! I have been cheated once or twice in that way,—this time no one has any idea what I am doing."

"No one? Not even Signor Varillo? "

"No," said Angela, smiling a little, " Not even Signor Varillo. I want to surprise him."

"In what way? " asked the Cardinal, rousing himself from his pensive reverie.

Angela blushed.

"By proving that perhaps, after all, a woman can do a great thing in art,—a really great thing! " she said, " Designed greatly, and greatly executed."

"Does he not admit that, knowing you? " asked Aubrey Leigh suggestively.

"Oh, he is most kind and sympathetic to me in my work," explained Angela quickly, vexed to think that she had perhaps implied some little point that was not quite in her beloved one's favour. " But he is like most men,—they have a preconceived idea of women, and of what their place should be in the world—"

" Unchanged since the early phases of civilization, when women were something less valuable than cattle? " said Leigh smiling.

" Oh, the cattle idea is not exploded, by any means! " put in Vergniaud. " In Germany and Switzerland, for example, look at the women who are ground down to toil and hardship there! The cows are infinitely prettier and more preferable, and lead much pleasanter lives. And the men for whom these poor wretched women work, lounge about in cafés all day, smoking and playing dominoes. The barbaric arrangement that a woman should be a man's drudge and chattel is quite satisfactory, I think, to the majority of our sex. It is certainly an odd condition of things that the mothers of men should suffer most from man's cruelty. But it is the work of an all-wise Providence, no doubt; and you, Mr. Leigh, will swear that it is all right! "

" It *is* all right," said Leigh quietly, " or rather I should say, it *will* be all right,—and it would have been all right long ago, if we had, as Emerson puts it, ' accepted the hint of each new experience.' But that is precisely what we will not do. Woman is the true helpmate of man, and takes a natural joy in being so whenever we will allow it,—whenever we will give her scope for her actions, freedom for her intelligence, and trust for her instincts. But for the present many of us still prefer to play savage,—the complete savage in low life,—the civilized savage in high. The complete savage is found in the dockyard labourer, who makes a woman bear his children and then kicks her to death,—the savage in high life is the man who equally kills the mother of his children, but in another way, namely, by neglect and infidelity, while he treats his numerous mistresses just as the Turk treats the creatures of his harem—merely as so many pretty soft animals, requiring to be fed with sweets and ornamented with jewels, and then to be cast aside when done with. All pure savagery! But we are slowly evolving from it into something better. A few of us there are, who honour womanhood,—a few of us believe in women as guiding stars in our troubled sky,—a few of us would work and climb to greatness for love of the one woman we adore,—would conquer all obstacles,—ay, would die for her if need be, or what is far more difficult, would live for her the life of a hero and martyr! Yes—such things are done,—and men can be found who will do such things—all for a woman's sake."

There was a wonderful passion in his voice,—a deep thrill of earnestness which carried conviction with sweetness. Cardinal Bonpré looked at him with a smile.

"You are perhaps one of those men, Mr. Leigh?" he said.

"I do not know,—I may be," responded Leigh, a flush rising to his cheeks;—"but,—so far, no woman has ever truly loved me, save my mother. But apart from all personalities, I am a great believer in women. The love of a good woman is a most powerful lever to raise man to greatness,—I do not mean by 'good' the goody-goody creature,—no, for that is a sort of woman who does more mischief in her so-called 'blameless' life than a very Delilah. I mean by 'good', a strong, pure, great soul in woman,—sincere, faithful, patient, full of courage and calm,—and with this I maintain she must prove a truly God-given helpmate to man. For we are rough creatures at best,—irritable creatures too!—you see," and here a slight smile lighted up his delicate features, "we really do try more or less to reach heights that are beyond us— we are always fighting for a heaven of some sort, whether we make it of gold, or politics, or art;—it is a 'heaven' or a 'happiness' that we want;—we would be as gods,— we would scale Olympus,—and sometimes Olympus refuses to be scaled! And then we tumble down, very cross, very sore, very much ruffled;—and it is only a woman who can comfort us then, and by her love and tenderness mend our broken limbs and put salve on our wounded pride."

"Well, then, surely the Church is in a very bad way," said Vergniaud smiling, "Think of the vow of perpetual celibacy!"

"Celibacy cannot do away with woman's help or influence," said Leigh, "There are always mothers and sisters, instead of sweethearts and wives. I am in favour of celibacy for the clergy. I think a minister of Christ should be free to work for and serve Christ only."

"You are quite right, Mr. Leigh;" said the Cardinal, "There is more than enough to do in every day of our lives if we desire to truly follow His commands. But in this present time, alas!—religion is becoming a question of form—not of heart."

"Dearest uncle, if you think that, you will not judge me too severely for my pictures," said Angela quickly, throwing herself on her knees beside him. "Do you not see? It is just because the ministers of Christ are so lax that I have taken to studying them in my way,—which is, I know, not your way;—still, I think we both mean one and the same thing!"

"You are a woman, Angela," said the Cardinal gently, "and as a woman you must be careful of offences——"

"Oh, a woman!" exclaimed Angela, her beautiful eyes flashing with mingled tenderness and scorn, and her whole face lighting up with animation, "Only a woman! *She* must not give a grand lesson to the world! *She* must not, by means of brush or pen, point out to a corrupt generation the way it is going! Why? Because God has created her to be the helpmate of man! Excellent reason! Man is taking a direct straight road to destruction, and she must not stop him by so much as lifting a warning finger! Again, why? Only because she is a woman! But I—were I twenty times a woman, twenty times weaker than I am, and hampered by every sort of convention and usage,—I would express my thoughts somehow, or die in the attempt!"

"*Bravissima!*" exclaimed Vergniaud, "Well said, *chère* Sovrani!—Well said! But I am the mocking demon always, as you know—and I should almost be tempted to say that you *will* die in the attempt! I do not mean that you will die physically,—no, you will probably live to a good old age; people who suffer always do!—but you will die in the allegorical sense. You will grow the stigmata of the Saviour in your hands and feet—you will bear terrible marks of the nails hammered into your flesh by your dearest friends! You will have to wear a crown of thorns, set on your brows no doubt by those whom you most love . . . and the vinegar and gall will be very quickly mixed and offered to you by the whole world of criticism without a moment's hesitation! And you will probably have to endure your agony alone,—

as nearly everyone runs away from a declared Truth, or if they pause at all, it is only to spit upon it and call it a Lie!"

"Do not prophesy so cruel a fate for the child!" said the Cardinal tenderly, taking Angela's hand and drawing her towards him. "She has a great gift,—I am sure she will use it greatly. And true greatness is always acknowledged in the end."

"Yes, when the author or the artist has been in the grave for a hundred years or more;" said Verginaud incorrigibly. "I am not sure that it would not be better for Donna Sovrani's happiness to marry the amiable Florian Varillo at once rather than paint her great picture! Do you not agree with me, Mr. Leigh?"

Leigh was turning over an old volume of prints in a desultory and abstracted fashion, but on being addressed, looked up quickly.

"I would rather not presume to give an opinion," he said somewhat coldly, "It is only on the rarest occasions that a woman's life is balanced between love and fame, —and the two gifts are seldom bestowed together. She generally has to choose between them. If she accepts love she is often compelled to forego fame, because she merges herself too closely into the existence of another to stand by her own individuality. If on the other hand, she chooses fame, men are generally afraid of or jealous of her, and leave her to herself. Donna Sovrani, however, is a fortunate exception,—she has secured both fame —and love."

He hesitated a moment before saying the last words, and his brows contracted a little. But Angela did not see the slight cloud of vexation that darkened his eyes,—his words pleased her, and she smiled.

"Ah, Mr. Leigh sees how it is with me!" she said, "He knows what good cause I have to be happy and to do the best work that is in me! It is all to make Florian proud of me!—and he *is* proud—and he will be prouder! You must just see this one more sketch taken from life, —it is the head of one of our most noted surgeons,—I call it for the present 'A Vivisectionist'."

It was a wonderful study,—perhaps the strongest of the three she had shown. It was the portrait of a thin, fine, intellectual face, which in its every line suggested

an intense, and almost dreadful curiosity. The brows
were high, yet narrow,—the eyes clear and cold, and pitiless in their straight regard,—the lips thin and compressed,—the nose delicate, with thin open nostrils, like
those of a trained sleuth-hound on the scent of blood. It
was a three-quarter-length picture, showing the hand of
the man slightly raised, and holding a surgeon's knife,—
a wonderful hand, rather small, with fingers that are generally termed " artistic "—and a firm wrist, which Angela had worked at patiently, carefully delineating the
practised muscles employed and developed in the vivisectionist's ghastly business.

Aubrey Leigh stood contemplating it intently.

" I think it is really the finest of all the types," he
said presently, " One can grasp that man's character so
thoroughly! There is no pity in him,—no sentiment—
there is merely an insatiable avidity to break open the
great treasure-house of Life by fair means or foul! It
is very terrible—but very powerful."

" I know the man," said Abbé Vergniaud, " Did he sit
to you willingly?"

" Very willingly indeed!" replied Angela, " He was
quite amused when I told him frankly that I wanted him
as a type of educated and refined cruelty."

" Oh, these fellows see nothing reprehensible in their
work," said Leigh, " And such things go on among them
as make the strongest man sick to think of! I know of
two cases now in a hospital; the patients are incurable,
but the surgeons have given them hope of recovery
through an ' operation ' which, however, in their cases,
will be no ' operation ' at all, but simply vivisection. The
poor creatures have to die anyhow, it is true, but death
might come to them less terribly,—the surgeons, however, will ' operate ', and kill them a little more quickly,
in order to grasp certain unknown technicalities of their
disease."

Angela looked at him with wide-open eyes of pain and
amazement.

" Horrible!" she murmured, " Absolutely horrible!
Can nothing be done to interfere with, or to stop such
cruelty?"

" Nothing, I fear," said Leigh, " I have been abroad
some time, studying various ' phases ', of its so-called

intellectual and scientific life, and have found many of these phases nothing but an output of masked barbarity. The savages of Thibet are more pitiful than the French or Italian vivisectionist,—and the horrors that go on in the laboratories would not be believed if they were told. Would not be believed! They would be flatly denied, even by the men who are engaged in them! And were I to write a plain statement of what I know to be true, and send it to an English journal, it would not be put in, not even in support of the Anti-Vivisection Society, lest it might ' offend ' the foreign schools of surgery, and also perhaps lest English schools might prove not altogether free from similar crimes. If, however, by chance, such a statement were published, it would be met with an indignant chorus of denial from every quarter of accusation! How, then, can justice be obtained from what I call the New Inquisition? The old-time Inquisitors tortured their kind for Religion's sake,—the modern ones do it in the name of Science,—but the inhumanity, the callousness, the inborn savage love of cruelty—are all the same in both instances."

Cardinal Bonpré shuddered as he heard.

"Lord Christ, where art thou!" he thought, "Where is Thy spirit of unfailing tenderness and care? How is Thy command of ' love one another ' obeyed!" Aloud he said, "Surely such deeds, even in the cause of surgical science, ought not to be permitted in a Christian city?"

"Christian city!" and Vergniaud laughed, "You would not apply that designation to Paris, would you? Paris is hopelessly, riotously pagan;—nay, not even pagan, for the pagans had gods and Paris has none! Neither Jove—nor Jupiter—nor Jehovah! As for the Christ,—He is made the subject of many a public caricature,—yes!—you may see them in the side-streets pasted upon the walls and hoardings!—and also of many a low lampoon;—but He is not accepted as a Teacher, nor even as an Example. His reign is over, in Paris at least!"

"Stop!" said the Cardinal, rising suddenly, "I forbid you, Vergniaud, to tell me these things! If they are true, then shame upon you and upon all the clergy of this unhappy city to stand by and let such disgrace to yourselves, and blasphemy to our Master, exists without protest!"

His tall spare figure assumed a commanding grandeur and authority,—his pale face flushed and his eyes sparkled —he looked inspired—superb—a very apostle burning with righteous indignation. His words seemed to have the effect of an electric shock on the Abbé,—he started as though stung by the lash of a whip, and drew himself up haughtily . . . then meeting the Cardinal's straight glance, his head drooped, and he stood mute and rigid. Leigh, though conscious of embarrassment as the witness of a strong reproof administered by one dignitary of the Church to another, yet felt deeply interested in the scene, —Angela shrank back trembling,—and for a few moments which, though so brief, seemed painfully long, there was a dead silence. Then Verginaud spoke in low stifled accents.

"You are perfectly right, Monseigneur! It *is* shame to me!—and to the priesthood of France! I am no worse than the rest of my class,—but I am certainly no better! Your reproach is grand,—and just! I accept it, and ask your pardon!"

He bent one knee, touched the Cardinal's ring with his lips, and then without another word turned and left the room. The Cardinal gazed after his retreating figure like a man in a dream, then he said gently,

"Angela, go after him!—Call him back!——"

But it was too late. Vergniaud had left the house before Angela could overtake him. She came back hurriedly to say so, with a pale face and troubled look. Her uncle patted her kindly on the shoulder.

"Well, well!—It will not hurt him to have seen me angry," he said smiling, "Anger in a just cause is permitted. I seem to have frightened you, Angela? Of a truth I have rather frightened myself! There, we will not talk any more of the evils of Paris. Mr. Leigh perhaps thinks me an intolerant Christian?"

"On the contrary I think you are one of the few 'faithful' that I have ever met," said Leigh, "Of course I am out of it in a way, because I do not belong to the Roman Church. I am supposed—I say 'supposed' advisedly—to be a Church of England man, or to put it more comprehensively, a Protestant, and I certainly am so much of the latter that I protest against all our systems altogether!"

" Is that quite just? " asked Bonpré gently.

" Perhaps not!—but what is one to do? I am not alone in my ideas! One of our English bishops has been lately deploring the fact that out of a thousand lads in a certain parish nine-hundred-and-ninety-nine of them never go to church! Well, what can you expect? I do not blame those nine-hundred and-ninety-nine at all. I am one with them. *I* never go to church."

" Why? "

" Simply because I never find any touch of the true Spirit of Christ there—and the whole tone of the place makes me feel distinctly un-Christian. The nine-hundred-and-ninety-nine youths possibly would sympathise with me. A church is a building more or less beautiful or ugly as the case may be, and in the building there is generally a man who reads prayers in a sing-song tone of voice, and perhaps another man who preaches without eloquence on some text which he utterly fails to see the true symbolical meaning of. There are no Charles Kingsleys nowadays,—if there were, I should call myself a ' Kingsleyite '. But as matters stand I am not moved by the church to feel religious. I would rather sit quietly in the fields and hear the gentle leaves whispering their joys and thanksgivings above my head, than listen to a human creature who has not even the education to comprehend the simplest teachings of nature, daring to assert himself as a teacher of the Divine. My own chief object in life has been and still is to speak on this and similar subjects to the people who are groping after lost Christianity. They need helping, and I want to try in my way to help them."

" Groping alter lost Christianity! " echoed the Cardinal, " Those words are a terrible indictment, Mr. Leigh! "

" Yet in your own soul your Eminence admits it to be true," returned Leigh quickly,—" I can see the admission in your eyes,—in the very expression of your face! You feel in yourself that the true spirit of Christ is lacking in all the churches of the present day,—that the sheep are straying for lack of the shepherd, and that the wolf is in the fold! You know it,—you feel it,—you see it! "

Cardinal Bonpré's head drooped.

" God help me and forgive me, I am afraid I do! " he

said sorrowfully. " I see the shadow of the storm before
it draws nigh,—I feel the terror of the earthquake before
it shakes down the edifice! No, the world is not with
Christ to-day!—and unhappily it is a fact that Christ's
ministers in recent years have done more to sever Him
from Humanity than any other power could ever have succeeded in doing. Not by action, but by inertia!—dumbness—lack of protest,—lack of courage! Only a few
stray souls stand out firm and fair in the chaos,—only
a few!"

"'I know thy works, that thou art neither cold nor
hot,—I would thou wert cold or hot! So because thou
art lukewarm and neither cold nor hot I will spew thee
out of my mouth!'" quoted Leigh, his eyes flashing and
his voice trembling with repressed earnestness, " That is
the trouble all through! Apathy,—dead, unproductive
apathy and *laissez-faire!*—Ah, I believe there are some
of us living now who are destined to see strange and terrible things in this new century!"

" For myself," said the Cardinal slowly, " I think there
is not much time left us! I feel a premonition of Divine
wrath threatening the world, and when I study the aspect of the times and see the pride, licentiousness, and
wealth-worship of men, I cannot but think the days are
drawing near when our Master will demand of us account
of our service. It is just the same as in the case of the
individual wrong-doer, when it seems as if punishment
were again and again retarded, and mercy shown,—yet
if all benefits, blessings and warnings are unheeded,
then at last the bolt falls suddenly and with terrific
effect. So with nations—so with churches—so with the
world!"

His voice grew feeble, and his eyes were clouded with
pain.

" You are fatigued," said Leigh gently, " And I ought
not to have stayed so long. I will bid you farewell now.
If I am in Rome when you are there, I trust you will permit me to pay my respects to you?"

" It will be a pleasure to see you, my son," answered
the Cardinal, pressing his hand and courteously prevent-
ing him from making the formal genuflection, " And let
me add that it will help me very much to hear from you
what progress you make in your intention of working for

Christ. For,—when you speak to the people as a teacher, it is in His name, is it not?"

"In His name, and I pray in His spirit," said Leigh, "But not through any church."

The Cardinal sighed, but said no more, and Leigh turned to Angela.

"Good-bye," he said, "I may come and see the picture in Rome?"

"You may indeed," and Angela gave him her hand in frank friendliness, "I shall feel the necessity of your criticism and the value of your opinion."

He looked at her intently for a moment.

"Be of good courage," he then said in a low tone, "'Work out your own salvation', it is the only way! Fulfil the expression of your whole heart and soul and mind, and never heed what opposing forces may do to hinder you. You are so clear-brained, so spiritually organised, that I cannot imagine your doing anything that shall not create a power for good. You are sometimes inclined to be afraid of the largeness of your own conceptions in the picture you are dreaming of,—I can see that,—but do not fear! The higher influences are with you and in you;—give yourself up to them with absolute confidence! Good-bye—God bless you!" He stooped and kissed her hand,—then left the room.

Angela looked after him, and a half sigh escaped her lips unconsciously. The Cardinal watched her with rather a troubled look. After a little silence he said,

"You must pardon me, my child, if I seemed over hasty in my judgment of your work . . ."

"Dearest uncle, do not speak of it!" exclaimed Angela, "You were pained and sorry to see such a 'servant of Christ' as the type I chose,—you could not help expressing your feeling——it was natural . . ."

"Yes, I was vexed,—I own it!—" went on Bonpré, "For I know many priests, poor, patient, simple men, who do their best for our Lord according to their measure and capability,—men who deserve all honour, all love, all respect, for the integrity of their lives,—still—I am aware that these are in the minority, and that men of the kind your sketch depicts, compose alas!—the majority. There is a frightful preponderance of evil influences in the world! Industry, and commerce, and science have advanced, and yet a noble and upright standard of conduct among men is sadly lacking. Men are seeking for happiness in Materialism, and find nothing but satiety and misery,—satiety and misery which become so insupportable that very often suicide presents itself as the only way out of such a tangle of wretchedness! Yes, child!—all this is true—and if you think you have a lesson to give which will be useful in these dark days, no one,—I least of all—should presume to hinder you from giving it. Still, remember that the results of work are not with the worker to determine—they rest with God."

"Truly I hope they do," said Angela fervently, "For then all bad work will pass away and only the good and necessary remain."

"That always is the rule," said the Cardinal, "No criticism can kill good work or vivify bad. So be happy, Angela *mia!* Paint your great picture with courage and hope—I will neither judge nor condemn, and if the world's verdict should be cruel, mine shall be kind!"

He smiled and stroked her soft hair, then taking her arm he leaned upon it affectionately as they left the studio together.

X.

THE next day, and the next after that, were passed by
the Cardinal in gratifying a certain eagerness shown by
his young foundling, Manuel, to see the churches and
great public buildings of Paris. The boy had a quiet,
straightforward way of expressing his wishes and opinions, and a certain marked individuality in his manner—
in fact, so simple and straight were his words, and so
much to the point, that they sometimes caused confusion
to his hearers. Once or twice he gave offence, as for
example, on visiting a great church where there were
numerous jewelled relics and priceless treasures of old
lace and embroidery, when he said suddenly:

"There is a woman just outside the door, very ill and
poor, with two little starving children;—would it not be
well to sell some of the jewels here and give her the
money?"

The custodian looked amazed, and the attendant priest
who was escorting Cardinal Bonpré through the building,
frowned.

"The treasures of the Church are not to be sold," he
said curtly. "The beggar outside is no doubt a trained
hypocrite."

"Christ would not say so," answered Manuel softly,—
"He would not, even if He knew her to be a hypocrite, retain anything of value for Himself, if by giving it to her,
He could ease her pain and poverty. I cannot understand why the Church should keep jewels."

"That is because you are ignorant," said the priest
roughly.

Manuel raised his grave blue eyes and fixed them steadily upon him.

"That may be," he said, "Yet I think it is nowhere
written in the Gospel that Christ cared for the world's
wealth or the world's possessions. When they are offered to Him did he not say, 'Get thee behind me, Satan'! The only gem he prized was the 'pearl of great
price,'—the pure and perfect human soul."

"The Church is the manufactory of those pearls," said the priest, with something between a grin and a sneer.

"Then the Church needs no other jewels" returned Manuel quietly, with a little gesture of his hand, "These glittering baubles you show, are out of place."

The priest glanced him over with angry contempt. Then he said to the Cardinal,

"Your Eminence will have trouble with that boy," he said. "His opinions are heretic."

The Cardinal smiled a little.

"You think so? Nay, there is something of truth in what he says, notwithstanding his simplicity of utterance, which is not perhaps in accordance with convention. I confess that I share his opinions somewhat. Certainly I esteem myself happy that in my far-off diocese there are none of the world's precious things, but only the un-prized prayers of the faithful."

The priest said nothing in reply,—but he was conscious of discomfort and uneasiness, and hurried through the rest of his duties with an ill-grace, annoyed, though he knew not why, by the very presence of Manuel. The boy, however, paid no heed to his angry glances, and noted everything in his own quiet meditative way,—a way which was a singularly winning one, graced as it was by an almost scholarly thoughtfulness united to the charm of youth. Once, before a magnificent priest's garment of lace, he paused, and touched the substance lightly.

"See," he said softly, looking wistfully up in the Cardinal's face, "See all the leaves and rosebuds worked in this by the needle,—and think how many human eyes have strained at it, and grown dull and blind over it! If one could only believe that the poor eyes were comforted at all in the following of the difficult thread!—but no,— the sunshine must have lessened and the days grown darker and darker, till death came and gently shut up the lids of the tired orbs of earthy vision, and opened those of the soul to Light indeed! This work speaks with a thousand tongues! I can hear them! Torture,—poverty, —pain,—pitilessness,—long hours,—scant reward,—tired fingers,—weary hearts!—and a priest of Christ wears this to perform Christ's service! Clad in a garment of human suffering, to preach mercy! Is it not strange?"

"You think too deeply, my child," said the Cardinal,

moved by the tender pity in Manuel's voice, " Nothing is accomplished without pain in this world,—our dear Lord Himself suffered pain."

" True," said Manuel, " But His pain was endured that there might be less of it for others! He asked His children in this world to love one another for His sake—not to grind each other down! Not to make unnecessary hardships for each other! But it seems as if He had asked in vain! "

He was silent after this, and refrained from remark even when, during their visit to Notre Dame, the treasury was unlocked for the Cardinal's inspection, and the relics formerly contained in the now disused " Sainte Chapelle," were shown,—including the fragments of the " crown of thorns," and a nail from the " true cross." The Cardinal was silent too. He had no remark to offer on these obvious " imaginations " of the priesthood. Then they went up together to the platform on the summit of the Cathedral, and looked at the great bell known as the " Bourdon de Notre Dame ";—and here they found a little wizened old man sitting carelessly on the edge of a balustrade, in a seemingly very dangerous position, who nodded and smiled familiarly as they appeared. He acted as cicerone of the summit of the North Tower, and was soon at their side explaining volubly all that was of interest.

" Tired,—oh yes, one gets tired! " he admitted, in response to a query from the Cardinal as to whether he did not find his duties fatiguing at his age, " But after all, I like the griffins and dragons and devils' faces up here, better than the griffins and dragons and devils down there, —below on the Boulevards! I call this Heaven, and down there in the streets, Hell. Yes, truly! It is wholesome up here,—the sky seems very near, and the sculptured beasts do no harm. But down in the streets one feels and smells the dirt and danger directly. I sit here all by myself for hours thinking, when no one comes to visit the tower,—for sometimes a whole day passes and no one wishes to ascend. And there is a moral in that, Monseigneur, if one has eyes to see it;—days pass, years, in the world,—and no one wishes to ascend!—to Heaven, I mean!—to go down to Hell is delightful, and everyone is ready for it! It is at night that the platform here is most beautiful,—oh yes, at night it is very fine, Monseigneur!—but it is only madmen and dreamers who call me up in the night hours, yet when they do I never refuse to go with them, for look you, I am a light sleeper and have no wife to bid me keep my bed. Yes,—if the authorities knew that I took anybody up to the tower at night they would probably dismiss me," and he chuckled like an old schoolboy with a sense of his own innate mischief and disobedience, " But you see they do not know! And I learn a great deal from the strange persons who come at night,—much more than from the strange persons who come by day. Now, the last so strange person that came here by night—you would not perhaps believe it, Monseigneur, but it was a priest! Yes," and the old fellow laughed, " a priest who had suddenly found out that the Church was not following its Master! Yes, yes! . . . just fancy killing himself for that!"

" Killing himself!" cried the Cardinal, " What do you mean?"

" You would like to hear the story?—ah, take care, *mon ange!*" he cried, as he perceived Manuel standing lightly near the brink of the platform, and stretching out his arms towards the city, " Thou art not a bird to fly from that edge in the air! What dost thou see?"

" Paris!" replied the boy in strangely sorrowful accents, turning his young, wistful face towards the Cardinal, his hair blown back in the light wind, " All Paris!"

" Ah!—'tis a fine sight, all Paris!" said the old guide —" one of the finest in the world, to judge by the outside of it. But the inside is a very different matter; and if Paris is not a doomed city, then there is no God, and I know nothing of the Bible. It has got all the old sins in a new shape, and revels in them. And of the story of the priest, if you would hear it;—ah!—that is well!" he said, as Manuel left the giddy verge of the platform where he had been standing, and drew near. " It is safer to be away from that edge, my child! And for the poor priest, it happened in this way,—it was a fair night, and the moon was high—I was dozing off in a chair in my room below, when the bell rang quickly, yet softly. I got up wth pleasure, for I said to myself, ' here is an artist or a poet,—one of those persons who are unlike anyone else ' —just as I am myself unlike anyone else—' and so we two

shall have a pleasant evening.' But when I opened the
door there was no one but a priest, and poor-looking even
at that; and he was young and pale, and very uneasy in
his manner, and he said to me, ' Jean Lapui '—(that is
my name)—' let me pass up to the platform.' ' Willingly,' said I, ' if I may go with you.' ' Nay, I would
rather be alone,' he answered. ' That may not be,' I told
him, ' I am as pleased to see the moonbeams shining on
the beasts and devils as any man,—and I shall do you no
harm by my company.' Well, he agreed to have me
then, and up we went the three hundred and seventy-eight
steps,—(it is a long way, Monseigneur;—)and he
mounted quickly, I slowly,—but always keeping my eye
upon him. At last we reached this platform, and the
moonlight was beautiful, and clear as day. Then my
little priest sat down and began to laugh. ' Ha, my
Lapui!' he said, ' Is it not droll that this should be all a
lie! All this fine building, and all the other fine buildings of the kind in Paris! Strange, my Lapui, is it not,
that this Cathedral should be raised to the worship of a
God whom no one obeys, or even thinks of obeying! All
show, my good Lapui! All to feed priests like me, and
keep them going—but God has nothing to do with it—
nothing at all, I swear to you!'—' You may be right, *mon
révérend,*' I said, (for I saw he was not in a mood to be
argued with)—" Yet truly the Cathedral has not always
been a place of holiness. In seventeen ninety-three there
was not much of our Lord or the blessed Saints in it.'
' No, you are right, Lapui!' he cried, ' Down came the
statue of the Virgin, and up went the statue of Liberty!
There was the crimson flare of the Torch of Truth!—and
the effigies of the ape Voltaire and the sensualist Rousseau, took the places of St. Peter and St. Paul! Ha!—
And they worshipped the goddess of Reason—Reason,
impersonated by Maillard the ballet-dancer! True to the
life, my Lapui!—that kind of worship has lasted in
Paris until now!—it goes on still—Reason,—man's idea
of Reason,—impersonated by a ballet dancer! Yes,—the
shops are full of that goddess and her portraits, Jean
Lapui! And the jewellers can hardly turn out sufficient
baubles to adorn her shrine!' He laughed again, and I
took hold of him by the arm. ' See here, petit père,' I
said, ' I fancy all is not well with you.' ' You are right,'

he answered, 'all is very ill!' 'Then will you not go
home and to bed?' I asked him. 'Presently—presently;' he said, 'if I may tell you something first!' 'Do
so by all means, *révérend père*,' said I, and I sat down
near him. 'It is just this, Lapui,' and he drew out a crucifix from his breast and looked at it very earnestly, 'I am
a priest, as you see; and this symbol represents my faith.
My mother told me that to be a priest and to serve God
was the highest happiness that could befall a man. I believed it,—and when I look at the stars up there crowd-
ing around us in such vast circles,—when I look at all
this moonlight and the majesty of creation around me, I
believe it still! Up here, it seems there *may* be a God;
down there,' and he pointed towards the streets, 'I know
there is a devil! But I have discovered that it is no use
telling the people about God, because they do not believe in Him. They think I am telling them a lie because it is my *métier* to tell lies. And also because they
think I have neither the sense nor the ability to do anything else. They know they are telling lies themselves
all day and every day. Some of them pretend to believe,
because they think it best to be on the safe side even by
feigning,—and they are the worst hypocrites. It drives
me mad, Lapui, to perform Mass for liars! If it were
only unbelievers! but liars!—liars! Liars who lie on
their death-beds, telling me with mock sighs of penitence
that they believe in God when they do not! I had a
dream last night—you shall tell me if I was mistaken in
it,—it was a dream of this very tower of Notre Dame. I
was up here as I am now—and the moonlight was around
me as it is now—and I thought that just behind the wing
of that third angel's head carved yonder—do you see?'
and he got up and made me get up too, and turned me
round with his hand on my shoulder—'a white dove had
made its resting-place. Is there a white dove there,
Lapui? If there is I shall be a happy man and all my
griefs will be at an end! Will you go and look—and tell
me if there is a white dove nestling there? Then I will
say good-night to you and go home.' God forgive me!—
I thought to humor him in his fancy, and so I left him to
walk those five steps—only five at the utmost—and see
if perhaps among the many doves that fly about the
towers, it might not be that a white one, as he said, should

have chosen to settle in the place he pointed out to me, 'for,' thought I, 'he will be quiet then and satisfied.' And like a blind fool I went——and when I came back the platform was empty!——Ah, Monseigneur!—he had said good-night indeed, and gone home!"

"You mean that he flung himself from this parapet?" said Bonpré, in a low, horrified tone.

"That was the way of it, Monseigneur," said Lapui commiseratingly,—"His body was found next day crushed to bits on the pavement below; but somehow no one troubled much about it, or thought he had thrown himself from the tower of Notre Dame. It was said that he had been murdered and thrown out of a window, but nobody knew how or when. Of course I could have spoken, but then I should have got into trouble. And I avoid trouble whenever I can. A very strange thing it is that no one has ever been suspected of leaping from Notre Dame into the next world since Victor Hugo's great story was written. 'It is against the rules,' say the authorities, 'to mount the towers at night.' True, but rules are not always kept. Victor Hugo's 'Quasimodo,' who never lived, is the only person the wiseacres associate with such a deed. And I,—I could tell many a strange story; only it is better to be silent! Life is hard living,—and when a priest of the Church feels there is no God in this world, why what is there left for him except to try and find out if there is in the next?"

"Suicide is not the way to find Heaven," said the Cardinal gravely.

"Maybe not,—maybe not," and the old custodian turned to lead the way down the steps of the tower, "But when the brain is gone all through grief at losing God, it may chance that God sees the conditions of things, and has mercy. Events happen in this world of such a kind as to make anyone who is not a saint, doubt the sense as well as the goodness of the Creator,—of course that is a wicked thing to say, for we make our own evils, no doubt——"

"That is very certain," said the Cardinal, "The unhappy man you have told me of should have trusted God to the end, whether those whom he preached to, believed his message or not. Their conduct was not his business, —his task was to declare, and not to judge."

" Now that is very well put!" and the old man paused on the stairway and looked round approvingly. "Of course that is said as only a wise man could say it, for after all, Christ Himself did not judge any one in any case. He came to save us all, not to punish us."

"Then why does not everyone remember that, and try to save one another rather than to condemn?" asked Manuel suddenly.

They had reached the bottom of the tower stairway, and old Jean Lapui, shading his eyes from the glare of the daylight with one wrinkled hand, looked at the boy with a smile of compassionate interest.

"Why does not everyone remember? Why does not everyone do as He did? Ah, that is a question! You are young, and you will find out many answers to it before you are much older. One fact is sure,—that if everybody *did* remember Him and lived exactly as He wished, we should have a new Heaven and a new Earth; and I will tell you something else," and the old fellow looked sly and mischievous, "No offence meant—no offence!—but there would be no churches and no priests! Believe me, I speak the truth! But this would be a great happiness; and is not to be our portion yet! Good-day, Monseigneur!—A thousand pardons for my wicked speech! Good-day!"

"Good-day!" responded the Cardinal gently, "Be careful of your night visitors, my friend! Do not for the future leave them alone to plunge into the Infinite without a warning!"

The old man smiled deprecatingly.

"Truly, Monseigneur, I am generally careful. I do not know when I have spoken so freely to anyone as I have to you; for I am generally in a bad humour with all Church dignitaries,—and of course I know you for a Cardinal by your dress, while you might truly be a saint from your manner;—so I should have held my tongue about the flight into the air of the little priest. But you will say nothing, for you are discreet; and even if you did, and I were asked about it, I should know nothing. Oh, yes, I can tell lies as fast as anybody else!—Yes, truly! I do not suppose anyone, not even an Archbishop himself, could surpass me in lying!"

"And are you not ashamed to lie?" asked Bonpré, with

an intense vibration of pain in his voice as he put the question.

"Heaven bless you, no, Monseigneur!" replied Lapui cheerfully, "For is not the whole world kept going by lies? Dear me, if we all told the truth there would be an end of everything! I am a philosopher in my way, Monseigneur,—and I assure you that a real serious truth told in Paris without any gloss upon it, would be like an earthquake in the city,—great houses would come down and numbers of people would be killed by it! Good-day, Monseigneur!—Good-day."

And still smiling and chuckling, the custodian of the North tower retired into his den there to await fresh visitors. The Cardinal walked slowly to the corner of the street where his carriage awaited him,—his head bent and his eyes downcast; Manuel stepped lightly along beside him, glancing at his pale face from time to time with a grave and tender compassion. When they were seated in the vehicle and driving homewards the boy spoke gently—

"You grieve too much for others, dear friend! You are now distressed because you have heard the story of one unhappy man who sought to find God by self-destruction; and you are pained also lest another man should lose God altogether by the deliberate telling of lies. All such mistakes and follies of the world weigh heavily on your heart, but they should not do so,—for did not Christ suffer all this for you when He was crucified?"

The Cardinal sighed deeply.

"Yes, my child; but He told us plainly *why* He suffered. It was that we might learn to follow Him, and that there should be less suffering for the future. And surely we have not obeyed Him, or there could not be so much pain and difficulty in the world as there is now."

"If He come again, you think He would be grieved and disappointed in His followers?" queried Manuel softly.

"If He came again, I fear He would not find much of His teaching in any of the creeds founded on His name! If He came again, then indeed might the churches tremble, totter and fall!"

"If He came again," pursued Manuel, still in the same soft, even voice, "how do you think He would come?"

"'Watch ye therefore for ye know not when He cometh,'" murmured the Cardinal,—" My dear child, I think if He came again it would be perhaps in the disguise of one who is poor and friendless ' despised and rejected of men,' as when He first glorified the earth by His presence; and I fear that in such plight He would find Himself, as before, unwelcome."

Manuel made no reply just then, as they had arrived at home. The servant who admitted them told them that Donna Sovrani had a visitor in her studio,—so that the Cardinal and his young attendant went straight to their own apartments.

" Read to me, Manuel," then said Bonpré, seating himself near the window, and looking out dreamily on the rich foliage of the woods and grassy slopes that stretched before him, " Find something in the Gospels that will fit what we have seen to-day. I am tired of all these temples and churches!—these gorgeous tombs and reliquaries; they represent penances and thank-offerings no doubt, but to me they seem useless. A church should not be a shrine for worldly stuff, unless indeed such things are used again for the relief of poverty and suffering; but they are not used; they are simply kept under lock and key and allowed to accumulate,—while human creatures dwelling perhaps quite close to these shrines, are allowed to die of starvation. Did you think this when you spoke to the priest who was offended with you to-day?"

" Yes, I thought it," replied Manuel gently, " But then he said I was a heretic. When one loves God better than the Church is one called a heretic?"

Cardinal Bonpré looked earnestly at the boy's inspired face,—the face of a dreaming angel in its deep earnestness.

" If so, then I am heretic," he answered slowly, " I love the Creator as made manifest to me in His works,—I love Him in every flower which I am privileged to look upon, —I find Him in every art and science,—I worship Him in a temple not made with hands,—His own majestic Universe! Above all churches,—above all formulated creeds and systems I love Him! And as declared in the divine humanity of Christ I believe in, and adore Him! If this makes me unworthy to be His priest and servant then I confess my unworthiness!"

He had spoken these words more to himself than Manuel, and in his fervour had closed his eyes and clasped his hands,—and he almost fancied that a soft touch, light as a falling rose-leaf, had for a second rested on his brow. He looked up quickly, wondering whether it was Manuel who had so touched him,—the boy was certainly near him,—but was already seated with the Testament open ready to read as requested. The Cardinal raised himself in his chair,—a sense of lightness, and freedom, and ease, possessed him,—the hopeless and tired feeling which had a few minutes since weighed him down with an undefinable languor was gone,—and his voice had gained new strength and energy when he once more spoke.

"You have found words of our Lord which will express what we have seen to-day?" he asked.

"Yes," replied Manuel, and he read in a clear vibrating tone, *"Woe unto you scribes and Pharisees, hypocrites; because ye build the tombs of the prophets and garnish the sepulchres of the righteous."* Here he paused and said, while the Cardinal gazed at him wonderingly, "Is not that true of Paris? There is their great Pantheon where most of their prophets lie,—their poets and their teachers whom they wronged and slandered in their lifetime——"

"My child," interrupted Bonpré gently, "Poets and so-called teachers are not always good men. One named Voltaire, who scoffed at God, and enunciated the doctrine of materialism in France, is buried there."

"Nevertheless he also was a prophet," persisted Manuel, in his quiet, half-childlike, half-scholarly way, "A prophet of evil. He was the incarnation of the future spirit of Paris. He lived as a warning of what was to come,—a warning of the wolves that were ready to descend upon the Master's fold. But Paris was then perhaps in the care of those 'hirelings' who are mentioned here as caring not for the sheep."

He turned a few pages and continued reading.

"'Well hath Esais prophesied of you, hypocrites, as it is written, This people honoureth me with their lips but their heart is far from me. Howbeit in vain do they worship me, *teaching for doctrine the commandments of man.'"*

He emphasised the last few words and looked up at the Cardinal, then he went on.

"'Whosoever will come after me let him deny himself and take up his cross and follow me. For whosoever will save his life shall lose it, but whosoever shall lose his life for my sake the same shall save it.'"

"Yes," said Cardinal Bonpré fervently, "It is all there! —'Whosoever will come after me let him deny himself,' *let him deny himself!* That is the secret of it. Self-denial! And this age is one of self-indulgence. We are on the wrong road, all of us, both Church and laity,—and if the Master should come He will not find us watching, but sleeping."

He broke off, as at that moment a knock came at the door and a servant entered the room bringing him a letter. It was from the Abbé Vergniaud, and ran as follows:—

"TRES CHER MONSIGNEUR! I preach the day after to-morrow at Notre Dame de Lorette, and if you wish to do a favour to a dying man you will come and hear me. I am moved to say things I have never said before, and it is possible I may astonish and perchance scandalise Paris. What inspires me I do not know,—perhaps your well-deserved reproach of the other day—perhaps the beautiful smile of the angel that dwells in Donna Sovrani's eyes, —perhaps the chance meeting with your Rouen foundling on the stairs as I was flying away from your just wrath. He had been gathering roses in the garden, and gave me one with a grace in the giving which made the flower valuable. It still lives and blooms in a glass on my writing-table at which I have been jotting down the notes of what I mean to say. *What I mean to say!* There is more in those words than there seems, if you could but guess all! I shall trust to the day itself for the necessary eloquence. The congregation that assembles at the Lorette is a curious and a mixed one. 'Artistes' of the stage and the café chantant are among the worshippers;— dames of rank and fashion who worship the male 'artistes,' and the golden youth of Paris who adore the very points of the shoes of the female ones,—are generally there also. It is altogether what 'perfide Albion,' or *Dame Grundee* would call a 'fast' audience. And the fact that I have arranged to preach there will draw a still greater mixture and 'faster' quality, as I am, alas!—a fashion in preachers. I pray you to come, or I shall think you have not forgiven me!

" VERGNIAUD."

Cardinal Bonpre folded the letter and put it aside with a curious feeling of compassion for the writer.

"Yes, I will go," he thought, "I have never heard him preach, though I know by report that he is popular. I was told once that he seems to be possessed by a very demon of mockery, and that it is this spirit which makes his attraction for the people; but I hope it is something more than that—I hope—" Here interrupting his meditations he turned to Manuel.

"So you gave the Abbé Vergniaud a rose the other day, my child?"

"Yes," replied Manuel, "He looked sad when I met him,—and sometimes a flower gives pleasure to a person in sorrow."

The Cardinal thought of his own roses far away, and sighed with a sensation of longing and homesickness.

"Flowers are like visible messages from God," he said, "Messages written in all the brightest and loveliest colours! I never gather one without finding out that it has something to say to me."

"There is a legend," said Manuel, "which tells how a poor girl who has lost every human creature she loved on earth, had a rose-tree she was fond of, and every day she found upon it just one bloom. And though she longed to gather the flower for herself she would not do so, but always placed it before the picture of the Christ. And God saw her do this, as He sees everything. At last, quite suddenly she died, and when she found herself in Heaven, there were such crowds and crowds of angels about her that she was bewildered, and could not find her way. All at once she saw a pathway edged with roses before her, and one of the angels said,' These are all the roses you gave to our Lord on earth, and He has made them into a pathway for you which will lead you straight to those you love!' And so with great joy she followed the windings of the path, seeing her roses blossoming all the way, and she found all those whom she had loved and lost on earth waiting to welcome her at the end!"

" A pretty fancy," said the Cardinal smiling, " And, as not even a thought is wasted, who knows if it might not prove true? "

" Surely the beautiful must be the true always! " said Manuel.

" Not so, my child,—a fair face may hide an evil soul."

" But only for a little while," answered the boy, " The evil soul must leave its impress on the face in time, if life lasts long enough."

" That is quite possible," said Bonpré, " In fact, I think it often happens,—only there are some people who simulate the outward show of goodness and purity perfectly, while inwardly ' they are as ravening wolves,' and they never seem to drop the mask. Others again——" Here he paused and looked anxiously at his young companion, " I wonder what you will be like when you grow up, Manuel! "

" But if I never grow up, what then? " asked Manuel with a smile.

" Never grow up? You mean——"

" I mean if I die," said Manuel, " or pass through what is called dying before I grow up? "

" God forbid! " said the Cardinal gently, " I would have you live——"

" But why," persisted Manuel, " since death is a better life? "

Bonpré looked at him wistfully.

" But if you grow up and are good and great, you may be wanted in the world," he said.

An expression of deep pain swept like a shadow across the boy's fair open brow.

" Oh no! " he said quietly, " the world does not want me! And yet I love the world—not because it is a world, for there are millions upon millions of worlds,—they are as numerous as flowers in a garden——but because it is a sorrowful world,—a mistaken world,—and because all the creatures in it have something of God in them. Yes, I love the world!—but the world does not love me."

He spoke in a tone of gentle pathos, with the resigned and patient air of one who feels the burden of solitude and the sense of miscomprehension. And closing the Testament he held he rested his clasped hands upon it, and for a moment seemed lost in sorrowful reverie.

"I love you," said the Cardinal tenderly, "And I will take care of you as well as I can."

Manuel looked up at him.

"And that will be well indeed, my lord Cardinal!" he said softly, "And you serve a Master who will hereafter say to you, remembering your goodness,—'Verily, in asmuch as ye have done it unto the least of my brethren ye have done it unto Me.'"

He smiled; and the Cardinal meeting his glance wondered whether it was the strong level light of the sinking sun through the window-pane that made such a glory shine upon his face, and gave such a brilliancy to his deep and steadfast eyes.

XI.

MEANWHILE, Angela Sovrani was detained in her studio by the fascinating company and bewildering chatter of a charming and very well-known personage in Europe, —a dainty, exquisitely dressed piece of femininity with the figure of a sylph and the complexion of a Romney "Lady Hamilton,"—the Comtesse Sylvie Hermenstein, an Austro-Hungarian of the prettiest and most bewitching type, who being a thorough bohémienne in spirit, and having a large fortune at her disposal, travelled everywhere, saw everything, and spent great sums of money not only in amusing herself, but in doing good wherever she went. By society in general, she was voted "thoroughly heartless,"—when as a matter of fact she had too much heart, and gave her "largesse" of sympathy somewhat too indiscriminately. Poor people worshipped her, —the majority of the rich envied her because most of them had ties and she had none. She might have married scores of times, but she took a perverse pleasure in "drawing on" her admirers till they were just on the giddy brink of matrimony,—then darting off altogether she left them bewildered, confused, and not a little angry.

"They tell me I cannot love, *cara mia,*" she was saying now to Angela who sat in pleased silence, studying her form, her colouring, and her animated expression, with all the ardour of an artist who knows how difficult it is to catch the swift and variable flashes of beauty on the face of a pretty woman, who is intelligent as well as personally charming, "They tell me I have no heart at all. Me—Sylvie!—no heart! Hèlas!—I am all heart! But to love one of those stupid heavy men, who think that just to pull a moustache and smile is sufficient to make a conquest—ah, no!—not for me! Yet I am now in love!—truly!—ah, you laugh!—" and she laughed herself, shaking her pretty head, adorned with its delicate "creation" in gossamer and feathers, which was supposed to be a hat——"Yes, I am in love with the Marquis

Fontenelle! Ah!—le beau Marquis! He is so extraordinary!—so beautiful!—so wicked! It must be that I love him, or why should I trouble myself about him?"

She spread out her tiny gloved hands appealingly, with a delightful little shrug of her shoulders, and again Angela laughed.

"He is good-looking, certainly," she said, "He is very like Miraudin. They might almost be brothers."

"Miraudin, ce cher Miraudin!" exclaimed the Comtesse gaily, "The greatest actor in Europe! Yes, truly!—I go to the theatre to look at him and I almost fancy I am in love with him instead of Fontenelle, till I remember he stage-manages;—ah!—then I shudder! ——and my shudder kills my love! After all it is only his resemblance to the Marquis that causes the love,— and perhaps the shudder!"

"Sylvie, Sylvie!" laughed Angela, "Can you not be serious? What do you mean?"

"I mean what I say," declared Sylvie, "Miraudin used to be the darling of all the sentimental old maids and little school-girls who did not know him off the stage. In Paris, in Rome, in Vienna, in Buda-Pesth—always a conqueror of ignorant women who saw him in his beautiful 'make-up'! Yes, he was perfectly delightful,— this big Miraudin, till he became his own manager and his own leading actor as well! Hèlas! What it is to be a manager! Do you know? It is to keep a harem like a grand Turk;—and woe betide the woman who joins the company without understanding that she is to be one of the many! The sultana is the 'leading lady'. Poor Miraudin!—he must have many little faggots to feed his flame! Oh, you look so shocked! But the Marquis is just like him,—he also stage-manages."

"In what way?"

"Ah, he has an enormous theatre,—the world! A big stage,—society! The harem is always being replenished! And he plays his part so well! He has what the wise-acres call 'perverted morals',—they are so charming!— and he will not marry. He says, 'Why give myself to one when I can make so many happy!' And why will not I, Sylvie Hermenstein, be one of those many? Why will I not yield to the embraces of Monsieur le beau Marquis? Not to marry him,—oh, no! so free a bird could not have his wings clipped! And why will I not see the force of this?——"

She stopped, for Angela sprang towards her exclaiming, "Sylvie! Do you mean to tell me that the Marquis Fontenelle is such a villain?——"

"*Tais-toi!* Dear little flame of genius, how you blaze!" cried Sylvie, catching her friend by the hand and kissing it, "Do not call Fontenelle a villain—he is too charming!—and he is only like a great many other men. He is a bold and passionate person; I rather like such characters,—and I really am afraid—afraid—" here she hesitated, then resumed, "He loves me for the moment, Angela, and I—I very much fear I love him for a little longer than that! *C'est terrible!* He is by no means worthy of it,—no, but what does that matter! We women never count the cost of loving—we simply love! If I see much of him I shall probably sink into the Quartier Latin of love—for there is a Quartier Latin as well as a high class Faubourg in the passion,—I prefer the Faubourg I confess, because it is so high, and respectable, and clean, and grand——but——"

"Sylvie," said Angela determinedly, "You must come away from Paris,——you must not see this man——"

"That is what I have arranged to do," said Sylvie, her beautiful violet eyes flashing with mirth and malice intermingled, "I am flying from Paris . . . I shall perhaps go to Rome in order to be near you. You are a living safety in a storm,—you are so serene and calm. And then you have a lover who believes in the ideal and perfect sympathy."

Angela smiled,—and Sylvie Hermenstein noted the warm and tender flush of pleasure that spread over her fair face.

"Yes, Florian is an idealist," she said, "There is nothing of the brute in him."

"And you think Fontenelle a brute?" queried Sylvie, "Yes, I suppose he is; but I have sometimes thought that all men are very much alike,—except Florian!" She paused, looking rather dubiously, and with a touch of compassion at Angela, "Well!—you deserve to be happy, child, and I hope you will be! For myself, I am going to run away from Monsieur le Marquis with as much speed as if I had stolen his watch!"

"It is the best thing you can do," said Angela with a little sigh of relief, "I am glad you are resolved."

Comtesse Sylvie rose from her chair and moved about the studio with a pretty air of impatience.

"If his love for me could last," she said, "I might stay! I would love him with truth and passion, and I would so influence him that he should become one of the most brilliant leading men of his time. For he has all the capabilities of genius,—but they are dormant,— and the joys of self-indulgence appeal to him more strongly than high ambition and attainment. And he could not love any women for more than a week or a month at most,—in which temperament he exactly resembles the celebrated Miraudin. Now I do not care to be loved for a week or a month——I wish to be loved for always,—for always!" she said with emphasis, "Just as your Florian loves you."

Angela's eyes grew soft and pensive.

"Few men are like Florian," she said.

Again Sylvie looked at her doubtfully, and there was a moment's silence. Then Sylvie resumed.

"Will you help me to give a little lesson to Monsieur le Marquis, Angela?"

"Willingly, if I can. But how?"

"In this way. It is a little drama! To-morrow is Saturday and you 'receive.' 'Tout Paris', artistic Paris, at any rate, flocks to your studio. Your uncle, the Cardinal Bonpré, is known to be with you, and your visitors will be still more numerous. I have promised Fontenelle to meet him here. I am to give him his answer——"

"To what?" enquired Angela.

"To his proposal."

"Of marriage?"

"Dear me, no!" And Sylvie smiled, but there was a look of pain in her eyes, "He has an idyllic house buried in the Forêt St. Germain, and he wants me to take possession . . . you know the rest! He is a villain? Yes —he is like Miraudin, who has a luxurious flat in Paris and sends each lady of his harem there in turn. How angry you look! But, my dear, I am not going to the house in the Forêt, and I shall not meet him here. He will come——looking charming as usual, and he will wait for me; but I shall not arrive. All I want you to do for me is to receive him very kindly, talk to him very sweetly, and tell him quite suddenly that I have left Paris."

"What good will that do?" enquired Angela, "Could you not write it to him?"

"Of course I could write it to him but——" Here Sylvie paused and turned away her head. Angela, moved by quick instinct, went to her and put her arm around her waist.

"Now there are tears in your eyes, Sylvie," she said, "You are suffering for this man's heartlessness and cruelty. For it *is* heartless,—it is insulting, and selfish, and cruel to offer you nothing but dishonour if he knows you love him."

Sylvie took out a tiny cobweb of a lace handkerchief and dried her tears.

"No, I will not have him called heartless, or cruel," she said, "He is merely one of his class. There are hundreds like him in Paris. Never mind my tears!—they are nothing. There are hundreds of women who would accept his proposals,—and he thinks I must be like them, —ready to fall into his arms like a ripe peach at a touch! He thinks all I say to him is an assumed affectation of virtue, and that he can easily break down that slight barricade. He tells me I am a charming preacher, but that he could never learn anything from sermons!" She laughed, "Oh, he is incorrigible! But I want you to let him know that for once he is mistaken. Will you? And you shall not have to say even the smallest figment of an untruth,—your news will be quite correct—for I leave Paris to-morrow morning."

She was very quiet now as she spoke—her brilliant eyes were dark with thought, and her delicate face wore a serious, almost melancholy expression.

"Dear Sylvie!" said Angela, kissing her soft cheek, "You really care for this wretched man?"

"I am not sure," she answered with a touch of hesitation in her voice, "I think I do—and yet despise myself for it!——but—who knows what wonders change of air and scene may work! You see, if I go away he will forget at once, and will trouble himself about me no more."

"Are you sure of that?"

Sylvie hesitated.

"Well, no, I cannot be quite certain,—you see no woman has ever avoided him,—it will be quite a new experience for him, and a strange one!" Her laughter rippled out musically on the air. "Positively I do not think he will ever get over it!"

"I begin to understand," said Angela, "You wish to make this callous man of the world realise that a woman may be beautiful, and brilliant, and independent, and yet live a pure, good life amid numerous temptations?"

"Yes,—I wish him to feel that all women are not to be led away by flattery, or even by the desire to be loved, which is the hardest temptation of all to resist! Nothing so hard as that, Angela! Nothing so hard! I have often thought what a contemptible creature Goëthe's Gretchen was to allow herself to be tempted to ruin with a box of jewels! Jewels! Worthless baubles! I would not cross the road to look at the biggest diamond in the world! But to be loved! To feel that you are all in all to one man out of the whole world! That would be glorious! That I have never felt—that I shall never know!"

Angela looked at her sympathetically,—what a strange thing it was, she thought, that this pretty creature, with her winsome, bright, bewitching ways, should be craving for love, while she, Angela Sovrani, was elected to the happiness of having the absolute devotion of such an ideal lover as Florian Varillo!

"But I am becoming quite tragic in my remarks," went on Sylvie, resuming her usual gaiety, "Melodramatic, as they say! If I go on in this manner I shall qualify to be the next 'leading lady' to Miraudin! *Quelle honneur!* Good-bye Angela;—I will not tell you where I am going lest Fontenelle should ask you,—and then you would have to commit yourself to a falsehood,—it is enough to say I have left Paris."

"Shall I see you again soon?" said Angela, holding her by both hands and looking at her anxiously.

"Yes, very soon, before the winter is over at any rate. You sweet, calm, happy Angela! I wonder if anything could ever whip you in a storm!"

"Would you like to see me in a stormy humour?" asked Angela, smiling.

"No, not exactly;—but,—you are *too* quiet,—too secure—too satisfied in your art and your surroundings;

and you do not enter at all into the passions and griefs of other people. You are absorbed in your love and your work,—a beautiful existence! Only I hope the gods will not wake you up some day!"

" I am not asleep," said Angela, " nor dreaming."

" Yes you are! You dream of beautiful things,—and the world is full of ugly ones; you dream of love and constancy, and purity,—and the world is full of spite, and hate, and bribery, and wickedness; you have a world of your own,—but Angela, it is a glass world!—in which only the exquisite colours of your own soul are reflected, take care that the pretty globe does not break!—for if it does you will never be able to put it together again! Adieu!"

"Adieu!" and Angela returned her loving embrace with equal affection, " I will announce your departure to the Marquis Fontenelle to-morrow."

" You will? Sweet Angela! And when you hear from me, and know where I am, you will write me a long, long letter and tell me how he looked, and what he said, and whether he seemed sorry or indifferent, or angry, or ashamed——or——"

Before she could finish the sentence the studio door was thrown open, and the servant announced, " Monsieur le Marquis Fontenelle!"

XII.

A MOMENT'S flashing glance of half-amused dismay at Angela, and the Comtesse Sylvie had vanished. Passing quickly behind one of the several tall tapestry screens that adorned the studio, she slipped away through a little private door at which Angela's "models" presented themselves, a door which led into the garden and then into the Bois, and making straight for her carriage which was in waiting round the corner, she sprang into it and was rapidly driven away. Meanwhile, Angela Sovrani, rather bewildered by her friend's swift departure, was left alone to face the Marquis, who entered almost on the heels of the servant who announced him, and in one swift survey of the studio saw that the object of his search was not there. Concealing his disappointment, however, under an admirable show of elegant indifference, he advanced towards Angela and saluted her with a courtly old-world grace that very well became his handsome face and figure.

"I must apologise for this intrusion," he said, speaking in deep, soft accents which gave a singular charm to his simplest words, "But—to be quite frank with you—I thought I should find the Comtesse Hermenstein here."

Angela smiled. In her heart she considered the man a social reprobate, but it was impossible to hear him speak, and equally impossible to look at him without a vague sense of pleasure in his company.

"Sylvie was here a moment ago," she answered, still smiling.

The Marquis took one or two quick impulsive steps forward—then checking himself, stopped short, and selecting a chair deliberately sat down.

"I understand!" he said, "She wished to avoid me, and she has done so. Well!—I would not run after her for the world. She must be perfectly free."

Angela looked at him with a somewhat puzzled air.

She felt herself in a delicate and awkward position. To be of any use in this affair now seemed quite impossible. Her commission was to have told the Marquis that Sylvie had left Paris, but she could not say that now as Sylvie was still in the city. Was she supposed to know anything about the Marquis's dishonourable proposals to her friend? Surely not! Then what was she to do? She stood hesitating, glancing at the fine, clear-cut, clean-shaven face of Fontenelle, the broad intellectual brows, and the brilliant hazel eyes with their languid, half-satirical expression, and her perplexity increased. Certainly he was a man with a grand manner,—the manner of one of those never-to-be-forgotten haughty and careless aristocrats of the "Reign of Terror" who half redeemed their vicious lives by the bravery with which they faced the guillotine. Attracted, yet repelled by him, Angela had always been,—even when she had known no more of him than is known of a casual acquaintance met at different parties and réunions, but now that she was aware of Sylvie's infatuation, the mingled attraction and revulsion became stronger, and she caught herself wishing fervently that the Marquis would rouse himself from his lethargy of pleasure, and do justice to the capabilities which Nature had evidently endowed him with, if a fine head and noble features are to be taken as exponents of character. Fontenelle himself, meanwhile, leaning carelessly back in the chair he had taken, looked at her with a little quizzical lifting of his eyebrows.

"You are very silent, mademoiselle," he broke out at last, "Have you nothing to say to me?"

At this straight question Angela recovered her equanimity.

"I *had* something to say to you, Marquis," she answered quietly, "but it was to have been said to-morrow."

"To-morrow? Ah, yes! You receive your world of art to-morrow," he said, "and I was to come and meet *la Comtesse,*—and of course she would not have been here! I felt that by a natural instinct! Something psychological—something occult! I saw her carriage pass my windows up the Champs Elysées,—and I followed in a common fiacre. I seldom ride in a common fiacre, but this time I did so. It was an excitement—*la chasse!* I saw the little beauty arrive at your door,—I gave her time to pour out all her confidences,—and then I arranged with myself and *le bon Dieu* to escort her home."

"You arranged well," said Angela, inclined to laugh at his easy audacity, " but *le bon Dieu* was evidently not of your opinion,—and you must remember that the most excellent arrangements are not always carried out."

"True!" and Fontenelle smiled, "In the case of the fascinating Sylvie, I do not know when I have had so much trouble about a woman. It is interesting, but vexatious. Sometimes I think I shall have to give up and gallop off the hunting-field altogether—"

"Excuse me, Marquis," said Angela coldly, " Sylvie Hermenstein is my friend——pray understand that I cannot allow her to be spoken of in the tone of badinage you are pleased to assume."

He looked up with a curious air of surprise and mock penitence.

"Pardon! But there is no badinage at all about the very serious position in which I find myself," he said, "You, mademoiselle, as a woman, have not the slightest idea of the anxiety and trouble your charming sex gives to ours. That is, of course, when you are charming—— which is not always. Now Sylvie, your friend Sylvie— is so distinctly charming that she becomes provoking and irritating. I am sure she has told you I am a terrible villain . . . "

"She has never said so,—never spoken one word against you!" interposed Angela.

"No? That is curious—very curious! But then Sylvie is curious. You see the position is this;——I wish to give her all I am worth in the world, but she will not have it,—I wish to love her, but she will not be loved—"

"Perhaps," said Angela, gaining courage to speak plainly, " Perhaps your love is not linked with honour?"

"Honour?" echoed the Marquis, lifting his finely arched eyebrows, "You mean marriage? No—I confess I am not guilty of so much impudence. For why should the brilliant Sylvie become the Marquise Fontenelle? It would be a most unhappy fate for her, because if there *were* a Marquise Fontenelle, my principles would oblige me to detest her!"

"You would detest your own wife!" said Angela surprised.

"Naturally! It is the fashion. To love one's wife would be *petite bourgoisie* —nothing more absurd! It is the height of good form to neglect one's wife and adore one's mistress,—the arrangement works perfectly and keeps a man well balanced,—perpetual complaint on one side, perpetual delight on the other."

He laughed, and his eyes twinkled satirically.

"Are you serious?" asked Angela.

"I never was more serious in my life," declared the Marquis emphatically, "With all my heart I wish to make the delicious pink and white Sylvie happy,—I am sure I could succeed in my way. If I should ever allow myself to do such a dull thing as to marry,—imagine it! —such a dull and altogether prosy thing!—my gardener did it yesterday;—I should of course choose a person with a knowledge of housekeeping and small details,— her happiness it would be quite unnecessary to consider. The maintenance of the establishment, the servants, and the ever increasing train of milliners and dressmakers would be enough to satisfy Madame la Marquise's ambitions. But for Sylvie,—half-fairy, half-angel as she is,—there must be poetry and moonlight, flowers, and romance, and music, and tender nothings,—marriage does not consort with these delights. If you were a little school-girl, dear Donna Sovrani, I should not talk to you in this way,—it would not be proper,—it would savour of Lord Byron, and Maeterlinck, and Heinrich Heine, and various other wicked persons. It would give you what the dear governesses would call ' *les idées folles* ', but being an artist, a great artist, you will understand me. Now, you yourself——you will not marry?"

"I am to be married next year if all is well, to Florian Varillo," said Angela, "Surely you know that?"

"I have heard it, but I will not believe it," said the Marquis airily, "No, no, you will never marry this Florian! Do not tell me of it! You yourself will regret it. It is impossible! You could not submit to matrimonial bondage. If you were plain and awkward I should say to you, marry, and marry quickly, it is the only thing for you!—but being what you are, charming and gifted, why should you be married? For protection? Every man who has once had the honour of meeting you will constitute himself your defender by natural instinct. For

respectability? Ah, but marriage is no longer respectable,—the whole estate of matrimony is as full of bribery
and corruption as the French War Office."

He threw himself back in his chair and laughed, running one hand through his hair with a provoking manner of indifferent ease and incorrigible lightheartedness.

"I cannot argue with you on the matter," said Angela, rather vexedly, "Your ideas of life never will be
mine,—women look at these things differently . . .":

"Poor dear women! Yes!—they do," said the Marquis, "And that is such a pity,—they spoil all the pleasure of their lives. Now, just think for a moment what
your friend Sylvie is losing! A devoted, ardent and passionate lover who would spare no pains to make her
happy,—who would cherish her tenderly, and make her
days a dream of romance! I had planned in my mind
such a charming boudoir for Sylvie, all ivory and white
satin,—flowers, and a soft warm light falling through
the windows,—imagine Sylvie, with that delicate face of
hers and white rose skin, a sylph clad in floating lace
and drapery, seen in a faint pink hue as of a late sunset!
You are an artist, mademoiselle, and you can picture the
fairy-like effect! I certainly am not ashamed to say that
this exquisite vision occupies my thoughts,—it is a suggestion of beauty and deliciousness in a particularly ugly
and irksome world,—but to ask such a dainty creature as
Sylvie to be my housekeeeper, and make up the trades-
men's books, I could not,—it would be sheer insolence
on my part,—it would be like asking an angel just out
of heaven to cut off her wings and go downstairs and
cook my dinner!"

"You please yourself and your own fanciful temperament by those arguments," said Angela,—"but they are
totally without principle. Oh, why," and raising her
eyes, she fixed them on him with an earnest look, "Why
will you not understand? Sylvie is good and pure,—why
would you persuade her to be otherwise?"

Fontenelle rose and took one or two turns up and down
the room before replying.

"I expect you will never comprehend me," he said at
last, stopping before Angela, "In fact, I confess sometimes I do not comprehend myself. Of course Sylvie is
good and pure——I know that;—I should not be so vio-

lently in love with her if she were not——but I do not see that her acceptance of me as a lover would make her anything else than good and pure. Because I know that she would be faithful to me."

"Faithful to you—yes!—while you were faithless to her!" said Angela, with a generous indignation in her voice, "You would expect her to be true while you amused yourself with other women. A one-sided arrangement truly!"

The Marquis seemed unmoved.

"Every relation between the sexes is one-sided," he declared, "It is not my fault! The woman gives all to one,—the man gives a little to many. I really am not to blame for falling in with this general course of things. You look very angry with me, Donna Sovrani, and your eyes positively abash me;—you are very loyal to your friend and I admire you for it; but after all, why should you be so hard upon me? I am no worse than Varillo."

Angela started, and her cheeks crimsoned.

"Than Varillo? What do you mean?"

"Well, Varillo has Pon-Pon,—of course she is useful——what he would do without her I am sure I cannot imagine,—still she *is* Pon-Pon."

He paused, checked by Angela's expression.

"Please explain yourself, Marquis," she said in cold, calm accents, "I am at a loss to understand you."

Fontenelle glanced at her and saw that her face had grown as pale as it was recently flushed, and that her lips were tightly set; and in a vague way he was sorry to have spoken. But he was secretly chafing at everything,—he was angry that Sylvie had escaped him,—and angrier still that Donna Sovrani should imply by her manner, if not by her words, that she considered him an exceptional villain, when he himself was aware that nearly all the men of his "Cercle" resembled him.

"Pon-Pon is Signor Varillo's model," he said curtly, "I thought you were aware of it. She appears in nearly all his pictures."

Angela breathed again.

"Oh, is that all!" she murmured, and laughed.

Fontenelle opened his eyes a little, amazed at her indifference. What a confiding, unsuspecting creature was this "woman of genius"! This time, however, he was discreet, and kept his thoughts to himself.

"That is all," he said, "But . . . artists have been known to admire their models in more ways than one."

"Yes," said Angela tranquilly, "But Florian is entirely different to most men."

The Marquis was moved to smile, but did not. He merely bowed with a deep and reverential courtesy.

"You have reason to know him best," he said, "and no doubt he deserves your entire confidence. For me— I willingly confess myself a *vaurien*—but I assure you I am not as bad as I seem. Your friend Sylvie is safe from me."

Angela's eyes lightened,—her mind was greatly relieved.

"You will leave her to herself——" she began.

"Certainly I will leave her to herself. She will not like it, but I will do it! She is going away to-morrow,— I found that out from her maid. Why will you beautiful ladies keep maids? They are always ready to tell a man everything for twenty or forty francs. So simple!—so cheap!—Sylvie's maid is my devoted adherent,—and why?—not only on account of the francs, but because I have been careful to secure her sweetheart as my valet, and he depends upon me to set him up in business. So you see how easy it is for me to be kept aware of all my fair lady's movements. This is how I learned that she is going away to-morrow——and this is why I came here to-day. She has given me the slip——she has avoided me and now I will avoid her. We shall see the result. I think it will end in a victory for me."

"Never!" said Angela, "You will never win Sylvie to your way of thinking, but it is quite possible she may win you!"

"That would be strange indeed," said the Marquis lightly, "The world is full of wonders, but that would be the most wonderful thing that ever happened in it! Commend me to the fair Comtesse, Mademoiselle, and tell her it is *I* who am about to leave Paris."

"Where are you going?" asked Angela impulsively.

"Ah, feminine curiosity!" said the Marquis laughing, "How it leaps out like a lightning flash, even through the most rigid virtue! Chére Mademoiselle,

where I am going is my own secret, and not even your
appealing looks will drag it out of me! But I am in no
hurry to go away; I shall not fly off by the midnight
train, or the very early one in the morning, as your romantic friend the Comtesse Sylvie will probably do,—I
have promised the Abbé Vergniaud to hear him preach
on Sunday. I shall listen to a farewell sermon and try
to benefit by it,—after that I take a long adieu of France;
——be good enough to say to the Countesse with my
humblest salutations!"

He bowed low over Angela's hand, and with a few
more light parting words took his graceful presence out
of the room, and went down the stairs humming a tune
as he departed.

After he had gone Angela sat for some minutes in silence thinking. Then she went to her desk and wrote a
brief note to the Comtesse as follows:—

" DEAR SYLVIE: Dismiss your maid. She is in the employ of Fontenelle and details to him all your movements. He has been here for half an hour and tells me
that he takes a long adieu of France after Sunday, and
he has promised me to *leave you to yourself*. I am sure
you are glad of this. My uncle and I go to Rome next
week.

                                    " ANGELA."

She sealed and marked the envelope " private ", and
ringing the bell for her man-servant requested him to deliver it himself into the hands of the Comtesse Hermenstein. This matter dismissed from her mind she went to
a portfolio full of sketches, and turned them over and
over till she came to one dainty, small picture entitled,
" Phillida et les Roses ". It was a study of a woman's
nude figure set among branching roses, and was signed
" Florian Varillo ". Angela looked at it long and earnestly,—all the delicate flesh tints contrasting with the
exquisite hues of red and white roses were delineated
with wonderful delicacy and precision of touch, and
there was a nymph-like grace and modesty about the
woman's form and the drooping poise of her head, which
was effective yet subtle in suggestion. Was it a portrait of Pon-Pon? Angry with herself Angela tried to

put the hateful but insinuating thought away from her,
—it was the first slight shadow on the fairness of her
love-dream,—and it was like one of those sudden clouds
crossing a bright sky which throws a chill and depression over the erstwhile smiling landscape. To doubt
Florian seemed like doubting her own existence. She
put the "Phillida" picture back in the portfolio and
paced slowly to and fro in her studio, considering deeply.
Love and Fame—Fame and Love! She had both,—and
yet Aubrey Leigh had said such fortune seldom fell to
the lot of a woman as to possess the two things together.
Might it not be her destiny to lose one of them? If so,
which would she prefer to keep? Her whole heart, her
whole impulses cried out, " Love " ! Her intellect and
her ambitious inward soul said, " Fame " ! And something higher and greater than either heart, intellect, or
soul whispered to her inmost self, " Work!—God bids
you do what is in you as completely as you can without
asking for a reward of either Love or Fame." " But,"
she argued with herself, " for a woman Love is so necessary to the completion of life." And the inward mon-
itor replied, " What kind of Love? Ephemeral or immortal? Art is sexless;—good work is eternal, no matter whether it is man or woman who has accomplished
it." And then a great sigh broke from Angela's lips as
she thought, " Ah, but the world will never own woman's
work to be great even if it be so, because men give the
verdict, and man's praise is for himself and his own
achievements always." " Man's praise," went on the interior voice, " And what of God's final justice? Have
you not patience to wait for that, and faith to work for
it?" Again Angela sighed; then happening to look up
in the direction of the music-gallery which occupied one
end of her studio where the organ was fitted, she saw a
fair young face peering down at her over the carved oak
railing, and recognised Manuel. She smiled;—her two
or three days' knowledge of him had been more than sufficient to win her affection and interest.

" So you are up there! " she said, " Is my uncle sleeping? "

" No," replied Manuel, " he is writing many letters to
Rome. Will you come and play to me? "

" Willingly! " and Angela went lightly up the winding

steps of the gallery, " But you have been out all day,—are you not tired?"

" No, not now. I *was* weary,—very weary of seeing and hearing so many false things . . . "

" False things?" echoed Angela thoughtfully, as she seated herself at the organ, " What were they?"

" Churches principally," said Manuel quietly; " How sad it is that people should come into those grand buildings looking for Christ and never finding Him!"

" But they are all built for the worship of Christ," said Angela, pressing her small white fingers on the organ keys, and drawing out one or two deep and solemn sounds by way of prelude, " Why should you think He is not in them?"

" He cannot be," answered Manuel, " They are all unlike Him! Remember how poor he was!—He told His followers to despise all riches and worldly praise!—and now see how the very preachers try to obtain notice and reward for declaring His simple word! The churches seem quite empty of Him,—and how empty too must be the hearts and souls of all the poor people who go to such places to be comforted!"

Angela did not reply,—her hands had unconsciously wandered into the mazes of a rich Beethoven voluntary, and the notes, firm, grand, and harmonious, rolled out in the silence with a warm deep tenderness that thrilled the air as with a rhythmic beat of angels' wings. Lost in thought, she scarcely knew what she played, nor how she was playing,—but she was conscious of a sudden and singular exaltation of spirit,—a rush of inward energy that was almost protest,—a force which refused to be checked, and which seemed to fill her to the very finger tips with ardours not her own,—martyrs going to the destroying flames might have felt as she felt then. There was a grave sense of impending sorrow hanging over her, mingled with a strong and prayerful resolve to overcome whatever threatened her soul's peace,—and she played on and on, listening to the rushing waves of sound which she herself evoked, and almost losing herself in a trance of thought and vision. And in this dreamy, supersensitive condition, she imagined that even Manuel's face fair and innocent as it was, grew still more beautiful,—a light, not of the sun's making, seemed to dwell like an aureole in his clustering hair and in his earnest eyes,—and a smile sweeter than any she had ever seen, seemed to tremble on his lips as she looked at him.

"You are thinking beautiful things," he said gently, "And they are all in the music. Shall I tell you about them?"

She nodded assent, while her fingers, softly pressing out the last chord of Beethoven's music, wandered of their own will into the melancholy pathos of a Schubert "Reverie."

"You are thinking of the wonderful plan of the world," he said,—"Of all the fair and glorious things God has made for those who love Him! Of the splendour of Faith and Hope and Courage,—of the soul's divine origin and responsibility,—and all the joy of being able to say to the Creator of the whole universe, 'Our Father!' You are thinking—because you know—that not a note of the music you are playing now fails to reach the eternal spheres,—echoing away from your touch, it goes straight to its mark,—sent with the soul's expression of love and gratitude, it flies to the centre of the soul's worship. Not a pulsation of true harmony is lost! You are thinking how grand it is to live a sweet and unsullied life, full of prayer and endeavour, keeping a spirit white and clean as the light itself, a spirit dwelling on the verge of earth but always ready to fly heavenward!— You are thinking that no earthly reward, no earthly love, no earthly happiness, though good in itself, can ever give you such perfect peace and joy as is found in loving, serving, and obeying God, and suffering His will to be entirely worked in you!"

Angela listened, deeply moved——her heart throbbed quickly,—how wonderfully the boy expressed himself! —with what sweetness, gentleness, and persuasion! She would have ceased playing, but that something imperative urged her to go on,—and Manuel's soft voice thrilled her strangely when he spoke again, saying—

"You know now—because your wise men are beginning to prove it—that you can in very truth send a message to heaven."

"To heaven!" murmured Angela, "That is a long way! We know we can send messages in a flash of light from one part of the world to another—but then there must be people to receive them—"

"And heaven is composed of millions of worlds," said Manuel, "'In my Father's house are many mansions!' And from all worlds to all worlds—from mansion to mansion, the messages flash! And there are those who receive them, with such directness as can admit of no error! And your wise men might have known this long ago if they had believed their Master's word, 'Whatsoever is whispered in secret shall be proclaimed on the housetops.' But you will all find out soon that it is true, and that everything you say, and that every prayer you utter God hears."

"My mother is in heaven," said Angela wistfully, "I wish I could send her a message!"

"Your very wish has reached her now!" said Manuel, "How is it possible that you in the spirit could ardently wish to communicate with one so beloved and she not know it! Love would be no use then, and there would be a grave flaw in God's perfect creation."

Angela ceased playing, and turned round to face the young speaker.

"Then you think we never lose those we love? And that they see us and hear us always?"

"They must do so," said Manuel, "otherwise there would be cruelty in creating the grace of love at all. But God Himself is Love. Those who love truly can never be parted,—death has no power over their souls. If one is on earth and one in heaven, what does it matter? If they were in separate countries of the world they could hear news of each other from time to time,—and so they can when apparent death has divided them."

"How?" asked Angela with quick interest.

"Your wise men must tell you," said Manuel, with a grave little smile, "I know no more than what Christ has said,—and He told us plainly that not even a sparrow shall fall to the ground without our Father. 'Fear not,' He said, 'Ye are more than many sparrows.' So, as there is nothing which is useless, and nothing which is wasted, it is very certain that love, which is the greatest of all things, cannot lose what it loves."

Angela's eyes filled with tears, she knew not why, "Love which is the greatest of all things cannot lose what it loves!"—How wonderfully tender was Manuel's voice as he spoke these words!

"You have very sweet thoughts, Manuel," she said, "You would be a great comfort to anyone in sorrow."

"That is what I have always wished to be," he answered, "But you are not in sorrow yet,—that is to come!"

She looked up quickly.

"You think I shall have some great trouble?" she asked, with a little tremour in her accents.

"Yes, most surely you will!" replied Manuel, "No one in the world ever tried to be good and great at the same time without suffering miscomprehension and bitter pain. Did not Christ say, 'In the world ye shall have tribulation'?"

"Yes,—and I have often wondered why," said Angela musingly.

"Only that you might learn to love God best," answered Manuel with a delicate inflexion of compassion in his voice, "And that you might know for certain and beyond all doubt that this life is not all. There is something better—greater—higher!—a glory that is worth winning because immortal. 'In the world ye shall have tribulation'—yes, that is true!—but the rest of the saying is true also—'Be of good cheer,—I have overcome the world'!"

Moved by an impulse she could not understand, Angela suddenly turned and extended her hands with an instinctive grace that implied reverence as well as humility. The boy clasped them lightly then let them go,—and without more words went softly away and left her.

XIII.

THE Church of Notre Dame de Lorette in Paris with its yellow stucco columns, and its hideous excess of paint and gilding, might be a ball-room designed after the newest ideas of a vulgar *nouveau riche* rather than a place of sanctity. The florid-minded Blondel, pupil of the equally florid-minded Regnault, hastily sketched in some of the theatrical frescoes in the " Chapel of the Euchar- ist," and a misguided personage named Orsel, splashed out the gaudy decorations of the " Chapel of the Virgin." The whole edifice glares at the spectator like a badly- managed limelight, and the tricky, glittering, tawdry effect blisters one's very soul. But here may be seen many little select groups out of the hell of Paris,—fresh from the burning as it were, and smelling of the brim- stone,—demons who enjoy their demonism,—satyrs, con- cerning whom, one feels that their polished boots are cleverly designed to cover their animal hoofs, and that skilful clothiers have arranged their garments so that their tails are not perceived. But that hoofs and tails are existent would seem to be a certainty. Here some- times will sing a celebrated tenor, bulky and brazen,— pouring out from his bull-throat such liquid devotional notes as might lift the mind of the listener to Heaven if one were not so positive that a moral fiend sang them; —here sometimes may be seen the stout *chanteuse* who is the glory of open-air cafés in the Champs Elysées, kneeling with difficulty on a velvet hassock and actually saying prayers. And one must own that it is an exhilar- ating and moving sight to behold such a woman pretend- ing to confess her sins, with the full delight of them written on her face, and the avowed intention of com- mitting them all over again manifesting itself in every turn of her head, every grin of her rouged lips, and every flash of her painted eyes! For these sections out of the French " Inferno," Notre Dame de Lorette is a good place

to play penitence and feign prayer;—the Madeleine is
too classic and serene and sombre in its interior to suggest anything but a museum, from which the proper custodian is absent,—Notre Dame de Paris reeks too much
with the blood of slain Archbishops to be altogether
comfortable,—St. Roch in its " fashionable " congregation, numbers too many little girls who innocently go to
hear the music, and who have not yet begun to paint their
faces, to suit those whose lives are all paint and mas-
querade,—and the " Lorette " is just the happy medium
of a church where, Sham being written on its walls, one
is scarcely surprised to see Sham in the general aspect of
its worshippers. Among the ugly columns, and against
the heavy ceiling divided into huge raised lumps of paint
and gilding, Abbé Vergniaud's voice had often re-
sounded,—and his sermons were looked forward to as a
kind of witty entertainment. In the middle or the afterwards of a noisy Mass,—Mass which had been " performed " with perhaps the bulky tenor giving the " Agnus Dei," with as sensually dramatic an utterance as
though it were a love-song in an opera, and the " basso,"
shouting through the " Credo," with the deep musical
fury of the tenor's jealous rival,—with a violin " inter-
lude," and a 'cello " solo,"—and a blare of trumpets at
the " Elevation," as if it were a cheap spectacle at a cir-
cus fair,—after all this melodramatic and hysterical excitement it was a relief to see the Abbé mount the pulpit stairs, portly but lightfooted, his black clerical surtout buttoned closely up to his chin, his round clean-
shaven face wearing a pious but suggestive smile, his
eyes twinkling with latent satire, and his whole aspect
expressing, " Welcome excellent humbugs! I, a humbug myself, will proceed to expound Humbug! " His
sermons were generally satires on religion,—satires delicately veiled, and full of the *double-entendres* so dear to
the hearts of Parisians,—and their delight in him arose
chiefly from never quite knowing what he meant to imply, or to enforce. Not that his hearers would have followed any counsel even if he had been so misguided as to
offer it; they did not come to hear him " preach " in the
full sense of the word,—they came to hear him " say
things,"—witty observations on the particular fad of the
hour—sharp polemics on the political situation—or what

was still more charming, neat remarks in the style of Rochefoucauld or Montaigne, which covered and found excuses for vice while seemingly condemning viciousness. There is nothing perhaps so satisfactory to persons who pride themselves on their intellectuality, as a certain kind of spurious philosophy which balances virtue and vice as it were on the point of a finger, and argues prettily on the way the two can be easily merged into each other, almost without perception. "If without perception, then without sin," says the sophist; "it is merely a question of balance." Certainly if generosity drifts into extravagance you have a virtue turned into a vice;—but there is one thing these spurious debaters cannot do, and that is to turn a vice into a virtue. That cannot be done, and has never been done. A vice is a vice, and its inherent quality is to "wax fat and gross," and to generally enlarge itself;—whereas, a virtue being a part of the Spiritual quality and acquired with difficulty, it must be continually practised, and guarded in the practice, lest it lapse into vice. We are always forgetting that we have been, and still are in a state of Evolution,—out of the Beast God has made Man,—but now He expects us, with all the wisdom, learning and experience He has given us, to evolve for ourselves from Man the Angel,—the supreme height of His divine intention. Weak as yet on our spiritual wings, we hark back to the Beast period only too willingly, and sometimes not all the persuasion in the world can lift us out of the mire wherein we elect to wallow. Nevertheless, there must be and will be a serious day of reckoning for any professing priest of the Church, or so-called "servant of the Gospel", who by the least word or covert innuendo, gives us a push back into prehistoric slime and loathliness,—and that there are numbers who do so, no one can deny. Abbé Vergniaud had flung many a pebble of sarcasm at the half-sinking faith of some of his hearers with the result that he had sunk it altogether. In his way he had done as much harm as the intolerant bigot, who when he finds persons believing devoutly in Christ, but refusing to accept Church-authority, considers such persons atheists and does not hesitate to call them so. The "Pharisees" in Christian doctrine are as haughty, hypocritical and narrow as the Pharisees whom Jesus calls "ravening wolves," and to whom He said, " Ye shut up the Kingdom of Heaven against men; for ye neither go in yourselves, *neither suffer ye them that are entering to go in,*" and " Even so ye also outwardly appear righteous unto men, but within ye are full of hypocrisy and iniquity." The last words, it may be said, will apply fittingly to more than one-half of the preachers of the Gospel at the present day!

It was a brilliant, soft autumnal Sunday morning when Cardinal Bonpré, mindful of Abbé Vergniaud's request that he should be present to hear him preach, took his slow and thoughtful way to the church of the Lorette, accompanied by his niece Angela and Manuel. The building was crammed, and had not the Abbé been previously careful to reserve seats, and to mention the Cardinal's name to the custodian, he would have scarcely obtained admission. As it was, however, he passed slowly up the centre aisle without hindrance, followed by Manuel and Angela, and watched by a good many inquisitive persons, who wondered as they looked, who the boy was that walked after His Eminence with such easy self-possession,—with such a noble and modest bearing, and with such a strangely thoughtful face. A few whispered and nudged each other as " the Sovrani" passed them, dressed in her usual quiet black, her head slightly bent and her eyes downcast. The Marquis Fontenelle, seated in an attitude which suggested a languid indifference to all persons and events, lifted his bright hazel eyes as she passed,—and a sudden wave of consciousness swept over him,—uneasy consciousness that perhaps this small slight woman despised him. This was not quite a pleasant reflection for a man and a Marquis to boot,— one who could boast of an ancient and honourable family pedigree dating back to the fighting days of Cœur-de-Lion and whose coat-of-arms was distinguished by three white lilies of France on one of its quarterings. The lilies of France!—emblems of honour, loyalty, truth, and chivalry!—what smudged and trampled blossoms they seem to day! He frowned as this fancy crossed his mind, and turned his eyes away from the following of Angela's slight form up the aisle; and his glance fell instead on a face he detested, because it was almost the counterpart of his own,—the face of the great French actor Miraudin. The same clean-shaven classic face and

clustering hair,—the same glittering, amorous hazel eyes,
—the same charming and kindly smile,—all these attributes were in Miraudin's face, indefinably coarsened,
while in Fontenelle's they remained refined and indicative of the highest breeding. The Marquis moved
uneasily in his seat,—he saw himself in the famous actor,—himself as he would be, if he continued his career of self-indulgence,—for Miraudin
though gifted with a genius that could move all Paris
to the wildest excesses of admiration, was in private life
known as a man of detestable reputation, whose
liaisons with women were endless, but who, in his extreme egotism and callousness had never been known
to yield to the saving grace of a " *grande passion,*"—
one of those faithful passions which sometimes make
the greatness of both man and woman concerned, and
adorn the pages of dull history with the brilliancy of
deathless romance. Was he, Guy Beausire de Fontenelle no better, no nobler, no higher, in his desires and
ambitions than Miraudin? What was he doing with the
three lilies emblazoned on his escutcheon? He thought
with a certain fretful impatience of Sylvie, of her captivating grace, her tender eyes, her sweet laughter, and
sweeter smile. She had seemed to him a mere slight
creation of the air and the moonbeams,—something dainty
that would have melted at a touch, and dropped into his
mouth, as it were, like a French bon-bon. So he, man-
like, had judged, and now lo!—the little ethereal creature
had suddenly displayed a soul of adamant—hard and
pure, and glittering as a diamond,—which no persuasion
could break or bend. She had actually kept her word!—
she had most certainly left Paris. The Marquis knew
that, by the lamentable story of her dismissed maid who
had come to him with hysterical tears, declaring that
" Madame " had suddenly developed a " *humeur incroy-
able* "—and had gone away alone,—alone, save for a little
dusky-skinned Arab boy whom she had once brought
away from Biskra and had trained as an attendant,—her
" gouvernante " and companion, Madame Bozier, and her
old butler who had known her from childhood. Fontenelle felt that the dismissal of the maid who had been
such a convenient spy for him, was due to Angela
Sovrani's interference, and though angry, he was con-

scious of feeling at the same time mean in himself, and miserable. To employ a servant to play the spy on her mistress, and report to him her actions and movements, might be worthy of a Miraudin, but was it quite the thing for a Marquis Fontenelle? Thinking over these things his handsome face grew flushed and anon pale again, as from time to time he stole a vexed side glance at the easy Miraudin,—so like him in features and—unfortunately so equally like him in morals! Meanwhile, the music of the Mass surged round him, in thunders of the organ, wailings of violins, groaning of 'cellos, and flutings of boys' and men's voices,—and as the cloudy incense rose upon the air he began to weave strange fancies in his mind, and to see in the beams of sunlight falling through the stained glass windows a vision of the bright face of Sylvie looking down upon him with a half-tender, half-reproving smile,—a smile that seemed to say, "If thou lovest me, set the grace of honour on thy love!" These were strange thoughts for him to entertain, and he was almost ashamed of them,—but as long as the melodies of the Mass kept rolling on and reverberating around him he could not help thinking of them; so that he was relieved when a pause came,—the interval for the sermon,—and Abbé Vergniaud, leisurely mounting the steps of the pulpit, stood surveying the congregation with the composed yet quizzical air for which he was celebrated, and waiting till the rustling, fidgeting, coughing, snuffing, toe-scraping noises of the congregation had settled down into comparative silence. His attitude during this interval was suggestive. It implied contempt, wearied patience, resignation, and a curious touch of defiance. Holding himself very erect he rested his left hand on the elaborate sculptured edge of the pulpit,—it was the hand on which he usually wore his ring, a diamond of purest lustre,—but on this occasion the jewel had been removed and the white, firm fingers, outlined against the pulpit edge, looked as though they had just relaxed their grasp of something that had been more or less of a trouble to retain. Nothing perhaps is so expressive as a hand,—the face can disguise itself,—even the eyes can lie,—but the hand never. Its shape, its movements, its attitude in repose, give a more certain clue to character and disposition than almost any other

human feature. Thus, with the Abbé, while his left hand
suggested a "letting go," his right hand, which held a
small black-bound Testament implied defiance, grip, resolve and courage. And when the people seated immediately around the pulpit lifted their eyes expectantly to
the popular preacher's face, several of the more observant
noticed something in his look and manner which was un-
familiar and curiously disconcerting. If it be true, as
there is every reason to believe it is, that each human being unconsciously gives out an "aura" of his interior
personality which is made more or less powerful to attract or repel by the nature of his intentions, and which
affects the "aura" of those with whom he is brought in
contact, then Abbé Vergniaud was this morning creating
all unawares to himself a very singular impression of
uneasiness. Some of the persons thus uncomfortably
influenced coughed violently in an instinctive attempt to
divert or frustrate the preacher's mood, but even the
most persistent cougher must cease coughing at some
time or another—and the Abbé was evidently determined to wait for an absolute silence before he spoke.
At last silence came, and he opened the Testament.
Holding it up to the view of the congregation, he began
with all that easy eloquence which the French tongue
gives to a cultured speaker,—his voice full and sonorous,
reaching distinctly to every part of the crowded church.

"This," he said, "is a small book which you all pretend to know. It is so small a book that it can easily be
read through in an hour. It is the Testament;—or the
Last Will and Command to the world of one Jesus
Christ, who was crucified on account of His Divinity
more than eighteen hundred years ago. I mention the
fact, in case any of you have forgotten it! It is generally understood that this book is the message of God
and the key of Faith;—upon it our churches and religious
systems are founded;—by its teaching we are supposed
to order our conduct of life—and yet,—though as I have
said, it is a very small book, and would not take you an
hour to read it—none of you know any thing about it!
That is a strange thing, is it not?"

Here he leaned over the pulpit edge, and his bright
eyes, coldly satiric, flashed a comprehensive glance over
the whole congregation.

"Yes, it is a strange thing, but I affirm it true,—that none of you know anything whatever about the contents of this small volume which is the foundation of the Christian Faith! You never read it yourselves,—and if we priests read it to you, you never remember it! It is a locked Mystery,—perhaps, for all we know, the greatest mystery in the world,—and the one most worth probing! For the days seem to be coming, if they have not already come, which were prophesied by St. John the Divine, whom certain 'clever' men of the time have set down as mad;—days which were described as 'shaking the powers of heaven and creating confusion on the earth.' St. John said some strange things; one thing in particular, concerning this very book, which reads thus; —'I saw in the right hand of Him that sat upon the throne a book sealed with seven seals. And I saw a strong angel proclaiming with a loud voice; Who is worthy to open and to loose the seals thereof? And no man in heaven or in earth was able to open the book neither to look thereon. And I wept much because no man was found worthy to open and to read the book, neither to look thereon.' But St. John the Divine was mad, we are told,—madness and inspiration being judged as one and the same thing. Well, if in these statements he is supposed to prove his madness, I consider a doubt must be set upon everyone's sanity. For his words are an exact description of the present period of the world's existence and its attitude towards the Gospel of Christ,— '*No man is found worthy to loose the seals of the book or to look thereon.*' But I am not going to talk to you about the seven seals. They adequately represent our favourite 'seven deadly sins,' which have kept the book closed since the days of the early martyrs;—and are likely to keep it closed still. Nor shall I speak of our unworthiness to read what we have never taken the trouble to rightly understand,—for all this would be waste of time. It is part of our social sham to pretend we know the Gospel,—and it is a still greater sham to assume that we have ever tried in the smallest degree to follow its teaching. What we know of these teachings has influenced us unconsciously, but the sayings in the Gospel of Christ are in very truth as enveloped in mystery to each separate individual reader as the oracles of the ancient Egyptians were to the outside multitude. And why? Merely because, to comprehend the teaching of Jesus we should have to think,—and we all hate thinking. It is too much exertion,—and exertion itself is unpleasant. A quarter of an hour's hard thinking will convince each one of us that he or she is a very worthless and ridiculous person, and we strongly object to any process which will, in itself, bring us to that conclusion. I say ' we ' object,—that is, I and you; particularly I. I admit at once that to appear worthless and ridiculous to the world has always seemed to me a distressing position, and one to be avoided. Worthless and ridiculous in my own eyes I have always been,—but that is not your affair. It is strictly mine! And though I feel I am not worthy ' to loose the seals of the book or look thereon,' there is one passage in it which strikes me as particularly applicable to the present day, and from it I will endeavour to draw a lesson for your instruction, though perhaps not for your entertainment."

Here he paused and glanced at his hearers with an indefinable expression of mingled scorn and humour.

" What an absurdity it is to talk of giving a ' lesson ' to you!—you who will barely listen to a friend's advice, —you who will never take a hint for your mental education or improvement, you who are apt to fly into a passion, or take to the sulks when you are ever so slightly contradicted. *Tiens, tiens! c'est drôle!* Now the words I am about to preach from, are supposed to have been uttered by Divine lips; and if you thoroughly believed this, you would of your own accord kneel down and pray that you might receive them with full comprehension and ready obedience. But you do not believe;— so I will not ask you to kneel down in mockery, or feign to pray when you are ignorant of the very spirit of prayer! So take the words,—without preparation, without thought, without gratitude, as you take everything God gives you, and see what you can make of them. ' The light of the body is the eye,—if therefore thine eye be single, thy whole body shall be full of light. But if thine eye be evil, thy whole body shall be full of darkness. If therefore the light that is in thee be darkness, how great is that darkness! ' "

Here he closed the Testament, and rested it edgewise

on the pulpit cushion, keeping one hand firmly clasped upon it as he turned himself about and surveyed the whole congregation.

" What is the exact meaning of the words, ' *If thine eye be single* '? It is an expressive term; and in its curt simplicity covers a profound truth. ' If thine eye,' namely, —the ability to see,—' be single,' that is straight and clear, without dimness or obliquity,—' thy whole body shall be full of light.' Christ evidently did not apply this expression to the merely physical capability of sight,—but to the moral and mental, or psychic vision. It matters nothing really to the infinite forces around us, whether physically speaking, we are able to see, or whether we are born blind; but spiritually, it is the chief necessity of our lives that we should be able to see straight morally. Yet that is what we can seldom or never do. Modern education, particularly education in France, provides us at once with a double psychic lens, and a side-squint into the bargain! Seeing straight would be too primitive and simple for us. But Christ says, ' If thine eye be evil, thy whole body shall be full of darkness.' Now this word ' evil,' as set in juxtaposition to the former term ' single,' evidently implies a double sight or perverted vision. With this ' evil,' or double sight, our whole body ' shall be full of darkness.' Very well, my friends, if this be true,—(and you surely must believe it true, otherwise you would not support churches for the exposition of the truth as spoken by the Founder of our Faith;—) then we are children of the dark indeed! I doubt if one amongst us,—for I include myself with you,—can be said to see clearly with a straight psychic vision. The straight psychic vision teaches us that God is the Creator of all things,—God is Light and Love,— God desires good from us, and from every particle of his creation;—but the double or perverted line of sight offers a different view and declares, ' This life is short and offers many pleasures. I cannot be sure of God because I have never seen Him;—the Universe is certainly very majestic, and somewhat startling to me in its exact mathematical proportions; but I have no more to do with it than has a grain of sand;—my lot is no more important than that of the midge in the sunbeam;—I live,—I breed—I die;—and it matters to no one but myself how I do these three things, provided I satisfy my nature.' This is the Philosophy of the Beast, and it is just now very fashionable. It is ' la haute mode ' both in France, and England, Italy, and Spain. Only young America seem to be struggling for a Faith,—a Christian Faith;—it has almost, albeit faintly and with a touching indecision, asked for such a Faith from the Pope,—who has however declared it to be impossible in these words addressed to Cardinal Gibbons, ' Discussion of the principles of the Church cannot be tolerated even in the United States. There can only be one interpreter, the Pope. In the matter of discipline, concessions may be allowed, but in doctrine none.' Mark the words, ' cannot be tolerated '! Consider what stability a Faith can have whose principles may not be discussed! Yet the authority of the Church is, we are told the authority of God Himself. How is this? We can discuss God and His principles. He 'tolerates ' us while we search for His laws, and stand amazed and confounded before His marvellous creation. The more we look for Him the more He gives Himself gloriously to us; and Christ declares ' Seek and ye shall find,'—the Church says ' Seek and ye shall not be tolerated '! How are we to reconcile these two assertions? We do not reconcile them; we cannot; it is a case of double sight,—oblique and perverted psychic vision. Christ spoke plainly;—the Church speaks obscurely. Christ gave straight commands,—we fly in the face of them and openly disobey them. Truth can always be ' discussed,' and Truth *must* be ' tolerated ' were a thousand Holy Fathers to say it nay! But note again the further words to America, ' There can only be one interpreter,—the Pope. In the matter of discipline, concessions may be allowed, but in doctrine none.' Let us examine into this doctrine. It is the doctrine of Christ, plain and straightforward; enunciated in such simple words that even a child can understand them. But the Church announces with a strident voice that there can only be one interpreter,—the Pope. Nevertheless Truth has a more resonant voice than even that of the Church. Truth cries out at this present day, ' Unless you will listen to Me who am the absolute utterance of God, who spake by the prophets, who spake through Christ,—who speaks through Christ and all things still,—your little systems, your uncertain churches, your inefficient creeds, your quarrelsome sects, shall crumble away into dust and ruins! For humanity is waiting for the true Church of Christ; the one pure House of Praise from which all sophistry, all superstition and vanity shall have fled, and only God in the Christ-Miracle and the perfection of His Creation shall remain!' And there is no more sure foundation for this much-needed House of Praise than the Catholic Church,—the word 'catholic' being applied in its widest sense, meaning a 'Universal' answering to the needs of all;—and I am willing to maintain that the *Roman* Catholic Church has within it the vital germ of a sprouting perfection. If it would utterly discard pomp and riches, if it would set its dignity at too high an estimate for any wish to meddle in temporal or political affairs, if it would firmly trample down all superstition, idolatry and bigotry, and 'use no vain repetition as the heathen do'—to quote Christ's own words, —if in place of ancient dogma and incredible legendary lore, it would open its doors to the marvels of science, the miracles and magnificence daily displayed to us in the wonderful work of God's Universe, then indeed it might obtain a lasting hold on mankind. It might conquer Buddhism, and Christianize the whole earth. But—'If thine eye be evil thy whole body shall be full of darkness,'—and while the Church remains double-sighted we are bound also to see double. And so we listen with a complete and cynical atheism to the conventional statement that 'one man alone' shall interpret Christ's teaching to us of the Roman following,—and this man an old frail teacher, whose bodily and intellectual powers are, in the course of nature, steadily on the decline. Why we ask, must an aged man be always elected to decide on the teaching of the ever-young and deathless Christ?—to whom the burden of years was unknown, and whose immortal spirit, cased for a while in clay, saw ever the rapt vision of 'old things being made new'? In all other work but this of religious faith, men in the prime of life are selected to lead,—men of energy, thought, action, and endeavour,—but for the sublime and difficult task of lifting the struggling human soul out of low things to lofty, an old man, weak, and tottering on the verge of the grave, is set before us as our 'infallible' teacher!

There is something appalling in the fact, that look where we may, no profession holds out much chance of power or authority to any man past sixty, but the Head of the Church may be so old that he can hardly move one foot before the other, yet he is permitted to be declared the representative of the ever-working, ever-helping, ever-comforting Christ, who never knew what it was to be old! Enough, however of this strange superstition which is only one of many in the Church, and which are all the result of double or perverted sight,—I come to the last part of the text which runs, ' If therefore the light in thee be darkness how great is that darkness.' *If therefore the light in thee be darkness!* My friends, that is exactly my condition, and has been my condition ever since I was twenty. The light in me has been darkness. The intellectual quality of my brain which has helped me to attain my present false position among you . . ."

Here he paused, for there was a distinct movement of surprise among his audience, which till now, had remained to a man so still that the buzz of a fly on the window-pane sounded almost as loud as the drone of a bag-pipe,—then with a faint smile on his lips he resumed,—

" I hope you all heard my words distinctly! I said, the false position I have attained among you. I repeat it lest there should be any mistake. It *is* a false position and always has been. I have never for an instant believed half what I have asked you to believe! And I have preached to you what I have never dreamed of practising! Yet I venture to say that I am not worse than most of my brethren. The intellectual men of France, whether clergy or laity, are in a difficult situation. Their brains are keen and clear; and, intellectually speaking, they are totally unable to accept the Church superstitions of the tenth and twelfth centuries. But in rejecting superstition it would have been quite possible to have held them fast to a sublime faith in God and an Immortal Future, had the Church caught them when slipping, and risen to the mental demand made upon her resources. But the old worn-out thunder of the Vatican, which lately made a feeble noise in America, has rolled through France with the same assertion, ' Discussion cannot be tolerated'; and what has been the result? Simply this,—that all the intellectual force of the country is arrayed against priestcraft;—and the spirit of an insolent, witty, domineering atheism and materialism rules us all. Even young children can be found by the score who laugh at the very idea of a God, and who fling a jeer at the story of the Crucifixion of Christ,—while vice and crime are tolerated and often excused. Moral restraint is being less and less enforced, and the clamouring for sensual indulgence has become so incessant that the desire of the whole country, if put into one line, might be summed up in the impotent cry of the Persian voluptuary Omar Khayyám to his god, ' Reconcile the law to my desires '. This is as though a gnat should seek to build a cathedral, and ask for the laws of architecture to be altered in order to suit his gnat-like capacity. The Law is the Law; and if broken, brings punishment. The Law makes for good, —and if we pull back for evil, destroys us in its outward course. Vice breeds corruption in body and in soul; and history furnishes us with more than sufficient examples of that festering diseases. It is plainly demanded of us that we should assist God's universe in its way towards perfection; if we refuse, and set a drag on the majestic Wheel, we are ourselves crushed in its progress. Here is where our Church errs in the present generation. It is setting itself as a drag on the Wheel. Meanwhile, Truth advances every day, and with no uncertain voice proclaims the majesty of God. Heaven's gates are thrown open;— the secrets of the stars are declared,—the mysteries of light and sound are discovered; and we are approaching possibly to the time when the very graves shall give up their dead, and the secrets of all men's hearts shall be made manifest. Yet we go on lying, deceiving, cajoling, humbugging each other and ourselves;—living a daily life of fraud and hypocrisy, with a sort of smug conviction in our souls that we shall never be found out. We make a virtue of animalism, and declare the Beast-Philosophy to be in strict keeping with the order of nature. We gloat over our secret sins, and face the world with a brazen front of assumed honour. Oh, we are excellent liars all! But somehow we never seem to think we are fools as well! We never remember that all we do and all we say, is merely the adding of figures to a sum which in the end must be made up to the grand total, and paid!

Every figure tells;—the figure 'nought' especially, puts an extra thousand on the whole quantity! But the light in us being darkness, how great is that darkness! So great that we refuse to look an inch before us! We will not see, we will not understand,—we utterly decline to accept any teaching or advice which might inflict some slight inconvenience on our own Ego. And so we go on day after day, till all at once a reckoning is called and death stares us in the face. What! So soon finished? All over? Must we go at once, and no delay? Must we really and truly drop all our ridiculous lies and conventions and be sent away naked-souled into the Living Unknown? Not the Dead Unknown remember!—for nothing is actually dead! The whole universe palpitates and burns with ever re-created life. What have we done with the past life?—and what shall we do with this other life? Oh, but there is no time to ask questions now,—we should have asked them before; the hour of departure is come, and there is not a moment's breathing time! Our dear friends (if we have any), and our paid doctors and servants stand around us awe-struck,—they watch out last convulsive shudder—and weep—not so much for sorrow sometimes as terror,—and then when all is over, they say we are 'gone'. Yes,—we are gone—but where? Well, we shall each of us find that out, my friends, when we pass away from Popes, Churches, Creeds, and Conventions to the majesty of the actual Glory! Shall we pray then? Shall we weep? Shall we talk of rituals? Shall we say this or that form of prayer was the true one?—this or that creed was the 'only' one? Shall we complain of our neighbours?—or shall we not suddenly realise that there never was but one way of life and progress through creation,—the good and pure, the truthful and courageous, as taught with infinite patience by the God-Man, and that wheresoever we have followed our own inclinations rather than His counsel, then our *own* action, not God's punishment, condemns us,—our *own* words, not God's, re-echo back our sins upon ourselves!"

He paused, looking everywhere around him,—all his hearers were listening with an almost breathless attention.

"Oh, yes! I know the charm of sin!" he continued

with mingled mockery and passion vibrating in his voice;
—" The singular fascination of pure devilry! All of you
know it too,—those of you who court the world's applause
on the stage, or in the *salons* of art and literature, and
who pretend that by your work you are elevating and
assisting humanity, while in your own private lives you
revel in such vice as the very dogs you keep might be
ashamed of! There is no beast so bestial as man at his
worst! And some of you whom I know, glory in being
seen at your worst always. There are many among you
here to-day whose sole excuse for a life of animalism is,
that it is your nature, ' I live according to my temperament,—my disposition,—I do not wish to change myself
—you cannot change me; I am as I am made ' ! So
might the thief argue as he steals his neighbour's money,
—so may the murderer console himself as he stabs his victim! ' It is my nature to stab and to steal—it is my
nature to live as a beast—I do not wish to change; you
cannot change me '. Now if these arguments were true,
and hold good, man would be still where he begun,—in
the woods and caves,—an uncouth savage with nothing
save an animal instinct to lead him where he could find
food. But even this earliest instinct, savage though it
was, taught him that something higher than himself had
made him, and so he began to creep on by slow degrees
towards that higher at once; hence instinct led to reason,
and reason to culture and civilization. And now having
touched as high a point of experience and knowledge as
the ancient Assyrians and Egyptians attained before their
decline, he is beginning even as they did, to be weary and
somewhat afraid of what lies beyond in the as yet un-
fathomed realms of knowledge; and he half wishes to
creep back again on all-fours to the days when he was
beast merely. The close contemplation of the Angel ter-
rifies him,—he dare not grow his wings! Further than
life, as life appears to him on its material side, he is
afraid to soar,—what lies in the far distance he dare not
consider! This is where the Pause comes in all progress,
—the hesitation, the doubt, the fear;—the moment when
the Creature draws so near to his Creator that he is dazzled and confounded. And it is a strange fact that he is
always left alone,—alone with his own Will, in every
such grand crisis. He has been helped so much by divine

influences, that he is evidently considered strong enough to decide his own fate. He *is* strong enough,—he has sufficient reason and knowledge to decide it for the Highest, if he would. But, with national culture goes national luxury,—the more civilised a community, the greater its bodily ease,—the more numerous the temptations against which we are told we must fight. Spirit flies forward— Body pulls back. But Spirit is one day bound to win! We have attained in this generation a certain knowledge of Soul-forces—and we are on a verge, where, if we hesitate, we are lost, and must recoil upon our own Ego as the centre of all desire. But if we go on boldly and leave our own Ego behind, we shall see the gates of Heaven opening indeed, and all the Mysteries unveiled! How often we pause on the verge of better things, doubting whether to rise or grovel! The light in us is darkness, and how great is that darkness! Such is the state of mind in which I, your preacher, have found myself for many years! I do not know whether to rise or grovel, —to sink or soar! To be absolutely candid with you, I am quite sure that I should not sink in your opinion for confessing myself to be as outrageous in my conceptions of mortality as many of you are. You would possibly pretend to be ashamed of me, but in your hearts you would like me all the better. The sinking or the soaring of my nature has therefore nothing whatever to do with you. It is a strictly personal question. But what I specially wish to advise you of this morning,—taking myself as an example,—is that none of you, whether inclined to virtue or to vice, should remain such arrant fools as to imagine that your sins will not find you out. They will,—the instant they are committed, their sole mission is to start on your track, and hunt you down! I cannot absolutely vouch to you that there is a God,—but I am positive there is a hidden process of mathematics going on in the universe which sums up our slightest human affairs with an exactitude which at the least is amazing. Twenty-five years ago I did a great wrong to a human creature who was innocent, and who absolutely trusted me. There is no crime worse than this, yet it seemed to me quite a trifling affair,—an amusement—a nothing! I was perfectly aware that by some excessively straight-laced people it might be termed a sin; but my ideas of sin were as easy and condoning as yours are. I never repented it,—I can hardly say I ever thought of it,—if I did I excused myself quickly, and assured my own conscience in the usual way, that the fault was merely the result of circumstances over which I had no control. Oh, those uncontrollable circumstances! How convenient they are! And what a weak creature they make of man, who at other times than those of temptation, is wont to assert himself master of this planet! Master of a planet and cannot control a vice! Excellent! Well,—I never, as I say, thought of the wrong I had done,—but if *I* forgot it, some One or some Thing remembered it! Yes— remembered it!—put it down—chronicled it with precision as to time and place,—and set it, a breathing fact, before me in my old age,—a living witness of my own treachery."

He paused, the congregation stirred,—the actor Miraudin looked up at him with a surprised half-smile. Angela Sovrani lifted her beautiful violet eyes towards him in amazed compassion,—Cardinal Bonpré, recalling the Abbé previous confession to him, bent his head, deeply moved.

"Treachery," resumed Vergniaud determinedly, "Is always a covert thing. We betray each other in the dark, with silent foot-steps and sibilant voices. We whisper our lies. We concoct our intrigues with carefully closed doors. I did so. I was a priest of the Roman Church as I am now; it would never have done for a priest to be a social sinner! I therefore took every precaution to hide my fault;—but out of my lie springs a living condemnation; from my carefully concealed hypocrisy comes a blazonry of truth, and from my secret sin comes an open vengeance . . ."

At the last words the loud report of a pistol sounded through the building . . . there was a puff of smoke, a gleam of flame, and a bullet whizzed straight at the head of the preacher! The congregation rose, *en masse*, uttering exclamations of terror,—but before anyone could know exactly what had happened the smoke cleared, and the Abbé Vergniaud was seen leaning against the steps of the pulpit, pale but uninjured, and in front of him stood the boy Manuel with arms outstretched, and a smile on his face. The bullet had split the pulpit immediately above him. An excited group assembled round them immediately, and the Abbé was the first to speak.

" I am not hurt!—" he said quickly—" See to the boy! He sprang in front of me and saved my life."

But Manuel was equally unhurt, and waived aside all enquiries and compliments. And while eager questions were poured out and answered, a couple of *gendarmes* were seen struggling in the centre of the church with a man who seemed to have the power of a demon, so fierce and frantic were his efforts to escape.

" *Ah, voilà!* The assassin!" cried Miraudin, hastening to give assistance.

" The assassin!" echoed a dozen other persons pressing in the same direction.

Vergniaud heard, and gave one swift glance at Cardinal Bonpré who, though startled by the rapidity and excitement of the scene that had occurred, was equal to the occasion, and understood his friend's appeal at once, even before he said hurriedly,

" Monseigneur! Tell them to let him go!——or—— bring him face to face with me!"

The Cardinal endeavoured to pass through the crowd, but though some made way for him on account of his ecclesiastical dignity, others closed in, and he found it impossible to move more than a few steps. Then Vergniaud, moved by a sudden resolve, raised himself a little, and resting one hand on the shoulder of Manuel, who still remained on the steps of the pulpit in front of him, he called,

" Let Monsieur the assassin come here to me! I have a word to say to him!"

Through the swaying, tumultuous, murmuring throng came a sudden stillness, and everyone drew back as the *gendarmes* responding to Abbé Vergniaud's command, pushed their way along, dragging and hustling their prisoner between them,—a young black-browed, black-eyed peasant with a handsome face and proud bearing, whose defiant manner implied that having made one fierce struggle for liberty and finding it in vain, he was now disdainfully resigned to the inevitable. When brought face to face with the Abbé he lifted his head, and flashed his dark eyes upon him with a look of withering contempt. His lips parted,—he seemed about to speak when his glance accidentally fell upon Manuel,—then something caused him to hesitate,—he checked himself on the very verge of speech and remained silent. The Abbé surveyed him with something of a quizzical half-admiring smile, then addressing the *gendarmes* he said,

" Let him go ! "

The men looked up astonished, doubting whether they had heard aright.

" Let him go ! " repeated the Abbé firmly, " I have no accusation to make against him. Had he killed me he would have been perfectly justified ! Let him go ! "

" Cher Abbé ! " remonstrated the Marquis Fontenelle, who had made himself one of the group immediately around the pulpit, " Is not this a mistake on your part? Let me advise you not to be so merciful . . ."

" ' Blessed are the merciful for they shall obtain mercy ' " ! quoted the Abbé with a strange smile, while his breath came and went quickly, and his face grew paler as he spoke. " Set him free, messieurs, if you please ! I decline to prosecute my own flesh and blood ! I will be answerable for his future conduct,—I am entirely answerable for his past ! He is my son ! "

XIV.

No one ever afterwards quite knew how the crowd in the church broke up and dispersed itself after this *dénouement*. For a few minutes the crush of people round the pulpit was terrific; all eyes were fixed on the young black-browed peasant who had so nearly been a parricide,—and on the father who publicly exonerated him,—and then there came a pressing towards the doors which was excessively dangerous to life and limb. Cardinal Bonpré, greatly moved by the whole unprecedented scene, placed himself in front of Angela as a shield and defence from the crowd; but before he had time to consider how he should best pilot her through the pushing and scrambling throng, a way was made for him by Manuel, who,—with a quiet step and unruffled bearing,—walked through the thickest centre of the crowd, which parted easily on either side of him, as though commanded to do so by some unheard but absolute authority. Admiring and wondering glances were turned upon the boy, whose face shone with such a grave peace and sweetness;—he had saved the Abbé's life, the people whispered, by springing up the steps of the pulpit, and throwing himself between the intended victim and the bullet of his assailant. Who was he? Where did he come from? No one knew;—he was merely the attendant of that tall ascetic-looking Cardinal, the uncle of the famous Sovrani. So the words ran from mouth to mouth, as Felix Bonpré and his niece moved slowly through the throng, following Manuel;—then, when they had passed, there came a general hubbub and confusion once more, and the people hustled and elbowed each other through the church regardless of consequences, eager to escape and discuss among themselves the sensation of the morning.

"*C'est un drâme! Un veritable drâme!*" said Miraudin, pausing, as he found himself face to face with the Marquis Fontenelle.

Fontenelle stared haughtily.

"Did you speak to me, Monsieur?" he enquired, glancing the actor up and down with an air of supreme disdain.

Miraudin laughed carelessly.

"Yes, I spoke to you, Marquis!" he replied, "I said that the public confession of our dear priest Vergniaud was a *veritable drâme!*"

"An unfortunate scandal in the Church!" said Fontenelle curtly.

"Yes!" went on the unabashed Miraudin, "If it were on the stage it would be taken as a matter of course. An actor's follies help to populate the world. But a priest's *petite faute* would seem to suggest the crushing down of a universe!"

"Custom and usage make the rule in these things," said Fontenelle turning away, "I have the honour to wish you good-day, Monsieur!"

"One moment!" said the actor smiling, "There is a curious personal resemblance between you and me, Monsieur le Marquis! Have you ever noticed it? We might almost be brothers by our looks——and also I believe by our temperaments!"

Fontenelle's hazel eyes flashed angrily.

"I think not!" he said coldly, "A certain resemblance between totally unrelated persons is quite common. For the rest, we are absolutely different—absolutely!"

Again Miraudin laughed.

"As you will, Marquis!" and he raised his hat with a light, half-mocking air, "Au revoir!"

Fontenelle scarcely acknowledged the salutation,—he was too much annoyed. He considered it a piece of insolence on Miraudin's part to have addressed him at all without previous introduction. It was true that the famous actor was permitted a license not granted to the ordinary individual,—as indeed most actors are. Even princes, who hedge themselves round with impassable barriers to certain of their subjects who are in all ways great and worthy of notice, unbend to the Mime who to-day takes the place of the Court-jester, and allow him to enter the royal presence, often bringing his newest wanton with him. And there was not the slightest reason for the Marquis Fontenelle to be at all particular in his choice of acquaintances. Yet somehow or other, he was.

The fine and sensitive instincts of a gentleman were in him, and though in the very depths of his own conscience he knew himself to be as much of a social actor as Miraudin was a professional one,—though he was aware that his passions were as sensual, and therefore as vulgar, (for sensuality is vulgarity), there was a latent pride in him which forbade him to set himself altogether on the same level. And now as he walked away haughtily, his fine aristocratic head lifted a little higher in air than usual, he was excessively irritated—with everything and everybody, but with himself in particular. Abbé Vergniaud's sermon had stung him in several ways, and the startling *finale* had vexed him still more.

" What folly ! " he thought, as he entered his luxuriously appointed flat, and threw himself into a chair with a kind of angry weariness, " How utterly stupid of Vergniaud to blazon the fact that he is no better than other men, in the full face of his congregation ! He must be mad ! A priest of the Roman Church publicly acknowledging a natural son ! * Has ever such a thing been heard of ! And the result is merely to create scandal and invite his own disgrace ! *A quoi bon !*"

He lit a cigarette and puffed at it impatiently. His particular " code " of morality had been completely upset ;—things seemed to have taken a turn for general offence, and the simplest thoughts became like bristles in his brain, pricking him uncomfortably in various sore and sensitive places. Then, added to his general sense of spleen was the unpleasant idea that he was really in love, where he had never meant to be in love. " In love ", is a wide term nowadays, and covers a multitude of poor and petty passing emotions,—and it is often necessary to add the word " really " to it, in order to emphasise the fact that the passion has perhaps,—and even then it is only

* ROME, August 19, 1899.—A grave scandal has just burst upon the world here. The *Gazetta di Venezia* having attacked the bishops attending the recent conclave of " Latin America," that is, Spanish-speaking America, as men of loose morality, the *Osservatore Cattolico*, the Vatican organ, replied declaring that the life of the bishops present at the conclave was above suspicion. The *Gazetta di Venezia* responds, affirming that the majority of the bishops brought with them to Rome their mistresses, and in some instances their children. The *Gazetta* offers to disclose the names of these bishops, and demands that the Pope shall satisfy the Catholic world by taking measures against them.— *Central News.*

a perhaps,—taken a somewhat lasting form. Why could
not Sylvie Hermenstein have allowed things to run their
natural course?—this natural course being according to
Fontenelle, to drop into his arms when asked, and leave
those arms again with equal alacrity also when asked!
It would have been quite pleasant and satisfactory to him,
the Marquis;—and for Sylvie—well!—for Sylvie, she
would soon have got over it! Now there was all this
fuss and pother about virtue! Virtue, quotha! In a
woman, and in Paris! At this time of day! Could anything be more preposterous and ridiculous!

"One would imagine I had stumbled into a convent
for young ladies," he grumbled to himself, "What with
Sylvie actually gone, and that pretty pattern of chastity,
Angela Sovrani, preaching at me with her big violet eyes,
—and now Vergniaud who used to be '*bon camarade et
bon vivant*', branding himself a social sinner——really
one would imagine that some invisible Schoolmaster was
trying to whip me into order . . ."

"*Peut-on entrer?*" called a clear voice outside at this
juncture, and without waiting for permission the speaker
entered, a very pretty woman in an admirably fitting riding habit, which she held daintily up with one gloved
hand, extending the other as she came to the Marquis
who gracefully bent over it and kissed it.

"*Charmé de vous voir, Princesse!*" he murmured.

"Not at all! Spare me your falsehoods!" was the gay
reply, accompanied by a dazzling smile, "You are not in
the least charmed, nothing,—nobody charms you,—I least
of all! Did you not see me in church? No! Where were
your eyes? On the courageous Vergniaud, who so nearly
gave us the melancholy task of arranging a '*chapelle
ardente*' for him this afternoon?" She laughed, and her
eyes twinkled maliciously,—then she went on, "Do you
know he is quite a delightful boy,—the peasant son and
assassin? I think of taking him to my Chateau and making something of him. I waited to see the whole play out,
and bring you the news. Papa Vergniaud has gone home
with his good-looking offspring——then Cardinal Bonpré——do you know the Cardinal Bonpré?"

"By reputation merely," replied the Marquis, setting
a chair for his fair visitor, "And as the uncle of Donna
Sovrani."

"Oh, reputation is nothing," laughed the lady, known as the Princesse D'Agramont, an independent beauty of great wealth and brilliant attainments, "Your butler can give you a reputation, or take it away from you! But the Cardinal's reputation is truly singular. It is goodness, merely! He is so good that he has become actually famous for it! Now I once thought that to become famous for goodness must surely imply that the person so celebrated had a very hypocritical nature,—the worst of natures indeed;—that of pretending to be what he was not,—but I was mistaken. Cardinal Bonpré *is* good. Absolutely sincere and noble—therefore a living marvel in this age!"

"You are pleased to be severe, Princesse," said the Marquis, "Is sincerity so difficult to find?"

"The most difficult of virtues!" answered the Princesse, lightly tapping out a little tune with the jewelled handle of her riding whip on the arm of her chair, "That is why I like horses and dogs so much—they are always honest. And for that reason I am now inclined to like Abbé Vergniaud whom I never liked before. He has turned honest! To-day indeed he has been as straightforward as if he were not a man at all!—and I admire him for it. He and his son will be my guests at the Chateau D'Agramont."

"What a very strange woman you are!" said Fontenelle, with a certain languid admiration beginning to glimmer in his eyes, "You always do things that nobody else would dare do—and yet . . . no lovers!"

She turned herself swiftly round and surveyed him with a bright scorn that swept him as with a lightning flash from head to heel.

"Lovers! Who would be bored by them! Such delightful company! So unselfish in their demands——so tender and careful of a woman's feelings! Pouf! *Cher ami!*—you forget! I was the wife of the late Prince D'Agramont!"

"That explains a great many of your moods certainly," said the Marquis smiling.

"Does it not? *Le beau* Louis!—romantic Louis!—poet Louis!—musician Louis!—Louis, who talked pretty philosophies by the hour,—Louis who looked so beautiful by moonlight,—who seemed fastidious and refined to a

degree that was almost ethereal!——Louis who swore,
with passion flashing in his eyes, that I was the centre
of the universe to him, and that no other woman had ever
occupied, would ever occupy, or *should* ever occupy his
thoughts!—yes, he was an ideal lover and husband indeed!" said the Princesse smiling coldly, " I gave him all
my life and love, till one day, when I found I was sharing
his caresses with my plumpest dairymaid, who called
him " *her* Louis " ! Then I thought it was time to put an
end to romance. *Tiens!*" and she gave a little shrug and
sigh, " It is sad to think he died of over-eating."

The Marquis laughed.

" You are incorrigible, *belle* Loyse!" he said, " You
should write these things, not speak them."

" Really! And do I not write them? Yes, you know
I do, and that you envy me my skill. The Figaro
is indebted to me for many admirable essays. At
the same time I do not give you permission to call me
Loyse."

" Forgive me!" and the Marquis folded his hands
with an air of mock penitence.

" Perhaps I will, presently," and she laughed, " But
meanwhile I want you to do something for me."

" *Toujours à votre service, madame!*" and Fontenelle
bowed profoundly.

" How theatrical you look! You are alarmingly like
Miraudin;—and one *must* draw the line at Miraudin!
This is a day of truth according to the Abbé Vergniaud;
how dare you say you are at my service when you do not
mean it?"

" Princesse, I protest . . ."

" Oh, protest as much as you like,—on the way to
Rome!"

The Marquis started.

" To Rome?"

" Yes, to Rome. I am going, and I want someone to
look after me. Will you come? All Paris will say we
have eloped together." She laughed merrily.

The Marquis stood perplexed and silent.

" Well, what is it?" went on the Princesse gaily, " Is
there some faint sense of impropriety stealing over you?
Not possible! Dear me, your very muscles are growing
rigid! You will not go?"

"Madame, if you will permit me to be frank with you,
—I would rather not!"

"*A la bonheur!*—then I have you!" And the
Princesse rose, a dazzling smile irradiating her features,
"You have thrown open your heart! You have begun
to reform! You love Sylvie Hermenstein—yes!—you
positively *love* her!"

"Princesse—" began the Marquis, "I assure you——"

"Assure me nothing!" and she looked him straight
in the eyes, "I know all about it! You will not journey
with me because you think the Comtesse Sylvie will hear
of it, and put a wrong construction on your courtesy.
You wish to try for once, to give her no cause for doubting you to be *sans peur et sans reproche.* You wish to
make her think you something better than a sort of
Miraudin whose amorous inclinations are not awakened
by one woman, but by women! And so you will not do
anything which, though harmless in itself, may seem
equivocal. For this you refuse the friendly invitation of
one of the best known 'society leaders' in Europe!
Cher Marquis!—it is a step in the right direction!
Adieu!"

"You are not going so soon," he said hurriedly, "Wait
till I explain . . ."

"There is nothing to explain!" and the pretty
Princesse gave him her hand with a beneficent air, "I
am very pleased with you. You are what the English
call 'good boy'! Now I am going to see the Abbé and
place the Chateau D'Agramont at his disposal while he
is waiting to be excommunicated,—for of course he will
be excommunicated——"

"What does it matter!—Who cares?" said the Marquis recklessly.

"It does not matter, and nobody cares—not in actual
Paris. But very very nice people in the suburbs, who are
morally much worse than the Abbé, will perhaps refuse
to receive him. That is why my doors are open to him,
and also to his son."

"Original, as usual!"

"Perfectly! I am going to write a column for the
Figaro on the amazing little scene of this morning. *Au
revoir!* My poor horse has been waiting too long already,—I must finish my ride in the Bois, and then go to

Angela Sovrani; for all the *dramatis personæ* of to-day's melodrama are at her studio, I believe."

"Who is that boy with the Cardinal?" asked the Marquis suddenly.

"You have noticed him? I also. A wonderful face! A little acolyte, no doubt. And so you will not go to Rome with me?"

"I think not," and Fontenelle smiled.

"*Comme il vous plaira!* I will tell Sylvie."

"The Comtesse Hermenstein is not in Paris."

"No!" and the Princesse laughed mischievously, "She is in Rome! She must have arrived there this morning. *Au revoir,* Marquis!" Another dazzling smile, and she was gone.

Fontenelle stood staring after her in amazement. Sylvie was in Rome then? And he had just refused to accompany the Princesse D'Agramont thither! A sudden access of irritation came over him, and he paced the room angrily. Should he also go to Rome? Never! It would seem too close a pursuit of a woman who had by her actions distinctly shown that she wished to avoid him. Now he would prove to her that he also had a will of his own. *He* would leave Paris;—he would go—yes, he would go to Africa! Everybody went to Africa. It was becoming a fashionable pasture-land for disappointed lives. He would lose himself in the desert,—and then— then Sylvie would be sorry when she did not know where he was or what he was doing! But also,—he in his turn would not know here Sylvie was, or what she was doing! This was annoying. It as certain that she would not remain in Rome a day longer than she chose to,—well!— then where would she go? In Africa he would find some difficulty in tracing her movements. On second thoughts he resolved that he would lose himself in another fashion ——and would go to Rome to do it!

"She shall not know I am there!" he said to himself, with a kind of triumph in his own decision, "I shall amuse myself——I shall see her—but she shall not see me."

Satisfied with this as yet vague plan of entertainment, he began at once making his arrangements for departure; —meanwhile, the Princesse D'Agramont riding gracefully through the Bois on her beautiful Arab, was amus-

ing herself with her thoughts, and weighing the *pros* and
cons of the different lives of her friends, without giving
the slightest consideration to her own. Here was a
strange nature,—as a girl she had been intensely loving,
generous and warm-hearted, and she had adored her
husband with exceptional faith and devotion. But the
handsome Prince's amours were legion, though he had
been fairly successful in concealing them from his wife,
till the unlucky day when she had found him making
desperate love to a common servant,—and after that her
confidence, naturally, was at an end. One discovery led
to another,—and the husband around whom she had
woven her life's romance, sank degraded in her sight,
never to rise again. She was of far too dignified and
proud a nature to allow her sense of outrage and wrong
to be made public, and though she never again lived with
D'Agramont as his wife, she carried herself through all
her duties as mistress of the household and hostess of his
guests, with a brave bright gaiety, which deceived even
the closest observer,—and the gossips of Paris used to
declare that she did not know the extent of her husband's
follies. But she did know,—and while filled with utter
disgust and loathing for his conduct she nevertheless gave
him no cause of complaint against herself. And when
he died of a fever brought on through over-indulgence
in vice, she conformed to all the strictest usages of society,
—wore her solemn widow's black for more than the accustomed period,—and then cast it off,—not to dash into
her fashionable " circle " again with a splurge of colour,
but rather to glide into it gracefully, a vision of refinement, arrayed in such soft hues as may be seen in some
rare picture; and she took complete possession of it by
her own unaided charm. No one could really tell whether
she grieved for D'Agramont's death or not; no one but
herself knew how she had loved him,—no one guessed
what agonies of pain and shame she had endured for his
sake, nor how she had wept herself half blind with despair when he died. All this she shut up in her own
heart, but the working of the secret bitterness within her
had made a great change in her disposition. Her nature, once as loving and confiding as that of a little child,
had been so wronged in its tenderest fibres that now she
could not love at all.

"Why is it," she would ask herself, "that I am totally unable to care for any living creature? That it is indifferent to me whether I see any person once, or often, or never? Why are all men like phantoms, drifting past my soul's immovability?"

The answer to her query would be, that having loved greatly once and been deceived, it was impossible to love again. Some women,—the best, and therefore the unhappiest—are born with this difficult temperament.

Now, as she rode quietly along, sometimes allowing her horse to prance upon the turf for the delight of its dewy freshness, she was weaving quite a brilliant essay on modern morals out of the scene she had witnessed at the Church of the Lorette that morning. She well knew how to use that dangerous weapon, the pen,—she could wield it like a wand to waken tears or laughter with equal ease, and since her husband's death she had devoted a great deal of time to authorship. Two witty novels, published under a *nom-de-plume* had already startled the world of Paris, and she was busy with a third. Such work amused her, and distracted her from dwelling too much on the destroyed illusions of the past. The *Figaro* snatched eagerly at everything she wrote; and it was for the *Figaro* that she busied her brain now, considering what she should say of the Abbé Vergniaud's confession.

"It is wisest to be a liar and remain in the Church? or tell the truth and go out of the Church?" she mused, "Unfortunately, if all priests told the truth as absolutely as the Abbé did this morning we should have hardly any of them left."

She laughed a little, and stroked her horse's neck caressingly.

"Good Rex! You and your kind never tell lies; and yet you are said to have no souls. Now I wonder why we, who are mean and cunning and treacherous and hypocritical should have immortal souls, while horses and dogs who are faithful and kind and honest should be supposed to have none."

Rex gave a gay little prance forward as one who should say, "Yes, but it is only you silly human beings who suppose such nonsense. We know what *we* know; —we have our own secrets!"

"Now the Church," went on Loyse D'Agramont, pursuing the tenor of her thoughts, " is in a bad way all over the world. It is possible that God is offended with it. It is possible, that after nearly two thousand years of patience He is tired of having come down to us to teach us the path of Heaven in vain. Something out of the common has surely moved the Abbé Vergniaud to speak as he spoke to-day. He was quite unlike himself and beyond himself; if all our preachers were seized by the spirit of frankness in like manner——"

Here she broke off for she had arrived at Angela Sovrani's door, and a servant coming out, assisted her to alight, and led her horse into the courtyard there to await her leisure. She was an old friend of Angela's and was accustomed to enter the house without announcement, but on this occasion she hesitated, and after ascending the first few steps leading to the studio paused and rang the bell. Angela herself answered the summons.

"Loyse! Is it you! Oh, I am so glad!" and Angela caught her by both hands,—"You cannot imagine the confusion and trouble we have been in this morning!"

"Oh yes, I can!" answered the Princesse smiling, as she put an arm round her friend's waist and entered the studio, "You have certainly had an excitement! What of the courageous Abbé? Where is he?"

"Here!" And Angela's eyes expressed volumes,— "Here, with my uncle. They are talking together—— and that young man——Cyrillon——the son, you know——"

"Is that his name?—Cyrillon?" queried the Princesse.

"Yes,—he has been brought up as a peasant. But he is not ignorant. He has written books and music, so it appears—yet he still keeps to his labour in the fields. He seems to be a kind of genius; another sort of Maeterlinck——"

"Oh, capricious Destiny!" exclaimed the Princesse, "The dear Abbé scandalises the Church by acknowledging his son to all men,—and lo!—the son he was ashamed of all these years, turns out a prodigy! The fault once confessed, brings a blessing! Angela, there is something more than chance in this, if we could only fathom it!"

"This Cyrillon is all softness and penitence now," Angela went on, "He is overcome with grief at his murderous attempt,—and has asked his father's pardon. And they are going away together out of Paris till——"

"Till excommunication is pronounced," said the Princesse, "Yes, I thought so! I came here to place my Chateau at the Abbé's disposal. I am myself going to Rome; so he and his son can be perfectly at home there. I admire the man's courage, and above all I admire his truthfulness. But I cannot understand why he was at such pains to keep silence all these years, and *then* to declare his fault? He must have decided on his confession very suddenly?"

Angela's eyes grew dark and wistful.

"Yes," she answered slowly,—then with a sudden eagerness in her manner she added, "Do you know, Loyse, I feel as if some very strange influence had crept in among us! Pray do not think me foolish, but I assure you I have had the most curious sensations since my uncle, Cardinal Bonpré arrived from Rouen—— bringing Manuel——"

"Manuel? Is that the boy I saw in the church this morning? The boy who threw himself as a shield between Verginaud and the flying shot? Yes? And do you not know who he is?"

"No," and Angela repeated the story of the way in which Manuel had been found and rescued by the Cardinal; "You see," she continued, "it is not possible to ask him any questions since he has declined to tell us more than we already know."

"Strange!" And the Princesse D'Agramont knitted her delicate brows perplexedly. "And you have had curious feelings since he came, you say? What sort of feelings?"

"Well, you will only laugh at me," replied Angela, her cheeks paling a little as she spoke, "but it really is as if some supernatural being were present who could see all my inward thoughts,—and not only mine, but the thoughts of everyone else. Someone too who impels us to do what we have never thought of doing before——"

The Princesse opened her eyes in amazement.

"My dear girl! You must have been over-working to get such strange fancies into your head! There is nothing supernatural left to us nowadays except the vague idea of a God,—and even that we are rather tired of!"

Angela trembled and grew paler than usual.

"Do not speak in that way," she urged, "The Abbé talked in just such a light fashion until the other day here,—yet this morning I think—nay, I am sure he believes in something better than himself at last."

The Princesse was silent for a minute.

"Well, what is to happen next?" she queried, "Excommunication of course! All brave thinkers of every time have been excommunicated, and many of our greatest and most valuable scientific works are on the Index Expurgatorius. It is my ambition to get into that Index, —I shall never rest till I win the honour of being beside Darwin's 'Origin of Species'!"

Angela smiled, but her thoughts were elsewhere.

"I hope the Abbé will go away at once," she said meditatively, "But you have no idea how happy and at ease he is! He seems to be ready for anything."

"What does Cardinal Bonpré think?" asked the Princesse.

"My uncle never thinks in any way except the way of Christ," replied Angela. "He says, 'Thy sins be forgiven thee; arise and walk', to every soul stricken with the palsy of pain and repentance. He helps the fallen; he does not strike them down more heavily."

"Ah, so! And is he fit to be a Cardinal?" queried the Princesse D'Agramont dubiously.

Angela gave her a quick look, but had no time to reply as at that moment a servant entered and announced, "Monsignor Moretti!"

Angela started nervously.

"Moretti!" she said in a low tone, "I thought he had left Paris!"

Before she had time to say any more the visitor himself entered, a tall spare priest with a dark narrow countenance of the true Tuscan type,—a face in which the small furtive eyes twinkled with a peculiarly hard brilliancy as though they were luminous pebbles. He walked into the room with a kind of aggressive dignity common to many Italians, and made a slight sign of the cross in air as the two ladies saluted him.

"Pardon me, Mesdames, for this intrusion," he said in a harsh metallic voice, "But I hear that the Abbé Vergniaud is in this house,—and that Cardinal Felix

Bonpré has received him here *since"* (and he emphasised the word " since ") " the shameful scene of this
morning. My business in Paris is ended for the moment; and I am returning to Italy to-night,—but I wish
to know if the Abbé has anything to say through me to
His Holiness the Pope in extenuation of his conduct
before I perform the painful duty of narrating this distressing affair at the Vatican."

" Will you see him for yourself, Monsignor? " said
Angela quietly, offering to lead the way out of the studio,
" You will no doubt obtain a more direct and explicit
answer from the Abbé personally."

For a moment Moretti hesitated. Princesse D'Agramont saw his indecision, and her smile had a touch of
malice in it as she said,

" It is a little difficult to know how to address the Abbé
to-day, is it not, Monsignor? For of course he is no
longer an Abbé—no longer a priest of Holy Church!
Hèlas! When anybody takes to telling the truth in public the results are almost sure to be calamitous! "

Moretti turned upon her with swift asperity.

" Madame, you are no true daughter of the Church,"
he said, " and my calling forbids me to enter into any
discussion with you! "

The Princesse gave him a charming upward glance
of her bright eyes, and curtsied demurely, but he paid
no heed to her obeisance, and moving away, went at once
with Angela towards the Cardinal's apartments. In the
antechamber he paused, hearing voices.

" Is there anyone with His Eminence, besides
Vergniaud? " he asked.

" The Abbé's son Cyrillon," replied Angela timidly.

Moretti frowned.

" I will go in alone," he said, " You need not announce
me. The Abbé knows me well, and—" he added with
a slight sneer, " he is likely to know me better! "

Without further words he signed to Angela to retire,
and passing through the antechamber, he opened the
door of the Cardinal's room and entered abruptly.

XV.

The Cardinal was seated,—he rose as Moretti appeared.

"I beg your Eminence to spare yourself!" said Moretti suavely, with a deep salutation, "And to pardon me for thus coming unannounced into the presence of one so highly esteemed by the Holy Father as Cardinal Bonpré!"

The Cardinal gave a gesture of courteous deprecation; and Monsignor Moretti, lifting his, till then, partially lowered eyelids, flashed an angry regard upon the Abbé Vergniaud, who resting his back against the book-case behind him, met his glance with the most perfect composure. Close to him stood his son and would-be murderer Cyrillon,—his dark handsome face rendered even handsomer by the wistful and softened expression of his eyes, which ever and anon rested upon his father with a look of mingled wonder and respect. There was a brief silence—of a few seconds at most,—and then Moretti spoke again in a voice which thrilled with pent-up indignation, but which he endeavoured to render calm and clear as he addressed the Cardinal.

"Your Eminence is without doubt aware of the cause of my visit to you. If, as I understand, your Eminence was present at Notre Dame de Lorette this morning, and witnessed the regrettable conduct of the faithless son of the Church here present——"

"Pardon! This is my affair," interposed Vergniaud, stepping forward, "His Eminence, Cardinal Bonpré, is not at all concerned in the matter of the difficult dispute which has arisen between me and my own conscience. You call me faithless, Monsignor,—will you explain what you mean by 'faithless' under these present conditions of argument?"

"It shows the extent and hopelessness of your retrogression from all good that you should presume to ask such a question," answered Moretti, growing white under the natural darkness of his skin with an impotency of rage he could scarcely suppress, " Your sermon this morning was an open attack on the Church, and the amazing scene at its conclusion is a scandal to Christianity!"

" The attack on the Church I admit," said the Abbé quietly, " I am not the only preacher in the world who has so attacked it. Christ Himself would attack it if He were to visit this earth again!"

Moretti turned angrily towards the Cardinal.

" Your Eminence permits this blasphemy to be uttered in your presence?" he demanded.

" Nay, wherever and whenever I perceive blasphemy, my son, I shall reprove it," said the Cardinal, fixing his mild eyes steadily on Moretti's livid countenance, " I cannot at present admit that our unhappy and repentant brother here has blasphemed. In his address to his congregation to-day he denounced social hypocrisy, and also pointed out certain failings in the Church which may possibly need consideration and reform; but against the Gospel of Christ, or against the Founder of our Faith I heard no word that could be judged ill-fitting. As for the conclusion which so very nearly ended in disaster and crime, there is nothing to be said beyond the fact that both the persons concerned are profoundly sorry for their sins."

" No sorrow can wipe out such infamy——" began Moretti hotly.

" Patience! Patience, my son!" and the Cardinal raised his hand with a slight gesture of authority, " Surely we must believe the words of our Blessed Lord, ' There is more joy in Heaven over one sinner that repenteth than over ninety and nine just persons which have no need of repentance '!"

" And on this old and well-worn phrase you excuse a confessed heretic?" said Moretti, with a sneer.

" This old and well-worn phrase is the saying of our Master," answered the Cardinal firmly, " And it is as true as the truth of the sunshine which, in its old and well-worn way, lights up this world gloriously every morning! I would stake my very life on the depth and the truth of Vergniaud's penitence! Who, seeing and knowing the brand of disgrace he has voluntarily burnt into his own social name and honour, could doubt his sincerity, or refuse to raise him up, even as our Lord would have done, saying, ' Thy sins be forgiven thee! Go, and sin no more!'?"

Moretti's furtive eyes disappeared for a moment under his discoloured eyelids, which quivered rapidly like the throbbings in the throat of an angry snake. Before he could speak again however, Vergniaud interposed.

"Why trouble His Eminence with my crimes or heresies?" he said quietly, "I am grateful to him from my soul for his gentleness and charity of judgment—but I need no defence—not even from him. I am answerable to God alone!—neither to Church nor Creed! It was needful that I should speak as I spoke to-day——"

"Needful to scandalize the Church?" demanded Moretti sharply.

"The Church is not scandalized by a man who confesses himself an unworthy member of it!" returned Vergniaud, "It is better to tell the truth and go out of the Church than to remain in it as a liar and a hypocrite."

"According to your own admission you have been a liar and a hypocrite for twenty-five years!" said Moretti bitterly, "You should have made your confession before, and have made it privately. There is something unnatural and reprehensible in the sudden blazon you have made to the public of your gross immorality."

"'A sudden blazon' you call it,—" said the Abbé, "Well, perhaps it is! But murder will out, no matter how long it is kept in. You are not entirely aware of my position, Monseigneur. Have you the patience to hear a full explanation?"

"I have the patience to hear because it is my duty to hear," replied Moretti frigidly, "I am bound to convey the whole of this matter to His Holiness."

"True! That is your duty, and who shall say it is not also your pleasure!" and Vergniaud smiled a little. "Well!—Convey to His Holiness the news that I, Denis Vergniaud, am a dying man, and that knowing myself to be in that condition, and that two years at the utmost, is my extent of life on this planet, I have taken it seriously into my head to consider as to whether I am fit to meet death with a clean conscience. Death, Monsignor, admits of no lying, no politeness, no elegant sophistries! Now, the more I have considered, the more I am aware of my

total unfitness to confront whatever may be waiting for
me in the Afterwards of death—(for without doubt there
is an afterwards,)—and being conscious of having done
at least one grave injury to an innocent person, I have
taken the best and quickest way to make full amends. I
wronged a woman—this boy's mother—" and he indicated with a slight gesture Cyrillon, who had remained
a silent witness of the scene, —"and the boy himself
from early years set his mind and his will to avenge his
mother's dishonour. I—the chief actor in the drama,—
am thus responsible for a woman's misery and shame;
and am equally responsible for the murderous spirit
which has animated one, who without this feeling, would
have been a promising fellow enough. The woman I
wronged, alas!—is dead, and I cannot reinstate her name,
save in an open acknowledgment of her child, my son.
I do acknowledge him,—I acknowledge him in your presence, and therefore virtually in the presence of His Holiness. I thus help to remove the stigma I myself set on
his name. Plainly speaking, Monsignor, we men have no
right whatever to launch human beings into the world
with the 'bar sinister' branded upon them. We have no
right, if we follow Christ, to do anything that may injure
or cause trouble to any other creature. We have no right
to be hasty in our judgment, even of sin."

"Sin is sin,—and demands punishment—" interrupted
Moretti.

"You quote the law of Moses, Monsignor! I speak
with the premise 'if'. *If* we follow Christ;—if we do
not, the matter is of course different. We can then twist
Scripture to suit our own purpose. We can organise
systems which are agreeable to our own convenience or
profit, but which have nothing whatever of Christ's Divine Spirit of universal love and compassion in them.
My action this morning was unusual and quixotic no
doubt. Yet, it seemed to me the only way to comport
myself under those particular circumstances. I did a
wrong—I seek to make amends. I believe this is what
God would have me do. I believe that the Supernal
Forces judge our sins against each other to be of a far
worse nature than sins against Church or Creed. I also
believe that if we try to amend our injustices and set
crooked things straight, death will be an easier business,

and Heaven will come a little nearer to our souls. As for my attack on the Church——"

"Ah truly! What of your attack on the Church?" said Moretti, his small eyes glistening, and his breath going and coming quickly.

"I would say every word of it again with absolute conviction," declared Vergniaud, "for I have said nothing but the truth! There is a movement in the world, Monsignor, that all the powers of Rome are unable to cope with!—the movement of an advancing resistless force called Truth,—the Voice of God,—the Voice of Christ! Truth cannot be choked, murdered and killed nowadays as in the early Inquisition! Rather than that the Voice of Truth should be silenced or murdered now at this period of time, God will shake down Rome!"

"Not so!" exclaimed Moretti hotly—"Every nation in the world shall perish before Rome shall lose her sacred power! She is the 'headstone of the corner'—and 'upon whomsoever that stone shall fall, it shall grind him to powder!'"

"You think so?" and Verginaud shrugged his shoulders ever so slightly—"Well! For me, I believe that material as well as spiritual forces combine to fight against long-concealed sin and practised old hypocrisies. It would not surprise me if the volcanic agencies which are for ever at work beneath the blood-stained soil of Italy, were to meet under the Eternal City, and in one fell burst of flame and thunder prove its temporary and ephemeral worth! The other day an earthquake shook the walls of Rome and sent a warning shock through St. Peter's. St. Peter's, with its vast treasures, its gilded shrines, its locked-up wealth, its magnificence,—a strange contrast to Italy itself!—Italy with its people ground down under the heel of a frightful taxation, starving, and in the iron bonds of poverty! 'The Pope is a prisoner and can do nothing'? Monsignor, the Pope is a prisoner by his own choice! If he elected to walk abroad among the people and scatter Peter's Pence among the sick and needy, he would then perhaps be *beginning* to do the duties our Lord enjoined on all His disciples!"

Moretti had stood immovable during this speech, his dark face rigid, his eyes downcast, listening to every word, but now he raised his hand with an authoritative gesture.

"Enough!" he said, "I will hear no more! You know the consequences of this at the Vatican?"

"I do."

"You are prepared to accept them?"

"As prepared as any of the truth-tellers who were burned for the love of Christ by the Inquisition," replied Vergniaud deliberately. "The world is wide,—there is room for me in it outside the Church."

"One would imagine you were bitten by the new 'Christian Democratic' craze," said Moretti with a cold smile, "And that you were a reader and follower of the Socialist, Gys Grandit!"

At this name, Verginaud's son Cyrillon stirred, and lifting his dark handsome head turned his flashing eyes full on the speaker.

"Did you address me, Monsignor?" he queried, in a voice rich with the musical inflexions of Southern France, "I am Gys Grandit!"

Had he fired another pistol shot in the quiet room as he had fired it in the church, it could hardly have created a more profound sensation.

"You—you—" stammered Moretti, retreating from him as from some loathsome abomination, "You—— Gys Grandit!"

"You, Cyrillon!—you!——you, my son!"——and the Abbé almost lost breath in the extremity of his amazement, while Cardinal Bonpré half rose from his chair doubting whether he had heard aright. Gys Grandit!— the writer of fierce political polemics and powerful essays that were the life and soul, meat and drink of all the members of the Christian Democratic party!

"Gys Grandit is my *nom-de-plume,*" pursued the young man, composedly, "I never had any hope of being acknowledged as Cyrillon Vergniaud, son of my father,— I had truly no name and resolved to create one. That is the sole explanation. My history has made me—not myself."

There was a dead pause. At last Moretti spoke.

"I have no place here!" he said, biting his lips hard to keep them from trembling with rage, "This house which I thought was the abode of a true daughter of the

Church, Donna Sovrani, is apparently for the moment a refuge for heretics. And I find these heretics kept in countenance by Cardinal Felix Bonpré, whose reputation for justice and holiness should surely move him to denounce them were he not held in check by some malignant spirit of evil, which seems to possess this atmosphere—"

" Monsignor Moretti," interposed the Cardinal with dignity, " it is no part of justice or holiness to denounce anything or anybody till the full rights of the case have been heard. I was as unaware as yourself that this young man, Cyrillon Vergniaud, was the daring writer who has sent his assumed name of ' Gys Grandit ' like a flame through Europe. I have read his books, and cannot justly denounce them, because they are expressed in the language of one who is ardently and passionately seeking for Truth. Equally, I cannot denounce the Abbé, because he has confessed his sin, declared himself as he is, to the public, saved his son from being a parricide, and has to some extent we trust, made his peace with God. If you can find any point on which, as a servant of Christ, I can denounce these two human beings who share with me the strange and awful privileges of life and death, and the promise of an immortal hereafter, I give you leave to do so. The works of Gys Grandit do not blaspheme Christ,—they call, they clamour, they appeal for Christ through all and in all——"

" And with all this clamour and appeal their writer is willing to become a murderer ! " said Moretti satirically.

Young Vergniaud sprang forward.

" Monsignor, in the name of the Master you profess to serve I would advise you to set a watch upon your tongue ! " he said, " Granted that I was willing to murder the man who had made my mother's life a misery, I was also willing to answer to God for it ! I saw my mother die—" here he gave a quick glance towards the Abbé who instinctively shrank at his words, " I shall pain you, my father, by what I say, but the pain is perhaps good for us both ! I repeat—I saw my mother die. She passed away uncomforted after a long life of patient loneliness and sorrow—for she was faithful to the last, ever faithful ! I have seen her weep in the silence of the night !——I have heard her ever since I was able to understand the sound of weeping ! Oh, those tears !—Do you not think God has seen them! She worked and toiled, and starved herself to educate me,—she had no friends, for she had ' fallen', they said, and sometimes she could get no employment, and often we starved together; and when I thought of the man who had done this thing, even as a young boy I said to myself, ' I will kill him!' She did not mean, poor mother, to curse her lover to me—but unconsciously she did,—her sorrow was so great—her loneliness so bitter!"

Moretti gave a gesture of impatience and contempt. Cyrillon noted it, and his dark eyes flashed, but he went on steadily,—

" And then I saw her die—she stretched her poor thin hard-working hands out to God, and over and over again she muttered and moaned in her fever the refrain of an old peasant song we have in Touraine, ' Oh, la tristesse d'avoir aimé!' If you had heard her—if you had seen her—if you had, or have a heart to feel, nerves to wrench, a brain to rack, blood to be stung to frenzy, you would, —seeing your mother perish thus,—have thought, that to kill the man who had made such a wreck of a sweet pure life, would be a just, aye even a virtuous deed! I thought so. But my intended vengeance was frustrated —whether by the act of God, who can say? But the conduct of the man whom I am now proud to call my father——"

" You have great cause for pride!" said Moretti sarcastically.

" I think I have "—said the young man, " In the close extremity of death at my hands, he won my respect. He shall keep it. It will be my glory now to show him what a son's love and pardon may be. If it be true as I understand, that he is attacked by a disease which needs must be fatal, his last hours will not be desolate! It may be that I shall give him more comfort than Churches,— more confidence than Creeds! It may be that the clasp of my hand in his may be a better preparation for his meeting with God,—and my mother,—than the touch of the Holy Oils in Extreme Unction!"

" Like all your accursed sect, you blaspheme the Sacraments "—interrupted Moretti indignantly—" And in the very presence of one of her chiefest Cardinals, you scorn the Church!"

Cyrillon gave a quick gesture of emphatic denial.

"Monsignor, I do not scorn the Church,—but I think that honesty and fair dealing with one another is better than any Church! Christ had no Church. He built no temples, He amassed no wealth,—He preached simply to those who would hear Him under the arching sky,—in the open air! He prophesied the fall of temples; 'In this place,' He said, 'is One greater than the temple.'* He sought to destroy long built-up hypocrisies. 'My house is called the house of prayer, but ye have made it a den of thieves.' Thieves, not only of gold, but of honour!— thieves of the very Gospel, which has been tampered with and twisted to suit the times, the conditions and opinions of varying phases of priestcraft. Who that has read, and thought, and travelled and studied the manuscripts hidden away in the old monasteries of Armenia and Syria, believes that the Saviour of the world ever condescended to 'pun' on the word Petrus, and say, 'On this Rock (or stone) I will build my Church,' when He already knew that He had to deal with a coward who would soon deny Him?"

"Enough! I will hear no further!" cried Moretti, turning livid with fury—"Cardinal Bonpré, I appeal to you . . ."

But Cyrillon went on unheedingly,—

"Beware of that symbol of your Church, Monsignor! It is a very strange one! It seems about to be expanded into a reality of dreadful earnest! 'I know not the man,' said Peter. Does not the glittering of the world's wealth piled into the Vatican,—useless wealth lying idle in the midst of hideous beggary and starvation,—proclaim with no uncertain voice, '*I know not the Man*'? The Man of sorrows,—the Man of tender and pitying heart,—the Man who could not send the multitude away without bread, and compassed a miracle to give it to them,—the Man who wept for a friend's death,—who took little children in His arms and blessed them,—who pardoned the unhappy outcast and said, 'Sin no more,'— who was so selfless, so pure, so strong, so great, that even sceptics, while denying His Divinity, are compelled to own that His life and His actions were more Divine than those of any other creature in human shape that

* Matt. xii. v. 6.

has ever walked the earth! Monsignor, there is no true representative of Christ in this world!"

"Not for heretics possibly," said Moretti disdainfully.

"For no one!" said Cyrillon passionately—"For no poor sinking, seeking soul is there any such visible comforter! But there is a grand tendency in Mankind to absorb His Spirit and His teaching;—to turn from forms and shadows of faith to the Faith itself,—from descriptions of a possible heaven to the *real* Heaven, which is being disclosed to us in transcendent glimpses through the jewel-gates of science! There were twelve gates in the visioned heaven of St. John,—and each gate was composed of one pearl! Truly do the scoffers say that never did any planetary sea provide such pearls as these! No,—for they were but prophetic emblems of the then undiscovered Sciences. Ah, Monsignor!—and what of the psychic senses and forces?—forces which we are just beginning to discover and to use,—forces which enable me to read your mind at this present moment and to see how willingly you would send me to the burning, Christian as you call yourself, for my thoughts and opinions! —as your long-ago predecessors did with all men who dared to reason for themselves! But that time has passed, Monsignor; the Spirit of Christ in the world has conquered the Church *there!*"

The words rushed from his lips with a fervid eloquence that was absolutely startling,—his eyes were aglow with feeling—his face so animated and inspired, that it seemed as though a flame behind it illumined every feature. Abbé Vergniaud, astonished and overcome, laid a trembling hand on the arm of the passionate speaker with a gesture more of appeal than restraint, and the young man caught that hand within his own and held it fast. Moretti for a moment fixed his eyes upon father and son with an expression of intense hatred that darkened his face with a deep shadow as of a black mask, —and then without a word deliberately turned his back upon both.

"Your Eminence has heard all this," he said coldly, addressing the Cardinal who sat rigidly in his chair, silent and very pale.

"I have," replied Bonpré in a low strained tone.

"And I presume your Eminence permits——?"

"Why talk of permission?" interrupted the Cardinal, raising his eyes with a sorrowful look, "Who is to permit or deny freedom of speech in these days? Have I —have you—the right to declare that a man shall not express his thoughts? In what way are we to act? Deny a hearing? We cannot—we dare not—not if we obey our Lord, who says, 'Whatsoever ye would that men should do unto you, do ye even so to them.' If we ask for ourselves to be heard, we must also hear."

"We may hear—but in such a case as the present one must we not also condemn?" demanded Moretti, watching the venerable prelate narrowly.

"We can only condemn in the case of a great sin," replied Bonpré gently, "and even then our condemnation must be passed with fear and trembling, and with full knowledge of all the facts pertaining to the error. 'Judge not that ye be not judged.' We are told plainly that our brother may sin against us not only seven times but seventy times seven, and still we are bound to forgive, to sustain, to help, and not to trample down the already fallen."

"These are your Eminence's opinions?" said Moretti.

"Most assuredly! Are they not yours?"

Moretti smiled coldly.

"No. I confess they are not! I am a faithful servant of the Church; and the Church is a system of moral government in which, if the slightest laxity be permitted, the whole fabric is in danger——"

"A house of cards then, which a breath may blow down!" interposed "Gys Grandit," otherwise Cyrillon Vergniaud, "Surely an unstable foundation for the everlasting ethics of Christ!"

"I did not speak to you, sir," said Moretti, turning upon him angrily.

"I know you did not. I spoke to you," answered the young man coolly, "I have as much right to speak to you, as you have to speak to me, or to be silent—if you choose. You say the Church is a system of moral government. Well, look back on the past, and see what it has done in the way of governing. In the very earliest days of Christianity, when men were simple and sincere, when their faith in the power of the Divine things was strong and pure, the Church was indeed a safeguard, and a powerful restraint on man's uneducated licentiousness and inherent love of strife. But when the lust of gain began to creep like a fever into the blood of those with whom worldly riches should be as nothing compared to the riches of the mind, the heart, and the spirit, then the dry-rot of hypocrisy set in—then came craftiness, cruelty, injustice, and pitilessness, and such grossness of personal conduct as revolts even the soul of an admitted sinner. Moral government? Where is it to day? Look at France—Italy—Spain! Count up the lies told by the priests in these countries to feed the follies of the ignorant! Did Christ ever tell lies? No. Then why, if you are His follower, do you tell them?"

"I repeat, I did not speak to you," said Moretti, his eyes sparkling with fury,—"To me you are a heretic, accursed, and excommunicate!—thrust out of salvation, and beyond my province to deal with!"

"Oh, that a man should be thrust out of salvation in these Christian days!" exclaimed Cyrillon with a flashing look of scorn, "And that he should find a servant of Christ to tell him so! Accursed and excommunicate! Then I am a kind of leper in the social community! And you, as a disciple of your Master, should heal me of my infirmity—and cleanse me of my leprosy! Loathsome as leprosy is whether of mind or body, Christ never thrust it out of salvation!"

"The leper must wish to be cleansed!" said Moretti fiercely, "If he does not himself seek to be healed of his evil, no miracle can help him."

"Oh but I do seek!" And young Vergniaud threw back his handsome head with a splendid gesture of appeal, "With all my soul, if I am diseased, I wish to be cleansed! Will *you* cleanse me? *Can* you? I wish to stand up whole and pure, face to face with the Divine in this world, and praise Him for His goodness to me. But surely if He is to be found anywhere it is in the Spirit of Truth! Not in any sort of a lie! Now, according to His own words the Holy Ghost is the Spirit of Truth. 'When the Spirit of Truth is come He will guide you into all Truth.' And what then? Monsignor, it is somewhat dangerous to oppose the Spirit of Truth, whether that Force speak through the innocent lips of a child or the diseased ones of a leper! 'For whosoever speaketh a word against the Son of Man it shall be forgiven him, *but whosoever speaketh against the Holy Ghost*'—or the Spirit of Truth, known sometimes as Inspiration . . . "*it shall not be forgiven him* in this world, neither in the world to come.' That is a terrible curse, which an ocean of Holy Water could scarcely wash away!"

"Your argument is wide of the mark," said Moretti, impatiently, yet forced in spite of himself to defend his position, "the Church is not opposed to Truth but to Atheism."

"Atheism! There is no such thing as a real atheist in the world!" declared Cyrillon passionately, "No reasoning human being alive, that has not felt the impress of the Divine Image in himself and in all the universe around him! He may, through apathy and the falsehoods of priestcraft, have descended into callousness, indifference and egotism, but he knows well that that impress cannot be stamped out—that he will have to account for his part, however small it be, in the magnificent pageant of life and work, for he has not been sent into it 'on chance.' Inasmuch as if there is chance in one thing there must be chance in another, and the solar system is too mathematically designed to be a haphazard arrangement. With all our cleverness, our logic, our geometrical skill, we can do nothing so exact! As part of the solar system, you and I have our trifling business to enact, Monsignor,—and to enact it properly, and with satisfaction to our Supreme Employer, it seems to me that if we are honest with the world and with each other, we shall be on the right road."

"For my part, I am perfectly honest with you," said Moretti smiling darkly, "I told you, and I tell you again, that to me you are a heretic, accursed and excommunicate. You will, as the democrat 'Gys Grandit,' no doubt feel a peculiar pleasure when your father is also declared accursed and excommunicate. I have said, and I say again, that the Church is a system of moral government, and that no laxity can be permitted. It is a system founded on the Gospel of our Lord, but to obey the commands of our Lord to the letter we should have to find another world to live in——"

"Pardon me—I ask for information," interposed

Cyrillon, "You of course maintain that Christ was God in Man?"

"Most absolutely!"

"And yet you say that to obey His commands to the letter we should have to find another world to live in! Strange! Since He made the world and knows all our capabilities of progress! But have you never fancied it possible that we may be forced to obey His commands to the letter, or perish for refusing to do so?"

Moretti made as though he would have sprung forward,—his face was drawn and rigid, his lips tightly compressed, but he had no answer to this unanswerable logic. He therefore took refuge in turning brusquely away as before and was about to address himself to Bonpré, but stopped short, as he perceived Manuel, who had entered while the conversation was going on, and who now stood quietly by the Cardinal's chair in an attitude of composed attention. Moretti glanced at him with a vexed sense of irritation and reluctant wonder; —then moistening his dry lips he began,

"I am bound to regret deeply that your Eminence has allowed this painful discussion to take place in your presence without reproof. But I presume you are aware of the responsibility incurred?"

The Cardinal slowly inclined his head in grave assent.

"In relating the scene of to-day to His Holiness, I shall be compelled to mention the attitude you have maintained throughout the conversation."

"You are at perfect liberty to do so, my son," said Bonpré with unruffled gentleness.

Moretti hesitated. His eyes again rested on Manuel.

"Pardon me," he said suddenly and irrelevantly, "This boy . . ."

"Is a foundling," said the Cardinal, "He stays with me till I can place him well in the world. He has no friends."

"He took some part in the affair of this morning, I believe?" queried Moretti, with a doubtful air.

"He saved my life," said Abbé Vergniaud advancing, "It was not particularly worth saving—but he did it. And I owe him much—for in saving me, he also saved Cyrillon from something worse than death."

"Naturally you must be very grateful," retorted Moretti satirically, " The affection of a son you have denied for twenty-five years must be exceedingly gratifying to you!" He paused—then said, " Does this boy belong to the Church?"

" No," said Manuel, answering for himself, " I have no Church."

" No Church!" exclaimed Moretti, " His Eminence must educate you, boy. You must be received."

" Yes," said Manuel, raising his eyes, and fixing them full on Moretti, " I must be received! I need education to understand the Church. And so,—for me to be received might be difficult!"

XVI.

As he thus spoke, slowly and with an exquisite soft-ness, something in his voice, manner, or words aroused a sudden and violent antipathy in Moretti's mind. He became curiously annoyed, without any possible cause, and out of his annoyance answered roughly.

"Ignorance is always difficult to deal with," he said, "But if it is not accompanied by self-will or obstinacy— (and boys of your age are apt to be self-willed and ob-stinate)—then much can be done. The Church has in-finite patience even with refractory sinners."

"Has it?" asked Manuel simply, and his clear eyes, turning slowly towards Vergniaud and his son, rested there a moment, and then came back to fix the same steady look upon Moretti's face. Not another word did he say,—but Moretti flushed darkly, and anon grew very pale. Restraining his emotions however by an effort, he addressed himself with cold formality once more to the Abbé.

"You have no explanation then to offer to His Holi-ness, beyond what you have already said?"

"None!" replied Vergniaud steadily. "The reasons for my conduct I think are sufficiently vital and earnest to be easily understood."

"And your Eminence has nothing more to say on this matter?" pursued Moretti, turning to the Cardinal.

"Nothing, my son! But I would urge that the Holy Father should extend his pardon to the offenders, the more so as one of them is on the verge of that land where we 'go hence and are no more seen.'"

Moretti's eyelids quivered, and his lips drew together in a hard and cruel line.

"I will assuredly represent your wishes to His Holi-ness," he replied, "But I doubt whether they will meet with so much approval as surprise and regret. I have the honour to wish your Eminence farewell!"

"Farewell, my son!" said the Cardinal mildly, "*Benedicite!*"

Moretti bent down, as custom forced him to do, under the gently uttered blessing, and the extended thin white hand that signed the cross above him. Then with a furtive under-glance at Manuel, whose quiet and contemplative observation of him greatly vexed and disturbed his composure, he left the room.

There was a short silence. Then Abbé Vergniaud, somewhat hesitatingly, approached Bonpré.

"I much fear, my dear friend, that all this means unpleasantness for you at the Vatican," he said, "And I sincerely grieve to be the means of bringing you into any trouble."

"Nay, there should be no trouble," said Bonpré quietly, "Nothing has happened which should really cause me any perplexity—on the contrary, events have arranged themselves so that there shall be no obstacle in the way of speaking my mind. I have journeyed far from my diocese to study and to discover for myself the various phases of opinion on religious matters in these days, and I am steadily learning much as I go. I regret nothing, and would have nothing altered,—for I am perfectly confident that in all the things I meet, or may have to consider, my Master is my Guide. All is well wherever we hear His Voice;—all things work for the best when we are able to perceive His command clearly, and have strength and resolution enough to forsake our sins and follow Him."

As he spoke, a tranquil smile brightened his venerable features, and seeing the fine small hand of Manuel resting on his chair, he laid his own wrinkled palm over it and clasped it tenderly. Cyrillon Vergniaud, moved by a quick impulse, suddenly advanced towards him.

"Monseigneur," he said, with unaffected deference, "You are much more than a Cardinal,—you are a good and honest man! And that you serve Christ purely is plainly evidenced in your look and bearing. Do me one favour! Extend your pardon to me for my almost committed crime of to-day,—and give me your blessing! I will try to be worthy of it!"

The Cardinal was silent for a few minutes looking at him earnestly.

"My blessing is of small value," he said, "And yet I do not think you would ask it for mere mockery of an old man's faith. I should like,——" here he paused—then slowly went on again," I should like to say a few words to you if I might—to ask you one or two questions concerning yourself——"

"Ask anything you please, Monseigneur," replied Cyrillon, " I will answer you frankly and fully. I have never had any mysteries in my life save one,—that of my birth, which up till to day was a stigma and a drawback;—but now, I feel I may be proud of my father. A man who sacrifices his entire social reputation and position to make amends for a wrong done to the innocent is worthy of honour."

"I grant it!" said the Cardinal, " But you yourself—why have you made a name which is like a firebrand to start a conflagration of discord in Europe?—why do you use your gifts of language and expression to awaken a national danger which even the strongest Government may find itself unable to stand against? I do not blame you till I hear,—till I know;—but your writings,—your appeals for truth in all things,—are like loud clarion blasts which may awaken more evil than good."

"Monseigneur, the evil is not of my making,—it exists!" replied Cyrillon, " My name, my writings,—are only as a spark from the huge smouldering fire of religious discontent in the world. If it were not *my* name it would be another's. If *I* did not write or speak, someone else would write and speak—perhaps better—perhaps not so well. At any rate I am sincere in my convictions, and write from the fulness of the heart. I do not care for money—I make none at all by literature,—but I earn enough by my labour in the fields to keep me in food and lodging. I have no desire for fame,—except in so far as my name may serve as an encouragement and help to others. If you care to hear my story——"

"I should appreciate your confidence greatly," said the Cardinal earnestly, " The Fates have made you a leading spirit of the time,—it would interest me to know your thoughts and theories. But if you would prefer not to speak——"

"I generally prefer not to speak," replied Cyrillon, " But to-day is one of open confession,—and I think too that it is sometimes advisable for men of the Church to understand and enter into the minds of those who are outside the Church,—who will have no Church,—not from disobedience or insubordination, but simply because they do not find God or Christ in that institution as it at present exists. And nowadays we are seeking for God strenuously and passionately! We have found Him too in places where the Church assured us He was not and could not be."

"Is there any portion of life where God is not?" asked Manuel gently.

Cyrillon's dark eyes softened as he met the boy's glance.

"No, dear child!—truly there is not,—but the priests do nothing to maintain or to prove that," he replied; "and the more the world lifts itself higher and higher into the light, the more we shall perceive God, and the less we will permit anything to intervene between ourselves and Him. But you are too young to understand——"

"No, not at all too young to understand!" answered Manuel, "Not at all too young to understand that God is love, and pardon, and patience;—and that wheresoever men are intolerant, uncharitable, and bigoted, there they straightway depart from God and know Him not at all."

"Truly that is how I understand Christianity," said Cyrillon, "But for so simple and plain a perception of duty one is called atheist and socialist, and one's opinions are branded as dangerous to the community. Truth is dangerous, I know—but why?"

"Would that not take a century to explain?" said the silvery voice of the Princesse D'Agramont, who entered with Angela at that moment, and made her deep obeisance before the Cardinal, glancing inquisitively as she did so at Manuel who still stood resting against the prelate's chair, "Pardon our abrupt appearance, Monseigneur, but Angela and I are moved by the spirit of curiosity!—and if we are swept out of the Church like straws before the wind for our impertinence, we care not! Monsignor Moretti has just left the house, wrapt up in his wrath like a bird of prey in a thunder-cloud, muttering menaces against 'Gys Grandit' the Socialist writer. Now what

in the world has Gys Grandit to do with him or with us?
Salut, cher Abbé!"—and she gave Vergniaud her hand
with charming friendliness; " I came here really to see
you, and place the Chateau D'Agramont at your disposal,
while I am away passing the winter in Italy. Pray make
yourself at home there—and your son also . . ."

"Madame," said the Abbé, profoundly touched by
the sincerity of her manner, and by the evident cordiality
of her intention, " I thank you from my heart for your
friendship at this moment when friendship is most
needed! But I feel I ought not to cast the shadow of my
presence on your house under such circumstances——and
as for my son——it would certainly be unwise for you
to extend your gracious hospitality to him . . . he is my
son——yes truly!—and I acknowledge him as such;
but he is also another person of his own making——
Gys Grandit!"

Angela Sovrani gave a slight cry, and a wave of colour
flushed her face,—the Princesse stood amazed.

"Gys Grandit!" she echoed in a low tone, "And
Vergniaud's son! *Grand Dieu!* Is it possible!" Then
advancing, she extended both her hands to Cyrillon, "Monsieur, accept my homage! You have a supreme genius,—and with it you command more than one-
half of the thoughts of France!"

Cyrillon took her hands,—lightly pressed, and released them.

"Madame, you are too generous!"

But even while he exchanged these courtesies with her,
his eyes were fixed on Angela Sovrani, who, moving
close to her uncle's chair, had folded her hands upon its
sculptured edge and now stood beside it, a graceful
nymph-like figure of statuesque repose. But her breath
came and went quickly, and her face was very pale.

"No wonder Monsignor Moretti was so exceedingly
angry," resumed the Princesse D'Agramont with a smile,
" I understand the position now. It is a truly remarkable
one. Monseigneur," this with a profound reverence to
the Cardinal, " you have found it difficult to be umpire in
the discussion."

"The discussion was not mine," said the Cardinal
slowly, " But the cause of the trouble is a point which
affects many,—and I am one of those who desire to hear

all before I presume to judge one. I have asked the son of my old friend Vergniaud to tell me what led him to make his assumed name one of such terror and confusion in the world; he is but six-and-twenty, and yet . . ."

"And yet people talk much of me you would say, Monseigneur," said Cyrillon, a touch of scorn lighting up his fine eyes, "True, and it is easy to be talked of. That is nothing. I do not wish for that, except in so far as it helps me to attain my ambition."

"And that ambition is?" queried the Princesse.

"To lead!" answered Cyrillon with a passionate gesture, "To gather the straying thoughts of men into one burning focus—and turn *that* fire on the world!"

They were all silent for a minute—then the Princesse D'Agramont spoke again—

"But——Pardon me! Then you were about to destroy all your own chances of the future in your wild impulse of this morning?"

"Oh, Madame, it was no wild impulse! When a man takes an oath by the side of a dead woman, and that woman his mother, he generally means to keep it! And I most resolutely meant to kill my father and make of myself a parricide. But I considered my mother had been murdered too—socially and morally—and I judged my vengeance just. If it had not been for the boy there——" and he glanced at Manuel, "I should certainly have fulfilled my intention."

"And then there would have been no Abbé Vergniaud, and no 'Gys Grandit,'" said the Princesse lightly, endeavouring to change the sombre tone of the conversation,— "and the 'Christian Democratic' party would have been in sackcloth and ashes!"

"The Christian Democratic party!" echoed the Cardinal, "What do they mean? What do they want?"

"Christianity, Monseigneur! That is all!" replied Cyrillon, "All—but so much! You asked me for my history—will you hear it now?"

There was an immediate murmur of assent, and the group around Cardinal Bonpré were soon seated—all save Manuel, who remained standing. Angela sat on a cushion at her uncle's feet, and her deep violet eyes were full of an eager, almost feverish interest which she could scarcely conceal; and the Abbé Vergniaud, vitally and painfully concerned as he was in the narrative about to be told, could not help looking at her, and wondering at the extraordinary light and beauty of her face thus transfigured by an excitation of thought. Was she a secret follower of his son's theories, he wondered? Composing himself in his chair, he sat with bent head, marvelling as he heard the story of the bold and fearless and philosophic life that had sprung into the world all out of his summer's romance with a little innocent girl, whom he had found praying to her guardian angel.

"It is not always ourselves," began Cyrillon in his slow, emphatic, yet musical voice, "who are responsible for the good or the evil we may do in our lives. Much of our character is formed by the earliest impressions of childhood—and my earliest impressions were those of sorrow. I started life with the pulse of my mother's broken heart beating in me,—hence my thoughts were sombre, and of an altogether unnatural character to a child of tender years. We lived—my mother and I—in a small cottage on the edge of a meadow outside the quaint old city of Tours—a meadow, full at all seasons, of the loveliest wild flowers, but sweetest in the springtime when the narcissi bloomed, lifting their thousand cups of sweet perfume like incense to the sky. I used to sit among their cool green stems,—thinking many thoughts, chief among which was a wonder why God had made my little mother so unhappy. I heard afterwards that God was not to blame,—only man, breaking God's laws of equity. She was a good brave woman, for despite her loneliness and tears, she worked hard;—worked to send me to school, and to teach me all she herself knew —which was little enough, poor soul,—but she studied in order to instruct me,—and often when I slept the unconscious sleep of healthy childhood, she was up through half the night spelling out abstruse books, difficult enough for an educated woman to master, but for a peasant —(she was nothing more)—presenting almost superhuman obstacles. I was very quick to learn, and her loving patience was not wasted upon me;—but when I was about eleven years old I resolved that I could no longer burden her with the expenses of my life—so without asking her consent, I hired myself out to a farmer, to clear weeds from his fields, and so began to earn my bread, which is the best and noblest form of knowledge existing in the world for all of us. With the earning of my body's keep came spiritual independence, and young as I was I began to read and consider for myself —till when I was about fifteen chance brought me across the path of a man whose example inspired me and decided my fate, named Aubrey Leigh."

Angela gave a slight exclamation of surprise, and Cyrillon turned his dark eyes upon her.

"Yes, mademoiselle!—I am aware that he has been in Paris lately. No doubt you know him. Certainly he is born to be a leader of men, and if a noble life and unsullied character, together with eloquence, determination, and steadfastness of purpose can help him to fulfil his mission, he will assuredly succeed. He is from America, though born of British parents, and the first thing I gathered from him was an overwhelming desire to study and to master the English language—not because it was English, but because it was the universal language spoken by America. I felt from what he said then,—and I feel still from what I have learnt and know now,—that America has all the future in the hollow of her hand. My intention, had I succeeded in my revengeful attempt this morning, was to escape to America immediately, and from there write under the *nom de plume* which I have already made known. I can write as easily in English as in French,—for my friend Aubrey Leigh was very kind and took a great liking to me, and stayed in Touraine for a year and a half, simply for the pleasure of instructing me and grafting his theories upon my young and aspiring mind. And now we are as one in our hopes and endeavours, and the years make little disparity between us. He was twenty-two when I was but fifteen,— but now that I am twenty-six and he thirty-three we are far better matched associates. From him I learnt much of the discontents,—ethical and religious,—of the world; from him I learnt how to speak in public. He was then an actor, a sort of wandering 'Bohemian,'—but he soon tired of the sordidness of the stage and aspired to higher platforms of work, and he had already begun to lead the people by his powers of oratory, as he leads them now. I heard him speak in French as fluently as in English; and

I resolved on my part to speak likewise in English as easily as he did in French. And when we parted it was with a mutual resolve *to lead!*—to lead—and ever still to lead!—we would starve on our theories, we said, but we would speak out if it cost us our very lives. To earn daily bread I managed to obtain steady employment as a labourer in the fields,—and I soon gained sufficient to keep my mother and myself. My friend Aubrey had imbued me thoroughly with the love of incessant hard work; there was no disgrace, he said, in digging the soil, if the brain were kept working as well as the hands. And I did keep my brain working; I allowed it also to lie fallow, and to absorb everything of nature that was complex, grand and beautiful,—and from such studies I learnt the goodness and the majesty of the Creator as they are never found in human expositions of Him made by the preachers of creeds. At eighteen I made my first public address,—and the next year published my first book in Tours. But though I won an instant success my soul was hampered and heavy with the burning thought of vengeance; and this thought greatly hindered the true conceptions of life that I desired to entertain. When my mother died, and her failing voice crooned for the last time, '*Ah, la tristesse d'avoir aimé!*' the spark of hatred I had cherished all the years of my life for my father burst into a flame, and leapt up to its final height this morning as you saw. Now it has gone out into dust and ashes—the way of all such flames! I have been spared for better things I hope. What I have written and done, France knows,—but my thoughts are not limited to France, they seek a wider horizon. France is a decaying nation—her doom is sealed. I work and write for the To-Be, not the Has-Been. Such as my life is, it has never been darkened or brightened by love of any sort, save that which my mother gave me. Your Eminence," and he turned towards the Cardinal, " asks me why I inculcate theories which suggest change, terror and confusion;—Monseigneur, terror and confusion can never be caused save among the ranks of those who have secret reason to be terrorised! There is nothing terrifying in Truth to those who are true! If I distract and alarm unworthy societies, revolting hypocrism, established shams and miserable conventions, I am only the wielder

of the broom that sweeps out the cobwebs and the dust
from a dirty house. My one desire is to make the habitation of Christian souls clean! Terror and confusion
there will be,—there must be;—the time is ripe for it—
none of us can escape it—it is the prophesied period of
'men's hearts failing them for fear, and looking after
those things which are coming on the earth.' I have
not made the time. I am born *of* it—one *with* it;—God
arranges these things. I am not working for self or for
money,—I can live on bread and herbs and water. I
want no luxurious surroundings,—no softnesses—no deli-
cacies—no tendernesses—no sympathies! I set my face
forward in the teeth of a thousand winds of opposition,
forward still forward! I seek nothing for my own personal needs! I know that nothing can hinder me or keep
me back! Nothing! Monseigneur, I voice the cry of
multitudes!—they have, as it were, been wandering in
the wilderness listening to the Gospel for many days,—
days which have accumulated to more than eighteen hundred years; just as they did of old,—only the Master did
not send them away hungry—He fed them lest they
should 'faint by the way.' He thought of *that* possibility!—we seldom care how many faint by the way, or
die in the effort to live! Monseigneur, I must—I will
speak for the dumb mouths of the nations! And every
unit that can so speak, or can so write, should hasten to
turn itself into a Pentecostal flame of fire to blaze and
burn a warning upon the verge of this new century,—
causing men to prophesy with divers tongues, of the
Truth of God,—not of the lies that have been made to
represent Him! "

Felix Bonpré raised one hand with a slight gesture en-
joining silence, and seemed wrapped for a moment in
painful meditation. Angela looking anxiously up at him
caught, not his glance, but that of Manuel, who smiled
at her encouragingly. Presently the Cardinal spoke,—
gently and with a kind of austere patience.

"Am I to understand from your speech, my son, and
the work of your life, that you consider the Church a lie?
I put the question plainly; but I do not ask it either to
reproach or intimidate you. I am well aware I can do
neither. Thought is free to the individual as well as to
the nations; and whereas, in past time we had one man

who could think and speak, we have now a thousand! We are unfortunately apt to forget the spread of education;—but a man who thinks as you do, and dares all things for the right to act upon his thought, should surely be able to clearly explain his reasons for arming himself against any outwardly expressed form of faith, which has received the acceptance and submission of the world?"

"Monseigneur, I do not attack any faith! Faith is necessary,—faith is superb! I honour this uplifting virtue,—whether I find it in the followers of the Talmud or the Koran, or the New Testament, and, personally speaking, I would die for my belief in the great name and ethical teaching of Christ. I attack the Church—yes,—and why? Because it has departed from the Faith! Because it is a mere system now,—corrupt in many parts, as all systems must naturally become when worn out by long usage. In many ways it favours stupid idolatries, and in others it remains deaf and blind and impervious to the approach of great spiritual and religious facts, which are being made splendidly manifest by Science. Why, there is not a miracle in the Testament that science will not make possible!—there is not a word Christ ever spoke that shall not be proved true! And may I not be called a Christian? I may,—I must, —I will be,—for I am! But hypocrisy, false measures, perverted aims, and low pandering to ignorance and brutality, vile superstition and intimidation—these things must be destroyed if the Church is to last with honour to itself and with usefulness to others. To-day, over in England, they are quarrelling with bitter acrimony concerning forms and outward symbols of religion, thus fulfilling the words of the Lord, ' Ye make clean the outside of the cup and of the platter but within ye are full of extortion and excess.' Now, if the Spirit of Christ were at all in these men who thus argue, there would be no trouble about forms or symbols of faith,—there would be too much of the faith itself for any such petty disputation. Monseigneur, I swear to you, I say nothing, teach nothing but what is the straight and true command of Christ! . . . no more, but also no less!"

Moved by the young man's eloquence, the Cardinal looked at him straightly in the eyes.

"You speak well," he said, "Some people would tell you that you have that fluency of tongue which is judged dangerous. But danger is after all only for those who have something to fear. If we of the Church are pure in our intent nothing should disturb our peace,—nothing should move us from our anchorage. Your ideas, you say, are founded on the Master's Word?"

"Entirely," replied Cyrillon, "I am working,—Aubrey Leigh is working,—we are all working for a House of Praise more than a Place of Prayer. We want to give thanks for what we are, and what, if we follow the sane and healthy laws of life, we may be,—rather than continue the clamour for more benefits when we have already received, and are receiving so much."

"Would you not pray at all then?" asked Bonpré.

"Yes—for others, not for ourselves! And then not as the Church prays. Her form of service is direct disobedience!"

"In what way?"

"Monseigneur, I always preface my remarks on these subjects with the words ' if we believe in Christ.' I say *if* we believe, we must accept His commands; and they are plain enough. '*When ye pray, use not vain repetitions as the heathen do, for they think they shall be heard for their much speaking. Be not ye therefore like unto them, for your Father knoweth what things ye have need of before ye ask him.*' Now if this is to be understood as the command of Christ, the Messenger of God, do we not deliberately act against it in all directions? Vain repetitions! The Church is full of them,—choked with them! The priests who order us to say ten or twenty ' Paternosters ' by way of penance, are telling us to do exactly what Christ commanded us *not* to do! The terrible Litany of the Protestant Church, with its everlasting ' Good Lord deliver us,' is another example of vain repetition. Again—think of these words—' When thou prayest, thou shalt *not be as the hypocrites are,* for they love to pray standing in the synagogues, and at the corners of the streets *that they may be seen of men.*' Is not all our churchgoing that we may be seen of men?"

"Then, my son, it seems that you would ·do away with the Church altogether in the extremity of your zeal!"

said the Cardinal gently, "There must surely be some outward seeming—some city set on a hill whose light cannot be hid—some visible sign of Christ among us——"

"True, Monseigneur, but such a sign must be of so brilliant and pure a nature,—so grand an uplifted Cross of unsullied light that it shall be as the sun rising out of darkness! Oh, I would have churches built gloriously, with every possible line of beauty and curve of perfect architecture in their fabrication;—but I would have no idolatrous emblems,—no superstitious ceremonies within them,—no tawdry reliquaries of gems—no boast of the world's wealth at all; but great Art,—the result of man's great Thought rendered and given with pure simplicity! I would have great music,—and more than all I would have thanksgiving always! And if valuables were brought to the altar for gifts, the gifts should be given out again to those in need—not kept,—not left untouched like a miser's useless hoard, while one poor soul was starving!"

"My son, such a scheme of purification as yours will take centuries to accomplish," murmured Bonpré slowly, "Almost it would need Christ to come again!"

"And who shall say He will not come!" exclaimed Cyrillon fervently, "Who shall swear He is not even now among us! Has he not told us all to 'watch,' because we know not the hour at which He cometh? No, Monseigneur!—centuries are not needed for Truth to make itself manifest nowadays! We hold Science by the hand, —she is becoming our familiar friend and companion, and through her guidance we have learned that the Laws of the Universe are Truth,—Truth which cannot be contradicted; and that only the things which move and work in harmony with those laws can last. All else must perish! *'Whosoever is not with me is against me,'*—or in other words, whosoever opposes himself to Eternal Laws must be against the whole system of the Universe, and is therefore a discord which is bound to be silenced. Monseigneur, Christ was a Divine Preacher of Truth;—and I, in my humble man's way endeavour to follow Truth. And if I ever fail now, after to-day's attempted crime, to honour the commands of Christ, and obey them as closely as I can, then pass your condemnation upon me, but not till then! Meanwhile, give me a good man's blessing!"

Deeply interested as he was, the Cardinal nevertheless still hesitated. To him, though the sayings and opinions of the famous "Gys Grandit" were not exactly new, there was something terrible in hearing him utter them with such bold and trenchant meaning. He sighed, and appeared lost in thought; till Manuel touched him gently on the arm.

"Dear friend, are you afraid to bless this man who loves our Father?"

"Afraid? My child, I am afraid of nothing—but there is grave trouble in my heart——"

"Nay, trouble should never enter there!" said Manuel softly, "Stretch out your hand!—let no human soul wait for a benediction!"

Profoundly moved, the Cardinal obeyed, and laid his white trembling hand on Cyrillon's bent head.

"May God forgive thee the intention of thy sin to-day!" he said, in a low and solemn tone—"May Christ guide thee out of all evil, and lead thee through the wildness of the world to Heaven's own peace, which passeth understanding!"

So gentle, so brave, so sweet and tender were the accents in which he spoke these few simple works, that the tears filled Angela's eyes, and Abbé Vergniaud, resting his head on one hand, felt a strange contraction in his throat, and began to think of possible happy days yet to be passed perchance in seclusion with this long-denied son of his, who had sprung out of the secret ways of love, first to slay and then to redeem him. Could there be a more plain and exact measuring out of law? If he had not confessed his sin he would have probably died in it suddenly without a chance of amendment or repentance—but lo!—on confession, his life had been saved as if by a miracle, and the very result of evil had been transformed into consolation! So he sat absorbed, wondering—musing—and while the Cardinal spoke his blessing with closed eyes, all heads were bent, and faces hidden. And in the reverent silence that followed, the gentle prelate gave a sign of kind dismissal and farewell to all, which they, understanding, accepted, and at once made their brief adieux, the Abbé Vergniaud only lingering a moment longer than the rest, to bend humbly down and kiss his Apostolic ring. Then they left him, alone with Manuel.

On their way out of the house, through Angela's studio, the Princesse D'Agramont paused for a few minutes to say further kind words to the Abbé respecting the invitation she had given him to her Château—, and while she was thus engaged, Angela turned hurriedly to Cyrillon.

"As 'Gys Grandit' you receive many letters from strangers, do you not?"

The young man regarded her earnestly, with unconcealed admiration glowing in his fine eyes.

"Assuredly, Mademoiselle! And some of these letters are very dear to me, because they make me aware of friends I might otherwise never have known."

"You have one correspondent who is deeply interested in your theories, and who sympathises keenly in all your religious views—" she went on, lowering her eyes—— "a certain Madame Angèle——"

He uttered a quick exclamation of pleasure.

"You know her?"

She looked up,—her eyes sparkled—and she laid a finger on her lips.

"Keep my secret!" she said——"I am so glad to meet you personally at last!"

He stared, bewildered.

"You——you . . . !"

"Yes. I!" and she smiled—"The mysterious and Christian-Democratic 'Angèle' is Angela Sovrani. So you see we have been unconscious friends for some time!"

His face grew radiant, and he made a quick movement towards her.

"Then I owe you a great debt of gratitude!" he said ——"For encouragement—for sympathy—for help in dark hours!——and how unworthy I have proved of your goodness . . . what must you think of me—you— so beautiful—so good——"

She moved back a little with a warning gesture—and his words were interrupted by the Abbé, who glancing from one to the other in a little surprise, said, as he bent reverently over her hand and kissed it,—

"We must be going, Cyrillon!"

Another few moments and Angela was left alone to think over, and try to realise the strange and rapidly-occurring events of the day. Whatever her thoughts were, they seemed for a long time to be of a somewhat April-like character, for her eyes brimmed over with tears even while she smiled.

XVII.

In one of the few remaining streets of Rome which the vandal hand of the modern builder and restorer has not meddled with, stands the "Casa D'Angeli", a sixteenth-century building fronted with wonderfully carved and widely projecting balconies—each balcony more or less different in design, yet forming altogether in their entirety the effect of complete sculptural harmony. The central one looks more like a cathedral shrine than the embrasure of a window, for above it angels' heads look out from the enfolding curves of their own tall wings, and a huge shield which might serve as a copy of that which Elaine kept bright for Lancelot, is poised between, bearing a lily, a cross, and a heart engraven in its quarterings. Here, leaning far forward to watch the intense gold of the Roman moon strike brightness and shadow out of the dark uplifted pinions of her winged stone guardians, stood Sylvie Hermenstein, who, in her delicate white attire, with the moonbeams resting like a halo on her soft hair, might have easily passed for some favoured saint whom the sculptured angels were protecting. And yet she was only one whom the world called "a frivolous woman of society, who lived on the admiration of men". So little did they know her,—so little indeed does the world know about any of us. It was true that Sylvie, rich, lovely, independent, and therefore indifferent to opinions, lived her own life very much according to her own ideas,—but then those ideas were far more simple and unworldly than anybody gave her credit for. She to whom all the courts of Europe were open, preferred to wander in the woods alone, reading some favourite book, to almost any other pleasure,—and as for the admiration which she won by a look or turn of her head wherever she went, nothing in all the world so utterly bored her as this influence of her own charm. For she had tried men and found them wanting. With all the pent-up passion of her woman's soul she longed

to be loved,—but what she understood by love was a
much purer and more exalted emotion than is common
among men and women. She was suffering just now
from an intense and overpowering ennui. Rome was
beautiful, she averred, but dull. Stretching her fair white
arms out over the impervious stone-angels she said this,
and more than this, to someone within the room, who answered her in one of the most delightfully toned voices
in the world—a voice that charmed the ear by its first
cadences, and left the listener fascinated into believing
that its music was the expression of a perfectly harmonious mind.

" You seem very discontented," said the voice, speaking
in English, " But really your pathway is one of roses! "

" You think so? " and Sylvie turned her head quickly
round and looked at her companion, a handsome little
man of some thirty-five years of age, who stretching
himself lazily full length in an arm-chair was toying
with the silky ears of an exceedingly minute Japanese
spaniel, Sylvie's great pet and constant companion. " Oh,
mon Dieu! You, artist and idealist though you are—or
shall I say as you are supposed to be," and she laughed
a little, " you are like all the rest of your sex! Just because you see a woman able to smile and make herself
agreeable to her friends, and wear pretty clothes, and
exchange all the *bon mots* of badinage and every-day
flirtation, you imagine it impossible for her to have any
sorrow! "

" There is only one sorrow possible to a woman," replied the gentleman, who was no other than Florian
Varillo, the ideal of Angela Sovrani's life, smiling as he
spoke with a look in his eyes which conveyed an almost
amorous meaning.

Sylvie left the balcony abruptly, and swept back into
the room, looking a charming figure of sylph-like slen-
derness and elegance in her clinging gown of soft white
satin showered over with lace and pearls.

" Only one sorrow! " she echoed, " And that is—? "

" Inability to win love, or to awaken desire! " replied
Varillo, still smiling.

The pretty Comtesse raised her golden head a little
more proudly, with the air of a lily lifting itself to the
light on its stem—her deep blue eyes flashed.

"I certainly cannot complain on that score!" she said, with a touch of malice as well as coldness—"But the fact that men lose their heads about me does not make me in the least happy."

"It should do so!" and Varillo set the little Japanese dog carefully down on the floor, whereupon it ran straight to its mistress, uttering tiny cries of joy, "There is no sweeter triumph for a woman than to see men subjugated by her smile, and intimidated by her frown;—to watch them burning themselves like moths in her clear flame, and dying at her feet for love of her! The woman who can do these things is gifted with the charm which makes or ruins life,—few can resist her,—she draws sensitive souls as a magnet draws the needle,—and the odd part of it all is that she need not have any heart herself —she need not feel one pulse of the passion with which she inspires others—indeed it is better that she should not. The less she is moved herself, the greater is her fascination. Love clamours far more incessantly and passionately at a closed gate than an open one!"

Sylvie was silent for a minute or two looking at him with something of doubt and disdain. The room they were in was one of those wide and lofty apartments which in old days might have been used for a prince's audience chamber, or a dining hall for the revelry of the golden youth of Imperial Rome. The ceiling, supported by eight slender marble columns, was richly frescoed with scenes from Ariosto's poems, some of the figures being still warm with colour and instinct with life—and on the walls were the fading remains of other pictures, the freshest among them being a laughing Cupid poised on a knot of honeysuckle, and shooting his arrow at random into the sky. Ordinarily speaking, the huge room was bare and comfortless to a degree,—but the Comtesse Sylvie's wealth, combined with her good taste, had filled it with things that made it homelike as well as beautiful. The thickest velvet pile carpets laid over the thickest of folded mattings, covered the marble floors, and deprived them of their usual chill,—great logs of wood burned cheerfully in the wide chimney, and flowers, in every sort of quaint vase or bowl, made bright with colour and blossom all dark and gloomy corners, and softened every touch of melancholy away. A grand piano stood open,—

a mandoline tied with bright ribbons, lay on a little table near a cluster of roses and violets,—books, music, drawings, bits of old drapery and lace were so disposed as to hide all sharp corners and forbidding angles,—and where the frescoes on the wall were too damaged to be worth showing even in outline, some fine old Flemish tapestry covered the defect. Sylvie herself, in the exquisite clothing which she always made it her business to wear, was the brilliant completion of the general picturesqueness,—and Florian Varillo seemed to think so as he looked at her with the practised underglance of admiration which is a trick common to Italians, and which some women accept as a compliment and others resent as an insult.

"Do you not agree with me?" he said persuasively, with a smile which showed his fine and even teeth to perfection, "When the chase is over the hunters go home tired! What a man cannot have, that very thing is what he tries most to obtain!"

"You speak from experience, I suppose," said Sylvie, moving slowly across the room towards the fire, and caressing her little dog which she held nestled under her rounded chin like a ball of silk, "And yet you, more than most men, have everything you can want in this world—but I suppose you are not satisfied—not even with Angela!"

"Angela is a dear little woman!" said Florian, with an air of emotional condescension, "The dearest little woman in the world! And she is really clever."

"Clever!" echoed Sylvie, "Is that all?"

"*Cara Contessa,* is not that enough?"

"Angela is a genius," averred Sylvie, with warmth and energy, "a true genius!—a great,—a sublime artist!"

"*Che che!*" and Varillo smiled, "How delightful it is to hear one woman praise another! Women are so often like cats spitting and hissing at each other, tearing at each other's clothes and reputations,—clothes even more than reputations,—that it is really quite beautiful to me to hear you admire my Angela! It is very generous of you!"

"Generous of me!" and the Comtesse Hermenstein looked him full in the eyes, "Why I think it an honour to know her—a privilege to touch her hand! All Europe admires her—she is one of the world's greatest artists."

"She paints wonderfully well,—for a woman," said

Varillo lazily, " But there is so much in that phrase, *cara Contessa*, ' for a woman '. Your charming sex often succeeds in doing very clever and pretty things; but in a man they would not be considered surprising. You fairy creatures are not made for fame—but for love ! "

The Comtesse glanced him up and down for a moment, then laughed musically.

" And for desertion, and neglect as well ! " she said, " And sometimes for bestowing upon *your* charming sex every fortune and every good blessing, and getting kicked for our pains ! And sometimes it happens that we are permitted the amazing honour of toiling to keep you in food and clothing, while you jest at your clubs about the uselessness of woman's work in the world ! Yes, I know ! Have you seen Angela's great picture ? "

Again Florian smiled.

" Great ? No ! I know that the dear little girl has fixed an enormous canvas up in her studio, and that she actually gets on a ladder to paint something upon it ;— but it is always covered,—she does not wish me to see it till it is finished. She is like a child in some things, and I always humour her. I have not the least desire to look at her work till she herself is willing to show it to me. But in myself I am convinced she is trying to do too much—it is altogether too large an attempt."

" What are *you* doing ? " asked Sylvie abruptly.

" Merely delicate trifles,—little mosaics of art ! " said Varillo with languid satisfaction, " They may possibly please a connoisseur,—but they are quite small studies."

" You have the same model you had last year ? " queried Sylvie.

Their eyes met, and Varillo shifted uneasily in his chair.

" The same," he replied curtly.

Again Sylvie laughed.

" Immaculate creature ! " she murmured, " The noblest of her sex, of course ! Men always call the women who pander to their vices ' noble '."

Varillo flushed an angry red.

" You are pleased to be sarcastic, fair lady," he said carelessly, " I do not understand——"

" No ? You are not usually so dense with me, though to those who do not know you as well as I do, you sometimes appear to be the very stupidest of men! Now be frank!—tell me, is not Pon-Pon one of the 'noble' women?"

"She is a very good creature," averred Varillo gently, and with an air that was almost pious,—"She supports her family entirely on her earnings."

"How charming of her!" laughed Sylvie, "And so exceptional a thing to do, is it not? My dressmaker does the same thing,—she 'supports' her family; but respectably! And just think!—if ever your right hand loses its cunning as a painter, Angela will be able to 'support' *you!*"

"Always Angela!" muttered Varillo, beginning to sulk, "Cannot you talk of something else?"

"No,—not for the moment! She is an interesting subject,—to *me!* She will arrive in Rome to-morrow night, and her uncle Cardinal Bonpré, will be with her, and they will all stay at the Sovrani Palace, which seems to me like a bit of the Vatican and an old torture-chamber rolled into one! And, talking of this same excellent Cardinal, they have almost canonized him at the Vatican,—almost, but not quite."

"For what reason?"

"Oh, have you not heard? It appears he performed a miracle in Rouen, curing a child who had been a cripple ever since babyhood, and making him run about as well and strong as possible. One prayer did it, so it is said,—the news reached the Vatican some days ago; our charming Monsignor Gherardi told me of it. The secretary of the Archbishop of Rouen brought the news personally to the Holy Father."

"I do not believe it," said Varillo indifferently, "The days of miracles are past. And from what I know, and from what Angela has told me of her uncle, Cardinal Bonpré, he would never lend himself to such nonsense."

"Well, I only tell you what is just now the talk at the Vatican," said Sylvie, "Your worthy uncle-in-law that is to be, may be Pope yet! Have you heard from Angela?"

"Every day. But she has said nothing about this miracle."

"Perhaps she does not know,"—and Sylvie began to

yawn, and stretch her white arms above her head lazily,
" Oh, *Dio mio!* How terribly dull is Rome! "

" How long have you been here, Contessa? "

" Nearly a week! If I am not more amused I shall go
away home to Budapest."

" But how is one to amuse you? " asked Varillo, sitting down beside her and endeavouring to take her hand.
She drew it quickly from him.

" Not in that way! " she said scornfully, " Is it possible that you can be so conceited! A woman says she is
dull and bored, and straightway the nearest man imagines
his uncouth caresses will amuse her! *Tiens tiens!*
When will you understand that all women are not like
Pon-Pon? "

Varillo drew back, chafed and sullen. His *amour
propre* was wounded, and he began to feel exceedingly
cross. The pretty laugh of Sylvie rang out like a little
peal of bells.

" Suppose Angela knew that you wished to ' amuse '
me in that particularly unamusing way? " she went on,
" You—who, to her, are *chevalier sans peur et sans
reproche!* "

" Angela is different to all other women," said Varillo quickly, with a kind of nervous irritation in his manner as he spoke, " and she has to be humoured accordingly. She is extremely fantastic—full of strange ideas
and unnatural conceptions of life. Her temperament is
studious and dreamy—self-absorbed too at times—and
she is absolutely passionless. That is why she will make
a model wife."

The Comtesse drew her breath quickly,—her blood
began to tingle and her heart to beat——but she repressed these feelings and said,

" You mean that her passionless nature will be her
safety in all temptation? "

" Exactly! " and Varillo, smiling, became good na-
tured again—" For Angela to be untrue would be a
grotesque impossibility! She has no idea of the stronger
sentiment of love which strikes the heart like a lightning
flash and consumes it. Her powers of affection are intellectually and evenly balanced,—and she could not be
otherwise than faithful because her whole nature is opposed to infidelity. But it is not a nature which, being

tempted, overcomes—inasmuch as there is no temptation which is attractive to her!"

"You think so?" and a sparkle of satire danced in Sylvie's bright eyes, "Really? And because she is self-respecting and proud, you would almost make her out to be sexless?—not a woman at all,—without heart?—without passion? Then you do not love her!"

"She is the dearest creature to me in all the world!" declared Florian, with emotional ardour, "There is no one at all like her! Even her beauty, which comes and goes with her mood, is to an artist's eye like mine, exquisite,—and more dazzling to the senses than the stereotyped calm of admitted perfection in form and feature. But, *cara Contessa,* I am something of an analyst in character—and I know that the delicacy of Angela's charm lies in that extraordinary tranquillity of soul, which, (*you* suggested the word!) may indeed be almost termed sexless. She is purer than snow—and very much colder."

"You are fortunate to be the only man selected to melt that coldness," said Sylvie with a touch of disdain, "Myself, I think you make a great mistake in calling Angela passionless. She is all passion—and ardour—but it is kept down,—held firmly within bounds, and devoutly consecrated to you. Pardon me, if I say that you should be more grateful for the love and trust she gives you. You are not without rivals in the field."

Florian Varillo raised his eyebrows smilingly.

"Rivals? *Veramente!* I am not aware of them!"

"No, I should say you had too good an opinion of yourself to imagine any rival possible!" said the Comtesse, "But such a person may exist!"

Varillo yawned, and flicked a grain of dust off his waistcoat with a fastidious thumb and finger.

"Impossible! No one could possibly fall in love with Angela now! She is an icicle,—no man save myself has the ghost of a chance with her!"

"Of course not," said Sylvie impatiently, "Because she is betrothed to you. But if things were not as they are——"

"It would make no difference, I assure you," laughed Varillo gaily, "Angela does not like men as a rule. She is fondest of romance—of dreams—of visions, out of which come the ideas for her pictures——"

"And she is quite passionless with all this, you think?" said Sylvie, "The 'stronger sentiment which strikes the heart like a flash of lightning, and consumes it', as you so poetically describe it—could never possibly disturb her peace?"

"I think not," replied Varillo, with a meditative air, "Angela and I glided into love like two children wandering by chance into a meadow full of flowers,—no storm struck us—no sudden danger signal flashed from our eyes—no trembling hurry of the blood bade us rush into each other's arms and cling!——nothing of this marvel touched us!——we loved with all the calm—— but without the glory!"

His voice,—the most fascinating quality attached to his personality,—rose and fell in this little speech with an exquisite cadence, half sad, half sweet,—and Sylvie, impressionable creature as she was, with her innate love of romance and poetry, was unconsciously moved by it to a faint sigh. There was nothing to sigh for, really,—it was just a mere melodious noise of words, in the making of which Florian Varillo was an adept. He had not an atom of serious thought in his remark, any more than in the dainty verses he was wont to append to his pictures —verses which he turned out with the lightest and swiftest ease, and which read like his spoken sentences, as if there were a meaning in them, when truly there was none. But Sylvie was just then in a curious state of mind, and slight things easily impressed her. She was in love— and yet she was not in love. The handsome face and figure of the Marquis Fontenelle, together with many of his undoubted good and even fine qualities, attracted her and held her in thrall, much more than the consciousness of his admiration and pursuit of her,—but—and this was a very interfering "but" indeed,—she was reluctantly compelled to admit to herself that there was no glozing over the fact that he was an incorrigibly "fast", otherwise bad man. His life was a long record of *liaisons* with women,—an exact counterpart of the life of the famous actor Miraudin. And though there is a saying that a reformed rake makes the best husband, Sylvie was scarcely sure of being willing to try this test,—besides, the Marquis had not offered himself in that capacity, but only as a lover. In Paris,—within reach of him, surrounded by his gracious and graceful courtesies everywhere, the pretty and sensitive Comtesse had sometimes felt her courage oozing out at her finger's ends,—and the longing to be loved became so strong and overwhelming in her soul that she had felt she must perforce one day yield to her persistent admirer's amorous solicitations, come what would of it in the end. Her safety had been in flight; and here in Rome, she had found herself, like a long-tossed little ship, suddenly brought up to firm anchorage. The vast peace and melancholy grandeur of the slowly dying " Mother of Nations ", enveloped her as with a sheltering cloak from the tempest of her own heart and senses, and being of an exquisitely refined and dainty nature in herself, she had, while employing her time in beautifying, furnishing and arranging her apartments in the casa D'Angeli, righted her mind, so to speak, and cleared it from the mists of illusion which had begun to envelop it, so that she could now think of Fontenelle quietly and with something of a tender compassion,—she could pray for him and wish him all things good,—but she could not be quite sure that she loved him. And this was well. For we should all be very sure indeed that we do love, before we crucify ourselves to the cross of sacrifice. Inasmuch as if the love in us be truly Love, we shall not feel the nails, we shall be unconscious of the blood that flows, and the thorns that prick and sting,—we shall but see the great light of Resurrection springing glorious out of death! But if we only *think* we love,—when our feeling is the mere attraction of the senses and the lighter impulses—then our crucifixion is in vain, and our death is death indeed. Some such thoughts as these had given Sylvie a new charm of manner since her arrival in Rome—she was less mirthful, but more sympathetic—less *riante,* but infinitely prettier and more fascinating. Florian Varillo studied her appreciatively in this regard after he had uttered his little meaningless melody of sentiment, and thought within himself—" A week or two and I could completely conquer that woman ! " He was mistaken—men who think these sort of things often are. But the thought satisfied him, and gave bold lustre to his eyes and brightness to his smile when he rose to take his leave. He had been one of the guests at a small and early dinner-party given by the Comtesse that evening,—and with the privilege of an old acquaintance, he had lingered thus long after all the others had gone to their respective homes.

"I will bid you now the *felicissima notte, cara e bella Contessa!*" he said caressingly, raising her small white hand to his lips, and kissing it with a lingering pressure of what he considered a peculiarly becoming moustache— "When Angela arrives to-morrow night I shall be often at the Palazzo Sovrani—shall I see you there?"

"Of course you will see me there," replied Sylvie, a little impatiently, "Am I not one of Angela's closest friends?"

"True! And for the sake of *la mia dolcézza,* you will also be a friend to me?"

"'*La mia dolcézza*'", repeated Sylvie, "Is that what you call her?"

"Yes—but I fear it is not original!" said Varillo smiling, "One Ariosto called his lady thus."

"Yes?" and Sylvie's eyes darkened and grew humid with a sudden tenderness of thought, "It is a pretty phrase!"

"It should be used to *you* always, by every man who has my present privilege!" said Varillo, gallantly, kissing her hand once more, "You will be my friend?"

Sylvie disengaged her hand from his.

"You must not depend upon me, Signor," she said with sudden coldness, "To be perfectly frank with you I am not sure that I like you. You are very charming and very clever—but I doubt your sincerity."

"*Ah, che sono infelice!*" murmured Varillo softly, "You are right, *bellissima Madama!* I am not myself with many people—but with you—you are one of the few who understand me . . . I am the very soul of candour!"

He fixed his eyes full upon her with an open and straight regard, adding, "Can *you* doubt me?" in a touching tone of wounded feeling.

The Comtesse laughed, and her face flushed.

"Well, I do not know!" she said, with a light gesture of her hands as though she threw something unpleasant away from her, "I shall judge of you by the happiness —or sorrow—of Angela!"

A slight frown contracted his brows—but it passed

quickly, and the candid smile illumined his mobile face once more.

"*Ebben! Buona notte, bella capricciosa!*" and bowing low he turned towards the door, "Thank you a thousand times for a very happy evening! Even when you are unkind to me you are still charming! *Addio!*"

She murmured an "addio" in response, and when he had gone, and the echo of his footfall down the great marble stairs had completely died away, she went out once more to the balcony and leaned among the sculptured angels, a dainty, slender, white figure, with her soft flower-like face turned up to the solemn sky, where the large moon marched like an Amazon through space, attended by her legions and battalions of stars. So slight, so fragile and sweet a woman!—with a precious world of love pent up in her heart . . . yet alone—quite alone on this night of splendid luminousness and majestic suggestions of infinity,—an infinity so monstrous and solitary to the one delicate creature, whose whole soul craved for a perfect love. Alas, for this "perfect love," of which all the dearest women dream! Where shall they find it? —and how shall they win it? Too often it comes when they may not have it; the cup of nectar is offered to lips that are forbidden to drink of it, because the world's convention stands between and turns the honey to gall. One of the many vague problems of a future life, offered for our consideration, is the one concerning the righteous satisfaction of love. Will not those who have been bound fast as prisoners in the bonds of matrimony without love, find those whose spirits are naturally one with theirs, but whom they have somehow missed in this life? For Byron's fine lines are eternally true,—

> "Few—none—find what they love or could have loved,—
> Though accident, blind contact, and the strong
> Necessity of loving, have removed
> Antipathies—but to recur ere long
> Envenom'd with irrevocable wrong."

And the "blind contact" is the worst of all influences brought to bear upon the mind and heart,—the most pernicious, and the most deeply weighted with responsibility. In this regard, Sylvie Hermenstein had acted wisely by removing herself from association, or "blind contact" with her would-be lover,—and yet, though she was aware

that her doing so had caused a certain dispersal of the
atmosphere which almost veered towards complete disillusion, she found nevertheless, that Rome as she had
said, was "dull"; her heart was empty, and longing for
she knew not what. And that deep longing she felt could
not have been completely gratified by the brief ardours of
Fontenelle. And so she sat thinking wearily,—wondering what was to become of her life. She had riches in
plenty, a fine estate and castle in Hungary,—servants at
her beck and call—and yet with all her wealth and beauty
and brilliancy, she felt that she was only loved by two
persons in the world, her old butler, and Madame Bozier,
who had been her first governess, and who now lived with
her, as a sort of *dame d'honneur* surrounded with every
comfort and luxury, and who certainly served her former
pupil with a faithful worship that would not have
changed, even if the direst poverty instead of riches had
been the portion of her beloved patroness. This elderly
lady it was who entered now with a soft and hesitating
step, and raising her glasses to her eyes, peered anxiously
through the lighted room towards the dark balcony where
Sylvie stood, like a fairy fallen out of the moon, and who
presently ventured to advance and call softly,

"Sylvie!"

The pretty Comtesse turned and smiled.

"Is it you, Katrine? Will you come out here? It is
not cold, and there is a lace wrap on the chair,—put it
round your dear old head and come and be romantic with
me!" and she laughed as the worthy Bozier obeyed her,
and came cautiously out among the angels' sculptured
wings. "Ah, dear Katrine! The happy days are gone
when a dark-eyed Roman lover would come strolling
down a street like this to strike the chords of his mandoline, and sing the dear old song,

> "'Ti voglio bene assai,
> E tu non pensi a me!'"

Without thinking about it, she sang this refrain suddenly in her sweet mezzo-soprano, every note ringing
clear on the silence of the night, and as she did so a man
of slim figure and medium height, stepped out of the dark
shadows and looked up. His half laughing eyes, piercing
in their regard, met the dreamy soft ones of the pretty

woman sitting among the angels' heads above him——
and pausing a moment he hesitated—then lifted his hat.
His face was excessively delicate in outline and very
pale, but a half mischievous smile softened and sweet-
ened the firm lines of his mouth and chin, and as the
moonbeams played caressingly on his close curling crop
of fair hair, he looked different enough to most of the
men in Rome to be considered singular as well as handsome. Sylvie, hidden as she was among the shadows,
blushed and drew back, a little vexed with herself,—the
worthy Madame Bozier was very properly scandalised.

"My dear child!" she murmured, "Remember—we
are in Rome. People judge things so strangely! What
an unfortunate error!——"

But Sylvie became suddenly unmanageable. Her love
of coquetry and mischief got the better of her, and she
thrust out her pretty head over the balcony once more.

"Be quiet, Katrine!" she whispered, "I was longing
for a romance, and here is one!" And detaching a rose
from her dress she tossed it lightly to the stranger below. He caught it—then looked up once more,

"Till we meet," he said softly in English,—and moving on among the shadows, disappeared.

"Now, who do you suppose *he* was?" enquired Sylvie, leaning back against the edge of the balcony, with
an arch glance at her *gouvernante*, "It was someone
unlike anyone else here, I am sure! It was somebody
with very bright eyes,—laughing eyes,—audacious eyes,
because they laughed at me! They sparkled at me like
stars on a frosty night! Katrine, have you ever been for
a sleigh-ride in America? No, I did not take you there,
—I forgot! You would have had the rheumatism, poor
dear! Well, when you are in America during the winter, you go for rides over the snow in a big sleigh, with
tinkling bells fastened to the horses, and you see the stars
flash as you pass—like the eyes of that interesting gentleman just now. His face was like a cameo—I wonder
who he is! I shall find out! I must do something desperate for Rome is so terribly dull! But I feel better
now! I like that man's eyes. They are *such* a contrast
to the sleepy tiger eyes of the Marquis Fontenelle!"

"My dear Sylvie!" remonstrated Madame Bozier,
"How can you run on in this way? Do you want to

break any more hearts? You are like a lamp for unfortunate moths to burn themselves in!"

"Oh no, not I," said Sylvie, shaking her head with
a touch of half melancholy scorn, "I am not a 'professional' beauty! The Prince of Wales does not select
me for his admiration,—hence it follows that I cannot
possibly be an attraction in Europe. I have not the
large frame, the large hands, and the still larger feet of
the beautiful English ladies, who rule royal hearts and
millionaires' pockets! Men scarcely notice me till they
come to know me—and then, pouf!—away go their
brains!—and they grovel at my small feet instead of the
large ones of the English ladies!" She laughed. "Now
how is that, Katrine?"

"*C'est du charme—toujours du charme!*" murmured
Madame Bozier, studying with a wistful affection the
dainty lines of Sylvie's slight figure, "And that is an even
more fatal gift than beauty, *chere petite!*"

"*Du charme!* You think that is it? Yes?—and so
the men grow stupid and wild!—some want me, and some
want my fortune—and some do not know what they want!
—but one thing is certain, that they all quarrel together
about me, and bore me to extinction!—Even the stranger
with the bright stars of an American winter for eyes,
might possibly bore me if I knew him!"

She gave a short sigh of complete dissatisfaction.

"To be loved, Katrine—really loved! What a delicious thing that would be! Have you ever felt it?"

The poor lady trembled a little, and gave a somewhat
mournful smile.

"No, you dear romantic child! I cannot say with
truth that I have! I married when I was very young,
and my husband was many years older than myself. He
was afflicted with chronic rheumatism and gout, and to
be quite honest, I could never flatter myself that he
thought of me more than the gout. There! I knew that
would amuse you!"—this, as Sylvie's pretty tender laugh
rippled out again on the air, "And though it sounds as
if it were a jest, it is perfectly true. Poor Monsieur
Bozier! He was the drawing master at the school where
I was assistant governess,—and he was very lonely; he
wanted someone to attend to him when the gouty par-
oxysms came on, and he thought I should do as well,

perhaps better than anyone else. And I—I had no time
to think about myself at all, or to fall in love—I was very
glad to be free of the school, and to have a home of my
own. So I married him, and did my best to be a good
nurse to him,—but he did not live long, poor man—you
see he always would eat things that did not agree with
him, and if he could not get them at home he went out
and bought them on the sly. There was no romance
there, my dear! And of course he died. And he left
me nothing at all,—even our little home was sold up to
pay our debts. Then I had to work again for my living,
—and it was by answering an advertisement in the *Times,*
which applied for an English governess to go to a family
in Budapest, that I first came to know you."

"And that is all your history!" said Sylvie, "Poor
dear Bozier! How uneventful!"

"Yes, it is," and the worthy lady sighed also, but hers
was a sigh of placid and philosophical comfort. "Still,
my dear, I am not at all sorry to be uninteresting! I
have rather a terror of lives that arrange themselves into
grand dramas, with terrible love affairs as the central
motives."

"Have you? I have not!" said Sylvie thoughtfully,—
"With all my heart I admire a ' *grande passion.*' Sometimes I think it is the only thing that makes history. One
does not hear nearly so much of the feuds in which Dante
was concerned, as of his love for Beatrice. It is always
so, only few people are capable of the strength and patience and devotion needed for this great consummation
of life. Now I——"

Madame Bozier smiled, and with tender fingers arranged one of the stray knots of pearls with which Sylvie's white gown was adorned.

"You dear child! You were made for sweetness and
caresses,—not suffering . . ."

"You mistake!" said Sylvie, with sudden decision,
"You, in your fondness for me, and because you have
seen me grow up from childhood, sometimes still view
me as a child, and think that I am best amused with friv-
olities, and have not the soul in me that would endure
disaster. But for love's sake I would do anything—yes!
. . . anything!"

"My child!"

"Yes," repeated Sylvie, her eyes darkening and lightening quickly in their own fascinating way, "I would consent to shock the stupid old world!—though one can scarcely ever shock it nowadays, because it has itself become so shocking! But then the man for whom I would sacrifice myself, must love *me* as ardently as I would love *him*! That is the difficulty, Katrine. For men do not love—they only desire."

She raised her face to the sky, and the moonbeams shed a golden halo round her.

"That," she said slowly, "is the reason why I have come here to avoid the Marquis Fontenelle. He does not love me!"

"He is a villain!" said Madame Bozier with asperity.

"Hélas! There are so many villains!" sighed Sylvie, still looking up at the brilliant heavens, "And sometimes if a villain really loves anybody he half redeems his villainy. But the Marquis loves himself best of anyone in the world . . . and I—I do not intend to be second in anyone's affections! So . . ." she paused, "Do you see that star, Katrine? It is as bright as if it were shining on a frosty night in America. And do you not notice the resemblance to the eyes of the stranger who has my rose? I daresay he will put it under his pillow to-night, and dream!" She laughed,—"Let us go in!"

Madame Bozier followed her as she stepped back into the lighted salon, where she was suddenly met by her little Arab page, carrying a large cluster of exquisite red and white roses. A card was attached to the flowers, bearing the words, "These many unworthy blossoms in return for one beyond all worth."

The Comtesse read and passed it in silence to Madame Bozier. A smile was on her face, and a light in her eyes.

"I think Rome is not so dull after all!" she said, as she set the flowers carefully in a tall vase of Etruscan ware, "Do you know, I am beginning to find it interesting!"

XVIII.

AUBREY LEIGH was a man who had chosen his own way of life, and, as a natural consequence of this, had made for himself an independent and original career. Born in the New World of America he had been very highly educated,—not only under the care of a strict father, and an idolising mother, but also with all the advantages one of the finest colleges in the States could give him. Always a brilliant scholar, and attaining his successes by leaps and bounds rather than by close and painstaking study, the day came,—as it comes to all finely-tempered spirits,—when an overpowering weariness of body and soul took possession of him,—when the very attainment of knowledge seemed absurd,—and all things, both in nature and art, took on a sombre colouring, and the majestic pageant of the world's progress appeared no more than a shadow too vain and futile to be worth while watching as it passed. Into a Slough of Despond, such as Solomon experienced when he wrote his famous "*Ecclesiastes,*" Aubrey sank unconsciously, and,—to do him justice,—most unwillingly. His was naturally a bright, vivacious, healthy nature—but he was over-sensitively organised,—his nerves did not resemble iron so much as finely-tempered steel, which could not but suffer from the damp and rust in the world's conventionalities. And some " little rift within the lute " chanced to him, as it often chances to many, so that the subtle music of his soul jarred into discord with the things of life, making harsh sounds in place of melody. There was no adequate cause for this,—neither disappointed love nor balked ambition shadowed his days;—it was something altogether indefinable—a delicate, vague discontent which, had he known it, was merely the first stirring of an embryo genius destined one day to move the world. He did not know what ailed him,—but he grew tired—tired of books—tired of music—tired of sifting the perplexing yet enchanting riddles of science—tired of even his home and his mother's anxious eyes of love that watched his moods too closely for his peace,—and one day, out of the merest boyish impulse, he joined a company of travelling actors and left America. Why he did this he could never tell, save that he was a student and lover of Shakespeare. Much to his own surprise, and somewhat to his disgust, he distinguished himself with exceptional brilliancy on the stage,—his voice, his manner, his physique and his bearing were all exceptional, and told highly in his favour,—but unfortunately his scholarly acumen and knowledge of literature went against him with his manager. This personage, who was densely ignorant, and who yet had all the ineffable conceit of ignorance, took him severely to task for knowing Shakespeare's meanings better than he did,—and high words resulted in mutual severance. Aubrey was hardly sorry when his theatrical career came thus untimely to an end. At first he had imagined it possible to become supreme in histrionic art, —one who should sway the emotions of thousands by a word, a look or a gesture,—he had meant to be the greatest Shakespearean actor of his day; and with his knowledge of French, which was as perfect as his knowledge of English, he had even foreseen the possibility of taking the French stage as well as the English by storm. But when he gradually came to discover the mean tricks and miserable treacheries used by his fellow-actors to keep a rising comrade down,—when he felt to the core of his soul the sordidness and uncleanness of his surroundings,—when he shudderingly repulsed the would-be attentions of the painted drabs called "ladies of the stage",—and above all, when he thought of the peace and refinement of the home he had, for a mere freak, forsaken,—the high tone of thought and feeling maintained there, the exquisite gracefulness and charm of womanhood, of which his mother had been, and was still a perfect embodiment, some new and far stronger spirit rose up within him, crying—"What is this folly? Am I to sink to the level of those whom I know and see are beneath me? With what I have of brain and heart and feeling, are these unworthy souls to drag me down? Shall I not try to feel my wings, and make one bold dash for higher liberty? And if I do so, whither shall I fly?"

He had come to England at this period,—and in the

small provincial town where his final rupture with the illiterate theatrical manager had taken place, there was a
curious, silent contest going on between the inhabitants
and their vicar. The vicar was an extremely unpopular
person,—and the people were striving against him, and
fighting him at every possible point of discussion. For
so small a community the struggle was grim,—and Aubrey for some time could not understand it, till one day
an explanation was offered him by a man engaged in
stitching leather, in a dirty evil-smelling little hole of a
shop under a dark archway.

"You see, sir, it's this way," he said, " Bessie Morton,
—she wor as good a girl as ever stepped—bright and
buxom and kind hearted—yes, that was Bessie, till some
black scoundrel got her love at a soft moment, and took
the better of her. Well!—I suppose some good Christian
folk would say she wor a bad 'un—but I'll warrant she
worn't bad at heart, but only just soft-like—and she an
orphan, with no one to look after her, or say she done ill
or well. And there was a little child born—the prettiest
little creature ye ever saw—Bessie's own copy—all blue
eyes and chestnut hair——and it just lived a matter of
fower year, and then it took sick and died. Bessie went
nigh raving mad; that she did. And now, what do you
think, sir? The passon refused to bury that there little
child in consecrated ground, cos 'twas born out of wedlock! What d'ye think of that for a follower of Jesus
with the loving heart? What d'ye think of that?"

"Think!" said Aubrey indignantly, with an involuntary clenching of his hand, " Why, that it is abominable
—disgraceful! I should like to thrash the brute!"

"So would a many," said his informant with an approving chuckle, " So would a many! But that's not all
—there's more behind—and worse too——"

"Why, what can be worse?"

"Well, sir, we thinks—we ain't got proofs to go on—
for Bessie keeps her own counsel—but we thinks the
passon hisself is the father of that there little thing he
winnot lay in a holy grave!"

"Good God!" cried Aubrey.

"Ay, ay—you may say ' Good God!' with a meaning,
sir," said the leather-seller——" And that's why, as we
ain't got no facts and no power with bishops, and we

ain't able to get at the passon anyhow, we're just making it as unpleasant for him in our way as we can. That's all the people can do, sir, but what they does, they means!"

This incident deeply impressed Aubrey Leigh, and proved to be the turning point in his career. Like a flash of light illumining some divinely written scroll of duty, he suddenly perceived a way in which to shape his own life and make it of assistance to others. He began his plan of campaign by going about among the poorer classes, working as they worked, living as they lived, and enduring what they endured. Disguised as a tramp, he wandered with tramps. He became for a time one of the " hands " in a huge Birmingham factory. After that he worked for several months at the coal pits among the lowest of the men employed there. Then he got a " job " in a dock-yard and studied the ways of shipping and humanity together. During this time of self-imposed probation, he never failed to write letters home to Canada, saying he was " doing well " in England, but how this " doing well " was brought about he never explained. And the actual motive and end of all his experiences was as yet a secret locked within his own heart. Yet when it was put into words it sounded simple enough,—it was merely to find out how much or how little the clergy, or so-called " servants of Christ ", obeyed their Master. Did they comfort the comfortless? Were they " wise as serpents, and harmless as dōves "? Were they long-suffering, slow to wrath, and forbearing one to the other? Did they truly " feed the sheep "? Did they sacrifice themselves, their feelings, and their ambitions to rescue what was lost? All these and sundry other questions Aubrey Leigh set himself to answer,—and by and by he found himself on an endless path of discovery, where at every step some new truth confronted him;—some amazing hypocrisy burned itself in letters of flame against the splendour of church altars;—some deed of darkness and bigotry and cruelty smirched the white robes of the " ordained to preach the Gospel ". Gradually he became so intently and vitally interested in his investigations, and his sympathy for the uncomforted people who had somehow lost Christ instead of finding Him, grew so keen that he resolved to give up his entire life to the work of beginning to try and remedy the evil. He had no independent means,— he lived from hand to mouth earning just what he could by hard labour,—till one day, when the forces in his own soul said "Ready!" he betook himself to one small room which he hired in a fisherman's cottage on the coast of Cornwall, and there sat down to write a book. Half the day he wrote, and half the day he earned his bread as a common fisherman, going out with the others in storm and shine, sailing through sleet and hail and snow, battling with the waves, and playing with Death at every turn of the rocks, which, like the teeth of great monsters, jagged the stormy shore. And he grew strong, and lithe, and muscular——his outward life of hard and changeful labour, accompanied by the inward life of intelligent and creative thought, gradually worked off all depression of soul and effeminacy of body,—his experience of the stage passed away, leaving no trace on his mind but the art, the colour and the method,—particularly the method of speech. With art, colour, and method he used the pen; —with the same art, colour, and method he used his voice, and practised the powers of oratory. He would walk for miles to any lonely place where he could be sure of no interruption,—and there he would speak aloud to the roaring waves and wide stretches of desolate land, and tell them the trenchant things he meant one day to thunder into human ears. Always of a fine figure, his bearing grew more dauntless and graceful,—the dangers of the sea taught him self-control,—the swift changes of the sky gave him the far-off rapt expression and keen flash of his eyes,—the pitiful sorrows of the poor, in which, as he had elected to be one of them, he was bound to share, had deepened the sympathetic lines round his delicate mouth, and had bestowed upon his whole countenance that look which is seldom seen save in the classic marbles—the look of being one with, and yet above mankind. All the different classes of people with whom he had managed to associate had called him "gentleman", a name he had gently but firmly repudiated. "Call me a Man, and let me deserve the title!" he would say smilingly, and his "mates" hearing this would eye each other askance, and whisper among themselves "that he *was* a gentleman for all that, though no doubt he had come

down in the world and had to work for his living. And
no shame to him as he gave himself no airs, and could
turn a hand to anything." And so the time moved on,
and he remained in the Cornish fishing village till his
book was finished. Then he suddenly went up to London;—and after a few days' absence came back again,
and went contentedly on with the fishing once more.

A month or so later, one night when the blackness of
the skies was so dense that it could almost be felt, it
chanced that he and his companions were far out at sea
in their little smack, which lay becalmed between two
darknesses—the darkness of the rolling water, and the
darkness of the still heaven. Little waves lapped heavily
against the boat's side, and the only glimpse of light at
all was the yellow flicker of the lamp that hung from the
mast of the vessel, casting a tremulous flicker on the
sombrous tide, when all at once a great noise like the
crash of thunder, or the roll of cannon, echoed through
the air, and a meteor more brilliant than an imperial
crown of diamonds, flared through the sky from height to
depth, and with a blazing coruscation of flying stars and
flame, dropped hissingly down into the sea. The fishermen startled, all looked up—the heavy black nets dropped
from their brown arms just as they were about to pull in.

"A sign of strife!" said one.

"Ay, ay! We shall hev a war maybe!"

Aubrey leaned far over the boat's side, and looked out
into the dense blackness, made blacker than ever by the
sudden coming and going of the flaming sky-phenome-
non,—and half unconsciously he murmured, "Think not
that I am come to send peace on earth,—I come not to
send peace, but a sword!" And he lost himself in dreams
of the past, present, and future,—till he was roused to
give a hand in the dragging up of the nets, now full of
glistening fish with silvery bodies and ruby eyes,—and
then his thoughts took a different turn and wandered off
as far back as the Sea of Galilee when the disciples, fishing thus, were called by the Divine Voice, saying "Follow me, and I will make you fishers of men!" And in
silence he helped to row the laden boat homewards, for
there was no wind to fill the sail,—and the morning gradually broke like a great rose blooming out of the east,
and the sun came peering through the rose like the calyx

of the flower,—and still in a dream, Aubrey walked
through all that splendour of the early day home to his
lodging,—there to find himself,—like Byron,—famous.
His book was in everyone's hand—his name on everyone's tongue. Letters from the publisher whom his visit
to London had made his friend, accompanied by a bundle
of the chief newspapers of the day, informed him that
he had in one bound taken his place at the very head
and front of opinion,—and, finest proof of power, the
critics were out like the hounds in full cry, and were already baying the noble quarry. The Church papers were
up in arms—indignant articles were being added to the
" weeklies " by highly respectable clergymen with a large
feminine " following ", and in the midst of all these written things, which in their silent print seemed literally to
make a loud clamour in the quiet of his room, Aubrey, in
his sea-stained fisherman's garb, with the sparkle of the
salt spray still glittering on his closely curling bright hair,
looked out at the clear horizon from which the sun had
risen up in all its majesty, and devoutly thanked God!

" I have written part of my message," he said to himself, " And now by-and-by I shall speak! "

But he lived on yet for a time in the remote fishing
village, waiting,—without knowing quite what he waited
for,—while the great Gargantuan mouth of London
roared his name in every imaginable key, high and low,
and gradually swept it across the seas to America and
Australia, and all the vast New World that is so swiftly
rising up, with the eternal balance of things, to overwhelm
the Old. And presently the rumour of his fame reached
those whom he had left behind in the quiet little town of
his birth and boyhood,—and his mother, reading the
frantic eulogies, and still more frantic attacks of the different sections of press opinion, wept with excitement and
tenderness and yearning; and his father, startled at the
strange power and authority with which this new Apostle
of Truth appeared to be invested, trembled as he read,
but nevertheless held himself more erect with a pride
in his own old age that he had never felt before, as he
said a hundred times a day in response to eager ques-
tioners—" Yes,—Aubrey Leigh is my son! " Then
mother and father both wrote to Aubrey, and poured
out their affectionate hearts to him and blessed him,

which blessing he received with that strange heaving of the heart and contraction of the throat, which in a strong man means tears. And still he waited on, earning his bread in the humble village which knew nothing of him, save as one of themselves,—for the inhabitants of the place were deaf and blind to the ways of the world, and read little save old and belated newspapers, so that they were ignorant of his newly celebrated personality,—till one day the Fates gave him that chance for which, though he was unconscious of it, he had been holding himself back, and counting the slow strokes of time;—time which seems to beat with such a laggard pulse when one sees some great thing needing to be done, and while feeling all the force to do it, yet has to control and keep back that force till the appointed hour strikes for action.

There had been a terrific storm at sea, and a herring smack had gone down within sight of land, sinking eight strong men with it, all husbands and fathers. One after the other, the eight bodies were thrown back from the surging deep in the sullen grey morning on the day after the catastrophe,—one after the other they were borne reverently up from the shore to the village, there to be claimed by shrieking women and sobbing children,—women, who from more or less contented, simple-hearted, hard-working souls, were transformed into the grandly infuriated forms of Greek tragedy—their arms tossing, their hair streaming, their faces haggard with pain, and their eyes blind with tears. Throughout the heart-rending scene, Aubrey Leigh worked silently with the rest—composing the stiff limbs of the dead, and reverently closing the glazed and staring eyes; gently he had lifted fainting women from the corpses to which they clung,—tenderly he had carried crying children home to their beds,—and with sorrowful eyes fixed on the still heaving and angry billows, he had inwardly prayed for ways and means to comfort these afflicted ones, and raised their thoughts from the gloom of the grave to some higher consummation of life. For they were inconsolable,—they could neither see nor understand any adequate cause for such grief being inflicted on them,—and the entire little population of the village wore a resentful attitude towards God, and God's inexorable law of death. When the funeral day came, and the bodies of the eight unfortunate victims were committed to the earth, it happened, as fate would have it, that the rector of the parish, a kindly, sympathetic, very simple old man, who really did his best for his parishoners according to the faint perception of holy things that indistinctly illumined his brain, happened to be away, and his place was taken by the assistant curate, a man of irritable and hasty temper, who had a horror of " scenes," and who always put away all suggestions of death from him whenever it was possible. It was very disagreeable to him to have to look at eight coffins,—and still more disagreeable to see eight weeping widows surrounded by forlorn and fatherless children—and he gabbled over the funeral service as quickly as he could, keeping his eyes well on the book lest he should see some sobbing child looking at him, or some woman dropping in a dead faint before he had time to finish. He was afraid of unpleasant incidents— and yet with all his brusque and nervous hurry to avoid anything of the kind, an unpleasant incident insisted on manifesting itself. Just as the fourth coffin was being lowered into the ground, a wild-haired girl rushed forward and threw herself upon it.

" Oh, my man, my man ! " she wailed, " My own sweetheart ! "

There was a moment's silence. Then one of the widows stepped out, and approaching the girl, laid her hand on her arm.

" Are ye making a mock of me, Mary Bell ? " she said, " Or is it God's truth ye're speaking to my husband lying there ? "

The distraught creature called Mary Bell looked up with a sudden passion glowing in her tear-wet eyes.

" It's God's truth ! " she cried, " And ye needn't look scorn on me !—for both our hearts are broken, and no one can ever mend them. Yes ! It's God's truth ! He was your husband, but my sweetheart ! And we'll neither of us see a finer man again ! "

The curate listened, amazed and aghast. Was nothing going to be done to stop this scandalous scene ? He looked protestingly from right to left, but in all the group of fisher-folk not a man moved. Were these two women going to fight over the dead ? He hummed and hawed —and began in a thin piercing voice—" My friends——"

when he was again interrupted by the passionate speech of Mary Bell.

"I'm sorry for ye," she said, lifting herself from the coffin to which she clung, and turning upon the widow of the drowned man, "and ye can be just as sorry for me! He loved us both, and why should we quarrel! A man is ever like that—just chancy and changeful—but he tried his honest hardest not to love me—yes, he tried hard!—it was my fault! for I never tried!—I loved him! —and I'll love him, till I go where he is gone! And we'll see who God'll give his soul to!"

This was too much for the curate.

"Woman!" he thundered, "Be silent! How dare you boast of your sin at such a time, and in such a place! Take her away from that coffin, some of you!"

So he commanded, but still not a man moved. The curate began to lose temper in earnest.

"Take her away, I tell you," and he advanced a step or two, "I cannot permit such a scandalous interruption of this service!"

"Patience, patience, measter," said one of the men standing by, "When a woman's heart's broke in two ways it ain't no use worrying her. She'll come right of herself in a minute."

But the curate, never famous for forbearance at any time, was not to be tampered with. Turning to his verger he said,

"I refuse to go on! The woman is drunk!"

But now the widow of the dead man suddenly took up the argument in a shrill voice which almost tore the air to shreds.

"She's no more drunk than you are!" she cried passionately, "Leave her alone! You're a nice sort of God's serving man to comfort we, when we're all nigh on losing our wits over this mornin' o' misery, shame on ye! Mary Bell, come here! If so be as my husband was your sweetheart, God forgive him, ye shall come home wi' me!—and we'll never have a word agin the man who is lying dead there. Come wi' me, Mary!"

With a wild cry of anguish, the girl rushed into her arms, and the two women clung together like sisters united in the same passionate grief. The curate turned a livid white.

"I cannot countenance such immorality," he said, addressing the verger, though his words were heard by all present, "Enough of the service has been said! Lower the coffins into the earth!" and turning on his heel he prepared to walk away. But Aubrey Leigh stopped him.

"You will not finish the service, sir?" he asked civilly, but with something of a warning in the flash of his eyes.

"No! The principal part of it is over. I cannot go on. These women are drunk!"

"They are not drunk, save with their own tears!" said Aubrey, his rich voice trembling with indignation. "They are not mad, except with grief! Is it not your place to be patient with them?"

"My place! My place!" echoed the curate indignantly, "Man, do you know to whom you are talking?"

"I think I do," answered Aubrey steadily, "I am talking to a professed servant of Christ,—Christ who had patience and pardon for all men! I am talking to one whose calling and vocation it is to love, to forgive, and to forbear—whose absolute protestation has been made at the altar of God that he will faithfully obey his Master. Even if these unhappy women were drunk, which they are not, their fault in conduct would not release you from the performance of your duty,—or the reverence you are bound to show towards the dead!"

Trembling with rage, the curate eyed him up and down scornfully.

"How dare you speak to me about my duty! You common lout! Mind your own business!"

"I will," said Aubrey, fixing his eyes full upon him, "And it shall be my business to see that you mind yours! Both your rector and bishop shall hear of this!"

He strode off, leaving the curate speechless with fury; and joining the little crowd of mourners who had been startled and interrupted by this unexpected scene, drew a prayer book from his pocket, and without asking anyone's permission read with exquisite gravity and pathos the concluding words of the funeral service,—and then with his own hands assisted the grave-diggers to lay the coffined dead tenderly to rest. Awestruck, and deeply impressed by his manner the fisher-folk mechanically obeyed his instructions, and followed his movements till all the sad business was over, and then they lingered about the churchyard wistfully watching him, while he in turn, standing erect and bare-headed near the open graves, looked at them with a strange pity, love and yearning.

"It'll be all right when our owld passon comes back," said one of the men addressing him, "It's just this half eddicated wastrel of a chap as doesn't know, and doesn't care for the troubles of common folk like we."

Aubrey was silent for a space. "Common folk like we!" The words were full of pathetic humility, and the man who spoke them was a hero of no mean type, who had often buffeted the winds and waves to save a human life at the risk of his own. "Common folk like we!" Aubrey laid his hand gently on his "mate's" shoulder.

"Ben, old boy, there are no common folk in God's sight," he said, "Look there!" and he pointed to the graves that were just beginning to be filled in, "Every creature lying there had as much of God in him as many a king, and perhaps more. In this majestic universe there is nothing common!"

Ben shuffled one foot before the other uneasily.

"Ay, ay, but there's few as argify the way o' life in they lines!" he said, "There's a many that think—but there's a main few that speak."

"That is true," said Aubrey, still keeping his hand on Ben's shoulder, "there's a main few that speak! Now, *I* want to speak, Ben,—I want to have a talk to you and the rest of our mates about——well!—about the dangers of the sea and other things. Will you meet me on the shore this evening near the quay and listen to a word or two?"

Ben looked surprised but interested, and a puzzled smile came into his eyes.

"Be ye a goin' to preach to us like the passon?" he said, "Or like the fellers in the porter's caps as calls themselves Salvationists?"

Aubrey smiled.

"No! I only want to say a few parting words to you all."

"Parting words!" echoed Ben with a stupefied air.

"Yes—I am going away to-morrow—going for good. I have got some other work to do. But I shall not forget you all . . . and you will hear of me often,—yes, you will hear of me!—and some day I will come back. But to-night . . . I should just like to say good-bye."

Ben was secretly much distressed. "Gentleman Leigh" as he was sometimes called, had greatly endeared himself to their little community, and that he should leave them was not at all a desirable thing, and would, as Ben well knew, cause universal regret. But there was no time just now for either argument or protestation, so Ben accepted the blow as he accepted all buffetings of fate, and merely said,

"All right! We'll be there to-night for sure!"

And then Aubrey, gravely content, walked slowly out of the little churchyard still bare-headed, his eyes dark with thought,—and the reluctant sun came out of the gray sky and shone on his pale face and bright hair—and one or two of the widowed women timidly touched his arm as he passed, and murmured, "God bless you!" And Mary Bell, the sorrowful and sinning, clinging to the waist of the woman she had wronged, looked up at him appealingly with the strained and hunted gaze of a lost and desperate creature, and as he met her eyes, turned shudderingly away and wept. And he, knowing that words were useless, and that even the kindliest looks must wound in such a case, passed on in silence, and when he reached his own lodging took some of the newspapers which spoke of himself and his book, and after marking certain passages, tied them up in a packet and sent them to the curate with whom he had crossed swords that morning, accompanied by a note which briefly ran thus:—

"You asked me how I 'dared' to speak to you about your duty. I reply—By the force of truth and the power of the pen I dare!—and I shall be ready to answer to God for it, as you must answer to him for leaving any part of *your* duty undone.

"AUBREY LEIGH."

And the day passed on, half in drifting clouds, half in glimpses of sunshine, till late afternoon, when the sky cleared altogether, and the waves sank to a dead calm;—and with the night a shield-like moon, all glistening pearl and silver, rose up out of the east with a royal air of white and wondering innocence, as though she pro-

claimed her entire blamelessness for any havoc wrought
by storm. And in the full radiance of that silvery splendour Aubrey Leigh, leaning against the sea-weed covered capstan of the quay, round which coils of wet rope
glistened like the body of a sleeping serpent, told to an
audience of human hearers for the first time the story
of his life, and adventures, and the varied experiences
he had gone through in order to arrive at some straight
and clear comprehension of "the Way, the Truth, and
the Life" of the Gospel of Love and Mutual Labour. His
practised voice, perfect in all modulation, inflexion, and
expression, carried each simple, well-chosen word home
to the hearts of his hearers,—not one so ignorant as not
to understand him—not one so blind as not to see the
beauty of work and creative effort as he depicted them,—
not one so insensate as not to feel the calm, the grandeur,
and repose of the strong soul of a man in complete
sympathy with his fellow-men. They listened to him almost breathlessly—their bronzed weather-beaten faces all
turned towards his; forgetting to smoke, they let their
pipes die out and drop from their hands—and no interruption broke the even flow and cadence of his earnest
language, save the slow ripple of the water beating
against the quay, and the faint, occasional sigh of a stirring wind. Silhouetted black against the radiant sky
were the masts of the fishing fleet, and the roofs of the
fishermen's cottages—dwellings so often made desolate
by death—and as Aubrey noted the fascinated attention
with which these rough men heard him, his heart grew
strong. "If a few listen, so will many," he said to himself, "The Master of our creed first taught His divine
ethics to a few fishermen,—to them the message was first
given . . . and by them again delivered,—and it is through
our having departed from the original simplicity of utterance that all the evil has crept in. So let me be content
with this night's work and await the future with patience." Then lifting up his voice once more he said,—

"You think your lot a hard one—you, friends and
brothers, who set the brown sails out to sea on a night
of threatening storm, and bid farewell to your homes
built safe upon the shore. You must meet all the horror
of white foam and cloud-blackness, to drag from the sea
its living spoil, and earn the bread to keep yourselves and

those who are dependent upon you,—you *must* do this, or the Forces of Life will not have you,—they will cast you out and refuse to nourish you. For so is your fate in life, and work ordained. Then where is God?—you cry, as the merciless billows rise to engulf your frail craft,—why should the Maker of man so deliberately destroy him? Why should one human unit, doing nothing, and often thinking nothing, enjoy hundreds of pounds a day, while you face death to win as many pence? Is there a God of Love who permits this injustice? Ah, stop there, friends! There is no such thing as injustice! Strange as it sounds to this world of many contradictions and perplexities, I repeat there is no such thing as injustice. There is what *seems* injustice—because we are all apt to consider the material side of things only. That is where we make our great mistake in life and conduct. We should all remember that this world, and the things of this world, are but the outward expression of an inward soul—the Matter evolved from Mind—and that unless we are ourselves in harmony with the Mind, we shall never understand the Matter. Your millionaire is surrounded with luxuries,—your fishermen has dry bread and herring,—your millionaire dies, with a famous doctor counting his pulse-beats, and a respectable clergyman promising him heaven on account of the money he has left to the church in his will; your fisherman goes down in a swirl of black water, without a prayer—for he has no time to pray—without leaving a penny behind him, inasmuch as he has no pence to leave; and for both these different creatures we judge the end is come? No,—the end is *not* come! It is the beginning only! If the millionaire has died with a thousand selfish sores in his mind,—if his life's privileges have been wasted in high feeding and self-indulgence,—if he has thought only of himself, his riches, his pride, his position, or his particular form of respectability, he will get the full result of that mental attitude! If the fisherman has been content with his earnings, and thanked God for them,—if he has been honest, brave, true, and unselfish, and has shared with others their joys and sorrows, and if at the last he goes down in the waves trying to save some other life while losing his own,—depend upon it he will rise to the full splendour of *that* mental attitude! For both millionaire and fisherman are but men, made on the same lines, of the same clay, and are each one, personally and separately responsible to God for the soul in them,—and when both of them pass from this phase of being to the next, they will behold all things with spiritual eyes, not material ones. And then it may be that the dark will be discovered to be the bright, and the fortunate prove to be the deplorable, for at present we ' see through a glass darkly, but then, face to face.' The friends whom we have buried to-day are not dead,—for death is not Death, but Life. And for those who are left behind it is merely a time of waiting, for as the Master said, ' There shall not a hair of your head perish. In your patience possess ye your souls.' "

He paused a moment,—the moon rays illumined his delicate features, and a half sorrowful smile rested on his lips.

"I am no clergyman, my friends! I have not been ' ordained '. I am not preaching to you. I will not ask you to be good men, for there is something effeminate in the sound of such a request made to brawny, strong fellows such as you are, with an oath ready to leap from your lips, and a blow prepared to fly from your fists on provocation. I will merely say to you that it is a great thing to be a Man!—a Man as God meant him to be, brave, truthful, and self-reliant, with a firm faith in the Divine Ordainment of Life as Life should be lived. There is no disgrace in work;—no commonness,—no meanness. Disgrace, commonness, and meanness are with those who pretend to work and never do anything useful for the world they live in. The king who amuses himself at the expense and ruin of his subjects is the contemptible person,—not the labourer who digs the soil for the planting of corn which shall help to feed his fellows. And the most despicable creature of our time and century, is not the man who doubts Christ, or questions God—for Christ was patient with the doubter, and God answers, through the medium of science, every honest question—it is the man who pretends to believe and lives on the pretence, while his conduct gives the lie to his profession! That is why you—and why thousands of others like you, are beginning to look upon many of the clergy with contempt, and to treat their admonitions with indifference. That is why thousands of the rising generation of men and women will not go to church. ' The parson does not do anything for me,' is a common every-day statement. And that the parson *should* do something is a necessary part of his business. His ' doing ' should not consist in talking platitudes from the pulpit, or in sending round a collection plate. And if he has no money, and will not ' sell half that he has and give to the poor ' as commanded, he can at any rate give sympathy. But this is precisely what he chiefly lacks. The parson's general attitude is one of either superiority or servility,—a ' looking down ' upon his poor parishoners—a ' looking up ' to his rich ones. A disinterested, loving observation of the troubles and difficulties of others never occurs to him as necessary. But this was precisely the example Christ gave us—an unselfish example of devotion to others—a supreme descent of the Divine into man to rescue and bless humanity. Now I know all your difficulties and sorrows,—I have worked among you, and lived among you—and I feel the pulse of your existence beating in my own heart. I know that when a great calamity overwhelms you all as it has done this week, you have no one to comfort you, —no one to assure you that no matter how strange and impossible it seems, you have been deprived of your associates for some *good* cause which will be made manifest in due season,—that they have probably been taken to save them from a worse fate than the loss of earth-consciousness in the sea. For that, scientifically speaking, is all that death means—the loss of earth-consciousness, —but the gain of another consciousness, whether of another earth or a heaven none can say. But there is no real death—inasmuch as even a grain of dust in the air will generate life. We must hold fast to the Soul of things—the Soul which is immortal, not the body which is mortal. ' What shall it profit a man if he gain the whole world and lose his own soul!' That is what each man of us must find, and hold, and keep,—his own soul! Apart from all creeds, and clergy, forms and rituals— that is the vital matter. Stand clear of all things,—all alone if need be, surrounded by the stupendous forces of this great universe,—let us find,—each man of us—his own soul; find and keep it brave, truthful, upright, and bound straight on for the highest,—the highest always!

And the very stars in their courses will help us—storms will but strengthen us—difficulties but encourage us—and death itself shall but give us larger liberty."

He ceased, and one by one the men drew closer to him, and thanked him, in voices that were tremulous with the emotion he had raised in them. The instinct which had led them to call him " Gentleman Leigh " had proved correct,—and there was not a man among them all who did not feel a thrill of almost fraternal pride in the knowledge that the dauntless, hard-working " mate " who had fronted tempests with them, and worked with them in all weathers, had without any boast or loquacious preparation, made his name famous and fit for discussion in the great world of London far away, a world to which none of them had ever journeyed. And they pressed round him and shook his hand, and gave him simple yet hearty words of cheer and goodwill, together with unaffected expressions of regret that he was leaving them,—" though for that matter," said one of them, " we allus felt you was a scholard-like, for all that you was so handy at the nets. For never did a bit of shell or weed come up from the sea but ye was a lookin' at it as if God had throwed it to yer for particular notice. And when a man takes to obsarvin' common things as if they were special birthday presents from the Almighty, ye may be pretty sure there's something out of the ordinary in him! "

Aubrey smiled, and pressed the hand of this roughly eloquent speaker,—and then they all walked with him up from the shore to the little cottage where he had lived for so many months, and at the gate of which he bade them farewell.

" But only for a time," he said, " I shall see you all again. And you will hear of me! "

" Ay, ay, we'll hear of ye—for we'll take the papers in just for news of yer! " said Ben, with a rough laugh which covered his deeper feelings, " And mebbe ye'll come back afore we's all drownded! "

And so with a few more kindly words they left him, and he stood at the gate watching their stalwart figures disappear down the different windings of the crooked and picturesque little street.

" God bless them all! " he murmured, " They have taught me many a grand lesson! "

The next day he took his quiet departure in the early morning before the village folks were up and stirring,—and a month later he addressed a large meeting in one of the poorest and most densely populated districts of London on "The Ethics of Christ versus the Clergy", which attracted universal attention and created an enormous sensation. His book began to sell in thousands where it had previously sold in hundreds, and he earned sufficient from the profits of the sale to keep him going in the simple fashion of clothes and food to which he had strictly disciplined himself, so that he felt free to plunge into the thick of the fight. And he straightway did so. His name became a terror to liars, and a clarion sound of alarm in the ears of social hypocrites. He wrote another book which obtained even a larger hearing than the first—and he spoke to the people on an average once a week, wherever he could assemble them together. All his addresses were made gratuitously, and he soon resembled a sort of blazing torch in the darkness, to which the crowds rushed for light and leading. In the midst of the sensation his writings and orations were creating, a noble lord, with several Church livings in his gift, asked him to stand for Parliament, and offered to pay the expenses of his election. At first Aubrey was sufficiently tempted by the offer to pause hesitatingly on the verge of acceptance, but twenty-four hours' hard thinking promptly pulled him together. " No," he said—" I see what you mean! You and your party wish to tie my hands—to gag my mouth, and make me as one of yourselves—no, I will not consent to it. I will serve the people with all my life and soul!—but not in *your* way!"

And to avoid further discussion he went straight out of England for a time, and travelled through Europe, making friends everywhere, and learning new phases of the " Christian Dispensation " at every turn in his road. Paris had held him fascinated for a long while, not only because he saw her doom written like that of Babylon in letters of fire, and Ruin, like a giant bird of prey hovering over her with beak and claw prepared to pick the very flesh from her bones,—but also because he had met Angela Sovrani, one of the most rarely-gifted types of womanhood he had ever seen. He recognised her genius at once, and marvelled at it. And still more did he mar-

vel at her engagement of marriage with Florian Varillo.
That such a fair, proud creature so splendidly endowed,
could consent to unite herself to a man so vastly inferior,
was an interesting puzzle to him. He had met Varillo
by chance in Naples one winter before he ever saw Angela, and knew that half his claim to the notice of the
social world there was the fact of his betrothal to the famous " Sovrani." And moved by a strange desire to
follow out this romance, and also because he was complet-
ing his studies of the Roman Church viewed as a " moral
support to the education and elevation of man," he, after
leaving Paris, and paying a brief visit to Florence on a
matter of business which could not be attended to otherwise than personally, went on as though drawn by some
invisible magnet to Rome. He had only been twenty-
four hours in the city, when chance had led him under the
balcony where the sculptured angels fronted the moon,
and from whence the sweet voice of Sylvie Hermenstein
had floated towards him with the words,—

> " Ti voglio ben assai,
> E tu non pensi a me."

And he who had faced crowds without a tremor, and had
flung thunderbolts of splendid defiance at shams, with the
manner of a young Ajax defying the lightning, now
found himself strangely put out and disturbed in his
usual composure by the innocent aspect, and harmless perfume of a rose,—a mere little pink petalled thing, with
not even a thorn on its polished green stalk! He had
placed it in a glass of water on his writing table, and his
eyes rested upon it the morning after he had received it
with almost a reproachful air. What was its golden-
hearted secret? Why, when he studied it, did he see
the soft hue of a fair cheek, the flash of a bright eye,
the drooping wave of a golden web of hair, the dainty
curve of a white arm on which the sparkle of diamonds
gleamed? How was it that he managed to perceive all
this in the leaves of a rose? He could not tell; and he
was angry with himself for his inability to explain the
puzzle. He reminded himself that he had business in
Rome—" business," he repeated sternly to his own conscience,—the chief part of which was to ascertain from
some one of the leading spirits at the Vatican the view

taken by the Papacy of the Ritualistic movement in England.

"If you can gauge correctly the real feeling, and render it in plain terms, apart from all conventional or social considerations," wrote his publisher in a letter which had just reached him—"that is, if you dare to do so much—and I think you will scarcely hesitate—you will undoubtedly give great and lasting help to Christian England." As he read this over for the second or third time he remembered that he had an appointment with a certain powerful personage, known as Monsignor Gherardi, that morning at eleven.

"And you," he said, apostrophising the rose with a protesting shake of his head, "were nearly making me forget it!" He lifted the flower out of the water and touched it with his lips. "She was a fair creature,—the woman who wore you last night!"— he said with a smile as he put it carefully back again in its glass, "In fact, she was very much like you! But though I notice you have no thorns, I dare say she has!" He paused a moment, lost in thought, the smile still giving warmth and light to his features; then with a quick movement of impatience at his own delaying, threw on his coat and hat and left the room, saying, "Now for Gherardi!"

XIX.

Set square and dark against the pale blue of the Italian sky the Palazzo Sovrani, seen for the first time, suggests a prison rather than a dwelling house,—a forbidding structure, which though of unsentient marble, seems visibly to frown into the light, and exhale from itself a cloud on the clearest day. Its lowest windows, raised several feet from the ground, and barred across with huge iron clamps, altogether deprive the would-be inquisitive stranger from the possibility of peering within, —the monstrous iron gate, richly wrought with fantastic scroll-work and heraldic emblems raised in brass, presents so cold and forbidding a front that some of the youthful ladies who were Angela's friends, were wont to declare that it gave them a palpitation of the heart to summon up the necessary courage required to ring the great bell. Within the house there was much of a similar gloom, save in Angela's own studio, which she had herself made beautiful with a brightness and lightness found in no other corner of the vast and stately abode. Her father, Prince Pietro Sovrani, was of a reserved and taciturn nature,—poor but intensely proud—and he would suffer no interference by so much as a word or a suggestion respecting the manner in which he chose to arrange or to order his household. His wife Gita Bonpré, the only sister of the good Cardinal, had been the one love of his life,—and when she died all his happiness had died with her,—his heart was broken, but he showed nothing of his grief to the outside world, save that in manner he was more silent and reserved than ever,—more difficult to deal with,—more dangerous to approach. People knew well enough that he was poor, but they never dared to mention it,—though once an English acquaintance, moved by the best intentions in the world, had suggested that he could make a good deal of money by having a portion of the Palazzo Sovrani redecorated, and modernized, to suit the comfort and convenience of travelling millionaires who might probably be disposed to pay a high rent for it during the Roman " season." But the proposal was disastrous in its results. Sovrani had turned upon his adviser like an embodied thunder-cloud.

" When a prince of the House of Sovrani lets out apartments," he said, " you may ask your English Queen to take in washing! "

And a saturnine smile, accompanied by the frowning bend of his white fuzzy eyebrows over his flashing black eyes, had produced such a withering, blistering effect on the soul of the unfortunate Englishman, whose practical ideas of utility had exceeded his prudence, that he had scarcely ever dared to look the irate Italian noble in the face again.

Just now, the Prince was in his library, seated in dignified uprightness like a king enthroned to give audience, in a huge high-backed chair, shadowed over by an ancient gilded baldacchino, listening with a certain amount of grim patience to his daughter's softly murmured narrative of her stay in Paris. He had received the Cardinal an hour ago on his arrival, with first, a humble genuflexion as became a son of the Church, and secondly with a kiss on both cheeks as became a brother-in-law. The Cardinal's youthful companion Manuel, he had scarcely remarked, even while giving him welcome. These two had gone to the suite of rooms prepared for the reception of His Eminence,—but Angela, after hastily changing her travelling dress, had come down to her father, anxious not only to give, but to hear news—— especially news of Florian Varillo. Prince Sovrani, however, was not a man given to much social observation,— nor did he ever break through his half cynical, half gloomy humour, to detail the gossip of Rw, and he therefore sat more or less unmoved, while Angela told him all she could think of that would interest him. At last with a little delicate hesitation, she related the strange story of Abbé Vergniaud, and added,

" And by this time, I suppose, the Holy Father has been told all! "

" Naturally," said the Prince, with a stern smile moving the hard muscles of his mouth, " Moretti's love of scandal is as deep as that of any old woman!—and the joy of excommunicating a soul from the salvation of the

Church must be too exquisite to admit of any delay! I am sorry for Vergniaud, but I do not think he will suffer much. These things are scarcely ever noticed in the press nowadays, and it will only be a very limited circle that even learns of his excommunication. Nevertheless, I am sorry—one is always sorry for brave men, even if they are reckless. And the son is Gys Grandit! *Corpo di Bacco!* What a dénouement!"

He considered it a moment, looking straight before him at the rows of ancient and musty books that adorned his walls,—then he gave a sudden exclamation.

"*Pesta!* I had nearly forgotten! I knew there was a curious thing I had to tell you, Angela,—but in the hurry of your arrival it had for the moment escaped my mind . . ."

"About Florian?" asked Angela anxiously.

The Prince bent his brows upon her quizzically.

"Florian! What should I know about Florian? He has not been near me since you left Rome. I fancy he will not be too attentive a son-in-law! No, it is not about Florian. It is about your uncle Felix. Have you heard of this miracle he has performed?"

Angela's eyes opened wide.

"A miracle! What do you mean by a miracle?"

"*Santissima Madonna!* A miracle is always a miracle," retorted her father testily, "A something out of the common, and an upsetting of the ordinary laws of nature. Did your uncle tell you nothing of his visit to Rouen?"

"Nothing," replied Angela, "Nothing but the story of Manuel."

"Manuel? Who is he?"

"The boy he has with him now. Uncle Felix found him lost at night near the Cathedral of Rouen, and has taken him under his protection ever since."

"*Altrò!* That is nothing!" said her father, "That is only one of Felix's quixotic ideas. There is no miracle in that. But when a child is a cripple from babyhood, and our Felix cures him by one simple prayer, and makes him strong and well again—*Gran Dio!*—it is not remarkable that such news creates a stir at the Vatican."

"But it cannot be true!" said Angela surprised,

"Uncle Felix never said a word about it. I am sure he knows nothing whatever of such a report!"

"*Ebben!* We will ask him presently,"—and the Prince raised himself stiffly and slowly out of his throne-like chair, "Personally I have considered Felix above any sort of priestly trickery; but after all, if he has an ambition for the Papacy, I do not see why he should not play for it. Others do!"

"Oh, father!" cried Angela, "How can you think such a thing of Uncle Felix! He is as nearly a saint as any mortal man can be!"

"So I always thought, child—so I always thought!" replied the Prince, with a vexed air, "But to perform such a miracle of healing as to cure a child with a twisted spine and bent legs, by the mere utterance of a prayer!—that is impossible!—impossible! It sounds like charlatanism—not like Felix!"

As he spoke he straightened himself and stood upright, a tall, spare, elegant figure of a man,—his dark complexioned face very much resembling a fine bronze cast of the Emperor Aurelius. Angela rose too and stood beside him, and his always more or less defiant eyes slowly softened as he looked at her.

"You grow very like your mother," he said, with just the faintest tremor in his voice—"*Ah, la mia Gita!*"

A sigh that was like a groan broke from his lips, and Angela laid her head caressingly against his breast in silence. He touched her soft hair tenderly.

"Very like your mother," he repeated, "Very like! But you will leave me soon, as she has left me,—not for Heaven, no!—but for that doubtful new life called marriage. It is not doubtful when there is love—love in both hearts;—and if there is any difference at all, the love should be greater on the man's side than on the woman's! Remember that, Angela *mia,* remember that! The true lover is always spiritually on his knees before the woman he loves; not only in passion, but in worship —in reverence!"

"And is not Florian so?" murmured Angela timidly.

"I do not know, child; he may be! Sometimes I think that he loves himself too much to love *you* as well as you deserve. But we shall see."

As he spoke a servant entered, carrying an exquisite

basket of flowers, and brought it to Angela who blushed and smiled divinely as she took it and opened the envelope fastened to its handle and addressed to her, which contained merely these words,—

"*A la mia dolcézza! Con voto d'eterno amore!*
"FLORIAN."

"Are they not lovely?" she said, bending over the blossoms tenderly as though she would have taken them all into her embrace, "Such a sweet welcome home!"

Her father nodded, but gave no verbal response to her enthusiasm. Presently he said,

"How about your picture? When will it be finished?"

"A month's work will be enough now," she replied, looking up quickly—"And then——"

"Then it will remain in one of the galleries unsold!" said Sovrani, with a touch of bitterness in his tone which he could not quell, "You have chosen too large a canvas. From mere size it is unsaleable,—for unless it were a marvel of the world no nation would ever purchase a woman's picture."

Angela's delicate head drooped,—she turned away to hide the tears that rushed to her eyes. Her father's words were harsh, yet eminently practical; she knew he did not mean them unkindly, but that the continual pinch of poverty was sometimes greater than he could endure with patience. Angela had earned considerable sums of money by the smaller pictures which had established her name; and the Prince had bitterly grudged the time she had given to the enormous canvas which had now remained so long in her studio covered up, even from his eyes—for he had made up his mind that it was one of those fantastic dreams of genius, which when they become realised into the substance of a book or a picture, terrify the timid conventions of the world so completely as to cause general avoidance.

"If Raffaelle were alive he would not paint a 'Transfiguration' now," he was wont to say, "The Church no longer employs great artists. It keeps its money for speculation purposes. If a Michael Angelo were in Rome he would find nothing to do."

Which statement was true enough. For the modern Italian loves money next to his own precious skin, and everything beautiful or sacred is sacrificed to this insatiable craze. There is no love, no honour, no patriotism in Italy without careful calculation as to the cost of indulging in these sentiments,—and what wreck of religion is left merely panders to the low melodramatic temper of an ignorant populace. Art is at its lowest ebb; it cannot live without encouragement and support—and it is difficult for even the most enthusiastic creator in marble or colour to carry out glorious conceptions for an inglorious country. But Angela Sovrani—ambitious Angela,—was not painting for Italy. She was painting for the whole world. She had dreams of seeing her great picture borne away out of Rome to Paris, and London, to be gazed upon by thousands who would take its lesson home to their hearts and lives. Italy was merely a village in the area of her aspiring mind; but she built her "castles in the air" alone; and never by so much as the smallest hint allowed anyone to guess the far reaching scope of her intentions. Truth to tell, she had obtained very little encouragement during her long days and months of work, though in the sweetness of her nature she pleased herself by imagining that Florian Varillo gave her a complete and perfect sympathy. Yet even with Florian, one or two casual remarks he had let fall lightly and unthinkingly, had vaguely startled her, and set her wondering, "Perhaps he does not think much of my abilities after all"—and had caused her for once to be closely reserved upon the subject and treatment of her work, and to refuse a glimpse of it even to him who was her elect Beloved. She had thought he would perhaps have been pained at this inviolate secrecy on her part,— she had feared he might take offence at finding the doors of her studio always locked,—but on the contrary he appeared quite amused at her uncommunicative humour, and jested about it as if she were a little child playing in a dark corner at some forbidden game. She was somewhat surprised at this,—the more so as he frequently spoke of the importance of his own pictures for the Roman "Art Season,"—pictures to which he really gave the attentive discussion and consideration a man always bestows on matters of his personal business—but often when Angela's work was spoken of, he smiled with a kindly tolerance, as one who should say, "Dear girl! How sweetly she embroiders her simple sampler!" And yet again, he never failed, when asked about it in Angela's presence, to say that he was " sure Donna Sovrani would astonish the world by what she was doing!" So that one never quite knew where to have him, his nature being that curious compound of obsequious servility and intense self-love which so often distinguishes the Italian temperament. Angela however put every shadow of either wonder or doubt as to his views, entirely aside,— and worked on with an earnest hand and trusting heart, faithfully and with a grand patience and self-control seldom found either in masculine or feminine heroes. Sometimes her spirit sank a little, as now, when her father told her that her picture would remain unsold in one of the galleries—but all the same, some force within her urged her to go on with her intention steadily, and leave all results to God. And the tears that had sprung to her eyes at the smart of old Sovrani's rough speech, soon returned to their source; and she was quite her composed sweet self again when her uncle the Cardinal, accompanied by Manuel, entered the room, holding an open letter in his hand, and looking strangely agitated.

"Brother, here is a matter which I cannot possibly understand," he said, "Monsignor Gherardi writes here to congratulate me upon a miracle I have worked in Rouen! —and summons me at once to the presence of His Holiness! What can it mean? I have performed no miracle! Surely some jest is being played with me,—and one most unbecoming to a man of Gherardi's position and influence!"

Prince Sovrani took the letter from Bonpré's hand and read it in silence.

"Yes——I have heard about it already," he said, "And if you indeed know nothing, it is strange! But can you not remember——is there no clue to such a report? Were there no sick children brought to you . . .?"

"Oh, for that," answered the Cardinal quickly, "a little boy named Fabien Doucet, was brought to me by the children of an inn-keeper of the Hotel Poitiers where I stayed two nights, and to grant their wishes, (and also because it is my duty to do what I can for the suffering and the afflicted), I laid my hands upon him and prayed to our Lord that he might be healed."

"*Ebbene!* Our Lord has then healed him," said Sovrani drily, " It is remarkable!—but if the cure is truly accomplished, we shall have to admit that the Deity does sometimes pay attention to our many prayers, though for the most part they appear to fall upon a deaf, dumb, and irresponsive Silence."

The Cardinal sat down, wearily resting his head on his hand.

" I do not like it!" he said, " It is altogether amazing to me; it seems like a snare set to catch my soul! For I have no power to perform miracles . . . I can only pray."

"And why should not your prayer be answered?" asked Manuel suddenly.

They had all forgotten the boy's presence in the room, and his voice startled them. His young face was pale, yet tranquil—and the deep tenderness that always dwelt in his eyes seemed deeper and softer at this moment than ever.

"Truly I do not see why," said Prince Sovrani, bending his fierce regard full on the lad as he spoke, and beginning to wonder like the rest at his fairness and beauty, " Only as a rule, *fanciuollo mio*—prayer is mere waste of breath—a demand without supply."

" Is that not perhaps the fault of the person who prays?" said Manuel, " May that person not lack faith and pure intention? May he not even be too self-absorbed to lift his soul high enough for an approach to God? When the disciples were vexed that they could not cure a child that was afflicted, and saw that their Master healed that child at once, they asked why they were unable to do what He did. And He told them plainly, ' Because of your unbelief. For verily I say unto you, if ye have faith as a grain of mustard seed ye shall say unto this mountain, remove from yonder place, and it shall remove, and nothing shall be impossible to you.' And I am sure that my lord the Cardinal's faith is greater than a grain of mustard seed!"

They were all silent. Cardinal Bonpré turned his eyes thoughtfully on the young speaker

" You were with me, child, when the little cripple sat on my knee and held my crucifix," he said in a low tone,

"You saw—you heard all.   What did I do?—what did I say?"

"You held him in your arms, even as Christ took little children in His arms and blessed them," replied Manuel, "And you prayed—and in your prayer you said—'King and Master of all such children, even as Thou wert a child Thyself, be pleased to heal him of his sad infirmity. For if Thou wilt, Thou canst make this bent body straight, and these withered muscles strong,—from death itself Thou canst ordain life, and nothing is impossible unto Thee!'"

There was a pause.   Then Manuel added,—

"That is what you said, my lord Cardinal;—and when the child went away, you told him that if the giving of your own life could make him strong, he should have that life willingly.   Some people might say that without meaning it,—but you meant what you said,—every word came straight from your heart.   And should it then surprise you that God has granted your prayer?"

Prince Sovrani listened to the dulcet young voice with a strange emotion.   Something holy and convincing seemed to emanate from the boy's very presence, and though he, as became a modern Italian, was thoroughly sceptical and atheistical, and would have willingly argued against the very words of Christ as written in the Gospel, some curious hesitation that was almost shamefacedness held him silent. But the Cardinal was even more strongly moved.   The earnest spirit of truth with which Manuel appeared always to be environed,—his simple and straight enunciation of the old, oft-quoted phrases used by the Divine Saviour of the world,—and then his unfaltering memory of the simple prayer that had been said for the comfort of the unfortunate little Fabien Doucet, together with this strange and unexpected announcement of the child's miraculous cure,—these things rushed over the mind of the good Bonpré like an overwhelming flood, and confused his brain——strange half-formed thoughts occurred to him that he dared not express, chief among which was a vague, a terrifying idea that the young boy beside him who spoke so sweetly, and almost so commandingly, must surely be an Angel!   Strange legends of the Church began to recur to him;—legends of old-time when angels had descended to walk with priests in their monastic seclusion, and instruct them as to the value of time, as in the "Legend Beautiful," when the monk Felix, being perplexed by the phrase "a day with God is as a thousand years," went to sleep in a garden, soothed by the singing of the birds at sunset, and woke up to find that in his slumber a century had rolled away! All manner of fantastic notions swept in upon him, and he grew suddenly blind and dizzy—rising from his chair totteringly he extended his hands—then suddenly sank back again in a dead faint. Sovrani caught him as he fell—and Angela ran for water, and tenderly bathed his forehead while Manuel took his hand and held it fast.

"Too long a journey, and too much excitement!" said the Prince,—"Our Felix is growing old,—he cannot stand fatigue. He is failing fast!"

"Oh, no," said Manuel brightly, "He is not failing! He is younger by far than he seems! He is too strong to fail!"

And as he spoke the Cardinal opened his eyes and smiled with an expression of perfect rapture.

"Why, what has ailed me?" he enquired, looking at Angela's anxious face, "I had but gone for a moment into the presence of my Lord!" Here he paused, and then gradually recovering himself entirely, sat upright.

"All is well with me!" he said, pressing the hand of Manuel in his own, and releasing it again, "Do not fret, Angela,—it was the merest passing faintness. Forgive me, brother, for alarming you thus foolishly! As for the letter from the Vatican concerning this miracle, I must needs present myself before His Holiness and assure him that I know nothing of it,—that I did no more than pray—that I left the crippled child still crippled— and that if indeed it be true he is healed, it is by the merciful act of God and the intervention of our Lord and Saviour Christ, to Whom be all the praise and glory!"

He rose up again from his chair and stood full height, —a grand and beautiful figure of noble old age, transfigured by the light of some never-aging thought, some glorious inspiration. And Angela, who had been startled and alarmed by his sudden fainting fit, was even more overcome by the sight of him thus radiant and self-possessed, and dropping on her knees she caught his hand and kissed it, her tears falling fast. He stooped and raised her.

"Child, why are you weeping?" he said tenderly, "Nay, I am not so ill as you think me! I am well—strong!—ready for the doing of many things in my Master's service! Pietro, take this dear girl and comfort her!" and he put her gently into her father's arms—"For myself, I have work to do—work to do!——" he repeated musingly,—"I see trouble ahead!—but I shall face it—and if God please—overcome it!" His eyes flashed, and after a moment he resumed, "I will write to Gherardi now——and to-morrow—to-morrow I will speak!"

"Can I help you, brother?" asked the Prince, taken out of himself by the air of splendour and sovereignty which seemed to surround the Cardinal as with a divine halo, "You are fatigued with your journey,—let me write for you!"

"No, Pietro! I must do this myself, and think well of all I should say." He paused, then added, "They tell me Claude Cazeau, secretary to the Archbishop of Rouen brought the news of this so-called miracle to Rome. I should have liked to have seen that man to-night."

"You will see him at the Vatican," said Sovrani, with a touch of irony, "That will be time enough! Oh, innocent Felix! Do you not see you will be confronted with Cazeau? And that Gherardi and his set will be there to note your every look and gesture, and privately judge as to whether you and the Archbishop of Rouen concocted the miracle between you! And that if you were to see this Cazeau to-night, that very meeting would be taken as a sign of conspiracy!"

Over the pale features of the Cardinal rushed a warm glow of indignation, but it died away as rapidly as it had come.

"True!" he said simply, "I forgot! If a good deed is done in the world by the force of the undefiled Spirit of Christ, it is judged as trickery,—and we must never forget that even the Resurrection of our Blessed Lord from the dead is believed by some to be a mere matter of conspiracy among His disciples. True—I forgot the blindness,—the melancholy blindness of the world! But we must always say, ' Father forgive them, for they know not what they do!' I will write to Gherardi,—and,—if you will permit me, I will remain in my own rooms to-night for I must think and pray,—I must be alone . . ."

"Without me, my lord Cardinal?" asked Manuel softly.

" No, not without you!" and Bonpré looked at him with a smile, " Not without you! I have no wish to be so much alone as your absence would make me. Come!"

And lifting the heavy velvet portiére at the door, he held it back for his " foundling " to pass,—and then slowly followed.

XX.

On the first floor of an ancient mansion, in a street which slopes down towards the Tiber, there is a suite of dreary old rooms which must evidently have once belonged to some great " Prince of the Church ", (to use the term which Cardinal Bonpré held so much in aversion,) if one may form any opinion from the ecclesiastical designs on the faded green hangings, which cling like moss to the damp walls, and give an additional melancholy to the general gloom. The " salon " or audience-chamber is perhaps the best in repair, and possesses a gorgeous, painted ceiling, bordered by a frieze of red and gold, together with one or two large pictures, which perhaps if cleaned might show the touch of some great Master, but which in their sad condition of long neglect, present nothing to the view but a dark blur of indistinct outlines. The rooms in their entirety composed the business, or town dwelling of Monsignor Gherardi, one of the cleverest, most astute, and most unscrupulous of men, to whom Religion was nothing more than a means of making money and gaining power. There was scarcely a Roman Catholic " community " in the world, in which Gherardi had not a share;—and he was particularly concerned in " miraculous shrines ", which were to him exactly in the same category as " companies " are to the speculator on the Stock Exchange. He had been cautious, prudent, and calculating from his earliest years,—from the time when, as the last male scion of the house of Gherardi he had been educated for the Ecclesiastical career at the " College of Nobles ". He had read widely; and no religious or social movement took place anywhere without his knowing of it, and admitting it into his calculations as a sort of new figure in his banking sum. He was an extensive shareholder in the " Lourdes " business; and a careful speculator in all the religious frenzies of the uneducated and superstitious. His career had been very successful so far. He had amassed a considerable fortune; and away out towards Frascati he had a superb Villa, furnished with every modern luxury and convenience, (not rented in his own name, but in that of a man whom he paid heavily to serve him as his tool and menial,) —where a beautiful Neapolitan *danseuse* condescended to live as his mistress;—he was a diplomat for himself if not for his country, and kept his finger on the pulse of European politics as well as on the fluctuating fevers of new creeds. But he never troubled himself seriously as to the possible growth of any "movement", or "society", or "crusade"; as experience had taught him that no matter how ardently thinkers may propound theories, and enthusiasts support them, there is always a dense and steady wave of opposition surging against everything new,—and that few can be found whose patience will hold out sufficiently long to enable them to meet and ride over that wet wall of dull resistance.

Monsignor Gherardi was a most useful man at the Vatican, as he never failed to comfort the Pope whenever that Holy Personage was cast down or afraid of brooding disasters. When the Representative of the ever-merciful Christ ventured to give it out as his Christian opinion that the unhappy and maltreated Dreyfus would be found guilty Monsignor Gherardi smilingly agreed with him. When His Holiness denounced Freemasonry as a wicked association, formed for atheistical and revolutionary purposes, Gherardi, though he knew well enough that it was a fraternity formed for the mutual help and sustainment of its members, denounced it too;—in the gardens of the Vatican, but not elsewhere. There was nothing really either in the way of Freemasonry or other sort of "society", that he was afraid of;—no anxiety whatever troubled his mind, except the possibility of losing money by some incautious speculation. In appearance he was an exceedingly handsome man,—tall, with a fine figure and commanding features,—physical advantages which greatly helped him to enforce his spiritual authority. As he sat in his high-backed, gilded chair, turning over papers on his desk, docketing this and marking that for reference, his dark eyes sparkling with avidity as he counted up certain dividends obtained from mysterious shares in "miracle" health resorts, and a smile of satisfaction playing on the firm, well-shaped curve of his intellectual but hard mouth, he looked an imposing personage enough, of the very type to awe the weak and timorous. He was much entertained on this particular morning,—one might almost say he was greatly amused. Quite a humorous little comedy was being played at the Vatican,—a mock-solemn farce, which had the possibility of ending in serious disaster to the innocent;—and he, as a student of the wily and treacherous side of human nature, was rather interested in its development. Cardinal Felix Bonpré, a man living far away in an obscure cathedral-town of France, where he had become renowned for good works and saintly living, had now, after many years, come out of his long voluntary retirement, and had performed a miracle!

"And very well done too!" murmured Monsignor Gherardi, smiling to himself, "Well prepared, well thought out, and successfully accomplished! Our good Felix is much cleverer than I gave him credit for. First, he wins a renown for good works,—then he starts travelling toward Rome, the Mother of our Faith,—and on his way to the sacred city performs a miraculous cure! An excellent move! I see a possibility of making the Cathedral of Rouen a popular shrine for healing. Yes, much can be done there! Only I am sorry that Felix has made a little mistake in Paris—just a little mistake!—in that matter of Vergniaud. And it is exceedingly unfortunate that the son should turn out to be Gys Grandit. No wonder the Holy Father is troubled: —no wonder! It is a little drama of the age, and will no doubt prove complex in its movement, and worth watching." Here his smile broadened,—and his eyes glittered more keenly than ever. "Yes!—it will be an excitement; and one wants a little excitement now and then in the general monotony. Since Agostino preached;——" here he paused, and a dark contraction knitted his brows,—"Let me see!—this morning, yes!— this morning I receive the English socialist Aubrey Leigh."

He turned in his chair, and glanced at the dial of a huge ticking clock behind him, and saw that the hands were close on the appointed hour of eleven. His smile slowly disappeared, and vanished altogether in a heavy

frown. "A dangerous man! I do not like his book——
it is written in melodramatic style, with heat and with enthusiasm, and will attract the vulgar. He must be suppressed—but how?"

He rose and paced the room slowly, his long white
hands clasped behind his back, and the frown on his brows
deepened;—how suppress a man who had announced
himself as free of every Church and Creed, and who was
resolved to stand by the moral ethics of Christ only? A
man who desired nothing for himself, not even money;
—— "But stop!" thought Gherardi,—"that is absurd!
Every man wants money! Every man must have it, and
the more he has, the more he seeks. There is no one in
the world who cannot be bought or bribed!"

At that moment the green hangings of the door were
lifted, and the Italian man-servant announced,—

"*Il Signor Aubri Lee!*"

Gherardi, who in his pacing to and fro had reached the
window, wheeled round abruptly and faced his entering
visitor. The light fell aslant upon his stately figure as he
drew himself up to his full height, and greeted Leigh
with a suavely condescending bow and smile, while Aubrey in turn glanced him up and down with a pleasurable
consciousness of his intellectual appearance, and evident
combative temperament.

"You are welcome, Mr. Leigh," said Gherardi, speaking English with a fluency of which he was pardonably
proud, "Your letter from Florence received my instant
attention, and as you see, I have made it a point to receive you at once—in spite of pressing business. Yes,—
in spite of pressing business! I confess I have been curious to see the writer who has made himself so obnoxious to our dear friends and brothers, the English
clergy!"

A smile that was brilliant, but which conveyed no
meaning whatever, illumined his features; but for all reply to these words Aubrey simply bowed and remained
silent. Gherardi glanced at him sharply. Was he intimidated already?—overawed at being in the presence
of one who was known to be a friend and confidant of the
Pope? No—there was nothing of fear or embarrassment in the composed attitude, proud manner, and reserved expression of this slim, muscular man, with the

bright hair and keen eyes,—and Gherardi dropped his tone of patronage for one of courtesy.

" Pray sit down! " he said, " I understand that you wish to obtain a private audience of the Holy Father. That of course is impossible! "

Aubrey drew a chair slowly towards the desk where Gherardi had resumed his own usual seat, and raised his eyes with a curious look of half satirical questioning.

" Impossible! " he said, " And why? "

Gherardi almost laughed.

" Why? My dear sir, is it necessary to ask? Your name is sufficiently well-known! and—I am sorry to tell you so,—but it is quite as unpleasant at the Vatican as that of Gys Grandit! "

" Gys Grandit is a friend of mine," responded Aubrey composedly, " In fact, I may almost say he is my disciple. I found him working in the fields as a little peasant lad,— the love child, or 'bastard,' to put it roughly, of some priest whose name he never told me. He was helping to earn daily bread for his deserted mother whose maiden name he then bore; and I helped to train his evident genius in the way it has since developed."

" I cannot congratulate you on your pupil! " said Gherardi, smiling coldly, " The offspring of a priest's sin is not likely to do the world any credit. The son of the renegade Abbé Vergniaud may become notorious, but never famous! "

Aubrey Leigh started up from his chair doubting whether he had heard aright.

" The son of Abbé Vergniaud! " he exclaimed, " Is it possible! No, you must surely be mistaken!—I know the Abbé,—I saw him in Paris but a fortnight ago! "

" Indeed! Well, since that time strange things have happened," said Gherardi, still preserving his calm inscrutability of demeanour, " We have had our news from Monsignor Moretti, an envoy of ours in Paris, on secret service. To put it briefly,—Vergniaud, for no particular cause whatever, save perhaps the idea —(which may be only an idea)—that he is going to die soon, has made a public confession of his twenty-five-year-old crime and hypocrisy, in a blasphemous address preached from the pulpit of Notre Dame de Lorette. The son, known to the world as Gys Grandit, was present in the church, and fired a pistol shot at his father, hoping to murder him,—then came the theatrical dénouement of the whole scene;—the Abbé ordered the *gendarmes* to release the assassin, pronouncing him to be his son. And finally—the saddest incident of all—there took place the mutual pardon and reconciliation of both parties in the presence of one of our most respected and beloved Princes of the Church, Cardinal Felix Bonpré, whose grave error in this matter is causing poignant and loving sorrow to the Holy Father!"

A curious expression began to appear in the delicate lines of Aubrey's face—an expression which some of his London audiences knew so well, and which generally meant war.

"You surprise me, Monsignor," he said in quiet accents,—"Events move quickly, I know, in a quickly moving age,—still your news is entirely unexpected. I never knew till now who the father of my friend Gys Grandit was;—but now that I do know I think the public confession you tell me of, was the only fitting reparation such a man as the Abbé could make to the dead woman who was his wife in the sight of God, as well as to his living son, and the public generally. I never quite liked or trusted the Abbé; but if all this be true, he has risen a hundred per cent. in my opinion! As for Cardinal Bonpré, one of the noblest and purest of men, you surely cannot be in earnest when you speak of his having committed a grave error!"

"You know the Cardinal?" asked Gherardi evading the question.

"I was presented to him in Paris the day before I left for Florence," replied Aubrey, "at the studio of his niece, Donna Angela Sovrani."

"Ah!" and Gherardi balanced a paper-knife lightly on the point of his long forefinger, "An unpleasant woman that! One of the female ' geniuses ' who presume nowadays to compete with men in art and literature."

"In Donna Sovrani's case there can be no question of competition," answered Leigh quietly, "She is by far and away the best artist of her time."

"You think so? Very good, very good!" and Gherardi laughed a little, "You are very chivalrous! You have a touch of the American in you, have you not?—

there is a tendency in the men of the New World to be always on their knees before women. Strange, very strange!"

"We begin our lives in that way," replied Leigh, "We kneel to our mothers!"

A slight flush reddened Gherardi's yellow paleness, but he kept his smile well in evidence.

"Charmingly expressed—very charmingly!" he said suavely, "And so you have met our dear St. Felix! Well, well! And did he tell you all about the wonderful miracle he performed at Rouen?"

A cloud of surprise intermingled with contempt darkened Leigh's intellectual brows.

"Never!" he said emphatically, "I should not have thought so much of him if he had laid any claim to such a pretence!"

Gherardi laughed again softly.

"What a pity," he observed, "What a pity you clever heretics are so violent! You think the power of the Church is a decaying one, and that our Lord has ceased to supply its ministers with the Spirit of Grace and the powers of healing? But this is where you are mistaken! The Church—the Roman Church—remains as it always was and always will be; impregnable!—the source of inspiration, the seat of miracle, the only clue and road to everlasting life! And as for its power——" here he closed his hand and dropped it on the table with a silent force which was strangely expressive, "its power is immeasurable! It reaches out in every direction—it grasps —it holds,—it keeps! Why will you and your co-workers 'kick' like St. Paul 'against the pricks'? It is quite useless! The Church is too strong for any one of you— aye, and for any army of you! Do you not hear the divine Voice from heaven calling daily in your ears, 'Why persecutest thou Me?'"

"Yes," answered Aubrey deliberately, "I hear that every time I enter a church! I hear it every time I see an ordained priest or minister of the Gospel misusing his time in construing to his own purposes the classic simplicity of Christ's doctrine. In some places of worship, such as the tawdry church of the 'Annunziata' in Florence that protest seems to reach its climax. When one sees the unwashen priests expectorating every five min-

utes or so * on the very altars where they perform Mass;
—when one notes the dirt, the neglect, the gim-
crackery;—the sickening and barbarous superstition
everywhere offered as being representative of sublime
Deity,—the Force which has raised the heaven above us
with its endless star-patterns of living universe,—then the
cry of ' Why persecutest thou Me?' seems to roll through
the arches like the thunder which sometimes precedes a
general earthquake!"

Leigh's clear penetrating voice, artistically modulated
to the perfectly musical expression of thought, was not
without its usual effect, even on a mind so callous as
that of Gherardi. He moved uneasily in his chair,—he
was inwardly fuming with indignation, and for one moment was inclined to assume the melodramatic pose of
the irate Churchman, and to make himself into the figure
of an approved " stage " dignitary of religion, with outstretched arm, menacing eyes, and words that were as
darts to wound and sting. But looking under his eyelids at the cold, half satirical tranquillity of Aubrey's pale,
clear-cut features, he felt that any attempt at " acting "
his part would be seen through in a second by a man who
was so terribly in earnest. So with a benevolent and re-
gretful air, he said,

" Yes!—no doubt things appear to you as they do not
appear to us. The spirit of faith enables us to see through
all unsatisfactory outward forms and ceremonies, to the
actual divine mysteries which they symbolise;—and heretics perceive incongruities, where we, by the grace of
God, see nothing but harmony! And though you, Mr.
Leigh, receive the information with incredulity and a
somewhat blameable indifference, it is a matter of re-
joicing to us that Cardinal Bonpré has performed this
miracle of healing at Rouen. It would have raised him
to a very high place indeed in the Holy Father's estimation, had it not been for the strange mistake he has unfortunately made with respect to the Abbé Vergniaud."

" One may cure a sick person then, but one must not
pardon a sinner?" suggested Aubrey, "' For whether is
it easier to say, Thy sins be forgiven thee;' or ' Arise and
walk?' The one is considered a miracle;—the other a
mistake!"

* A fact

Gherardi's cold eyes glittered.

"We will not go into the technicalities of the question," he said frigidly, "We will return to the point from whence we diverged. Your wish expressed in this letter," and he drew one from a packet on the table and glanced it over in a business-like way, "was to obtain a private audience from the Pope. I repeat that to a mere civilian and socialistic writer like yourself, that is impossible!"

Aubrey sat unmoved.

"I suppose if I were a prince of the blood-royal I should not be refused an audience?" he said.

Gherardi's thick dark eyebrows went up with a movement of surprise at such an irrational remark.

"That would make a difference certainly," he answered smiling, "The claims of diplomacy have to be considered!"

"If a prince of the blood-royal whose private life was a scandal to the world"—went on Aubrey, "who was guilty of every vice known in the calendar,—who was neither intelligent nor sympathetic,—whose whole career was one of self and self-indulgence,—I say if he were to seek a private audience of the man who is declared to be the representative of Christ in Christendom, he would obtain it! On the other hand, if a man who had denied himself every personal gratification, and had sacrificed his whole life in working for his fellow men, and to the following of the teachings of the Gospel as far as it was possible, —but who yet had got no further in world's wealth than to be earning from his writings a few hundreds a year, he could *not* be received! Monsignor, this may be diplomacy, but it is not Christianity!"

"I cannot enter into these matters with you——" began Gherardi impatiently.

"No, you cannot, because you dare not!" said Aubrey boldly. "Man, you are not a Christian! Why pretend to be one? Is it not time you left off feigning what you do not feel? Is it not preposterous that you, at your years, should consent to make your life a lie in the face of Omnipresent Deity?"

Gherardi rose up pale and trembling.

"Mr. Leigh, if you have come here to insult me——"

"Insult you!" echoed Aubrey, "Not I! I would make a man of you if I could,—but that is too late!

You are a witness of imposture and a supporter of it,—
and we are none of us worthy to be called men if we do
either of these two things. You know as well as I do,
that there is no representative of the blameless Christ at
the Vatican,—you know there is only a poor weak old
man, whose mind is swayed by the crafty counsels of the
self-seeking flatterers around him, and who passes his
leisure hours in counting up money, and inventing new
means of gaining it through forms of things that should
be spiritual and divine. If you *believe* Christ was God
Incarnate, how dare you tamper with such a Supernal
Mystery?"

Gherardi turned his head slowly and looked round at
Aubrey,—then recovering his composure, sat down and
pretended to turn over some documents on the table, but
Aubrey went on undeterred by his aspect of frigidity,
"How dare you, I say? The God in Man! Do you realize the stupendous meaning of such a phrase? Do you
not see that it means *a Divine Life palpitating through
every atom of creation?* A Force so great, so pure and
majestic, so absolute in Its working for good, and yet so
deliberate in Its movements that It will give Its creature Man whole centuries of chance to find and save his
own soul before utterly destroying him? What has this
sublime Power in common with the Pope, who shuts
himself up in his palace, a voluntary prisoner,
all forsooth because he is denied temporal power!
Temporal power! What is temporal power compared to spiritual power! If he were the true representative of Christ he would move the world by
deeds of benevolence, goodness, and sanctity! In such a
case as that of the unhappy Dreyfus for instance, he
would have issued a solemn warning and earnest reproach
to the French nation for their misguided cruelty;—he
would have travelled himself to Rennes to use his personal influence in obtaining an innocent man's release
with honour! That would have been Christian! That
would have been a magnificent example to the world!
But what did he do? Shut comfortably up in his luxurious palace where no harm could touch him, where no
crucifixion of the heart or soul could torture him, he announced to his myrmidons his opinion that the wretched
martyr would be found guilty! And who can tell but

that his utterance thus unchristianly proclaimed did not help to sway the minds of the Rennes Court-martial? Again, why are there so many poor in Italy? If the Pope were the father indeed of those who are immediately around him, the land should be like the fabled Paradise, flowing with milk and honey. The Vatican is full of money and jewels. 'Sell half that thou hast and give to the poor,' was the command of Christ.—Does the Pope do that? Why does he not go out among the people and work in active sympathy with them? Christ did so! Christ was never borne with solemn flourish of trumpets, like a mummy in a chair, under canopies of cloth of gold, to give a blessing to a crowd who had got admission to see him by paid ticket! Man, man! The theatrical jugglery of Rome is a blasphemy in the sight of heaven:—and most truly did St. John declare this city, throned on its seven hills, to be, ' MYSTERY, THE MOTHER OF HARLOTS AND ABOMINATIONS OF THE EARTH.' And most clearly does God say at this period of our time, ' Come out of her My people, that ye be not partakers of her sins, and that ye receive not of her plagues. For her sins have reached unto heaven, and God hath remembered her iniquities!' The days of evil are drawing to an end; Rome must fall!"

Gherardi's breath came and went quickly,—but he kept up the outward appearance of cold composure.

"You rant very well, Mr. Leigh!" he said, "You would make an excellent Hyde Park orator! You have all the qualities which attract the vulgar; but we—we of the Church know quite well how to deal with men of your class,—their denunciations do not affect us at all. They amuse us occasionally; and sometimes they pain us, for naturally we grieve for the backslidings of refractory brethren. We regret the clamourings of ignorance which arise from a strong personal desire for notoriety. That passage in the Revelation of St. John, has been quoted scores of times as being applicable to Rome, though as a matter of fact it distinctly mentions Babylon." Here he smiled suavely. "And thanks to the workings of an All-wise Influence, Rome was never more powerful than she is at the present moment. Her ramifications are everywhere; and in England she has obtained a firm footing. Your good English Queen has never uttered one word of reproach against the spread of our Holy Religion among her subjects! Our prayers for the conversion of England will yet be granted!"

"Not while I live!" said Aubrey firmly, "Not while I can hold back but a handful from such a disaster, and that handful shall hold back yet another handful! The hand of Roman priestcraft shall never weigh on England while there are any honest men left in it! The conversion of England! The retrogression of England! Do you think such a thing is likely to happen because a few misguided clerics choose to appeal to the silly sentimentality of hysterical women with such church tricks and rags of paganism as incense and candles! Bah! Do not judge the English inward heart by its small outward follies, Monsignor! There are more honest, brave, and sensible folk in the British Islands than you think. And though our foreign foes desire our fall, the seed of *their* decay is not yet in us!"

XXI.

GHERARDI sat for two or three minutes in absolute silence. Only the twitching of his eyelids and a slight throbbing in the muscles of his throat showed with what difficulty he suppressed his rising fury. But his astute and crafty powers of reasoning taught him that it would be worse than ridiculous to give way to anger in the presence of this cool, determined man, who, though he spoke with a passion which from its very force seemed almost to sound like " the mighty wind " which accompanied the cloven tongues of fire at the first Pentecost, still maintained his personal calm,—that immovable calmness which is always the result of strong inward conviction. A dangerous man!—yes, there was no doubt of that! He was one of those concerning whom Emerson wrote, " let the world beware when a Thinker comes into it." Aubrey Leigh was a thinker,—and more than that, he was a doer. He was of the strong heroic type of genius that turns its dreams into facts, its thoughts into deeds. He did not talk, in common with so many men, of what they considered *ought* to be done, without exerting themselves to *do* it;—he was sincerely in earnest, and cared nothing for any personal loss or inconvenience he might suffer from carrying out his intentions. And Gherardi saw that there was little or no possibility of moving such a man from the firm ground of truth which he had elected to stand on. There is nothing so inconvenient in this world as an absolutely truthful person, who can both speak and write, and has the courage of his convictions. One can always arrange matters with liars, because they, being hampered by their own deceits, are compelled to study ways, means, and chances for appearing honest. But with the man or woman who holds truth dearer than life, and honour more valuable than advancement, there is nothing to be done, now that governments cannot insist on the hemlock-cure, as in the case of Socrates. Gherardi, looking furtively under his eyelids at Leigh's strong lithe figure, and classic head, felt he could have willingly poisoned or stabbed him. For there were, and *are* great interests at stake in the so-called " conversion of England,"—it is truly one of the largest financial schemes ever set afloat in the world, if those whose duty it is to influence and control events could only be brought to see the practical side of the matter, and set a check on its advancement before it is too late. Gherardi knew what great opportunities there were in embryo of making large fortunes;—and not only of making large fortunes but of obtaining incredible power. There was a great plan afoot of drawing American and English wealth into the big Church-net through the medium of superstitious fear and sentimental bigotry,—and an opposer and enemy like Aubrey Leigh, physically handsome, with such powers of oratory as are only granted to the very few, was capable of influencing women as well as men—and women, as Gherardi well recognised, are the chief supporters of the Papal system. Uneasily he thought of a certain wealthy American heiress whom he had persuaded into thinking herself specially favoured and watched over by the Virgin Mary, and who, overcome by the strong imaginary consciousness of this heavenly protection, had signed away in her will a million of pounds sterling to a particular " shrine " in which he had the largest share of financial profit. Now, suppose she should chance to come within the radius of Leigh's attractive personality and teaching, and revoke this bequest? Deeply incensed he sat considering, yet he was conscious enough of his own impotency to persuade or move this man a jot.

" I am very sorry," he said at last without raising his eyes, and carefully preserving an equable and mild tone of voice, " I am sorry you are so harsh in your judgments, Mr. Leigh;—and still more sorry that you appear to be bent on opposing the Roman Catholic movement in England. I will do you the justice to believe that you are moved by a sincere though erroneous conviction,—and it is out of pure kindness and interest in you that I warn you how useless you will find the task in which you have engaged. The force of Rome is impregnable!—the interpretation of the Gospel by the Pope infallible. Any man, no matter how gifted with eloquence, or moved by what he imagines to be truth—(and alas! how often error is mistaken for truth and truth for error!)—must be crushed in the endeavour to cope with such a divinely ordained power."

"The Car of Juggernaut was considered to be divinely ordained," said Aubrey, "And the wretched and ignorant populace flung themselves under it in the fit of hysterical mania to which they were excited by the priests of the god, and so perished in their thousands. Not *they* were to blame; but the men who invented the imposture and encouraged the slaughter. *They* had an ideal;—the priests had none! But Juggernaut had its end—and so will Rome!"

"You call yourself a Christian?" asked Gherardi, with a touch of derision.

"Most assuredly I do," replied Aubrey, "Most assuredly I am! I love and honour Christ with every fibre of my being. I long to see that Divine Splendour of the ages stand out white and shining and free from the mud and slime with which His priests have bespattered Him. I believe in Him absolutely! But I can find nowhere in His Gospel that He wished us to turn Religion into a sort of stock-jobbing company managed by sacerdotal directors in Rome!"

"What do you know about the 'sacerdotal directors' as you call them, of Rome?" asked Gherardi slowly, his eyes narrowing at the corners, and his whole countenance expressing ineffable disdain, "Do you think we give out the complex and necessary workings of our sacred business to the uneducated public?"

"No, I do not," replied Aubrey, "For you keep the public in the dark as much as you can. Your methods of action are precisely those of the priests of ancient Egypt, who juggled with what they were pleased to call their sacred 'mysteries' in precisely the same way as you do. Race copies race. Roman Christianity is grafted upon Roman Paganism. When the Apostles were all dead, and their successors (who had never been in personal touch with Christ) came on to the scene of action, they discovered that the people of Rome would not do without the worship of woman in their creed, so they cleverly substituted the Virgin Mary for Venus and Diana. They turned the statues of gods and heroes into figures of

Apostles and Saints. They knew it would be unwise to deprive the populace of what they had been so long accustomed to, and therefore they left them their swinging censers, their gold chalices, and their symbolic candles. Thus it is that Roman Catholicism became, and is still, merely a Christian form of Paganism which is made to pay successfully, just as the feasts and Saturnalia of ancient days were made to pay as spectacular and theatrical pastimes. I should not blame your Church if it declared itself to be an offshoot of Paganism at once,—Paganism, or any other form of faith, deserves respect as long as its priests and followers are sincere; but when their belief is a mere pretence, and their system degenerates into a scheme of making money out of the fond faiths of the ignorant, then I consider it is time to protest against such blasphemy in the presence of God and all things divine and spiritual!"

Gherardi had listened to these words very quietly, his countenance gradually relaxing and smoothing into an amiable expression of forbearance. He looked up now at Aubrey with a smile that was almost benignant.

"You are quite right, Mr. Leigh!" he said gently, "I begin to understand you now! I see that you have studied deeply, and you have thought still more. If you will continue your studies and your thinking also, you will see how difficult it is for us to move as rapidly with the times as you would have us do. You must remember that it would be quite possible for Holy Mother Church to rise at once to the high scientific and psychical position you wish her to adopt, if it were not for the mass of the ignorant, with whom one must have patience! You are a man in the prime of life—you are zealous—eager for improvement,—yes!—all that is very admirable and praiseworthy. But you forget the numerous and widely differing interests with which we of the Church have to deal. For the great majority of persons it would be useless, for example, to give them lessons on the majesty of God's work in the science of Astronomy. They would be confused, bewildered, and more or less frightened out of faith altogether. They must have something tangible to cling to—for instance,"—and he pressed the tips of his fingers delicately together, "there are grades of intelligence just as there are grades of creation; you cannot instruct a caterpillar as you instruct a man. Now there are many human beings who are of the caterpillar quality of brain—what are you to do with them? They would not understand God as manifested in the solar system, but they would try to please some favourite Saint by good conduct. Is it not better that they should believe in the Saint than in nothing?"

"I cannot think it well for anyone to believe in a lie," said Aubrey slowly, taken aback despite himself by Gherardi's sudden gentleness, "There is a magnificent simplicity in truth;—truth which, the more it is tested, the truer it proves. Where is there any necessity of falsehood? Surely the marvels of nature could be explained with as much ease as the supposed miracles of a Saint?"

"I doubt it!" answered Gherardi smiling, "You must admit, my dear sir, that our scientific men are a great deal too abstruse for the majority;—in some cases they are almost too abstruse for themselves! You spoke just now of the priests of Egypt;—the oracles of Memphis were clear reading compared to the involved sentences of some of our modern scientists! Scientific books are hard nuts to crack even for the highly educated; but for the uneducated, believe me, the personality of a Saint is much more consoling than the movements of a star. Besides, Humanity must have something human to love and to revere. The infinite gradations of the Mind of God through Matter, appeal to none but those of the very highest intellectual capability."

Aubrey was silent a moment, then he said,

"But even the most ignorant can understand Christ,—Christ as He revealed Himself to the world in perfect beauty and simplicity as 'a Man of sorrows and acquainted with grief.' There needs no Vatican, no idolatry of the Pope, no superstitious images, no shrines of healing and reliquaries to explain His sublime intention!"

"I am afraid, Mr. Leigh, you entertain a very optimistic view of mankind," said Gherardi, "Unfortunately Christ is not enough for many people. Christ was an Incarnation of God, and though He became Man he 'knew not sin.' He therefore stands apart; an Example, but not a Companion. There are a certain class of sinners who like to think of Saints;—human beings constituted like themselves, who have committed errors, even crimes, and repented of them. This is a similar spirit to that of the child who catches hold of any convenient support he can find to guide his first tottering steps across the floor to his mother,—the Saint helps the feeble-footed folk to totter their way towards Christ. I assure you, our Church considers everything that is necessary for the welfare of its weakest brethren."

"Yes,—I grant you that it is full of subtle means for approaching and commanding the ignorant," said Aubrey, "But to the intellectual forces it offers no progress."

"The intellectual forces can clear their own way!" declared Gherardi, rising to his full imposing height, and beaming sovereign benevolence on his visitor, "and can, if they choose, make their own Church. This is the age of freedom, and no restraint is placed on the action of the intellectually free. But the ignorant must always form the majority; and in their ignorance and helplessness, will do wisely to remain like obedient children under the sway of Rome!"

Aubrey rose also, and could not forbear an involuntary glance of reluctant admiration at the stately figure and commanding attitude of the man who confronted him with such a pride in the persistent Jesuitical conviction that even a Lie may be used in religion for the furtherance of conversion to the Truth.

"I do not see," Gherardi went on, smiling blandly, "why after all, you should not be received by the Holy Father. I will try to arrange it for you. But it would avail you very little, I imagine, as he is not strong, and would not be capable of conversing with you for more than a few minutes. I think it would serve your purpose much more to carefully study the movements, and the work of what you call 'the stock-jobbing company of sacerdotal directors,'" and here his smile became still more broadly benevolent, "and take note of their divisions and subdivisions of influence which extend from the very poorest and most abandoned to the very highest and most cultured. You will then understand why I maintain that Rome as a power is impregnable;—and why some of the more far-sighted and prophetic among us look upon the Conversion of England as an almost accomplished fact!"

Aubrey smiled; but he was not without the consciousness that from his own particular point of view Gherardi had some excuse for his belief.

"According to your own written opinions," went on Gherardi, "for I have read your books,—the Church of England is in a bad way. Its Ritualistic form is very nearly Roman. Some of your Archbishops confess to a liking for incense! You admit that the stricter forms of Protestantism do not comfort the sick soul in times of need; well, what would you Socialists and Freethinkers have? Would you do without a Church altogether?"

"No," said Aubrey quickly, "But we would have a purified Church,—a House of Praise to God—without any superstition or dogma."

"You must have dogma," said Gherardi complacently, "You must formulate something out of a chaos of opinion. As for superstition, you will never get rid of that weakness out of the human composition. If the Church gives nothing for this particular mood of man to feed on, man will invent something else *outside* the Church. My dear sir, we have thought of all these difficulties for ages! In religion one cannot appeal solely to the intellect. One must touch the heart—the emotions. Music, painting, colour, spectacle, all these are permitted us to use for the good purpose of lifting the soul of a sinner to contemplate something better than himself. Women and little children enter the Church as well as men,—would you have *them* find no comfort? Must a woman with a broken heart take her sorrows to the vast Silence of an unreasonable God among universes of star systems? Or shall she find hope, and a gleam of comfort in a prayer to a woman of the same clay as herself in the person of the Virgin Mary? And remember, there is something very beautiful in the symbol of the Virgin as applied to womanhood! The Mother of God! Does it not suggest to your poetical mind that woman is destined always to be the Mother of the God?—that is, mother of the perfect man when that desirable consummation shall be accomplished?"

"I have never doubted it!" said Aubrey, "The Mother of Christ is to me a symbol of womanhood for all time!"

Gherardi smiled.

"Good! Then in spite of your denunciations you come very near to our faith!"

"I never denied the beauty, romance, or mysticism of the Roman Catholic Faith," said Aubrey, "If it were purified from the accumulated superstition of ages, and freed from intolerance and bigotry, it would perhaps be the grandest form of Christianity in the world. But the rats are in the house, and the rooms want cleaning!"

"In every house there are those rats—in every room there is dirt!" said Gherardi, "Presuming that you speak in a moral sense. What of your Houses of Parliament? What of the French Senate? What of the Reichstag? What of the Russian Autocracy?—the American Republic? In every quarter the rats squeal, and the dirt gathers! The Church of Rome is purity itself compared to your temporal governments! My dear sir," and approaching, he laid a kindly hand on Aubrey's arm, "I would not be harsh with you for the world! I understand your nature perfectly. It is full of enthusiasm and zeal for righteousness,—your heart warms to the sorrows of the human race,—you would lift up the whole world to God's footstool; you would console—you would be a benefactor—you would elevate, purify, rejuvenate, inspire! Yes! This is a grand mood—one which has fired many a would-be reformer before you,—but you forget! It is not the Church against which you should arm yourself—it is the human race! It is not one or many religious systems with which you should set yourself to contend—it is the blind brutishness of humanity!" As he spoke, his tall form appeared to tower to an even greater height,—his eyes flashed, and the intellectual pride and force of his character became apparent in every feature of his face. "If humanity in the mass asked us for Christ only; if men and women would deny themselves the petty personal aim, the low vice, the crawling desire to ingratiate themselves with Heaven, the Pharisaical affectation of virtue—if they would themselves stand clear of 'vain repetition' and obstinate egoism, and would of themselves live purely, the Church would be pure! May I venture to suggest to you that men make the Church, not the Church the men? We try to supply the spiritual needs of the human being, such as his spiritual needs at present are,—when he demands more we will give him more. At present his needs are purely personal, and therefore low and tainted with sensuality,—yet we drag him along through these emotions as near to the blameless Christ as we can. When he is impersonal enough, unselfish enough, loyal-hearted enough, to stand face to face with the glorious manifestation of the Deity unaided, we can cast away his props, such as superstitious observances, Saints and the like, and leave him,—but then the Millennium will have come, and there will be new heavens and a new earth!"

He spoke well, with force and fervour, and Aubrey Leigh was for a moment impressed. After a slight pause however, he said,

"You admit the ignorance of human beings, and yet—you would keep them ignorant?"

"Keep them ignorant!" Gherardi laughed lightly. "That is more than any of us can do nowadays! Every liberty is afforded them to learn,—and if they still remain barbarous it is because they elect to be so. But *our* duty is to look after the ignorant more than the cultured! Quite true it is that the Pope lost a magnificent opportunity in the Dreyfus affair,—if he had spoken in favour of mercy and justice he would have won thousands of followers; being silent he has lost thousands. But this should be a great satisfaction to you, Mr. Leigh! For if the Holy Father had given an example to the Catholic clergy to act in the true Christian spirit towards Dreyfus, the Conversion of England might have been so grafted on enthusiastic impulse as to be a much nearer possibility than it is now!"

Aubrey was silent.

"Now, Mr. Leigh, I think you have gained sufficient insight into my views to judge me with perhaps greater favour than you were inclined to do at the beginning of our interview," continued Gherardi, "I assure you that I shall watch your career with the greatest interest! You have embarked in a most hopeless cause,—you will try to help the helpless, and as soon as they are rescued out of trouble, they will turn and rend you,—you will try to teach them the inner mysteries of God's working, and they will say you are possessed of a devil! You will endeavour to upset shams and hypocrisies, and the men of your press will write you down and say you are seeking advertisement and notoriety for yourself. Was there ever a great thinker left unmartyred? Or a great writer that has not been misunderstood and condemned? You wish to help and serve humanity! Enthusiast! You would do far better to help and serve the Church! For the Church rewards; humanity has cursed and killed every great benefactor it ever had *including Christ!*"

The terrible words beat on Aubrey's ears like the brazen clang of a tocsin, for he knew they were true. But he held his ground.

" There are worse things than death," he said simply.

Gherardi smiled kindly.

" And there are worse things than life!" he said, " Life holds a good many harmless enjoyments, which I am afraid you are putting away from you in your prime, for the sake of a mere chimera. But—after all, what does it matter! One must have a hobby! Some men like horse-racing, others book-collecting,—others pictures, —and so forth—you like the religious question! Well, no doubt it affords you a great many opportunities of studying character. I shall be very happy—" here he extended his hand cordially, " to show you anything that may be of interest to you in Rome, and to present you to any of our brethren that may assist you in your researches. I can give you a letter to Rampolla——"

Aubrey declined the offered introduction with a decided negative shake of his head.

" No," he said, " I know Cardinal Bonpré; that is enough!"

" But there is a great difference between Rampolla and Bonpré," said Gherardi, with twinkling eyes, " Bonpré is scarcely ever in Rome. He lives a life apart—and has for a long while been considered as a kind of saint from the privacy and austerity of his life. But he has heralded his arrival in the Eternal City triumphantly—by the performance of a miracle! What do you say to this?—you who would do away with things miraculous?"

" I say nothing till I hear," answered Aubrey, " I must know what the nature of the so-called miracle is. I am a believer in soul-forces, and in the exhalation of spiritual qualities affecting or influencing others; but in this there is no miracle, it is simply natural law."

" Well, you must interview the Cardinal yourself," said Gherardi indulgently, " and tell me afterwards what you think about it, if indeed you think anything. But you will

not find him at home this morning. He is summoned to
the Vatican."

"On account of the miracle?—or the scandal affecting
the Abbé Vergniaud?" asked Aubrey.

"Both matters are under discussion, I believe," replied
Gherardi evasively, "But they are not in my province.
Now, can I be of any further service to you, Mr. Leigh?"

"No. I am sorry to have taken up so much of your
time," said Aubrey, "But I think I understand your
views——"

"I hope you do," interrupted Gherardi, "And that you
will by and by grasp the fact that my views are shared
by almost everyone holding any Church authority. But
you must go about in Rome, and make enquiries for yourself . . . now, let me see! Do you know the Princesse
D'Agramont?"

"No."

"Oh, you must know her,—she is a great friend of
Donna Sovrani's, and a witty and brilliant personage in
herself. She is rather of your way of thinking, and so
is out of favour with the Church. But that will not matter to you; and you will meet all the dissatisfied and enthusiastic of the earth in her salons! I will tell her to send
you a card."

Aubrey said something by way of formal acknowledgment, and then took his leave. He was singularly depressed, and his face, always quick to show traces of
thought, had somewhat lost its former expression of eager
animation. The wily Gherardi had for the time so influenced his sensitive mind as to set it almost to the tune
of the most despairing of Tennyson's "Two Voices",

> "A life of nothings, nothing worth,
> From that first nothing ere his birth,
> To that last nothing under earth."

What was the use of trying to expound a truth, if the
majority preferred a lie?

> "Will one bright beam be less intense,
> When thy peculiar difference
> Is cancelled in the world of sense?"

And Gherardi noted the indefinable touch of fatigue
that gave the slight droop of the shoulders and air of lan-

guor to the otherwise straight slim figure as it passed from his presence,—and smiled. He had succeeded in putting a check on unselfish ardour, and had thrown a doubt into the pure intention of enthusiastic toil. That was enough for the present. And scarcely had Aubrey crossed the threshold—scarcely had the echo of his departing footsteps died away—when a heavy velvet curtain in the apartment was cautiously thrust aside, and Monsignor Moretti stepped out of a recess behind it, with a dignity and composure which would have been impossible to any but an Italian priest convicted of playing the spy. Gherardi faced him confidently.

"Well?" he said, with a more exhaustive enquiry expressed in his look than in the simple ejaculation.

"Well!" echoed Moretti, as he slowly advanced into the centre of the room, "You have not done as much as I expected you would. Your arguments were clever, but not—to a man of his obstinacy, convincing."

And sitting down, he turned his dark face and gleaming eyes full on his *confrère,* who with a shrug of his massive shoulders expressed in his attitude a disdainful relinquishment of the whole business.

"You have not," pursued Moretti deliberately, "grasped anything like the extent of this man Leigh's determination and indifference to results. Please mark that last clause,—indifference to results. He is apparently alone in the world,—he seems to have nothing to lose, and no one to care whether he succeeds or fails;—a most dangerous form of independence! And in his persistence and eloquence he is actually stopping—yes, I repeat it,—stopping and putting a serious check on the advancement of the Roman Catholic party. And of course any check just now means to us a serious financial loss both in England and America,—a deficit in Vatican revenues which will very gravely incommode certain necessary measures now under the consideration of His Holiness. I expected you to grasp the man and hold him,—not by intimidation but by flattery."

"You think he is to be caught by so common a bait?" said Gherardi, "Bah! He would see through it at once!"

"Maybe!" replied Moretti, "But perhaps not if it were administered in the way I mean. You seem to have forgotten the chief influence of any that can be brought to bear upon the heart and mind of a man,—and that is, Woman."

Gherardi laughed outright.

"Upon my word I think it would be difficult to find the woman suited to this case!" he said. "But you who have a diplomacy deeper than that of any Jew usurer may possibly have one already in view?"

"There is now in Rome," pursued Moretti, speaking with the same even deliberation of accent, "a faithful daughter of the Church, whose wealth we can to a certain extent command, and whose charm is unquestionable,— the Comtesse Sylvie Hermenstein——"

Gherardi started. Moretti eyed him coldly.

"You are not stricken surely by the childlike fascination with which this princess of coquettes rules her court?" he enquired sarcastically.

"I?" echoed Gherardi, shifting his position so that Moretti's gaze could not fall so directly upon him. "I? You jest!"

"I think not!" said Moretti, "I think I know something about women—their capabilities, their passions, their different grades of power. Sylvie Hermenstein possesses a potent charm which few men can resist, and I should not wonder if you yourself had been occasionally conscious of it. She is one of those concerning whom other women say 'they can see nothing in her'. Ah!" and Moretti smiled darkly, "What a compliment that is from the majority of women to one! This woman Sylvie is unique. Where is her beauty? You cannot say—yet beauty is her very essence. She cannot boast perfection of features,—she is frequently hidden away altogether in a room and scarcely noticed. And so she reminds me of a certain flower known to the Eastern nations, which is difficult to find, because so fragile and small that it can scarcely be seen, but when it *is* found, and the scent of it unwittingly inhaled, it drives men mad!"

Gherardi looked at him with a broadly wondering smile.

"You speak so eloquently," he said, "that one would almost fancy——"

"Fancy nothing!" retorted Moretti quickly, "Fancy and I are as far apart as the poles, except in the putting together of words, in which easy art I daresay I am as great an adept as Florian Varillo, who can write verses on love or patriotism to order, without experiencing a touch of either emotion. What a humbug by the way, that fellow is!—" and Moretti broke off to consider this new point—" He rants of the honour of Italy, and would not let his finger ache for her cause! And he professes to love the ' Sovrani ' while all Rome knows that Pon-Pon is his mistress! "

Gherardi wisely held his peace.

" The Comtesse Sylvie Hermenstein is the little magic flower you must use; " resumed Moretti, emphasising his words with an authoritative movement of his hand, " Use her to madden Aubrey Leigh. Bring them together;— he will lose his head as surely as all men do when they come under the influence of that soft deep-eyed creature, with the full white breast of a dove, and the smile of an angel,—and remember, it would be an excellent thing for the Church if he could be persuaded to marry her,— there would be no more preaching then!——for the thoughts of love would outweigh the theories of religion."

" You think it? " queried Gherardi dubiously.

" I know it! " replied Moretti rising, and preparing to take his departure, " But,—play the game cautiously! Make no false move. For—understand me well, this man Leigh must be silenced,——or we shall lose England! "

And with these last words he turned abruptly on his heel and left the apartment.

XXII.

CARDINAL FELIX BONPRE sat alone in the largest and loneliest room of the large and lonely suite of rooms allotted to him in the Palazzo Sovrani,—alone at a massive writing table near the window, his head resting on one hand, and his whole figure expressive of the most profound dejection. In front of him an ancient silver crucifix gleamed in the flicker of the small wood fire which had been kindled in the wide cavernous chimney—and a black-bound copy of the Gospels lay open as if but lately consulted. The faded splendour of certain gold embroidered hangings on the walls added to the solemn and melancholy aspect of the apartment, and the figure of the venerable prelate seen in such darkening gloom and solitude, was the crowning completion of an expressive and pathetic picture of patient desolation. So might a martyr of the Inquisition have looked while the flames were getting ready to burn him for the love of the gentle Saviour; and something of the temper of such a possible predecessor was in the physically frail old man, who just now was concentrating all the energies of his mind on the consideration of a difficult question which is often asked by many hearts in secret, but is seldom voiced to the public ear;—" Christ or the Church? Which must I follow to be an honest man?"

Never had the good Cardinal been in such a strange predicament. Living away from the great centres of thought and action, he had followed a gentle and placid course of existence, almost unruffled, save by the outside murmurs of a growing public discontent which had reached him through the medium of current literature, and had given him cause to think uneasily of possible disaster for the religious world in the near future,—but he had never gone so far as to imagine that the Head of the Church would, while being perfectly conscious of existing threatening evils, deliberately turn his back to appeals for help,—shut his ears to the cry of the " lost sheep of the House of Israel ", and even endeavour, with an impotence of indignation which was as pitiable as useless, to shake a rod of Twelfth-century menace over the advancement of the Twentieth!

"For the onward movement of Humanity is God's work," said the Cardinal, "And what are we—what is even the Church—when it does not move side by side in perfect and pure harmony with the order of Divine Law?"

And he was bitterly troubled in spirit. He had spent the whole morning at the Vatican, and the manner of his reception there had been so curiously divided between flattery and reproach that he had not known what to make of it. The Pope had been tetchy and querulous,— precisely in such a humour as one naturally expects so aged a man to be when contradicted on any matter, whether trivial or important. For with such advanced years the faculties are often as brittle as the bones, and the failing powers of the brain are often brought to bear with more concentration on inconsiderable trifles than on the large and important affairs of life. He had questioned the Cardinal closely concerning the miraculous cure performed at Rouen, and had become excessively angry when the honest prelate earnestly disclaimed all knowledge of it. He had then confronted him with Claude Cazeau, the secretary of the Archbishop of Rouen, and Cazeau had given a clear and concise account of the whole matter, stating that the child, Fabien Doucet, had been known in Rouen since his babyhood as a helpless cripple, and that after Cardinal Bonpré had prayed over him and laid hands on him, he had been miraculously cured, and was now to be seen running about the city as strong and straight as any other healthy child. And Bonpré listened patiently;—and to all that was said, merely reiterated that if the child *were* so cured, then it was by the special intervention of God, as he personally had done no more than pray for his restoration. But to his infinite amazement and distress he saw plainly that the Holy Father did not believe him. He saw that he was suspected of playing a trick,—a trick, which if he had admitted, would have been condoned, but which if he denied, would cause him to be looked upon with distrust by all the Vatican party. He saw that even the man Cazeau suspected him. And then,—when the public con-

fession of the Abbé Vergniaud came under discussion,
—the Pope had gathered together all the visible remains
of physical force his attenuated frame could muster, and
had hurled himself impotently against the wall of opposing fact with such frail fury as almost to suggest the
celebrated simile of " a reed shaken with the wind ". In
vain had the Cardinal pleaded for Vergniaud's pardon ; in
vain had he urged that after all, the sinner had branded
himself as such in the sight of all men ; what further need
to add the ban of the Church's excommunication against
one who was known to be within touch of death ? Would
not Christ have said, " Go, and sin no more " ? But this
simple quotation from the Gospels seemed to enrage the
representative of St. Peter more violently than before,
and when Bonpré left the Holy Presence he knew well
enough that he was, for no fault of his own, under the
displeasure of the Vatican. How had it all come about?
Nothing could have been simpler than his life and actions since he left his own Cathedral-town,—*he had
prayed for a sick child,—he had sympathised with a sorry
sinner,—that was all.* And such deeds as these were commanded by Christ. Yet—the Head of the Church for
these same things viewed him with wrath and suspicion !
Wearily he sat, turning over everything in his mind, and
longing, with a weakness which he fully admitted to his
own conscience, to leave Rome at once and return to his
own home, there to die among his roses at peace. But
he saw it would never do to leave Rome just yet. He
was bound fast hand and foot. He was " suspect " ! In
his querulous fit the Pope had ordered Claude Cazeau to
return to Rouen without delay, and there gather further
evidence respecting the Cardinal's stay at the Hotel Poitiers, and if possible, to bring the little Fabien Doucet
and his mother back to Rome with him. Pending the arrival of fresh proof, Bonpré, though he had received no
actual command, knew he was expected to remain where
he was. Weary and sick at heart, the venerable prelate
sighed as he reviewed all the entangling perplexities,
which had, so unconsciously to himself, become woven
like a web about his innocent and harmless personality,
and so absorbed was he in thought that he did not hear
the door of his room open, and so was not aware that his
foundling Manuel had stood for some time silently watch-

ing him.　Such love and compassion as were expressed in
the boy's deep blue eyes could not however radiate long
through any space without some sympathetic response,—
and moved by instinctive emotion, Cardinal Felix looked
up, and seeing his young companion smiled,—albeit the
smile was a somewhat sad one.

"Where have you been, my child?" he asked gently,
"I have missed you for some hours."

Manuel advanced a little, and stood between the pale
afternoon light reflected through the window, and the
warmer glow of the wood fire.

"I have been to the strangest place in all the world!"
he answered, "The strangest,—and surely one of the
most wicked!"

The Cardinal raised himself in his chair, and bent an
anxious wondering look upon the young speaker.

"One of the most wicked!" he echoed, "What place
are you talking of?"

"St. Peter's!" answered Manuel, with a thrill of passion in his voice as he uttered the name, "St. Peter's,—
the huge Theatre misnamed a Church!　Oh, dear friend!
—do not look at me thus!　Surely you must feel that what
I say is true?　Surely you know that there is nothing of
the loving God in that vast Cruelty of a place, where
wealth and ostentation vie with intolerant officialism, bigotry and superstition!—where even the marble columns
have been stolen from the temples of a sincerer Paganism,
and still bear the names of Isis and Jupiter wrought in
the truthful stone;—where theft, rapine and murder have
helped to build the miscalled Christian fane!　You cannot in your heart of hearts feel it to be the abode of
Christ; your soul, bared to the sight of God, repudiates
it as a Lie! Yes!"——For, startled and carried away by
the boy's fervour, Cardinal Felix had risen, and now stood
upright, making a feeble gesture with his hands, as though
seeking to keep back the crushing weight of some too
overwhelming conviction,—"Yes—you would silence me!
—but you cannot!—I read your heart!　You love God
. . . and I—I love Him too!　You would serve Him!—and
I—I would obey Him!　Ah, do not struggle with yourself,
dear and noble friend!　If you were thrice crowned a
martyr and saint you could not see otherwise than clearly
—you could not but accept Truth when Truth is mani-

fested to you,—you could not swear falsely before God!
Would the Christ not say now as He said so many centuries ago—'My House is called the house of prayer,
but ye have made it a den of thieves!' Is it not truly
a den of thieves? What has the Man of Sorrows to do
with all the evil splendour of St. Peter's?—its bronzes,
its marbles, its colossal statues of dead gods, its glittering
altars, its miserable dreary immensity, its flaring gilding
and insolent vulgarity of cost! Oh, what a loneliness is
that of Christ in this world! What a second Agony in
Gethsemane!"

The sweet voice broke—the fair head was turned away,
—and Cardinal Felix, overcome by such emotion as he
found it impossible to explain, suddenly sank on his
knees, and stretched out his arms to the young slight
creature who spoke with such a passion and intensity of
yearning.

"Child!" he said, with tremulous appeal in his accents, "For God's sake!—you who express your thoughts
with such eloquence and fervent pain!—tell me, *Who are
you?* My mind is caught and controlled by your words,
—you are too young to think as you do, or to speak as
you do,—yet some authority you seem to possess, which
I submit to, not knowing why; I am very old, and maybe
growing foolish in my age——many troubles are gathering about me in these latter days,—do not make them
more than I can bear!"

His words were to himself incoherent, and yet it seemed
as if Manuel understood them. Suffering himself to be
clasped for a moment by the old man's trembling hands,
he nevertheless gently persuaded and assisted him to rise,
and when he was once more seated, stood quietly by his
side, waiting till he should have recovered from his sudden agitation.

"Dear friend, you are weary and troubled in spirit,"
he said tenderly then, "And my words seem to you only
terrible because they are true! If they grieve you, it is
because the grief in your heart echoes mine! And if I do
think and speak more seriously than I should, it is for
the reason that I have been so much alone in the world,
—left to myself, with my own thoughts of God, which
are not thoughts such as many care for. I would not
add to your sorrows,—I would rather lighten them if I

could—but I feel and fear that I shall be a burden upon you before long!"

"Never!" exclaimed Bonpré fervently, "Never a burden on me, child! Surely while I live you will not leave me?"

Manuel was silent for a little space. His eyes wandered from the Cardinal's venerable worn features to the upstanding silver crucifix that gleamed dully in the glow of the wood-embers.

"I will not leave you unless it is well for you that I should go," he answered at last, "And even then, you will always know where to find me."

The Cardinal looked at him earnestly, and with a searching interrogation,—but the boy's face though sweetly composed, had a certain gravity of expression which seemed to forbid further questioning. And a deep silence fell between them,—a silence which was only broken by the door opening to admit Prince Sovrani who, pausing on the threshold, said,

"Brother, if you will allow yourself to be disturbed, Angela would like to see you in her studio. There are several people there,—her *fiancé*, Varillo among the number,—and I think the girl would be glad of your presence."

The Cardinal started as from a dream, and rose from his chair.

"I will come at once—yes—I will come," he said, "I must not be selfish and think only of my own troubles!" He stood erect,—he was still in the scarlet robes in which he had made his appearance at the Vatican, and they fell regally about his tall dignified form, the vivid colour intensifying the pallor of his thin features. A servant entering at the moment with two large silver candelabra ablaze with lights, created an effect of luminance in the room that made him appear to even greater advantage as an imposing figure of ecclesiastical authority, and Prince Pietro looked at him with the admiring affection and respect which he, though a cynic and sceptic, had always felt for the brother of his wife,—affection and respect which had if anything become intensified since that beloved one's untimely death.

"You were well received at the Vatican?" he said tentatively.

" Not so well as I had hoped," replied the Cardinal patiently—" Not so well! But the cloud will pass. I will go with you to the studio,—Manuel, will you stay here?"

Manuel bent his head in assent; he had just closed the before open copy of the Gospels, and now stood with his hand upon the Book.

" I will wait till you call me, my lord Cardinal," he replied.

Prince Pietro then led the way, and Cardinal Bonpré followed, his scarlet robes sweeping behind him with a rich rustling sound, and as the two entered the large lofty studio, hung with old tapestries, and panelled with deeply carved and gilded oak, the room which was Angela Sovrani's special *sanctum,* all the persons there assembled rose from their different sitting or lounging attitudes, and respectfully bent their heads to the brief and unostentatious benediction given to them by the venerable prelate of whom all present had heard, but few had seen, and everyone made way for him as Angela met and escorted him to a seat on one of the old, throne-like chairs with which the Sovrani palace was so amply supplied. When he was thus installed, he made the picturesque centre of a brilliant little scene enough,—one of those vivacious and bright gatherings which can be found nowhere so perfectly blended in colour and in movement as in a great art-studio in Rome. Italians are not afraid to speak, to move, to smile,—unlike the Anglo-Saxon race, their ease of manner is inborn, and comes to them without training, hence there is nothing of the stiff formality and awkward gloom which too frequently hangs like a cloud over English attempts at sociality,—and that particular charm which is contained in the brightness and flashing of eyes, creates a dazzling effect absolutely unknown to colder northern climes. Eyes,—so potent to bewitch and to command, are a strangely neglected influence in certain forms of social intercourse. English eyes are too often dull and downcast, and wear an inane expression of hypocrisy and prudery; unless they happen to be hard and glittering and meaningless; but in southern climes, they throw out radiant invitations, laughing assurances, brilliant mockeries, melting tendernesses, by the thousand flashes, and make a fire of feeling in the coldest air. And so in Angela's beautiful studio, among the whiteness of classic marbles, and the soft hues of richly falling draperies, fair faces shone out like flowers, lit up by eyes, whose light seemed to be vividly kindled by the heat of an amorous southern sun,—Venetian eyes blue as a corn-flower, Florentine eyes brown and brilliant as a russet leaf in autumn, Roman eyes black as night, Sicilian eyes of all hues, full of laughter and flame—and yet among all, no sweeter or more penetratingly tender eyes than those of Sylvie Hermenstein ever shot glances abroad to be-wilder and dazzle the heart of man. Not in largeness, colour or brilliancy lay their charm, but in deep, langour-ous, concentrated sweetness,—a sweetness so far-reach-ing from the orb to the soul that it was easy to sink away into their depths and dream,—and never wish to wake. Sylvie was looking her fairest that afternoon,—the weather was chilly, and the close-fitting black velvet dress with its cape-like collar of rich sables, well became her figure and delicately fair complexion, and many a spiteful little whisper concerning her went round among more showy but less attractive women,—many an involuntary but low murmur of admiration escaped from the more cautious lips of the men. She was talking to the Princesse D'Agramont, who with her brilliant dark beauty could afford to confess ungrudgingly the charm of a woman so *spirituelle* as Sylvie, and who, between various careless nods and smiles to her acquaintance, was detailing to her with much animation the account of her visit to the Marquis Fontenelle before leaving Paris.

"He must be very *épris!*" said the Princesse laugh-ing, "For he froze into a rigid statue of virtue when I suggested that he should escort me to Rome! I did not wait to see the effect of my announcement that *you* were already there!"

Sylvie lowered her eyes, and a faint colour crimsoned her cheeks.

"Then he knows where I am?" she asked.

"If he believes *me,* he knows," replied Loyse D'Agra-mont, "But perhaps he does not believe me! All Paris was talking about the Abbé Vergniaud and his son 'Gys Grandit', when I left, and the Marquis appeared as in-terested in that *esclandre* as he can ever be interested in anything or anybody. So perhaps he forgot my visit as soon as it was ended. Abbé Vergniaud is very ill by the way. His self-imposed punishment, and his unexpected reward in the personality of his son, have proved a little too much for him,—both he and ' Grandit ' are at my Chateau," here she raised her lorgnon, and peered through it with an inquisitive air, " *Tiens!* There is the dear Varillo making himself agreeable as usual to all the ladies! When does the marriage come off between him and our gifted Sovrani?"

" I do not know," answered Sylvie, with a little dubious look, " Nothing is contemplated in that way until Angela's great picture is exhibited."

The Princesse D'Agramont looked curiously at the opposite wall where an enormous white covering was closely roped and fastened across an invisible canvas, which seemed to be fully as large as Raffaelle's " Transfiguration ".

" Still a mystery? " she queried, " Has she never shown it even to you? "

Sylvie shook her head.

" Never! " and then breaking off with a sudden exclamation she turned in the direction of the door where there was just now a little movement and murmur of interest, as the slim tall figure of a man moved slowly and with graceful courtesy through the assemblage towards that corner of the studio where the Cardinal sat, his niece standing near him, and there made a slight yet perfectly reverential obeisance.

" Mr. Leigh! " cried Angela, " How glad I am to see you! "

" And I too," said the Cardinal, extending his hand, and kindly raising Aubrey before he could complete his formal genuflection, " You have not wasted much of your time in Florence! "

" My business was soon ended there," replied Aubrey. " It merely concerned the saving of a famous religious picture—but I find the modern Florentines so dead to beauty that it is almost impossible to rouse them to any sort of exertion . . . " Here he paused, as Angela with a smile moved quickly past him saying,

" One moment, Mr. Leigh! I must introduce you to one of my dearest friends! "

He waited, with a curious sense of impatience, and full beating of his heart, answering quite mechanically one or two greetings from Florian Varillo and other acquaintances who knew and recognised him—and then felt, rather than saw, that he was looking into the deep sweet eyes of the woman who had flung him a rose from the balcony of the angels, and that her face, sweet as the rose itself, was smiling upon him. As in a dream he heard her name, "The Comtesse Sylvie Hermenstein" and his own, "Mr. Aubrey Leigh"; he was dimly aware of bowing, and of saying something vague and formal, but all the actuality of his being was for the moment shaken and transfigured, and only one strong and overwhelming conviction remained,—the conviction that, in the slight creature who stood before him gracefully acknowledging his salutation, he had met his fate. Now he understood as he had never done before what the poet-philosopher meant by "the celestial rapture falling out of heaven";—for that rapture fell upon him and caught him up in a cloud of glory, with all the suddenness and fervour which must ever attend the true birth of the divine passion in strong and tender natures. The calculating sensualist can never comprehend this swiftly exalted emotion, this immediate radiation of light through all life, which is like the sun breaking through clouds on a dark day. The sensualist has by self-indulgence, blunted the edge of feeling, and it is impossible for him to experience this delicate sensation of exquisite delight,—this marvellous assurance that here and now, face to face, stands the One for whom all time shall be merged into a Song of Love, and upon whom all the sweetest thoughts of imagination shall be brought to bear for the furtherance of mutual joy! Aubrey's strong spirit, set to stern labour for so long, and trained to toil with but scant peace for reward, now sprang up as it were to its full height of capability and resolution,—yet its power was tempered with that tender humility which, in a noble-hearted man, bends before the presence of the woman whose love for him shall make her sacred. All his instincts bade him recognise Sylvie as the completion and fulfilment of his life, and this consciousness was so strong and imperative that it made him more than gentle to her as he spoke his first few words, and obtained her consent to escort her to a seat not far off from the Cardinal, yet removed sufficiently from the rest of the people to enable them to converse uninterruptedly for a time. Angela watched them, well pleased;—she too had quick instincts, and as she noted Sylvie's sudden flush under the deepening admiration of Aubrey's eyes, she thought to herself, " If it could only be ! If she could forget Fontenelle—if———"

But here her thoughts were interrupted by her own "ideal",—Florian Varillo who, catching her hand abruptly, drew her aside for a moment.

"*Carissima mia,* why did you not introduce the Princesse D'Agramont to Mr. Leigh rather than the Comtesse Hermenstein? The Princesse is of his way of thinking,—Sylvie is not!" and he finished his sentence by slipping an arm round her waist quickly, and whispering a word which brought the colour to her cheeks and the sparkle to her eyes, and made her heart beat so quickly that she could not speak for a moment. Yet she was supposed by the very man whose embrace thus moved her, to be "passionless!"

"You must not call her 'Sylvie'," she answered at last, "She does not like such familiarity—even from you!"

"No? Did she tell you so?" and Florian laughed, "What a confiding little darling you are, Angela! I assure you, Sylvie Hermenstein is not so very particular— but there!—I will not say a word against any friend of yours! But do you not see she is already trying to make a fool of Aubrey Leigh?"

Angela looked across the room and saw Leigh's intellectual head bending closely towards the soft gold of Sylvie's hair, and smiled.

"I do not think Sylvie would willingly make a fool of anyone," she answered simply, "She is too loyal and sincere. I fancy you do not understand her, Florian. She is full of fascination, but she is not heartless."

But Florian entertained a very lively remembrance of the recent rebuff given to himself by the fair Comtesse, and took his masculine vengeance by the suggested innuendo of a shrug of his shoulders and a lifting of his eyebrows. But he said no more just then, and merely contented himself with coaxingly abstracting a rose out of Angela's bodice, kissing it, and placing it in his own buttonhole. This was one of his "pretty drawing-room tricks" according to Loyse D'Agramont, who always laughed unmercifully at these kind of courtesies. They had been the stock-in-trade of her late husband, and she knew exactly what value to set upon them. But Angela was easily moved by tenderness, and the smallest word of love, the lightest caress made her happy and satisfied for a long time. She had the simple primitive notions of an innocent woman who could not possibly imagine infidelity in a sworn love. Looking at her sweet face, earnest eyes, and slim graceful figure now, as she moved away from Florian Varillo's side, and passed glidingly in and out among her guests, the Princesse D'Agramont, always watchful, wondered with a half sigh how she would take the blow of disillusion if it ever came; would it crush her, or would she rise the nobler and stronger for it?

"Many a one here in this room to-day," mused the Princesse, "would be glad if she fell vanquished in the hard fight! Many a man—shameful as it seems—would give a covert kick to her poor body. For there is nothing that frets and irks some male creatures so much as to see a woman attain by her own brain and hand a great position in the world, and when she has won her crown and throne they would deprive her of both, and trample her in the mud if they dared! *Some* male creatures— not all. Florian Varillo for instance. If he could only get the world to believe that he paints half Angela's pictures he would be quite happy. I daresay he does persuade a few outsiders to think it. But in Rome we know better. Poor Angela!"

And with another sigh she dismissed the subject from her mind for the moment, her attention being distracted by the appearance of Monsignor Gherardi, who just then entered and took up a position by the Cardinal's chair, looking the picture of imposing and stately affability. One glance of his eyes in the direction of Aubrey Leigh, where he sat absorbed in conversation with the Comtesse Hermenstein, had put the wily priest in an excellent humour, and nothing could exceed the deferential homage and attention he paid to Cardinal Bonpré, talking with him in low, confidential tones of the affairs which principally occupied their attention,—the miraculous cure of Fabien Doucet, and the defection of Vergniaud from the Church. Earnestly did the good Felix, thinking Gher-

ardi was a friend, explain again his utter unconsciousness
of any miracle having been performed at his hands, and
with equal fervour did he plead the cause of Vergniaud,
in the spirit and doctrine of Christ, pointing out that the
erring Abbé was, without any subterfuge at all, truly
within proximity of death, and that therefore it seemed
an almost unnecessary cruelty to set the ban of excommunication against a repentant and dying man.   Gherardi
heard all, with a carefully arranged facial expression of
sympathetic interest and benevolence, but gave neither
word nor sign of active partisanship in any cause. He had
another commission in charge from Moretti, and he
worked the conversation dexterously on, till he touched
the point of his secret errand.

"By the way," he said gently, "among your many
good and kindly works, I hear you have rescued a poor
stray boy from the streets of Rouen—and that he is
with you now. Is that true?"

"Quite true," replied the Cardinal, "But no particular goodness can be accredited to any servant of
the Gospel for trying to rescue an orphan child from
misery."

"No—no, certainly not!" assented Gherardi——
"But it is seldom that one as exalted in dignity as yourself
condescends——ah, pardon me!—you do not like that
word I see!"

"I do not understand it in *our* work," said the Cardinal, "There can be no 'condescension' in saving the
lost."

Gherardi was silent a moment, smiling a little to himself.   "What a simpleton is this Saint Felix!" he
thought.   "What a fool to run amuck at his own chances
of distinction and eminence!"

"And the boy is clever?" he said presently in kindly
accents—"Docile in conduct?—and useful to you?"

"He is a wonderful child!" answered the Cardinal
with unsuspecting candour and feeling, "Thoughtful beyond his years,—wise beyond his experience."

Gherardi shot a quick glance from under his eyelids
at the fine tranquil face of the venerable speaker, and
again smiled.

"You have no further knowledge of him?—no clue to
his parentage?"

"None."

Just then the conversation was interrupted by a little movement of eagerness,—people were pressing towards the grand piano which Florian Varillo had opened,—the Comtesse Sylvie Hermenstein was about to grant a general request made to her for a song. She moved slowly and with a touch of reluctance towards the instrument, Aubrey Leigh walking beside her.

"You are a musician yourself?—" she said, glancing up at him, "You play—or you sing?"

"I do a little of both," he answered, "But I shall be no rival to you! I have heard *you* sing!"

"You have? When?"

"The other night, or else I dreamed it," he said softly, "I have a very sweet echo of a song in my mind with words that sounded like '*Ti volglio bene*', and a refrain that I caught in the shape of a rose!"

Their eyes met—and what Emerson calls "the deification and transfiguration of life" began to stir Sylvie's pulses, and set her heart beating to a new and singular exaltation. The warm colour flushed her cheeks—the lustre brightened in her eyes, and she looked sweeter and more bewitching than ever as she loosened the rich sables from about her slim throat, and drawing off her gloves sat down to the piano. Florian Varillo lounged near her—she saw him not at all,—Angela came up to ask if she could play an accompaniment for her,—but she shook her bright head in a smiling negative, and her small white fingers running over the keys, played a rippling passage of a few bars while she raised her clear eyes to Aubrey and asked him,—

"Do you know an old Brittany song called '*Le Palais D'Iffry*'? No? It is just one of those many songs of the unattainable,—the search for the 'Fortunate Isles', or the 'Fata Morgana' of happiness."

"Is happiness nothing but a 'Fata Morgana'?" asked Aubrey gently, "Must it always vanish when just in sight?"

His eyes grew darkly passionate as he spoke, and again Sylvie's heart beat high, but she did not answer in words, —softening the notes of her prelude she sang in a rich mezzo-soprano, whose thrilling tone penetrated to every part of the room, the quaint old Breton ballad,

" Il serait un roi !
Mais quelqu'un a dit,
  ' Non !—Pas pour toi !
' Reste en prison,—ecoute le chant d'amour,
' Et le doux son des baisers que la Reine a promit
' A celui qui monte, sans peur et sans retour
  Au Palais D'Iffry !'
    Hélas, mon ami,
  C'est triste d'ecouter le chanson sans le chanter aussi ! "

Aubrey listened to the sweet far-reaching notes—
"*Sans peur, et sans retour, au Palais D'Iffry*" ! Thither
would he climb—to that enchanted palace of love with its
rainbow towers glittering in the " light that never was on
sea or land "—to the throne of that queen whose soft
eyes beckoned him—whose kiss waited for him—everything now must be for her—all the world for her sake,
willingly lost or willingly won! And what of the work
he had undertaken? The people to whom he had pledged
his life? The great Christ-message he had determined to
re-preach for the comfort of the million lost and sorrowful? His brows contracted,—and a sudden shadow
of pain clouded the frank clearness of his eyes. Gherardi's words came back to his memory,—" You have embarked in a most hopeless cause ! You will help the helpless, and as soon as they are rescued out of trouble they
will turn and rend you,—you will try to teach them the
inner mysteries of God's working and they will say you
are possessed of a devil ! " Then he thought of another
and grander saying—" Whoso, putting his hand to the
plough, looketh back, is not fit for the Kingdom of
God!—" and over all rang the enchanting call of the
siren's voice—

  " Et le doux son des baisers que la Reine a promit
  A celui qui monte, sans peur et sans retour
    Au Palais D'Iffry ! "

and he so lost himself in a tangle of thought that he did
not observe how closely Monsignor Gherardi was studying every expression of his face, and he started as if he
had been awakened from a dream when Sylvie's song
ceased, and Sylvie herself glanced up at him.

" Music seems to make you sad, Mr. Leigh! " she said
timidly.

"Not music—but sometimes the fancies which music engenders, trouble me," he answered, bending his earnest searching eyes upon her, and wondering within himself whether such a small, slight gossamer thing of beauty, brilliant as a tropical humming-bird, soft and caressable as a dove, could possibly be expected to have the sweet yet austere fortitude and firmness needed to be a true "helpmeet" to him in the work he had undertaken, and the life he had determined to lead. He noted all the dainty trifles of her toilette half doubtingly, half admiringly,—the knot of rich old lace that fastened her sables,—the solitary star-like diamond which held that lace in careless position—the numerous little touches of taste and elegance which made her so unique and graceful among women—and a pang shot through his heart as he thought of her wealth, and his own poverty. She meanwhile, on her part, was studying him with all the close interest that a cultured and refined woman feels, who is strongly conscious of having awakened a sudden and masterful passion in a man whom she secretly admires. A triumphant sense of her own power moved her, allied to a much more rare and beautiful emotion—the sense of soul-submission to a greater and higher life than her own. And so it chanced that never had she looked so charming—never had her fair cheeks flushed a prettier rose—never had her easy fascination of manner been so bewitchingly troubled by hesitation and timidity—never had her eyes sparkled with a softer or more irresistible languor. Aubrey felt that he was fast losing his head as he watched her move, speak, and smile,—and with a sudden bracing up of his energies resolved to make his *adieux* at once.

"I must be going,—" he began to say, when his arm was touched from behind, and he turned to confront Florian Varillo, who smiled with all the brilliancy his white and even teeth could give him.

"Why must you be going?" asked Varillo cheerily, "Why not stay and dine with my future father-in-law, and Angela, and the eminent Cardinal? We shall all be charmed!"

"Thanks, no!—I have letters to write to England . . ."

"Good-bye!" said the Comtesse Hermenstein at this

juncture,—" I am going to drive the Princesse D'Agramont round the Pincio, will you join us, Mr. Leigh? The Princesse is anxious to know you—may I introduce you?"

And without waiting for a reply, as the Princesse was close at hand, she performed the ceremony of introduction at once in her own light graceful fashion.

" Truly a strange meeting!" laughed Varillo, " You three ought to be very good friends! The Comtesse Hermenstein is a devout daughter of the Roman Church —Madame la Princesse is against all Churches—and you, Mr. Leigh, are making your own Church!"

Aubrey did not reply. It was not the time or place to discuss either his principles or his work, moreover he was strangely troubled by hearing Sylvie described as " a devout daughter of the Roman Church."

" I am charmed!" said the Princesse D'Agramont, " Good fortune really seems to favour me for once, for in the space of a fortnight I have met two of the most distinguished men of the time, ' Gys Grandit ', and Aubrey Leigh!"

Aubrey bowed.

" You are too kind, Madame! Grandit and I have been friends for some years, though we have never seen each other since I parted from him in Touraine. But we have always corresponded."

" You have of course heard who he really is? The son of Abbé Vergniaud?" continued the Princesse.

" I have heard—but only this morning, and I do not know any of the details of the story."

" Then you must certainly come and drive with us," said Loyse D'Agramont, " for I can tell you all about it. I wrote quite a brilliant essay on it for the *Figaro,* and called it ' Church Morality '!" She laughed. " Come,— we will take no denial!"

Aubrey tried to refuse, but could not,—the attraction, —the ' will o' the wisp' magnetism of Sylvie's dainty personality drew him on, and in a few minutes, after taking respectful leave of the Cardinal, Prince Sovrani, and Angela, he left the studio in the company of the two ladies. Passing Monsignor Gherardi on the way out he received a wide smile and affable salute from that personage.

"A pleasant drive to you, Mr. Leigh," he said, "The view from the Pincio is considered extremely fine!"

Aubrey made some formal answer and went his way. Gherardi returned to the studio and resumed his confidential talk with Bonpré, while one by one the visitors departed, till at last the only persons left in the vast room were Angela and Florian Varillo, Prince Pietro, and the two dignitaries of the Church. Florian was irritated, and made no secret of his irritation to his fair betrothed, with whom he sat a little apart from the others in the room.

"Do you want a love affair between Sylvie Hermenstein and that fellow Leigh?" he enquired, "If so, it is probable that your desire will be gratified!"

Angela raised her delicate eyebrows in a little surprise.

"I have no wish at all in the matter," she answered, "except to see Sylvie quite happy."

"How very romantic is the friendship between you two women!" said Varillo somewhat sarcastically, "You wish to see Sylvie happy,—and the other day she told me she would form her judgment of me by *your* happiness! Really, it is most admirable and touching!"

Angela began to feel somewhat puzzled. Petulance and temper were not in her character, and she was annoyed to see any touch of them in her lover.

"Are you cross, Florian?" she asked gently, "Has something worried you to-day?"

"Oh, I am often worried!" he replied;—and had he spoken the exact truth he would have confessed that he was always seriously put out when he was not the centre of attraction and the cynosure of women's eyes—"But what does it matter! Do not think at all about me, *cara mia!* Tell me of yourself. How goes the picture?"

"It is nearly finished now," she replied, her beautiful violet eyes dilating and brightening with the fervour that inspired her whenever she thought of her work, "I rise very early, and begin to paint with the first gleam of daylight. I think I shall have it ready sooner than I expected. The Queen has promised to come and see it here before it is exhibited to the public."

"Margherita di Savoja is very amiable!" said Florian, with a tinge of envy he could not wholly conceal, "She is always useful as a patron."

A quick flush of pride rose to Angela's cheeks.

"I do not need any patronage, Florian," she said simply yet with a little coldness, "You know that I should resent it were it offered to me. If my work is not good in itself, no 'royal' approval can make it so. Queen Margherita visits me as a friend—not as a patron."

"There now! I have vexed you!" And Florian took her hand and kissed it. "Forgive me, sweetest!—Look at me—give me a smile!—Ah! That is kind!" and he conveyed an expression of warm tenderness into his eyes as Angela turned her charming face upon him, softened and radiant with the quick affection which always moved her at his voice and caress. "I spoke foolishly! Of course my Angela could not be patronised—she is too independent and gifted. I am very glad the Queen is coming!"

"The Queen is coming?" echoed Gherardi, who just then advanced. "Here? To see Donna Sovrani's picture? Ah, that will be an excellent advertisement! But it would have been far better, my dear young lady, had you arranged with me, or with some other one of my confrères, to have the picture sent to the Vatican for the inspection of His Holiness. The Popes, as you know, have from time immemorial been the best patrons of art!"

"My picture would not please the Pope," said Angela quietly, "It would more probably win his denunciation than his patronage."

Gherardi smiled. The idea of a woman—a mere woman imagining that anything which she could do was powerful enough to bring down Papal denunciation! The strange conceit of these feminine geniuses! He could almost have laughed aloud. But he merely looked her over blandly and forbearingly.

"I am sorry," he said, "very sorry you should consider such a thing as possible of your work. But no doubt you speak on impulse. Your distinguished uncle, the Cardinal Bonpré, would be sadly distressed if your picture should contain anything of a nature to bring you any condemnation from the Vatican,—and your father . . ."

"Leave me out of it, if you please!" interrupted Prince Pietro, "I have nothing whatever to do with it! Angela works with a free hand; none of us have seen what she is doing."

"Not even you, Signor Varillo?" enquired Gherardi affably.

"Oh, I?" laughed Florian carelessly, "No indeed! I have not the least idea of the subject or the treatment!"

"A mystery then?" said Gherardi, still preserving his bland suavity of demeanour, "But permit me, Donna Sovrani, to express the hope that when the veil is lifted a crown of laurels may be disclosed for you!"

Angela thanked him by a silent inclination of her head, and in a few minutes the stately Vatican spy had taken his leave. As he disappeared the Cardinal rose from his chair and moving somewhat feebly, prepared to return to his own apartments.

"Dearest uncle, will you not stay with us to-night? Or are you too tired?" asked Angela as she came to his side.

He raised her sweet face between his two wrinkled hands and looked at her long and earnestly.

"Dear child!" he said, "Dear brave little child! For you must always be nothing more than a child to me,—tell me, are you sure you are moved by the right spirit in the painting of your picture?"

"I think so!" answered Angela gently, "Indeed, indeed, I think so! I know that according to the teaching of our Master Christ, it is a *true* spirit!"

Slowly the Cardinal released her, and slowly and with impressive earnestness traced the Cross on her fair brows.

"God bless you!" he said, "And God help you too! For if you work by 'the Spirit of Truth, the Comforter', remember it is the same Spirit which our Lord tells us 'the world cannot receive because it seeth Him not, neither knoweth Him.' And to testify of a Spirit which the world cannot receive makes the world very hard to you!"

And with these words he gently leaned on the arm she proffered and left the studio with her, the rich glow and voluminous folds of his scarlet robes contrasting vividly with the simple black gown which Angela wore without other adornment than a Niphétos rose to relieve its sombreness. As she went with her uncle she looked over her shoulder and smiled an adieu to Florian,—he, in his turn lightly kissed his hand to her, and then addressed Prince Pietro, who, with the care of a man to whom expense is a consideration, was putting out some of the tall lamps that had illumined the dusk of the late afternoon.

"The good Cardinal is surely breaking up," he said carelessly, "He looks extremely frail!"

"Young men sometimes break up before old ones!" returned the Prince drily, "Felix is strong enough yet. You dine with us to-night?"

"If you permit—" said Varillo, with a graceful salutation.

"Oh, my permission does not matter!" said Sovrani eyeing him narrowly, "Whatever gives pleasure to Angela must needs please me. She is all that is left to me now in an exceedingly dull world. *A riverderci!* At eight we dine."

Florian nodded,—and took his departure, and the Prince for a moment stood hesitating, looking at the great white covering on the wall which concealed his daughter's mysterious work. His tall upright figure stiff and sombre, looked as if cast in bronze in the half light shed by the wood fire,—one lamp was still burning, and after a pause he moved from his rigid attitude of gloomy consideration, and extinguished it, then glancing round to see that all was in order, he left the studio, closing its great oaken door behind him. Five minutes after he had gone a soft step trod the polished floor, and the young Manuel, holding a lighted taper, entered all alone. The flame of the little torch he carried cast a soft golden glow about him as he walked noiselessly through the great empty room, his blue eyes lifted to the marble heads of gods and heroes which occupied their different positions on the gilded and oaken brackets set against the tapestried walls,—and presently he paused in front of Angela's hidden work. It was but a moment's pause; and then, still with the same light step, and the same bright glow reflected from the flame that glittered in his hand, he passed through the room, lifted the velvet portière at the other end where there was another door leading to the corridor connected with the Cardinal's apartments, and so unnoticed, disappeared.

XXIII.

Meanwhile, the Marquis Fontenelle had been nearly a fortnight in Rome, living a sufficiently curious sort of life, and passing his time in a constant endeavour to avoid being discovered and recognised by any of his numerous acquaintances who were arriving there for the winter. His chief occupation was of course to watch the Comtesse Sylvie,—and he was rewarded for his untiring pains by constant and bewitching glimpses of her. Sometimes he would see her driving, wrapped in furs, her tiny Japanese dog curled up in a fold of her sables, and on her lap a knot of violets, the fresh scent of which came to him like a sweet breath on the air as she passed. Once he almost met her, face to face in the gardens of the Villa Borghese, walking all alone, and reading a book in which she seemed to be deeply interested. He made a few cautious enquiries about her, and learnt that she lived very quietly,— that she received certain " great " people,—especially Cardinals and Monsignori, notably Monsignor Gherardi, who was a constant visitor. But of any closer admirer he never gathered the slightest rumour, till one afternoon, just when the sun was sinking in full crimson glory behind the dome of St. Peter's, he saw her carriage come to a sudden halt on the Pincio and she herself leaned out of it to shake hands with, and talk to a tall fair man, who seemed to be on exceptionally friendly terms with her. It is true she was accompanied in the carriage by the famous Sovrani,—but that fact did not quell the sudden flame of jealousy which sprang up in Fontenelle's mind —for both ladies appeared equally charmed with the fair man, and their countenances were radiant with pleasure and animation all the time they were in conversation with him. When the carriage resumed its round again, the Marquis sauntered by a side path where he could take quiet observation of his apparent rival, who walked past him with a firm light step, looking handsome, happy, and amazingly confident. There was an old man raking the path, and of him Fontenelle asked carelessly,

"Do you know who that gentleman is?"

The gardener looked up and smiled.

"*Ah, si, si! Il Signor Inglese! Molto generoso! Il Signor Aubri Lee!*"

Aubrey Leigh! A "celebrity" then,—an English author;—not that all English authors are considered "celebrities" in Rome. Italian society makes very short work of spurious art, and closes its doors ruthlessly against mere English "Grub Street". But Aubrey Leigh was more than an author,—he was an influential power in the world, as the Marquis well knew.

"A great religious reformer! And yet a victim to the little Sylvie!" he mused, "Well! The two things will not work together. Though truly Sylvie would captivate a John Knox or a Cromwell. I really think,—I really do begin to think, that rather than lose her altogether, I must marry her!"

And he went back to the obscure hotel where he had chosen temporarily to reside in a meditative mood, and as he entered, was singularly annoyed to see a flaring poster outside, announcing the arrival of Miraudin and his whole French Company in Rome for a few nights only. The name "MIRAUDIN" glared at him in big, fat, red letters on a bright yellow ground; and involuntarily he muttered,

"D——n the fellow! Can I go nowhere in the world without coming across him!"

Irritated, and yet knowing his irritation to be foolish,— for after all, what was the famous actor to him?—what was there in his personality to annoy him beyond the trivial fact of a curious personal resemblance?—he retired to his room in no pleasant humour, and sitting down began to write a letter to Sylvie asking her to be his wife. Yet somehow the power of expression seemed lacking, and once or twice he laid down his pen in a fit of abstraction, wondering why, when he had sought Sylvie as a lover only, he had been able to write the most passionate love phrases, full or ardour and poetry, and now, when he was about to make her the offer of his whole life, his sentences were commonplace and almost cold. And presently he tore up what he had beeen writing, and paced the room impatiently.

"The fact is I shall make a bad husband, and I know it!" he said candidly to himself, "And Sylvie will make a great mistake if she accepts me!"

He walked to the window and looked out. His hotel was not in a fashionable or frequented quarter of Rome, and the opposite view of the street was anything but en-livening. Dirty, frowsy women,—idle men, lounging along with the slouching gait which is common to the 'unemployed' Italian,—half-naked children, running hither and thither in the mud, and screaming like tortured wild animals,—this kind of shiftless, thriftless humanity, pictured against the background of ugly modern houses, such as one might find in a London back slum, made up a cheerless prospect, particularly as the blue sky was clouded and it was beginning to rain. One touch of col-our brightened the scene for a moment, when a girl with a yellow handkerchief tied round her head passed along, carrying a huge flat basket overflowing with bunches of purple violets, and as Fontenelle caught the hue, and im-agined the fragrance of the flowers, he was surprised to feel his eyes smart with a sudden sting of tears. The pic-ture of Sylvie Hermenstein, with her child-like head, fair hair, and deep blue eyes, floated before him,—she was fond of violets, and whenever she wore them, their odour seemed to be the natural exhalation of her sweet and *spirituelle* personality.

"She is much too good for me!" he said half aloud, "To be perfectly honest with myself, I know I have no stability of character, and I cannot imagine myself re-maining constant to any woman for more than six months. And the best way is to be perfectly straight-forward about it."

He sat down again, and without taking any more thought wrote straight from the heart of his present humour, addressing her by the name he had once play-fully bestowed upon her.

"*Enchanteresse!* I am here in Rome, and this brief letter is to ask, without preamble or apology, whether you will do me the infinite honour to become my wife. I con-fess to you honestly that I am not worth this consideration on your part, for I am not to be relied upon. I repose no confidence in myself, therefore I will leave it to you to measure my audacity in making the suggestion that you should place a lifetime's confidence in me. But with all my heart, (as much as I know of it at the present), I desire to show you what respect so poor a life as mine can give to one who deserves all tenderness, as well as trust. If I may hope that you will pardon my past follies and *libertinage* with regard to you,—if you can love me well enough to wear my not too exalted name, and preserve my remaining stock of honour, summon me to your presence, and I will endeavour, by such devotion and fidelity as in me lies, to atone for whatsoever offence I may have given you previously by my too passionate pursuit of your beauty. Yours, unless you decide my fate otherwise,

" GUY BEAUSIRE DE FONTENELLE. "

Thrusting this note into an envelope he hastily sealed it, but decided not to post it till late at night, in order that Sylvie might only receive it with the early morning, when her mind was fresh, and unswayed by any opinions or events of a long day. And to pass the time he strolled out to one of the many " *osterie*," or winehouses which abound in Rome,—a somewhat famous example of its kind in the Via Quattro Fontane. Choosing a table where he could sit with his back turned towards the door, so as to avoid being seen by either strangers or possible friends, he took up the *Giornale Romano*, and ordered a " *mezzo-litro* " of the " Genzano " wine, for which that particular house has long been celebrated. He sat there about half an hour thus quietly reading,— scarcely hearing the loud voices and louder laughter of the men who came and went around him, when suddenly the name " Sylvie Hermenstein " caught his ear. It was spoken carelessly and accompanied with a laugh. Quietly laying down his newspaper, he sat very still in his chair, keeping his back turned to the groups of wine drinkers who were gathering in large numbers as the evening advanced, and listened.

" The most delicious little *bonbon* in the whole box! *Jolie à craquer!* " said a man's voice.

"*Chocolat fondant! Garantie très pure!*" cried another, his words being followed by a shout of laughter.

Fontenelle gripped the arm of his chair, and held himself rigid, but ready to spring.

"The Church always knows where to find the prettiest women," said the first man who had spoken, "from the Santissima Madonna downwards! What would become of the Pope if it were not for the women!"

"Bah! The Pope is only one man, but what would become of all the *Monsignori?*" asked a voice different to the rest in mellowness and deep quality, but with a touch of insolent mockery in its tone.

Another burst of laughter answered him.

Fontenelle turned in his chair and looked at the last speaker, and to his amazement saw the actor, Miraudin. He was leaning carelessly against the wine counter, a half-emptied "*fiaschetto*" in front of him, and a full glass of wine in his hand.

"The Monsignori would be all desolate bachelors!" he went on, lazily, "And the greatest rascal in the Vatican, Domenico Gherardi, would no longer be the fortunate possessor of the wealth, the influence, and the dear embraces of the fascinating Hermenstein!"

Scarcely had he spoken when the glass he held was dashed out of his hand, and Fontenelle, white with fury, struck him smartly and full across the face. A scene of the wildest confusion and uproar ensued. All the men in the wine-shop crowded around them, and for a moment Miraudin, blinded by the blow, and the wine that had splashed up against his eyes, did not see who had struck him, but as he recovered from the sudden shock and stared at his opponent, he broke into a wild laugh.

"*Diantre! Bon soir, Monsieur le Marquis!* Upon my life, there is something very strange in this! Fate or the devil, or both! Well! What now!"

"You are a liar and a blackguard!" said Fontenelle fiercely, "And unless you apologise for your insult to the lady whose name you have presumed to utter with your mountebank tongue——"

"Apologise! I! *Moi!—génie de France!* Never!" retorted Miraudin with an air of swaggering audacity, "All women are alike! I speak from experience!"

White to the lips, the Marquis Fontenelle looked around.

"Are there any *men* here?" he asked, eying the crowd about him with ineffable hauteur.

A young fellow stepped forward. "At your command, Marquis! You served me once—I shall be happy to serve you now!"

Quickly Fontenelle shook hands with this timely friend. He recognised in him a young Italian officer, named Ruspardi, an acquaintance of some years back, to whom he had chanced to be useful in a pressing moment of need.

"Thanks! Arrange everything for me, will you, Ruspardi? And as quickly as possible!"

"It is nearly midnight now," said Ruspardi in a low tone, "Shall we say five or six in the morning?"

"Yes—anything you like—but quickly!"

Then raising his head haughtily, he addressed Miraudin in distinct tones.

"Monsieur Miraudin, you have greatly insulted and falsely slandered a lady whom I have the honour to know. I have struck you for your lie; and consider you worthy of no further treatment save a horsewhipping in public. Gentlemen do not as a rule condescend to meet their paid servants—actors and the like,—in single combat—but I will do you that honour!"

And with these words he bowed haughtily to all present, and left the scene of noisy disorder.

Out in the streets the moonlight lay in broad silver bands, like white glistening ribbon spread in shining strips across the blackness, and there was a moisture in the air which,—dropped as it were fresh, from the surrounding hills,—cooled Fontenelle's flushed face and burning brows. He walked rapidly,—he had a vague, unformed desire in his mind to see Sylvie again if possible. He knew where she lived, and he soon turned down the street where the quaint old central balcony of the Casa D'Angeli thrust itself forwand into the moon-rays among the sculptured angels' wings,—and he saw that the windows were open. Pausing underneath he waited, hesitating—full of strange thoughts and stranger regrets. How poor and valueless seemed his life as he regarded it now!—now when he had voluntarily placed it in jeopardy! What had he done with his days of youth and prime? Frittered away every valuable moment,—thrown to the winds every costly opportunity,—spent his substance on light women who had kissed and clung to him one day, and repulsed him the next. Well—and after? His heart beat thickly, —if he could only see Sylvie for a moment! Hush! There was a murmur—a voice—a ripple of sweet laughter; and moving cautiously back into the shadows, he looked up—yes!—there she was—clad in some soft silvery stuff that gathered a thousand sparkles from the light of the moon,—her fair hair caught up in a narrow circlet of diamonds, and her sweet face purely outlined against the dark worn stone of one of the great carved angel-wings. But someone was with her,—someone whom Fontenelle recognised at once by the classic shape of his head and bright curly hair,—the man whom he had seen that very day on the Pincio,—Aubrey Leigh. With a jealous tightening at his heart, Fontenelle saw that Leigh held the soft plume of downy feathers which served Sylvie for a fan, and that he was lightly waving it to and fro as he talked to her in the musical, all-potent voice which had charmed thousands, and would surely not be without its fascination for the sensitive ears of a woman. Moving a little closer he tried to hear what was being said,—but Leigh spoke very softly, and Sylvie answered with equal softness, so that he could catch no distinct word. Yet the mere tone of these two voices melted into a harmony more dulcet and perfect than could be endured by Fontenelle with composure, and uttering an impatient exclamation at his own folly he hastily left his retreat, and with one parting glance up at the picture of fair loveliness above him walked swiftly away. Returning to his hotel he saw the letter that he had written to Sylvie lying on the table, and he at once posted it. Then he began to prepare for his encounter with Miraudin. He dressed quickly,—wrote a few business letters,—and was about to lie down for a rest of an hour or so when the swift and furious galloping of a horse's hoofs awoke the echoes of the quiet street, and almost before he had time to realise what had happened, his friend Ruspardi stood before him, breathless and wild with excitement.

" Marquis, you are tricked! " he cried, " Everything is

prepared—seconds,—pistols,—all! But your man—your man has gone!"

"Gone!" exclaimed Fontenelle furiously, "Where?"

"Out of Rome! In a common *fiacre*—taking his latest mistress, one of the stage-women with him. They were seen driving by the Porta Pia towards the Campagna half an hour ago! He dare not face fire—bully and coward that he is!"

"I will go after him!" said Fontenelle promptly, "Half an hour ahead, you say! Good!—I will catch him up. Can I get a horse anywhere?"

"Take mine," said Ruspardi eagerly, "he is perfectly fresh—just out of the stable. Have you weapons?"

"Yes," and the Marquis unlocked a case, and loading two, placed them in a travelling holder. Then, turning to Ruspardi he shook hands.

"Thanks, a thousand times! There are a few letters here—see to them if I should not come back."

"What are you going to do?" asked Ruspardi, his excitement beginning to cool a little, now that he saw the possible danger into which Fontenelle was voluntarily rushing.

"Persuade the worthy mountebank either to come back or fight at once on whatever ground I find him, and assume to be a gentleman—for once!" said Fontenelle, carelessly. "*Addio!*"

And without further words he hurried off, and tossing a twenty-franc piece to the sleepy hotel porter who was holding Ruspardi's horse outside, he flung himself into the saddle and galloped away. Ruspardi, young and hot-blooded, was of too mercurial a disposition to anticipate any really serious results of the night's adventure;—his contempt for a coward was far greater than his fear of death, and he was delighted to think that in all probability the Marquis would use his riding-whip on Miraudin's back rather than honour him by a pistol shot. And so dismissing all fears from his mind he took Fontenelle's letters in his charge, and went straight out of the hotel singing gaily, charmed with the exciting thought of the midnight chase which was going on, and the possible drubbing and discomfiture of the "celebrated" Miraudin.

Meanwhile, under the flashing stars, and through the

sleeping streets of Rome, the Marquis galloped with almost breakneck haste. He was a daring rider, and the spirited animal he bestrode soon discovered the force of his governing touch,—the resolve of his urging speed. He went by the Porta Pia, remembering Ruspardi's hurried description of the route taken by the runaway actor, and felt, rather than saw the outline of the Villa Torlonia, as he rushed past, and the Basilica of St. Agnese Fuori le Mura, which is supposed to cover the tomb of the child-martyr St. Agnes,—then across the Ponte Nomentano, till, two miles further on, in the white radiance of the moon, he perceived, driving rapidly ahead of him, the vehicle of which he was in pursuit. Letting the reins fall loosely on the neck of his straining steed, he raised himself in his stirrups, and by his own movements assisted the animal's now perfectly reckless gallop,—and at last, hearing the flying hoofs behind, the driver of the *fiacre* became seized with panic, and thinking of possible brigands and how to pacify them, he suddenly pulled up and came to a dead halt. A head was thrust out of the carriage window,—Miraudin's head,—and Miraudin's voice shouted in bad Italian,

"What are you stopping for, rascal! On with you! On with you! Five hundred francs for your best speed!"

Scarcely had he uttered the words when the Marquis gained the side of the vehicle, and pulling up his horse till it almost fell in rearing backwards, he cried furiously,

"*Lache! Tu vas te crêver sur terre avant je te quitte!*"

And he struck his riding-whip full in the actor's face.

Springing out of the *fiacre* Miraudin confronted his antagonist. His hat was off—and his countenance, marked as it was with the crimson line of the lash, lightened with laughter.

"Again! *Monsieur le Marquis, je vous salue!*" he said, "*Kismet!* One cannot escape it! Better to fight with you, *beau sire*, than with destiny! I am ready!"

Fontenelle at once dismounted, and tied his horse to the knotted bough of a half-withered tree. Taking his pistols out of their holder he proffered them to Miraudin.

"Choose!" he said curtly, "Or use your own if you have any,—but mine are loaded,—take care yours are!

Play no theatrical tricks on such a stage as this!" And
then he gave a comprehensive wave of his hand towards
the desolate waste of the Campagna around them, and
the faint blue misty lines of the Alban hills just rimmed
with silver in the rays of the moon.

At the first sight of the pistols the driver of the *fiacre,*
who had been more or less stupefied till now, by the suddenness of the adventure, gave a sort of whining cry, and
climbing down from his box fell on his knees before
Miraudin, and then ran a few paces and did the same
thing in front of the Marquis, imploring both men not
to fight,—not to get killed, on account of the trouble it
would cause to him, the coachman;—and with a high fal-
setto shriek a lady flung herself out of the recesses of the
closed vehicle, and clung to the actor's arm.

"*Mon Dieu! Mon Dieu!* What is it you would do?"
she cried, "Be killed out here on the Campagna? and not
a soul in sight—not a house—not a shelter? And what
is to become of me!—Me!—Me!—" and she tapped her
heaving bosom in melodramatic style, "Have you thought
of *me?*"

"You—you!" laughed Miraudin, tearing off the lace
veil which she wore wrapped loosely round her head and
shoulders, "You, Jeanne Richaud! What is to become
of you? The same fate will attend you that attends all
such little moths of the footlights! Perhaps à dozen
more lovers after me—then old age, and the care of a
third-class lodging-house for broken-down actors!"
Here he chose his weapon. "At your service, Marquis!"

Jeanne Richaud, a *soubrette,* whose chief stock-in-trade
had been her large dark eyes and shapely legs, uttered a
desperate scream, and threw herself at the feet of the
Marquis Fontenelle.

"*Monsieur! Monsieur!* Think for a moment! This
combat is unequal—out of rule! You are a gentleman,
—a man of honour!—would you fight without seconds?
It is murder—murder——!"

Here she broke off, terrified in spite of herself by the
immovability of Fontenelle's attitude, and the coldness of
his eyes.

"I regret to pain you, Madame," he said stiffly, "This
combat was arranged according to rule between Monsieur Miraudin and myself some hours since—and though

it seems he did not intend to keep his engagement I intend to keep mine! The principals in the fight are here, —seconds are, as their name implies, a secondary matter. We must do without them."

"By no means!" exclaimed Miraudin, "We have them! Here they are! You, Jeanne, will you be my second—how often you have seconded me in many a devil's game—and you—*cochon d'un cocher!*—you will for once in your life support the honour of a Marquis!"

And with these words he seized the unhappy Roman cab-driver by the collar of his coat, and flung him towards Fontenelle, who took not the slightest notice of him as he lay huddled up and wailing on the grass, but merely stood his ground, silently waiting. Mademoiselle Jeanne Richaud however was not so easily disposed of. Throwing herself on the cold ground, thick with the dust of dead Cæsars, she clung to Miraudin, pouring out a torrent of vociferous French, largely intermixed with a special slang of the Paris streets, and broken by the hysterical yells when she saw her "protector" throw off his coat, and, standing in his shirt-sleeves, take close observation of the pistol he held.

"Is this your care of me?" she cried, "*Mon Dieu!* What a thing is a man! Here am I alone in a strange country—and you endanger your life for some quarrel of which I know nothing,—yet you pretend to love me! *Nom de Jésus!* What is your love!"

"You do well to ask," said Miraudin, laughing carelessly, "What is my love! A passing fancy, *chére petite!* We actors simulate love too well to ever feel it! Out of the way, *jou-jou!* Your life will be amusing so long as you keep a little *beauté de diable*. After that—the lodging-house!"

He pushed her aside, but she still clung pertinaciously to his arm.

"Victor! Victor!" she wailed, "Will you not look at me—will you not kiss me!"

Miraudin wheeled round, and stared at her amazed.

"Kiss you!" he echoed, "*Pardieu!* Would you care! Jeanne! Jeanne! You are a little mad,—the moonlight is too much for you! To-morrow I will kiss you, when the sun rises—or if I am not here—why, somebody else will!"

"Who is the woman you are fighting for?" she suddenly demanded, springing up from her crouching position with flushed cheeks and flashing eyes. Miraudin looked at her with nonchalant admiration.

" I wish you would have looked like that sometimes on my stage," he said, " You would have brought down the house! ' Woman!' No ' woman ' at all, but *women!* The glamour of them—the witchery of them—women!— the madness of them! Women!—The *one* woman saves when the *one* woman exists, but then,—we generally kill *her!* Now, once more, Jeanne,—out of the way! Time flies, and *Monsieur le Marquis* is in haste. He has many fashionable engagements! "

He flashed upon her a look from the bright amorous hazel eyes, that were potent to command and difficult to resist, and she cowered back, trembling and sobbing hysterically as the Marquis advanced.

" You are ready? " he enquired civilly.

" Ready! "

" Shall we say twelve paces? "

" Excellent! "

Deliberately Fontenelle dug his heel into the ground and measured twelve paces from that mark between himself and his antagonist. Then with cold courtesy he stood aside for Miraudin to assure himself that the measurement was correct. The actor complied with this formality in a sufficiently composed way, and with a certain grace and dignity which Fontenelle might almost have taken for bravery if he had not been so convinced that the man was " acting " still in his mind, and was going through a " part " which he disliked, but which he was forced to play. And with it all there was something indefinable about him—something familiar in the turn of his head, the glance of his eye, the movement of his body, which annoyed Fontenelle, because he saw in all these little personal touches such a strong resemblance to himself. But there was now no time to think, as the moment for the combat drew near. Jeanne Richaud was still weeping hysterically and expostulating with the cab-driver, who paid no attention whatsoever to her pleadings, but remained obstinately on his knees out of harm's way, begging the " Santissima Madonna " and all his " patron saints " to see him safely with his *fiacre* back to the city. That was all he cared for.

"We have no one to give us a signal," said Miraudin lightly, "But there is a cloud on the moon. When it passes, shall we fire?"

The Marquis bowed assent.

For a moment the moon-rays were obscured,—and a faint sigh from the wind stirred the long dry grass. A bat flew by, scurrying towards the Catacombs of Alexander,—a shadow lay upon the land. The combatants,—so singularly alike in form and feature,—stood rigidly in position, their weapons raised,—their only witnesses a cabman and a wanton, both creatures terrified out of their wits for themselves and their own safety. Swiftly the cloud passed—and a brilliant silver glory was poured out on hill and plain and broken column,—and as it shone, the two shots were fired simultaneously—the two bullets whizzed through the air. A light puff of smoke rose in the moonbeams——it cleared—and Miraudin reeled backwards and fell heavily to the ground. Fontenelle stood upright, but staggered a little,—instinctively putting his hand to his breast. Jeanne Richaud rushed to the side of her fallen lover.

"Victor! Victor!"

Miraudin struggled up to a half sitting position—— the blood was welling up thickly from a wound in his lungs. Half suffocated as he was, he made a strong effort to speak, and succeeded.

"Not you—not you!" he gasped, "Do not touch me! Do not come near me! Him!——him!" And he pointed to Fontenelle who still stood erect, swaying slightly to and fro with a dazed far-off look in his eyes— but now—as the frenzied *soubrette* beckoned him, he moved unsteadily to the side of his mortally wounded opponent, and there, through weakness, not emotion, dropped on his knees. Miraudin looked at him with staring filmy eyes.

"How I have hated you, *Monsieur le Marquis!*" he muttered thickly, "How I have hated you! Yes—as Cain hated Abel! For we—we are brothers as they were ——born of the same father—ah! You start!" for Fontenelle uttered a gasping cry——"Yes—in spite of your pride, your lineage, your insolent air of superiority —*your* father was *my* father!—the late Marquis was no more satisfied with one wife than any of us are!—and had no higher code of honour! *Your* mother was a *grande dame,—mine* was a ' light o' love ' like this feeble creature! " and he turned his glance for a moment on the shuddering, wailing Jeanne Richaud. " *You* were the legal Marquis—*I* the illegal genius! . . . yes—genius——! "

He broke off, struggling for breath.

" Do you hear me? " he whispered thickly, " Do you hear? "

" I hear," answered Fontenelle, speaking with difficulty, " You have hated me, you say——hate me no more!—for hate is done with——and love also!——I am——dying! "

He grasped the rank grass with both hands in sudden agony, and his face grew livid. Miraudin turned himself on one arm.

" Dying! You, too! By Heaven! Then the Marquisate must perish! I should have fired in the air——but——but the sins of the fathers . . . what is it? " Here a ghastly smile passed over his features, " The sins of the fathers—are visited on the children! What a merciful Deity it is, to make such an arrangement!—and the excellent fathers!—when all the children meet them ——I wonder what they will have to say to each other—— I wonder . . ." A frightful shudder convulsed his body and he threw up his arms.

> " ' Un peu d'amour,
> Et puis—bon soir ! '

C'est ça! Bon soir, Marquis! "

A great sigh broke from his lips, through which the discoloured blood began to ooze slowly—he was dead. And Fontenelle, whose wound bled inwardly, turned himself wearily round to gaze on the rigid face upturned to the moon. His brother's face! So like his own! He was not conscious himself of any great pain——he felt a dizzy languor and a drowsiness as of dreams—but he knew what the dreaming meant,—he knew that he would soon sleep to wake again——but where? He did not see that the woman who had professed to love Miraudin had already rushed away from his corpse in terror, and was entreating the cabman to drive her quickly from the scene of combat,—he realised nothing save the white moonbeams on the still face of the man who in God's sight had been his brother. Fainter and still fainter grew his breath——but he felt near his heart for a little crumpled knot of filmy lace which he always carried—a delicate trifle which had fallen from one of Sylvie's pretty evening gowns once, when he had caught her in his arms and sworn his passion. He kissed it now, and inhaled its violet perfume——as he took it from his lips he saw that it was stained with blood. The heavy languor upon him grew heavier—and in the dark haze which began to float before his eyes he saw women's faces, some beautiful, some devilish, yet all familiar,—he felt himself sinking—sinking into some deep abyss of shadows, so dark and dreary that he shuddered with the icy cold and horror, till Sylvie came, yes!—Sylvie's soft eyes shone upon him, full of the pity and tenderness of some divine angel near God's throne,—an angel of sweetness—an angel of forgiveness——ah!—so sweet she was, so childlike, so trusting, so fair, so enticing in those exquisite ways of hers which had pleaded with him, prayed to him, tried to draw him back from evil, and incite him to noble thought; "ways" that would have persuaded him to cleanse his flag of honour from the mud of social vice and folly, and lift it to the heavens white and pure! Ah, sweet ways!—sweet voice!—sweet woman!—sweet possibilities of life now gone forever! Again that sinking,—that icy chill! His eyes were closing—yet he forced himself to open them as he sank back heavily on the truf, and then——then he saw the great white moon descending on him as it seemed, like a shield of silver flung down to crush him, by some angry god!

"Sylvie!—Sylvie!" he muttered, "I never knew—how much I loved you——till—now! Sylvie!"

His eyes closed—a little smile flickered on his mouth for a moment—and then the Shadow fell. And he lay stark and pallid in the moonlight, close to the brother he had never known till the last hour of life had revealed the bond of blood between them. Side by side they lay, —strangely alike in death,—men to whom the possibilities of noble living had been abundantly given, and who had wasted all their substance on vanity. For Victor Miraudin, despite his genius and the brilliancy of his art, was

not likely to be longer remembered or mourned than the
Marquis Fontenelle. The fame of the actor is even less
than that of the great noble,—the actor's name is but a
bubble on the air which a breath disperses,—and the
heir to a proud house is only remembered by the flattering
inscription on his tombstone. Forgotten Cæsars, greater
than any living monarch, had mixed their bones with the
soil where these two sons of one father lay dead,—the
bright moon was their sanctuary lamp,—the stars their
funeral torches,—the width of the Campagna their bier,
and the heavens their pall. And when the two terrified
witnesses of the fatal fight realised the position, and saw
that both combatants had truly perished, there were no regrets, no lamentations, no prayers, no thought of going
for assistance. With the one selfish idea uppermost,—
that of escaping immediate trouble—Jeanne Richaud rallied her scattered wits, and dragging the praying and
gesticulating cab-driver up from his knees, she bade him
mount his box and drive her back to the city. Tremblingly he prepared to obey, but not without unfastening
the horse which the dead Marquis had so lately ridden,
and taking some trouble to attach it to his vehicle for his
own uses.

"For if we do this, they will never know!" he muttered with chattering teeth, "A horse is always a horse
—and this is a good animal, more valuable than the men;
—and when they find the men that is none of our business.
In—in with you, *Madama!* I will drive you into the
city,—that is, if you give me a thousand francs instead of
the five hundred your man promised me! Otherwise I
will leave you here!"

"A thousand!" shrieked Richaud, "Oh, thief! You
know I am a poor stranger—Oh, *mon Dieu!* Do not
murder me!" This, as the driver, having hustled her
into the vehicle and shut the door, now shook his dirty
fist at her threateningly. "Oh!—what a night of horror!
Yes—yes!—a thousand!—anything!—only take me back
to Rome!"

Satisfied in his own mind that he had intimidated her
sufficiently to make her give him whatever he demanded,
the driver who, despite his native cupidity, was seriously
alarmed for his own safety, hesitated no longer, and the
noise of the dashing wheels and the galloping hoofs woke

loud echoes from the road, and dull reverberations from the Ponte Nomentano, as the equipage, with two horses now instead of one, clattered out of sight. And then came silence,—the awful silence of the Campagna—a silence like no other silence in the world—brooding like darkness around the dead.

XXIV.

THE next morning dawned with all the strange half mystical glow of light and colour common to the Italian sky,—flushes of pink warmed the gray clouds, and dazzling, opalescent lines of blue suggested the sun without declaring it,—and Sylvie Hermenstein, who had passed a restless and wakeful night, rose early to go on one of what her society friends called her "eccentric" walks abroad, before the full life of the city was up and stirring. She, who seemed by her graceful *mignonne* fascinations and elegant toilettes, just a butterfly of fashion and no more, was truly of a dreamy and poetic nature, —she had read very deeply, and the griefs and joys of humanity presented an ever-varying problem to her refined and penetrative mind. She was just now interesting herself in subjects which she had never studied so closely before,—and she was gradually arriving at the real secret of the highest duty of life,—that of serving and working for others without consideration for oneself. A great love was teaching her as only a great love can;—a love which she scarcely dared to admit to herself, but which nevertheless was beginning to lead her step by step, into that mysterious land, half light, half shadow, which is the nearest road to Heaven,—a land where we suffer gladly for another's sorrow, and are joyous in our own griefs, because another is happy! To love *one* greatly, means to love *all* more purely,—and to find heart-room and sympathy for the many sorrows and perplexities of those who are not as uplifted as ourselves. For the true mission of the divine passion in its divinest form, is that it should elevate and inspire the soul, bringing it to the noblest issues, and for this it must be associated with respect, as well as passion. No true soul can love what it does not sincerely feel to be worthy of love. And Sylvie—the brilliant little caressable Sylvie, whose warm heart had been so long unsatisfied, was, if not yet crowned by the full benediction of love, still gratefully aware of the wonderful colour and interest which had

suddenly come into her life with the friendship of Aubrey
Leigh.   His conversation, so different to the " small talk "
of the ordinary man, not only charmed her mind, but
strengthened and tempered it,—his thoughtful and tender
personal courtesy filled her with that serenity which is
always the result of perfect manner,—his high and pure
ideas of life moved her to admiration and homage,—and
when she managed to possess herself of every book he had
written, and had read page after page, sentence after sentence, of the glowing, fervent, passionate language, in
which he denounced shams and glorified truth,—the firmness and fearlessness with which he condemned religious
hypocrisy, and lifted pure Christianity to the topmost
pinnacle of any faith ever known or accepted in the world,
her feelings for him, while gaining fresh warmth, grew
deeper and more serious, merging into reverence as well
as submission.   She had a book of his with her as a companion to her walk this very morning, and as she entered
the Pamphili woods, where she had a special " permesso "
to go whenever she chose, and trod the mossy paths,
where the morning sun struck golden shafts between the
dark ilex-boughs, as though pointing to the thousands of
violets that blossomed in the grass beneath, she opened it
at a page containing these lines:—

" Who is it that dares assert that his life or his thoughts
are his own? No man's life is his own! It is given to
him in charge to use for the benefit of others,—and if he
does not so use it, it is often taken from him when he
least expects it. *Thou fool, this night thy life shall be
required of thee!'* No man's thoughts even, are his own.
They are the radiations of the Infinite Mind of God which
pass through every living atom. The beggar may have
the same thought as the Prime Minister,—he only lacks
the power of expression. The more helpless and inept
the beggar, the greater the responsibility of the Premier.
For the Premier has received education, culture, training, and the choice of the people, and to him is given
the privilege of voicing the beggar's thought. And not
only the beggar's thought, but the thoughts of all in the
nation who have neither the skill nor the force to speak.
If he does not do what he is thus elected to do, he is but
an inefficient master of affairs. And what shall we say

of the ministers of Religion who are 'ordained' to voice
the Message of Christ? To echo the Divine!—to repeat
the grand Ethics of Life,—the Law of Love and Charity
and Forbearance and Pity and Forgiveness! When one
of these highly destined servants of the Great King fails
in his duty,—when he cannot pardon the sinner,—when
he looks churlishly upon a child, or condemns the innocent
amusements of the young and happy,—when he makes the
sweet Sabbath a day of penance instead of praise—of
tyranny instead of rest,—when he has no charity for back-
sliders, no sympathy for the sorrowful, no toleration for
the contradictors of his own particular theory——do
we not feel that his very existence is a blasphemy, and
his preaching a presumption!"

Here Sylvie raised her eyes from the book. She was
near an ancient cedar-tree whose dark spreading boughs,
glistening with the early morning dew, sparkled like a
jewelled canopy in the sun,—at her feet the turf was
brown and bare, but a little beyond at the turn of the
pathway, a cluster of white narcissi waved their graceful
stems to the light wind. There was a rustic bench close
by, and she sat down to rest and think. Very sweet
thoughts were hers,—such thoughts as sweet women
cherish when they dream of Love. Often the dream
vanishes before realisation, but this does not make the
time of dreaming less precious or less fair. Lost in a
reverie which in its pleasantness brought a smile to her
lips, she did not hear a stealthy footstep on the grass behind her, or feel a pair of dark eyes watching her furtively from between the cedar-boughs,—and she started
with surprise, and something of offence also, as Monsignor Gherardi suddenly appeared and addressed her,—
"Buon giorno, Contessa!"
She rose from her seat and saluted him in silence, instinctively grasping the book she held a little closer. But
Gherardi's quick glance had already perceived the title
and the name of its author.
"You improve the time!" he said, sarcastically, pacing slowly beside her. "To one of your faith and devotion that book should be accursed!"
She raised her clear eyes and looked at him straightly.
"Is the sunlight accursed?" she said, "The grass or

the flowers? The thoughts in this book are as pure and beautiful as they!"

Gherardi smiled. The enthusiasm of a woman's unspoilt nature was always a source of amusement to him.

"Your sentiments are very pretty and poetic!" he said, "But they are exaggerated. That book is on the 'Index'!"

"Yes, of course it would be!" answered Sylvie quietly, "I have often wondered why so much fine literature is condemned by the Church,—and do you know, it occurred to me the other day that if our Lord had *written* what He said in the form of a book, it might be placed on the 'Index' also?"

Gherardi lifted his eyes from their scrutiny of the ground, and fixed them upon her with a look of amazement that was almost a menace. But she was not in the least intimidated,—and her face, though pale as the narcissi she had just seen in blossom, was very tranquil.

"Are you the Comtesse Hermenstein?" said Gherardi then, after an impressive pause, "The faithful, gentle daughter of Holy Church? or are you some perverted spirit wearing her semblance?"

Sylvie laughed.

"If I am a perverted spirit you ought to be able to exorcise me, Monsignor!" she said,—"With the incense of early Mass clinging to you, and the holy water still fresh on your hands, you have only to say, '*Retro me Sathanas!*' and if I am *not* Sylvie Hermenstein I shall melt into thin air, leaving nothing but the odour of sulphur behind me! But if I *am* Sylvie Hermenstein, I shall remain invincible and immovable,—both in myself and in my opinions!"

Gherardi controlled his rising irritation, and was silent for some minutes, reflecting within himself that if the fair Countess had suddenly turned restive and wayward, it was probably because she was falling in love with the author whose works she defended, and taking this into consideration, he judged it would be wisest to temporise.

"Invincible you always are!" he said in softer tones, "As many unhappy men in Europe can testify!"

"Are you among them?" queried Sylvie mischievously, the light of laughter beginning to twinkle and flash in her pretty eyes.

"Of course!" answered Gherardi suavely, though his heart beat thickly, and the secret admiration he had always felt for the delicate beauty of this woman who was so utterly out of his reach, made his blood burn with mingled rage and passion. "Even a poor priest is not exempt from temptation!"

Sylvie hummed a little tune under her breath, and looked up at the sky.

"It will be a lovely day!" she said—"There will be no rain!"

"Is that the most interesting thing you can say to me?" queried Gherardi.

"The weather is always interesting," she replied, "And it is such a safe subject of conversation!"

"Then you are afraid of dangerous subjects?"

"Oh no, not at all! But I dislike quarrelling,—and I am afraid I should get very angry if you were to say anything more against the book I am reading"—here she paused a moment, and then added steadily, "or its author!"

"I am aware that he is a great friend of yours," said Gherardi gently, "And I assure you, *Contessa*—seriously I assure you, I should be the last person in the world to say anything against him. Indeed, there is nothing to say, beyond the fact that he is, according to our religion, a heretic—but he is a brilliant and intellectual heretic,— *well worth redeeming!*"

He emphasised the words, and shot a meaning glance at her; but she did not appear to take his hint or fathom his intention. She walked on steadily, her eyes downcast,—her tiny feet, shod in charming little French walking shoes, peeping in and out with a flash of steel on their embroidered points, from under the mysterious gleam of silk flounces that gave a soft "swish," as she moved,— her golden hair escaping in one or two silky waves from under a picturesque black hat, fastened on by velvet ribbons, which were tied in a captivating knot under the sweetest of little white chins, a chin whose firm contour almost contradicted the sensitive lines of the kissable mouth above it. A curious, dull sense of anger teased the astute brain of Domenico Gherardi, as with all the dignified deportment of the stately churchman, he walked on by her side. What was all his scheming worth, he began to think, if this slight feminine creature proved herself more than a match for him? The utmost he could do with his life and ambitions was to sway the ignorant, cram his coffers with gold, and purchase a change of mistresses for his villa at Frascati. But love, —real love, from any human creature alive he never had won, and knew he never should win. Sylvie Hermenstein was richer far than he,—she had not only wealth and a great position, but the joys of a natural existence, and of a perfect home-life were not denied to her. Presently, seeing that they were approaching the gates of exit from the Pamphili, he said,—

"*Contessa*, will you give me the favour of an hour's conversation with you one afternoon this week? I have something of the very greatest importance to say to you."

"Can you not say it now?" asked Sylvie.

"No, it would take too long,—besides, if walls have ears, it is possible that gardens have tongues! I should not presume to trouble you, were it not for the fact that my business concerns the welfare of your friend, Mr. Aubrey Leigh, in whose career I think you are interested, —and not only Mr. Leigh, but also Cardinal Bonpré. You will be wise to give me the interview I seek,—unwise if you refuse it!"

"*Monsignor*, you have already been well received at my house, and will be well received again,"—said Sylvie with a pretty dignity, "Provided you do not abuse my hospitality by calumniating my *friends*, whatever you may think of myself,—you will be welcome! What day, and at what hour shall I expect you?"

Gherardi considered a moment.

"I will write," he said at last, "I cannot at this moment fix the time, but I will not fail to give you notice. *A riverderci! Benedicite!*"

And he left her abruptly at the gates, walking rapidly in the direction of the Vatican. Full of vague perplexities to which she could give no name, Sylvie went homewards slowly, and as she entered her rooms, and responded to the affectionate morning greetings of Madame Bozier, she was conscious of a sudden depression that stole over her bright soul like a dark cloud on a sunny day, and made her feel chilled and sad. Turning over the numerous letters that waited her perusal, she recognised the handwriting of the Marquis Fontenelle on one, and took it up with a strange uneasy dread and beating of the heart. She read it twice through, before entirely grasping its meaning, and then—as she realised that the man who had caused her so much pain and shame by his lawless and reckless pursuit of her in the character of a libertine, was now, with a frank confession of his total unworthiness, asking her to be his wife,—the tears rushed to her eyes, and a faint cry broke from her lips.

"Oh, I cannot . . . I cannot!" she murmured, "Not now——not now!"

Madame Bozier looked at her in distress and amazement.

"What is the matter, dear?" she asked, "Some bad news?"

Silently Sylvie handed her Fontenelle's letter.

"Dear me! He is actually in Rome!" said the old lady, "And he asks you to be his wife! Well, dear child, is not that what you had a right to expect from him?"

"Yes——perhaps——but I cannot—not now!—Oh no, not now!" murmured Sylvie, and her eyes, wet with tears, were full of an infinite pain.

"But—pardon me, dear—do you not love him?"

Sylvie stood silent—gazing blankly before her, with such perplexity and sorrow in her face that her faithful *gouvernante* grew anxious and troubled.

"Child, do not look like that!" she exclaimed, "It cuts me to the heart! You were not made for sorrow!"

"Dear Katrine,—we were all made for sorrow," said Sylvie slowly, "Sorrow is good for us. And perhaps I have not had sufficient of it to make me strong. And this is real sorrow to me,—to refuse Fontenelle!"

"But why refuse him if you love him?" asked Madame Bozier bewildered.

Sylvia sat down beside her, and put one soft arm caressingly round her neck.

"Ah, Katrine,—that is just my trouble," she said, "I do *not* love him now! When I first met him he attracted me greatly, I confess,—he seemed so gentle, so courteous, and above all, so true! But it was 'seeming' only, Katrine!—and he was not anything of what he seemed. His courtesy and gentleness were but a mask for licentiousness,—his apparent truth was but a disguise for mere reckless and inconstant passion. I had to find this out, bit by bit,—and oh, how cruel was the disillusion! How I prayed for him, wept for him, tried to think that if he loved me he might yet endeavour to be nobler and truer for my sake. But his love was not great enough for that. What he wanted was the body of me, not the soul. What *I* wanted of him was the soul, not the body! So we played at cross purposes,—each with a different motive,— and gradually, as I came to recognise how much baseness and brutality there is in mere libertinism,—how poor and paltry an animal man becomes when he serves himself and his passions only, my attraction for him diminished, —I grew to realise that I could never raise him out of the mud, because he had lived by choice too long in it, —I could never persuade him to be true, even to himself, because he found the ways of falsehood and deceit more amusing. He did unworthy things, which I could not, with all my admiration for him, gloze over or excuse;— in fact, I found that in his private life and code of honour he was very little better than Miraudin,—and Miraudin, as you know, one *cannot* receive!"

"He is in Rome also," said Madame Bozier, "I saw his name placarded in the streets only yesterday, and also outside one of the leading theatres. He has brought all his Parisian company here to act their *repertoire* for a few nights before proceeding to Naples."

"How strange he should be here!" said Sylvie, "How very strange! He is so like the Marquis Fontenelle, Katrine! So very like! I used to go to the theatre and frighten myself with studying the different points of resemblance! Every feature of Miraudin's face seemed to be the rough copy of Fontenelle's,—and I always saw in the actor what the gentleman would be if he continued to live as he was doing. Miraudin, whose *amours* are a disgrace, *even* to the stage!—Miraudin, who in his position of actor-manager, takes despicable advantage of all the poor ignorant, struggling creatures who try to get into his company, and whose vain little heads are turned by a stray compliment,—and to think that the Marquis Fontenelle should be merely the better-born copy of so mean a villain! Ah, what useless tears I have shed about it,—how I have grieved and worried myself all in vain! —and now . . . "

"Now he asks you to marry him," said Madame Bozier gently, "And you think it would be no use? You could not perhaps make him a better man?"

"Neither I nor any woman could!" said Sylvie, "I do not believe very much in 'reforming' men, Katrine. If they need to reform, they must reform themselves. We make our own lives what they are."

"Dear little philosopher!" said Madame Bozier tenderly, taking Sylvie's small white hand as it hung down from her shoulder and kissing it, "You are very depressed to-day! You must not take things so seriously! If you do not love the Marquis as you once did——"

"As I once did——ah, yes!" said Sylvie, "I did love him. I thought he could not be otherwise than great and true and noble-hearted——but——"

She broke off with a sigh.

"Well, and now that you know he is not the hero you imagined him, all you have to do is to tell him so," said the practical Bozier cheerfully, "Or if you do not want to pain him by such absolute candour, give him his refusal as gently and kindly as you can."

Sylvie sighed again.

"I am very sorry," she said, "If I could have foreseen this——perhaps——"

"But did you not foresee it?" asked Madame Bozier persistently, "Did you not realise that men always want what they cannot have——and that the very fact of your leaving Paris increased his ardour and sent him on here in pursuit?"

Sylvie Hermenstein was of a very truthful nature, and she had not attempted to deny this suggestion.

"Yes—I confess I did think that if I separated myself altogether from him it might induce him to put himself in a more honourable position with me—but I did not know then——" she paused, and a deep flush crimsoned her cheeks.

"Did not know what?" queried Madame Bozier softly.

Sylvie hesitated a moment, then spoke out bravely.

"I did not know then that I should meet another man whose existence would become ten times more interesting and valuable to me than his! Yes, Katrine, I confess it! There is no shame in honesty! And so, to be true to myself, however much the Marquis might love me now, I could never be his wife."

Madame Bozier was silent. She guessed her beloved pupil's heart's secret,—but she was too tactful to dwell upon the subject, and before the brief, half-embarrassed pause between them had ended, a servant entered, asking,

"Will the *Signora Contessa* receive the *Capitano* Ruspardi?"

Sylvie rose from her seat with a look of surprise.

"Ruspardi?—I do not know the name."

"The business is urgent;—the Capitano is the bearer of a letter to the *Signora Contessa.*"

"Remain with me, Katrine," said Sylvie after a pause, —then to the servant—" Show Captain Ruspardi in here."

Another moment, and a young officer in the Italian uniform entered hurriedly,—his face was very pale,—and as the Comtesse Hermenstein received him in her own serene sweet manner which, for all its high-bred air had something wonderfully winning and childlike about it, his self-control gave way, and when after a profound salute he raised his eyes, she saw they were full of tears. Her heart began to beat violently.

"You bring some bad news?" she asked faintly.

"*Madama,* I beg you not to distress yourself——this letter—" and he held out a sealed envelope,—" was given to me specially marked, among others, by my friend, the Marquis Fontenelle——last night before—before he went to his death!"

"His death!" echoed Sylvie, her eyes dilating with horror——" His death! What do you mean?"

Madame Bozier came quickly to her side, and put a hand gently on her arm. But she did not seem to feel the sympathetic touch.

"His death!" she murmured. And with trembling fingers she opened and read the last lines ever penned by her too passionate admirer.

"SWEETEST SYLVIE! Dearest and purest of women! If you ever receive this letter I shall be gone beyond the reach of your praise or your blame. For it will not be given to you at all unless I am dead. Dead, dear Sylvie! That will be strange, will it not? To be lying quite still, cold and stiff, out of the reach of your pretty warm white

arms,—deprived for ever and ever of any kiss from your
rose-red lips,—ah, Sylvie, it will be very cold and lonely!
But perhaps better so! To-night I saw you, up in your
balcony, with someone who is a brave and famous man,
and who no doubt loves you. For he cannot fail to love
you, if he knows you. God grant you may be happy when
I am gone! But I want you to feel that to-night—to-
night *I* love you!—love you as I have never loved you or
any woman before—without an evil thought,—without
a selfish wish!—to the very height and breadth of love,
I love you, my queen, my rose, my saving grace of sweetness!—whose name I shall say to God as my best prayer
for pardon, if I die to-night!

FONTENELLE."

Sylvie shuddered as with icy cold . . . a darkness
seemed to overwhelm her . . . she staggered a little, and
Ruspardi caught her, wondering at the lightness and delicacy and beauty of her, as he assisted Madame Bozier to
lead her to a deep fauteuil where she sank down, trembling in every nerve.

"And—he is dead?" she asked mechanically.

Ruspardi bowed a grave assent. She paused a moment—then forced herself to speak again.

"How did it happen?"

In brief, concise words Ruspardi gave the account of
the quarrel with Miraudin,—and Sylvie shrank back as
though she had received a blow when she heard that her
name had been the cause of the dispute.

"And this morning, hearing no news," continued Ruspardi, " I made enquiries at the theatre. There I found
everything in confusion; Miraudin and a *soubrette* named
Jeanne Richaud, had left Rome the previous evening so
the box-keeper said, and there was no news of either of
them beyond a note from the girl saying she had returned
alone to Paris by the first morning train. Nothing had
been heard of Miraudin himself;—I therefore, knowing
all the circumstances, drove out to the Campagna by the
Porte Pia, the way that Miraudin had gone, and the way
I bade the Marquis follow;—but on the Ponte Nomentano
I met some of the Miserecordia carrying two corpses on
the same bier,—two corpses so strangely alike that they

might almost have been brothers!—they were the bodies of the Marquis Fontenelle and,—Miraudin!"

Sylvie uttered a low cry and covered her face with her hands.

"Miraudin!" exclaimed Madame Bozier in horrified tones. "Miraudin! Is he killed also?"

"Yes, *Madame!* Both shots must have been fired with deadly aim. They had no seconds. Miraudin had hired a common *fiacre* to escape in from the city, and the police will offer a reward for the discovery of the driver. My horse, which my unfortunate friend Fontenelle rode, is gone, and if it could be discovered, its possessor might furnish a clue;—but I imagine it will be difficult, if not impossible to trace the witnesses of the combat. The woman Richaud is on her way to Paris. But by this time all Rome knows of the death of Miraudin; and in a few hours all the world will know!"

"And what of the Marquis Fontenelle?" asked Madame Bozier.

"*Madama,* I posted all the letters he entrusted to my charge. The one I have brought to the Contessa was enclosed in an envelope to me and marked 'To be personally delivered in case of my death'. But among the letters for the post was one to the Marquis's only sister, the Abbess of a convent in Paris—she will probably claim her brother's remains."

He was silent. After a pause Sylvie rose unsteadily, and detached a cluster of violets she wore at her neck.

"Will you——" her voice faltered.

But Ruspardi understood, and taking the flowers, respectfully kissed the little hand that gave them.

"They shall be buried with him," he said. "His hand was clenched in death on a small knot of lace—you perhaps might recognise it,—yes?——so!—it shall be left as it was found."

And,—his melancholy errand being done,—he bowed profoundly once more, and retired.

Sylvie gazed around her vaguely,—the letter of her dead admirer grasped in her hand,—and his former letter, proposing marriage, lying still open on the table. Her old *gouvernante* watched her anxiously, the tears rolling down her cheeks.

"You are crying, Katrine!" she said, "And yet you

knew him very little,—he never loved you! I wish—I wish *my* tears would come! But they are all here—aching and hurting me—" and she pressed her hand to her heart—— " You see—when one is a woman and has been loved by a man, one cannot but feel sorry——for such an end! You see he was not altogether cruel!——he defended my name——and he has died for my sake! For my sake!——Oh, Katrine! For *my* sake! So he *did* love me—at the last! . . . and I——I——Oh, Katrine!—I wish——I wish the tears would come! "

And as she spoke she reeled——and uttering a little cry like that of a wounded bird, dropped senseless.

XXV.

THE death of the famous actor Miraudin was a nine days' wonder, and about a three weeks' regret. He had made no reputation beyond that of the clever Mime,— he was not renowned for scholarship,—he had made no mark in dramatic literature,—and his memory soon sank out of sight in the whirling ocean of events as completely as though he had never existed. There was no reality about him, and as a natural consequence he went the way of all Shams. Had even his study of his art been sincere and high—had he sought for the best, the greatest, and most perfect work, and represented that only to the public, the final judgment of the world might perhaps have given him a corner beside Talma or Edmund Kean,—but the conceit of him, united to an illiterate mind, was too great for the tolerance of the universal Spirit of things which silently in the course of years pronounces the last verdict on a man's work. Only a few of his own profession remembered him as one who might have been great had he not been so little ;—and a few women laughed lightly, recalling the legion of his " amours ", and said, *"Ce pauvre coquin,* Miraudin ! " That was all. And for the mortal remains of Guy Beausire de Fontenelle, there came a lady, grave and pale, clothed in deep black, with the nun's white band crossing her severe and tranquil brows,—and she, placing a great wreath of violets fresh gathered from the Pamphili woods, and marked, " In sorrow, from Sylvie Hermenstein ", on the closed coffin, escorted her melancholy burden back to Paris, where in a stately marble vault, to the solemn sound of singing, and amid the flare of funeral tapers, with torn battle banners drooping around his bier, and other decaying fragments of chivalry, the last scion of the once great house of Fontenelle was laid to rest with his fathers. Little did the austere Abbess, who was the chief mourner at these obsequies, guess that the actor Miraudin, whose grave had been hastily dug in Rome, had also a right to be laid

in the same marble vault;—proud and cold and stern as
her heart had grown through long years of pain and disappointment, it is possible that had she known this, her
sufferings might have been still more poignant. But the
secret had died with the dead so far as the world went;
—there remained but the Eternal Record on which the
bond of brotherhood was inscribed,—and in that Eternal
Record some of us do our best not to believe, notwithstanding the universal secret dread that we shall all be
confronted with it at last.

Meanwhile, events were moving rapidly, and the net
of difficult circumstance was weaving itself round the
good Cardinal Bonpré in a manner that was strangely
perplexing to his clear and just mind. He had received
a letter from Monsignor Moretti, worded in curtly civil
terms, to the effect that as the Cardinal's miracle of healing had been performed in France, he, as on Vatican service in Paris, found it his duty to enquire thoroughly into
all the details. For this cause, he, Monsignor Moretti,
trusted it would suit the Cardinal's convenience to remain in Rome till the return of Monsieur Claude Cazeau,
secretary to the Archbishop of Rouen, who had been despatched back to that city on the business connected with
this affair. Thus Monsignor Moretti;—and Cardinal
Bonpré, reading between the lines of his letter, knew that
the displeasure of Rome had fallen upon him as heavily
as it did upon the eloquent and liberal-minded Padre
Agostino when he made the mistake of asking a blessing
from Heaven on the King and Queen of Italy for their
works of charity among the poor. And he easily perceived where the real trouble lay,—namely, in the fact
of his having condoned the Abbé Vergniaud's public confession. Out of the one thing there was an effort being
made to contrive mischief with the other,—and Bonpré,
being too frail and old to worry his brain with complex
arguments as to the how and why and wherefore of the
machinations carried on at the Vatican, resigned himself
to God, and contenting his mind with meditation and
prayer, waited events patiently, caring little how they
ended for himself, provided they did not involve others in
any catastrophe. Moreover, there was a certain consolation contained in his enforced waiting,—for his niece
Angela had confided to him that the work of her great

picture had advanced more swiftly than she had imagined possible, and that it was likely she would be able to show it to her relatives and private friends in the course of a week or so.

"But Florian must see it first," she said, "Of course you know that! Florian must always be first!"

"Yes," and the Cardinal stroked her hair tenderly, while his eyes rested on her with rather a troubled look —"Yes—of course—Florian first. I suppose he will always be first with you, Angela?—after God?"

"Always!" she answered softly, "Always—after God!"

And Felix Bonpré sighed—he knew not why—except that he was always sorry for women who loved men with any very great exaltation or devotion. That curiously tender adoration of a true woman's heart which is so often wasted on an unworthy object, seemed to him like lifting a cup of gold to a swine's snout. He found no actual fault with Florian Varillo,—he was just a man as men go, with nothing very pronounced about him, except a genius for fine mosaic-like painting. He was not a great creator, but he was a delicate and careful artist,—a man against whom nothing particular could be said, except perhaps that his manner was often artificial, and that his conduct was not always sincere. But he had a power of fascinating the opposite sex,—and Angela had fallen a willing victim to his candid smile, clear eyes, charming voice, and courteous ways,—and with that strange inconsistency so common to gifted women, she was so full of "soul" and "over-soul" herself, that she could not imagine "soul" lacking in others;—and never dreamed of making herself sure that it elevated the character or temperament of the man she loved.

> "Alas, the love of women! it is known
>   To be a lovely and a fearful thing ;
> For all of theirs upon that die is thrown
> And, if 'tis lost, life hath no more to bring ! " *

During the time that matters were thus pending in Rome, Claude Cazeau, well satisfied with himself, and the importance of being entrusted with a special message from the Vatican to the Archbishop of Rouen, returned

* Byron.

to the Normandy capital with many ambitious specula-
tions rife in his brain, and schemes for improving the position of confidence with which he had, by the merest
chance, and the fluctuations of the Pope's humour, been
suddenly thrust. He took the Patoux family by surprise
on the evening of his arrival in Rouen, and much to his
secret satisfaction found Martine Doucet in their company. The children were gone to bed, and the appearance
of Cazeau in Papa Patoux's kitchen was evidently not altogether the most agreeable circumstance that could have
happened at the Hotel Poitiers. He was civilly received,
however, and when he expressed his pleasure at seeing
Madame Doucet present, that worthy female lifted her
eyes from her knitting and gave him a suspicious glance
of exceeding disfavour.

"I do not see what pleasure my company can give you,
Monsieur," she said curtly, "I am only a poor market-
woman!"

"But you have been singularly favoured by the protection and confidence of a great Cardinal,——" began
Cazeau.

"Protection—confidence——!" echoed Martine snap-
pishly, *"Nom de Jésus!* What is the man talking about!
I never set eyes on the Cardinal in my life. But that he
cured my Fabien is enough to make me think of him as a
saint for ever,—though it seems there are some that
would almost make him out to be a devil for having done
a good deed! And ever since my boy was cured I have
lived a life of torture and trouble—yes, truly!—torn between two things, our Blessed Lord and the Church! But
I am trying my best to keep fast hold of our Lord, whatever the Church may do to me!"

"Dear me!" said Cazeau blandly, turning with a smile
and propitiatory air to Patoux who sat silently smoking,
"Madame Doucet seems a little——what shall we say?
—unduly excited? Yet surely the recovery of her child
should fill her with thanksgiving and make her a faithful and devout servant——"

"Pardon, Monsieur," interrupted Madame Patoux,
"Believe me, Martine is thankful enough, and devout
enough,—but truly it has been very hard for her to suffer
the things that have been said to her of late,—how that
the child could never have been really crippled at all, but

simply shamming,—how that it was all a trick got up between herself and the priests for the purpose of bringing
visitors and their money to Rouen,—for of course since
the miracle was noised abroad there have been many pil-
grimages to Notre Dame, it having got about that there
was some mysterious spirit or angel in one of the shrines,
—for look you, our Archbishop, when he came to visit the
Cardinal here in this very hotel, distinctly remembers that
His Eminence assured him he had heard strange music
in the Cathedral, when truly there was no organ unlocked,
and no organist on duty,—and then there was something
about the boy that His Eminence found lost that
night . . . ."

" Stop! Stop!" said Cazeau, growing impatient,
" Your eloquence is so impressive, Madame, and you say
so much that is excellent in one breath, that you must
pardon my inferior capacity in not being able to follow
you quite coherently! There are conflicting statements,
you say——"

" No, there are none," said Patoux himself, drawing
his pipe out of his mouth slowly, and looking intently at
its well-sucked stem—" It is all the same sort of thing.
A child is sick—a child is cured—and it is either God or
the Devil who has done it. Some people prefer to think
it is the Devil,—some give the praise to God. It was exactly like that whenever our Lord did a good deed. Half
the folks said he was God,—the other half that he had a
devil. Jerusalen was like Rouen, Rouen is like Jerusalem. Jerusalem was ancient and wicked; Rouen is modern and wickeder,—that's all! As for music in the
church, we have only the Archbishop's warrant that the
Cardinal ever said anything about hearing music."

" ' Only' the Archbishop's warrant!" echoed Cazeau
meaningly.

" I said ' only', Monsieur!—Make the best of it!" answered Patoux, sticking his pipe into his mouth again, and
resuming his smoke with undisturbed tranquillity.

Cazeau hummed and hawed,—he was irritated yet
vaguely amused too at the singular self-assertion of these
common folk who presumed to take their moral measurement of an Archbishop! It is a strange fact, but these
same common folk always *do* take these sorts of measurements.

" The inconsistencies—(if there are any—) in the story will soon be cleared up," he said, with a benevolent assumption of authority, " At least, I hope so! I am glad to say that I am entrusted with a message to the Archbishop from our Holy Father, the Pope,—and I have also His Holiness's instructions to request you, Madame Doucet, together with your son Fabien, to accompany me back to Rome!"

Martine Doucet bounced up from her chair, and let fall her knitting.

" Me—me!" she cried, "*Me* go to Rome! Never! Wild horses will not drag me there, nor shall you take my Fabien either! What should I do in Rome?"

" Testify personally to the truth of the Cardinal's miracle," answered Cazeau, gazing coldly at her excited face as though he saw something altogether strange and removed from human semblance. " And bring your child into the Holy Presence and relate his history. It will be nothing but an advantage to you,—for you will obtain a patient hearing, and the priceless boon of the Papal benediction!"

" *Grand merci!*" said Martine, " But I have lived more than half my time without the Papal benediction, and I can work out the rest of my days in the same way! Look you!—there is a great English Duke I am told, who has an only son sorely afflicted, and he has taken this son to every place in the world where the Church is supposed to work miracles for the healing of the sick and the helpless,—all to no use, for the poor boy is as sick and helpless as ever. How is that? What has the Papal benediction done for him?"

" Woman, your tongue overrules your senses!" said Cazeau, with rising temper, " You rail against the Church like an ungrateful heathen, even though you owe your son's recovery to the Church! For what is Cardinal Bonpré but a Prince of the Church?"

Martine stuck her arms akimbo, and surveyed him disdainfully.

" *Oh-hé!*" she cried, " My tongue overrules my senses, Monsieur Claude Cazeau! Take care that your cunning does not overrule yourself! Did I ever deny the worth and the goodness of Cardinal Bonpré? Though if I were to speak the whole truth, and if I were to believe the nonsense-talk of a child, I should perhaps give the credit of the miracle to the stray boy whom the Cardinal found outside the Cathedral door——" Cazeau started—" For Fabien says that he began to feel strong the moment that little lad touched him!"

" The boy!" exclaimed Cazeau—" The boy!"

A curious silence ensued. Jean Patoux lifting his drowsy eyes gazed fixedly at the whitewashed ceiling,— Madame, his wife, stood beside him watching the changes on Cazeau's yellow face—and Martine sat down to take breath after her voluble outburst.

" The boy!" muttered Cazeau again——then he broke into a harsh laugh.

" What folly!" he exclaimed, " As if a little tramp of the streets could have anything to do with a Church miracle! Martine Doucet, if you were to say such a thing at the Vatican——"

" *I* have not said it," said Martine angrily, " I only told you what my Fabien says. I am not answerable for the thoughts of the child! That he is well and strong— that he has the look and the soul of an angel, is enough for me to praise God all my life. But I shall never say the *Laus Deo* at the Vatican,—you will have no chance to trap me in that way!"

Cazeau stared at her haughtily.

" You must be mad!" he said, " No one wishes to ' trap ' you, as you express it! The miracle of healing performed on your child is a very remarkable one,—it should not be any surprise to you that the Head of the Church seeks to know all the details of it thoroughly, in order to ratify and confirm it, and perhaps bestow new honour on the eminent Cardinal——"

" I rather doubt that!" interposed Patoux slowly, " For I gather from our Archbishop that the Holy Father was suspicious of some trick rather than an excess of sanc-tity!"

Cazeau reddened through his pallid skin.

" I know nothing of that!" he said curtly, " But my orders are imperative, and I shall seek the assistance of the Archbishop to enforce and carry them out! For the moment I have the honour to wish you good-night, Mon-sieur Patoux!—and you also, Mesdames!"

And he departed abruptly, in an anger which he was at

no pains to disguise. Personally he cared nothing about the miracle or how it had been accomplished, but he cared very much for his own advancement,—and he saw, or thought he saw, a chance of very greatly improving his position among the ecclesiastical authorities if he only kept a cool head and a clear mind. He recognised that there was a desire on the part of the Pope to place Cardinal Bonpré under close observance and restraint on account of his having condoned the Abbé Vergniaud's confession to his congregation in Paris; and he rightly judged that anything he could do to aid the accomplishment of that end would not be without its reward. And the few words which Martine Doucet had let drop concerning the stray boy who now lived under the Cardinal's protection, had given him a new idea which he resolved to act upon when he returned to Rome. For it was surely very strange that an eminent Prince of the Church should allow himself to be constantly attended by a little tramp rescued from the street! There was something in it more than common,—and Cazeau decided that he would suggest a close enquiry being made on this point.

Crossing the square opposite the Hotel Poitiers, he hesitated before turning the corner of the street which led towards the avenue where the Archbishop's house was situated. The night was fine and calm—the air singularly balmy,—and he suddenly decided to take a stroll by the river before finally returning to his rooms for the night. There is one very quiet bit of the Seine in Rouen where the water flows between unspoilt grassy banks, which in summer are a frequent resort for lovers to dream the dreams which so often come to nothing,—and here Cazeau betook himself to smoke and meditate on the brilliancy of his future prospects. The river had been high in flood during the week, and the grass which sloped towards the water was still wet, and heavy to the tread. But Cazeau limited his walk to the broad summit of the bank, being aware that the river just below flowed over a muddy quicksand, into which, should a man chance to fall, it would be death and fast burial at one and the same moment. And Cazeau set a rather exorbitant value on his own life, as most men do whose lives are of no sort of consequence to the world. So he was careful to walk where there was the least danger of slipping,—and as he lit an excellent cigar, and puffed the faint blue rings of smoke out into the clear moonlit atmosphere, he was in a very agreeable frame of mind. He was crafty and clever in his way,—one of those to whom the Yankee term "cute" would apply in its fullest sense,—and he had the happy knack of forgetting his own mistakes and follies, and excusing his own sins with as much ease as though he were one of the "blood-royal" of nations. Vices he had in plenty in common with most men,—except that his particular form of licentiousness was distinguished by a callousness and cruelty in which there was no touch of redeeming quality. As a child he had loved to tear the wings off flies and other insects, and one of his keenest delights in boyhood had been to watch the writhings of frogs into whose soft bodies he would stick long pins,— the frogs would live under this treatment four and five hours—sometimes longer, and while observing their agonies he enjoyed "that contented mind which is a per- petual feast." Now that he was a man, he delighted in torturing human beings after the same methods applied mentally, whenever he could find a vulnerable part through which to thrust a sharp spear of pain.

"The eminent Cardinal Bonpré!" he mused now, "What is he to me! If I could force the Archbishop of Rouen into high favour at the Vatican instead of this foolish old Saint Felix, it would be a better thing for my future. After all, it was at Rouen that the miracle was performed—the city should have some credit! And Bon- pré has condoned a heretic . . . he is growing old and feeble—possibly he is losing his wits. And then there is that boy . . ."

He started violently as a fantastic shadow suddenly crossed his path in the moonlight, and a peal of violent laughter assailed his ears.

"*Enfin! Toi, mon Claude!—enfin!—Grace a Dieu! Enfin!*"

And the crazed creature, known as Marguerite, "La Folle", stood before him, her long black hair streaming over her bare chest and gaunt arms, her eyes dilated, and glowing with the mingled light of madness and despair.

Cazeau turned a livid white in the moon-rays;—his blood grew icy cold. What! After two years of dodging about the streets of Rouen to avoid meeting this wretched woman whom he had tricked and betrayed, had she found him at last!

"When did you come back from the fair?" cried the girl shrilly, "I lost you there, you know—and you managed to lose *me*—but I have waited!—waited patiently for news of you! . . . and when none came, I still waited, making myself beautiful! . . . see!—" And she thrust her fingers through her long hair, throwing it about in wilder disorder than ever. "You thought you had killed me—and you were glad!—it makes all men glad to kill women when they can! But I—I was not killed so easily, —I have lived!——for this night—just for this night! Listen!" and she sprang forward and threw herself violently against his breast, "Do you love me now? Tell me again—as you told me at the fair—you love me?"

He staggered under her weight—and tried for a moment to thrust her back, but she held him in a grip of iron, looking up at him with her great feverish dark eyes, and grasping his shoulders with thin burning hands. He trembled;—he was beginning to grow horribly afraid. What devil had sent this woman whom he had ruined so long as two years ago, across his path to-night? Would it be possible to soothe her?

"Marguerite—" he began.

"Yes, yes, Marguerite! Say it again!" she cried wildly, "Marguerite! Say it again! Sweet—sweet and tenderly as you said it then! Poor Marguerite! Your pale ugly face seemed the face of a god to her once, because she thought you loved her—we all find men so beautiful when we think they love us! Yes—your cold eyes and cruel lips and hard brow!—it was quite a different face at the fair! So was mine a different face—but you!—*you* have made mine what it is now!—look at it! What!—you thought you could murder a woman and never be found out! You thought you could kill poor Marguerite, and that no one would ever know——"

"Hush, hush!" said Cazeau, his teeth chattering with the cold of his inward terror, "I never killed you, Marguerite!—I loved you—yes, listen!" For she was looking up at him with an attentive, almost sane expression in her eyes. "I meant to write to you after the fair,— and come to you . . ."

"Hush, hush!" said the girl, "Let me hear this!—

this is strange news! He meant to write to me——yet
he let me die by inches in an agony of waiting!—till I
dropped into the darkness where I am now! He meant
to come to me——oh, it was very easy to come if he had
chosen to come,—before I wandered away into all this
strangeness—this shadow—this confusion and fire! But
you see, it is too late now," and she began to laugh again,
" Too late! I have a strange idea that I am dead, though
I seem alive—I am in my grave; and so you must die also
and be buried with me! Yes, you must certainly die!—
when one is cruel and false and treacherous one is not
wanted in the world!—better to go out of it—and it is
quite easy,—see!—this way!——"

And before he realised her intention she sprang back
a step—then drew a knife from her bosom, and with a
sort of exultant shriek, stabbed him furiously once—
twice——thrice . . . crying out——" This for your lie!
This for my sorrow!—This for your love!—"

Reeling back with the agony of her murderous blows
he made a fierce effort to tear the knife from her hands,
but she suddenly threw it a long way from her towards
the river, where it fell with a light splash, and rushing at
him twined her arms close about his neck, while her mad
laughter, piercing and terrible, rang out through the
quiet air.

" Together!" she said, " That day at the fair we were
together, and now——we shall be together again! Come!
—Come! I have waited long enough!——your promised
letter never came——you have kept me waiting a long
long while——but now I will wait no longer! I have
found you!—I will never let you go!"

Furiously, despite his wounds, he fought with her,—
tried to thrust her away from him,—and beat her backwards and downwards,—but she had the strength of ten
women in her maddened frame, and she clung to him with
the tenacity of some savage beast. All around them was
perfectly quiet,—there was not a soul in sight,—there was
no place near where a shout for help could have been
heard. Struggling still, dizzy, blind and breathless, he
did not see that they were nearing the edge of the slippery
bank—all his efforts were concentrated in an endeavour
to shake off the infuriated creature, made more powerful
in her very madness by the just sense of her burning

wrong and his callous treachery——when all at once his foot slipped and he fell to the ground. She pounced on him like a tigress, and fastened her fingers on his throat,—clutching his flesh and breathlessly muttering, "Never!——never! Never can you hide away from me any more! Together—together! I will never let you go!—" till, as his eyes rolled up in agony and his jaw relaxed, she uttered a shout of ecstasy to see him die! He sank heavily under her fierce grasp which she never relaxed for an instant, and his dead weight dragged her unconsciously down—down!—she not heeding or knowing whither she was moving,—down—still down!—till, as she clung to his inert body, madly determining not to let it go, she fell,—fast grappling her betrayer's corpse,—into the ominous stillness of the river. The flood opened, as it were, to receive the two,—the dead and the living—there was a slight ripple as though a mouth in the water smiled —then the usual calm surface reflected the moon once more, and there was no sign of trouble. Nothing struggled,—nothing floated,—all was perfectly tranquil. The bells chimed from all the churches in the city a quarter to midnight, and their pretty echoes were wafted across the water,—no other sound disturbed the silence,—not a trace of the struggle was left, save just one smeared track of grass and slime, which, if examined carefully, might have been found sprinkled with blood. But with the morning the earth would have swallowed those drops of human life as silently as the river-quicksand had sucked down the bodies of the betrayed and the betrayer;—in neither case would Nature have any hint to give of the tragedy enacted. Nature is a dumb witness to many dramas,—and it may be that she has eyes and ears and her own way of keeping records. Sometimes she gives up long-buried secrets, sometimes she holds them fast;— biding her time until the Judgment Day, when not only the crime shall be disclosed but the Cause of the crime's committal. And it may chance in certain cases, such as those of men who have deliberately ruined the lives of trusting and loving women, that the Cause may be proved a more criminal thing than the crime!

That night Martine Doucet slept badly, and had horrible dreams of being dragged by force to Rome, and there taken before the Pope who at once deprived her of her

son Fabien, and ordered her to be shot in one of the public squares for neglecting to attend Mass regularly. And
Jean Patoux and his wife, reposing on their virtuous
marital couch, conversed a long time about the unexpected and unwelcome visit of Claude Cazeau, and the
mission he had declared himself entrusted with from the
Vatican,—" And you may depend upon it," said Madame
sententiously, " that he will get his way by fair means or
foul! I am thankful that neither of *our* children were
subjects for a Church-miracle!—the trouble of the remedy
seems more troublesome than the sickness! "

" No, no," said her husband, " Thou dost not judge
these things rightly, my little one! God worked the
remedy, as He works all good things,—and there would
be no trouble about it if it were not for the men's strange
way of taking it. Did ever our Lord do a good or a kind
deed without being calumniated for it? Did not all those
men-fools in Jerusalem go about ' secretly seeking how
they might betray him '? That is a lesson for us all,—
and never forget, *petite,* that for showing them the
straight way to Heaven He was crucified! "

The next day a telegram was despatched from the
Archbishop of Rouen to Monsignor Moretti at the Vatican :—

" Claude Cazeau visited Hotel Poitiers last night, but
has since mysteriously disappeared. Every search and
enquiry being made. Strongly suspect foul play."

XXVI.

NOVEMBER was now drawing to a close, and St. Cecilia's Day dawned in a misty sunrise, half cloud, half light, like smoke and flame intermingled. Aubrey Leigh, on waking that morning, had almost decided to leave Rome before the end of the month. He had learned all that was necessary for him to know;—he had not come to study the antiquities, or the dark memories of dead empires, for he would have needed to live at least ten years in the city to gain even a surface knowledge of all the Romes, built one upon another, in the Rome of to-day. His main object had been to discover whether the Holy See existed as a grand and pure institution for the uplifting and the saving of the souls of men; or whether it had degenerated into an unscrupulous scheme for drawing the money out of their pockets. He had searched this problem and solved it. He had perceived the trickery, the dissimulation and hypocrisy of Roman priestcraft. He had seen the Pope officiate at High Mass in the Sistine Chapel, having procured the "introduction from very high quarters" which, even according to ordinary guide-books, is absolutely necessary,—the "high quarters" in this instance being Monsignor Gherardi. Apart from this absurdity,—this impious idea of needing an "introduction" to a sacred service professedly held for the worship of the Divine, by the Representative of Christ on earth, he had watched with sickening soul all the tawdry ceremonial so far removed from the simplicity of Christ's commands, —he had stared dully, till his brows ached, at the poor, feeble, scraggy old man with the pale, withered face and dark eyes, who was chosen to represent a "Manifestation of the Deity" to his idolatrous followers;—and as he thought of all the poverty, sorrow, pain, perplexity, and bewilderment of the "lost sheep" who were wandering to and fro in the world, scarcely able to fight the difficulties of their daily lot, and unable to believe in God because they were never allowed to understand or to experience any of His goodness, such a passion of protest arose in him, that he could have sprung on the very steps of the altar and cried aloud to the aged Manager of the Stage-scene there, " Away with this sham of Christianity! Give us the true message of Christ, undefiled! Sell these useless broidered silks,—these flaunting banners;—take the silver, gold, and bank-notes which hysterical pilgrims cast at your feet!—this Peter's Pence, amounting to millions, whose exact total you alone know,—and come out into the highways and byways of the cities of all lands,—call to you the lame, the halt, the blind, the sickly, and diseased,—give comfort where comfort is needed,—defend the innocent—protect the just, and silence the *Voce de la Verita* which published under your authority, callously advocates murder! "

And though he felt all this, he could only remain a dumb spectator of the Show in which not the faintest shadow of Christianity according to Christ, appeared—and when the theatrical pageant was over, he hurried out into the fresh air half stupefied with the heavy sense of shame that such things could be, and no man found true enough to the commands of the Divine Master to shake the world with strong condemnation.

" Twelve fishermen were enough to preach the Gospel," he thought, " Yet now there cannot be found twelve faithful souls who will protest against its falsification! "

And on St. Cecilia's morning he was in sad and sober mood,—too vexed with himself to contemplate his future work without a sense of pain and disappointment and loneliness. He loved Sylvie Hermenstein, and admitted his passion for her frankly to his own soul, but at the same time felt that a union with her would be impossible. He had seen her nearly every day since their first introduction to each other, and had realised to the height of soul-intoxication the subtle charm of her delicate beauty, and the sweetness of her disposition. But—(there was a but in it,—there always is!) he was not sure of her constancy. The duel between the Marquis Fontenelle and the actor Miraudin had furnished food for gossip at all the social gatherings in Rome, and Sylvie's name, freely mentioned as the cause of the dispute, had been thus given an unpleasant notoriety. And though Aubrey Leigh was far too chivalrous and noble-natured to judge and con-

demn a woman without seeking for the truth from her
own lips, he was indescribably annoyed to hear her spoken
of in any connection with the late Marquis. He had a
strong desire to ask Angela Sovrani a few questions concerning the affair, but hesitated, lest his keen personal
anxiety should betray the depth of his feelings. Then,
too, he was troubled by the fact that the Hermenstein
family had been from time immemorial devout Roman-
ists, and he felt that Sylvie must perforce be a firm adherent to that faith.

"Better to leave Rome!" he said to himself, "Better
to shake off the witchery of her presence, and get back
to England and to work. And if I cannot kill or quell
this love in me, at any rate it shall serve me to good purpose,—it shall make me a better and a braver man!"

He had promised to meet the Princesse D'Agramont
that morning at the Catacombs of St. Callistus, to see the
illumination of the tomb of St. Cecilia, which takes place
there annually on the Saint's Feast-Day, and he knew
that Angela Sovrani and the Comtesse Hermenstein were
to be of the Princesse's party. He was somewhat late in
starting, and hired a *fiacre* to drive him along the Via
Appia to his destination, but when he arrived there Mass
had already commenced. A Trappist monk, tall and grim
and forbidding of aspect, met him at the entrance to the
Catacombs with a lighted taper, and escorted him in
silence through the gloomy "Oratorium" and passage of
tombs,—the torch he carried flinging ghastly reflections
on the mural paintings and inscriptions, till, on reaching
the tomb of St. Cecilia where the murdered saint once
lay, though her remains are now enshrined in the Church
of St. Cecilia in Trastevere, the Trappist suddenly left
him at a corner to attend to other incoming visitors, and
disappeared. Aubrey looked around him, vaguely
touched and awed by the solemnity of the scene;—the
damp walls on which old Byzantine paintings of the
seventh century were still visible, though crumbling
fast away,—the glimmering lights,—the little crowd of
people pressed together,—the brilliantly illuminated altar,
—the droning accents of the officiating priests;—and
presently the sound of a boy's exquisite young voice rose
high and pure, singing the *Agnus Dei*. St. Cecilia herself might have been enraptured by such sweet harmony,

—and Aubrey Leigh instinctively bent his head, moved strongly by the holy and tender fervour of the anthem. Growing accustomed to the flickering lights, he presently perceived the Princesse D'Agramont a little in front of him,—and beside her were her two friends, Angela Sovrani and Sylvie Hermenstein. Sylvie was kneeling, and her face was hidden. Angela was seated,—and her eyes, full of the radiance of thought and dreaming genius, were fixed on the altar. Gradually he moved up till he reached the rough bench where they were all together,— the Princesse D'Agramont saw him at once, and signed to him to take a vacant place next to Sylvie. He sat down very gently—afraid to disturb the graceful figure kneeling within touch of his hand—how devout she seemed, he thought! But as the *Agnus Dei* ceased, she stirred, and rose quietly,—as quietly as a bent flower might lift itself in the grass after the rush of the wind,— and gave him a gentle salute, then sat down beside him, drooping her soft eyes over her prayer-book, but not before he had seen that they were wet with tears. Was she unhappy he wondered? It seemed impossible! Such a woman could never be unhappy! With beauty, health, and a sunny temperament,—wealth and independence, what could she know of sorrow! It is strange how seldom a man can enter into the true comprehension of a woman's grief, though he may often be the cause of the trouble. A woman, if endowed with beauty and charm, ought never, in a man's opinion, to *look* sad, whatever she may *feel*. It is her business to smile, and shine like a sunbeam on a spring morning for his delectation always. And Aubrey Leigh, though he could thoroughly appreciate and enter into the sordid woes of hard-worked and poverty-stricken womankind, was not without the same delusion that seems to possess all his sex,—namely, that if a woman is brilliantly endowed, and has sufficient of this world's goods to ensure her plenty of friends and pretty toilettes, she need never be unhappy. Sylvie's tears were therefore a mystery to him, except when a jealous pang contracted his generally liberal and tender soul, and he thought, " Perhaps she is grieving for the Marquis Fontenelle!" He glanced at her every now and again dubiously,—while the service went on, and the exquisite music beat rhythmic waves against the ancient walls and roof of the murdered Saint's tomb,—but her face, fair and childlike, was a puzzle to his mind,—he could never make out from its expression whether she were thoughtful or frivolous. Strange mistakes are often made in physiognomy. Often the so-called "intellectual" face,—the "touch-me-not" dignity—the "stalking-tragedy" manner, covers a total lack of brain, —and often a large-featured, seemingly "noble" face, has served as a mask for untold depths of villainy. The delicate, small face of Nelson suggested nothing of the giant heroism in his nature, and many a pretty, and apparently frivolous woman's face, which suggests nothing but the most thoughtless gaiety, is a disguise for a strong nature capable of lofty and self-sacrificing deeds. There is nothing likely to be so deceptive as a human countenance,—for with the exception of a few uncomfortably sincere persons, we all try to make it disguise our feelings as much as we can.

The service concluded, and St. Cecilia solemnly commended once more to her eternal rest, the people all rose and wandered like black ghosts, through the darkness of the Catacombs, following the flicker of the torches carried by the Trappist monks, who always perform the duty of guides on this occasion,—and, once out in the open air, in the full blaze of the sunshine which had now broken brilliantly through the mist of the previously threatening rain-clouds, Aubrey Leigh saw with pain that Sylvie looked very pale and ill. He ventured to say something solicitous concerning this to the Princesse D'Agramont, whose bright dark eyes flashed over him with an enigmatical look, half wonder, half scorn.

"What strange creatures men are!" she said satirically, "Even you, clever, and gifted with an insight into human nature, seem to be actually surprised that our poor, pretty little Sylvie looks ill! With half Rome declaring that she *was* the mistress of Fontenelle, and the other half swearing itself black in the face that she *is* the mistress of Gherardi, she certainly ought to be very happy, ought she not? Indeed, almost dancing with the joy and consolation of knowing how pleasant her 'Society' friends are making her life for her!"

Aubrey's heart beat violently.

"Princesse," he said, in a low tone of vibrating earnestness, " If I thought—if I could think such abominable lies were told of her . . . "

" *Chût!* " And the Princesse smiled rather sadly,— " It is not like you to ' pretend,' Mr. Leigh—You *do* know,—you *must* know—that a coarse discussion over her name was the cause of the duel between the Marquis Fontenelle and that miserable *vaurien* of the stage, Miraudin,—gossip generously lays the two deaths at her door—and the poor child is as innocent of harm as the lilies we have just seen left to die in the darkness of St. Cecilia's tomb. The fact is, she came to Rome to escape the *libertinage* and amorous persecution of Fontenelle; and she never knew till the day she heard of his death, that he had followed her. Nor did I. In fact, I asked him to be my escort to Rome, and he refused. Naturally I imagined he was still in Paris. So we were all in the dark, —and as often happens in such cases, when the world does not know whom to blame for a disaster, it generally elects to punish the innocent. All the Saints we have heard about this morning, bear witness to *that* truth! "

Aubrey lifted his eyes and looked yearningly at the sylph-like figure of Sylvie walking a little ahead of him with her friend Angela.

" I thought," he said hesitatingly,—" I confess, I thought there might have been something between her and the late Marquis . . . "

" Of course there was something! " answered the Princesse impatiently, " Oh, *mon Dieu! Plus de sottises!* There always *is* something where Sylvie is, Mr. Leigh! She cannot smile or sing, or turn her head, or raise her eyes, or smell a bunch of violets, without some one of your audacious sex conceiving the idea of making himself agreeable and indispensable to her. And when she will not compromise herself—(is that not your convenient little phrase?)—she is judged much more severely than if she had done so! And do you know why? Because you men can never endure defeat in love-matters! You would rather spread abroad the rumour that you had conquered, than confess that your libertinism had been perceived and repulsed with indignation and scorn! And I will tell you another thing if you do not know it. In the frequent destruction of an innocent woman's reputation, it is a rejected suitor who generally starts the first rumour and hands the lie over to debased women, knowing that *they* may be trusted to keep it up!"

Aubrey flushed, and winced under the lash of her cutting words.

"You are very cruel, Princesse!" he said, "Surely unnecessarily bitterly cruel!"

"*Cher philosophe,* I have loved!" she replied, "And that is why I am cruel. I have loved and have been deceived in love,—and that kind of thing often turns the most patient Griselda into an exceptionally fierce tiger-cat! I am not quite a tiger-cat,—but I confess I do not like one-sidedness in anything, Nature's tendency being to equalise—equalise—till we are all flattened down into one level,—the grave! At the present moment we are treading on a mixture of kings and saints and heroes, —all one soil you see, and rather marshy,—badly in need of draining at all times!" She laughed a little. "Frankly, I assure you, it is to me the most deplorable arrangement that a true woman should be destined to give all the passion and love of her life to one man, while the same man scatters his worthless affections about like halfpence among dozens of drabs! My dear Mr. Leigh, do not frown at me in that tragic way! I am not blaming *you!* I am not in the least inclined to put you in the general category,—at least not at present. You do not look like the ordinary man, though you may be for all that! Expression is very deceptive!" She laughed again, then added, "Think of our sweet Angela, for instance! Unless a merciful Providence intervenes, she will marry Florian Varillo,—and no doubt he will make her invite Mademoiselle Pon-Pon to her house to dine and sleep!"

"She loves him!" said Aubrey simply.

"Yes, she loves him, because she deludes herself with the idea that he is worthy of love. But if she were to find him out her whole soul would indignantly repulse him. If she knew all *I* know of him, she would rather embrace the mildewy skeleton of San Carlo Borromeo, with the great jewels glistening in his ghastly eye-sockets, than the well-fed, fresh coloured Florian Varillo!"

"If you fear for her happiness, why not warn her?" asked Aubrey.

"Warn her against the one creature she loves in the world?" said the Princesse, "Thanks very much! I would rather not. She would never speak to me again, and I should lose every chance of comforting or helping her when affliction comes—as of course it is bound to come! Each individual man or woman makes his or her own life,—we poor 'friends' can only stand and look on, waiting till they get into the muddle that we have always foreseen, and then doing our best to drag them out of it; but God Himself I think, could not save them from falling into the muddle in the first place. As for Sylvie, I have advised her to leave Rome and go back to Budapest at once."

Aubrey started.

"Why?"

"Why? Can you ask? Because she is misjudged here on account of Fontenelle's death, and calumniated and wronged; because the women hate her for her beauty and wealth, and the men hate her too because she will not flatter them by accepting their ridiculous attentions. She will be much happier in her own home,—such a grand old castle it is!—a cluster of towers and broad battlements, with purple mountains in the background, and tall pine-trees everywhere . . . "

"It must be lonely for her!" said Aubrey quickly, "She is so *mignonne*—so caressable—so made for love and care and tenderness——" Here he broke off, vexed with himself for having said so much,—and his face flushed warmly. The Princesse stopped in her walk and looked at him straightly.

"Mr. Leigh," she said, "I think—I hope you are an honest man! And do you know the best advice I can give you?"

He answered no word, but his eyes questioned her meaning.

"Remain honest!" she said, smiling an answer to his look, "Be true to your own instincts and highest impulses. Do not allow yourself to be swayed by opinion or rumour; stand clear of both,—and treat *even* a woman as you would treat a man!—squarely—candidly—faithfully!"

She moved on and rejoined her companions, and Aubrey followed. The Comtesse Hermenstein's carriage

was waiting for her, and the Comtesse herself was just
entering it with Angela Sovrani as he came up.

"Good-bye, Mr. Leigh," she said gently, extending
her hand, "I may not see you again perhaps. I am going home to Buda this week."

"Must you go?" he asked, looking earnestly into the
lovely eyes, lovelier than ever in their present sorrowful
languor.

"I think so," she answered, "I may wait to see Angela's great picture, but——"

"Do not hurry your departure," said Aubrey, speaking
in a softer tone——"Tell me—may I come and see you
this evening,—just for a few moments?"

His eyes rested on her tenderly, and at the passion of
his glance her own fell.

"If you like——yes," she murmured. And just then
the Princesse D'Agramont approached.

"May I drive you home, Mr. Leigh?" she asked.

"Thank you!" And Aubrey smiled as he accepted
the invitation.

And presently the carriages started, Sylvie's light vic-
toria leading, and the Princesse D'Agramont's landeau
following. Half way back to Rome a picturesque little
beggar, whose motley-coloured rags scarcely clothed his
smooth brown limbs, suddenly sprang out of a corner
where he had been in hiding with a great basket of violets, and threw the whole fragrant heap dexterously into
Sylvie's carriage, crying out,

"*Bellissima Signora! Bellissima! Bellissima! Un
soldo! Un soldo!*"

Laughingly Sylvie threw out four or five francs, but
Aubrey, carried beyond all prudence by catching a
glimpse of Sylvie's pretty head gleaming above the great
purple cluster of violets she had caught and held, tossed a
twenty-franc piece to the clever little rascal who had by
"suiting the action to the word, and the word to the action" as Italians so often do, gained a week's earnings in
one successful morning.

And the evening came, misty but mild, with the moon
peering doubtfully through a fleecy veil of fine floating
vapour, which, gathering flashes of luminance from the
silver orb, turned to the witch-lights of an opal,—and
Aubrey made his way to the Casa D'Angeli, which in his

own mind he called the "Palais D'Iffry," in memory of
the old Breton song, Sylvie had sung. On giving his
name he was at once shown up into the great *salon*, now
made beautiful by the picturesque and precious things accumulated there, and arranged with the individuality and
taste of the presiding spirit. She was quite alone, seated
in a deep easy chair near the fire,—and her dress, of some
faint shell-pink hue, clung about her in trailing soft folds
which fell in a glistening heap of crushed rose-tints at
her feet, making a soft rest for her tiny dog who was
luxuriously curled therein. The firelight shed a warm
glow around her,—flickering brightly on her fair hair, on
her white arms, and small hands where one or two diamonds flashed like drops of dew,—and Aubrey, as he entered, was conscious of an overpowering sense of weakness, poverty of soul, narrowness of mind, incompetency
of attainment,—for the tranquillity and sweet perfection
of the picture his eyes rested upon—a picture lovelier
than even the Gretchen which tempted Goëthe's Faust to
Hell,—made him doubtful of his own powers—mistrust-
ful of his own worth. In his life of self-renunciation
among the poorer classes, he had grown accustomed to
pity women,—to look upon them more or less as frail,
broken creatures needing help and support,—sometimes
to be loved, but far more often to be despised and neglected. But Sylvie, Comtesse Hermenstein, was not of
these,—he knew, or thought he knew that she needed
nothing. Beauty was hers, wealth was hers, independence of position was hers; and if she had given a smile
or nod of encouragement, lovers were hers to command.
What was he that he should count himself at all valuable
in her sight, even as the merest friend? These despond-
ent thoughts were doubly embittered by the immense
scorn he now entertained for himself that he should have
been such a fool as to listen for a moment to the silly and
malignant gossip circulated among the envious concerning a woman who was admittedly the superior of those
who calumniated her. For clearest logic shows that wherever superiority exists, inferiority rises up in opposition,
and the lower endeavours to drag the higher down.
Such vague reflections, coursing rapidly through his
brain, gave him an air of embarrassment and awkward-
ness not by any means common to him, as he advanced,

and Sylvie, half rising from her chair, greeted him in her turn with a little touch of shyness which sent a wave of soft colour over her face, and made her look ten times prettier than ever.

" I am glad to find you alone——" he began.

" Yes? I am generally alone," answered Sylvie with a little smile——" except for Katrine——she would be here to welcome you this evening, but she has a very bad neuralgic headache——"

" I am very sorry," murmured Aubrey, with hypocritical earnestness, all the while devoutly blessing Madame Bozier's timely indisposition. " She is a great sufferer from neuralgia, I believe?"

" Yes . . ." and Sylvie, to divert the cloud of embarrassment that seemed to be deepening rather than dispersing for them both, rang the bell with a pretty imperativeness that was rather startling to Aubrey's nerves.

" What is that for?" he enquired irrelevantly.

" Only for coffee!"

Their eyes met,—the mutual glance was irresistible, and they both laughed. Sylvie's Arab page entered in response to her summons, a pretty dusky-skinned lad of some twelve years old, picturesquely arrayed in scarlet, and bearing a quaintly embossed gilt salver with coffee prepared in the Arabian fashion.

" Do you like coffee made in this way?" asked Sylvie, as she handed Aubrey his cup.

Aubrey's eyes were fixed on the small white hand that looked so dainty, curled over the trifle of Sèvres china that was called a coffee-cup,—and he answered vaguely,

" This way? Oh, yes——of course—any way!"

A faint smile lifted the rosy corners of Sylvie's mouth as she heard this incoherent reply—and the Arab page rolled his dark eyes up at his fair mistress with a look of dog-like affectionate enquiry, as to whether perhaps some fault in his serving had caused that little playful enigmatical expression on the face which he, in common with many others of his sex, thought the fairest in the world. The coffee dispensed and the page gone, there followed a spell of silence. The fire burned cheerily in the deep chimney, and the great logs cracked and spluttered as much as to say, "If these two curious people can find nothing to talk about, we can!" And then, just as luck would have it, a burning ember suddenly detached itself from the rest and fell out blazing on the hearth—Sylvie sprang up to push it back, and Aubrey to assist her,—and then, strange to relate—only the occult influences of attraction know how it happened—the little difficulty of the burning ember brought those two other burning embers of humanity together—for Aubrey, hardly conscious of what he did, caught Sylvie's swaying, graceful figure as she rose from bending over the fire, closely in his arms, with a passion which mounted like a wave to tempest height, and knew no further hesitation or obstacle.

"Sylvie! Sylvie! I love you!—my darling! I love you!——"

No answer came, for there was none needed. Her face was hidden on his breast—but he felt rather than saw the soft white arms and dainty hands moving tremblingly upwards, till they closed round him in the dear embrace which meant for him from henceforth the faith and love and devotion of one true heart through all the sorrows and perplexities as well as the joys and triumphs of life. And when, with his heart beating, and all his pulses thrilling with the new ecstacy that possessed him, he whispered a word or two that caused the pretty golden head to raise itself timidly—the beautiful dark blue eyes to grow darker with the tenderness that overflowed the soul behind them, and the sweet lips to meet his own in a kiss, as soft and fragrant as though a rose had touched them, it was small blame to him that for a moment he lost his self-possession, and drawing her closer in his arms, showered upon her not only kisses, but whispered words of all that tender endearment which is judged as "foolish" by those who have never had the privilege of being made the subject of such priceless and exquisite "fooling." And when they were calmer, and began to think of the possibility of the worthy Bozier suddenly recovering from her neuralgia and coming to look after her pupil,—or the undesired but likely entrance of a servant to attend to the lamps, or to put fresh wood on the fire, they turned each from the other, with reluctance and half laughing decorum,—Sylvie resuming her seat by the fire, and Aubrey flinging himself

with happy recklessness in a low fauteuil as near to
her as could be permitted for a gentleman visitor, who
might be considered as enthusiastically expounding literature or science to a fascinating hostess. And somehow,
as they talked, their conversation did gradually drift from
passionate personalities into graver themes affecting
wider interests, and Aubrey, warming into eloquence,
gave free vent to his thoughts and opinions, till noticing
that Sylvie sat very silent, looking into the fire somewhat
gravely, he checked himself abruptly, fancying that perhaps he was treading on what might be forbidden ground
with her whose pleasure was now his law. As he came
to this sudden pause, she turned her soft eyes towards him
tenderly, with a smile.

" Well!" she said, in the pretty foreign accent which
distinguished her almost perfect English, " And why do
you stop speaking? You must not be afraid to trust me
with your closest thoughts,—because how can our love
be perfect if you do not?"

" Sweetheart!" he answered, catching the white hand
that was so temptingly near his own, " Our love *is* perfect!—and so far as I am concerned there shall never be
a cloud on such a dazzling sky!"

She smiled.

" Ah, you talk romance just now!" she said, " But Aubrey, I want our love to be something more than romance
—I want it to be a grand and helpful reality! If I am
not worthy to be the companion of your very soul, you
will not, you cannot love me long. Now, no protestations!" For he had possessed himself of the dear little
hand again, and was covering it with kisses—" You see,
it is very sweet just now to sit by the fire together, and
look at each other, and feel how happy we are—but life
does not go on like that. And your life, my Aubrey, belongs to the world . . ."

" To you!—to you!" said Aubrey passionately, " I
give it to you! You know the song?—

> I set my life in your hand
> Mar it or make it sweet,—
> I set my life in your hand,
> I lay my heart at your feet!"

Sylvie rose impulsively, and leaning over his chair
kissed his forehead.

"Yes, I know! And I know you mean what you say! I could not imagine you telling an untruth,—not even in making love!" and she laughed, "Though there are many of your sex who think any amount of lies permissible under similar circumstances! And it is just because I have found men such practised liars, that I have the reputation of being heartless. Did you ever think me heartless?"

Aubrey hesitated a moment.

"Yes," he admitted at last, frankly, "I did till I knew better. I was told——"

"Stop! I know all you were told!" said Sylvie, drawing her slim figure up with a pretty dignity as she moved back to her place by the fire—"You were told that I was the cause of the death of the Marquis Fontenelle. So I was, unhappily—but not through my own fault. The actor Miraudin,—known to be one of the most coarse-minded and brutal of men,—slandered me in public,—the Marquis defended me. Hence the combat and its fatal end, which no one has deplored more bitterly than I. Miraudin was never a gentleman,—Fontenelle could have been one had he chosen. And I confess I cared very much for him at one time!"

"You loved him," said Aubrey, trying to master a pang of jealousy.

"Yes! I loved him!—till he proved himself unworthy of love."

There was a silence.

"I tell you all this," said Sylvie then slowly and emphatically, "that you may know me at once as I am. I wish to hide nothing from you. I have read all your books—I know your views of life—your hatred of dissimulation—your contempt of a lie! In your love for me, you must have complete knowledge of my nature, and confidence in my truth. I would never give my life to any man unless he trusted me absolutely,—unless I was sure he felt I was a real helpmate for him. I love you—but I also love your work and your aims; and I go with all your thoughts and wish to share all your responsibilities. But I must feel that you will never misjudge me,—never set me down on the level of mean and small-natured women, who cannot sacrifice themselves or their personal vanities for another's sake. It is not for me to say that the calumnies circulated concerning me are untrue,—it is for my life to show and *prove* they are not! But I must be trusted—not suspected; and if you give me your life as you say, I will give mine to help make yours happier, asking from you in return just your faith —your *faith* as well as your love!"

Like a fair queen she stood, royal in her look, bearing and attitude, and Aubrey bent his head low in reverence before her as he once more kissed her hand.

"My wife!" he said simply.

And the silence that followed was as that of God's benediction on that perfect marriage which is scarcely ever consummated in all the world,—the marriage of two souls, which like twin flames, unite and burn upward clear to Heaven, as One.

XXVII

SOCIETY soon learned the news of the Countess Hermenstein's betrothal to the " eccentric Englishman," Aubrey Leigh,—and with its million tongues discussed the affair in all tones,—most people preferring to say, with the usual " society " kindness, that—" Leigh was not quite such a self-sacrificing idealist as he seemed to be,—he was going to marry for money." Some few ventured to remark that Sylvie Hermenstein was charming in herself and well worth winning,—but the more practical pooh-poohed this view of the case at once. " Pretty women are to be had by the score," they said, " It is the money that tells ! " Aubrey Leigh caught these rumours, and was in a manner stung by them,—he said very little however, and to all the congratulations he received, merely gave coldly civil thanks. And so the gossips went to work again in their own peculiar way, and said, " Well ! She will have an iceberg for a husband, that is one thing ! A stuck up, insolent sort of chap !—not a bit of go in him ! " Which was true,—Aubrey had no " go." " Go " means, in modern parlance, to drink oneself stupid, to bet on the most trifling passing events, and to talk slang that would disgrace a stable-boy, as well as to amuse oneself with all sorts of mean and vulgar intrigues which are carried on through the veriest skulk and caddishness ;—thus Aubrey was a sad failure in " tip-top " circles. But the " tip-top " circles are not a desirable heaven to every man ;—and Aubrey did not care much as to what sort of comments were passed on himself, provided he could see Sylvie always " queen it " over her inferiors in that graceful, gracious way of conquest which was her special peculiarity and charm. Among her friends no one perhaps was happier in Sylvie's happiness than Angela Sovrani ; her nature was of that rare quality which vibrates like a harp to every touch, and the joy of others swept over her with a gladness which made her more glad than if she had received some priceless boon for her own benefit. Florian Varillo was exceedingly angry at the whole affair,—and whenever Sylvie's betrothal was spoken of he assumed an expression of pained and personal offence which was almost grotesque.

"Such a marriage is ridiculous!" he declared,— "Everyone can see how utterly unsuited the two are in tastes, habits and opinions! They will rue the day they ever met!"

And not all the gentle remonstrances of his own *fiancée* Angela, could soothe his ruffled humour, or make him accept the inevitable with grace. Angela was exceedingly troubled and puzzled by his almost childish waywardness,—she did not yet understand the nature of a man who was to himself all in all, and who could not endure the idea that any woman whom he personally condescended to admire should become the possession of another, no matter how completely that woman might be beyond his own reach. Poor Angela! She was very simple—very foolish indeed;—she never imagined it could be possible for a man to carry on five or six love-affairs at once, and never be found out. Yet this was the kind of life her "ideal" found the most suitable to his habit and temperament,—and he had made a mental note of Sylvie Hermenstein as one whom he proposed to add to his little list of conquests. So that her engagement of marriage to one who, though reserved in manner and without "go," was yet every inch a gentleman, and a determined opposer of sophistry and humbug, had considerably disturbed his little plans, and the unsettlement of anything he had set his heart upon greatly displeased him. He generally had his own way in most things, and could not at all comprehend why he was not to have it now. But among all the people who discussed the intended marriage there were two who were so well satisfied as to be almost jubilant, and these were the Monsignori Moretti and Gherardi. These worthies met together in one of the private chambers set apart for the use of the Papal court in the Vatican, and heartily congratulated each other on the subjugation and enthralment of Aubrey Leigh, which meant, as they considered, the consequent removal of a fierce opponent to the Roman Catholic movement in England.

"Did I not tell you," said Moretti, as he untied some

papers he had been carrying, and sat down at a table to glance over them, " Did I not tell you that when all other arguments fail, the unanswerable one of woman can be brought in to clinch every business? "

Gherardi, though in a way contented, was not altogether so sure of his goal. He remembered, with an uncomfortable thrill of doubt, the little skirmish of words he had had with the fair Sylvie in the Pamphili woods.

" You take your thoughts for deeds, and judge them as fully accomplished while they are still in embryo! " he said, " It is true that the engagement of marriage is settled,—but can you be certain that in religious matters the wife may not go with her husband? "

" What! " exclaimed Moretti, opening his dark eyes quickly, as a flash of hell-fire illumined them at the very idea, " Do you suggest that Sylvie Hermenstein,—the last of her race—a race which, back to its earliest source, has been distinguished for its faithful allegiance to Mother-Church, and has moreover added largely to the Papal revenues—could be otherwise than our obedient and docile daughter? *Per la Santissima Madonna!*—if I thought she could turn against us her marriage should never take place! "

And he brought his fist down with a fierce blow on the papers before him.

" The marriage should never take place! " echoed Gherardi, " How could you prevent it? "

" The Pope himself should intervene! " said Moretti, with increasing fury, losing a little of his self-control, " *Gran Dio!* Conceive for a moment the wealth of the Hermensteins being used to promulgate the reformer Leigh's threadbare theories, and feed his rascal poor! Do you know what Sylvie Hermenstein's fortune is? No, I suppose you do not! But I do! She tries to keep it a secret, but I have made it my business to find out! It is enormous!—and it is ever increasing. With all the fanciful creature's clothes and jewels and unthinking way of living her life, she spends not a quarter, nor half a quarter of her income,—and yet you actually venture to suggest that her power is so slight over the man who is now her promised husband, that she would voluntarily allow him to use all that huge amount of money as he pleased, *outside* the Church? "

Moretti spoke with such passionate insistence that Gherardi thought it prudent not to irritate him further by argument. So he merely said,

"You expect her to persuade him to embrace our faith?"

"Naturally!" answered Moretti, "And she can, and will do so. If she cannot or will not, she must be *made* to do so!"

He bent over his papers again and rustled them impatiently, but his hand trembled. The pale December sunlight glittered through a stained-glass window above him, and cast deep violet rays about his chair,—Gherardi stood where the same luminance touched his pale face with a crimson glow as of fire.

"This is a busy morning with us," said Moretti, without looking up, "The excommunication of Denis Vergniaud will be pronounced to-day,—and, what is even more important,—Cardinal Bonpré is summoned by His Holiness's command to wait upon him this afternoon, bringing the boy,—that boy who is always with him—"

"Ah, there is a history there!" interrupted Gherardi, "It should be remembered that this boy was a witness of the miracle in Rouen, and he was also present at the Vergniaud scandal in Paris——he should have been sent for ere now. He, more than anyone, must surely know how the miracle was accomplished,—for the worthy Felix tells me he is 'wise beyond his years'!"

"So! His wisdom will be put to the test to-day!" said Moretti coldly, "Do you not think it strange"— here he raised his eyes from his papers, "and somewhat incriminating too—always supposing the miracle is a case of conspiracy—that no trace has been discovered of the man Claude Cazeau?"

Gherardi had moved to a book-case, and was standing close to it, turning over a vellum-bound manuscript.

"Yes—the whole business looks as black as murder!" he said.

Moretti looked at him sharply.

"Murder? You suppose——"

"That Claude Cazeau has been murdered? Certainly I suppose it! It is more than a week now since we heard that he had mysteriously disappeared, and still there is no news. What can it be but murder? But I do not for a moment suppose that our good Saint Felix is concerned in it!"

And he smiled, turning over the vellum volume carelessly.

Moretti knitted his dark brows.

"No—no!" he said musingly, "That would not be possible! Cardinal Bonpré is not that kind of man—he would rather bear the heaviest weight of punishment for himself than allow another to suffer. That I *know* of him;—and though I do not admire his extreme views on this point, and do not think them politic, I give him full credit for this particular and uncommon form of—eccentricity!"

"Or Christianity!" said Gherardi, still smiling.

Moretti pushed aside his papers, and leaning his head on one hand frowned meditatively at the amethyst light which streamed radiantly through the jewel-like window above him.

"Yes—or Christianity, if you like!" he said, "For Christianity *pur et simple, would* be eccentricity. In its primitive simplicity it is an impossible creed. Founded by the Divine it needs divine beings to comprehend and follow it,—beings not of this world nor addicted to the things of this world. And to exist in the world, made of the world's clay, and the world's inherited associations, and yet not be of it, is to be judged crazed! True, there have been saints and martyrs,—there are saints and martyrs now, unknown and unheard of, but nevertheless consumed by flames more cruel perhaps than those which physically burn the flesh;—idealists, thinkers, dreamers, heralds of future progress,—and how are they estimated? As madmen all! To be human, and yet above humanity, is the supreme sin! For that very affront the multitude cried out, 'Not this man, but Barabbas!' And to this day we all prefer Barabbas to Christ. Hence the power of the Church!"

Gherardi put back the volume he had been glancing at, on its shelf, and looked at his *confrère* with a certain amount of admiring respect. He had been long an interested student of the various psychological workings of Moretti's mind,—and he knew that Moretti's scheming brain was ever hard at work designing bold and almost martial plans for securing such conversions to the Church as would seriously trouble the peace of two or three great nations. Moretti was in close personal touch with every crowned head in Europe; he was acquainted more closely than anyone alive with the timidities, the nervous horrors, the sudden scruples, the sickening qualms of conscience, and the overwhelming fears of death which troubled the minds of certain powerful personages apparently presenting a brave front to the world,—and he held such personages in awe by the very secrets which they had, in weak moments, entrusted to him. Gherardi even was not without his own fears,—he instinctively felt that Moretti knew more about himself than was either safe or convenient.

"We all live for Barabbas," pursued Moretti, an ironical smile playing on his thin lips, "Not for Christ! Barabbas, in the shape of the unscrupulous millionaire, robs the world!—and we share the spoils, pardon his robberies, and set him free. But whosoever lives outside Dogma, serving God purely and preaching truth,—him we crucify!—but our Robber,—our murderer of Truth, we set at liberty! Hence, as I said before, the power of the Church!"

Carried away by his thoughts, he rose, and pacing the room, talked more to himself than to Gherardi.

"The Church supports the robber, because he is always a coward and cannot stand alone. The murderer of his fellow-men's good name is naturally a liar, and fears lest his lies should find him out. Fear! That is the keynote on which we of Rome play our invincible march of triumph! The Church appeals to the ignorant, the base, the sensual, the false, and the timorous; and knowing that they never repent, but are only afraid, retains them by fear!—fear, not love! Christ taught love —but hate is the more popular virtue! Hence again, the power of the Church!"

"Your argument is perfectly orthodox!" said Gherardi, with a smile.

"Hate is a grand, a strong quality!" went on Moretti, "It makes nations, it builds up creeds! If men loved one another what should they need of a Church? But Hate! —the subtle sense which makes the ultra-respectable thank God that he is not as other men are!—the fierce emotion which almost touches ecstacy when the wronged individual thinks his enemy will go to hell!—the fine fever which sets father against son, creed against creed, nation against nation!—hate is the chief mainspring of human motives! From hate and envy spring emulation and conquest—and we of the Church encourage the haters to hate on! They make Us!—they emulate each other in the greed of their gifts to us, which give them notoriety and advertise their generosity,—*we* fan the flame and encourage the fury! For the world must have a religion—it crucified Christ, but the Church, built up in His name, takes just and daily revenge for His murder! We do not save—we kill! We do not rescue—we trample down! We humiliate,—we crush wherever we can, and it is well and fitting we should do so! For Humanity is a brute beast, and serves us best under the lash. Rome made many a blunder in the old days of barbarity and ignorance—but now we have a thousand forces put into our hands instead of one or two,—forces to terrorise—forces to compel!——and the power of Rome wielded by the Popes of the days to come, shall be indeed a power irresistible!"

He stood enrapt,—his hand upraised, his eyes flashing; then recalling himself, turned abruptly on Gherardi with an impatient gesture.

"You can repeat all this," he said sarcastically, "in your next eloquent discourse with Aubrey Leigh! It will save you the trouble of thinking! His influence with the English masses will be but a brief phenomenon,—the blind and brutal stupidity of the people he seeks to serve will soon dishearten and discourage him, and then he will come to us through his wife, and his conversion will be a triumph worth winning,—a step in the right direction. And now to other matters. These papers," and he sat down at the table once more, "are, I think, sufficiently in order to be placed before His Holiness. But you may as well look through them with me first. Later on, the affair of Cardinal Bonpré will occupy all our time . . ."

"It is an 'affair' then?" asked Gherardi, "The 'saint' is in trouble?"

"All 'saints' get into trouble!" answered Moretti, "It is only sinners who receive honour! Cardinal Bonpré has made the fatal mistake of reading Jesus Christ's Gospel instead of Church Doctrine! His creed is Love,—his duty, as I have just explained to you, if he would be a faithful son of the Church, is Hate!"

"Love forms no part of your nature then?" asked Gherardi, hardly knowing why he put the question, yet curious as to the answer.

"I am of the world!" replied Moretti coldly, "And I hate accordingly. I hate, and in my hate, aspire to crush those who in turn hate me! That is the human code, and one that must be strictly practised by all who would rule mankind. Never do anything for those who can do nothing for you! Firmly oppose those who oppose you! Revenge yourself on those who despitefully use you! We do revenge ourselves,—and we reward all who help us to our revenge! For example, Denis Vergniaud has cast opprobrium on his calling, and made a scandal and a shame of the Church before his congregation in Paris;— we excommunicate him! It is no use, but we do it on principle. And we are still unable to explain away, or offer any excuse for Cardinal Bonpré's mistake in condoning and pardoning his offence. Therefore it follows as you say, that the 'saint' is in trouble!"

"Notwithstanding the miracle?"

"Notwithstanding the miracle!" echoed Moretti, "For the miracle is doubtful. The Holy Father is not satisfied of its truth. Yes—there is no doubt about it, Saint Felix is in trouble! It would be better for him had he never come out of his long retirement. But perhaps he was compelled to look after his Rouen foundling!"

A smile flickered faintly over Gherardi's face, but he said not a word in answer. Discovering an error in one of the documents he was examining, he called Moretti's attention to it, and the conversation drifted to everyday trivial subjects. But the thoughts of both men were elsewhere, and not even the news received that morning of the bequest of one hundred thousand pounds to the Shrine of Lourdes from a deluded believer in the miraculous Virgin there, absorbed so much of their reflective brain powers as the imminent trial—for it was little else —of Cardinal Bonpré, in the presence of the boy to whom he so openly gave his confidence and protection.

Meanwhile, the good Felix himself was very sorely

troubled. During his sojourn in Rome, he had grown thinner and paler, and the fine, spiritual delicacy of his features had become more intensified, while his clear blue eyes shone from under their deeply arched brows with a flashing luminance that was almost unearthly. Often, when about to enter his room with unthinking haste, his brother-in-law, Prince Pietro, would see him kneeling before his crucifix absorbed, one might almost say entranced, in prayer. And he would softly move away again with a deep sense of awe, and a feeling that some higher power than any on earth, sustained the venerable prelate, and inspired both his words and actions. But with all his patient, sometimes passionate prayer, earnest meditations, and constant study of the Gospels, the Cardinal himself was more or less heavy-hearted,—and his Master's phrase—" My soul is exceeding sorrowful even unto death! " was one which he often breathed in the solitude and extremity of his own position. The news of the disappearance of Claude Cazeau had materially added to his difficulties—and now he had been commanded, with a certain peremptoriness in the summons, to wait upon the Sovereign Pontiff in a private audience, bringing with him the boy who could, or would give no further account of himself than that of a world's waif and stray. Prepared for this visit and arrayed in all the splendour befitting his rank in the Church, the gentle old man looked paler and more fragile than ever, and the vague trouble he felt at the express injunction laid upon him concerning Manuel, showed itself in the deep furrows of anxiety marked upon his brow, and the pain in his thoughtful eyes. Prince Pietro's own man-servant had assisted him to dress for the impending ceremonial, and just as the last folds of his regal attire were being set in place a knock was heard at the door of his apartment, and Prince Pietro himself entered.

"A telegram for you, brother Felix," he said, " I have brought it myself, thinking it may perhaps immediately concern your visit to the Pope to-day."

The Cardinal, with a gentle word of thanks, opened the envelope handed to him.

" Praise be to God! " he said simply, as he read its contents, " Vergniaud has passed to the Higher tribunal! "

And he crossed himself reverently on brow and breast.

"Dead?" exclaimed Sovrani.

"To this world, yes!" answered Bonpré, "He died peacefully last night. This message is from his son."

A faint ironical smile flickered over Sovrani's dark features.

"The ban of excommunication has not been declared!" he said, "It will be a somewhat belated announcement!"

Cardinal Bonpré folded the telegram, ready to take with him to the Vatican.

"The Church can excommunicate even the dead!" he said sorrowfully, "If such an extreme measure is judged politic it will doubtless be carried out!"

"Wonderful Christian charity," murmured Sovrani under his breath, "to excommunicate a corpse! For that is all they can do. The Soul of the man is God's affair!"

Cardinal Bonpré answered nothing, for just then the young Manuel entered the room, in readiness to accompany his venerable protector and friend to the Vatican, and the old man's eyes rested upon him with a wistful, wondering trouble and anxiety which he could not conceal. Manuel smiled up at him—that rare and beautiful smile which was like sunshine in darkness—but the Cardinal's sad expression did not alter.

"The Abbé Vergniaud is no more," he said gently, as the boy drew near, "His sins and sufferings are ended!"

"And his joys have begun!" answered Manuel, "For he set his life right with the world before he left it!"

"Child, you talk as a very wise man might!" said Prince Sovrani, his rugged brows smoothing into a kindly smile. "But the unfortunate Abbé is not likely to be judged in that way. It will be said of him that he scandalized the world before he left it!"

"When truth is made scandal, and right is made wrong," said Manuel, "It will surely be a God-forgotten world!"

"*Will* be? I think it is already!" said Prince Pietro. "It is said that the patience of the Almighty is unwearied,—but I do not feel sure of that in my own mind. Science teaches us that many a world has been destroyed before now,—and sometimes I feel as if our turn were soon coming!"

Here the man-servant having completely finished arranging the Cardinal's attire, made respectful obeisance and left the room, and the Cardinal himself proceeded into the adjoining *salon,* where he found his niece Angela waiting to see him.

"Dearest uncle," she said, making her pretty genuflection as he approached her, "I must ask you to forgive me for coming to your rooms just now when your time is so much taken up, and when I know you have to go to the Vatican,—but I want to tell you one thing that may perhaps please you,—my picture is finished!"

"Finished!" echoed the Cardinal——then tenderly taking her hands, he added, "I congratulate you, dear child, with all my heart!—and I pray that the reward of your long and patient toil may be worthy of you. And when are we to see your work?"

"To-morrow!" answered Angela, and her cheeks flushed, and her eyes sparkled, "I shall be busy all to-day arranging it for exhibition in the best light. To-morrow morning Florian is to see it first,—then my father will come, and you——and Manuel!" and she smiled as she met the boy's gentle look,—"And Queen Margherita has promised to be here at mid-day."

"Florian first! And then your father!" said Prince Pietro, with a touch of melancholy in his tone, "Ah well, Angela *mia!*—I suppose it must always be so! The lover's love—the stranger's love,—is greater than the love of years, the love of home! Yet sometimes, I fancy that the lover's love often turns out to be a passing impulse more than a real truth, and that the home-love reasserts itself afterwards with the best and the holiest power!"

And not trusting himself to say more, he abruptly left the room. Angela looked after him, a little troubled. The Cardinal took her hand.

"He is your father, dear girl!" he said gently, "And he cannot but feel it hard—at first—to be relegated to a second place in your affections."

Angela sighed.

"I cannot help it!" she said, "Florian is my very life! I should have no ambition—no joy in anything if he did not love me!"

Over the Cardinal's fine open face there came an expression of great pain.

"That is idolatry, Angela!" he said gravely, "We make a grievous mistake when we love human beings too deeply,—for they are not the gods we would make of them. Like ourselves, they are subject to sin, and their sins often create more unhappiness for us than our own!"

"Ah! But we can save our beloved ones from sin!" answered Angela, with a beautiful upward look of exaltation,—"That is love's greatest mission!"

"It is a mission that cannot always be fulfilled"—said the Cardinal sorrowfully,—then, after a pause he added—"The Abbé Vergniaud is dead."

"Dead!" And Angela turned very pale. "His son——"

"His son sends the message——" and he handed her the telegram he had received. She read it, and returned it to him,—then made the sign of the cross.

"May he rest in peace!" He died true!"

"Yes, he died true. But remember, child, neither Truth nor Love are spared their crown of thorns. Love cannot save—would that it could! It may warn—it may pray—it may watch—it may hope,—but if despite its tenderness, the sinner sins, what can love do then?"

"It can pardon!" said Angela softly.

Deeply moved, the good Felix took her hand and patted it gently.

"Dear child, God grant your powers of forgiveness may never be put to the test!" he ejaculated fervently. "The one unforgivable sin according to our Lord, is treachery;—may *that* never come your way!"

"It can never come my way through Florian!" answered Angela smiling,—"and for the rest—I do not care!"

Manuel stood by silently, with thoughtful, downcast eyes—but at these last words of hers he raised his head and looked full at her with a touch of melancholy in his straight regard.

"Ah, that is wrong!" he said, "You *should* care!—you *must* care for the rest of the world. We must all learn to care for others more than ourselves. And if we will not learn, God sometimes takes a hard way of teaching us!"

Angela's head drooped a little. Then she said,

"I *do* care for others,—I think perhaps my picture will prove that for me. But the tenderness I have for the sorrows of the world is impersonal; and perhaps if I analysed myself honestly, I feel even that through my love for Florian. If he were not in the world, I am afraid I should not love the world so much!"

The Cardinal said no more, for just then a servant entered and announced that His Eminence's carriage was in waiting. Angela bending low once more before her uncle, kissed his apostolic ring, and said softly—" To-morrow!"

And Manuel echoed the word, " To-morrow!" as she bade them both a smiling " *addio* " and left the apartment. When she had gone, and he was left alone with his foundling, the Cardinal stood for a few minutes absorbed in silent meditation, mechanically gathering his robes about him. After a pause of evident hesitancy and trouble, he approached the boy and gently laid a hand upon his shoulder.

" Manuel," he said, " Do you understand whom it is that you are going to see?"

" Yes," replied Manuel quickly, " The Head of the Church. One who holds an office constituted by man long after Christ. It was founded upon the name and memory of the Apostle Peter, who publicly denied all knowledge of His Master. That is how I understand the person I am to see to-day!"

Cardinal Bonpré's face was a study of varying expressions as he heard these words.

" My child, you must not say these things in the Pope's presence!"

Manuel lifted his radiant eyes with a look of calm confidence.

" Dear friend, you must trust me!" he said, " They have sent for me, have they not, to this place you call the Vatican? They desire to see me, and to question me. That being so, whatever God bids me say, I will say; fearing nothing!"

A strong tremour shook the Cardinal's nerves,—he essayed to find words of wisdom and instruction, but somehow language failed him,—he felt blinded and strengthless, and warned by this impending sense of feebleness, made an instant effort to brace himself up and master the strange fainting that threatened to overwhelm him as it had frequently done before. He succeeded, and without speaking again to Manuel, but only bending one earnest

look upon him, he quitted his rooms and proceeded slowly
down the great marble staircase of the Palazzo Sovrani,—
a staircase famous even in Rome for its architectural
beauty—Manuel stepping lightly at his side—and reaching his carriage, entered it with his foundling, and was
rapidly driven away.

Arrived at the Vatican, the largest palace in the world,
which contains, so historians agree in saying, no less than
eleven thousand different apartments with their courts
and halls and corridors, they descended at the Portone di
Bronzo,—the Swiss Guard on duty saluting as the Cardinal passed in. On they went into the vestibule, chilly
and comfortless, of the Scala Pia;—and so up the stone
stairs to the Cortile do San Damaso, and thence towards
the steps which lead to the Pope's private apartments.
Another Guard met them here and likewise saluted,—
in fact, almost at every step of the way, and on every landing, guards were on duty, either standing motionless, or
marching wearily up and down, the clank, clank of their
footsteps waking dismal echoes from the high vaulted
roofs and uncarpeted stone corridors. At last they
reached the Sala Clementina, a vast unfurnished hall, rich
only with mural decorations and gilding, and here another
Guard met them who, without words, escorted the Cardinal and his young companion through a number of
waiting-rooms, made more or less magnificent by glorious
paintings, wonderful Gobelin tapestries, and unique sculp-
tures, till they reached at last what is called the *anti-
camera segreto*, where none but Cardinals are permitted
to enter and wait for an audience with the Supreme
Pontiff. At the door of this " Holy of Holies " stood a
Guarda Nobile on sentry duty,—but he might have been
a figure of painted marble for all the notice he took of
their approach. As they passed into the room, which was
exceedingly high and narrow, Monsignor Gherardi rose
from a table near the window, and received the Cardinal
with a kind of stately gravity which suitably agreed with
the coldness and silence of the general surroundings. A
small lean man, habited in black, also came forward, ex-
changing a few low whispered words with Gherardi as he
did so, and this individual, after saluting the Cardinal,
mysteriously disappeared through a little door to the
right. He was the Pope's confidential valet,—a person-

age who was perhaps more in the secrets of everybody and everything than even Gherardi himself.

"I am afraid we shall have to keep you waiting a little while," said Gherardi, in his smooth rich voice, which despite its mellow ring had something false about it, like the tone produced by an invisible crack in a fine bell, "Your young friend," and here he swept a keen, inquisitive glance over Manuel from face to feet, and from feet to face again, "will perhaps be tired?"

"I am never tired!" answered Manuel.

"Nor impatient?" asked Gherardi with a patronising air.

"Nor impatient!"

"Wonderful boy! If you are never tired or impatient, you will be eminently fitted for the priesthood," said Gherardi, his lip curling with a faint touch of derision, "For even the best of us grow sometimes weary in well-doing!"

And turning from him with a movement which implied both *hauteur* and indifference, he addressed himself to Bonpré, whose face was clouded, and whose eyes were troubled.

"The unfortunate affair of our friend Vergniaud will be settled to-day," he began, when the Cardinal raised one hand with a gentle solemnity.

"It is settled!" he returned, "Not even the Church can intervene between Vergniaud and his Maker now!"

Gherardi uttered an exclamation of undisguised annoyance.

"Dead!" he ejaculated, his forehead growing crimson with the anger he inwardly repressed——"Since when?"

"Last night he passed away," replied the Cardinal, "according to the telegram I have just received from ——his son. But he has been dying for some time, and what he told me in Paris was no lie. I explained his exact position to you quite recently, on the day you visited my niece at her studio. He had a serious valvular disease of the heart,—he might, as the doctors said, have lived, at the utmost, two years—but the excitement of recent events has evidently proved too much for him. As I told you, he felt that his death might occur at any moment, and he did not wish to leave the world under a false impression of his character. I trust that now the Holy Father may be inclined to pardon him, in death, if not in life!"

Gherardi walked up and down the narrow room impatiently.

"I doubt it!" he said at last, "I very much doubt it! The man may be dead, but the scandal he caused remains. And his death has made the whole position very much more difficult for you, my lord Cardinal! For as Vergniaud is not alive to endure the penalty of his offence, it is probable *you* may have to suffer for having condoned it!"

Felix Bonpré bent his head gently.

"I shall be ready and willing to suffer whatever God commands!" he answered, "For I most faithfully believe that nothing can injure my soul while it rests, as I humbly place it, in His Holy keeping!"

Gherardi paused in his pacing to and fro, and gazed at the frail figure, and fine old face before him, with mingled compassion and curiosity.

"You should have lived in the early days of the Faith," he said, "You are too literal—too exact in your following of Christian ethics. That sort of thing does not work nowadays. Dogma must be maintained!"

"What is dogma?" asked Manuel suddenly.

Gherardi gave him a careless glance.

"Cardinal Bonpré must teach you that *in extenso!*" he replied, with a little smile—"But briefly,—dogma is an opinion or theory derived from the Gospels, and formulated as doctrine, by the Church."

"An opinion or theory of man, founded on the words of Christ?" said Manuel.

"Just so!"

"But if Christ was divine, should any man presume to formulate a theory on what He Himself said?" asked Manuel. "Are not his own plain words enough?"

Gherardi stared at the young speaker half angrily.

"His own plain words enough?" he repeated mechanically. "What do you mean, boy?"

"I mean," answered Manuel simply, "that if He were truly a Manifestation of God in Himself, as the Church declares Him to be, *I wonder that man can dare to formulate mere dogma on God's own utterance!*"

There was a dead pause. After a few minutes of chill silence Gherardi addressed the Cardinal.

"Your young friend has a dangerous tongue!" he said sternly, "You had best warn or command him that he set a guard upon it in the Holy Father's presence!"

"There is no need to either warn or command me!" said Manuel, a smile irradiating his fair face as he met the angry eyes of Gherardi with the full calmness of his own—"I have been sent for, and I am here. Had I not been sent for I should not have come. Now that I have been called to answer for myself I will answer,—with truth and without fear. For what can any man cause me to suffer if I am to myself true?"

Another heavy pause ensued. An invisible something was in the air,—a sense of that vast supernatural which is deeply centered at the core of the natural universe,—a grave mystery which seemed to envelop all visible things with a sudden shadow of premonitory fear. The silence prevailing was painful—almost terrible. A great ormolu clock in the room, one of the Holy Father's "Jubilee" gifts, ticked the minutes slowly away with a jewel-studded pendulum, which in its regular movements to and fro sounded insolently obtrusive in such a stillness. Gherardi abstractedly raised his eyes to a great ivory crucifix which was displayed upon the wall against a background of rich purple velvet,—Manuel was standing immediately in front of it, and the tortured head of the carven Christ drooped over him as though in a sorrow-stricken benediction. A dull anger began to irritate Gherardi's usually well-tempered nerves, and he was searching in his mind for some scathing sentence wherewith to overwhelm and reprove the confident ease of the boy, when the door leading to the Pope's apartments was slowly pushed open to admit the entrance of Monsignor Moretti. Cardinal Bonpré had not seen him since the day of the Vergniaud scandal in Paris,—and a faint colour came into his pale cheeks as he noted the air of overbearing condescension and authority with which Moretti, here on his own ground, as one of the favorites of the Pope, greeted him.

"The Holy Father is ready to receive you," he said, "But I regret to inform your Eminence that His Holiness can see no way to excuse or condone the grave offence of the Abbé Vergniaud,—moreover, the fact of the sin-begotten son being known to the world as Gys Grandit, makes it more than ever necessary that the ban of excommunication should be passed upon him. Especially, as those uninstructed in the Faith, are under the delusion that the penalty of excommunication has become more or less obsolete, and we have now an opportunity for making publicly known the truth that it still exists, and may be used by the Church in extreme situations, when judged politic and fitting."

"Then in this case the Church must excommunicate the dead!" said the Cardinal quietly.

Moretti's face turned livid.

"Dead?" he exclaimed, "I do not believe it!"

Silently Bonpré handed him the telegram received that morning. Moretti read it, his eyes sparkling with rage.

"How do I know this is not a trick?" he said, "The accursed atheist of a son may have telegraphed a lie!"

"I hardly think he would condescend to that!" returned the Cardinal calmly, "It would not be worth his while. You must remember, that to one of his particular views, Church excommunication, either for his father or himself, would mean nothing. He makes himself responsible for his conduct to God only. And whatever his faults he certainly believes in God!"

Moretti read through the telegram again.

"We must place this before His Holiness," he said, "And it will very seriously annoy him! I fear your Eminence," here he gave a quick meaning look at Bonpré, "will be all the more severely censured for having pardoned the Abbé's sins."

"Is it wrong to forgive sinners?" asked Manuel, his clear young voice breaking through the air like a silver bell rung suddenly,—"And when one cannot reach the guilty, should one punish the innocent?"

Moretti scowled fiercely at the fair candid face turned enquiringly near his own.

"You are too young to ask questions!" he said roughly —"Wait to be questioned yourself—and think twice—aye three times before you answer!"

The bright expression of the boy's countenance seemed to become intensified as he heard.

"'Take no thought how or what ye shall speak, for

it shall be given you in that same hour what ye shall speak!'" he said softly—"'For it is not ye that speak, but the Spirit of your Father which speaketh in you!'"

Moretti flushed angrily, and his hand involuntarily clenched.

"Those words were addressed by our Lord to His Apostles," he retorted—"Apostles, of whom our Holy Father the Pope is the one infallible representative.   They were not spoken to an ignorant lad who barely knows his catechism!"

"Yet were not the Apostles themselves told," went on Manuel steadily, "to be humble as ignorant children if they would enter the Kingdom of Heaven?   And did not Christ say, ' Whoso offendeth one of these little ones which believe in Me, it were better for him that a millstone were hanged about his neck, and that he were drowned in the depths of the sea!'   I am sure there are many such little ones who believe in Christ,—perhaps too, without knowing any catechism,—and even Apostles must beware of offending them!"

"Does this boy follow *your* teaching in the quoting of Scripture with so glib a tongue?" asked Moretti, turning sharply round upon the Cardinal.

Bonpré returned his angry look with one of undisturbed serenity.

"My son, I have taught him nothing!" he replied, "I have no time as yet—and I may add—no inclination, to become his instructor.   He speaks from his own nature."

"It is a nature that needs training!" said Gherardi, smiling blandly, and silencing by a gesture Moretti's threatening outburst of wrath, "To quote Scripture rashly, without due consideration for the purpose to which it is to be applied, does not actually constitute an offence, but it displays a reprehensible disregard and ignorance of theology.   However, theology," here he smiled still more broadly, "is a hard word for the comprehension of the young!   This poor little lad cannot be expected to grasp its meaning."

Manuel raised his bright eyes and fixed them steadily on the priest's countenance.

"Oh, yes!" he said quietly, "I understand it perfectly! Originally it meant the Word or Discourse of God,—it has now come to mean the words or discourses, or quarrels and differences of men on the things of God! But God's Word remains God's Word—eternally, invincibly! No man can alter it, and Christ preached it so plainly that the most simple child cannot fail to understand it!"

Moretti was about to speak when again Gherardi interrupted him.

"Patience! Patience!" he said soothingly, "Perchance we must say"—this with a flash of derision from his dark crafty eyes, "that a prophet hath arisen in Israel! Listen to me, boy! If Christ spoke as plainly as you say, and if all He preached could be understood by the people, why should He have founded a Church to teach His doctrine?"

"He did not found a Church," answered Manuel, "He tried to make a Human Brotherhood. He trusted twelve men. They all forsook Him in His hour of need, and one betrayed Him! When He died and arose again from the dead, they sought to give themselves a Divine standing on His Divinity. They preached His Word to the world—true!—but they preached their own as well! Hence the Church!"

Moretti's angry eyes rolled in his head with an excess of wrath and amazement.

"Surely some evil spirit possesses this boy!" he exclaimed irately, "*Retro me Sathanas!* He is a rank heretic—a heathen! And yet he lives in the companionship of Cardinal Felix Bonpré!"

Both priests looked at the Cardinal in angry astonishment, but he stood silent, one wrinkled hand holding up the trailing folds of his scarlet robe,—his head slightly bent, and his whole attitude expressive of profound patience and resignation. Manuel turned his eyes upon him and smiled tenderly.

"It is not the fault of Cardinal Bonpré that I think my own thoughts," he said, "or that I speak as I have spoken from the beginning. He found me lost and alone in the world,—and he sheltered me, knowing not whom he sheltered! Let what blame there is in me therefore be mine alone, and not his or another's!"

His young voice, so full of sweetness, seemed to melt the cold and heavy silence into vibrations of warm feeling, and a sudden sense of confusion and shame swept over the callous and calculating minds of the two men, miscalled priests, as they listened. But before they could determine or contrive an answer, the door was thrown open, and the lean man in black entered, and pausing on the threshold bowed slightly,—then raising his hand with a gesture which invited all to follow him, turned again and walked on in front,—then crossing a small antechamber, he drew aside a long curtain of purple damask heavily fringed with gold, and opened a farther door. Here he stood back, and allowed Cardinal Bonpré to pass in first, attended by Manuel,—Monsignori Gherardi and Moretti followed. And then the valet, closing the door behind them, and pulling the rich curtain across, sat down himself close outside it to be within call when the Holy Father should summon his attendance by means of a bell which hung immediately over his head. And to while away the time he pulled from his pocket that day's issue of a well-known Republican paper,—one of the most anti-Papal tendency, thereby showing that his constant humble attendance upon the Head of the Church had not made him otherwise than purely human, or eradicated from his nature that peculiar quality with which most of us are endowed, namely, the perversity of spirit which leads us often to say and do things which are least expected of us. The Pope's confidential valet was not exempt from this failing. He like the Monsignori, enjoyed the exciting rush and secret risk of money speculation,—he also had his little schemes of self-advancement; and, as is natural to all who are engaged in a certain kind of service, he took care to read everything that could be said by outsiders against the person or persons whom he served. Thus, despite the important capacity he filled, he was not a grade higher than the ordinary butler, who makes it his business to know all the peccadilloes and failings of his master. " No man is a hero to his valet " is a very true axiom,—and even the Head of the Church, the Manifestation of the Divine, the " Infallible in Council," was a mere Nothing to the little man in black who had the power to insist on His Holiness changing a soiled cassock for a clean one.

XXVIII.

THERE are certain moments in life which seem weighted with the history of ages—when all the past, present and future merge into the one omnipresent Now,—moments, which if we are able to live through them with courage, may decide a very eternity of after-glory—but which, if we fail to comprehend their mission, pass, taking with them the last opportunity of all good that shall ever be granted to us in this life. Such a moment appeared, to the reflective mind of Cardinal Bonpré, to have presented itself to him, as for the second time in ten days, he found himself face to face with the Sovereign Pontiff, the pale and aged man with the deep dark eyes set in such cavernous sockets, that as they looked out on the world through that depth of shadow, seemed more like great jewels in the head of a galvanised skeleton than the eyes of a living human being. On this occasion the Pope was enthroned in a kind of semi-state, on a gilded chair covered with crimson velvet; and a rich canopy of the same material, embroidered and fringed with gold, drooped in heavy folds above him. Attired in the usual white,—white cassock, white skull cap, and white sash ornamented with the emblematic keys of St. Peter, embroidered in gold thread at the ends,—his unhandsome features, pallid as marble, and seemingly as cold,—bloodless everywhere, even to the lips,—suggested with dreadful exactitude a corpse in burial clothes just lifted from its coffin and placed stiffly upright in a sitting position. Involuntarily Cardinal Bonprè, as he made the usual necessary genuflections, thought, with a shrinking interior sense of horror at the profanity of his own idea, that the Holy Father as he then appeared, might have posed to a painter of allegories, as the frail ghost of a dead Faith. For he looked so white and slender and fragile and transparent,—he sat so rigidly, so coldly, without a movement or a gesture, that it seemed as if the touch of a hand might break him into atoms, so brittle and delicate a figure of clay was he.

When he spoke, his harsh voice, issuing from the long thin lips which scarcely moved, even in utterance, was startling in its unmelodious loudness, the more so when its intonation was querulous, as now.

"It is regrettable, my lord Cardinal," he said slowly, keeping his dark eyes immovably fixed on the venerable Felix,—"that I should be compelled to send for you so soon again on the same matters which, since your arrival in Rome, have caused me so much anxiety. This miracle, —of which you are declared to be the worker,—though for some inscrutable reason, you persist in denying your own act,—is not yet properly authenticated. And, to make the case worse, it seems that the unfortunate man, Claude Cazeau, whom we entrusted with our instructions to the Archbishop of Rouen, has suddenly disappeared, leaving no trace. Naturally there are strong suspicions that he has met with a violent death,—perhaps at the hands of the Freemasons, who are ever at work conspiring against the Faith,—or else through the intrigues of the so-called 'Christian Democrats,' of whom 'Gys Grandit' is a leader. In any case, it is most reprehensible that you, a Cardinal-prince of the Church, should have permitted yourself to become involved in such a doubtful business. The miracle may have taken place,—but if so, you should have no cause to deny your share in it; and however much you may be gifted with the power of healing, I cannot reconcile your duty to us with the Vergniaud scandal! Since you were here last, I have investigated that matter thoroughly,—I have read a full report of the blasphemous address the Abbé preached from his pulpit in Paris, and I cannot, no I cannot"—here the Pope raised his thin white hand with a gesture of menace that was curiously powerful for one so seemingly frail— "I cannot forgive or forget the part you have taken in this deplorable affair!"

The Cardinal looked up with a touch of pain and protest.

"Holy Father, I strove to obey the command of Christ —'Forgive that ye may be forgiven'!—I cannot be sorry that I did so obey it;—for now the offender is beyond the reach of either punishment or absolution. He must answer for his deeds to God alone!"

The Pope turned his eyes slowly round in his waxen-like head to Gherardi—then to Moretti—and seeing confirmation of the news in their looks, fixed them again as immovably as before upon the Cardinal. The faint shadow of a cold smile flickered on his long slit-like mouth.

"Dead!" he murmured, and he nodded slowly, and beat with one finger on the back of the other hand, as though keeping time mechanically to some funeral march in his brain. "Dead! A fortunate thing for him! An escape from worse than death, so far as this life is concerned! But what of the next?—'where the worm dieth not and the fire is not quenched!'" And here the representative of St. Peter smiled pallidly. "Dead!—but his works live after him; and his sin-begotten son also lives, to spread his pernicious writings through the world, and incite the already disobedient to further license. Therefore the Church must still publicly condemn his memory, as a warning to the faithful. And you, Cardinal Bonpré, must receive from us a necessary measure of correction, for having pardoned one who in his last discourse to humanity attacked the Church and slandered it. To one of your eminence and reputation, the lesson may seem hard, but a chastening reproof can but purify the spirit, and free it from that pride which apes humility!"

The Cardinal bent his head patiently and remained silent.

Monsignor Moretti advanced a step towards the Papal throne.

"The boy"—he began.

A slight animation warmed the chill lifelessness of the Pope's features.

"True! I had almost forgotten!" he said. Then to the Cardinal, "Where is the boy you rescued from the streets, who lives with you, and who witnessed the miracle at Rouen?"

Manuel had till now stood aside, half hidden in the shadow of the crimson damask which, falling from ceiling to floor in rich luxurious folds, draped the corners of the room, but at these words he advanced at once.

"I am here!" he said.

Fronting the Pope, with his fair head thrown back, and his blue eyes flashing with all the soul-light of a swift, unwarped intelligence, he stood,—and the white shrunken figure of the old man in the gilded chair raised itself as if by some interior electric force, slowly, slowly—higher and higher—the deep-set old eyes staring into the brilliant youthful ones—staring—staring till they seemed to protrude and tremble under their shelving brows, like the last sparks of a flame about to fall into extinction. Gherardi made a quick step forward.

"My lord Cardinal!" he said significantly, "Should not your waif and stray have been taught how to comport himself before he came here? He does not kneel to the Holy Father!"

The Cardinal opened his lips to speak, but Manuel stayed him by a slight gesture.

"I may not kneel to any man!" he said, "But to God only! For it is written, 'Call no man your Father upon the earth, for One is your Father which is in Heaven. Neither be ye called Masters, for One is your Master, even Christ.' How then," and he came nearer to the Pope's foot-stool, "can you be called 'Father'? or 'Holy'? For there is none Holy but God!"

The deep silence which had fallen like a spell upon them all in the antechamber, fell now with redoubled impressiveness. The Pope, gripping the arms of his gilded chair, forced himself fully upright, and his lips trembled.

"Whence came you, and of what parentage are you?" he asked slowly, enunciating his words with even more than his usual harsh distinctness.

"That is my own secret!" answered the boy—"The Cardinal accepted me without question!"

"Which is but a fresh proof of the Cardinal's unwisdom," said the Pope severely, "And we shall not follow his example in this or in any other matter!" And turning to Moretti he enquired, "Does this boy understand he is here as a witness to the miracle effected at Rouen?"

"As a witness to the Truth—yes! I understand!" said Manuel quickly, before Moretti could answer. "The miracle was no miracle!"

"No miracle!" exclaimed the Pope, moved at last from his usual inflexibility, "Do you hear that, Domenico?" turning excitedly to Gherardi, "No miracle!"

"No miracle!" repeated Manuel, steadily—"Nothing but the law of Nature working in response to the law of

God, which is Love! The child was healed of his infirmity by the power of unselfish prayer. Are we not told
'Ask and ye shall receive'? But the asking must be
pure! The prayer must be untainted by self-interest!
God does not answer prayer that is paid for in this world's
coin! No miracle was ever wrought for a fee! Only
when perfect love and perfect faith exist between the
creature and the Creator, are all things possible!"

A nervous twitching of the Pope's features showed his
suppressed irritation at this reply.

"The boy jests with us!" he said angrily, "He de-
fends his benefactor, but he either does not understand,
or else is regardless of our authority!"

"What, do you not also believe?" asked Manuel, placing one foot on the first step of the Pope's throne, and
looking him straightly in the face, "Do you not even
affirm that God answers prayers? Do *you* not pray? Do
you not assert that you yourself are benefited and helped
—nay, even kept alive by the prayers of the faithful?
Then why should you doubt that Cardinal Bonpré has, by
his prayer, rescued one life—the life of a little child? Is
not your Church built up for prayer? Do you not command it? Do you not even insist upon the 'vain repetitions' which Christ forbade? Do you not summon the
people to pray in public?—though Christ bade all who
truly sought to follow Him to pray in secret? And amid
all the false prayers, the unthinking, selfish petitions, the
blasphemous demands for curses and confusion to fall
upon enemies and contradictors, the cowardly cryings for
pardon from sinners who do not repent, that are sent up
to the throne of the Most High,—is it marvellous that
one prayer, pure of all self and sophistry, ascending to
God, simply to ask for the life of a child should be heard
and granted?"

His voice rang through the silence with a pure intonation, unlike any human voice in the world—and as he
spoke, the Pope slowly drew back in his chair, further
and further away from the young, beautiful face that
confronted his own so steadily. The dumb sense of
stupefaction that had before possessed Gherardi and
Moretti in the presence of this child, seized them
again now,—and slow tears welled up into the Cardinal's eyes, as, clasping his withered hands, he waited

in fear and awe, listening and wondering,—overwhelmed by the strangeness of the scene. Like a shrunken white mummy set in a gilded sarcophagus, the representative of St. Peter huddled himself together, reflections of the daylight on the crimson hangings around him casting occasional gleams of crimson athwart his bony hands and cadaverous features;—while on the first step of his throne the aerial form of the beautiful boy, with his fair face, full flashing eyes, and radiant hair, stood like an Angel suddenly descended at the portal of the mummy's tomb.

"Faith must surely be weaker in these days than in the days of Christ," continued Manuel, "The disciples were not always wise or brave; but they believed in the power of their Master! You,—with so many centuries of prayer behind you,—will surely not say as John did— 'Master, we saw one casting out devils in Thy name, and he followeth not us!' Because this miracle is unexpected and exceptional, do you say of your good Cardinal, 'He followeth not us'? Remember how Christ answered,—'Forbid him not, for there is no man which shall do a miracle in my name that can speak evil of me!'"

Still the same silence reigned. A shaft of sunlight falling through the high oriel window, touched the boy's hair with a Pentecostal flame of glory.

"You sent for me," he went on, "and I have come! They say I must be taught. Will you teach me? I would know many things! Tell me for one, why are You here, shut away from the cities, and the people? Should you not be among them? Why do you stay here all alone? You must be very unhappy!"

A sudden quivering light illumined the jewel-like dark eyes of the seeming mummy in the chair—its lips moved —but no sound came from them.

"To be here all alone!" went on Manuel, "And a whole world outside waiting to be comforted! To have vast wealth lying about you unused—with millions and millions of poor, starving, struggling, dying creatures, near at hand, cursing the God whom they have never been taught to know or to bless! To be safely sheltered while others are in danger! To know that even kings and emperors are trembling on their thrones because of the evil days that are drawing near in punishment for evil deeds!——to feel the great pulsating ache of the world's heart beating through every hour of time, and never to stretch forth a hand of consolation! Surely this must make you very sad! *Will you not come out with me?*"

With a strong effort the Pope raised himself and looked into the pleading Angel-face. With his sudden movement, Gherardi and Moretti also stirred from their frozen attitudes of speechless amazement, and would have approached, but that the Pope signed them away with so fierce and impatient a gesture that they shrank back appalled. And still he gazed at Manuel as if his very soul were passing through his eyes.

"Come out with you!" he said, in a hoarse, faint whisper——"Come out with you!"

"Yes!—come out with me!" repeated Manuel, his accents vibrating with a strange compelling sweetness, "Come out and see the poor lying at the great gates of St. Peter's—the lame, the halt, the blind——come and heal them by a touch, a prayer! You can, you must, you shall heal them!—if you *will!* Pour money into the thin hands of the starving!—come with me into the miserable places of the world,—come and give comfort! Come freely into the courts of kings, and see how the brows ache under the crowns!—and the hearts break beneath the folds of velvet and ermine! Why stand in the way of happiness, or deny even emperors peace when they crave it? Your mission is to comfort, not to condemn! You need no throne! You want no kingdom!—no settled place—no temporal power! Enough for you to work and live as the poorest of all Christ's ministers,—without pomp, without ostentation or public ceremonial, but simply clothed in pure holiness! So shall God love you more! So shall you pass unscathed through the thick of battle, and command Brotherhood in place of Murder! Go out and welcome Progress!—take Science by the hand!—encourage Intellect!—for all these things are of God, and are God's gifts divine! Live as Christ lived, teaching the people personally and openly;—loving them, pitying them, sharing their joys and sorrows, blessing their little children! Deny yourself to no man;—and make of this cold temple in which you now dwell self-imprisoned, a home and refuge for the friendless and the poor! *Come out with me!*"

As he thus spoke, with a living, breathing enthusiasm of entreaty, which might have moved even the dry bones in the valley of the prophet's vision to rise up and become a great standing army, the Pope's figure seemed to grow more and more attenuated,—his worn white hands grasping the gilt arms of his chair, looked like the claws of a dead bird—and his face, shrunken and withered, like a Chinese ivory carving of some forgotten idol.

" Come out with me and minister with your own hands to the aged and dying!" pursued Manuel, " And so shall you grow young! Command that the great pictures, the tapestries, the jewels, the world's trash of St. Peter's, be sold to the rich, who can afford to set them in free and open places where all the poorest may possess them! But do not You retain them! You do not need them—your treasure must be sympathy for all the world! Not *one* section of the world,—not *one* form of creed,—but for all!—if you are truly the Dispenser of Christ's Message to the earth! Come—unprotected, save by the Cross! Come with no weapon of defence—' heal the sick, cleanse the lepers, raise the dead, cast out devils! Freely ye have received, freely give! Provide neither gold nor silver nor brass in your purse,'—come, and by your patience—your gentleness—your pardon—your love to all men, show that ' the Kingdom of Heaven is at hand!' Walk fearless in the thick of battles, and your very presence shall engender peace! For the Holy Spirit shall surround and encompass you; the fiercest warriors shall bend before you, as they never would if you assumed a world's throne or a world's sovereignty! Come, uncrowned, defenceless; —but strong in the Spirit of God! Think of all the evil which has served as the foundation for this palace in which you dwell! Can you not hear in the silence of the night, the shrieks of the tortured and dying of the Inquisition? Do you never think of those dark days, ten and twelve hundred years after Christ, when no virtue seemed left upon the earth?—when the way to this very throne was paved by poison and cold steel?—when those who then reigned here, and occupied Your place, led such infamous lives that the very dogs might have been ashamed to follow in their footsteps!—when they professed to be able to sell the Power of the Holy Ghost for so much gold and silver? Remember the words, 'Whoso shall blaspheme against the Holy Ghost it shall not be forgiven him, either in this world or in the world to come.' Look back upon the Past—and look out upon the Present! Try to understand the sufferings of the forsaken people!—the pain—the bewilderment—the groping for life in death!—and come out with me! Come and preach Christ as He lived and died, and *was,* and *is! Come out with me!"*

The dreadful, dumb spell remained unbroken. The room seemed invested with a strange solemnity—the figures of the human beings in it were like images frozen into rigidity—even Cardinal Bonpré appeared stricken by this mental paralysis, and not a fold of his rich attire stirred with so much as a pulsation of natural breath. Only Manuel seemed truly alive—his slight boyish figure was instinct with ardour—his face was radiant, and his eyes brilliant as stars. And now, withdrawing himself a little from the motionless creature seated stiffly on the Papal throne, with its deep, dark eyes alone giving sign of life by their unwearied stare and feverish glitter, he raised his head with a royal gesture of mingled appeal and warning.

"Come out with me!" he exclaimed, "For there are wonderful things in the world to-day!—wonderful, beautiful, and terrible! Take your share in them, and find God in every glory! For with all the wisdom and the splendour,—with all the flashing light of Heaven poured out upon the darkness of the Sorrowful Star, its people are weary,—they are lost in the confusion and clamour of their own desires—they would fain serve God, but know not where to find Him, because a thousand, aye a million churches stand in the way!—churches, which are like a forest of dark trees, blocking out the radiance of the Sun! God, who manifests His power and tenderness in the making of the simplest leaf, the smallest bird, is lost to the understanding and affection of humanity in the multitude of Creeds! Come out with me,—simple and pure, gentle and strong! Tell all the lost and the wandering that there never was, and never will be but one God supreme and perfect, whose name is Love, whose work is Love!—and whose Messenger, Christ, pro-

nounced the New Commandment Love instead of Hate!
Come out with me while it is yet day, for the night cometh
when no man can work! Come and lift up the world by
your very coming! Stretch out your hands in benediction over kings and beggars alike!—there are other roses
to give than Golden ones to Queens! There are poor
women who share half they earn with those still poorer—
there are obscure lives which in their very obscurity, are
forming the angel-nature, and weaving the angel's crown!
—look for these in the world—give *them* your Golden
Roses! Leave rulers and governments alone, for you
should be above and beyond all rulers and governments!
You should be the Herald of peace,—the Pardoner of
sin, the Rescuer of the fallen, and the Refuge of the distressed! Come out with me, and be all this to the world,
so that when the Master comes He may truly find you
working in His vineyard!"

Another dead pause ensued. Not a sound, not a breath
disturbed the heavy silence which seemed to have grown
deeper than before. And Manuel, looking eagerly again
and closely into the Pope's face, went on with increasing
ardour and passion.

"Come out with me!" he said, "Or if you will not
come,—then beware of the evil days which are at hand!
The people are wandering to and fro, crossing all lands,
struggling one against the other, hoarding up useless
gold, and fighting for supremacy!—but 'the day of the
Lord shall come like a thief in the night, and blessed is
he who shall be found watching!' Watch! The hour
is growing dark and full of menace!—the nations are as
frightened children, losing faith, losing hope, losing
strength! Put away,—put away from you the toys of
time!—quench in your soul the thirst for gold, for of this
shall come nothing but corruption! Why trifle with the
Spirit of holy things? Why let your servants use the
Name of the Most High to cover hypocrisy? Why crave
for the power of temporal things which passes away in
the dust of destroyed kingdoms? For the Power of the
Spirit is greater than all! And so it shall be proved! The
Spirit shall work in ways where it has never been found
before!—it shall depart from the Churches which are
unworthy of its Divine inspiration!—it shall invest the
paths of Science!—it shall open the doors of the locked

stars! It shall display the worlds invisible;—the secrets
of men's hearts, and of closed graves!—there will be
terror and loss and confusion and shame to mankind,—
and this world shall keep nothing of all its treasures but
the Cross of Christ! Rome, like Babylon, shall fall!—
and the Powers of the Church shall be judged as the
Powers of Darkness rather than of Light, because they
have rejected the Word of their Master, and 'teach for
doctrine the commandments of men!' Disaster shall
follow swift upon disaster, and the cup of trembling
shall be drained again to its last dregs, as in the olden
days, unless,—unless perchance——you will come out
with me!"

With the last words a sort of galvanic shock seemed
to be imparted to the rigid figure in the chair. Springing
upright suddenly, his voice rang out like a clarion, dis-
cordantly yet clearly.

"In the name of God," he cried, "Who and what is
this boy! How came he with Cardinal Bonpré? And
you, Domenico!—do you stand by and permit this affront to me!——the living Head of the Church! From
a child!—a tramp of the streets!—who dares to speak
to me!——who dares to reproach, to prophesy—aye, to
blaspheme!——and teach Me,——"

"As One having authority,—and not as the Scribes!"
said Manuel, with one swift flashing glance, which like
a shaft of lightning seemed to pierce through flesh and
bone,—for, as he met that radiant and commanding look,
the jewel-like eyes of the Pope lost their lustre and became fixed and glassy,——he put his hand to his throat
with a choking gasp for breath,——and like a dead
body which had only been kept in place by some secret
mechanical action, he fell back in his chair senseless, his
limbs stretching themselves out with a convulsive shudder
into stark immovability.

Gherardi started from his stupor, and rushed to his
assistance, ringing the bell violently which summoned
the valet from the antechamber,—and Moretti, with a
fierce oath, pushing Manuel aside, rushed to the chair
in which the Pope's fainting figure lay,—all was confusion;——and in the excitement and terror which had
overwhelmed Cardinal Bonpré at the unprecedented
scene, Manuel suddenly touched him on the arm.

"Follow me!" he said, "We are no longer needed here! Come!—let us go hence!"

Hardly knowing what he did the old man obeyed, trembling in every limb as Manuel, grasping him firmly by the hand, led him from the apartment, and on through the winding corridors of the huge building, out into the open air. No one questioned them,—no one interfered with their progress. Benediction was being sung in one of the many chapels of St. Peter's, and the solemn sound of the organ reached them, softened and mellowed by distance, as they stood on the steps of the Vatican, where the Cardinal, pausing to recover breath and equanimity, gazed at his strange foundling in alarm and bewilderment.

"Manuel!" he murmured feebly, "Child!—what have you done!"

"Only what I am bound to do!" replied Manuel simply, "I have said no more than it is right to say, if Christ's words are true! Dear friend, be at peace! You will not suffer misjudgment long!"

The music stealing out from the distant chapel, floated round them in large circles of solemn melody,—and the glow of sunset lit the clear sky with a warm red radiance, flecked with golden clouds of glory.

"He would not come with me!" said Manuel, with a slight gesture backward to the sombre portals they had just passed, "And he will never come! But *you* will!"

And smiling,—with his fair face turned to the radiant sky,—he rested his hand lightly on the Cardinal's arm as they descended the broad marble steps, and left the great Palace of the Popes together.

XXIX.

WHILE the foregoing scene was taking place at the Vatican, Angela Sovrani, left to herself for some hours, took the opportunity to set her great picture " on view " for the coming morrow. Locking both doors of her studio, she began to arrange the room; her huge canvas was already on a movable easel supplied with wheels, which ran lightly and easily over the polished floor without making any sound. At its summit a brass rod was attached, and on this a curtain of golden-coloured silk was hung, the folds of which at present concealed the painting from view. The top-light of the studio was particularly good on this special afternoon, as the weather was clear, and the Roman sky translucent and bright as an opal, and Angela, as she wheeled her " great work " into position, sang for pure lightness of heart and thankfulness that all was done. In her soul she had the consciousness that what she had produced from her brain and hand was not altogether unworthy. For, though to the true artist, no actual result can ever attain to the beauty of the first thought or ideal of the thing to be performed, there is always the consolation that if one's best and truest feeling has been earnestly put into the work, some touch, however slight, of that ideal beauty must remain. The poet's poem is never so fine as the poet's thought. The thought is from the immortal and invincible soul,—the poem has to be conveyed through the grosser body, clothed in language which must always be narrow and inadequate. Hence the artist's many and grievous limitations. To the eyes of the spirit all things appear transfigured, because lifted out of the sphere of material vision. But when we try to put these " beautiful things made new, for the delight of the sky-children " on paper or canvas, in motionless marble or flexible rhyme,—we are weighted by grosser air and the density of bodily feeling. So it was with Angela Sovrani, in whose compact little head were folded the splendid dreams of genius like sleeping fairies in a magic cave;—and thoughtful and brilliant though she was, she could not, in her great tenderness for her affianced lover Florian Varillo, foresee that daily contact with his weaker and smaller nature, would kill those dreams as surely as a frost-wind kills the buds of the rose,—and that gradually, very gradually, the coarser fibre of his intelligence mingling with hers, would make a paltry and rough weaving of the web of life, instead of a free and gracious pattern. She never thought of such possibilities—she would have rejected the very idea of them with scorn and indignation. She would have declared that her love for Florian was the very root and source of her art,— that for him she worked—for him she lived. So indeed she believed, in her finely-fervent self-delusion,—but it was not ordained that this glamour should last,—for hers was a nature too rare and valuable to be sacrificed, and the Higher destinies had begun to approve her as precious. Therefore, as is the case with all precious things, the furnace was preparing for the shaping of the gold,— the appointed Angel of her Fate was already hovering near, holding ready the cup of bitterness which all must drain to the dregs, before knowing what it is to drink of "the new wine in the Kingdom of God."

"I wonder," thought the girl now, as she stepped lightly from one corner of her studio to the other, rearranging a vase here—a bust there—and imparting to the whole room that indefinable air of grace and luxury which can only be bestowed by the trained hand of a practised artist,—"I wonder if Florian will be proud? People will certainly talk of my picture,—some will praise and some will condemn; and this mixture of praise and condemnation is what is called Fame. But will my beloved love me more? Will he be glad that I am found worthy in the world's sight?—or will he think I am usurping his place? Ah!" and she paused in her work, looking vaguely before her with thoughtful, wondering eyes, "That is where we women workers have to suffer! Men grudge us the laurel, but they forget that we are trying to win it only that we may wear the rose more fittingly! A woman tries to do a great and a noble thing, not that she may vex or humiliate a man by superiority,—but that she may be more worthy to be his mate and helper in the world,—and also, that her children may reverence her for something more than the mere animal duties of nursing and tenderness. How proud to-day would be any man or woman who could point to Rosa Bonheur and say, 'She was my mother!' And yet perhaps this idea of mine is too fantastic,—the Brownings left a son—and he has nothing of their genius or their enthusiasm."

She moved to the grand piano and set it open; as she did so a thought of Sylvie came across her mind, and she smiled.

"Dear little rose-bud of a woman!" she mused, "How glad I am that she is happy! And how delightful it is to see the pride she takes in Aubrey Leigh!—how she studies his books, and pores over his statistics and theories! I really believe she knows them all by heart! And what wonderful schemes she is building up in her mind for the people in whom he is so interested! What a sensation she will make if she intends to work with her husband as thoroughly and devotedly as her ideas imply! Her marriage will be an immense disappointment to certain persons I could name!" and she smiled, "Dear Sylvie! With all her goodness, and grace and beauty, her name will sound more obnoxious at the Vatican than even the name of Gys Grandit!"

She had lifted a cluster of lilies from a vase to regroup them, and as her thoughts turned in this direction she bent her eyes upon their large white blooms meditatively, and a faint rose flush warmed her cheeks.

> "Ce sont des fleurs étranges,
> Et traîtresses, avec leurs airs de sceptres d'anges,
> De thyrses lumineux pour doigts de séraphins ;
> Leurs parfums sont trop forts, tout ensemble, et trop fins."

"It is strange," she thought, "that I should have corresponded so many months with 'Gys Grandit' through my admiration for his books—and that he should turn out to be the son of poor Abbé Vergniaud! Cyrillon! It is a pretty name! And since we met—since that terrible scene in the church in Paris,—since he knew who I was, he has not written. And, and for his poor father's death, . . . I suppose he thought it was sufficient to telegraph the news of the death to my uncle. But I am sorry he does not write to me any more!——I valued his letters——they were such brilliant essays on all the movements and politics of the time. It was just a little secret of mine;—it was pleasant to think I was in correspondence with such a genius. However, he has had so much to think of since then, . . ." She set the lilies in their vase again, inhaling their delicious odour as she did so.

"The flowers of the saints and martyrs!" she said, "I do not wonder that the artists chose them for that purpose; they are so white—and pure—and passionless, . . ."

A slight crash disturbed her self-communion, and she hastened to see what had fallen. It was a small clay figure of "Eros",—a copy of a statuette found in the ruins of Pompeii. The nail supporting its bracket had given way. Angela had been rather fond of this little work of art, and as she knelt to pick up the fragments she was more vexed at the accident than she cared to own. She looked wistfully at the pretty moulded broken limbs of the little god as she put them all in a heap together.

"What a pity!" she murmured, "I am not at all superstitious, yet I wish anything in the room had come to grief rather than this! It is not a good omen!"

She moved across the floor again and stood for a moment inert, one hand resting lightly on the amber silk draperies which veiled her picture.

"There was no truth at all in that rumour about Florian's 'Phillida';—'Pon-Pon,' as they call her," she thought, "She serves as a model to half the artists in Rome. Unfortunate creature. She is one of the most depraved and reckless of her class, so I hear—and Florian is far too refined and fastidious to even recognise such a woman, outside his studio. The Marquis Fontenelle only wished to defend himself by trying to include another man in the charge of *libertinage*, when he himself was meditating the most perfidious designs on Sylvie. Poor Fontenelle! One must try and think as kindly as possible of him now—he is dead. But I cannot think it was right of him to accuse my Florian!"

Just then she heard a soft knocking. It came from the door at the furthest end of the studio, one which communicated with a small stone courtyard, which in its turn opened out to a narrow street leading down to the Tiber. It was the entrance at which models presented themselves whenever Angela needed them.

"Angela!" called a melodious voice, which she recognised at once as the dearest to her in the world. "Angela!"

She hurried to the door but did not open it.

"Florian!" she said softly, putting her lips close to the panel, "Florian, *caro mio!* Why are you here?"

"I want to come in," said Florian, "I have news, Angela! I must see you!"

She hesitated a moment longer, and then she undid the bolt, and admitted him. He entered with a smiling and victorious air.

"I am all alone here," she said at once, before he could speak, "Father is at Frascati on some business—and my uncle the Cardinal is at the Vatican. Will you not come back later?"

For all answer, Florian took her in his arms with quite a reverent tenderness, and kissed her softly on brow and lips.

"No, I will stay!" he said, "I want to have you all to myself for a few minutes. I came to tell you, sweetest, that if I am to be the first to see your picture and pass judgment on it, I had better see it now, for I am going away to-morrow!"

"Going away!" echoed Angela, "Where?"

"To Naples," he answered, "Only for a little while. They have purchased my picture 'Phillida et les Roses' for one of the museums there, and they want me to see if I approve of the position in which it is to be placed. They also wish to honour me by a banquet or something of the kind—an absurdly unnecessary affair, but still I think it is perhaps advisable that I should go."

He spoke with an affectation of indifference, but any observer of him whose eyes were not blinded by affection, could have seen that he exhaled from himself an atmosphere of self-congratulation at the banquet proposition. Little honours impress little minds;—and a faint thrill of pain moved Angela as she saw him thus delighted with so poor and ordinary a compliment. In any other man it would have moved her to contempt, but in Florian——well!—she was only just a little sorry.

"Yes, perhaps it might look churlish of you not to accept," she said, putting away from her the insidious suggestion that perhaps if Florian loved her as much as he professed, an invitation to a banquet at Naples would have had no attraction for him as compared with being present at the first view of her picture on the morning she had herself appointed——"I think under the circumstances you had better not see the picture till you come back!"

"Now, Angela!" he exclaimed vexedly, "You know I will not consent to that! You have promised me that I shall be the first to see it—and here I am!"

"It should be seen by the morning light," said Angela, a touch of nervousness beginning to affect her equanimity,—"This light is pale and waning, though the afternoon is so clear. You cannot see the coloring to the best advantage!"

"Am I not a painter also?" asked Varillo playfully, putting his arm round her waist,—"And can I not guess the effect in the morning light as well as if I saw it? Come, Angela *mia!* Unveil the great prodigy!" and he laughed,—"You began it before we were affianced;— think what patience I have had for nearly two years!"

Angela did not reply at once. Somehow, his light laugh jarred upon her.

"Florian," she said at last, raising her truthful, beautiful eyes fully to his, "I do not think you quite understand! This picture has absorbed a great deal of my heart and soul—I have as it were, painted my own life blood into it—for I mean it to declare a truth and convey a lesson. It will either cover me with obloquy, or crown me with lasting fame. You speak jestingly, as if it were some toy with which I had amused myself these three years. Do you not believe that a woman's work may be as serious, as earnest, and strongly purposeful as a man's?"

Still clasping her round the waist, Florian drew her closer, and pressing her head against his breast, he looked down on her smiling.

"What sweet eyes you have!" he said, "The sweetest, the most trusting, the most childlike eyes I have ever seen! It would be impossible to paint such eyes, unless one's brushes were Raffaelle's, dipped in holy water!

Not that I believe very much in holy water as a painter's medium!" He laughed,—he had a well-shaped mouth and was fond of smiling, in order that he might show his even pearly teeth, which contrasted becomingly with his dark moustache. "Yes, my Angela has beautiful eyes, —and such soft, pretty hair!" and he caressed it gently, "like little golden tendrils with a beam of the sunlight caught in it! Is not that a pretty compliment? I think I ought to have been a poet instead of a painter!"

"You are both," said Angela fondly, with a little sigh of rest and pleasure as she nestled in his arms—"You will be the greatest artist of your time when you paint large subjects instead of small ones."

His tender hold of her relaxed a little.

"You think 'Phillida et les Roses' a small subject?" he asked, with a touch of petulance in his tone, "Surely if a small study is perfect, it is better than a large one which is imperfect?"

"Of course it is!" replied the girl quickly—"By small-ness I did not mean the size of the canvas,—I meant the character of the subject."

"There is nothing small in the beauty of woman!" de-clared Varillo, with an enthusiastic air—"Her form is divine! Her delicious flesh tints—her delicate curves— her amorous dimples—her exquisite seductiveness—com-bined with her touching weakness—these qualities make of woman the one,—the only subject for a painter's brush, when the painter is a man!"

Involuntarily Angela thought of "Pon-Pon," who had posed for the "Phillida," and a little shiver ran over her nerves like a sudden wind playing on the chords of an Æolian harp. Gently she withdrew herself from her lover's embrace.

"And when the painter is a woman, should the only subject for her brush be the physical beauty of man?" she asked.

Varillo gave an airy gesture of remonstrance.

"*Carissima mia!* You shock me! How can you sug-gest such a thing! The two sexes differ in tastes and aspirations as absolutely as in form. Man is an unfet-tered creature,—he must have his liberty, even if it reaches license; woman is his dependent. That is Na-ture's law. Man is the conqueror—woman is his conquest! We cannot alter these things. That is one reason for the prejudice existing against woman's work—if it excels that of man, we consider it a kind of morbid growth—an unnatural protuberance on the face of the universe. In fact, it is a wrong balance of the intellectual forces, which in their action, should always remain on the side of man."

"But if man abuses his power, may it not be taken from him altogether?" suggested Angela tranquilly, "If man, knowing that a life of self-indulgence destroys his intellectual capacity, still persists in that career, and woman, studying patiently to perfect herself, refuses to follow his example of vice, may it not happen that the intellectual forces may range themselves on the side of right rather than wrong, and invest woman with a certain supremacy in the end? It is a problem worth thinking of!"

Varillo looked sharply at her. Had she heard anything of his private life in Rome?—a life he kept carefully concealed from everyone who might be likely to report his little amusements at the Palazzo Sovrani? A slight, very slight touch of shame pricked him, as he noted the grace of her figure, the dainty poise of her head on her slim white throat—the almost royal air of dignity and sweetness which seemed to surround her,—there was no doubt whatever of her superiority to the women he generally consorted with, and for a moment he felt remorseful,—but he soon dismissed his brief compunction with a laugh.

"No, sweet Angela," he said gaily, "it is not worth thinking of! Believe me! I will not enter into any such profound discussions with you. My present time is too short, and your attractions too many! Why did you slip out of my arms so unkindly just now? Surely you were not offended? Come back! Come, and we will go up to the great picture as lovers should, together—entwined in each other's arms!—and you shall then draw the mysterious curtain,—or shall I?"

She still hesitated. Then after a pause, she came towards him once more, the soft colour alternately flushing and paling her cheeks, as she laid her hand on his arm.

"You did not answer me," she said, "when I asked you just now if you believed that a woman's work could be as purposeful as a man's—sometimes indeed more so. You evaded the question. Why?"

"Did I evade it?" and Varillo took her hand in his own and kissed it,—"*Dolcèzza mia*, I would not pain you for the world!

A slight shadow clouded her face.

"You will not pain me," she answered, "except by not being true to yourself and to me. You know how I have worked,—you know how high I have set my ambition for your sake—to make myself more worthy of you; but if you do honestly think that a woman's work in art must always be inferior to a man's, no matter how ardently she studies—no matter even if she has so perfected herself in drawing, anatomy, and colouring as to be admitted the equal of men in these studies—if the result must, in your mind, be nevertheless beneath that of the masculine attainment, why say so,—because then——then—"

"Then what, my sweet philosopher?" asked Florian lightly, again kissing the hand he held.

She fixed her eyes fully on him.

"Then," she replied slowly, "I should know you better—I should understand you more!"

An unpleasant twinge affected his nerves, and his eyelids quivered and blinked as though struck by a sudden shaft of the sun. This was the only facial sign he ever gave of the difficulty he at times experienced in meeting the straight, clear glance of his betrothed.

"You would know me more, and love me less? Is that it?" he said carelessly. "My dear girl, why do you press the point? If you will have it, I tell you frankly, I think women are growing very clever, much too clever in fact, —and that the encouragement and impetus given to them in the Arts is a very great mistake. Because they are not all geniuses like my Angela! You are one in a thousand—or rather one in a million,—and for one Angela Sovrani we shall have a world of female daubers calling themselves artists and entering into competition with us, as if we had not already quite enough competition among our own sex! I honestly believe that with very rare exceptions woman's work is decidedly inferior and mediocre as compared to man's."

Quickly Angela disengaged herself from his hold, her lips trembling—her eyes were full of a strange fire and brilliancy,—her slight figure seemed to grow taller as she stood for a moment like a queen, regarding him steadfastly from under her fair, level brows.

"Then come and see!" she said, "I am not proud—I make no boast at all of what I have done—and no one perceives or deplores the faults of my work more than I do—but I know I have not altogether failed!"

She moved away from him and stood opposite her veiled canvas,—then as Florian followed and joined her, with a swift action which had something of defiance as well as grace in it, she swept aside the concealing curtain. Florian recoiled with an involuntary cry,—and then remained motionless and silent,—stricken dumb and stupid by the magnificent creation which confronted him. This Angela's masterpiece! A woman's work! This stupendous conception! This perfect drawing! This wondrous colouring! Fully facing him, the central glory of the whole picture, was a figure of Christ—unlike any other Christ ever imagined by poet or painter——an etherealised Form through which the very light of Heaven itself seemed to shine,—supreme, majestic, and austerely God-like;—the face was more beautiful than any ever dreamed of by the hewers of the classic marbles —it was the face of a great Archangel,—beardless and youthful, yet kingly and commanding. Round the broad brows a Crown of Thorns shone like a diadem, every prickly point tipped with pale fire,—and from the light floating folds of intense white which, cloud-like, clung about the divine Form, faint flashes of the lightning gleamed. Above this grand Christ, the heavens were opened, pouring out a rain of such translucent purity of colour and radiance as never had been seen in any painted canvas before—but beneath, the clouds were black as midnight—confused, chaotic, and drifting darkly on a strong wind as it seemed into wierd and witch-like shapes, wherein there were seen the sun and moon revolving pallidly, like globes of fire lost from their orbits and about to become extinct. And among those shifting black films were a crowd of human creatures, floating and falling into unknown depths of darkness, and striking out wild arms of appeal and entreaty and despair,—the faces of these were all familiar, and were the life-like portraits of many of those pre-eminent in the history of the time. Chief among them was the Sovereign Pontiff, waxen and wan and dark-eyed,—he was depicted as fastening fetters of iron round the body of a beautiful youth, laurel-crowned, the leaves of the laurel bearing faint gold letters which spelt the word " Science." Huddled beside him was a well-known leader of the Jesuits, busily counting up heaps of gold,—another remarkable figure was that of a well-known magnate of the Church of England, who, leaning forward eagerly, sought to grasp and hold the garment of the Pope, but was dragged back by the hand of a woman crowned with an Imperial diadem. After these and other principal personages came a confusion of faces—all recognisable, yet needing study to discern;—creatures drifting downwardly into the darkness,—one was the vivisectionist whose name was celebrated through France, clutching at his bleeding victim and borne relentlessly onwards by the whirlwind,— and forms and faces belong to men of every description of Church-doctrine were seen trampling underneath them other human creatures scarcely discernible. And over all this blackness and chaos the supernal figure of the Christ was aërially poised,—one hand was extended and to this a woman clung—a woman with a beautiful face made piteous in its beauty by long grief and patient endurance. In her other arm she held a sleeping child—and mother and child were linked together by a garland of flowers partially broken and faded. Her entreating attitude,—the sleeping child's helplessness—her worn face,—the perishing roses of earth's hope and joy, —all expressed their meaning simply yet tragically, and as the Divine Hand supported and drew her up out of the universal chaos below, the hope of a new world, a better world, a wiser world, a holier world, seemed to be distantly conveyed. But the eyes of the Christ were full of reproach, and were bent on the Representative of St. Peter binding the laurel-crowned youth, and dragging him into darkness,—and the words written across the golden mount of the picture, in clear black letters, seemed to be actually spoken aloud from the vivid color and movement of the painting. " Many in that day will call upon Me and say, Lord, Lord, have we not prophesied in Thy name, and in Thy name cast out devils, and done many wonderful works?"

"Then will I say to them, I never knew you! Depart from me all ye that work iniquity!"

As an Allegory the picture was a daring yet sublime reproach to the hypocrisy of the religious world,—as a picture it was consummate in every detail, and would have been freely admitted as a masterpiece of Raffaelle had Raffaelle been fortunate enough to paint it. Still Varillo kept silence. Angela's heart beat so loudly that she could almost hear it in the deep silence of the room. Every fine little nerve in her body was strained to the utmost height of suspense,—she was afraid to look at her lover, or disturb the poise of his mental judgment by the lightest movement. And he? Thoughts, black as the chaos of cloud she had so powerfully portrayed, were stirring in his soul,—thoughts, base and mean and cowardly, which, gradually gathering force as he dwelt upon them, began to grow and spring up to a devilish height, worked into life and being by a burning spark of jealousy, which, long smouldering in his nature, now leaped into a flame. No trace of the wicked inner workings of his mind, however, darkened the equanimity of his features, or clouded the serene, soft candour of his eyes, as he at last turned towards the loving, shrinking woman, who stood waiting for his approval, as simply and sweetly as a rose might wait for the touch of the morning sun. Slowly, and like little pellets of ice, his first words fell from his lips,—

"Did you do it all yourself?"

The spell was disturbed—the charm broken. Angela turned very white—she drew a deep breath—and the tension on her nerves relaxed,—her heart gave one indignant bound—and then resumed its usual quiet beating, as with a strong effort she gathered all her dignity and force together, and replied simply,

"Can you ask?"

He looked at her. What an embodied insult to the arrogance of man she was! She!—a mere woman!—and the painter of the finest picture ever seen since Raffaelle and Michael Angelo left the world to work elsewhere. "Chaste as ice, pure as snow, thou shalt not escape calumny!" In his imagination he saw the world crowning her with imperishable bays—he heard the denunciation of the Vatican and the condemnation of the

Churches, thunder uselessly against the grand lesson of her work, while crowds gathered adoringly before the most perfect Christ ever painted!—and he saw her name written up in letters of gold on the scroll of those whom history numbers as immortal! It should not be! It should never be! And again he spoke, enunciating his words with difficulty, for his lips were dry.

"It is very fine! Quite marvellous, in fact!—almost unprecedented! That is why I ask, 'did you do it all yourself?' You must not be offended, Angela! I mean so well! You see the conception—the breadth of treatment—the gradation and tone of colour—are all absolutely masculine. Who first suggested the idea to you?"

Still very pale, breathing quickly yet lightly, and maintaining an air of calm which was almost matter of fact, she answered,—

"No one! Though perhaps, if it is traced to its source, it arose in my mind from seeing the universal dissatisfaction which most intelligent people feel with religion, as administered to them by the Churches. That, and a constant close study of the New Testament, set the thought in my brain,—a thought which gradually expressed itself in this form. So far as any work belongs to the worker, it is entirely my own creation. I am sorry you should have implied any doubt of it!"

Here her voice trembled a little, but she quickly steadied it. He smiled—a little difficult smile—and slipping his right hand between his coat and vest, felt for something he always carried there. It should never be!

"My dear Angela!" he said, with a gracious tranquillity that was almost dignity, "I do not doubt you in the least!—I merely *suggest* what all the world will *say!* There is not an art-critic alive who will accept this—this extraordinary production——as the work of a woman! It is the kind of thing which might have been produced hundreds of years ago by a great master setting his pupils to work at different sections of the canvas,—but that one woman, painting all alone for three years, should have designed and executed such a masterpiece—yes!—I will admit it *is* a masterpiece!—is an unheard of and altogether an extraordinary thing, and you must not wonder if competent judges reject the statement with incredulity!"

"It does not matter to me," said Angela, "what they reject or accept. You admit it is a masterpiece—that is enough for me. It is my own work, and you know it is!"

"Dear little one!" he said, laughing forcedly, "How do I know? You have never admitted me into the studio once while you were at work!"

"Florian!"

The exclamation broke from her lips like a cry of physical pain.

"That was a mistake of yours!" he went on recklessly, his eyes beginning to glitter with the fever raging in his mind, "You should not have shut the doors against your lover, my beloved! Nor would you admit your father either! That looks very strange!"

White as a snowflake, yet with blazing eyes, Angela turned upon him.

"Florian!" she said, "Do you—you of all people in the world—you to whom I have given all my love and confidence—mean to suggest that my work is not my own?"

He looked at her, smiling easily.

"Sweet Angela, not I! I know your genius—I worship it! See!" and with a light grace he dropped on one knee, and snatching her hand, kissed it—then springing up again, he said, "You are a great creature, my Angela! —the greatest artist in the world,—*if we can only make the world believe it!*"

Something in his voice, his manner, moved her to a vague touch of dread. Earnestly she looked at him,— wonderingly, and with a passionate reproach in her pure, true eyes. And still he smiled, while the fiends of envy and malice made havoc in his soul.

"My glorious Angela!" he said, "My bride, my beautiful one! A veritable queen, to whom nations shall pay homage!" He threw one arm round her waist and drew her somewhat roughly to him. "You must not be vexed with me, sweetheart!—the world is a cruel world, and always doubts great ability in woman! I only prepare you for what most people will say. But *I* do not doubt!—I know your power, and triumph in it!" He paused a moment, breathing quickly,—his eyes were fixed on the picture,—then he said, "If I may venture to criticise—

there is a shadow—there, at the left hand side of the canvas—do you not see?"

She disengaged herself from his clasp.

"Where?" she asked, in a voice from which all spirit and hopefulness had fled.

"You are sad? My Angela, have I discouraged you? Forgive me! I do not find fault,—this is a mere nothing, —you may not agree with me,—but does not that dark cloud make somewhat too deep a line near the faded roses? It may be only an effect of this waning light,— but I do think that line is heavy and might be improved. Be patient with me!—I only criticise to make perfection still more perfect!"

Listlessly she moved closer to the picture, turning away from him as she did so.

"Just the slightest softening of the tone—the finishing touch!" he murmured in caressing accents; while to himself he muttered—"It shall not be! It shall never be!" Then with a swift movement his hand snatched at the thing he always carried concealed near his breast—— a flash of pointed steel glittered in the light,—and with one stealthy spring and pitiless blow, he stabbed her full and furiously in the back as she stood looking at the fault he had pretended to discover in her picture! One choking cry escaped her lips—

"Florian——you! *You*—Florian!" Then reeling, she threw up her arms and fell, face forwards on the floor, insensible.

He stood above her, dagger in hand,—and studied the weapon with strange curiosity. It was crimson and wet with blood. Then he stared at the picture. A faint horror began to creep over him. The great Christ in the centre of the painting seemed to live and move, and float towards him on clouds of blinding glory. His breath came and went in uneasy gasps.

"Angela!" he muttered thickly,—"Angela!"

She lay prone and horribly still. He was afraid to touch her. What had he done? Murdered her? Oh no!—he had done nothing—nothing at all,—she had merely fainted—she would be well presently! He smiled foolishly at this, still gazing straight at the picture, and holding the sharp blood-stained blade in his hand.

"My love!" he said aloud,—then listened—as though

waiting for an answer. And still he stared persistently at the glorious figure of the Christ, till the Divine eyes seemed to flash the fire of an everlasting wrath upon his treacherous soul.

"To destroy the work? Or claim it?" he mused, "Either would be easy! That is, if she were dead!——." he paused,—amazed at his own thought. "If she were dead, it would be easy to swear *I* had painted the picture! If she were dead!" Again he listened. "Angela!" he whispered.

A door banging in the house startled him from his semi-stupor. His eyes wandered from the picture to the inanimate form lying at his feet.

"Sweet Angela!" he said, a cold smile flickering on his lips, "You were always unselfish! You wished me to be the greatest artist of my time!—and perhaps I shall be! —now *you* are dead! My love!"

A sudden clatter of horses' hoofs and rolling wheels wakened hollow echoes from the great stone courtyard below. It was the Cardinal returning from the Vatican. A panic seized him—his teeth chattered as with icy cold. He sprang swiftly to the door by which Angela had admitted him, and opened it cautiously,—then slinking out, locked it carefully behind him, took the key,—and fled. Once in the street, he never paused till he reached the corner of a dark projecting wall over-looking the Tiber, and here, glancing nervously round lest he should be observed, he flung his murderer's dagger and the key of the studio both into the water. Again he paused and listened—looking up at the frowning windows of the Palazzo Sovrani which could be dimly seen from where he stood. He had not meant to kill Angela. Oh no! He had come to the studio, full of love, prepared to chide her tenderly for the faults in her work,—till he saw that it was faultless; to make a jest of her ambition,—till he realized her triumph! And then,—then the devil had seized him—then——! A scarlet slit in the western horizon showed where the sun had sunk,—a soft and beautiful after-glow trembled over the sky in token of its farewell. A boy came strolling lazily down the street eating a slice of melon, and paused to fling the rind over the wall. The innocent, unconscious glance of the stripling's eyes was sufficient to set up a cowardly trembling in his body,—and turning round abruptly so that even this stray youth might not observe him too closely, he hurried away. And the boy, never regarding him at all, strolled on with the mellow taste of the fruit he had just enjoyed in his mouth, and presently, as if inspired thereby, awoke the slumbering echoes of the street with his high, fluting young treble, singing,

"Che faro senza Eurydice!"

XXX.

MEANWHILE Cardinal Bonpré had once more reached his own apartments, thankful enough to be there after his difficult experience at the Vatican. But he was neither fatigued nor depressed by what had occurred,—on the contrary he was conscious of an extraordinary vigour and lightness of heart, as though he had suddenly grown young again. Changing his scarlet robes of office for his every-day cassock, he seated himself restfully, and with a deep sigh of relief, in his easy chair near the writing-table, and first of all closing his eyes for a moment, while he silently prayed for guidance to the Supreme Judge of all secret intentions, he called Manuel to his side.

" My child," he said gently, " I want you to listen to me very attentively. I do not think you quite understand what you have done to-day, do you? "

Manuel raised his eyes with a clear look of confidence.

" Yes. I have spoken to the Head of the Church of Rome," he answered,—" That is all. I have said to him, as Christ once said to the very Peter whom he represents, ' Thou savourest not the things that be of God, but those that be of men.' "

The Cardinal regarded him straightly.

" True! But for you, a mere child, to say to the Head of the Church what Christ said to St. Peter, will be judged as blasphemy. I have never urged you, as you know, to tell me who you are, or where you came from. I do not urge you now. For I feel that you have been sent to me for some special purpose,—that young as you are, you have been entrusted by a Higher Power with some mission to me—for you possess the spirit of inspiration, prophecy and truth. I dare not question that spirit! Wherever I find it, in the young, in the old, in the wise or the ignorant I give it welcome. For you have uttered not only what I have myself thought, but what half the world is thinking, though you are only one

of those 'babes and sucklings out of whose mouth the
Lord hath ordained wisdom.' But what you have said
at the Vatican will be judged as heresy—and I shall be
counted heretic for having permitted you to speak thus
boldly."

" Your permission was not asked," said Manuel simply,
" I was summoned to the Vatican, but I was not told
what to say to the Pope. I spoke as I felt. No one interrupted me. The Pope listened to all my words. And
I said no more than is true."

" Truth is judged as libel nowadays in the world," answered the Cardinal, " And we have to confront the fact
that we have incurred the displeasure, and have also invited the vengeance of the Sovereign Pontiff. Thus we
must expect to suffer."

" Then he who is called the visible Head of Christianity
objects to the truth, and is capable of vengeance!" said
Manuel, " That is a strange contradiction! But I will
suffer whatever he pleases to inflict upon me. You shall
suffer nothing!"

The Cardinal smiled gravely.

" My child, I am old, and whatever trouble is in store
for me cannot last long. But I must guard you from
harm with all the remaining powers of my life. Having
constituted myself your protector and defender, I must
continue to protect and defend. And so, Manuel, to-
morrow or the next day I shall take you away to England. So far, at least, I will defy the powers of Rome!"

His eyes flashed, and his whole person seemed to be
invested with sudden strength, dignity and command.
He pointed to the crucifix on the table before him.

" He, the Holy One of the Heavens, was crucified for
speaking the truth,—I can do no better than follow His
divine example! If my soul is stretched on the cross-
beams of injustice—if every tender emotion of my heart
is tortured and slain—if I am stripped of honour and exposed to contempt, what matter! My glorious Master
suffered likewise."

Manuel was silent. He stood near the great chimney
where the wood fire burned and crackled, casting a ruddy
glow through the room. After a few minutes he turned
his fair head towards the Cardinal with an earnest,
scrutinising gaze in his expressive eyes.

"Then, dear friend, you are not angry? You do not reproach me for what I have done?"

"Reproach you? I reproach no one!" said Bonpré, —"Least of all, a child! For you speak unconsciously— as genius speaks;—you cannot weigh the meaning of your words, or the effect of what you say on the worldly or callous minds which have learned to balance motives and meanings before coining them into more or less ambiguous language. No!—I have nothing to reproach you with, Manuel,—I am thankful to have you by my side!"

His eyes rested again upon the crucifix for a moment, and he went on, more to himself than to the boy,—

"In the early days of our Lord, He spoke to the wise men in the Temple, and they were 'astonished at his understanding and answers.' But they did not reprove Him,—not then,—on the contrary, they listened. How often in our own days do young children ask us questions to which we cannot reply, and which they themselves perchance could easily answer if they but knew how to clothe their thoughts with speech! For the Spirit of God is made manifest in many ways, and through many methods;—sometimes it whispers a hint or a warning to us in the petals of the rose, sometimes in the radiance of the sunset on the sea, sometimes in the simple talk of a child younger even than you are,—'Except ye become as little children——!'"

He paused in his dreamy utterance, and turned in his chair listening. "What is that?" There was a noise of hurrying footsteps and murmuring voices,—that sort of half-muffled confusion in a household which bodes something wrong,—and all at once Prince Sovrani threw open the door of the Cardinal's apartments without ceremony, crying out as he entered,—

"Where is Angela?"

The Cardinal rose out of his chair, startled and alarmed.

"Angela?" he echoed, "She is not here!"

"Not here!" Prince Sovrani drew a sharp breath, and his face visibly paled,—"It is very strange! Her studio is locked at both entrances—yet the servants swear she has not passed out of the house! Besides she never goes out without leaving word as to where she has gone and when she is coming back!"

"Her studio is locked on both sides!" repeated the Cardinal, "But that is quite easy to understand—her picture is unveiled, and no one is to be permitted to see it until to-morrow."

"Yes—yes—" said the Prince Pietro impatiently, "I know all that,—but where is Angela herself? There is no sign of her anywhere! She cannot have gone out. Her maid tells me she was not dressed to go out. She was in her white working gown when last seen. *Santissima Madonna!*"—and old Sovrani gave a wild gesture of despair—"If any harm has happened to the child . . ."

"Harm? Why what harm could happen? What harm could happen?" said the Cardinal soothingly,— "My dear brother, do not alarm yourself needlessly——"

"Let us go to the studio," interposed Manuel suddenly —"She may not have heard you call her."

He moved in his gentle light way out of the room, and without another word they followed. Outside the studio door they paused, and Prince Sovrani tried again and again to open it, calling "Angela!" now loudly, now softly, now entreatingly, now commandingly, all to no purpose. The servants had gathered on the landing, afraid of they knew not what, and one old man, the Prince's valet, shook his head dolefully at the continued silence.

"Why not break open the door, Eccellenza?" he asked anxiously, "I know the trick of those old locks— if the Eccellenza will permit I can push back the catch with a strong chisel."

"Do so then," replied his master, "I cannot wait— there is something horrible in the atmosphere!—something that chokes me! Quick! This suspense will kill me!"

The old valet hurried away, and in two or three minutes, during which time both Prince Sovrani and the Cardinal knocked and called again outside the door quite uselessly, he returned with a strong iron chisel which he forced against the lock. For some time it resisted all efforts—then with appalling suddenness gave way and flew back, the door bursting wide open with the shock. For one instant the falling shadows of evening made the interior of the room too dim to see distinctly—there was a confused blur of objects,—the carved summit of a great easel,—a gold picture-frame shining round a wonderful mass of colouring on canvas——then gradually they discerned the outline of a small figure lying prone at the foot of the easel, stiff and motionless. With a dreadful cry of despair Sovrani dashed into the room.

"Angela! Angela!"

Falling on his knees he raised the delicate figure in his arms,—the little head drooped inanimate on his shoulder, and with the movement a coil of golden hair became unbound, and fell in soft waves over his trembling hands—the fair face was calm and tranquil—the eyes were closed, —but as the distracted man clasped that inert, beloved form closer, he saw what caused him to spring erect with a terrible oath, and cry for vengeance.

"Murdered!" he exclaimed hoarsely—"Murdered! Brother, come close!——see here! Will you talk to me of God *now!* My last comfort in life—the last gift of my Gita, murdered!"

The affrighted Cardinal tottered forward, and looking, saw that a deep stain of blood oozed over the soft white garments of the lifeless girl, and he wrung his hands in despair.

"My God! My God!" he moaned, "In what have we offended Thee that Thou shouldst visit us with such heavy affliction? Angela, my child!—my little girl!—Angela!"

The servants had by this time clustered round, a pale and terrified group, sobbing and crying loudly,—only the old valet retained sufficient presence of mind to light two or three of the lamps in the studio. As this was done, and the sudden luminance dispersed some of the darker shadows in the room, the grand picture on the easel was thrown into full prominence,—and the magnificent Christ, descending in clouds of glory, seemed to start from the painted canvas and move towards them all. And even while he wrung his hands and wept, the Cardinal's glance was suddenly caught and transfixed by this splendour,—he staggered back amazed, and murmured feebly—"Angela! *This* is her work!——this her great picture, and she—she is dead!"

Sovrani suddenly clutched him by the arm, and drew

him close to the couch where he had just laid the body of his daughter down.

" Now, where was this God you serve, think you, when this happened? " he demanded, in a hoarse whisper, while his aged eyes glittered feverishly, and his stern dark face under the tossed white hair was as a frowning mask of vengeance,—" Is the world so rich in sweet women that *she* should be slain? "

Half paralysed with grief, the unhappy Cardinal sank on his knees beside the murdered girl,—taking the passive hand he kissed it, the tears flowing down his furrowed cheeks. Her magnificent picture shone forth, a living presence in the room, but the thoughts of all were for the dead only, and the distracted Sovrani saw nothing but his child's pale, set face, closed eyes, and delicate figure, lying still with the red stain of blood spreading through the whiteness of her garments. None of them thought of Manuel—and it was with a shock of surprise that the Cardinal became aware of him, and saw him approaching the couch, raising his hand as he came, warningly.

" Hush, hush! " he said, very gently, " It may be that she is not dead! She will be frightened when she wakes if she sees you weeping! "

Prince Sovrani caught the words.

" When she wakes! " he cried, " Poor boy, you do not know what you say! She will never wake! She is dead! "

But Manuel was bending closely over the couch, and looking earnestly into Angela's quiet face. Cardinal Bonpré watched him wonderingly. And the old Prince stood, arrested as it were in the very midst of his wrath and sorrow by some force more potent than even the spirit of vengeance. The sobbing servants held their breath—and all stared as if fascinated at the young boy, as after a pause, he took Angela's hand that hung so inertly down, in one of his own, and with the other felt her heart. Then he spoke.

" She is not dead! " he said simply,—" She has only swooned. Let someone fetch a physician to attend her —see!—she breathes! "

With a wild, half-smothered cry Prince Sovrani sprang forward to see for himself if this blessed news was true.

He and the Cardinal both, seized with a passionate anxiety, gazed and gazed at the fair beloved face in hope, in fear and longing,—and still Manuel stood beside the couch, stroking the small hand he held with thoughtful care and tenderness. All at once a faint sigh parted the sweet lips,—the bosom heaved with a struggle for breath. Her father fell on his knees, overcome, and hiding his face in his hands sobbed aloud in the intensity of his relief and joy, while the Cardinal murmured a devout 'Thank God!' A few minutes passed, and still the fluttering uncertain breathings came and went, and still Manuel stood by the couch, quietly watchful. Presently the closed eyelids quivered and lifted,—and the beautiful true eyes shone star-like out upon the world again! She stirred, and tried to raise herself, but sank back exhausted in the effort. Then seeing the Cardinal, she smiled,—and her gaze wandered slowly to the bent, white-haired figure crouching beside her, whose whole frame was shaken by sobs.

"Father!" she murmured—"Dearest father! What is it?"

He lifted his tear-stained, agonised face, and seeing that the tender eyes regarding him were full of fear and wonder as well as love, he instantly controlled himself, and rising from his knees, kissed her gently.

"I thought you were dead, my darling!" he said softly—— "Hush now—do not speak! Lie quite still! You are hurt a little,—you must rest!—you will be better, —much better presently!"

But Angela's looks had again wandered, and now they were fixed on Manuel. Over her whole face there came a sudden life and radiance.

"Manuel!" she said eagerly—"Manuel, stay with me! Do not leave me!"

Manuel smiled in answer to her appealing eyes, and came nearer.

"Do not fear!" he said—"I will stay!"

She closed her eyes again restfully, and her breathing grew lighter and easier. Just then one of the servants entered with the physician who was accustomed to attend the Sovrani household. His arrival roused Angela completely,—she became quite conscious, and evidently began to remember something of what had happened.

The doctor raised her to see where she was injured, and quickly cutting away her blood-stained vesture, tenderly and carefully examined the wound.

" I cannot understand how it is that she is not dead!" he said at last—" It is a miracle! This is a stab inflicted with some sharply pointed instrument,—probably a dagger—and was no doubt intended to be mortal. As it is, it is dangerous—but there is a chance of life." Then he addressed himelf to Angela, who was looking at him with wide-open eyes and a most piteous expression. " Do you know me, my child?"

" Oh, yes, doctor!" she murmured faintly.

" Do you suffer much pain?"

" No."

" Then can you tell me how this happened? Who stabbed you?"

She shuddered and sighed.

" No one!—that I can remember!"

Her eyes closed—she moved her hands about restlessly as though seeking for something she had lost.

" Manuel!"

" I am here!" answered the boy gently.

" Stay with me! I am so tired!"

Again a convulsive trembling shook her fragile body from head to foot, and again she sighed as though her heart were breaking,—then she lay passively still, though one or two tears crept down her cheeks as they carried her tenderly up to her own room and laid her down on her simple little white bed, softly curtained, and guarded by a statue of the Virgin bending over it. There, when her cruel wound was dressed and bandaged, and the physician had given her a composing draught, she fell into a deep, refreshing slumber, and only Manuel stayed beside her as she slept.

Meanwhile, down in the studio, Prince Sovrani and the Cardinal stayed together, talking softly, and gazing in fascinated wonder, bewilderment, admiration and awe at Angela's work unveiled. All the lamps in the room were now lit, and the great picture—a sublime Dream resolved into sublime Reality—shone out as much as the artificial light would permit,—a jewel of art that seemed to contain within itself all the colour and radiance of a heaven unknown, unseen, yet surely near at hand. The figure and face of the approaching Saviour, instinct with life, expressed almost in positive speech the words, " Then shall ye see the Son of Man coming in the clouds with great power and glory "!—and if Cardinal Bonpré had given way to the innermost emotions of his soul, he could have knelt before the exalted purity of such a conception of the Christ,—a god-like ideal, brought into realization by the exalted imagination, the holy thoughts, and the faithful patient work of a mere woman!

" This—" he said, in hushed accents—" This must be the cause of the dastardly attempt made to murder the child! Some one who knew her secret,—some one who was aware of the wonderful power and magnificence of her work,—perhaps the very man who made the frame for it,——who can tell? "

Prince Pietro meditated deeply, a frown puckering his brows,—his countenance was still pale and drawn with the stress of the mingled agony and relief he had just passed through, and the anxiety he felt concerning Angela's immediate critical condition.

" I cannot hold the position yet!—" he said, at last— " That is to say, I am too numb and stricken with fear to realize what has happened! See you! That picture is marvellous!—a wonder of the world!—it will crown my girl with all the laurels of a lasting fame,—but what matter is it to me,—this shouting of the public,—if she dies? Will it console me for her loss, to call her a Raffaelle? "

" Nay, but we must not give up hope! "—said the Cardinal soothingly—" Please God, you will not lose her! Be glad that she is not dead,—and remember that it is almost by a miracle that she lives! "

" That is true—that is true! " murmured old Sovrani, ruffling his white hair with one hand, while he still stared abstractedly at his daughter's picture—" You are very patient with me, brother!—you have all the kindness as well as all the faithfulness of your sister,—the sweetest woman the sun was ever privileged to shine on! Well. well! What did you say to me? That this picture must have been the cause of the attempted murder? Maybe. —but the poor hard-working fellow who made the frame for it, could not have done such a deed,—he has been a pensioner of Angela's for many a long day, and she has given him employment when he could not obtain it from others. Besides, he never saw the picture. Angela gave him her measurements, and when the frame was finished he brought it to her here. But he had nothing whatever to do with setting the canvas in it,—that I know, for Angela herself told me. No, no!—let us not blame the innocent; rather let us try to find the guilty."

At that moment a servant entered with a large and exquisitely arranged basket of lilies-of-the-valley, and a letter.

"For Donna Sovrani," he said, as he handed both to his master.

The Prince took the basket of lilies, and moved by a sudden fancy, set it gently in front of Angela's great work. Glancing at the superscription of the letter, he said,—

"From Varillo. I had better open it and see what he says."

He broke the seal and read the following:

"SWEETEST ANGELA,—I am summoned to Naples on business, and therefore, to my infinite regret, shall not be able to see the great picture to-morrow. You know,—you can feel how sorry I am to disappoint both you and myself in a pleasure which we have so long lovingly anticipated, but as the Queen has promised to make her visit of inspection, I dare not ask you to put off the exhibition of your work till my return. But I know I shall come back to find my Angela crowned with glory, and it will be reserved for me to add the last laurel leaf to the immortal wreath! I am grieved that I have no time to come and press my 'addio' on your sweet lips,—but in two or three days at most, I shall be again at your feet.

Un bacio di

FLORIAN."

"Then he has left for Naples?" said Bonpré, to whom Prince Pietro had read this letter—"A sudden departure, is it not?"

"Very sudden!"

"He will not know what has happened to Angela——"

"Oh he will be sure to hear that!" said the Prince—"To-night it will be in all the newspapers both of Rome and Naples. Angela's light cannot be hidden under a bushel!"

"True. Then of course he will return at once."

"Naturally. If he hears the news on his way, he will probably be back to-night—" said Sovrani, but his fuzzy brows were still puckered. Some uncomfortable thought seemed to trouble him,—and presently, as if moved by a sudden inexplicable instinct, he took the basket of lilies away from where he had set it in front of his daughter's picture, and transferred it to a side-table. Cardinal Bonpré, always observant, noticed his action.

"You will not leave the flowers there?" he queried.

"No. The picture is a sacred thing!—it is an almost living Christ!—in whom Varillo does not believe!"

The Cardinal lifted his eyes protestingly.

"Yet you let the child marry him?"

Sovrani passed one hand wearily across his brows.

"Let us not talk of marriage," he said—"Death is nearer to us to-day than life! I am opposed to the match —I always have been,—and who knows——who knows what may not yet prevent it——" He paused, thinking,—then turning a solicitous glance on his brother-in-law's frail figure he said—"Felix, you look weary,—let me attend you to your own rooms, that you may rest. We need you with us,—it may be that we shall need you more than we have ever done! Pray for us, brother!—Pray for my Angela, that she may be spared——"

His harsh voice broke,—and tears trickled down his furrowed cheeks.

"See you!" he said, pointing in a kind of despair to the magnificent "Coming of Christ"—"If Raffaelle or Angelo had dared to paint this in their day, the world would be taking a lesson from it now! If it were a modern man's work, that man would be a centre for hero-worship! But that a *woman* should create such a masterpiece!—and that woman my Angela! Do you know what it means, Felix?—what Fame always means, what it always must mean—for a woman? Just what has already happened,—the murderous dagger-thrust—the coward stab in the back—and the little child's cry of the tender broken heart we heard just now—— 'Stay with me!—I am so tired!'"

The Cardinal pressed his hand sympathetically, too profoundly moved himself to speak.

" This picture will bring down the thunders of the Vatican!—" went on Sovrani—" And those thunders will awaken a responsive echo from the world ! But not from the Old World—the New ! The New World !—yes—my Angela's work is for the living present, the coming future—not for the decayed Past ! "

As he spoke, he dropped the silken curtain before the picture and hid it from view.

" We will raise it again when the painter lives—or dies ! " he said brokenly.

They left the studio, Prince Pietro extinguishing the lights, and giving orders to his servant to put a strong bar across the door they had forced open,—and the Cardinal, feeling more lonely than he had done for many days, owing to the temporary absence of Manuel who was keeping watch over Angela, returned to his own apartments full of grave thoughts and anxious trouble. He had meant to leave Rome at once,—but now, such a course seemed more than impossible. Yet he knew that the scene which had, through himself indirectly, occurred at the Vatican, would have its speedy results in some decisive and vengeful action, if not on the part of the Supreme Pontiff, then through his ministers and advisers, and Bonpré was sufficiently acquainted with the secret ways of the Church he served, to be well aware of its relentlessness in all cases where its authority was called into question. The first step taken, so he instinctively felt, would be to deprive him of Manuel's companionship,—the next perhaps, to threaten him with the loss of his own diocese. He sighed heavily,—yet in his own tranquil and pious mind he could not say that he resented the position his affairs had taken. Accustomed as he was always, to submit the whole daily course of his life to the ruling of a Higher Power, he was framed and braced as temperately for adversity as for joy,—and nothing seemed to him either fortunate or disastrous except as concerned the attitude in which the soul received the announcement of God's will. To resent affliction was, in his opinion, sinful ; to accept it reverently and humbly as a means of grace, and endeavour to make sweetness out of the seeming bitterness of the divine dispensation, appeared to him the only right and natural way of duty,—hence his clear simplicity of thought, his patience, plain faith, and purity of aim. And even now, perplexed and pained as he was, much more for the sorrow which had befallen his brother-in-law, than for any trouble likely to occur personally to himself, he was still able to disentangle his thoughts from all earthly cares—to lift up his heart, unsullied by complaint, to the Ruler of all destinies—and to resign himself with that Christian philosophy, which when truly practised, is so much more powerful than all the splendid stoicism of the heroic pagans, to those

> " Glorious God-influences,
> Which we, unseeing, feel and grope for blindly,
> Like children in the dark, knowing that Love is near ! "

Meanwhile Prince Pietro, moved by conflicting sentiments and forebodings which he was unable to explain to himself, and only strongly conscious of the desire to be avenged on his daughter's cowardly assailant, whoever it might be, muffled himself in a well-worn " Almaviva " cloak, his favourite out-door garment, pulled his hat down over his eyes, and so, looking like a fierce old brigand of the mountains, went out, not quite knowing why he went, but partly impelled by a sense of curiosity. He wanted to hear something,—to find something,—and yet he could not agree with himself as to the nature of the circumstance he sought to discover. There was a lurking suspicion in his mind to which he would not give a name, —a dark thought that made him tremble with mingled rage and horror,—but he put it away from him as a hint offered by the Evil One—an insidious suggestion as hideous as it was unnatural. The afternoon had now closed into night, and many stars were glistening bravely in the purple depths of the clear sky,—the air was mild and balmy,—and as he crossed the road to turn down the little side street leading to the Tiber, where Florian Varillo had stood but a few hours previously, a flower-girl met him with a large basket of white hyacinths and held them up to his eyes.

"*Ecco la primavera, Signor!*" she said, with a smile.

He shook his head, and turned abruptly away,—as he did so, his foot struck against some slight obstacle. Stooping to examine it, he saw it was the empty leathern sheath of a dagger. He picked it up, and studied it intently. It was elaborately adorned with old rococco work, and was evidently the ornamental covering of one of those small but deadly weapons which Italians, both men and women, so often wear concealed about their persons, for the purpose of taking vengeance, when deemed necessary, on an unsuspecting enemy. Slipping the thing into his pocket, the Prince looked about him, and soon recognised his bearings,—he was standing about six yards away from the private back-entrance to his daughter's studio. He walked up to the door and tried it,—it was fast locked.

"Yes——I remember!——the servants told me—— both doors were locked,——and from this they said the key was gone,—" he muttered, then paused.

Presently, actuated by a sudden impulse, he turned and walked swiftly with long impatient strides through the more populated quarters of Rome towards the Corso, and he had not proceeded very far in this direction before he heard a frenzied and discordant shouting which, though he knew it did not yet bear the truth in its harsh refrain, yet staggered him and made his heart almost stand still with an agony of premonitory fear.

"*Morte di Angela Sovrani!*"

"*Assassinamènto di Angela Sovrani!*"

"*Morte subito di Angela Sovrani!*"

"*Assassinamènto crudele della bella Sovrani!*"

Prince Pietro held his breath in sharp pain, listening. How horrible was the persistent cry of the newsvendors! —hoarse and shrill—now near—now far!—

"*Morte di Angela Sovrani!*"

How horrible!—how horrible! He put his hands to his ears to try and shut out the din. He had not expected any public outcry—not so soon——but ill news travels fast, and no doubt the very servants of his own household were responsible for having, in the extremity of their terror, given away the report of Angela's death. The terrible shouts were like so many cruel blows on his brain, —yet—half-reeling with the shock of them, he still went on his way,—straight on to the house and studio of Florian Varillo. There, he rang the bell loudly and impatiently. A servant opened the door in haste, and stared aghast at the tall old man with the white hair and blazing eyes, who was wrapped in a dark cloak, the very folds of which seemed to tremble with the suppressed rage of the form it enveloped.

"*Il Principe Sovrani!*" he stammered feebly, falling back a little from the threshold.

"Where is your master?" demanded Sovrani.

"*Eccellenza*, he has gone to Naples!"

"When did he leave?"

"But two hours ago, *Eccellenza!*"

Prince Pietro held up the dagger-sheath he had just found.

"This—belongs—to—him—does it not?" he asked slowly, detaching his words with careful directness.

The man answered readily and at once.

"Yes, *Eccellenza!*"

Sovrani uttered a terrible oath.

"Let me pass!"

The servant made a gesture of protest.

"But——*Eccellenza*——my master is not here! . . . "

Prince Pietro paying no heed to him, strode into the house, and brusquely threw open the door of a room which he knew to be Varillo's own specially private retreat. A woman with a mass of bright orange-gold hair, half-dressed in a tawdry blue peignoir trimmed with cheap lace, was sprawling lazily on a sofa smoking a cigarette. She sprang up surprised and indignant,—but shrank back visibly as she recognised the intruder, and met the steady tigerish glare of the old man's eyes.

"Where is your lover?" he asked.

"*Eccellenza!* You amaze——you insult me——!"

"*Basta!*" and Sovrani came a step nearer to her, his wrath seeming to literally encompass him like a thunder-cloud—"Play me no tricks! This is not the time for lying! I repeat my question—where is he? You, the companion of his closest thoughts,—you, his 'model'—you, Mademoiselle Pon-Pon, his mistress—you must know all his movements. Tell me then, where he is—or by heaven, if you do not, I will have you arrested for complicity in murder!"

She fell back from him trembling, her full red mouth half open,—and her face paling with terror.

"Murder!" she whispered——"*Dio mio! Dio mio!*"

"Yes—murder!" and the Prince thrust before her

wide-opened eyes the dagger-sheath he held—" What!
Have you not heard? Not yet? Not though the whole
city rings with the news? What news? That Angela
Sovrani is dead! That she—my daughter—the sweetest,
purest, most innocent and loving of women as well as the
greatest and most gifted—has been mortally stabbed in
her own studio this very day by some cowardly fiend
unknown! Unknown did I say? Not so—known! This
sheath belongs to Florian Varillo. Where is he? Tell me
at once—if only to save *yourself* trouble! "

Overcome by fear, and to do her justice, horror as well,
the miserable Pon-Pon threw herself on her knees.

" I swear he has gone to Naples! " she cried—" On my
word!—as I live!—I swear it!—he has gone! He seemed
as usual,—he was not in any haste—he left no message
—he said he would be back in two or three days——he
sent flowers to la Donna Sovrani——he wrote to her
. . . *O Santissima Virgine!* . . . I swear to you I know
nothing! "

The Prince eyed her with grim attention.

" They are shouting it in the streets—" he said—
" Listen! " He held up one hand,—she cowered on the
floor—she could hear nothing, and she stared at him in
fascinated terror—" They are telling all Rome of the
death of my child! First Rome—and then—the world!
The world shall hear of it! For there is only one Angela
Sovrani,—and earth and heaven cry out for justice in her
name! Tell this to the devil who has bought you for his
pleasure! I leave the message with you,—tell him that
when the world clamours for vengeance upon her murderer, *I know where to find him!* "

With that, he put the dagger-sheath back in his breast-
pocket with jealous care, and left her where she crouched,
shivering and moaning. Walking as in a dream he
brushed past the astonished and frightened servant unseeingly, and went out of the house into the street once
more. There he paused dizzily,—the stars appeared to
rock in the sky, and the houses seemed moving slowly
round him in a sort of circular procession. The shouting
of the newsvendors which had ceased for a while, began
again with even louder persistency.

" *Morte di Angela Sovrani!* "
" *La bella Sovrani!——Assassinamènto crudele!* "

The old man's heart beat in strong hammer-strokes,—he listened vaguely,—his tall figure shaking a little with the storm pent-up within him, till all at once as if the full realization of the position had only just burst upon him, he uttered a sharp cry—

"Her lover! Her promised husband! One whom she trusted and loved more than her own father! The hope of her life!—the man whose praise was sweeter to her than the plaudits of the whole world!—he—even he—her *murderer!* For even if she lives in body, he has murdered her soul!"

He looked up at the deep starlit heavens, his dark face growing livid in the intensity of his wrath and pain.

"May God curse him!" he whispered thickly—"May all evil track his footsteps, and the terrors of a cursed conscience hound him to his death! May he never know peace by day or night!——may the devils in his own soul destroy him! God curse him!"

He clenched his fist and raised it threateningly,—and gathering his cloak about him tried to walk on,—but there was a black mist before his eyes . . . he could not see——he stumbled forward blindly, and would have fallen, had not a strong arm caught him and held him upright. He turned a dazed and wondering look on the man whose friendly grasp supported him,——then, with an exclamation, made a trembling attempt to raise his hat.

"*Il Rè!*" he murmured feebly—"*Il Rè!*"

King Humbert—for it was he—held him still more closely.

"Courage, *amico!*" he said kindly.——"Courage!——yes——yes!—I know—I have heard the news! All Italy will give you vengeance for your child! We will spare no pains to discover her murderer. But now——you are ill—you are weary——do not try to speak——come with me! Let me take you home—come!"

A great sob broke from the old man's breast as he yielded to his Sovereign's imperative yet gentle guidance, and before he could realize the situation, he was in the King's own carriage, with the King beside him, being rapidly driven back to his own house. Arrived at the Palazzo Sovrani, a strange sight greeted them. The great *porte-cochere* was wide open, and, pressing through it, and surrounding the stately building at every point

was a vast crowd,—densely packed and almost absolutely
silent. Quite up to the inner portico these waiting thousands pressed,—though, as they recognised the Royal
liveries, they did their best to make immediate way, and
a low murmur arose *" Evviva il Rè! "* But there was no
loud shouting, and the continued hush was more distinctly recognisable than the murmur. Prince Sovrani
gazed bewilderedly at the great throng as the carriage
moved slowly through, and putting his hand to his head
murmured—

"What—what is this! I do not understand——why
are these people here?"

The King pressed his hand.

"All the world honours and loves your daughter, my
friend!" he said, "And Rome, the Mother of Nations,
mourns the loss of her youngest child of genius."

"No—no, not loss!——she is not dead—" began Sovrani stammeringly,—"I should have told your Majesty
——she is grievously wounded——but not dead . . ."

At that moment the carriage stopped. The door of the
Sovrani palace was open, and in the centre of a group
of people that had gathered within, among whom were
Aubrey Leigh, Sylvie Hermenstein, and the Princesse
D'Agramont, stood Cardinal Bonpré and Manuel. Manuel was a little in advance of the rest, and as the King
and Prince Sovrani alighted, he came fully forward, his
eyes shining, and a smile upon his lips.

"She will recover!" he said, "She is sleeping peacefully,—and all is well!"

His voice rang clear and sweet, and was heard by
everyone on the outskirts of the crowd. The good news
ran from mouth to mouth, till all the people caught it up
and responded with one brief, subdued, but hearty cheer.
Then, without bidding, they began to disperse, and the
King, baring his head in the presence of Cardinal Bonpré, gave up his self-imposed charge of old Sovrani,
who, faint and feeble, grasped Aubrey Leigh's quickly
proffered arm, and leaned heavily upon it.

"He needs care," said Humbert gently,—"The shock
has moved him greatly!"

"Your Majesty is ever considerate of the sorrows of
others," said the venerable Felix with emotion, "And God
will bless you as He blesses all good men!"

The King bowed reverently to the benediction. Then he looked up with a slight smile.

"It is not wise of your Eminence to say so,—in Rome!" he observed,—"But I thank you, and am grateful!"

His keen eyes rested for a moment on Manuel,—and the fair aspect of the boy seemed to move him to a sense of wonder—but he did not speak. With a light salute to all present he re-entered his carriage and was driven away—and Aubrey Leigh led Prince Sovrani into his own library where, when he was seated, they all waited upon him eagerly, the fair Sylvie chafing his cold hands, and the Princesse D'Agramont practically making him drink a glass of good wine. Gradually, warmth and colour and animation came back to his pale features,—his fears were soothed,—his heart relieved, and a smile crossed his lips as he met Sylvie's earnest, anxious eyes.

"What a pretty rosebud it is!" he said softly,—"Full of sunshine——and love!"

With returning strength he gathered up the forces of his native pride and independence and rose from his chair.

"I am well—quite well again now!" he said, "Where is the boy, Manuel?"

"Gone back to Angela," replied the Cardinal, "He said he would watch her until she wakes."

"An angel watching an angel!" then said the Prince musingly, "That is as it should be!" He paused a moment, "The King was very kind. And you, Princesse—and you, *bella Contessina!*" and he courteously bent over Sylvie's little hand and kissed it,—"You are all much too good to an old man like me! I am strong again——I shall be ready to speak——when Angela bids. But I must wait. I must wait!" He ruffled his white hair with one hand and looked at them all very strangely. "That was a great crowd outside—all waiting to hear news of my girl! If——if they knew who it was that stabbed her——"

"Do you know?" cried Aubrey quickly.

"*Per Dio!*" And Sovrani smiled, "I thought Englishmen were phlegmatic, and here is one ablaze, and ready to burst like a bomb! No!—I did not say I knew! —but I say, if the crowd had known, they would have

lynched him! Yes, they would have torn him to pieces!
. . . and he would have deserved it! He will deserve it!
—If he is ever found! Come—we will all sup here together this evening—sorrow strengthens the bonds of
friendship . . . and I will tell you . . . "

He paused, and again the strange far-off look came
into his eyes.

" I will tell you—" he went on slowly—" how I found
my Angela lying dead, as I thought—dead at the feet of
Christ!"

XXXI.

MEANWHILE Florian Varillo had not gone to Naples. He had been turned back by a spectre evoked from his own conscience—coward fear. He was on his way to the station when he suddenly discovered that he had lost the sheath of his dagger. A cold perspiration broke out on his forehead as this fact flashed upon him. What had he done with it? Surely he had drawn the weapon out and left the sheath in his breast pocket as usual—but no!—search as he would, he could not find it. It must have dropped on the floor of Angela's studio! If that were so, he would be traced!—most surely traced—as the sheath was of curious and uncommon workmanship, and many of his friends had seen it. He had told everybody he was going to Naples, and of course he would be followed there. Then, he would not go! But he went to the station as if bent on the journey, and took a ticket for Naples. Then, setting down his portmanteau on a bench, he surreptitiously tore off the label on which his name was written, and tearing it up in small bits scattered the fragments on the line. After this, he walked away leisurely, leaving the portmanteau behind him for there was nothing in it by which he could be traced, and sauntered slowly out of the station into the streets of Rome once more. Hailing the first *fiacre* he saw, he told the driver to take him to Frascati. The man was either lazy or sulky.

" Why not take the train, *Signor?* "

" Because I wish to drive! " replied Varillo. " What is your fare? "

" Twenty-five francs for half the way! " said the man, showing his white teeth in a mischievous grin.

" Good! "

The driver was surprised, as he had not thought his terms would be accepted. But he made no further demur, and Varillo jumped into the vehicle, his teeth chattering with an inward terror he could not control.

"Drive quickly!" he said.

The man shouted an affirmative, and they clattered away through the streets, Varillo shrinking back in the carriage overcome by panic. What a fool he had been! —what a fool! He ought to have told Pon-Pon. If the dagger-sheath were found and taken to his residence, it would be recognised instantly! And all Rome would rise against Angela Sovrani's murderer. Murderer! Yes,— that was what he had chosen to make of himself!

"It was all an impulse," he muttered,—"Just a hot impulse, nothing more! Just a sudden hatred of her which made me stab her! It was enough to make any man angry to see such a picture as that painted by a woman! Her fame would have ruined mine! But I never meant to kill her——no—no, I never meant to kill her!"

Shuddering and whimpering, he huddled himself in a corner of the carriage, and did not dare to look out of the window to see which way he was being driven. He only rallied a little when the wheels moved more quietly and smoothly, and he knew that he was on the open road, and out of Rome. Suddenly, after jolting along a considerable time, the vehicle stopped, and the driver shouted to him. Varillo dashed down the window and put his head out, almost beside himself with rage.

"What are you stopping for! What are you stopping for!" he yelled. "Go on—go on—we are not half way to Frascati yet! Go on, I tell you!"

"*Ma-che! Eccellenza,* I only stopped to ask a question!"

"What question—what? Is this a time for asking questions?" cried Varillo,—"The night is falling,—I want to get on!"

"But we are going on as fast as we can!" expostulated the driver,—"It is only this—there is an *albergo* on the way—where we can get food and wine. Would the *Eccellenza* like to stop there? It is as far as I can go, for I am wanted to-night in Rome."

"Very well—stop where you like—only get on now!" said Varillo, pulling his head in with a jerk. And sinking back in his seat again he wiped his hot face and cursed his miserable destiny. It would have been all right if he had only remembered that sheath! No one would have got on such a track of suspicion as that he, the lover and affianced husband of Angela, was her brutal assassin!

"I wrote a loving letter and sent her flowers," he argued with himself, "when I knew she would be dead! But her father would have got them, and he would have wired to me in Naples, and I should have come back overcome with sorrow,—and then I should have told them all how the picture was a secret between my Angela and myself,—how *I* had painted the greater part of it, and how she in her sweetness had wished me to surprise the world,——the plan was perfect, but it is all spoiled!—spoiled utterly through that stupid blunder of the sheath!"

Such a trifle! It seemed to him incredible—unjust—that so slight a thing could intervene between him and the complete success of his meditated treachery. For notwithstanding the fact that he had been a great reader and student of books, he now, in this particular hour of his own emergency, completely forgot what all the most astute and learned writers have always expounded to an inattentive world—namely, the fact that crime holds within itself the seed of punishment. Sometimes that seed ripens quickly,—sometimes it takes years to grow,—but it is always there. And it generally takes root in a mere, slight circumstance, so very commonplace and casual as to entirely escape the notice of the criminal, till the network of destiny is woven so closely about him that he can no longer avoid it,—and then he is shown from what a trifling cause the whole result has sprung. Varillo's present state of mind was one of absolute torture, for he felt that whoever found the sheath of his dagger would at once recognise it and declare the owner. If Angela had only been wounded,—if *she* had found it—she would never have given up the name of its possessor,—the miserable man knew her straight, pure soul intimately enough for that!

"If she heard, she would shield me and defend me at the cost of her own life!" he said—"She was always like that! *She* would never listen to anything that was said against me,—and if she lived, she would love me still, and never say that I had tried to kill her!" and he actually smiled at the thought. "How strangely some women are constituted!—especially women like Angela, who set up an exalted standard of life, and accommodate their daily conduct to it! They are sublime fools!—and so useful to men! We can do anything we like with them. We can ruin them—and they bear their shame in silence. We can laugh away their reputations over a game at billiards, and they are too pure and proud to even attempt to defend themselves. We can vilify whatever work they do, and they endure the slander,—we can murder them——" he paused, "Yes, we can murder them, and they die, without so much as leaving a curse behind them! Extraordinary!—angelic—superb!—and a wise Fate has ordained that we men shall never sacrifice ourselves for *such* women, or go mad for the love of them! We love the virago better than the saint; we are afraid of the woman who nags at us and gives us trouble—who screams vengeance upon us if we neglect her in a trifle—who clamours for our money, and insists on our gifts—and who keeps our lives in a perpetual fever of excitement and terror. But the innocent woman we hate—very naturally! Her looks are a reproach to us, and we like to kill her when we can—and we often succeed morally,—but *that* is not called murder. The other way of killing is judged as a crime——and—then——the punishment is death!"

As this word passed his lips in a whisper, he trembled violently. Death! It had a chill sound—yet he had not thought so when he associated it with Angela. For of course Angela was dead. Was she not? Surely she must be—he had driven the dagger straight home!

"She could not possibly live," he muttered—"Not after such a well directed blow. And that amazing picture! If I could but claim it as my work, I should be the greatest artist in the world! It would be quite easy to make out a proof—only that cursed dagger-sheath is in the way!"

He was startled out of his reverie by another stoppage of the carriage, and this time the driver jumped down from his box and came to the door.

"This is as far as I can take you, *Signor,*" he said, looking curiously at his passenger,—"It is quite half way to Frascati. There is the inn I told you of—where those lights are," and he pointed towards the left,—"The carriage road does not go up to it. It is a great place for artists!"

"I am not an artist!" said Varillo brusquely.

"No? But artists are merry company, *Eccellenza!*—" suggested the driver, wishing to make up for his previous sulkiness by an excess of amiability—"And for a night, the *albergo* is a pleasant resting place on the way to Frascati, for even the brigands who sup there are good-natured!"

"Ah! There are brigands, are there?" said Varillo, getting out of the *fiacre* and beginning to recover something of his usual composure,—"And I daresay you are one of them if the truth were known! Here is your money." And he gave the man two gold pieces, one of twenty francs, the other of ten.

"*Eccellenza,* I have no change——"

"I want none!" said Varillo airily,—"You asked twenty-five francs—there are thirty. And now—as you say you have business in Rome, be off with you!"

The man needed no second bidding; delighted with his thirty francs, he called a gay "*Buona notte, Signor!*" and turning his horse's head jogged down the road at a tolerably smart pace. The horse knew as well as the driver, that the way now lay homeward, and lost no time. Varillo, left to himself, paused a moment and looked about him. The Campagna! How he hated it! Should he pass the night at that *albergo,* or walk on? He hesitated a little—then made for the inn direct. It was a bright, cosy little place enough, and the *padrona,* a cheery, dark-eyed woman seated behind the counter, bade him smiling welcome.

Lodging—oh yes! she said, there was a charming room at the Signor's disposal, with a view from the windows which in the early morning was superb! The Signor was an artist?

"No!" said Varillo, almost fiercely——"I am a tourist——travelling for pleasure!"

Ah! Then the view would enchant the Signor, because it would be quite new to him! The room should be prepared at once! Would the Signor take supper?

Yes,—the Signor would take supper. And the Signor went and sat in a remote corner of the common-room, with a newspaper of a week old, pretending to read its contents. And supper was soon served to him,—a tasty meal enough, flavoured with excellent wine,—and while he was drinking his third glass of it, a man entered, tall and broad-shouldered, wrapped in a heavy cloak, which he only partially loosened as he leaned against the counter and asked for a cup of coffee. But as he caught sight of the dark face, Varillo shrank back into his corner, and put up his newspaper to shield himself from view,—for he saw that the new-comer was no other than Monsignor Gherardi. His appearance seemed to create a certain amount of excitement and vague alarm in the little inn; the *padrona* evidently knew him well, and hastened to serve him herself with the coffee he asked for.

" Will you not sit down, *Eccellentissima?* " she murmured deferentially.

" No, I am in haste! " replied Gherardi, glancing carelessly about him—" My carriage waits outside. There is strange news in Rome to-night! The famous artist, Angela Sovrani, has been found in her studio, murdered! "

The *padrona* uttered a little cry.

" Murdered! "

" So it seems! Here are the papers from which they cry the news. I will leave them with you. It is perhaps the judgment of Heaven on the Sovrani's uncle, Cardinal Bonpré! "

The mistress of the inn crossed herself devoutly.

" *Guiosto cielo!* Would Heaven punish a Cardinal? "

" Certainly! If a Cardinal is a heretic! "

The stout *padrona* clasped her hands and shuddered.

" Not possible! "

" Quite possible! " And Gherardi drained his coffee-cup. " And when so great a personage of the Church is a renegade, he incurs two punishments—the punishment of God and the punishment of the Church! The one comes first—the other comes—afterwards! *Buona notte!* "

And throwing down the money for his refreshment, Gherardi cast another glance around him, muffled himself up in his coat and went out into the night. Florian Varillo breathed again. But he was not left in peace for long. The *padrona* summoned her husband from the kitchen where he performed the offices of cook, to read the halfpenny sheets of news her visitor had left with her.

" Look you! " she said in a low voice, " The wicked Monsignor who has thee, my poor Paolo, in his clutches for debt, has just passed by and left evil tidings!—that beautiful girl who painted the famous pictures in Rome, has been murdered! Do you not remember seeing her once with her father at Frascati?"

Paolo, a round-faced, timid-looking little Piedmontese, nodded emphatically.

"That do I!" he answered—"Fair as an angel—kind-hearted too,—and they told me she was a wonder of the world. *Che, che!* Murdered! And who could have murdered her? Someone jealous of her fame! Poor thing—she is engaged to be married too, to another artist named Florian Varillo. *Gran Dio!* He will die of this misery!" And they bent their heads over the paper together and read the brief announcement headed "*Assassinamènto di Angela Sovrani!*"

A sudden crash startled them. Varillo had sprung up from his table in haste and overset his glass. It fell, shivering to atoms on the floor.

"Pardon!" he exclaimed, laughing forcedly,—"A thousand apologies! My hand slipped—it was an accident——"

"Do not trouble yourself, Signor," said the landlord, Paolo, cautiously going down on his fat knees to pick up the fragments—"It was an accident as you say. And truly one's nerves get shaken nowadays by all the strange things one is always hearing! Myself, I tremble to think of the murder of the Sovrani——the poor girl was so innocent of evil—and see you!—we might all be murdered in our beds with such villains about . . . "

He broke off, surprised at the angry oath Varillo uttered.

"*Per Dio!* Can you not talk of something else?" he said hoarsely,—"There is a murder nearly every day in Rome!"

Without waiting for a reply he hastily strode out of the inn, banging the door behind him. He had engaged his room there for the night—true!—but——after all this foolish gabble he resolved he would not go back. They would still talk of murder, if he did! Murder was in the air! Murder seemed written in letters of fire against the clear sky now luminous with the moon and stars! He was in a fever and a fury—he walked on and on, little heeding where he went. What the devil had brought

Gherardi to that particular inn at that particular time of night? He could not imagine. For though he knew most scandals in Rome, the scandal of the priest's "*villa d'amour*" at Frascati, was a secret too closely guarded for anyone save the sharpest of professional detectives to discover, and he was totally ignorant of it. He wondered restlessly whether the crafty Vatican spy had seen him while pretending not to see? If that were so, then he was lost! He could not satisfy himself as to whether he had really escaped observation, and tormented by this reflection he walked on and on, the burning impetus of his thoughts hastening his footsteps. A cold wind began to rise,—a chill, damp breath of the Campagna, bringing malaria with it. He felt heated and giddy, and there was a curious sense of fulness in his veins which oppressed him and made him uncertain of his movements. Presently he stopped, and stood gazing vaguely from left to right. He was surely not on the road to Frascati? There was a tall shadowy building not far from him, surrounded with eucalyptus trees—he tried to locate it, but somehow though, as a native of Rome and an artist, he was familiar with most of the Campagna, he did not recognise this part of it. How bright the stars were! Living points of fire flashing in dense purple!—one could never paint them! The golden round of the moon spreading wide reflections on the road, seemed to his excited mind like a magic ring environing him, drawing him in, pointing him out as the one criminal for whom all the world was seeking. He had no idea of the time,—his watch had stopped. He began to count up hours. He remembered that when he had gone to see Angela, it was about four o'clock. He had known perfectly well that she was alone, for he had seen the Cardinal drive past him in the streets on the way to the Vatican, and he had heard at his "Cercolo" or club, that Prince Sovrani had gone out of Rome for a few hours. And, thus informed, he had timed his visit to Angela well. Then, had he meant to kill her? No. He was quite certain that he never had had any such intention. Then what had been his purpose? First, to see her picture, and then to condemn it. Not harshly, but gently—with the chill toleration and faint commiseration of the critic who pretends to judge everything. He knew—none better—the glowing ardour and enthusiasm of the genius which was as much a part of Angela as colour is part of a rose,—his intention had been to freeze all that warmth with a few apparently kind words. For he had never thought it possible that she,—a mere woman,—could evolve from her own brain and hand, such a poetic, spiritual and magnificent conception as " The Coming of Christ." And when he saw what she had done, he bitterly envied her her power,—he realized the weakness of his own efforts as compared with her victorious achievement, and he hated her accordingly, as all men hate the woman who is intellectually superior to themselves. After all, there was no way out of it, but the way he had chosen,—to kill her and make an end! To kill her and make an end! He muttered these words over and over to himself, as he stood irresolutely watching the broad patterns of the moonlight, and thinking confusedly about the time. Yes,—it was four o'clock when he went to Angela's studio,—it must have been five, or past that hour when he left it,—— when he slunk down the side-street which led to the river, and threw the key and his dagger together into the muddy tide. After that he had gone home,—and had superintended his valet, while that individual packed his portmanteau for Naples——and then—and then? Yes,— then he had written to Angela,—one of the pretty gracious little notes she was accustomed to receive from him,—— how strange it was to write to a dead girl!——and he had gone out to the nearest florist's shop, and chosen a basket of lilies to send to her,——lilies were for dead maidens always,——and he had sent the flowers and his love letter together. Then surely it must have been about half-past six? He tried to fix the hour, but could not, and again his thoughts went rambling on. After sending the lilies, he had returned to his own house, and Pon-Pon had prepared a "*petit café*" for him, and he had partaken of it, and had smoked a couple of cigarettes with her, and then had said a leisurely good-bye, and had started for the railway-station *en route* for Naples. What train had he intended to go by? The eight o'clock express. He remembered that. But on the way, he had discovered that loss of the dagger-sheath,—an unforeseen fatality that had turned him back, and brought him to where he now stood meditating. How long did the driver of that *fiacre*

he hired, take to bring him to the wayside inn on the road
.o Frascati? This he could not determine,—but to his
uncertain memory it seemed to have been an unusually
tedious and tiresome journey. And now——here he was
——with no habitation in sight save the solitary building
whose walls loomed darkly through the eucalyptus trees.
He went towards it after a while, walking slowly and almost mechanically;—he was extremely tired, and an op-
pressive sense of heat and weariness combined made him
anxious to obtain a night's lodging somewhere,—no matter in what sort of place. Anything would be better than
sleeping out on the Campagna, an easy prey to the worst
form of fever. As he approached more nearly to the
house among the trees, he saw that it was surrounded by
a very high, closely intertwisted iron railing,—and when
he came within a few paces of what appeared to be the
entrance, he was startled by the sudden heavy clang of
a bell, which, striking through the still air, created such
harsh clamour that he instinctively shivered at the
sound. He paused,—and again the dismal boom crashed
on his ears,——then as its echo died away another deep
monotone, steadily persistent, began to stir the silence
with words,—words, which to Florian Varillo in his nervous excitation of mind sounded hellish and horrible.

" Libera me Domine, de morte æterna! "
   " In die illa tremenda ! "
" Quando coeli movendi sunt et terra ! "
   " Dum veneris judicare sæculum per ignem ! "

He listened, and a cold sweat broke out on his forehead. With that strange weakness and effeminacy which
often distinguishes the artistic, and particularly the Italian artistic temperament, he was excessively superstitious, and this unexpected chanting of a psalm of death
seemed to him at the moment, of supernatural and pre-
determined origin, devised on purpose to intensify the
growing terrors of his coward conscience.

" Tremens factus sum ego ! "
  Et timeo, dum discussio venerit, atque venerit ira ! "

Once more the great bell tolled heavily, and its discordant tone seemed to tear his brain. He uttered an involuntary cry,—every weak impulse in his soul was

aroused,—and in the excess of a miserable self-pity he longed to excuse himself for his crime of treachery and cruelty to the innocent woman who loved him,—to throw the blame on someone else,—if he could only find that someone else! Anything rather than own himself to be the mean wretch and traitor that he was. For he was a cultured and clever man,—a scholar,—an artist,—a poet; —these things were not consistent with murder! A man who painted beautiful pictures,—a man who wrote exquisite verses,—he could never be suspected of stabbing a helpless trusting woman in the back out of sheer jealousy, like a common hired assassin! No no! He could never be suspected! Why had he not thought of his intellectual gifts,—his position in the world of art, before? No one in their senses could possibly accuse him in the way he had imagined!—and even if the dagger-sheath were found, some explanation might be given,—someone else might be found guilty . . .

> " Quando coeli movendi sunt et terra;
> Dum veneris judicare sæculum per ignem ! "

Again that horrible bell! Moved by a sudden desperate determination to find out what this mysterious chanting was, and where it came from, he braced himself up and walked resolutely and quickly on to a great gateway, cross-barred and surmounted with tall spikes,—and there seized by fresh panic, he clung to the grating for support and stared through it affrightedly, his teeth chattering and his whole frame shaking as with an ague fit. What were those dark terrible figures he saw? Were they phantoms or men? Gaunt and black and tall, they swayed to and fro, now bending, now rising, in the misty splendour of the moonlight,—they were busy with the ground, digging it and casting out shovels full of earth in heaps beside them. Each ghostly figure stood by itself apart from its companions,—each one worked at its task alone, —and only their voices mingled in harsh dismal unison as, with the next stroke of the solemn bell, they chanted

> " Dies illa dies iræ,
> Calamitatis et miseriæ ! "

"No!" shrieked Varillo suddenly, shaking the gateway like an infuriated madman——"What are you doing

in there? Who told you to sing my mass or prepare my
grave? I am not ready, I tell you! Not ready! I have
done nothing to deserve death—nothing!—I have not
been tried!—you must wait—you must wait till you
know all——you must wait! . . . "

His voice choked in utterance, and thrusting one hand
through the grating he made frantic gesticulations to the
spectral figure nearest him. It paused in its toil and
lifted its head,—and from the dark folds of a drooping
cowl, two melancholy deep-set eyes glittered out like the
eyes of a famished beast. The other spectres paused also,
but only for a moment,—the bell boomed menacingly over
their heads once more, and again they dug and delved, and
again they chanted in dreary monotone—

" Dies magna et amara valde,
    Dum veneris judicare!
    Libera nos Domine, de morte æterna, in die illa tremenda !"

Wild with terror Varillo shook the gate more furiously
than before.

" Stop I tell you!" he cried—" It is too soon! You
are burying me before my time. You have no proof
against me—none! I am young,—full of life and strength
—the world loves me—wants me!——and I—I will not
die!—no I will not!—not yet! Not yet—I am not ready!
Stop—stop! You do not know what you are doing—
stop! You are driving me mad with your horrible singing!" And he shrieked aloud. " Mad, I tell you!
—mad!"

For one hazy moment he saw some of the dark figures begin to move towards him——he clutched at them
—fought with them—tore at their garments,—he would
have killed them all, he thought, if the moonlight had not
come in between him and them, and shut him up in a
cold silver circle of ice from which he could not escape,
—yet he went on struggling and talking and shrieking,
contending sometimes, as he fancied, with swords and
daggers, and trying to find his way through strange
storms of mingled fire and snow—till all at once some
strong invisible force swooped down upon him, lifted him
up and carried him away—and he remembered no more.

XXXII.

Away in Paris, a vast concourse of people were assembled round an open grave in Père-la-Chaise, wherein the plain coffin of the Abbé Vergniaud had just been lowered. The day was misty and cold, and the sun shone fitfully through the wreaths of thin vapour that hung over the city, occasionally gleaming on the pale fine face of the famous " Gys Grandit ", who, standing at the edge of the grave spoke his oration over the dead.

" To this, to this," he cried, " oh people of Paris, we all must come! Our ambitions, our hopes, our dreams, our grand reforms, our loves and joys end here, so far as this world is concerned! He whom we have just laid in the earth was skilled in many devious ways of learning,—gifted with eloquence, great in scholarship, quick with the tongue as with the pen, he was a man whom perchance all France would have called famous had it not been for me! I am the blot on my father's name! I am the sin for which he has made the last expiation! People of Paris, for years he lived and worked among you,—outwardly smiling, witty of speech and popular with you all,—but inwardly a misery to himself in his own conscience, because he knew his life was not what he professed it to be. He knew that he did not believe what he asked *you* to accept as true. He knew that he had guilt upon his soul,—he knew that all the sins which none of you could guess at, God saw. For there is a God! Not the God of the priests, but the God of the Universe and of man's natural and spiritual instinct. He from whom nothing escapes,—He who ordains where every drop of dew shall fall,—He whose omnipresent vision perceives the flight of every small bird in the air and predetermines the building of its nest, and the manner of its end,—He is the God whom none can deceive. Those who dream they can play false with Him are mistaken. This dead man, my father, living among you for years, was contented for years to seem like you,—yes!—for you all

474

have something which you think you can cover up from
the searching eye of Fate; and many of you pretend to be
what you are not,—while many more wear the aspect of
men over the souls of beasts. My father who rests here
to-day at our feet, was a priest of the Roman Church. In
that capacity he should have been clothed with sanctity.
Human, yet removed from common frailty. Yet reckless
of his order, heedless of his vows, he, priest as he was,
turned libertine, and betrayed an innocent woman. He
destroyed her name—killed her honour—broke her heart!
Libertines of all classes from kings to commoners, do this
kind of thing every day, and deem it but a small fault of
character. Nevertheless it is a crime!—and for a crime
there is always punishment! For everything that is
false,—for everything that is mean,—for everything that
is contemptible and cowardly, punishment comes,—if not
soon, then late. In this case vengeance was forestalled,
—for the sinner, repenting in time, took his vengeance on
himself. He confessed his sin before you all! That was
brave! How many of you here to-day would have such
courage! How many of you would throw off your cloaks
of virtue and admit your vices?—or having admitted
them, try to amend them? But this is what my father
did. And for this he should be honoured! He told you all
fully and frankly that his professions of faith were false
and vain and conventional; and that he had seemed to you
what he was not. Now the committal of a sin is one
thing,—but the frankly repentant confession of that sin
is another. Some of you will say—Who am I that I
should judge my father? Why truly I am nothing!—
and should have been nothing but the avenger of my
mother's life and broken-hearted misery. For that I lived,
—for that I was ready to die! What a trivial object of
existence it must seem to you Parisians nowadays!—to
avenge a mother's name! Much better to fight a duel for
some paltry dancer! Yes!—but I am not so constituted.
From my childhood I worked for two things—vengeance
and ambition; I put ambition second, for I would have
sacrificed it all to the fiercer passion. But when I sought
to fulfil my vengeance, the man on whom I would have
taken it, himself changed it into respect, pity, admiration,
affection,—and I loved what I had so long hated! So
even I, bent on cruelty, learned to be kind. But not so

the Church! The Church of Rome cannot forgive the dead priest whom we have laid in all-forgiving Mother Earth to-day! Had he lived, the sentence of excommunication would have been pronounced against him,—now that he is dead, it is quite possible it may still be pronounced against his memory. But what of that? We who know, who feel, who think,—we are not led by the Church of Rome, but by the Church of Christ! The two things are as different as this grave differs from high Heaven! For we believe that when Magdalen breaks a precious box of perfume at the feet of Christ 'she hath wrought a good work'. We also believe that when a man stands 'afar off', saying 'Lord, be merciful to me a sinner!' he goes back to his house again justified more than he who says 'Lord, I thank Thee I am not as other men!' We believe that Right is right, and that nothing can make it wrong! And simply speaking, we know it is right to tell the truth, and wrong to tell a lie. For a lie is opposed to the working forces of Nature, and those forces sooner or later will attack it and overcome it. They are beginning now in our swiftly advancing day, to attack the Church of Rome. And why? Because its doctrine is no longer that of Christ, but of Mammon! This is what my father felt and knew, when he addressed his congregation for the last time in Notre Dame de Lorette. He knew that he was doomed by disease to a speedy death,—though he little guessed how soon that death would be. But feeling the premonition of his end, he resolved to speak out,—not to condone or excuse himself for having preached what he could not believe all those years,—but merely to tell you how things were with him, and to trust his memory to you to be dealt with as you choose. He has left a book behind him,—a book full of great and noble thoughts expressed with most pathetic humility; hence I doubt not that when you see the better soul of him unveiled in his expressed mind, you will yet give him the fame he merits. His Church judges him a heretic and castaway for having confessed his sin at last to the people whom he so long deceived,—but I for this, judge him as an honest man! And I have some little right to my opinion, for as Gys Grandit I have sought to proclaim the thoughts of many——"

He paused till the murmur of enthusiasm at mention

of the name by which he was known through France should have ceased. It rose on the air in a sort of bee-like humming monotone, and then died away, while many people stood on tip-toe and craned their necks eagerly over each other's shoulders to catch a glimpse of the daring writer whose works threatened to upset a greater power than any throne, the Roman Church.

"I have tried," he resumed quietly, "as I say, to proclaim the thoughts of many! The people of France, like the peoples of many other nations, are losing God in a cloud of priest-craft. Look up to this broad canopy of heaven,—look up to yonder driving clouds heavy with rain, through which the great sun gleams like a golden shield,—that is the temple of the real God! That sparkling roof of air through which the planets roll in their tremendous orbits, bends over the wise and the foolish, the just and the unjust; the sun shines as kindly on the face of the street outcast as on that of the great lady who is often more soiled in soul than her miserable sister. The rich man can provide for himself no finer quality of light than is vouchsafed to the poor. The flowers in the field spring up as graciously under the feet of the beggar as the king. The Church of the true God is Equality! —the altar, the sacrament, the final resting-place of the dead, Equality! Your revolutionary cry was and is still,—Liberty, Equality, and Fraternity!—but when you shout those words, you know not what you are calling for. Your demand is instinctive,—the cry of a child for its parents. It is not for temporal things that you clamour, as the foolish imagine,—it is for eternal things! Liberty of thought,—Equality in work—Fraternity in faith! But your political leaders, ever at work for themselves, misread these words for you, even as your priests misread Christ's Gospel. They make out for you that you want Liberty of action—Equality of riches, Fraternity in position. These things are by Nature's law, impossible. They are not wanted,—and reasonable consideration will prove to you that you do not want them,—otherwise you would be asking for a disordered universe, a chaos instead of a world! The strong must always prevail,—but by strong, I do not mean the strong liar or the strong evil-doer. No! For a lie contains in itself the germ of rottenness which shall kill—and the evil-doer is not strong but weak, because cowardly. There is no strength in fear; no power in disease! Hence I repeat again, the strong must prevail—and by the strong, I mean the Good! Evil is always weak,—it flourishes for a day, a month, a year, or if you will, a thousand years, for a thousand years are but a moment in the sight of Heaven; but for ever and ever justice is done,—for ever and ever Right comes uppermost, and the Strong which is God, than whom is none stronger, and who is all Goodness—prevails! Liberty of thought should be the privilege of every human creature, but we must never mistake it for Liberty of action. Liberty of action is restrained by law in the world of nature, and must be equally restrained in the world of men. But insist on Equality in work! What do I mean by Equality in work? I mean this,—that every man's work is entitled to consideration and respect, in every phase of life. The road-mender works well and makes a smooth way for men and horses;—he deserves my honour for his skill,—he has it,—he shall have it,—for I know he can teach me many things of which I am ignorant. The chief of the State works well,—organizes;—puts grave matters in order and establishes necessary government— he also shall have my respect,—he has it,—he deserves his carriage and pair as fully as the road-mender deserves his dinner. We should not grudge or envy either man the reward due to their separate positions. The nightingale has a sweet voice,—the peacock screams —the one is plain in colour, the other gorgeous,—and there is no actual equality; yet the one bird does not grudge the other its position, inasmuch as though there is no Equality there is Compensation. So it is with men. There is always Compensation in every lot. So it should be; so it must be. Equality in work means simply, respect for every kind of work done, and contempt for none except for him who does no work at all! And lastly the word 'Fraternity.' Glorious word, meaning so much!— holding suggestions of peace, joy and purity in its mere utterance! Not a Fraternity of possession—for then should we become lower than the beasts, who have their own separate holes, their separate mates, their separate young—but Fraternity of Faith!—the one Faith that teaches us to cry 'Abba Father,'—that makes us under-

stand Christ as our Brother—and all of us the children of
one family,—one creation moving on in process of evolve-
ment to greater things! Let any priest tell me that I am
not a child of God, and I will retort that he, by such an
utterance, has proved himself a child of the devil. Ignorant, sinful, full of miserable imperfections as I am, I am
of God as the ant is, the worm, the fly!—and if I have no
more of God in me than such insects, still I am thankful to
have so much! What priest shall dare to say how much
or how little of God there was in the composition of this
man lying in the grave at our feet, who was my father?
Excommunication! Who can excommunicate the soul
from its Creator? Who can part the sunbeam from the
sun? Excommunication! The human being who, on what
he calls Church authority, shall thrust his brother away
from any form of communion which he himself judges
and accepts as valuable, is one of those whom Christ declared to be ' in danger of hell-fire.' For there is no man
who can, if he be true to himself, condemn his brother
man, or say to him, ' Stand back! I am holier than
thou!' Therefore, for him whom we lay down to rest
to-day, let there be pardon and peace! Let us remember
that for all his sins he atoned, by full confession;—by
publicly branding himself in the sight of that society in
whose estimation he had till then seemed something superior,—by voluntarily resigning himself to the wrath of
the Church of which he was a professed servant. Cursed
by his Creed, he may now perchance be blessed by his
Creator! For he died, clean-souled and true—washed of
hypocrisy,—with no secret vice left unhidden for others
to rake up and expose to criticism. Whatsoever wrong
he did, he openly admitted—whatever false things he said,
he retracted. I believe—and I am sure we all believe,
that his spirit thus purified, is acceptable to God. He
has left no lies behind him—no debts—no wrongs to be
avenged. He told you all, people of Paris, what he was
before he left you,—and, looking down into this dark
grave, we know what he is. A senseless, sightless, stif-
fening form of clay, from which the soul that animated
it into action has fled. Let the Church excommunicate
this poor corpse of my father,—let it muster its forces
against his memory as it will, I swear before you all, that
memory shall live! Yes—for I, his son, will guard it;

I whom he so late acknowledged as his own flesh and blood, will be a shield of defence for his name till I die! If priests would attack him, they must attack him through me!—and I, despite a thousand Churches, a thousand Creeds, a thousand Sacraments, will firmly maintain that a man who frankly repents his sins and is openly honest with the world before he leaves it, is a better Christian than he, who for the sake of mere appearances and conventionality, juggles with death and passes to his Maker's presence in a black cloud of lies! Better to be crucified with Christ, than live with the High Priests and Pharisees of the modern Jerusalem of our social conditions! Truth may seem to perish on the Cross of injustice——it may be buried in a sealed sepulchre, the entrance to which may be closed up by a great stone of Mammon-bulk and heaviness—but the moment must come when the Angel descends from Heaven—when the stone is rolled away—and the eternal, living God rises again and walks the world in the glory of a new dawn!"

He ended—and for a moment there was a deep silence. There had been no funeral service, for no priest would attend the burial of the heretic Abbé. So, after a brief pause, Cyrillon knelt down by the grave,—and carried away by the solemnity of the scene, as well as by their own emotional excitement, more than half the crowd knelt with him, as, bending his head reverently over his clasped hands, he prayed aloud—

"Oh God of Love, whose tenderness and care for Thy creation is everywhere disclosed to us, from the smallest atom of dust, to the stupendous majesty of Thy million worlds in the air,—give we beseech Thee, to this perished clay which once was man, the beauty which transforms vile things to virtuous, and endows our seeming death with life! Let Thy eternal Law of Resurrection so work upon this senseless body that it may pass through Earth to Heaven, and there find finer grades of being, higher forms of development, greater opportunities of perfection. And for the Soul, which is Thine own breath of fire, O God, receive it, purified from sin, and make it worthy of the final purpose for which Thou hast destined it from the beginning! And grant unto us, left here to still work out our own salvation on this the planet Thou hast chosen for our trial, the power to comprehend

Thy laws, and faithfully to obey them,—to forgive as we would be forgiven,—to love as we would be loved,— and to lift our thoughts from the appearance of this grave to the Reality of Thy beneficence, which hath ordained Light out of Darkness, and out of Death, Life, as proved most gloriously to us by Christ our Brother, our Teacher and our Master! Amen!"

His prayer finished, the young man rose, and taking a wreath of ivy, which he had travelled to Touraine himself to bring from the walls of the simple cottage where his mother had lived and worked and died, he dropped it gently on the coffin and signed to the grave-diggers to fill in the earth. Then turning to the crowd, he said,

" My friends, I thank you all for the sympathy which has brought you here to-day. ' It is finished.' The dead man is at rest! And now as you go,—as you return to your own homes,—homes happy or unhappy as the case may be, I will only ask you to remember that there is no permanence or virtue in falsehood whether it be falsehood religious or falsehood political;—and he who dies truthfully dealing with his fellow-men, lives again with God, and is not, as Scripture says ' dead in his sins,' but born again to a new and more hopeful existence!"

With the last words he gave the sign of dismissal. The people began to disperse slowly and somewhat reluctantly, every member of the crowd being curious to obtain a nearer view of the young orator who not only spoke his thoughts fearlessly, but whose pen was as a scythe mowing down a harvest of shams and hypocrisies, and whose frank utterance from the heart was so honest as to be absolutely convincing to the public. But he, after giving a few further instructions to the men who were beginning to close in his father's grave, walked away with one or two friends, and was soon lost to sight in one of the many winding paths that led from the cemetery out into the road, so that many who anxiously sought to study his features more nearly, were disappointed. One person there was, who had listened to his oration in wonder and open-mouthed admiration,—this was Jean Patoux. He had taken the opportunity offered him in a " cheap excursion " from Rouen to Paris, to visit a cousin of his who was a small florist owning a shop in the Rue St. Honoré,—and by chance, he and this same cousin, while

quietly walking together down one of the boulevards, had
got entangled in the press of people who were pouring
into Père-la-Chaise on this occasion, and had followed
them out of curiosity, not at all knowing what they were
going to see.   But the florist, known as Pierre Midon,
soon realised the situation and explained it all to his provincial relative.

"It is the Abbé Vergniaud they are burying," he said,
—"He was a wonderful preacher!   All fashionable Paris
used to go and hear him till he made that pretty scandal
of himself a month or so ago.   He was a popular and a
social favourite; but one fine morning he preached a sermon to his congregation all against the Church, and for
that matter against himself too, for he then and there confessed before everybody that he was no true priest.   And
as he preached,—what think you?—a young man fired a
pistol shot at him for his rascality, as everyone supposed,
and when the gendarmes would have taken the assassin,
this same Abbé stopped them, and refused to punish *his
own son!*   What do you think of that for a marvel?   And
something still more marvellous followed, for that very
son who tried to kill him was no other than Gys Grandit,
the man we have just heard speaking, though nobody
knew it till a week afterwards.   Such a scene you never
saw in a church!—Paris was wild with excitement for a
dozen hours, which is about as long as its fevers last,—
and the two of them, father and son, went straight away
to a famous Cardinal then staying in Paris,—and he, by
the way, was in the church when the Abbé publicly confessed himself——Cardinal Bonpré——"

"Ah!" interrupted Patoux excitedly, "This interests
me!   For that most eminent Cardinal stayed at my inn in
Rouen before coming on here!"

"So!"   And Cousin Pierre looked rather surprised.
"Without offence to thee, Jean, it was a poor place for a
Cardinal, was it not?"

"Poor, truly,—but sufficient for a man of his mind!"
replied Patoux tranquilly,—"For look you, he is trying
to live as Christ lived,—and Christ cared naught for
luxury."

Pierre Midon laughed.

"By my faith!   If priests were to live as Christ lived,
Paris might learn to respect them!" he said,—"But we

know that they will not,—and that few of them are better than the worst of us! But to finish my story—this Abbé and the son whom he so suddenly and strangely acknowledged, went to this Cardinal Bonpré for some reason—most probably for pardon, though truly I cannot tell you what happened—for almost immediately, the Abbé went out of Paris to the Château D'Agramont some miles away, and his son went with him, and there the two stayed together till the old man died. And as for Cardinal Bonpré, he went at once to Rome with his niece, the famous painter, Angela Sovrani,—I imagine he may have interceded with the Pope, or tried to do so for the Abbé, but whatever happened, there they are now, for all I know to the contrary. And we heard that the Church was about to excommunicate, or had already excommunicated Vergniaud, though I suppose Cardinal Bonpré had nothing to do with that?"

"Not he!" said Patoux firmly, "He would never excommunicate or do any unkind thing to a living soul—that I am pretty sure of. He is the very Cardinal who performed the miracle in my house that has caused us no end of trouble,—and he is under the displeasure of the Pope for it now, if all I hear be true."

"That is strange!" said Pierre with a laugh,—"To be under the displeasure of the Pope for doing a good deed!"

"Truly, it seems so," agreed Patoux,—"But you must remember there was no paying shrine concerned in it! Mark you that, my Pierre! Even our Lady of Bon Secours, near to Rouen as she is, was not applied to. The miracle took place in the poor habitation of an unknown little inn-keeper,—that is myself,—and there was no solemnity at all about it—no swinging of incense—no droning of prayers—no lighting of candles—no anything, but just a good old man with a crippled child on his knee, praying to the Christ whom he believed was able to help him. And—and——"

He broke off suddenly and crossed himself. Pierre Midon stared at the action.

"What ails thee, Jean?" he asked brusquely,—"Hast thou remembered a dead sin, or a passing soul?"

"Neither," replied Patoux slowly, "But only just the thought of another child—a waif and stray whom the good Cardinal found in the streets of Rouen, outside our great Cathedral door. A gentle lad!—my wife was greatly taken with him;—and he was present in my house too, when the miracle of healing was performed."

"And for that, is there any need to cross thyself like a mumbling old woman afraid of the devil?" enquired his cousin.

Patoux smiled a slow smile.

"Gently, Pierre—gently!" he said. "Thou art of Paris,—I of the provinces. That makes all the difference in the way we look at life. There are very few holy things in great cities,—but there are many in the country. Every day when I am at home I go out of the town to work in my field,—and I feel the clean breath of the wind, the scent of the earth and the colours of the sky and the flowers,—and I know quite well there is a God, or these blessings could not be. For if there were only Chance and a Man to manage the universe, a pretty muddle we should have of it! And when I see or think of a holy thing, I sign the cross out of old childhood's habit,—so just now, when I remembered the boy whom the Cardinal rescued from the streets, I knew I was thinking of a holy thing; and that explains my action."

"How dost thou prove a waif of the streets a holy thing?" enquired Pierre curiously.

Patoux shrugged his shoulders, and gave a wide deprecatory wave of both hands.

"Ah, that is more than I can tell you!" he said,—"It is a matter beyond my skill. But the boy was a fair-faced boy,—I never saw him myself——"

Midon laughed outright.

"Never saw him thyself!" he cried,—"And yet thou dost make the sign of the cross at the thought of him! Diantre! Patoux, thou art crazy!"

"Maybe—maybe," said Patoux mildly,—they were walking together out of the cemetery by this time in the wake of the rapidly dispersing crowd,—"But I have always taken my wife's word,—and I take it now. And she has said over and over again to me that the boy had a rare sweet nature. And then—the child whom the Cardinal healed,—Fabien Doucet,—will always insist upon it that it was the touch of that same boy which truly cured him and not the Cardinal at all!"

"Mere fancy!" said Pierre carelessly,—"And truly if it were not for knowing thee to be honest, I should doubt the miracle altogether!"

"And thou wouldst be of the majority!" said Patoux equally—"For our house has been a very bee-hive of buzz and trouble ever since a bit of good was done in it—and Martine Doucet, the mother of the cured child, has led the life of the damned, thanks to the kindness of her neighbours and friends! And will you believe me, the Archbishop of Rouen himself took the trouble to walk into the market-place and assure her she was a wicked woman,—that she had taught her boy to play the cripple in order to excite pity,—and I believe he thinks she is concerned in the strange disappearance of his clerk, Claude Cazeau. For this same Cazeau came to our house one night when Martine was there, and told her he had instructions to take her to Rome to see the Pope, and her child with her, for the purpose of explaining the miracle in her own words, and giving the full life-history of herself and the little one. And she was angry,—ah, she can be very angry, poor Martine!—she has a shrill tongue and a wild eye, and she said out flatly that she would not go, and furthermore that she would not be caught in a priest's trap, or words to that effect. And this clerk, Cazeau,—a miserable little white-livered rascal, crawled away from my door in a rage with us all, and was never seen again. The police have hunted high and low for trace of him, but can find none. But I have my suspicions——"

"What are they?" enquired Midon,—"That he went out like Judas, and hanged himself?"

"Truly he might have done that without loss or trouble to anyone!" said Patoux tranquilly,—"But he thought too well of himself to be quite so ready for a meeting with le bon Dieu! No!—I will tell you what I think. There was a poor girl who used to roam about the streets of our town, called Marguerite; she was once a sensible, bright creature enough, the only daughter of old Valmond the saddler, who died from a kick from his favourite horse one day, and left his child all alone in the world. She was a worker in a great silk-factory, and was happy and contented, so it seemed, till—well! It is the old story—a man with a woman, and the man is most often the devil in it. Anyway, this Marguerite went mad on her love-affair,—and we called her 'La Folle,'—not harshly—for all the town was kind to her. I mentioned her name once in the presence of this man Cazeau, and he started as if an adder had bitten him. And now—he has disappeared —and strange to say, so has she!"

"So has she!" echoed Midon, opening his eyes a little wider—"Then what do you suppose?——"

"Just this," said Patoux, emphasizing his words by marking them out with a fat thumb on the palm of the other hand——"That Cazeau was the villain of the piece as they say in the theatres, and that she has punished him for his villainy. She used to swear in her mad speech that if ever she met the man who had spoilt her life for her, she would kill him; and that is just what I believe she has done!"

"But would she kill herself also?" demanded Pierre —"And what has become of one or both bodies?"

"Ah! There thou dost ask more than I can answer!" said Patoux. "But what is very certain is, that both bodies, living or dead, have disappeared. And as I said to my wife when she put these things into my head,—for look you, my head is but a dull one, and if my wife did not put things into it, it would be but an emptiness alto-gether,—I said to my wife that if she were right in her suspicions—and she generally is right—this Marguerite had taken but a just vengeance. For you will not prove to me that there is any man living who has the right to take the joy out of a woman's soul and destroy it."

"It is done every day!" said Midon with a careless shrug,—"Women give themselves too easily!"

"And men take too greedily!" said Patoux obsti-nately—"What virtue there is in the matter is on the woman's side. For she mostly gives herself for love's sake,—but the man cares naught save for his own selfish pleasure. As a man myself, I am on the side of the woman who revenges herself on her betrayer."

"For that matter so am I!" said Midon. "Women have a hard time of it in this world, even under the best of circumstances,—and whatever man makes it harder for them, should be horse-whipped within an inch of his life, if I had my way. I have a wife—and a young daughter—and my old mother sits at home with us, as cheery and bright a body as you would find in all France,—and so I know the worth of women. If any rascal were to insult my girl by so much as a look, he would find himself in the ditch with a sore back before he had time to cry ' Dieu merci!' "

He laughed;—Patoux laughed with him, and then went on,—

" I told thee of the miracle in my house, and of the boy the Cardinal found in the streets,—well!—these things have had their good effect in my own family. My two children, Henri and Babette—ah! What children! God be praised for them! As bright, as kind as the sunlight, —and their love for me and their mother is a great thing —a good thing, look you!—one cannot be sufficiently grateful for it. For nowadays, children too often despise their parents, which is bad luck to them in their after days; but ours, wild as they were a while ago, are all obedience and sweetness. I used often to wonder what would become of them as they grew up—for they were wilful and angry-tempered, and ofttimes cruel in speech—but I have no fear now. Henri works well at his lessons, and Babette too,—and there is something better than the learning of lessons about them,—something new and bright in their dispositions which makes us all happy. And this has come about since the Cardinal stayed with us; and also since the pretty boy was found outside the Cathedral! "

" That boy seems to have impressed thee more than the Cardinal himself! " said Midon—" but now I remember well—on the day the Abbé Vergniaud preached his last sermon, and was nearly shot dead by his own son, there was a rumour that his life had been saved by some boy who was an attendant on the Cardinal, and who interposed himself between the Abbé and the flying bullet, —that must have been the one you mean? "

" No doubt—no doubt! " said Patoux, nodding gravely —" There was something about him that seemed a sort of shield against evil—or at least, so said my wife,—and so say my children. Only the other day, my boy Henri —he is big and full of mischief as boys will be—was playing with two or three younger lads, and one of them like a little sneak, stole up behind him and gave him a blow with a stick, which broke in two with the force of the way the young rascal went to work with it. Now, thought I, there will be need for me to step out and stop this quarrel, for Henri will beat that miserable little wretch into a jelly! But nothing of the sort! My boy turned round with a bright laugh—picked up the two pieces of the stick and gave them back to the little coward with a civil bow ' Hit in front next time! " he said. And the little wretch turned tail and began to boo-hoo in fine fashion—crying as if he had been hurt instead of Henri. But they are the best friends in the world now. I asked Henri about it afterwards, and he turned as red as an apple in the cheeks. ' I wanted to kill him, father,' he said,—' but I knew that the boy who was with Cardinal Bonpré would not have done it—and so I did not!' Now look you, for a rough little fellow such as Henri, that was a great victory over his passions—and there is no doubt the Cardinal's little foundling was the cause of his so managing himself."

Pierre Midon had nothing to say in answer,—the subject was getting beyond him, and he was a man who, when thought became difficult, gave up thinking altogether.

And while these two simple-minded worthies were thus talking and strolling together home through the streets of Paris, Cyrillon Vergniaud, having parted from the few friends who had paid him the respect of their attendance at his father's grave, was making his way towards the Champs Elysées in a meditative frame of mind, when his attention was suddenly caught and riveted by a placard set up in front of one of the newspaper kiosks at the corner of a boulevard, on which in great black letters, was the name " Angela Sovrani." His heart gave one great bound—then stood still—the streets of the city reeled round him, and he grew cold and sick. " Meurtre de la célèbre Angela Sovrani! "

Hardly knowing what he was about, he bought the paper. The news was in a mere paragraph briefly stating that the celebrated artist had been found stabbed in her studio, and that up to the present there was no trace of the unknown assassin.

Passionate and emotional as his warm nature was, the great tears rushed to Cyrillon's eyes. In one moment he realized what he had been almost unconsciously cherishing in his own mind ever since Angela's beautiful smile had shone upon him. When in the few minutes of speech he had had with her she admitted herself to be the mysterious correspondent who had constantly written to him as " Gys Grandit," fervently sympathising with his theories, and urging him on to fresh and more courageous effort, he had been completely overcome, not only with surprise, but also with admiration. It had taken him some time to realize that she, the greatest artist of her day, was actually his unknown friend of more than two years' correspondence. He knew she was engaged to be married to her comrade in art, Florian Varillo, but that fact did not prevent him from feeling for her all the sudden tenderness, the instinctive intimacy of spirit with spirit, which in the highest natures means the highest love. Then,—they had all been brought together so strangely!—his father, and himself, with Cardinal Bonpré,—and she—the Cardinal's fair niece, daughter of a proud Roman house,—she had not turned away from the erring and repentant priest whom the Church had cast out; she had given him her hand at parting, and had been as sweetly considerate of his feelings as though she had been his own daughter. And when he was ill and dying at the Château D'Agramont, she had written to him two or three times in the kindest and tenderest way, and her letters had not been answered, because the Abbé was too ill to write, and he, Cyrillon, had been afraid——lest he should say too much! And now—she was dead?—murdered? No!—he would not believe it!

" God is good! " said Cyrillon, crushing the paper in his hand and raising his eyes to the cloudy heavens—" He does nothing that is unnecessarily cruel. He would not take that brilliant creature away till she had won the reward of her work—happiness! No!—something tells me this news is false!—she cannot be dead! But I will start for Rome to-night."

He returned to the cheap *pension* where he had his room, and at once packed his valise. With all his fame he was extremely poor; he had for the most part refused to take payment for his books and pamphlets which had been so freely spread through France, preferring to work for his daily bread in the fields of an extensive farm near his birthplace in Touraine. He had begun there as a little lad, earning his livelihood by keeping the birds away from the crops—and had steadily risen by degrees, through his honesty and diligence, to the post of superintendent or bailiff of the whole concern. No one was more trusted than he by his employers,—no one more worthy of trust. But his wages were by no means considerable,—and though he saved as much as he could, and lived on the coarsest fare, it was a matter of some trouble for him to spare the money to take him from Paris to Rome. What cash he had, he carried about him in a leathern bag, and this he now emptied on the table to estimate the strength of his finances. Any possibility of changing his mind and waiting for further news from Rome did not occur to him. One of his chief characteristics was the determined way he always carried through anything he had set his mind upon. In one of his public speeches he had once said—" Let all the powers of hell oppose me, I will storm them through and pass on ! For the powers of Heaven are on *my* side ! "—the audacity and daring of this utterance carrying away his audience in a perfect whirlwind of enthusiasm. And though it is related of a certain cynical philosopher, that when asked by one of his scholars for a definition of hell, he dashed into the face of his enquirer an empty purse for answer, the lack of funds was no obstacle to Cyrillon's intended journey.

" Because if I can go no other way, I will persuade the guard to let me ride in the van, or travel in company with a horse or dog—quite as good animals as myself in their way," he thought.

With a characteristic indifference to all worldly matters he had entirely forgotten that the father whom he had just buried had died wealthy, and that his entire fortune had been left to the son whom he had so lately and strangely acknowledged. And when,—while he was still engaged in counting up his small stock of money,—a knock came at the door, and a well-dressed man of business-like appearance entered with a smiling and propitiatory air, addressing him as " Monsieur Vergniaud," Cyrillon did not know at all what to make of his visitor. Sweeping his coins together with one hand, he stood up, his flashing eyes glancing the stranger over carelessly.

"Your name, sir?" he demanded—"I am not acquainted with you."

The smiling man unabashed, sought about for a place to put down his shiny hat, and smiled still more broadly.

"No!" he said—"No! You would not be likely to know me. I have not the celebrity of Gys Grandit! I am only André Petitot—a lawyer, residing in the Boulevard Malesherbes. I have just come from your father's funeral."

Cyrillon bowed gravely, and remained silent.

"I have followed you," pursued Monsieur Petitot affably, "as soon as I could, according to the instructions I received, to ask when it will be convenient for you to hear me read your father's will?"

The young man started.

"His will!" he ejaculated. He had never given it a thought.

"Yes. May I take a chair? There are only two in the room, I perceive! Thanks!" And the lawyer sat down and began drawing off his gloves,—"Your father had considerable means,—though he parted with much that he might have kept, through his extraordinary liberality to the poor——"

"God bless him!" murmured Cyrillon.

"Yes—yes—no doubt God will bless him!" said Monsieur Petitot amicably—"According to your way of thinking, He ought to do so. But personally, I always find the poor extremely ungrateful, and God certainly does not bless *me* whenever I encourage them in their habits of idleness and vice! However, that is not a question for discussion at present. The immediate point is this—your father made his will about eighteen months ago, leaving everything to you. The wording of the will is unusual, but he insisted obstinately on having it thus set down——"

Here the lawyer drew a paper out of his pocket, fixed a pair of spectacles on his nose, and studied the document intently——"Yes!—it reads in this way;—'Everything of which I die possessed to my son, Cyrillon Vergniaud, born out of wedlock, but as truly my son in the sight of God, as Ninette Bernadin was his mother, and my wife, though never so legalised before the world, but fully acknowledged by me before God, and before the Church which I have served and disobeyed.' A curious wording!" said Petitot, nodding his head a great many times—"Very curious! I told him so—but he would have it his own way,—moreover, I am instructed to publish his will in any Paris paper that will give it a place. Now this clause is to my mind exceedingly disagreeable, and I wish I could set it aside."

"Why?" asked Cyrillon quietly.

"My dear young man! Can you ask? Why emphasise the fact of your illegitimacy to the public!"

"Why disguise it?" returned Cyrillon. "You must remember that I have another public than the merely social,—the people! They all know what I am, and who I am. They have honoured me. They shall not despise me. And they would despise me if I sought to hold back from them what my father bade me tell. Moreover, this will gives my mother the honour of wifehood in the sight of God,—and I must tell you, *monsieur l'avocat,* that I am one of those who care nothing what the world says so long as I stand more or less clear with the world's Creator!"

His great dark eyes were brilliant,—his face warm with the fire of his inward feeling. Monsieur Petitot folded up his document and looked at him with an amiable tolerance.

"Wonderful—wonderful!" he said—"But of course eccentricities *will* appear in the world occasionally!—and you must pardon me if I venture to think that you are certainly one of them. But I imagine you have not grasped the whole position. The money—I should say the fortune—which your father has left to you, will make you a gentleman——"

He paused, affrighted. Drawing himself up to his full height, young Vergniaud confronted him in haughty amazement.

"Gentleman!" he cried—"What do you mean by the term? A loafer?—a lounger in the streets?—a leerer at women? Or a man who works for daily food from sunrise to sunset, and controls his lower passions by hard and honest labour! Gentleman! What is that? Is it to live lazily on the toil of others, or to be up and working one's self, and to eat no bread that one has not earned? Will you answer me?"

"My dear sir, you must really excuse me!" said Petitot nervously—"I am quite unable to enter into any sort of discussion with you on these things! Please recollect that my life as a lawyer, depends entirely on men's stupidities and hypocrisies,—if they all entertained your views I should have to beg in the streets, or seek another profession. In my present business I should have nothing whatever to do. You perceive the position? Yes, of course you do!" For Cyrillon with one of the quick changes of mood habitual to him, smiled, as his temporary irritation passed like a cloud, and his eyes softened——"You see, I am a machine,—educated to be a machine; and I am set down to do certain machine-like duties, —and one of these duties is,—regardless of your fame, your eccentric theories, your special work which you have chosen to make for yourself in the world,—to put you in possession of the money your father left you——"

"Can you now—at once—" said Cyrillon suddenly—"give me enough money to go to Rome to-night?"

Monsieur Petitot stared.

"To go to Rome to-night?" he echoed—"Dear me, how very extraordinary! I beg your pardon! . . . of course—most certainly! I can advance you any sum you want—would ten thousand francs suffice?"

"Ten thousand francs!" Cyrillon laughed. "I never had so much money in all my life!"

"No? Well, I have not the notes about me at the moment, but I will send you up that sum in an hour if you wish it. Your father's will entitles you to five million francs, so you see I am not in any way endangering myself by advancing you ten thousand."

Cyrillon was quite silent. The lawyer studied him curiously, but could not determine whether he was pleased or sorry at the announcement of his fortune. His handsome face was pale and grave,—and after a pause he said simply—

"Thank you! Then I can go to Rome. If you will send me the money you speak of I shall be glad, as it will enable me to start to-night. For the rest,—kindly publish my father's will as he instructed you to do,— and I—when I return to Paris, will consult you on the best way in which I can dispose of my father's millions."

"Dispose of them!" began Petitot amazedly. Young Vergniaud interrupted him by a slight gesture.

"Pardon me, Monsieur, if I ask you to conclude this interview! For the present, I want nothing else in the world but to get to Rome as quickly as possible!—après ça, le deluge!"

He smiled—but his manner was that of some great French noble who gently yet firmly dismisses the attentions of a too-officious servant,—and Petitot, much to his own surprise, found himself bowing low, and scrambling out of the poorly furnished room in as much embarrassment as though he had accidentally stumbled into a palace where his presence was not required.

And Cyrillon, left to himself, gathered up all the coins he had been counting out previous to the lawyer's arrival, and tied them again together in the old leathern bag; then having closed and strapped his little travelling valise, sat down and waited. Punctually to the time indicated, that is to say, in one hour from the moment Petitot had concluded his interview with the celebrated personage whom he now mentally called "an impossible young man," a clerk arrived bringing the ten thousand francs promised. He counted the notes out carefully,—Cyrillon watching him quietly the while, and taking sympathetic observation of his shabby appearance, his thread-bare coat, and his general expression of pinched and anxious poverty.

"You will perceive it is all right, Monsieur," he said humbly, as he finished counting.

"What are you, *mon ami?*" asked Cyrillon; scarcely glancing at the notes but fixing a searching glance on the messenger who had brought them.

"I?" and the clerk coughed nervously and blushed,— "Oh, I am nothing, Monsieur! I am Monsieur Petitot's clerk, that is all!"

"And does he pay you well?"

"Thirty francs a week, Monsieur. It is not bad,— only this—I was young a few years ago, and I married— and two dear little ones came—so it is a pull at times to make everything go as it should—not that I am sorry for myself at all, oh no! For I am well off as the people go——"

Cyrillon interrupted him.

"Yes—as the people go! That is what you all say,

you patient, brave souls! See you, my friend, I do not want all this money—" and he took up a note for five hundred francs—" Take this and make the wife and little ones happy!"

" Monsieur!" stammered the astonished clerk—" How can I dare——!"

" Dare! Nay, there is no daring in freely taking what your brother freely gives you! You must let me practise what I preach, my friend, otherwise I am only a fraud and unfit to live. God keep you!"

The clerk still stood trembling, afraid to take up the note, and unable through emotion to speak a word, even of thanks. Upon which, Cyrillon folded up the note and put it himself in the man's pocket.

" There!—go and make happiness with that bit of paper!" he said—" Who can tell through what dirty usurer's hand it has been, carrying curses with it per-chance on its way! Use it now for the comfort of a woman and her little children, and perhaps it will bring blessing to a living man as well as to a departed soul!"

And he literally put the poor stupefied fellow outside his door, shutting it gently upon him.

That night he left for Rome. And as the express tore its grinding way along over the iron rails towards the south, he repeated to himself over and over again as in a dream—

" No—Angela Sovrani is not dead! She cannot be dead! God is too good for that. He will not let her die before she knows——before she knows I love her!"

XXXIII.

THE chain of circumstance had lengthened by several links round the radiant life of Sylvie Hermenstein since that bright winter morning when she had been startled out of her reverie, in the gardens of the Villa Borghese, by the unexpected appearance of Monsignor Gherardi. The untimely deaths of the Marquis Fontenelle and the actor Miraudin in the duel over her name, had caused so much malicious and cruel gossip, that she had withdrawn herself almost entirely from Roman society, which had, with one venomous consent, declared that she was only marrying Aubrey Leigh to shield herself from her *esclandre* with the late Marquis. And then the murderous attack on her friend Angela Sovrani, which occurred almost immediately after her engagement to Aubrey was announced, had occupied all her thoughts—so that she had almost forgotten the promise she had made to grant a private interview to Gherardi whenever he should seek it. And she was not a little vexed one morning when she was talking to her betrothed concerning the plans which were now in progress for their going to England as soon as possible, to receive a note reminding her of that promise, and requesting permission to call upon her that very afternoon.

"How very unfortunate and tiresome!" said Sylvie, with a charming pout and upward look at her lover, who promptly kissed the lips that made such a pretty curve of disdain—" I suppose he wants to give me a serious lecture on the responsibilities of marriage! Shall I receive him, Aubrey? I remember when I met him last that he had something important to say about Cardinal Bonpré."

"Then you must certainly give him an audience," answered Aubrey—" You may perhaps find out what has happened to bring the good Cardinal into disfavour at the Vatican, for there is no doubt that he is extremely worried and anxious. He is strongly desirous of leaving Rome at once with that gentle lad Manuel, who, from all

I can gather, has said something to displease the Pope.
Angela is out of danger now—and I am trying to persuade the Cardinal to accompany us to England, and be
present at our marriage."

"That would be delightful!" said Sylvie with a smile,
—"But my Aubrey, where are we going to be married?"

"In England, as I said—not here!" said Aubrey firmly
—"Not here, where evil tongues have spoken lies against
my darling!" He drew her into his arms and looked at
her fondly. "I want you to start for England soon, Sylvie—and if possible, I should like you to go, not only
with the faithful Bozier, but also in the care of the Cardinal. I will precede you by some days, and arrange
everything for your reception. And then we will be
married——in *my* way!"

Sylvie said nothing—she merely nestled like a dove in
the arms of her betrothed, and seemed quite content to
accept whatever ordinance he laid down for the ruling of
her fate.

"I think you must see Gherardi," he resumed—"Write
a line and say you will be happy to receive him at the
hour he appoints."

Sylvie obeyed—and despatched the note at once to the
Vatican by her man-servant.

Aubrey looked at her intently.

"I wonder——Sylvie, I wonder——" he began, and
then stopped.

She met his earnest eyes with a smile in her own.

"You wonder what, *caro mio?*" she enquired.

"I wonder whether you could endure a very great trial
—or make a very great sacrifice for my sake!" he said,
—then as he saw her expression, he took her little hand
and kissed it.

"There! Forgive me! Of course you would!—only
you look such a slight thing—such a soft flower of a
woman—like a rose-bud to be worn next the heart always—that it seems difficult to picture you as an inflexible
heroine under trying circumstances. Yet of course you
would be."

"I make no boast, my Aubrey!" she said gently.

He kissed her tenderly,—reverently,—studying her
sweet eyes and delicate colouring with all the fond scrutiny of a love which cannot tire of the thing it loves.

"Are you going round to see Angela this morning?" he asked.

"Yes, I always go. She is much better—she sits up a little every day now."

"She says nothing of her assassin?"

"Nothing. But I know him!"

"We all know him!" said Aubrey sternly—"But she will never speak—she will never let the world know!"

"Ah, but the world will soon guess!" said Sylvie—"For everyone is beginning to ask where her *fiancé* is—why he has shown no anxiety—why he has not been to see her—and a thousand other questions."

"That does not matter! While she is silent, no one dare accuse him. What a marvellous spirit of patience and forgiveness she has!"

"Angela is like her name—an angel!" declared Sylvie impulsively, the tears springing to her eyes—"I could almost worship her, when I see her there in her sick-room, looking so white and frail and sad,—quiet and patient—thanking us all for every little service done—and never once mentioning the name of Florian—the man she loved so passionately. Sometimes the dear old Cardinal sits beside her and talks—sometimes her father,—— Manuel is nearly always with her, and she is quite easy and content, one would almost say happy when he is there, he is so very gentle with her. But you can see through it all the awful sorrow that weighs upon her heart,—you can see she has lost something she can never find again,—her eyes look so wistful—her smile is so sad —poor Angela!"

Aubrey was silent a moment. "What of the Princesse D'Agramont?"

"Oh, she is simply a treasure!" said Sylvie enthusiastically—"She and my dear old Bozier are never weary in well-doing! As soon as Angela can be moved, the Princesse wants to take her back to Paris,—because then Rome can be allowed to pour into her studio to see her great picture."

"What does Angela say to that?"

"Angela seems resigned to anything!" answered Sylvie. "The only wish she ever expresses is that Manuel should not leave her."

"There is something wonderful about that boy," said

Aubrey slowly—" From the first time I saw him he impressed me with a sense of something altogether beyond his mere appearance. He is a child—yet not a child—and I have often felt that he commands me without my realising that I am so commanded."

" Aubrey! How strange! "

" Yes, it is strange!—" and Aubrey's eyes grew graver with the intensity of his thought—" There is some secret —but——" he broke off with a puzzled air——" I cannot explain it, so it is no use thinking about it! I went to Varillo's studio yesterday and asked if there had been any news of him—but there was none. I wonder where the brute has gone! "

" It would be well if he had made exit out of the world altogether," said Sylvie—" But he is too vain of himself for that! However, his absence creates suspicion—and even if Angela does not speak, people will guess for themselves what she does not say. He will never dare to show himself in Rome! "

Their conversation was abruptly terminated here by the entrance of Madame Bozier with a quantity of fresh flowers which she had been out to purchase, for Sylvie to take as usual on her morning visit to her suffering friend; and Aubrey took his leave, promising to return later in the afternoon, after Monsignor Gherardi had been and gone.

But he had his own ideas on the subject of Gherardi's visit to his fair betrothed,—ideas which he kept to himself, for if his surmises were correct, now was the time to put Sylvie's character to the test. He did not doubt her stability in the very least, but he could never quite get away from her *mignonne* child-like appearance of woman, to the contemplation of the spirit behind the pretty exterior. Her beauty was so *riante,* so dazzling, so dainty, that it seemed to fire the very air as a sunbeam fires it,—and there was no room for any more serious consideration than that of purely feminine charm. Walking dreamily, almost unseeingly through the streets, he thought again and yet again of the sweet face, the rippling hair, the laughing yet tender eyes, the sunny smile. Behind that beautiful picture or earth-phantom of womanhood, is there that sword of flame, the soul?—the soul that will sweep through shams, and come out as bright and glittering at

the end of the fight as at the beginning?—he mused;—
or is it not almost too much to expect of a mere woman
that she can contend against the anger of a Church?

He was still thinking on this subject, when someone
walking quickly came face to face with him, and said—

"Aubrey!" He started and stared,—then uttered a
cry of pleasure.

"Gys Grandit!"

The two men clasped each other's hands in a warm,
strong grasp—and for a moment neither could speak.

"My dear fellow!" said Aubrey at last—"This is indeed an unexpected meeting! How glad I am to see you!
When did you arrive in Rome?"

"This morning only," said Cyrillon, recovering his
speech and his equanimity together—"And as soon as I
arrived, I found that my hopes had not betrayed me—
she is not dead!"

"She?" Aubrey started——"My dear Grandit! Or
rather I must call you Vergniaud now——who is the
triumphant 'she' that has brought you thus post haste to
Rome?"

Cyrillon flushed—then grew pale.

"I should not have spoken!" he said—"And yet,
why not! You were my first friend!—you found me
working in the fields, a peasant lad, untrained and sullen,
burning up my soul with passionate thoughts which, but
for you, might never have blossomed into action,—you
rescued me—you made me all I am! So why should I
not confess to you at once that there is a woman I love!
—yes, love with all my soul, though I have seen her but
once!—and she is too far off, too fair and great for me;
she does not know I love her——but I heard she had
been murdered——that she was dead——"

"Angela Sovrani!" cried Aubrey.

Cyrillon bent his head as a devotee might at the shrine
of a saint.

"Yes—Angela Sovrani!"

Aubrey looked at his handsome face glowing with enthusiasm, and saw the passion, the tenderness, the devotion of a life flashing in his fine eyes.

"Love at first sight!" he said with a smile—"I believe
it is the only true fire! A glance ought to be enough to
express the recognition of one soul to its mate. Well!

Angela Sovrani is a woman among ten thousand—the love of her alone is sufficient to make a man better and nobler in every way—and if you can win her——"

"Ah, that is impossible! She is already affianced——"

Aubrey took his arm.

"Come with me, and I will tell you all I know," he said——" For there is much to say,—and when you have heard everything, you may not be altogether without hope."

They turned, and went towards the Corso, which they presently entered, and where numbers of passers-by paused involuntarily to look at the two men who offered such a marked contrast to each other,—the one brown-haired and lithe, with dark, eager eyes,—the other with the slim well set up figure of an athlete, and the fair head of a Saxon king. And of the many who so looked after them, none guessed that the one was destined in a few years' time to create a silent and bloodless French Revolution, which should give back to France her white lilies of faith and chivalry,—or that the other was the upholder of such a perfect form of Christianity as should soon command the following of thousands in all parts of the world.

And while they thus walked through the Roman crowd, the two women they severally loved were talking of them. In Angela's sick-room, softly shaded from the light, with a cheery wood fire burning, Sylvie sat by her friend, telling her all she could think of that would interest her, and rouse her from the deep gravity of mood in which she nearly always found her. The weary days of pain and illness had given Angela a strange, new beauty,—her face, delicate and pale, seemed transfigured by the working of the soul within,—and her eyes, tired as they were and often heavy with tears, had a serenity in their depths which was not of earth, but all of Heaven. She was able now to move from her bed, and lie on a couch near the fire,—and her little white hands moved caressingly and with loving care among the bunches of beautiful flowers which Sylvie had laid on her coverlet,—daffodils, anemones, narcissi, violets, jonquils, and all the sweet-scented flowers of early spring which come to Rome in December from the blossoming fields of Sicily.

"How sweet they are!" she said with a half sigh,—" They almost make me in love with life again!"

Sylvie said nothing, but only kissed her.

"How good you are to me, dearest Sylvie!" she then said—"You deserve to be very happy!"

"Not half so much as you do!" responded Sylvie tenderly—"I am of no use at all to the world; and you are! The world would not miss me a bit, but it would not find an Angela Sovrani again in a hurry!"

Angela raised a cluster of narcissi and inhaled their fine and delicate perfume. There were tears in her eyes, but she hid them with a spray of the flowers.

"Ah, Sylvie, you think too well of me! To be famous is nothing. To be loved is everything!"

Sylvie looked at her earnestly.

"You are loved," she said.

"No, no!" she said—"No, I am not loved. I am hated! Hush, Sylvie!—do not say one word of what is in your mind, for I will not hear it!"

She spoke agitatedly, and her cheeks flushed a sudden feverish red.

Sylvie made haste to try and soothe her.

"My darling girl, I would not say anything to vex you for the world! You must not excite yourself——"

"I am not excited," said Angela, putting her arms round her friend and drawing her fair head down till it was half hidden against her own bosom—"No——but I must speak—bear with me for a minute, dear! We all have our dreams, we women, and I have had mine! I dreamt there was such a beautiful thing in the world as a great, unselfish love,—I fancied that a woman, if gifted with a little power and ability above the rest of her sex, could make the man she loved proud of her— not jealous!—I thought that a lover delighted in the attainments of his beloved——I thought there was nothing too high, too great, too glorious to attempt for the sake of proving oneself worthy to be loved! And now—I have found out the truth, Sylvie!—a bitter truth, but no doubt good for me to know,—that men will kill what they once caressed out of a mere grudge of the passing breath called Fame! Thus, Love is not what I dreamed it; and I, who was so foolishly glad to think that I was loved, have wakened up to know that I am hated!—hated to the very extremity of hate, for a poor gift of brain and hand which I wish—I wish I had never had!"

Sylvie raised her head and gently put aside the weak trembling little hands that embraced her.

"Angela, Angela! You must not scorn the gifts of the gods! No, No!—you will not let me say anything—you forbid me to express my thoughts fully, and I know you are not well enough to hear me yet——but one day you *will* know!—you will hear,—you will even be thankful for all the sorrow you have passed through,—and meanwhile, dear, dearest Angela, do not be ungrateful!"

She said the word boldly yet hesitatingly, bending over the couch tenderly, her eyes full of light, and a smile on her lips. And taking up a knot of daffodils she swept their cool blossoms softly across Angela's burning forehead, murmuring—

"Do not be ungrateful!"

"Ungrateful——!" echoed Angela,—and she moved restlessly.

"Yes, darling! Do not say you wish you never had received the great gifts God has given you. Do not judge of things by Sorrow's measurement only. I repeat—you *are* loved—though not perhaps where you most relied on love. Your father loves you—your uncle loves you—— Manuel loves you . . ."

Angela interrupted her with a protesting gesture.

"Yes—I know," she murmured, "but——"

"But you think all this love is worthless, as compared with a love that was no love at all?" said Sylvie. "There! We will not speak about it any more just now,—you are not strong, and you see things in their darkest light. Shall I talk to you about Aubrey?"

"Ah! That is a subject you are never tired of!" said Angela with a faint smile. "Nor am I."

"Well, you ought to be," answered Sylvie gaily, "for I am too blindly, hopelessly in love to know when to stop! I see nothing else and know nothing else—it is Aubrey, Aubrey all the time. The air, the sunlight, the whole world, seem only an admirable exposition of Aubrey!"

"Then how would you feel if he did not love you any more?" asked Angela.

"But that is not possible!" said Sylvie. "Aubrey could not change. It is not in him. He is not like our poor friend Fontenelle."

"Ah! That love of yours was only fancy, Sylvie!"

"We all have our fancies!" answered the pretty Comtesse, looking very earnestly into Angela's eyes. "We are not always sure that what we first call love is love. But I had much more than a fancy for the Marquis Fontenelle. If he had loved me—as I think he did at the last——I should certainly have married him. But during all the time I knew him he had a way of relegating all women to the same level—servants, actresses, ballet-dancers, and ladies alike,—he would never admit that there is as much difference between one woman and another as between one man and another. And this is a mistake many men make. Fontenelle wished to treat me as Miraudin would have treated his 'leading lady';—he judged that quite sufficient for happiness. Now Aubrey treats me as his comrade,—his friend as well as his love, and that makes our confidence perfect. By the way, he spoke to me a great deal yesterday about the Abbé Vergniaud, and told me all he knew about his son Cyrillon."

"Ah, the poor Abbé!" said Angela. "They are angry with him still at the Vatican—angry now with his dead body! But 'Gys Grandit' is not of the Catholic faith, so they can do nothing with him."

"No. He is what they call a 'free-lance,'" said Sylvie. "And a wonderful personage he is! You have seen him?"

A faint colour crept over Angela's pale cheeks.

"Yes. Once. Just once, in Paris, on the day his father publicly acknowledged him. But I wrote to him long before I knew who he really was."

"Angela! You wrote to him?"

"Yes. I admired the writings of Gys Grandit—I used to buy all his books as they came out, and study them. I wrote to him—as many people will write to a favourite author—not in my own name of course—to express my admiration, and he answered. And so we corresponded for about two years, not knowing each other's identity till that scene in Paris brought us together——"

"How *very* curious,—ve—ry!" said Sylvie, with a little mischievous smile. "And so you are quite friends?"

"I think so—I believe so—" answered Angela—"but since we met, he has ceased to write to me."

Sylvie made a mental note of that fact in her own

mind, very much to the credit of "Gys Grandit," but said nothing further on the subject. Time was hastening on, and she had to return to the Casa D'Angeli to receive Monsignor Gherardi.

"I am going to be lectured I suppose," she said laughingly. "I have not seen the worthy Domenico since my engagement to Aubrey was announced!"

Angela looked at her intently.

"Are you at all prepared for what he will say?"

"Not in the least. What *can* he say?"

"Much that may vex you," said Angela. "Considering Aubrey Leigh's theories, he may perhaps reproach you for your intended marriage—or he may bring you information of the Pope's objection."

"Well! What of that?" demanded Sylvie.

"But you are a devout Catholic——"

"And you? With a great Cardinal for your uncle you paint 'The Coming of Christ'! Ah!—I have seen that picture, Angela!"

"But I am different,—I am a worker, and I fear nothing," said Angela, her eyes beginning to shine with the latent force in her that was gradually resuming its dominion over her soul—"I thought long and deeply before I put my thought into shape——"

"And *I* thought long and deeply before I decided to be the companion of Aubrey's life and work!" said Sylvie resolutely. "And neither the Pope or a whole college of Cardinals will change my love or prevent my marriage. *A riverderci!*"

"*A riverderci!*" echoed Angela, raising herself a little to receive the kiss her friend tenderly pressed on her cheeks. "I shall be anxious to know the result of your interview!"

"I will come round early to-morrow and tell you all," promised Sylvie, "for I mean to find out, if I can, what happened at the Vatican when Cardinal Bonpré last went there with Manuel."

"My uncle is most anxious to leave Rome," said Angela musingly.

"I know. And if there is any plot against him he *must* leave Rome—he *shall* leave it! And we will help him!"

With that she went her way, and an hour or so later

stood, a perfect picture of grace and beauty, in the grand old rooms of the Casa D'Angeli, waiting to receive Gherardi. She had taken more than the usual pains with her toilette this afternoon, and had chosen to wear a "creation" of wonderful old lace, with knots of primrose and violet velvet caught here and there among its folds. It suited her small lissom figure to perfection, and her only ornaments were a cluster of fresh violets, and one ring sparkling on her left hand,—a star of rose brilliants and rubies, the sign of her betrothal.

Punctual to the hour appointed, Gherardi arrived, and was at once shown into her presence. There was a touch of aggressiveness and irony in his manner as he entered with his usual slow and dignified step, and though he endeavoured to preserve that suavity and cold calmness for which he was usually admired and feared by women, his glance was impatient, and an occasional biting of his lips showed suppressed irritation. The first formal greetings over, he said—

"I have wished for some time to call upon you, *Contessa,* but the pressure of affairs at the Vatican——"

He stopped abruptly, looking at her. How provokingly pretty she was!—and how easily indifferent she seemed to the authoritative air he had chosen to assume.

"I should, I know, long ere this have offered you my felicitations on your approaching marriage——"

Sylvie smiled bewitchingly, and gave him a graceful curtsey.

"Will you not sit down, Monsignor?" she then said. "We can talk more at our ease, do you not think?"

She seated herself, with very much the air of a queen taking possession of a rightful throne, and Gherardi was vexedly aware that he had not by any means the full possession of his ordinary dignity or self-control. He took a chair opposite to her and sat for a moment perplexed as to his next move. Sylvie did not help him at all. Ruffling the violets among the lace at her neck, she looked at him attentively from under her long golden-brown lashes, but maintained a perfect silence.

"The news has been received by the Holy Father with great pleasure," he said at last. "His special benediction will grace your wedding-day."

Sylvie bent her head.

"The Holy Father is most gracious!" she replied quietly. "And he is also more liberal than I imagined, if he is willing to bestow his special benediction on my marriage with one who is considered a heretic by the Church."

He flashed a keen glance at her,—then forced a smile. "Mr. Leigh's heresy is of the past," he said—"We welcome him—with you—as one of us!"

Sylvie was silent. He waited, inwardly cursing her tranquillity. Then, as she still did not speak, he went on in smooth accents—

"The Church pardons all who truly repent. She welcomes all who come to her in confidence, no matter how tardy or hesitating their approach. We shall receive the husband of our daughter Sylvie Hermenstein, with such joy as the prodigal son was in old time received—and of his past mistakes and follies there shall be neither word nor memory!"

Then Sylvie looked up and fixed her deep blue eyes steadily upon him.

"*Caro Monsignor!*" she said very sweetly. "Why talk all this nonsense to me? Do you not realise that as the betrothed wife of Aubrey Leigh I am past the Church counsel or command?"

Gherardi still smiled.

"Past Church counsel or command?" he murmured with an indulgent air, as though he were talking to a very small child. "Pardon me if I am at a loss to understand——"

"Oh, you understand very well!" said Sylvie. "You know perfectly—or you should—that a wife's duty is to obey her husband,—and that in future *his* Church,—not yours,—must be hers also."

"Surely you speak in riddles?" said Gherardi, preserving his suave equanimity. "Mr. Leigh is (or was) a would-be ardent reformer, but he has no real Church."

"Then I have none!" replied Sylvie.

There was a moment's silence. A black rage began to kindle in Gherardi's soul,—rage all the more intense because so closely suppressed.

"I am still at a loss to follow you, Contessa," he said coldly. "Surely you do not mean to imply that your marriage will sever you from the Church of your fathers?"

"Monsignor, marriage for me means an oath before God to take my husband for better or for worse, and to be true to him under all trial and circumstances," said Sylvie. "And I assuredly mean to keep that oath! Whatever his form of faith, I intend to follow it,—as I intend to obey his commands, whatever they may be, or wherever they may lead. For this, to me, is the only true love,—this to me, is the only possible 'holy' estate of matrimony. And for the Church—a Church which does not hesitate to excommunicate a dying man, and persecute a good one,—I will leave the possibility of its wrath, together with all other consequences of my act—— to God!"

For one moment Gherardi felt that he could have sprung upon her and throttled her. The next, he had mastered himself sufficiently to speak,—this woman, so slight, so beautiful, so insolent should not baffle him, he resolved!—and bending his dark brows menacingly, he addressed her in his harshest and most peremptory manner.

"You talk of God," he said, "as a child talks of the sun and moon, with as little meaning, and less comprehension! What impertinence it is for a woman like yourself,—vain, weak and worldly,—to assert your own will—your own thought and opinion—in the face of the Most High! What! *You* will desert the Church? *You* whose ancestors have for ages been devout servants of the faith? *You*, the last descendant of the Counts Hermenstein, a noble and loyal family, will degrade your birth by taking up with the rags and tags of humanity— the scarecrows of life? And by your sheer stupidity and obstinacy, you will allow your husband's soul to be dragged to perdition with your own! You call it love— to keep him an infidel? You call it marriage—to be united to him without the blessings of Holy Church? Where is your reason?—Where is your judgment?— Where your faith?"

"Not in my bank, Monsignor!" replied Sylvie coldly. "Though that is the place where you would naturally expect to find these virtues manifested, and the potency of their working substantially proved! Pardon!—I have no wish to offend—but your manner to *me* is offensive, and unless you are disposed to discuss this matter temperately, I must close our interview!"

Gherardi flushed a dark red, then grew pale. After all, the Countess Hermenstein was in her own house,—she had the right to command his exit if she chose. Small and slight as she was, she had a dignity and power as great as his own, and if anything was to be gained from her it was necessary to temporize. Among many other qualifications for the part he had to play in life, he was an admirable actor, and would have made his fortune on the legitimate stage,—and this " quick change " ability served him in good stead now. He rose from his chair as though moved by uncontrollable agitation, and walked to the window, then turned again and came slowly and with bent head towards her.

"Forgive me!" he said simply. "I was wrong!"

Sylvie, easily moved to kindness, was touched by this apparent humility on the part of a man so renowned for unflinching hauteur, and she at once gave him her hand.

"I shall forget your words!" she said gently. "So there is nothing to pardon."

"Thank you for your generosity," he said, still standing before her and preserving his grave and quiet demeanour. "In my zeal for Holy Church, my tongue frequently outruns my prudence. I confess you have hurt me,—cruelly! You are a mere child to me—young, beautiful, beloved,—and I am growing old; I have sacrificed all the joys of life for the better serving of the faith—but I have kept a few fair dreams—and one of the fairest was my belief in *you!*"

Sylvie looked at him searchingly, but his eyes did not flinch in meeting hers.

"I am sorry you are disappointed, Monsignor," she began, when he raised his hand deprecatingly.

"No—I am not disappointed as yet!" he said, with an affectation of great kindness. "Because I do not permit myself to believe that you will allow me to be disappointed! Just now you made a passing allusion—and I venture to say a hasty and unworthy one—to your ' bank,' as if my whole soul were set on retaining you as a daughter of the Church for your great wealth's sake only! Contessa, you are mistaken! Give me credit for higher and nobler motives! Grant me the right to be a little better—a little more disinterested, than perhaps popular rumour describes me,——believe me to be at least your friend——"

He paused—his voice apparently broken by emotion, and turning away his head he paced the room once more and finally sat down, covering his eyes with one hand, in an admirably posed attitude of fatigue and sorrow.

Sylvie was perplexed, and somewhat embarrassed. She had never seen him in this kind of humour before. She was accustomed to a certain domineering authority in his language, rendered all the more difficult to endure by the sarcasm with which he sometimes embittered his words, as though he had dipped them in gall before pronouncing them,—but this apparent abandonment of reserve, this almost touching assumption of candour, were phases of his histrionical ability which he had never till now displayed in her presence.

"Monsignor," she said after a little silence, "I sincerely ask your pardon if I have wronged you, even in a thought! I had no real intention of doing so, and if anything I have said has seemed to you unduly aggressive or unjust, I am sorry! But you yourself began to scold" —and she smiled—"and I am not in the humour to be scolded! Though, to speak quite frankly, I have always been more or less prepared for a little trouble on the subject of my intended marriage with Mr. Aubrey Leigh,— I have felt and known all along that it would incur the Pope's displeasure . . ."

Here Gherardi uncovered his eyes and looked at her fully.

"But there you are mistaken!" he said gently, with a smile that was almost paternal. "I know of nothing in recent years that has given the Holy Father greater satisfaction!"

She glanced at him quickly but said nothing, whereat he was secretly annoyed. Why did she not express her wonder and delight at the Pope's lenity, as almost any other woman in her position would have done? Her outward appearance was that of child-like ultra-femininity, —how was it then that he felt as if she were mentally fencing with him, and that her intellectual sword-play threatened to surpass his own?

" Nothing," he repeated suavely, " has given the Holy Father greater satisfaction! For very naturally, he looks upon you as one of his most faithful children, and rejoices that by the power of perfect love—love which is an emanation of the Divine Spirit in itself—you have been chosen by our Lord to draw so gifted and brilliant a man as Aubrey Leigh out of the error of his ways and bring him into the true fold!"

XXXIV.

STILL the Countess Sylvie was silent. Bending a quick scrutinising glance upon her, he saw that her eyes were lowered, and that the violets nestling near her bosom moved restlessly with her quickened breath, and he judged these little signs of agitation as the favourable hints of a weakening and hesitating will.

"Aubrey Leigh," he went on slowly, "has long been an avowed enemy of our Church. In England especially, where many of the Protestant clergy, repenting of their recusancy—for Protestantism is nothing more than a backsliding from the true faith—are desirous of gradually, through the gentler forms of Ritualism, returning to the Original source of Divine Inspiration, he has taken a great deal too much upon himself in the freedom of his speeches to the people. But we are bound to remember that it is not against *our* Church only that he has armed himself at all points, but seemingly against all Churches; and when we examine, charitably and with patience, into the sum and substance of his work and aim, we find its chief object is to purify and maintain—not to destroy or deny—the Divine teaching of Christ. In this desire we are one with him—we are even willing to assist him in the Cause he has espoused—and we shall faithfully promise to do so, when we receive him as your husband. Nay, more—we will endeavour to further his work among the poor, and carry out any scheme for their better care, which he may propose to us, and we may judge as devout and serviceable. The Church has wide arms,—she stretches far, and holds fast! The very fact of a man like Aubrey Leigh voluntarily choosing as his wife the last scion of one of the most staunch Roman Catholic families in Europe, proves the salutary and welcome change which your good influence has brought about in his heart and mind and manner and judgment,—wherefore it follows, my dear child, that in his marriage with you he becomes one of us, and is no longer outside us!"

With a swift and graceful imperiousness, Sylvie suddenly rose and faced him.

"It is time we understood each other, Monsignor," she said quietly. "It is no good playing at cross purposes! With every respect for you, I must speak plainly. I am fully aware of all you tell me respecting my descent and the traditions of my ancestors. I know that the former Counts Hermenstein were faithful servants of the Church. But they were all merely half-educated soldiers; brave, yet superstitious. I know also that my father, the late Count, was apparently equally loyal to the Church,—though really only so because it was too much trouble for him to think seriously about anything save hunting. But I—Sylvie—the last of the race, do not intend to be bound or commanded by the trammels of any Church, in the face of the great truths declared to the world to-day! My faith in God is as my betrothed husband's faith in God, —my heart is his,—my life is his! From henceforth we are together; and together we are content to go, after death, wherever God shall ordain, be it Hell or Heaven!"

"Wait!" said Gherardi in low fierce accents, his eyes glittering with mingled rage and the admiration of her beauty which he could ill conceal. "Wait! If you care nothing for yourself in this matter, is it possible that you care nothing for him? Have you thought of the results of such rashness as you meditate? Listen!" and he leaned forward in his chair, his dark brows bent and his whole attitude expressive of a relentless malice—" Your marriage, without the blessing of the Church of your fathers, shall be declared illegal!—your children pronounced bastards! Wherever the ramifications of the Church are spread (and they are everywhere) you, the brilliant, the courted, the admired Sylvie Hermenstein, shall find yourself not only outside the Church, but outside all Society! You will be considered as 'living in sin';—as no true wife, but merely the mistress of the man with whom you have elected to wander the world! And he, when he sees the finger of scorn pointed at you and at his children, he also will change—as all men change when change is convenient or advantageous to themselves;—he will in time weary of his miserable Christian-Democratic theories,—and of you!—yes, even of you!" And Gherardi suddenly sprang up and drew nearer to her. "Even of *you*, I say! He will weary of your beauty—that delicate fine loveliness which makes *me* long to possess it!—me, a priest of the Mother-Church, whose heart is supposed to beat only for two things— Power and Revenge! Listen—listen yet a moment!" and he drew a step nearer, while Sylvie held her ground where she stood, unflinchingly, and like a queen, though she was pale to the very lips—"What of the friend you love so well, Angela Sovrani, who has dared to paint such a picture as should be burnt in the public market-place for its vile heresy! Do you think *she* will escape the wrath of the Church? Not she! We in our day use neither poison nor cold steel—but we know how to poison a name and stab a reputation! What! You shrink at that? Listen yet—listen a moment longer! And remember that nothing escapes the vigilant eye of Rome! At this very moment I can place my hand on Florian Varillo, concerning whom there is a rumour that he attempted the assassination of his betrothed wife,—an inhuman deed that no sane man could ever have perpetrated"—here Sylvie uttered a slight exclamation, and he paused, looking at her with a cold smile—"Yes, I repeat it!—a deed *which no sane man could have perpetrated!* The unfortunate, the deeply wronged Florian Varillo, is prepared to swear, and *I am prepared to swear with him,* that he is guiltless of any such vile act or treachery—and also that he painted more than half of the great picture this woman Sovrani claims as her own work! Whilst strongly protesting against its heresy and begging her to alter certain figures in the canvas, still he gave her for love's sake, all his masculine ability. The blasphemous idea is hers—but the drawing, the colouring, the grouping, are *his!*"

"He is a liar!" cried Sylvie passionately. "Let him prove his lie!"

"He shall have every chance to prove it!" answered Gherardi calmly. "*I* will give him every chance! *I* will support what you call his lie! *I say it is a truth!* No woman could have painted that picture! And mark you well—the mere discussion will be sufficient to kill the Sovrani's fame!"

Heedless of his ecclesiastical dignity—reckless of

everything concerning herself—Sylvie rushed up to him and laid one hand on his arm.

"What! Are you a servant of Christ," she said half-whisperingly, "or a slave of the devil?"

"Both," he answered, looking down upon her fair beauty with a wicked light shining in his eyes. "Both!" and he grasped the little soft hand that lay on his arm and held it as in a vice. "You are not wanting in courage, Contessa, to come so close to me!—to let me hold your hand! How pale you look! If you were like other women you would scream—or summon your servants, and create a scandal! You know better! You know that no scandal would ever be believed of a priest attached to the Court of Rome! Stay there—where you are—I will not hurt you! No—by all the raging fire of love for you in my heart, I will not touch more than this hand of yours! Good!—Now you are quite still—I say again, you have courage! Your eyes do not flinch—they look straight into mine—what brave eyes! You would search the very core of my intentions? You shall! Do you not think it enough for me—who am human though priest—to give you up to the possession of a man I hate! ——A man who has insulted me! Is it not enough, I say, to immolate my own passion thus, without having to confront the possibility of your deserting that Church for whose sake I thus resign you? For had this Aubrey Leigh never met you, I would have *made* you mine! Still silent?—and your little hand still quiet in mine?—I envy you your nerve! You stand torture well, but I will not keep you on the rack too long! You shall know the worst at once—then you shall yourself judge the position. You shall prove for yourself the power of Rome! To escape that power you would have, as the Scripture says, to 'take the wings of the morning and fly into the uttermost parts of the sea.' Think well!—the fame and reputation of Angela Sovrani can be ruined at my command,—and equally, the sanctity and position of her uncle, Cardinal Bonpré!"

With a sudden movement Sylvie wrenched her hand away from his, and stood at bay, her eyes flashing, her cheeks crimsoning.

"Cardinal Bonpré!" she cried. "What evil have you in your mind against him? Are you so lost to every sense of common justice as to attempt to injure one who is greater than many of the Church's canonized saints in virtue and honesty? What has he done to you?"

Gherardi smiled.

"You excite yourself needlessly, Contessa," he said. "He has done nothing to me personally,—he is simply in my way. That is his sole offence! And whatever is in my way, I remove! Nothing is easier than to remove Cardinal Bonpré, for he has, by his very simplicity, fallen into a trap from which extrication will be difficult. He should have stopped in his career with the performance of his miracle at Rouen,—then all would have been well; he should not have gone on to Paris, there to condone the crime of the Abbé Vergniaud, and *then* come on to Rome. To come to Rome under such circumstances, was like putting his head in the wolf's mouth! But the most unfortunate thing he has done on his ill-fated journey, is to have played protector to that boy he has with him."

"Why?" demanded Sylvie, growing pale as before she had been flushed.

"Do not ask why!" said Gherardi. "For a true answer would only anger you. Suffice it for you to know that whatever is in the way of Rome must be removed, —*shall* be removed at all costs! Cardinal Bonpré, as I said before, is in the way—and unless he can account fully and frankly for his strange companionship with a mere child-wanderer picked out of the streets, he will lose his diocese. If he persists in denying all knowledge of the boy's origin he will lose his Cardinal's hat. There is nothing more to be said! But—there is one remedy for all this mischief—and it rests with *you!*"

"With me?" Sylvie trembled,—her heart beat violently. She looked as though she were about to swoon, and Gherardi put out his arm to support her. She pushed him away indignantly.

"Do not touch me!" she said, her sweet voice shaken with something like the weakness of tears. "You tempt me to kill you,—to kill you and rid the world of a human fiend!"

His eyes flashed, and narrowed at the corners in the strange snake-like way habitual to them.

"How beautiful you are!" he said indulgently. "There are some people in the world who do not admire slight little creatures like you, all fire and spirit enclosed in sweetness—and in their ignorance they escape much danger! For when a man stoops to pick up a small flower half hidden in the long grass, he does not expect it to half-madden him with its sweetness—or half-murder him by its sting! That is why you are irresistible to me, and to many. Yes—no doubt you would like to kill me, *bella Contessa!*—and many a man would like to be killed by you! If I were not Domenico Gherardi, servant of Mother-Church, I would willingly submit to death at your hands. But being what I am, I must live! And living, I must work—to fulfil the commands of the Church. And so faithful am I in the work of our Lord's vineyard, that I care not how many grapes I press in the making of His wine! I tell you plainly that it rests with you to save your friend Angela Sovrani, and the saintly Cardinal likewise. Keep to the vows you have sworn to Holy Church,—vows sworn for you in infancy at baptism, and renewed by yourself at your confirmation and first Communion,—bring your husband to Us! And Florian Varillo's mouth shall be closed—the Sovrani's reputation shall shine like the sun at noonday; even the rank heresy of her picture shall be forgiven, and the Cardinal and his waif shall go free!"

Sylvie clasped her hands passionately together and raised them in an attitude of entreaty.

"Oh, why are you so cruel!" she cried. "Why do you demand from me what you know to be impossible?"

"It is not impossible," answered Gherardi, watching her closely as he spoke. "The Church is lenient,—she demands nothing in haste—nothing unreasonable! I do not even ask you to bring about Aubrey Leigh's conversion before your marriage. You are free to wed him in your own way and in his,—provided that one ceremonial of the marriage takes place according to our Catholic rites. But after you are thus wedded, you must promise to bring him to Us!—you must further promise that any children born of your union be baptized in the Catholic faith. With such a pledge from you, in writing, I will be satisfied;—and out of all the entanglements and confusion at present existing, your friends shall escape unharmed. I swear it!"

He raised his hand with a lofty gesture, as though he

were asserting the truth and grandeur of some specially noble cause. Sylvie, letting her clasped hands drop asunder with a movement of despair, stood gazing at him in fascinated horror.

"The Church!" he went on, warming with his own inward fervour. "The Rock, on which our Lord builds the real fabric of the Universe!" And his tall form dilated with the utterance of his blasphemy. "The learning, the science, the theoretical discussions of men, shall pass as dust blown by the breath of a storm-wind—but the Church shall remain, the same, yesterday, to-day and forever! It shall crush down kings, governments and nations in its unmoving Majesty! The fluctuating wisdom of authors and reformers—the struggle of conflicting creeds—all these shall sink and die under the silent inflexibility of its authority! The whole world hurled against it shall not prevail, and were all its enemies to perish by the sword, by poison, by disease, by imprisonment, by stripes and torture, this would be but even justice! 'For many are called—but few are chosen.'"

He turned his eyes, flashing with a sort of fierce ecstasy, upon the slight half-shrinking figure of Sylvie opposite to him. "Yes, *bella Contessa!* What the Church ordains, must be; what the Church desires, that same the Church will have! There is no room in the hearts or minds of its servants for love, for pity, for pardon, for anything human merely,—its authority is Divine! —and 'God will not be mocked'! Humanity is the mere food and wine of sacrifice to the Church's doctrine,—nations may starve, but the Church must be fed. What are nations to the Church? Naught but children,—docile or rebellious;—children to be whipped, and coerced, and *forced* to obey! Thus for you, one unit out of the whole mass, to oppose yourself to the mighty force of Rome, is as though one daisy out of the millions in the grass should protest against the sweep of the mower's scythe! You do not know me yet! There is nothing I would hesitate to do in the service of the Church. I would consent to ruin even *you*, to prove the fire of my zeal, as well as the fire of my love!"

He made a step towards her,—she drew herself to the utmost reach of her elfin height, and looked at him straightly. Pale, but with her dark blue eyes flashing like jewels, she in one sweeping glance, measured him with a scorn so intense that it seemed to radiate from her entire person, and pierce him with a thousand arrowy shafts of flame.

"You have stated your intentions," she said. "Will you hear my answer?"

He bent his head gravely, with a kind of ironical tolerance in his manner.

"There is nothing I desire more!" he replied, "for I am sure that in the unselfish sweetness of your nature you will do all you can to serve—and save—your friends!"

"You are right!" she said, controlling the quickness of her breathing, and forcing herself to speak calmly. "I will! But not in your way! Not at your command! You have enlightened me on many points of which I was hitherto ignorant—and for this I thank you! You have taught me that the Church, instead of being a brotherhood united in the Divine service of Christ, who was God-in-Man, is a mere secular system of avarice and tyranny! You pretend to save souls for God! What do you care for *my* soul! You would have me wed a man with fraud in my heart,—with the secret intent to push upon him the claims of a Church he abhors,—and this after he has made me his wife! You would have me tell lies to him before the Eternal! And you call that the way to salvation? No, Monsignor! It is the wealth of the Hermensteins you desire!—not the immortal rescue or heavenly benefit of the last of their children! You will support the murderer Varillo in his lie to ruin an innocent woman's reputation! You would destroy the honour and peace of an old man's life for the sake of furthering your own private interests and grudges! And you call yourself a servant of Christ! Monsignor, if you are a servant of Christ, then the Church you serve must be the shadow of a future hell! —not the promise of a future heaven! I denounce it,—I deny it!—I swear by the Holy Name of our Redeemer that I am a Christian!—not a slave of the Church of Rome!"

Such passion thrilled her, such high exaltation, that she looked like an inspired angel in her beauty and courage, and Gherardi, smothering a fierce oath, made one stride towards her and seized her hands.

"You defy me!" he said in a hoarse whisper. "You dare me to my worst?"

She looked up at his dark cruel face, his glittering eyes, and shuddered as with icy cold,—but the spirit in that delicate little body of hers was strong as steel, and tempered to the grandest issues.

"I dare you to do your worst!" she said, half-sobbingly,—half-closing her eyes in the nervous terror she could not altogether control. "You can but kill me—I shall die true!"

With a sort of savage cry, Gherardi snatched her round the waist, but scarcely had he done so when he was flung aside with a force that made him reel back heavily against the wall, and Aubrey Leigh confronted him.

"Aubrey!" cried Sylvie. "Oh, Aubrey!"

He caught her as she sprang to him, and held her fast, —and with perfect self-possession he eyed the priest disdainfully up and down.

"So this," he said coldly, "is the way the followers of Saint Peter fulfil the commands of Christ! Or shall we say this is the way in which they go on denying their Master? It is a strange way of retaining disciples,— a still stranger way of making converts! A brave way too, to intimidate a woman!"

Gherardi, recovering from the shock of Aubrey's blow, drew himself up haughtily.

"I serve the Church, Mr. Leigh!" he said proudly. "And in that high service all means are permitted to us for a righteous end!"

"Ah!—the old Jesuitical hypocrisy!" And Aubrey smiled bitterly. "Lies are permitted in the Cause of Truth! One word, Monsignor! I have no wish to play at any game of double-dealing with you. I have heard the whole of your interview with this lady. It is the first time I have ever played the eavesdropper—but my duty was to protect my promised wife, if she needed protection —and I thought it was possible she might need it—from *you!*"

Gherardi turned a livid paleness, and drew a quick breath.

"I know your moves," went on Aubrey quietly, "and it will be my business as well as my pleasure to frustrate them. Moreover, I shall give your plot into the care of the public press——"

"You will not dare!" cried Gherardi fiercely. "But —after all, what matter if you do!—no one will believe you!"

"Not in Rome, perhaps," returned Aubrey coolly. "But in England,—in America,—things are different. There are many honest men who dislike to contemplate even a distant vision of the talons of Rome hovering over us—we look upon such mischief as a sign of decay,—for only where the carcasses of nations lie, does the vulture hover! We are not dead yet! And now, Monsignor,— as your interview with the Countess is ended—an interview to which I have been a witness—may I suggest the removal of your presence? You have made a proposition—she has rejected it—the matter is ended!"

Civilly calm and cold he stood, holding Sylvie close to him with one embracing arm, and Gherardi, looking at the two together thus, impotently wished that the heavy sculptured and painted ceiling above them might fall and crush them into a pulp before him. No shame, no sense of compunction moved him,—if anything, he raised his head more haughtily than before.

"Aubrey Leigh," he said, "Socialist, reformer, revolutionist—whatever you choose to call yourself!—you have all the insolence of your race and class,—and it is beneath my dignity to argue with you. But you will rue the day you ever crossed my path! Not one thing have I threatened, that shall not be performed! This unhappy lady whose mind has been perverted from Holy Church by your heretical teachings, shall be excommunicated. Henceforth we look upon her as a child of sin, and we shall publicly declare her marriage with you illegal. The rest can be left with confidence, to—Society!"

And with a dark smile which made his face look like that of some malignant demon, he turned, and preserving his proud inflexibility of demeanour, without another look or gesture, left the apartment.

Then Aubrey, alone with his love, drew her closer, and lifted her fair face to his own, looking at it with passionate tenderness and admiration.

"You brave soul!" he said. "You true woman! You angel of the covenant of love! How shall I ever tell you how I worship you—how I revere you—for your truth and courage!"

She trembled under the ardour of his utterance, and her eyes filled with tears.

"I was not afraid!" she said. "I should have called Katrine,—only I knew that if I once did so, she also would be involved, and he would be unscrupulous enough to ruin my name with a few words in order to defend himself from all suspicion. But you, Aubrey?—how did it happen that you were here?"

"I was here from the first!" he replied triumphantly. "I followed on Gherardi's very heels. Your Arab boy admitted me—he was in my secret. He showed me into the anteroom just outside, where by leaving a corner of the door ajar I could see and hear everything. And I listened to your every word! I saw every bright flash of the strong soul in your brave eyes! And now those eyes question me, sweetheart,—almost reproachfully they seem to ask me why I did not interfere between you and Gherardi before? Ah, but you must forgive me for the delay! I wanted to drink all my cup of nectar to the dregs—I could not lose one drop of such sweetness! To see you, slight fragile blossom of a woman, matching your truth and courage against the treachery and malice of the most unscrupulous priestly tool ever employed by the Vatican, was a sight to make me strong for all my days!" He kissed her passionately. "My love! My wife! How can I ever thank you!"

She raised her sweet eyes wonderingly.

"Did you doubt me, Aubrey?"

"No! I never doubted you. But I wondered whether your force would hold out, whether you might not be intimidated, whether you might not temporize, which would have been natural enough—whether you might not have used some little social art or grace to cover up and disguise the absoluteness of your resolve—but no! You were a heroine in the fight, and you gave your blows straight from the hilt, without flinching. You have made me twice a man, Sylvie! With you beside me I shall win all I might otherwise have lost, and I thank God for you, dear!—I thank God for you!"

He drew her close again into his arms, pressing her to his heart which beat tumultously with its deep rejoic-

ing,—no fear now that they two would ever cease to be
one! No danger now of those miserable so-called "religious" disputes between husband and wife, which are
so eminently anti-Christian, and which make many a
home a hell upon earth,—disputes which young children
sometimes have to witness from their earliest years, when
the mother talks "at" the father for not going to Church,
or the father sneers at the mother for being "a rank
Papist"! Nothing now, but absolute union in spirit
and thought, in soul and intention—the rarest union
that can be consummated between man and woman, and
yet the only one that can engender perfect peace and un-
changing happiness.

And presently the lovers' trance of joy gave way to
thought for others; to a realization of the dangers hovering over the good Cardinal, and the already ill-fated
Angela Sovrani, and Aubrey, raising the golden head
that nestled against his breast, kissed the sweet lips once
more and said—

"Now, my Sylvie, we must take the law into our own
hands! We must do all we can to save our friends. The
Cardinal must be thought of first. If we are not quick to
the rescue he will be sent 'into retreat,' which can be
translated as forced detention, otherwise imprisonment.
He must leave Rome to-night. Now listen!"

And sitting down beside her, still holding her hand, he
gave her an account of his meeting with Cyrillon Vergniaud, otherwise "Gys Grandit," and told her of the sudden passion for Angela that had fired the soul of that
fiery writer of the fiercest polemics against priestcraft
that had as yet startled France.

"Knowing now all the intended machinations of Gherardi," continued Aubrey, "what I suggest is this,—that
you, my Sylvie, should confide in the Princesse D'Agramont, who is fortunately for us, an enemy of the Vatican. Arrange with her that she persuades Angela to
return under her escort at once to Paris. Angela is well
enough to travel if great care be taken of her, and the
Princesse will not spare that. Cyrillon can go with
them—I should think that might be managed?"

He smiled as he put this question. Sylvie smiled in
answer and replied demurely—

"I should think so!"

"But the Cardinal," resumed Aubrey, "and—and Manuel—must go to-night. I will see Prince Sovrani and arrange it. And Sylvie—will you marry me to-morrow morning?"

Her eyes opened wide and she laughed.

"Why yes, if you wish it!" she said. "But—so soon?"

"Darling, the sooner the better! I mean to take every possible method of making our marriage binding in the sight of the world, before the Vatican has time to launch its thunders. If you are willing, we can be married at the American Consulate to-morrow morning. You must remember that though born of British parents, I do not resign my American citizenship, and would not forego being of the New World for all the old worlds ever made! The American Consul knows me well, and he will begin to make things legal for us to-morrow if you are ready."

"*Begin* to make things legal?" echoed Sylvie smiling. "Will he do no more than begin?"

"My sweetheart, he cannot. He will make you mine according to American law. In England, you will again be made mine according to English law. And then afterwards we will have our religious ceremony!"

Sylvie looked at him perplexedly, then gave a pretty gesture of playful resignation.

"Let everything be as you wish and decide, Aubrey," she said. "I give my life and love to you, and have no other will but yours!"

He kissed her.

"I accept the submission, only to put myself more thoroughly at your command," he said tenderly,—"You are my queen,—but with powerful enemies against us, I must see that you are rightfully enthroned!"

A few minutes' more conversation,—then a hurried consultation with Madame Bozier, and Sylvie, changing her lace gown for a simple travelling dress, walked out of the Casa D'Angeli with the faithful Katrine, and taking the first carriage she could find, was driven to the Palazzo where the Princesse D'Agramont had her apartments. Allowing from ten to fifteen minutes to elapse after her departure, Aubrey Leigh himself went out, and standing on the steps of the house, looked up and down carelessly, drawing on his gloves and humming a tune.

His quick glance soon espied what he had been almost certain he should see, namely, the straight black-garmented figure of a priest, walking slowly along the street on the opposite side, his hands clasped behind his back, and his whole aspect indicative of devout meditation.

" I thought so!" said Aubrey to himself. " A spy set on already! No time to lose—Cardinal Bonpré must leave Rome at nightfall."

Leisurely he crossed the road, and walking with as slow a step as the priest he had noticed, came opposite to him face to face. With impenetrable solemnity the holy man meekly moved aside,—with equally impenetrable coolness, Aubrey eyed him up and down, then the two passed each other, and Aubrey walked with the same unhasting pace, to the end of the street,—then turned—to see that the priest had paused in his holy musings to crane his neck after him and watch him with the most eager scrutiny. He did not therefore take a carriage at the moment he intended, but walked on into the Corso, —there he sprang into a *fiacre* and drove straight to the Sovrani Palace. The first figure he saw there, strolling about in the front of the building, was another priest, absorbed in apparently profound thoughts on the sublimity of the sunset, which was just then casting its red glow over the Eternal City. And with the appearance of this second emissary of the Vatican police, he realised the full significance of the existing position of affairs.

Without a moment's loss of time he was ushered into the presence of the Cardinal, and there for a moment stood silent on the threshold of the apartment, overcome by the noble aspect of the venerable prelate, who, seated in his great oaken chair, was listening to a part of the Gospel of Saint Luke, read aloud in clear sweet accents by Manuel.

" A good man out of the good treasure of his heart bringeth forth that which is good; and an evil man out of the evil treasure of his heart bringeth forth that which is evil; for of the abundance of the heart his mouth speaketh.

" And why call ye me, Lord, Lord, and do not the things which I say?

" Whosoever cometh to me, and heareth my sayings, and doeth them, I will show you to whom he is like:

"He is like a man which built an house, and digged deep, and laid the foundation on a rock: and when the flood arose, the stream beat vehemently upon that house, and could not shake it: for it was founded upon a rock.

"But he that heareth, and doeth not, is like a man that without a foundation built an house upon the earth; against which the stream did beat vehemently, and immediately it fell; *and the ruin of that house was great.*"

And emphasizing the last line, Manuel closed the book; then at a kindly beckoning gesture from the Cardinal, Aubrey advanced into the room, bowing with deep reverence and honour over the worn old hand the prelate extended.

"My lord Cardinal," he said without further preface, "you must leave Rome to-night!"

The Cardinal raised his gentle blue eyes in wondering protest.

"By whose order?"

"Surely by your own Master's will," said Aubrey with deep earnestness. "For he would not have you be a victim to treachery!"

"Treachery!" And the Cardinal smiled. "My son, traitors harm themselves more than those they would betray. Treachery cannot touch me!"

Aubrey came a step nearer.

"Monsignor, if you do not care for yourself you will care for the boy," he said in a lower tone, with a glance at Manuel, who had withdrawn, and was now standing at one of the windows, the light of the sunset appearing to brighten itself in his fair hair. "He will be separated from you!"

At this the Cardinal rose up, his whole form instinct with resolution and dignity.

"They cannot separate us against the boy's will or mine," he said. "Manuel!"

Manuel came to his call, and the Cardinal placed one hand on his shoulder.

"Child," he said softly, "they threaten to part me from you, if we stay longer here. Therefore we must leave Rome!"

Manuel looked up with a bright flashing glance of tenderness.

"Yes, dear friend, we must leave Rome!" he said. "Rome is no place for you—or for me!"

There was a moment's silence. Something in the attitude of the old man and the young boy standing side by side, moved Aubrey deeply; a sense of awe as well as love overwhelmed him at the sight of these two beings, so pure in mind, so gentle of heart, and so widely removed in years and in life,—the one a priest of the Church, the other a waif of the streets, yet drawn together as it seemed, by the simple spirit of Christ's teaching, in an almost supernatural bond of union. Recovering himself presently he said,

"To-night then, Monsignor?"

The Cardinal looked at Manuel, who answered for him.

"Yes, to-night! We will be ready! For the days are close upon the time when the birth of Christ was announced to a world that does not yet believe in Him! It will be well to leave Rome before then! For the riches of the Pope's palace have nothing to do with the poor babe born in a manger,—and the curse of the Vatican would be a discord in the angels' singing—'Glory to God in the highest, and on earth *peace, goodwill towards men'!*"

His young voice rang out, silver clear and sweet, and Aubrey gazed at him in wondering silence.

"To-night!" repeated Manuel, smiling and stretching out his hand with a gentle authoritative gesture. "To-night the Cardinal will leave Rome, and *I* will leave it too—perchance for ever!"

XXXV.

During these various changes in the lives of those with whom he had been more or less connected, Florian Varillo lay between life and death in the shelter of a Trappist monastery on the Campagna. When he had been seized by the delirium and fever which had flung him, first convulsed and quivering, and then totally insensible, at the foot of the grim, world-forgotten men who passed the midnight hours in digging their own graves, he had been judged by them as dying or dead, and had been carried into a sort of mortuary chapel, cold and bare, and lit only by the silver moonbeams and the flicker of a torch one of the monks carried. Waking in this ghastly place, too weak to struggle, he fell a-moaning like a tortured child, and was, on showing this sign of life, straightway removed to one of the cells. Here, after hours of horrible suffering, of visions more hideous than Dante's Hell, of stupors and struggles, of fits of strong shrieking, followed by weak tears, he woke one afternoon calm and coherent,—to find himself lying on a straight pallet bed in a narrow stone chamber, dimly lighted by a small slit of window, through which a beam of the sun fell aslant, illumining the blood-stained features of a ghastly Christ stretched on a black crucifix directly opposite him. He shuddered as he saw this, and half-closed his eyes with a deep sigh.

"Tired—tired!" said a thin clear voice beside him. "Always tired! It is only God who is never weary!"

Varillo opened his eyes again languidly, and turned them on a monk sitting beside him,—a monk whose face was neither old nor young, but which presented a singular combination of both qualities. His high forehead, white as marble, had no furrows to mar its smoothness, and from under deep brows a pair of wondering wistful brown eyes peered like the eyes of a lost and starving child. The cheeks were gaunt and livid, the flesh hanging in loose hollows from the high and prominent bones, yet the mouth was that of a youth, firm, well-outlined and sweet in expression, and when he smiled as he did now, he showed an even row of small pearly teeth which might have been envied by many a fair woman.

"Only God who is never weary!" he said, nodding his head slowly, "but we—you and I—we are soon tired!"

Varillo looked at him dubiously; and a moment's thought decided him to assume a certain amount of meekness and docility with this evident brother of some religious order, so that he might obtain both sympathy and confidence from him, and from all whom he might be bound to serve. Ill and weak as he was, the natural tendency of his brain to scheme for his own advantage, was not as yet impaired.

"Ah, yes!" he sighed, "I am very tired!—very ill! I do not know what has happened to me—nor even where I am. What place is this?"

"It is a place where the dead come!" responded the monk. "The dead in heart! the dead in soul—the dead in sin! They come to bury themselves, lest God should find them and crush them into dust before they have time to say a prayer! Like Adam and his wife, they hide themselves 'from the presence of the Lord among the trees of the garden.'"

Varillo raised himself on one elbow, and stared at the pale face and smiling mouth of the speaker in fear and wonder.

"'A place where the dead come!'" he echoed. "But you are alive—and so am I!"

"You may be—I am not," said the monk quietly. "I died long ago! People who are alive say we are men, though we know ourselves to be ghosts merely. This place is called by the world a Trappist monastery,—you will go out of it if indeed you are alive—you must prove that first! But we shall never come out, because we are dead. One never comes out of the grave!"

With an effort Varillo tried to control the tremor of his nerves, and to understand and reason out these enigmatical sentences of his companion. He began to think —and then to remember,—and by and by was able to conjure up the picture of himself as he had last been conscious of existence,—himself standing outside the gates of a great building on the Campagna, and shaking the iron bars to and fro. It was a Trappist monastery then?—and he was being taken charge of by the Trappist Order? This fact might possibly be turned to his account if he were careful. He lay down once more on his pillow and closed his eyes, and under this pretence of sleep, pondered his position. What were they saying of him in Rome? Was Angela buried? And her great picture? What had become of it?

"How long have I been here?" he asked suddenly.

The monk gave a curious deprecatory gesture with his hands.

"Since you died! So long have you been dead!"

Varillo surveyed him with a touch of scorn.

"You talk in parables—like your Master!" he said with a feeble attempt at a laugh. "I am not strong enough to understand you! And if you are a Trappist monk, why do you talk at all? I thought one of your rules was perpetual silence?"

"Silence? Yes—everyone is silent but me!" said the monk—"I may talk—because I am only Ambrosio,—mad Ambrosio!—something wrong here!" And he touched his forehead. "A little teasing demon lives always behind my eyes, piercing my brain with darts of fire. And he obliges me to talk; he makes me say things I should not—and for all the mischief he works upon me I ‚wear this——see!"—And springing up suddenly he threw aside the folds of his garment, and displayed his bare chest, over which a coarse rope was crossed and knotted so tightly, that the blood was oozing from the broken flesh on either side of it. "For every word I say, I bleed!"

Varillo gave a nervous cry and covered his eyes.

"Do not be afraid!" said Ambrosio, drawing his robe together again, "It is only flesh—not spirit—that is wounded! Flesh is our great snare,—it persuades us to eat, to sleep, to laugh, to love—the spirit commands none of these things. The spirit is of God—it wants neither food nor rest,—it is pure and calm,—it would escape to Heaven if the flesh did not cramp its wings!"

Varillo took his hand from his eyes and tossed himself back on his pillow with a petulant moan.

"Can they do nothing better for me than this?" he ejaculated. "To place me here in this wretched cell alone with a madman!"

Ambrosio stood by the pallet bed looking down upon him with a sort of child-like curiosity.

"No better than this?" he echoed. "Would you have anything better? Safe—safe from the world,—no one can find you or follow you—no one can discover your sin——"

"Sin! What sin!" demanded Varillo fiercely. "You talk like a fool—as you own yourself to be! I have committed no sin!"

"Good—good!" said Ambrosio. "Then you must be canonized with all the rest of the saints! And St. Peter's shall be illuminated, and the Pope shall be carried in to see you and to lay his hands upon you, and they shall shout to him, '*Tu es Petrus!*' and no one will remember what kind of a bruised, bleeding, tortured, broken-down Head of the Church stood before the multitude when Pilate cried '*Ecce homo!*'"

Varillo stared at him in unwilling fascination. He seemed carried beyond himself,—it was as though some other force spoke through him, and though he scarcely raised his voice, its tone was so clear, musical, and penetrative that it seemed to give light and warmth to the cold dullness of the cell.

"You must not mind me!" he went on softly, "My thoughts have all gone wrong, they tell me,—so have my words. I was young once—and in that time I used to study hard and try to understand what it was that God wished me to do with my life. But there were so many things—so much confusion—so much difficulty—and the end is——here!" He smiled. "Well! It is a quiet end,—they say the devil knocks at the gate of the monastery often at midnight, but he never enters in,—never—unless perchance you are he!"

Varillo turned himself about pettishly.

"If I were he, I should not trouble you long," he said. "Even the devil might be glad to make exit from such a hole as this! Who is your Superior?"

"We have only one Superior,—God!" replied Ambrosio. "He who never slumbers or sleeps—He who troubles Himself to look into everything, from the cup of a flower to the heart of a man! Who shall escape the lightning of His glance, or think to cover up a hidden vileness from the discovery of the Most High?"

" I did not ask you for pious jargon," said Varillo, beginning to lose temper, yet too physically weak to contend with the wordy vagaries of this singular personage who had evidently been told off to attend upon him.   " I asked you who is the Head or Ruler of this community?   Who gives you the daily rule of conduct which you all obey?"

Ambrosio's brown eyes grew puzzled, and he shook his head.

" I obey no one," he said.   " I am mad Ambrosio!—I walk about in my grave, and speak, and sing, while others remain silent.   I would tell you if I knew of anyone greater than God,—but I do not!"

Varillo uttered an impatient groan.   It was no good asking this creature anything,—his answers were all wide of the mark.

" God," went on Ambrosio, turning his head towards the light that came streaming in through the narrow window of the cell, " is in that sunbeam!   He can enter where He will, and we never know when we shall meet Him face to face!   He may possess with His spirit the chaste body of a woman, as in our Blessed Lady,—or He may come to us in the form of a child, speaking to the doctors in the temple and arguing with them on the questions of life and death.   He is in all things; and the very beggar at our gates who makes trial of our charity, may for all we know, be our Lord disguised!   Shall I tell you a strange story?"

Varillo gave a weary sign of assent, half closing his eyes.   It was better this crazed fool should talk, he thought, than that he should lie there and listen, as it were, to the deadly silence which in the pauses of the conversation could be felt, like the brooding heaviness of a thick cloud hanging over the monastery walls.

" It happened long ago," said Ambrosio.   " There was a powerful prince who thought that to be rich and strong was sufficient to make all the world his own.   But the world belongs to God,—and He does not always give it over to the robber and spoiler.   This prince I tell you of, had been the lover of a noble lady, but he was false-hearted; and the false soon grow weary of love!   And so, tiring of her beauty and her goodness, he stabbed her mortally to death, and thought no one had seen him do the deed.   For the only witness to it was a ray of moonlight falling through the window—just as the sunlight falls now!—see!" And he pointed to the narrow aperture which lit the cell, while Florian Varillo, shuddering in spite of himself, lay motionless. "But when the victim was dead, this very ray of moonlight turned to the shape of a great angel, and the angel wore the semblance of our Lord,—and the glory and the wonder of that vision was as the lightning to slay and utterly destroy! And from that hour for many years, the murderer was followed by a ray of light, which never left him; all day he saw it flickering in his path,—all night it flashed across his bed, driving sleep from his eyes and rest from his brain!—till at last maddened by remorse he confessed his crime to a priest, and was taken into a grave like this, a monastery, —where he died, so they say, penitent. But whether he was forgiven, the story does not say!"

"It is a stupid story!" said Varillo, opening his eyes, and smiling in the clear, candid way he always assumed when he had anything to hide. "It has neither point nor meaning."

"You think not?" said Ambrosio. "But perhaps you are not conscious of God. If you were, that sunbeam we see now should make you careful, lest an angel should be in it!"

"Careful? Why should I be careful?" Varillo half raised himself on the bed. "I have nothing to hide!"

At this Ambrosio began to laugh.

"Oh, you are happy—happy!" he exclaimed. "You are the first I ever heard say that! Nothing to hide! Oh, fortunate, fortunate man! Then indeed you should not be here—for we all have something to hide, and we are afraid even of the light,—that is why we make such narrow holes for it; we are always praying God not to look at our sins,—not to uncover them and show us what vile souls we are—we men who could be as gods in life, if we did not choose to be devils——"

Here he suddenly broke off, and a curious grey rigidity stole over his features, as if some invisible hand were turning him into stone. His eyes sparkled feverishly, but otherwise his face was the face of the dead. The horrible fixity of his aspect at that moment, so terrified Varillo that he gave a loud cry, and almost before he knew he had uttered it, another monk entered the cell.

Varillo gazed at him affrightedly, and pointed to Ambrosio. The monk said nothing, but merely took the rigid figure by its arm and shook it violently. Then, as suddenly as he had lost speech and motion, Ambrosio recovered both, and went on talking evenly, taking up the sentence he had broken off—" If we did not choose to be as devils, we might be as gods!" Then looking around him with a smile, he added, " Now you are here, Filippo, you will explain!"

The monk addressed as Filippo remained silent, still holding him by the arm, and presently quietly guiding him, led him out of the cell. When the two brethren had disappeared, Varillo fell back on his pillows exhausted.

" What am I to do now?" he thought. " I must have been here many days!—all Rome must know of Angela's death—all Rome must wonder at my absence—all Rome perhaps suspects me of being her murderer! And yet—this illness may be turned to some account. I can say that it was caused by grief at hearing the sudden news of her death—that I was stricken down by my despair——but then——I must not forget—I was to have been in Naples. Yes—the thing looks suspicious—I shall be tracked!—I must leave Italy. But how?"

Bathed in cold perspiration he lay, wondering, scheming, devising all sorts of means of escape from his present surroundings, when he became suddenly aware of a tall dark figure in the cell,—a figure muffled nearly to its eyes, which had entered with such stealthy softness and silence as to give almost the impression of some supernatural visitant. He uttered a faint exclamation—the figure raised one hand menacingly.

" Be silent!" These words were uttered in a harsh whisper. " If you value your life, hold your peace till I have said what I come to say!"

Moving to the door of the cell, the mysterious visitor bolted it across and locked it—then dropped the disguising folds of his heavy mantle and monk's cowl, and disclosed the face and form of Domenico Gherardi. Paralysed with fear Varillo stared at him,—every drop of blood seemed to rush from his heart to his brain, turning him sick and giddy, for in the dark yet fiery eyes of the priest, there was a look that would have made the boldest tremble.

" I knew that you were here," he said, his thin lips widening at the corners in a slight disdainful smile. " I saw you at the inn on the road to Frascati, and watched you shrink and tremble as I spoke of the murder of Angela Sovrani! You screened your face behind a paper you were reading,—that was not necessary, for your hand shook,—and so betrayed itself as the hand of the assassin!"

With a faint moan, Varillo shudderingly turned away and buried his head in his pillow.

" Why do you now wish to hide yourself?" pursued Gherardi. " Now when you are an honest man at last, and have shown yourself in your true colors? You were a liar hitherto, but now you have discovered yourself to be exactly as the devil made you, why you can look at me without fear—we understand each other!"

Still Varillo hid his eyes and moaned, and Gherardi thereupon laid a rough hand on his shoulder.

" Come, man! You are not a sick child to lie cowering there as though seized by the plague! What ails you? You have done no harm! You tried to kill something that stood in your way,—I admire you for that! I would do the same myself at any moment!"

Slowly Varillo lifted himself and looked up at the dark strong face above him.

" A pity you did not succeed!" went on Gherardi, " for the world would have been well rid of at least one feminine would-be ' genius,' whose skill puts that of man to shame! But perhaps it may comfort you to know that your blow was not strong enough or deep enough, and that your betrothed wife yet lives to wed you—if she will!"

" Lives!" cried Florian. " Angela lives!"

" Ay, Angela lives!" replied Gherardi coldly. " Does that give you joy? Does your lover's heart beat with ecstasy to know that she—twenty times more gifted than you, a hundred times more famous than you, a thousand times more beloved by the world than you—lives, to be crowned with an immortal fame, while you are relegated to scorn and oblivion! Does that content you?"

A dull red flush crept over Varillo's cheeks,—his hand clenched the coverlet of his bed convulsively.

" Lives!" he muttered. " She lives! Then it must be

by a miracle! For I drove the steel deep . . . deep home!"

Gherardi looked at him curiously, with the air of a scientist watching some animal writhing under vivisection.

"Perhaps Cardinal Felix prayed for her!" he said mockingly, "and even as he healed the crippled child in Rouen he may have raised his niece from the dead! But miracle or no miracle, she lives. That is why I am here!"

"Why—you—are—here?" repeated Varillo mechanically.

"How dull you are!" said Gherardi tauntingly. "A man like you with a dozen secret intrigues in Rome, should surely be able to grasp a situation better! Angela Sovrani lives, I tell you,—I am here to help you to kill her more surely! Your first attempt was clumsy,—and dangerous to yourself, but—murder her reputation, amico, murder her reputation!—and so build up your own!"

Slowly Varillo turned his eyes upon him. Gherardi met them unflinchingly, and in that one glance the two were united in the spirit of their evil intention.

"You are a man," went on Gherardi, watching him closely. "Will you permit yourself to be baffled and beaten in the race for fame by a woman? Shame on you if you do! Listen! I am prepared to swear that you are innocent of having attempted the murder of your affianced wife, and I will also assert that the greater part of her picture was painted by you, though you were, out of generosity and love for her, willing to let her take the credit of the whole conception!"

Varillo started upright.

"God!" he cried. "Is it possible! Will you do this for me?"

"Not for you—No," said Gherardi contemptuously. "I will do nothing for you! If I saw you lying in the road at my feet dying for want of a drop of water, I would not give it to you! What I do, I do for myself— and the Church!"

By this time Varillo had recovered his equanimity. A smile came readily to his lips as he said—

"Ah, the Church! Excellent institution! Like charity, it covers a multitude of sins!"

"It exists for that object," answered Gherardi with a

touch of ironical humor. "Its own sins it covers,—and shows up the villainies of those who sin outside its juris-diction. Angela Sovrani is one of these,—her uncle the Cardinal is another,—Sylvie Hermenstein——"

"What of her?" cried Varillo, his eyes sparkling. "Is her marriage broken off?"

"Broken off!" Gherardi gave a fierce gesture. "Would that it were! No! She renounces the Church for the sake of Aubrey Leigh—she leaves the faith of her fathers——"

"And takes the wealth of her fathers with her!" fin-ished Varillo, maliciously. "I see! I understand! The Church has reason for anger!"

"It has reason!" echoed Gherardi. "And we of the Church choose you as the tool wherewith to work our vengeance. And why? Because you are a born liar!—because you can look straight in the eyes of man or woman, and swear to a falsehood without flinching!—be-cause you are an egotist, and will do anything to serve yourself—because you have neither heart nor conscience—nor soul nor feeling,—because you are an animal in de-sires and appetite,—because of this, I say, we yoke you to our chariot wheels, knowing you may be trusted to drive over and trample down the creatures that might be val-uable to you if they did not stand in your way!"

Such bitterness, such scorn, such loathing were in his accents, that even the callous being he addressed was stung, and made a feeble gesture of protest.

"You judge me harshly," he began——

Gherardi laughed.

"Judge you! Not I! No judgment is wanted. I read you like a book through and through,—a book that should be set on Nature's Index Expurgatorius, as unfit to meet the eyes of the faithful! You are a low creature, Florian Varillo,—and unscrupulous as I am myself, I despise you for meanness greater than even I am capable of! But you are a convenient tool, ready to hand, and I use you for the Church's service! If you were to refuse to do as I bid you, I would brand you through the world as the murderer you are! So realize to the full how thoroughly I have you in my power. Now understand me,—you must leave this place to-morrow. I will send my carriage for you, and you shall come at once to me, to me in Rome as my guest,—my *honoured* guest!" And he emphasized the word sarcastically. "You are weak and ill yet, they tell me here,—so much the better for you. It will make you all the more interesting! You will find it easier to play the part of injured innocence! Do you understand?"

"I understand," answered Varillo with a faint shudder, for the strong and relentless personality of Gherardi over-powered him with a sense of terror which he could not wholly control.

"Good! Then we will say no more. Brief words are best on such burning matters. To-morrow at six in the afternoon I will send for you. Be ready! Till then—try to rest—try to sleep without dreaming of a scaffold!"

He folded his mantle around him again and prepared to depart.

"Sleep," he repeated. "Sleep with a cold heart and quiet mind! Think that it is only a woman's name—a woman's work—a woman's honour, that stand in your way,—and congratulate yourself with the knowledge that the Church and her Divine authority will help you to re-move all three! Farewell!"

He turned, and unlocked the door of the cell. As he threw it open, he was confronted by the monk Ambrosio, who was outside on the very threshold.

"What are you doing here?" he demanded sus-piciously. "I had a permit from the Superior to speak to your charge alone."

"And were you not alone?" returned Ambrosio smil-ing. "I was not with you! I was here as sentinel, to prevent anyone disturbing you. Poor Ambrosio—mad Ambrosio! He is no good at all except to guard the dead!"

Gherardi looked at him scrutinizingly, and noted the lack-lustre eyes, the helpless childish expression, of the half-young, half-old face confronting his own.

"Guard the dead as much as you please," he said harshly. "But take heed how you spy on the living! Be careful of the sick man lying yonder—we want him back with us in Rome to-morrow."

Ambrosio nodded.

"Back in Rome—good—good!" he said. "Then he is living after all! I thought he was dead in his sins as I am,—but you tell me he lives,and will go back to Rome!—

Oh yes—I will take care of him——good care!—do not
fear! I know how to guard him so that he shall not
escape you!"

Gherardi looked at him again sharply, but he was playing with his long rosary and smiling foolishly, and there
seemed no use in wasting further speech upon him. So,
muffling himself in his cloak, he strode away, and Ambrosio entered the cell.

"You shall have meat and wine presently," he said,
approaching the bed where Florian lay. "The devil has
given orders that you shall be well fed!"

Varillo looked up and smiled kindly. He could assume
any expression at command, and it suited his purpose just
now to be all gentleness.

"My poor friend!" he said compassionately. "Your
wits are far astray! Devil? Nay—he who has just left
us is more of a saint!"

Ambrosio's brown eyes flashed, but he maintained a
grave and immovable aspect.

"The devil has often mocked us in saint's disguise,"
he said slowly. "I tell the porter here every night to
keep the gates well locked against him,—but this time it
was no use; he has entered in. And now we shall have
great work to get him out!"

Varillo resting his head on one arm, studied him curiously.

"You must have lived a strange life in the world!" he
said. "That is if you were ever in the world at all. Were
you?"

"Oh yes, I was in the world," replied Ambrosio calmly.
"I was in the midst of men and women who passed their
whole lives in acts of cruelty and treachery to one another.
I never met a man who was honest; I never saw a woman
who was true! I wondered where God was that He permitted such vile beings to live and take His name in vain.
He seemed lost and gone,—I could not find Him!"

"Ah!" ejaculated Florian languidly. "And did you
discover Him here? In this monastery?"

"No—He is not here, for we are all dead men," said
Ambrosio. "And God is the God of the living, not the
God of the dead! Shall I tell you where I found him?"
And he advanced a step or two, raising one hand warn-
ingly as though he were entrusted with some message of

doom—" I found Him in sin! I tried to live a life of truth in a world of lies, but the lies were too strong for me,—they pulled me down! I fell—into a black pit of crime—reckless, determined, conscious wickedness,—and so found God——in my punishment!"

He clasped his hands together with an expression of strange ecstasy.

" Down into the darkness!" he said. " Down through long vistas of shadow and blackness you go, glad and exultant, delighting in evil, and thinking ' God sees me not!' And then suddenly at the end, a sword of fire cuts the darkness asunder,—and the majesty of the Divine Law breaks your soul on the wheel!"

He looked steadfastly at Varillo.

" So you will find,—so you must find, if you ever go down into the darkness."

" Ay, if I ever go," said Florian gently. " But I shall not."

" No?—then perhaps you are there already?" said Ambrosio smiling, and playing with his rosary. " For those who say they will never sin have generally sinned!"

Varillo held the same kind look of compassion in his eyes. He was fond of telling his fellow-artists that he had a " plastic" face,—and this quality served him well just now. He might have been a hero and martyr, from the peaceful and patient expression of his features, and he so impressed by his manner a lay-brother who presently entered to give him his evening meal, that he succeeded in getting rid of Ambrosio altogether.

" You are sure you are strong enough to be left without an attendant?" asked the lay-brother solicitously, quite captivated by the gentleness of his patient. " There is a special evening service to-night in the chapel, and Ambrosio should be there to play the organ—for he plays well—but this duty had been given to Fra Filippo——"

" Nay, but let Ambrosio fulfil his usual task," said Varillo considerately. " I am much better—much stronger,—and as my good friend Monsignor Gherardi desires me to be in Rome to-morrow, and to stay with him till I am quite restored to health, I must try to rest as quietly as I can till my hour of departure."

" You must be a great man to have Domenico Gherardi for a friend!" said the lay-brother wistfully.

Here Ambrosio suddenly burst into a loud laugh.

"You are right! He is a great man!——one of the greatest in Rome, or for that matter in the world! And he means to be yet greater!" And with that he turned on his heel and left the cell abruptly.

Varillo, languidly sipping the wine that had been brought to him with his food, looked after him with a pitying smile.

"Poor soul!" he said gently.

"He was famous once," said the lay-brother, lowering his voice as he spoke. "One of the most famous sculptors in Europe. But something went wrong with his life, and he came here. It is difficult to make him understand orders, or obey them, but the Superior allows him to remain on account of his great skill in music. On that point at least he is sane."

"Indeed!" said Varillo indifferently. He was beginning to weary of the conversation, and wished to be alone. "It is well for him that he is useful to you in some regard. And now, my friend, will you leave me to rest awhile? If it be possible I shall try to sleep now till morning."

"One of us will come to you at daybreak," said the lay-brother. "You are still very weak—you will need assistance to dress. Your clothes are here at the foot of the bed. I hope you will sleep well."

"Thank you!" said Varillo, conveying an almost tearful look of gratitude into his eyes—"You are very good to me! God bless you!"

The lay-brother made a gentle deprecatory gesture of his hands and retired, and Varillo was left to his own reflections. He lay still, thinking deeply, and marvelling at the unexpected rescue out of his difficulties so suddenly afforded him.

"With Gherardi to support me, I can say anything!" he mused, his heart beating quickly and exultingly. "I can say anything and swear anything! And even if the sheath of my dagger has been found, it will be no proof, for I can say it is not mine. Any lie I choose to tell will have Gherardi's word to warrant it!—so I am safe—unless Angela speaks!"

He considered this possibility for a moment, then smiled.

"But she never will! She is one of those strange

women who endure without complaint,—she is too lofty and pure for the ways of the world, and the world naturally takes vengeance upon her. There is not a man born that does not hate too pure a woman; it is his joy to degrade her if he can! This is the way of Nature; what is a woman made for except to subject herself to her master! And when she rises superior to him—superior in soul, intellect, heart and mind, he sees in her nothing but an abnormal prodigy, to be stared at, laughed at, despised—but never loved! The present position of affairs is Angela's fault, not mine. She should not have concealed the work she was doing from her lover, who had the right to know all her secrets!"

He laughed,—a low malicious laugh, and then lay tranquilly on his pillows gazing at the gradually diminishing light. Day was departing—night was coming on,—and as the shadows lengthened, the solemn sound of the organ began to vibrate through the walls of the monastery like far-off thunder growing musical. With a certain sensuous delight in the beautiful, Varillo listened to it with pleasure; he had no mind to probe the true meaning of music, but the mere sound was soothing and sublime, and seemed in its gravity, to match the "tone" of the light that was gradually waning. So satisfied was he with that distant pulse of harmony that he began weaving some verses in his head to "His Absent Lady,"—and succeeded in devising quite a charming lyric to her whose honour and renown he was ready to kill. So complex, so curious, so callous, yet sensuous, and utterly egotistical was his nature, that had Angela truly died under his murderous blow, he would have been ready now to write such exquisite verses in the way of a lament for her loss, as should have made a world of sentimental women weep, not knowing the nature of the man.

The last glimpse of day vanished, and the cell was only illuminated by a flickering gleam which crept through the narrow crevice of the door from the oil lamp outside in the corridor. The organ music ceased—to be followed by the monotonous chanting of the monks at their evening orisons,—and in turn, these too came to an end, and all was silent. Easily and restfully Florian Varillo, calling himself in his own mind poet, artist, and lover of all women rather than one, turned on his pillow and slept peacefully,—a calm deep sleep such as is only supposed to visit the innocent and pure of conscience, but which in truth just as often refreshes the senses of the depraved and dissolute, provided they are satisfied with evil as their good. How many hours he slept he did not know, but he was wakened at last by a terrible sense of suffocation, and he sat up gasping for breath, to find the cell full of thick smoke and burning stench. The flickering reflection of the lamp was gone, and as he instinctively leaped from his bed and grasped his clothes, he heard the monastery bell above him swinging to and fro, with a jarring heavy clang. Weak from the effects of his illness, and scarcely able to stand, he dragged on some of his garments, and rushing to the door threw it open, to be met with dense darkness and thick clouds of smoke wreathing towards him in all directions. He uttered a loud shriek.

" Fire ! "

The bell clanged on slowly over his head, but otherwise there was no response. Stumbling along, blinded, suffocated, not knowing at any moment whether he might not be precipitated down some steep flight of stairs or over some high gallery in the building, he struggled to follow what seemed to be a cooling breath of air which streamed through the smoke as though blowing in from some open door, and as he felt his way with his hands on the wall he suddenly heard the organ.

" Thank God ! " he thought, " I am near the chapel ! The fire has broken out in this part of the building—the monks do not know and are still at prayer. I shall be in time to save them all ! . . ."

A small tongue of red flame flashed upon his eyes— he recoiled—then pressed forward again, seeing a door in front of him. The organ music sounded nearer and nearer; he rushed to the door, half choked and dizzy, and pushing it open, reeled into the organ loft, where at the organ, sat the monk Ambrosio, shaking out such a storm of music as might have battered the gates of Heaven or Hell. Varillo leaped forward——then, as he saw the interior of the chapel, uttered one agonized shriek, and stood as though turned to stone. For the whole place was in flames!—everything from the altar to the last small statue set in a niche, was ablaze, and only the organ, raised like a carven pinnacle, appeared to be intact, set high above the blazing ruin. Enrapt in his own dreams, Ambrosio sat, pouring thunderous harmony out of the golden-tubed instrument which as yet, with its self-acting machinery, was untouched by the flames, and Varillo half-mad with terror, sprang at him like a wild beast.

"Stop!" he cried. "Stop, fool! Do you not see—can you not understand—the monastery is on fire!"

Ambrosio shook him off; his brown eyes were clear and bright,—his whole expression stern and resolved.

"I know it," he replied. "And we shall burn—you and I—together!"

"Oh, mad brute!" cried Varillo. "Tell me which way to go!—where are the brethren?"

"Outside!" he answered. "Safe!—away at the farther end of the garden, digging their own graves, as usual! Do you not hear the bell? We are alone in the building!—I have locked the doors,—the fire is kindled inside! We shall be dead before the flames burst through!"

"Madman!" shrieked Varillo, recoiling as the thick volumes of smoke rolled up from the blazing altar. "Die if you must!—but I will not! Where are the windows?—the doors?——"

"Locked and bolted fast," said Ambrosio, with a smile of triumph. "There is no loophole of escape for you! The world might let you go free to murder and betray,—but I——Ambrosio,——a scourge in the Lord's hand—I will never let you go! Pray—pray before it is too late! I heard the devil tempt you—I heard you yield to his tempting! You were both going to ruin a woman—that is devil's work. And God told me what to do—to burn the evil out by flame, and purify your soul! Pray, brother, pray!—for in the searching and tormenting fire it will be too late! Pray! Pray!"

And pressing his hands again upon the organ he struck out a passage of chords like the surging of waves upon the shore or storm-winds in the forest, and began to sing,

> " Confutatis maledictis
> Flammis acribus addictis
> Voca me cum benedictis ! "

Infuriated to madness, but too physically weak to struggle with one who, though wandering in brain, was sound in body, Varillo tried to drag him from his seat,—but the

attempt was useless. Ambrosio seemed possessed by a
thousand electric currents of force and resolution combined. He threw off Varillo as though he were a mere
child, and went on singing—

> " Oro supplex et acclinis
>   Cor contritum quasi cinis :
>   Gere curam mei finis.
>
> Lacrymosa dies illa,—"

Driven to utter desperation, Varillo stood for a moment inert,—then, suddenly catching sight of a rope
hanging from one of the windows close at hand, he rushed
to it and pulled it furiously. The top of the window
yielded, and fell open on its hinge—the smoke rushed
up to the aperture, and Florian, still clinging to the rope,
shouted, " Help!—Help! " with all the force he could
muster. But the air blowing strongly against the smoke
fanned the flames in the body of the chapel,—they leaped
higher and higher,—and—seeing the red glow deepening
about him, Ambrosio smiled.——

" Cry your loudest, you will never be heard! " he said
—" Those who are busy with graves have done with life!
You had best pray while you have time—let God take
you with His name on your lips! "

And as the smoke and flame climbed higher and higher
and began to wreathe itself about the music gallery, he
resumed his solemn singing.

> " Lacrymosa dies illa,
>   Qua resurgat ex favilla
>   Judicandus homo reus
>   Huic ergo parce, Deus :
>   Pie Jesu Domine
>   Dona eis requiem ! "

But Varillo still shrieked " Help! " and his frenzied
cries were at last answered. The great bell overhead
ceased ringing suddenly,—and its cessation created an
effect of silence even amid the noise of the crackling fire
and the continued grave music of the organ. Then came
a quick tramp of many feet—a hubbub of voices——and
loud battering knocks at the chapel door. Ambrosio
laughed triumphantly.

" We are at prayers! " he cried—" We admit no one!
The devil and I are at prayers! "

Varillo sprang at him once more.

"Madman! Show me the way!" he screamed. "Show me the way down from this place or I will strangle you!"

"Find your own way!" answered Ambrosio—"Make it—as you have always made it!——and follow it——to Hell!"

As he spoke the gallery rocked to and fro, and a tall flame leaped at the organ like a living thing ready to seize and devour. Still the knocking and hammering continued, and still Ambrosio played wild music—till all at once the chapel door was broken open and a group of pale spectral faces in monk's cowls peered through the smoke, and then retreated again.

"Help!" shrieked Varillo—"Help!"

But the air rushing through the door and meeting with that already blowing through the window raised a perfect pyramid of flame which rose straight up and completely encircled the organ. With a frightful cry Varillo rushed to Ambrosio's side, and cowering down, clung to his garments.

"Oh, God!—Oh, God! Have mercy!——"

"He will have mercy!" said Ambrosio, still keeping his hands on the organ-keys and drawing out strange plaintive chords of solemn harmony—"He will have mercy——be sure of it! Ambrosio will ask Him to be merciful!—Ambrosio has saved you from crime worse than death,——Ambrosio has cleansed you by fire! Ambrosio will help you to find God in the darkness!"

Smoke and flame encircled them,—for one moment more their figures were seen like black specks in the wreathing columns of fire——for one moment more the music of the organ thundered through the chapel,—then came a terrific crash—a roar of the victorious flames as they sprang up high to the roof of the building, and then ——then nothing but a crimson glare on the Campagna, seen for miles and miles around, and afterwards described to the world by the world's press as the "Burning Down of a Trappist Monastery" in which no lives had been lost save those of one Fra Ambrosio, long insane, who was supposed to have kindled the destructive blaze in a fit of mania,—and of a stranger, sick of malarial fever, whom the monks had sheltered, name unknown.

XXXVI.

THE same night which saw the red glare of the burning monastery reflected from end to end of the Campagna, like the glow of some gigantic pagan funeral pyre, saw also the quiet departure of Cardinal Bonpré and his "foundling" Manuel from Rome. Innocent of all evil, their escape was after the manner of the guilty; for the spies of the Vatican were on guard outside the Sovrani Palace, and one priest after another "relieved the watch" in the fashion of military sentries. But like all too cunning schemers, these pious detectives overreached the goal of their intention, and bearing in mind the fact of the Cardinal's unsuspecting simplicity, it never occurred to them to think he had been put on his guard so soon, or that he would take advantage of any secret way of flight. But the private door of Angela's studio through which Florian Varillo had fled, and the key of which he had thrown into the Tiber, had been forced open, and set in use again, and through this the harmless prelate, with his young companion, passed without notice or hindrance, and under the escort of Aubrey Leigh and Cyrillon Vergniaud, reached the railway station unintercepted by any message or messenger from the Papal court, and started for Paris and London. When the train, moving slowly at first from the platform, began to rush, and finally darted swiftly out of sight, Aubrey breathed more easily.

"Thank God!" he said. "They are safe for the present! England is a free country!"

"Is it?" And Vergniaud smiled a little. "Are you sure? England cannot dispute the authority of the Vatican over its own sworn servants. Are you not yourself contending against the power of Rome in Great Britain?"

"Not only against Rome do I contend," replied Aubrey. "My battle is against all who seek to destroy the true meaning and intention of Christianity. But so far as Romanism is concerned,—we have a monarch whose proudest title is Defender of the Faith—that is Defender of the Faith against Papal interference."

"Yes? And yet her bishops pander to Rome? Ah, my dear friend!—your monarch is kept in ignorance of the mischief being worked in her realm by the Papal secret service! Cardinal Bonpré in London is as much under the jurisdiction of the Pope as if he still remained in Rome, and though he may be able to delay the separation between himself and the boy he cherishes, he will scarcely avert it!"

"Why should they wish to part that child from him I wonder!" said Aubrey musingly.

Cyrillon shrugged his shoulders.

"Who can tell! They have their reasons, no doubt. Why should they wish to excommunicate Tolstoi? But they do! Believe me, there is a time of terror coming for the religious world—especially in your great English Empire. And when your good Queen dies, the trouble will begin!"

Aubrey was silent for some minutes.

"We must work, Cyrillon!" he said at last, laying a hand on his friend's shoulder. "We must work and we must never leave off working! One man may do much,—all history proves the conquering force of one determined will. You, young as you are, have persuaded France to listen to you,—I am doing my best to persuade England to hear me. We are only two—but others will follow. I know it is difficult!—it is harassing and often heart-breaking to insist on Truth when the whole world's press is at work bolstering up false gods, false ideals, false art, false sentiment,—but if we are firm—if we hold an unflinching faith, we shall conquer!"

"You are brave!" said Cyrillon with a glance of mingled trust and admiration. "But you are an exception to the majority of men. The majority are cruel and treacherous, and stupid as well. Dense stupidity is hard to fight against! Who for example, do you suppose, will understand the lesson of Donna Sovrani's great picture?"

"All the New World!" said Aubrey, with enthusiasm, —"It is for the New World—not the Old. And that reminds me—to-day the picture is on view to the art-critics and experts for the first time. I prophesy it will be sold at once!"

"That would make her father happy," said Cyrillon slowly. "But she—she will not care!"

Aubrey looked at him attentively.

"Have you seen her?"

"Yes. For a moment only. I called at the Sovrani Palace and her father received me. We talked for some time together. I think he knows who dealt the murderous blow at his daughter, but he says nothing positive. He showed me the picture. It is great—sublime! I could have knelt before it! Then he took me to see Her —and I would have knelt still more readily! But—she is changed!"

"And—are you?" asked Aubrey with a slight smile.

"Changed? I? No—I shall never change. I loved her at first sight—I love her still more now. Yet I see the truth—she is broken-hearted!"

"Time and great tenderness will heal the wound," said Aubrey gently. "Meanwhile have patience!"

Cyrillon gave him a look more eloquent than speech, and by mutual consent they said no more on the subject of Angela just then.

Next morning at the American Consulate, Sylvie, Comtesse Hermenstein, was quietly married by civil law to Aubrey Leigh. The ceremony took place in the presence of the Princesse D'Agramont, Madame Bozier, and Cyrillon Vergniaud. When it was over the wedded lovers and their friends returned to the Sovrani Palace, there to join Angela who had come down from her sick room to grace the occasion. She looked as fair and fragile as the delicate "Killmeny" of the poet's legend, just returned from wondrous regions of "faery," though the land poor Angela had wandered away from was the Land of Sweet Delusion, which enchanted garden she would never enter again. Pale and thin, with her beautiful eyes drooping wearily under their dreamy tired lids, she was the very ghost of her former self;—and the child-like way in which she clung to her father, and kept near her father always, was pathetic in the extreme. When Sylvie and Aubrey entered, with their three companions, she advanced to greet them, smiling bravely, though her lips quivered.

"All happiness be with you, dear!" she said softly, and she slipped a chain of fine pearls round Sylvie's neck. "These were my mother's pearls,—wear them for my sake!"

Sylvie kissed her in silence,—she could not say anything, even by the way of thanks,—her heart was too full.

"We shall be very lonely without you, darling," went on Angela. "Shall we not, father?" Prince Pietro came to her side, and taking her hand patted it consolingly ——"But we shall know you are happy in England—and we shall try and come and see you as soon as I get strong, —I want to join my uncle and Manuel. I miss Manuel very much,—he and my father are everything to me now!"

She stretched out her hand to Aubrey, who bent over it and kissed it tenderly.

"You are happy now, Mr. Leigh?" she said smiling.

"Very happy!" said Aubrey. "May you be as happy soon!"

She shook her head, and the smile passed from her eyes and lips, leaving her face very sorrowful.

"I must work," she said. "Work brings content—if it does not insure joy." Her gaze involuntarily wandered to her great picture, "The Coming of Christ," which now, unveiled in all its splendour, occupied one end of her studio, filling it with a marvellous colour and glow of light. "Yes, I must work! That big canvas of mine will not sell I fear! My father was right. It was a mistake"—and she sighed—" a mistake altogether,—in more ways than one! And what is the use of painting a picture for the world if there is no chance to let the world see it?"

Prince Pietro looked at her benevolently.

"Your father was right, you think? Well, Angela mia, I think I had better be the first to own that your father was wrong! The picture is already sold;—that is if you consent to sell it!"

Angela turned very white. "If I consent to sell it? Sell it——to whom?"

Sylvie put a caressing arm around her. "Your father had the news this morning," she said, "and we all decided to tell it to you as soon as we came back from the Consulate. A wedding-surprise on our parts, Angela!

You know the picture was on view for the first time yesterday to some of the critics and experts in Rome?"

Angela made a faint sign of assent. Her wistful eyes were full of wonder and anxiety.

"Well, among them was a purchaser for America— Oh, you need not look at me, my dear!—I have nothing to do with it! You shall see the letter your father received—and you shall decide; but the end of the whole matter is, Angela, that if you consent, the picture will be bought, not by any private purchaser, but by the American nation."

"The American nation!" repeated Angela. "Are you really, really sure of this?"

"Quite sure!" said Sylvie joyously. "And you must say good-bye to it and let it go across the wide ocean—out to the New World all alone with its grand and beautiful message,—unless you go with it and show the Americans something even more perfect and beautiful in yourself than the picture!—and you must be content to take twenty thousand pounds for it, and be acknowledged as the greatest painter of the age as well! This will be hard work, Angela!——but you must resign yourself!"

She laughed for pure delight in her friend's triumph, —but Angela turned at once to her father.

"Dearest father!" she said softly. "I am glad—for your sake!"

He folded her in his arms, too deeply moved to speak, and then as he felt her trembling, he led her to a chair and beckoned to Cyrillon Vergniaud who had stood apart, watching the little scene in silence.

"Come and talk to this dear girl!" he said. "She is not at all a good hostess to-day! She ought to entertain the bride and bridegroom here,—but it seems as if she needed to be entertained herself!" And then, as Cyrillon obeyed him, and drew near the idol of his thoughts with such hesitating reverence as might befit a pilgrim approaching the shrine of a beloved saint, he turned away and was just about to speak to the Princesse D'Agramont when a servant entered and said hurriedly—

"Monsignor Gherardi desires to see Cardinal Bonpré!"

There was a dead pause. The group of friends looked at one another in embarrassment. Angela rose from her

chair trembling and glanced instinctively at her picture
—and for a moment no one seemed quite certain what
should be done next. The Princesse D'Agramont was
the first to recover her self-possession.

"Angela must not be here," she said. "She is not
strong enough to stand a scene. And no doubt Gherardi
has come to make one! We will leave him to you, Mr.
Leigh—and to Gys Grandit!"

She withdrew at once with Angela, and in another moment Gherardi was ushered in. He glanced quickly
around him as he made his formal salutation,—his eyes
rested for a moment on Sylvie and Aubrey Leigh—then
he addressed himself to Prince Pietro.

"I am sorry to intrude upon you, Prince!" he said.
"I have an urgent matter to discuss with Cardinal Bonpré, and must see him at once."

"I regret that it is not in my power to gratify your desire, Monsignor," said Prince Sovrani with stiff courtesy.
"My brother-in-law the Cardinal left Rome last night."

"Left Rome! Left Rome!" exclaimed Gherardi.
"Who gave him permission to leave Rome?"

"Was permission necessary?" asked Aubrey, stepping
forward.

"I did not address you, sir," returned Gherardi haughtily. "I spoke to Prince Sovrani."

"Prince Sovrani might well decline to answer you,"
said Aubrey undauntedly. "Were I to make him acquainted with the fiendish plot you have contrived against
his daughter's fame and honour, he would scarcely allow
you to cross his threshold!"

Gherardi stood still, breathing quickly, but otherwise
unmoved.

"Plot?" he echoed. "You must be mad! I have no
plot against anyone. My business is to uphold the cause
of truth and justice, and I shall certainly defend the name
of the great artist who painted that picture"—and he
pointed to Angela's canvas—"Florian Varillo! Dead as
he is, his memory shall live!"

"Dead!" cried Prince Sovrani, springing forward.
"Dead! Make me sure of that, and I will praise God
even for your lying tongue, if it could for once speak
such a welcome truth!"

Gherardi drew back amazed, instinctively recoiling

from the flashing eyes and threatening figure of the irate nobleman.

"Speak!" cried Sovrani again. "Tell me that the murderer of my child's youth and joy is dead and gone to hell—and I will sing a Laus Deo at St. Peter's! I will pay you a thousand pounds in masses to keep his soul safe with the devil to whom it has gone!"

"Prince Sovrani, you are in ignorance of the facts," said Gherardi coldly. "And you speak in an anger, which if what you suspect were true, would be natural enough, but which under present circumstances is greatly misplaced. The unfortunate Florian Varillo has been ill for many days at a Trappist monastery on the Campagna. He had gone out towards Frascati on a matter connected with some business before starting for Naples, and as he was returning, he was suddenly met by the news of the assassination of his betrothed wife——"

"And he knew nothing of it——" interposed Sovrani grimly. "Of course——he knew nothing!"

"He knew nothing—how should he know!" responded Gherardi calmly—"The terrible shock threw him into a delirium and fever——he was found in a dead swoon and taken into the monastery for shelter. I saw him there only yesterday."

He paused. No one spoke.

"He was to have come to Rome to-day, and a full explanation of his absence would have been given. But last night the monastery was set on fire——"

"Thank God!" said Sovrani.

Gherardi looked at him with an air of admirably affected sorrowful reproach.

"I grieve for your injustice and cruelty, Prince!" he said—"Some natural regret there should surely be in your mind at the tragic end of one so highly gifted—one whom you had accepted as your future son-in-law. He met with a terrible death! The monastery was set on fire, as I have told you—but the doors had all been previously locked within, it is supposed by one of the monks named Ambrosio, who was subject to fits of insanity—with the tragic result that he and Varillo perished in the flames, there being no possibility of rescue."

"Then the guillotine is saved unnecessary soiling," said Sovrani fiercely. "And you, Monsignor Gherardi, should have a special 'Jubilate' sung for the world being well-rid of an exceptionally damned and damnable villain!'"

There was something terrific in the aspect of Sovrani's face and threatening attitude, and for a moment Gherardi hesitated to go on with his prepared sequence of lies. Rallying his forces at last with an effort he made a very good assumption of his most authoritative manner.

"Prince, I must ask you to be good enough to hear me patiently," he said. "Your mind has been grossly abused, and you are not aware of the true position of affairs. You imagine with some few gossips in Rome, that Florian Varillo, your daughter's betrothed husband, was guilty of the murderous attack upon her life——you are mistaken!"

"Mistaken!" Prince Pietro laughed scornfully. "Prove my mistake!—prove it!"

"I give you my word!" said Gherardi. "And I also swear to you that the picture yonder, which, though offensive to the Church and blasphemous in its teaching, is nevertheless a great masterpiece of painting, is the work of the unfortunate dead man you so greatly wrong!"

"Liar!" And Cyrillon Vergniaud sprang forward, interposing himself between Sovrani and the priest. "Liar!"

Gherardi turned a livid white.

"Who is this ruffian?" he demanded, drawing his tall form up more haughtily than before. "A servant of yours?"

"Ay, a servant of his, and of all honest men!" returned Cyrillon. "I am one whom your Church has learned to fear, but who has no fear of you!—one whom you have heard of to your cost, and will still hear of,—Gys Grandit!"

Gherardi glanced him up and down, and then turned from him in disgust as from something infected by a loathly disease.

"Prince Sovrani!" he said. "I cannot condescend to converse with a street ranter, such as this misguided person, who has most regrettably obtained admission to your house and society! I came to see your brother-in-law

Cardinal Bonpré,—who has left Rome, you tell me—therefore my business must be discussed with you alone. I must ask you for a private audience."

Sovrani looked at him steadily.

"And I must refuse it, Monsignor! If in private audience you wish to repeat the amazing falsehood you have just uttered respecting my daughter's work—I am afraid I should hardly keep my hands off you! Believe me you are safest in company!"

Monsignor Gherardi paused a moment,—then turned towards Sylvie.

"Contessa," he said very deliberately. "You can perhaps arrange this matter better than I can. Florian Varillo is dead—as I have told you; and for stating what I believe to be the truth regarding him I have been subjected to insult in your presence. I have known you for many years and I knew your father before you,—I have no wish to either distress or offend you,—do you understand? I am in your hands!"

Sylvie looked him full in the face. "My husband will answer you, Monsignor," she said. "I am in *his* hands!"

Gherardi turned as crimson as he had before been pale. "Your husband!" He strode forward with a threatening movement—then stopped short, as he confronted Aubrey Leigh. "Your husband! So! You are married then!"—and he laughed fiercely—"Married by the law, and excommunicated by the Church! A pleasant position for the last of the Hermensteins! Contessa, by your own act you have ruined the fortunes of your friends! I would have held my peace at your will,—but now all Rome shall know the truth!"

"The truth according to the convenience of papal Rome?" queried Aubrey Leigh—"The truth, as expounded to the Comtesse Hermenstein in your interview with her yesterday?"

Gherardi looked him over with superb indifference.

"My interview with the Comtesse Hermenstein was a private one"—he said,—"And if a spy was present, he must prove himself a spy. And we of the Church do not accept a spy's testimony!"

White with indignation Aubrey sprang forward,—— but Cyrillon Vergniaud restrained him.

" Patience ! " he said in a low tone—" Let him have his way for the moment——it will then be my turn ! "

" My word is law in Rome ! "—went on Gherardi—" Whatsoever I choose to say will be confirmed and ratified by the greatest authority in the world—the Pope ! I am ready to swear that Florian Varillo painted that picture,—and the Pope is ready to believe it ! Who will admit such a masterpiece to be a woman's work ? No one ! Each member of the house of Sovrani can bear witness to the fact that no one ever saw Angela Sovrani painting it ! But I know the whole story—I was the last to see Florian Varillo before his death—and he confessed the truth —that he had worked for his betrothed wife in order to give her the greater fame ! So that he was not, and could not have been her assassin——"

" Then her assassin must be found ! " said Prince Pietro suddenly. " And the owner of this sheath—the sheath of the dagger with which she was stabbed—must claim his property ! " And holding up the sheath in question before Gherardi he continued—

" This *I* found ! This *I* traced ! Varillo's servant admitted it to be his master's—Varillo's mistress recognised it as her lover's—a slight thing, Monsignor !—but an uncomfortable witness ! And if you dare to promulgate your lie against my daughter and her work, I will accuse you in the public courts of complicity in an attempted murder ! And I doubt whether the Pope will judge it politic, or a part of national diplomacy, to support you then ! "

For a moment Gherardi was baffled. His dark brows met in a frown of menace and his lips tightened with his repressed fury. Then,—still managing to speak with the utmost composure, he said,

" You will permit me to look at this dagger-sheath— this proof on which you place so much reliance ? "

In the certainty of his triumph, old Sovrani was ready to place it in the priest's extended hand, when young Vergniaud interposed and prevented him.

" No ! You can admire it from a distance, Monsignor ! You are capable in your present humour of tearing it to atoms and so destroying evidence ! As the ' servant ' of Prince Sovrani, it is my business to defend him from this possibility ! "

Gherardi raised his dark eyes and fixed them, full of bitterest scorn, on the speaker.

"So *you* are Gys Grandit!" he said in accents which thrilled with an intensity of hatred. "You are the busy Socialist, the self-advertising atheist, who, like a yelping cur, barks impotently under the wheels of Rome! You —Vergniaud's bastard——"

"Give that name to your children at Frascati!" cried Cyrillon passionately. "And own them as yours publicly, as my father owned me before he died!"

With a violent start, Gherardi reeled back as though he had been dealt a sudden blow, and over his face came a terrible change, like the grey pallor of creeping paralysis. White to the lips, he struggled for breath . . . he essayed to speak,—then failing, made a gesture with his hands as though pushing away some invisible foe. Slowly his head drooped on his breast, and he shivered like a man struck suddenly with ague. Startled and awed, everyone watched him in fascinated silence. Presently words came slowly and with difficulty between his dry lips.

"You have disgraced me!" he said hoarsely——"Are you satisfied?" He took a step or two close up to the young man. "I ask you—are you satisfied? Or—do you mean to go on——do you want to ruin me?——" Here, moved by uncontrollable passion he threw up his hands with a gesture of despair. "God! That it should come to this! That I should have to ask you——you, the enemy of the Church I serve, for mercy! Let it be enough I say!——and I——I also will be silent!"

Cyrillon looked at him straightly.

"Will you cease to persecute Cardinal Bonpré?" he demanded. "Will you admit Varillo's murderous treachery?"

Gherardi bent his head.

"I will!" he answered slowly, "because I must! Otherwise——" He clenched his fist and his eyes flashed fire—then he went on—"But beware of Lorenzo Moretti! He will depose the Cardinal from office, and separate him from that boy who has affronted the Pope. He is even now soliciting the Holy Father to intervene and stop the marriage of the Comtesse Sylvie Hermenstein with Aubrey Leigh,—and——they are married!

No more—no more!—I cannot speak—let me go—let me go—you have won your way!—I give you my promise!"

"What is your promise worth?" said Vergniaud with disdain.

"Nothing!" replied Gherardi bitterly. "Only in this one special instance it is worth all my life!—all my position! You—even you, the accursed Gys Grandit!—you have me in your power!"

He raised his head as he said this,—his face expressed mingled agony and fury; but meeting Cyrillon's eyes he shrank again as if he were suddenly whipped by a lash, and with one quick stride, reached the door, and disappeared.

There was a moment's silence after his departure. Then Aubrey Leigh spoke.

"My dear Grandit! You are a marvellous man! How came you to know Gherardi's secrets?"

"Through a section of the Christian-Democratic party here"—replied Cyrillon—"You must not forget that I, like you, have my disciples! They keep me informed of all that goes on in Rome, and they have watched Domenico Gherardi for years. We all know much—but we have little chance to speak! If England knew of Rome what France knows, what Spain knows,—what Italy knows, she would pray to be given a second Cromwell! For the time is coming when she will need him!"

XXXVII.

A few days later the fashionable world of Europe was startled by the announcement of two things. One was the marriage of Sylvie, Countess Hermenstein, to the "would-be reformer of the clergy," Aubrey Leigh, coupled with her renunciation of the Church of her fathers. There was no time for that Church to pronounce excommunication, inasmuch as she renounced it herself, of her own free will and choice, and made no secret of having done so. Some of her Hungarian friends were, or appeared to be, scandalized at this action on her part, but the majority of them treated it with considerable leniency, and in some cases with approval, on the ground that a wife's religion ought to be the same as that of her husband. If love is love at all, it surely means complete union; and one cannot imagine a perfect marriage where there is any possibility of wrangling over different forms of creed. The other piece of news, which created even more sensation than the first, was the purchase of Angela Sovrani's great picture, "The Coming of Christ," by the Americans. As soon as this was known, the crowd of visitors to the artist's studio assumed formidable proportions, and from early morning till late afternoon, the people kept coming and going in hundreds, which gradually swelled to thousands. For by-and-by the history of the picture got about in disjointed morsels of information and gossip which soon formed a consecutive and fairly correct narration. Experts criticized it,—critics "explained" it—and presently nothing was talked of in the art world but "The Coming of Christ" and the artist who painted it, Angela Sovrani. A woman!—only a woman! It seemed incredible—impossible! For why should a woman think? Why should a woman dare to be a genius? It seemed very strange! How much more natural for her to marry some decent man of established position and be content with babies and plain needlework! Here was an abnormal prodigy

in the ways of womanhood,—a feminine creature who
ventured to give an opinion of her own on something else
than dress,—who presumed as it were, to set the world
thinking hard on a particular phase of religious history! Then, as one after the other talked and whispered
and commented, the story of Angela's own private suffering began to eke out bit by bit,—how she had been
brutally stabbed in her own studio in front of her own
picture by no other than her own betrothed husband Florian Varillo, who was moved to his murderous act by a
sudden impulse of jealousy,—and how that same Varillo
had met with his deserts in death by fire in the Trappist
monastery on the Campagna. And the excitement over
the great picture became more and more intense,—especially when it was known that it would soon be taken
away from Rome never to be seen there again. Angela
herself knew little of her rapidly extending fame,—she
was in Paris with the Princesse D'Agramont who had
taken her there immediately after Monsignor Gherardi's
visit to her father. She was not told of Florian Varillo's
death till she had been some days in the French capital,
and then it was broken to her as gently as possible. But
the result was disastrous. The strength she had slowly
regained seemed now to leave her altogether, and she
was stricken with a mute despair which was terrible to
witness. Hour after hour, she lay on a couch, silent and
motionless,—her large eyes fixed on vacancy, her little
white hands clasped close together as though in a very
extremity of bodily and mental anguish, and the Princesse
D'Agramont, who watched her and tended her with the
utmost devotion, was often afraid that all her care would
be of no avail, and that her patient would slip through
her hands into the next world before she had time to
even attempt to save her. And Cyrillon Vergniaud, unhappy and restless, wandered up and down outside the
house, where this life, so secretly dear to him, was poised
as it were on the verge of death, not daring to enter, or
even enquire for news, lest he should hear the worst.

One cold dark afternoon however, as he thus paced to
and fro, he saw the Princesse D'Agramont at a window
beckoning him, and with a sickening terror at his heart,
he obeyed the signal.

"I wish you would come and talk to her!" said the

Princesse as she greeted him, with tears in her bright eyes. "She must be roused from this apathy. I can do nothing with her. But I think *you* might do much if you would!"

"I will do anything—anything in the wide world!" said Cyrillon earnestly. "Surely you know that!"

"Yes—but you must not be too gentle with her! I do not mean that you should be rough—God forbid!—but if you would speak to her with authority——if you could tell her that she owes her life and her work to the world ——to God——"

She broke off, not trusting herself to say more. Cyrillon raised her hand to his lips.

"I understand!" he said. "You know I have hesitated—because—I love her! I cannot tell her not to grieve for her dead betrothed, when I myself am longing to take his place!"

The Princesse smiled through her tears.

"The position is difficult I admit!" she said, with a returning touch of playfulness—"But the very fact of your love for her should give you the force to command her back to life. Come!"

She took him into the darkened room where Angela lay—inert, immovable, with always the same wide-open eyes, blank with misery and desolation, and said gently,

"Angela, will you speak to Gys Grandit?"

Angela turned her wistful looks upon him, and essayed a poor little ghost of a smile. Very gently Cyrillon advanced and sat down beside her,—and with equal gentleness, the Princesse D'Agramont withdrew. Cyrillon's heart beat fast; if he could have lifted that frail little form of a woman into his arms and kissed away the sorrow consuming it, he would have been happy,—but his mission was that of a friend, not lover, and his own emotions made it hard for him to begin. At last he spoke.

"When are you going to make up your mind to get well, dear friend?"

She looked at him piteously.

"Make up my mind to get well? I shall never be well again!"

"You will if you resolve to be," said Cyrillon. "It rests with you!"

She was silent.

"Have you heard the latest news from Rome?" he asked after a pause.

She made a faint sign in the negative.

Cyrillon smiled.

"The Church has with all due solemnity anathematized your picture as an inspiration of the Evil One! But it is better that it should be so anathematized than that it should be reported as not your own work. Between two lies, the emissaries of the Vatican have chosen the one least dangerous to themselves."

Angela sighed wearily.

"You do not care?" queried Cyrillon. "Neither anathema nor lie has any effect on you?"

She raised her left hand and looked dreamily at the circlet of rubies on it—Florian Varillo's betrothal ring.

"I care for nothing," she said slowly. "Nothing—now he is gone!"

A bitter pang shot through Cyrillon's heart. He was quite silent. Presently she turned her eyes wistfully towards him.

"Please do not think me ungrateful for all your kindness!—but—I cannot forget!"

"Dear Donna Sovrani, may I speak to you fully and frankly—as a friend? May I do so without offence?"

She looked at him and saw how pale he was, how his lips trembled, and the consciousness that he was unhappy moved her to a faint sense of compunction.

"Of course you may!" she answered gently. "I know you do not hate me."

"Hate you!" Cyrillon paused, his eyes softening with a great tenderness as they rested upon her. "Who could hate you?"

"Florian hated me," she said. "Not always,—no! He loved me once! Only when he saw my picture, then his love perished. Ah, my Florian! Had I known, I would have destroyed all my work rather than have given him a moment's pain!"

"And would that have been right?" asked Cyrillon earnestly. "Would not such an act have been one of selfishness rather than sacrifice?"

A faint color crept over her pale cheeks.

"Selfishness?——"

"Yes! Your love for him was quite a personal matter,—but your work is a message to the world. You would have sacrificed the world for his sake, even though he had murdered you!"

"I would!" she answered, and her eyes shone like stars as she spoke. "The world is nothing to me; love was everything!"

"That is your way of argument," said Cyrillon. "But it is not God's way!"

She was silent, but her looks questioned him.

"Genius like yours," he went on, "is not given to you for yourself alone. You cannot tamper with it, or play with it, for the sake of securing a little more temporal happiness or peace for yourself. Genius is a crown of thorns,—not a wreath of flowers to be worn at a feast of pleasure! You wished your life to be one of love,—God has chosen to make it one of suffering. You say the world is nothing to you,—then my dear friend, God insists that it shall be something to you! Have you the right—I ask you, have you the right to turn away from all your fellow mortals and say—'No—because I have been disappointed in my hope and my love, then I will have nothing to do with life—I will turn away from all who need my help—I will throw back the gifts of God with scorn to the Giver, and do nothing simply because I have lost what I myself specially valued!'"

Her eyes fell beneath his straight clear regard, and she moved restlessly.

"Ah you do not know—you do not understand!" she said. "I am not thinking of myself—indeed I am not! But I feel as if my work—my picture—had killed Florian! I hate myself!—I hate everything I have ever done, or could ever possibly do. I see him night and day in those horrible flames!—Oh God! those cruel flames!—he seems to reproach me,—even to curse me for his death!"

She shuddered and turned her face away. Cyrillon ventured to take her hand.

"That is not like you, dear friend!" he said, his rich voice trembling with the pity he felt for her. "That is not like your brave spirit! You look only at one aspect of grief—you see the darkness of the cloud, but not its brighter side. If I were to say that he whom you loved so greatly has perhaps been taken to save him from even

a worse fate, you would be angry with me. You loved
him—yes; and whatever he did or attempted to do, even
to your injury, you would have loved him still had he
lived! That is the angel half of woman's nature. You
would have given him your fame had he asked you for it,
—you would have pardoned him a thousand times over
had he sought your pardon,—you would have worked for
him like a slave and been content to die with your genius
unrecognized if that would have pleased him. Yes I
know! But God saw your heart—and his—and with
God alone rests the balance of justice. You must not
set yourself in opposition to the law; you,—such a harmonious note in work and life,—must not become a
discord!"

She did not speak. Her hand lay passively in his, and
he went on.

"Death is not the end of life. It is only the beginning
of a new school of experience. Your very grief,—your
present inaction, may for all we know, be injuring the soul
of the man whose loss you mourn!"

She sighed.

"Do you think that possible——?"

"I do think it very possible," he answered. "Natural
sorrow is not forbidden to us,—but a persistent dwelling
on cureless grief is a trespass against the law. Moreover
you have been endowed with a great talent,—it is not
your own—it is lent to you to use for others, and you have
no right to waste it. The world has taken your work with
joy, with gratitude, with thanksgiving; will you say that
you do not care for the world?—that you will do nothing
more for it?—Because one love—one life, has been taken
from you, will you discard all love, all life? Dear friend,
that will not be reasonable,—not right, nor just, nor
brave!"

A wistful longing filled her eyes.

"I wish Manuel were here!" she said plaintively. "He
would understand!"

"Manuel is with Cardinal Bonpré in London," replied Cyrillon. "I heard from Aubrey yesterday that
they are going about together among the poor, doing
good everywhere. Would you like to join them? Your
friend Sylvie would be glad to have you stay with her, I
am sure."

She gave a hopeless gesture.

"I am not strong enough to go——" she began.

"You will be strong enough when you determine to be," said Cyrillon. "Your frightened soul is making a coward of your body!"

She started and drew her hand away from his gentle clasp.

"You are harsh!" she said, looking at him straightly. "I am not frightened—I never was a coward!"

Something of the old steady light came back to her eyes, and Cyrillon inwardly rejoiced to see it.

"My words seem rough," he said, "but truly they are not so. I repeat, your soul is frightened—yes! frightened at the close approach of God! God is never so near to us as in a great sorrow; and when we feel His presence almost within sight and touch, we are afraid. But we must not give way to fear; we must not grovel in the dust and hide ourselves as if we were ashamed! We must rise up and grow accustomed to His glory, and let Him lead us where He will!"

He paused, for Angela was weeping. The sound of her low sobbing smote him to the heart.

"Angela——Angela!" he whispered, more to himself than to her. "Have I hurt you so much?"

"Yes, yes!" she murmured between her tears. "You have hurt me!—but you are right——you are quite right! I am selfish—weak—cowardly—ungrateful too;—but forgive me,—have patience with me!—I will try—I will try to bear it all more bravely—I will indeed!"

He rose from her side and paced the room, not trusting himself to speak. She looked at him anxiously and endeavoured to control her sobs.

"You are angry?"

"Angry!" He came back, and lifting her suddenly, but gently like a little child, he placed her in an easy sitting position, leaning cosily among her pillows. "Come!" he said smiling, as the colour flushed her cheeks at the swiftness of his action—"Let the Princesse D'Agramont see that I am something of a doctor! You will grow weaker and weaker lying down all day—I want to make you strong again! Will you help me?"

He looked into her eyes, and her own fell before his earnest, reverent, but undisguisedly tender glance.

" I will try to do what you wish," she said. " If I fail you must forgive me——but I will honestly try ! "

" If you try, you will succeed "—said Cyrillon, and bending down, he kissed the trembling little hands—" Ah ! forgive me ! If you knew how dear your life is——to——to many, you would not waste it in weeping for what cannot be remedied by all your tears ! I will not say one word against the man you loved—for *you* do not say it, and you are the most injured ;—he is dead—let him rest ;—but life claims you,—claims me for the moment ;—our fellow-men and women claim our attention, our work, our doing for the best and greatest while we can,—our duty is to them, —not to ourselves ! Will you for your father's sake—for the world's sake—if I dared say, for *my* sake !—will you throw off this torpor of sorrow ? Only you can do it,— only you yourself can command the forces of your own soul ! Be Angela once more !—the guiding angel of more lives than you know of !—"

His voice sank to a pleading whisper.

" I will try ! " she answered in a low voice——" I promise !—"

And when the Princess D'Agramont entered she was surprised and overjoyed to find her patient sitting up on her couch for the first time in many days, talking quietly with the Perseus she had sent to rescue the poor Andromeda from the jaws of a brooding Melancholia which might have ended in madness or death. With her presence the conversation took a lighter tone—and by-and-by Angela found herself listening with some interest to the reading of her father's last letter addressed to her kind hostess.

" Angela's picture is gone out of Rome "—he wrote— " It was removed from the studio in the sight of an enormous crowd which had assembled to witness its departure. The *Voce Della Verita* has described it as a direct inspiration of the devil, and suggests the burning-down of the studio in which it was painted, as a means of purifying the Sovrani Palace from the taint of sulphur and brimstone. *La Croix* demands the excommunication of the artist, which by the way is very likely to happen. The *Osservatore Romano* wishes that the ship specially chartered to take it to America, may sink with all on board. All of which kind and charitable wishes on the part of the Vatican press have so augmented the fame of 'The Coming of Christ' that the picture could hardly be got through the crush of people craning their necks to get a glimpse of it. It is now en route via Bordeaux for London, where it is to be exhibited for six weeks. As soon as I have finished superintending the putting by of a few home treasures here, I shall join you in Paris, when I hope to find my dear girl nearly restored to her usual self. It will please her to know that her friend the charming Sylvie is well and very happy. She was married for the second time before a Registrar in London, and is now, as she proudly writes, 'well and truly' Mrs. Aubrey Leigh, having entirely dropped her title in favour of her husband's plainer, but to her more valuable designation. Of course spiteful people will say she ceased to be Countess Hermenstein in order not to be recognized too soon as the 'renegade from the Roman Church,' but that sort of thing is to be expected. Society never gives you credit for honest motives, but only for dishonest ones. We who know Sylvie, also know what her love for her husband is, and that it is love alone which inspires all her actions in regard to him. Her chief anxiety at present seems to be about Angela's health, and she tells me she telegraphs to you every day for news——"

"Is that true?" asked Angela, interrupting the reading of her father's letter. "Does Sylvie in all her new happiness, actually think of me so much and so often?"

"Indeed she does!" replied the Princess D'Agramont. "Chère enfant, you must not look at all the world through the cloud of one sorrow! We all love you!—we are all anxious to see you quite yourself again!"

Angela's eyes filled with tears as they rested on her friend's kindly face, a face usually so brilliant in its animated expression, but now saddened and worn by constant watching and fatigue.

"You are far too good to me," she said in a low voice— "And I am most unworthy of all your attention."

Loyse D'Agramont paid no heed to this remark, but resumed reading the Prince Sovrani's epistle——

"Let me see! . . . Sylvie—yes——here it is—'She telegraphs to you every day for news, which is apparently the only extravagance she is guilty of just now. She and her husband have taken rooms in some very poor neighbourhood of London, and are beginning work in real earnest. Our good Felix and his cherished foundling have been with them into many wretched homes, cheering the broken-hearted, comforting the sick, and assuring all those who doubt it that there is a God in spite of priest-craft,—and I have received an English paper which announces that Mr. Aubrey Leigh will give one of his famous " Addresses to the People " on the last day of the year. I should like to hear him, though my very slight knowledge of English would be rather against me in the comprehension of what he might say. For all other news you must wait till we meet. Expect me in Paris in a few days, and ask my Angela to rouse herself sufficiently to give her old father a smile of welcome. My compliments to " Gys Grandit," and to you the assurance of my devoted homage. Pietro Sovrani.' "

The Princesse folded up the letter and looked wistfully at Angela.

" You will give him the smile of welcome he asks for, will you not, little one? " she asked. " You are all he has in the world, remember! "

" I do remember," murmured Angela. " I know! "

" Aubrey and his wife are ' beginning work in real earnest ' ! " said Cyrillon. " And how much their work will mean to the world! More than the world can at present imagine or estimate! It seems to be a settled thing that the value of great work shall never be recognised during the worker's lifetime, but only afterwards—when he or she who was so noble, so self-sacrificing, or so far-seeing, shall have passed beyond the reach of envy, scorn and contumely, into other regions of existence and development. The finest deeds are done without acknowledgment or reward, and when the hero or heroine has gone beyond recall, the whole world stands lamenting its blindness for not having known or loved them better. Donna Sovrani "—and his voice softened—" will also soon begin again to work, like Aubrey and Sylvie, ' in real earnest.' Will she not? "

Angela raised her eyes, full of sadness, yet also full of light.

" Yes," she said. " I will! I will work my grief into a glory if I can! And the loss of world's love shall teach me to love God more! "

Loyse D'Agramont embraced her.

"That is my Angela!" she said. "That is what I wanted you to feel——to know——for I too have suffered!"

"I know you have—and I should have remembered it!" said Angela, penitently. "But—I have been frozen with grief——paralysed in brain and heart, and I have forgotten so many things!" She trembled and closed her eyes for a moment,—then went on—"Give me a little time—a few more days!—and I will prove that I am not ungrateful for your love——" She hesitated, and then turning, gave her hand to Cyrillon,——"or for your friendship."

He bent over the little hand and kissed it reverently, and soon afterwards took his leave, more light of heart, and more hopeful in spirit, than he had been for many days. He felt he could now go on with his work, part of which was the task of distributing the money his father had left him, among the poor of Paris. He considered that to leave money to the poor after death is not half such a Christian act as to give it while alive. Distributors, secretaries, lawyers, and red-tapeism come in with the disposal of wealth after we are gone ;—but to give it to those in need with our own hands—to part with it freely and to deny ourselves something in order to give it,—that is doing what Christ asked us to do. And whether we are blessed or cursed by those whom we seek to benefit, none can take away from us the sweet sense of peace and comfort which is ours to enjoy, when we know that we have in some small measure tried to serve our Divine Master, for the "full measure" of content, "pressed down and running over" which He has promised to those who "freely give," has never yet been known to fail.

And Cyrillon Vergniaud was given this happiness of the highest, purest kind, as with the aid of the wondering and reluctant Monsieur André Petitot, he gave poor families comfort for life, and rescued the sick and the sorrowful,—and all he reserved to himself from his father's large fortune was half a million francs. For he learned that most of the money he inherited had come to the late Abbé through large bequests left to him by those who had believed in him as a righteous priest of spotless reputation, and Cyrillon's conscience would not allow him to take advantage of money thus obtained, as he sternly told himself, " on false pretences."

" My father would not have wished me to keep it after his public confession," he said. " And I will not possess more than should have been spared in common justice to aid my mother's life and mine. The rest shall be used for the relief of those in need. And I know,—if I told Angela—she would not wish it otherwise ! "

So he had his way. And while his prompt help and personal supervision of the distribution of his wealth brought happiness to hundreds of homes, he was rewarded by seeing Angela grow stronger every day. The hue of health came gradually back to her fair cheeks,— her eyes once more recovered their steadfast brightness and beauty, and as from time to time he visited her and watched her with all the secret passion and tenderness he felt, his heart grew strong within him.

" She will love me one day if I try to deserve her love," he thought. " She will love me as she has never loved yet ! No woman can understand the true worth of love, unless her lover loves her more than himself ! This is a joy my Angela has not yet been given,—it will be for me to give it to her ! "

XXXVIII.

WITH the entry of Angela's great picture " The Coming of Christ" into London, where it became at once the centre of admiration, contention and general discussion, one of the most singular " religious " marriage ceremonies ever known, took place in a dreary out-lying district of the metropolis, where none but the poorest of the poor dwell, working from dawn till night for the merest pittance which scarcely pays them for food and lodging. It was one of Aubrey Leigh's "centres," and to serve his needs for a church he had purchased a large wooden structure previously used for the storing of damaged mechanical appliances, such as worn-out locomotives, old railway carriages, and every kind of lumber that could possibly accumulate anywhere in a dock or an engine yard. The building held from three to four thousand people closely packed, and when Leigh had secured it for his own, he was as jubilant over his possession as if the whole continent of Europe had subscribed to build him a cathedral. He had the roof mended and made rain-proof, and the ground planked over to make a decent flooring,—then he had it painted inside a dark oak colour, and furnished it with rows of benches. At the upper end a raised platform was erected, and in the centre of that platform stood a simple Cross of roughly carved dark wood, some twelve or fifteen feet in height. There was no other adornment in the building,—the walls remained bare, the floor unmatted, the seats uncushioned. No subscriptions were asked for its maintenance; no collection plate was ever sent around, yet here, whenever Leigh announced a coming " Address," so vast a crowd assembled that it was impossible to find room for all who sought admittance. And here, on one cold frosty Sunday morning, with the sun shining brightly through the little panes of common glass which had been inserted to serve as windows, he walked through a densely packed and expectant throng of poor, ill-clad, work-worn, yet evidently earnest and reverent men and women, leading his fair wife Sylvie, clad in bridal white, by the hand, up to the platform, and there stood facing the crowd. He was followed by Cardinal Bonpré and—Manuel. The Cardinal wore no outward sign of his ecclesiastical dignity,—he was simply attired in an ordinary priest's surtout, and his tall dignified figure, his fine thoughful face and his reverend age, won for him silent looks of admiration and respect from many who knew nothing of him or of the Church to which he belonged, but simply looked upon him as a friend of their idolized teacher, Aubrey Leigh. Manuel passed through the crowd almost unnoticed, and it was only when he stood near the Cross, looking down upon the upturned thousands of faces, that a few remarked his presence. The people had assembled in full force on this occasion, an invitation having gone forth in Leigh's name asking them " to be witnesses of his marriage," and the excitement was intense, as Sylvie, veiled as a bride, obeyed the gentle signal of her husband, and took her seat on the platform by the side of the Cardinal on the left hand of the great Cross, against which Manuel leaned lightly like a child who is not conscious of observation, but who simply takes the position which seems to him most natural. And when the subdued murmuring of the crowd had died into comparative silence, Aubrey, advancing a little to the front of the Cross, spoke in clear ringing tones, which carried music to the ears and conviction to the heart.

" My friends ! I have asked you all here in your thousands, to witness the most sacred act of my human life —my marriage ! By the law of this realm,—by the law of America, the country of my birth,—that marriage is already completed and justified,—but no ' religious ' ceremony has yet been performed between myself and her whom I am proud and grateful to call wife. To my mind however, a ' religious ' ceremony is necessary, and I have chosen to hold it here,—with you who have listened to me in this place many and many a time,—with you as witnesses to the oath of fidelity and love I am about to take in the presence of God ! There is no clergyman present— no one to my knowledge of any Church denomination except a Cardinal of the Church of Rome who is my guest and friend, but who takes no part in the proceedings.

The Cross alone stands before you as the symbol of the
Christian faith,—and what I swear by that symbol means
for me a vow that shall not be broken either in this world,
or in the world to come! I need scarcely tell you that this
is not the usual meaning of marriage in our England of to-
day. There is much blasphemy in the world, but one of
the greatest blasphemies of the age is the degradation of
the sacrament of matrimony,—the bland tolerance with
which an ordained priest of Christ presumes to invoke the
blessing of God upon a marriage between persons whom
he knows are utterly unsuited to each other in every way,
who are not drawn together by love, but only by worldly
considerations of position and fortune. I have seen these
marriages consummated. I have seen the horrible and
often tragic results of such unholy union. I have known
of cases where a man, recognized as a social blackguard
of the worst type, whose ways of life are too odious to be
named, has been accepted as a fitting mate for a young
innocent girl just out of school, because he is a Lord or
a Duke or an Earl. Anything for money! Anything for
the right to stand up and crow over your neighbours!
When an inexperienced girl or woman is united for life to
a loathsome blackguard, an open sensualist, a creature far
lower than the beasts, yet possessed of millions, she is
'congratulated' as being specially to be envied, when as a
matter of strict honesty, it would be better if she were in
her grave. The prayers and invocations pronounced at
such marriages are not 'religious,'—they are mere profanity! The priest who says 'Those whom God hath joined
together let no man put asunder,' over such immoral
wedlock, is guilty of a worse sacrilege than if he trampled
on the bread and wine of Christ's Communion! For
marriage was not intended to be a mere union of bodies,
—but a union of souls. It is the most sacred bond of
humanity. From the love which has created that bond,
is born new life,—life which shall be good or evil according to the spirit in which husband and wife are wedded.
'The sins of the fathers shall be visited on the children,'
—and the first and greatest sin is bodily union without
soul-love. It is merely a form of animal desire,—and
from desire alone no good or lofty thing can spring. We
are not made to be 'as the beasts that perish'—though
materialists and sensualists delight in asserting such to be

our destiny, in order to have ground whereon to practise their own vices. This planet, the earth, is set under our dominion; the beasts are ours to control,—they do not control us. Our position therefore is one of supremacy. Let us not voluntarily fall from that position to one even lower than the level of beasts! The bull, the goat, the pig, are moved by animal desire alone to perpetuate their kind —but we,—we have a grander mission to accomplish than theirs—we in our union are not only responsible for the Body of the next generation to come, but for the brain, the heart, the mind, and above all the Soul! If we wed in sin, our children must be born in sin. If we make our marriages for worldly advantage, vanity, blind desire, or personal convenience, our children will be moulded on those passions, and grow up to be curses to the world they live in. Love, and love only of the purest, truest, and highest kind, must be the foundation of the marriage Sacrament,—love that is prepared to endure all the changes of fate and fortune—love that is happy in working and suffering for the thing beloved—love that counts nothing a hardship,—neither sickness, nor sorrow, nor poverty, provided it can keep its faith unbroken!"

He paused—there was a slight stir among the audience, but otherwise not a sound. Sylvie sat quiet, a graceful, nymph-like figure, veiled in her cloudy white—Cardinal Bonpré's mild blue eyes raised to the speaker's face, were full of rapt attention—and Manuel still leaning against the great Cross seemed absorbed in dreamy and beautiful thoughts of his own.

"I should like," went on Aubrey with increasing warmth and passion, "to tell you what I mean by 'faith unbroken.' It is the highest form of love,—the only firm rock of friendship. It leaves no room for suspicion,—no place for argument—no cause for contradiction. It is the true meaning of the wedding-ring. Apart from marriage altogether, it is the only principle that can finally civilize and elevate man. So long as we doubt God and mistrust our fellows, so long must corruption sway business, and wars move nations. The man who gives us cause to suspect his honesty,—the man who forces us to realize the existence of treachery, is a worse murderer than he who stabs us bodily to death; for he has tainted our soul; he has pushed us back many steps on our journey Godward, and has made us wonder and question whether in truth a God can exist who tolerates in His universe such a living lie! It is only when we have to contemplate a broken faith that we doubt God! For a broken faith is an abnormal prodigy in the natural scheme of the universe—a discord in the eternal music of the stars! There are no treacheries, no falsifying of accounts, in the Divine order of the Law. The sun does not fail to rise each morning, whether clouds obscure the sky or not,—the moon appears at her stated seasons and performs her silver-footed pilgrimage faithfully to time—the stars move with precision in their courses,—and so true are they to their ordainment, that we are able to predict the manner in which they will group themselves and shine, years after we have passed away. In the world of Nature the leaves bud, and the birds nest at the coming of Spring; the roses bloom in Summer—the harvest is gathered in Autumn,—the whole marvellous system moves like a grand timepiece whose hands are never awry, whose chimes never fail to ring the exact hour,—and in all the splendour of God's gifts to us there is no such thing as a broken faith! Only we,—we, the creatures He has endowed with 'His own image,'—Free-will,—break our faith with Him and with each other. And so we come to mischief, inasmuch as broken faith is no part of God's Intention. And when two persons, man and woman, swear to be true to each other before God, so long as life shall last, and afterwards break that vow, confusion and chaos result from their perjury, and all the pestilential furies attending on a wrong deed whip them to their graves! In these times of ours, when wars and rumours of wars shake the lethargic souls of too-exultant politicians and statesmen with anxiety for themselves if not for their country, we hear every day of men and women breaking their marriage vows as lightly as though God were not existent,—we read of princes whose low *amours* are a disgrace to the world—of dukes and earls who tolerate the unchastity of their wives in order that they themselves may have the more freedom,—of men of title and position who even sell their wives to their friends in order to secure some much-needed cash or social advantage,—and while our law is busy night and day covering up 'aristocratic' crimes from publicity, and showing forth the far smaller sins of hard-working poverty, God's law is at work in a totally different way. The human judge may excuse a king's vices,—but before God there are neither kings nor commoners, and punishment falls where it is due! Christ taught us that the greatest crime is treachery, for of Judas He said 'it were better for that man that he had never been born,' and for the traitor and perjurer death is not the end, but the beginning, of evils. Against the man who accepts the life of a woman given to him in trust and love, and then betrays that life to misery, all Nature arrays itself in opposition and disaster. We, as observers of the great Play of human existence, may not at once see, among the numerous shifting scenes, where the evil-doer is punished, or the good man rewarded,—but wait till the end!—till the drop-curtain falls—and we shall see that there is no mistake in God's plan—no loophole left for breaking faith even with a child,—no 'permit' existing anywhere to destroy the life of the soul by so much as one false or cruel word! It is with a deep sense of the exact balance of God's justice, that I stand before you to-day, my friends, and ask you without any accepted ritual or ceremonial to hear my vows of marriage. She to whom I pledge my word and life, is one who in the world's eyes is accounted great, because rich in this world's goods,—but her wealth has no attraction for me, and for my own self I would rather she had been poor. Nevertheless, were she even greater than she is,—a crowned queen with many kingdoms under her control, and I but the poorest of her servants, nothing could undo the love we have for each other,—nothing could keep our lives asunder! Love and love only is our bond of union—sympathy of mind and heart and spirit; wealth and rank would have been but causes of division between us if love had not been greater. The world will tell you differently—the world will say that I have married for money—but you who know me better than the world, will feel by my very words addressed to you to-day that my marriage is a true marriage, in which no grosser element than love can enter. My wife's wealth remains her own—settled upon her absolutely and always, and I am personally as poor as when I first came among you and proved to you that hard work was a familiar friend. But I am rich in the possession of the helpmate God has given me, and with the ut-

most gratitude and humility I ask you to bear witness to
the fact that this day before you and in the presence of
the symbol of the Christian faith, I take my oath to be
true to her and only her while life shall last!"

Here going to where Sylvie stood, he took her by the
hand, and led her to the front of the platform. Then he
turned again to his eager and expectant audience.

"In your presence, my friends, and in the presence of
God and before the Cross, I take Sylvie Hermenstein to
be my wedded wife! I swear to devote myself to her,
body and soul,—to cherish her first and last of all human
creatures,—to be true to her in thought, word and deed,
—to care for her in sickness as in health, in age as in
youth,—to honour her as my chiefest good,—and to die
faithful to her in this world,—hoping by the mercy of
God to complete a more perfect union with her in the
world to come! In the name of Christ, Amen!"

And then Sylvie threw back her veil and turned her
enchanting face upon the crowd,—a face fairer than ever,
irradiated by the love and truth of her soul,—and the people gazed and wondered, and wondering held their breath
as her clear accents rang through the silence.

"In your presence, and in the presence of God and before the Cross, I take Aubrey Leigh to be my wedded
husband! I swear to devote myself to him body and soul,
to cherish him first and last of all human creatures,—to
be true to him in thought, word and deed,—to care for
him in sickness as in health, in age as in youth,—to honour
him as my chiefest good,—and to die faithful to him in
this world,—praying God in His mercy to complete a
more perfect union with him in the world to come. In the
name of Christ, Amen!"

Then Aubrey, taking his wife's hand, placed for the
first time on her finger the golden wedding-ring.

"In the presence of you all, before God, I place this
ring upon my wife's hand as a symbol of unbreaking faith
and loyalty! I pledge my life to hers; and promise to defend her from all evil, to shelter her, to work for her, and
to guard her with such tenderness as shall not fail! I
swear my faith; and may God forsake me if I break my
vow!"

And Sylvie without hesitation, responded in her sweet
clear voice.

"In the presence of you all, before God, I take this ring and wear it as a symbol of my husband's trust in me, and a token of his love! I pledge my life to his; and promise to uphold the honour of his name,—to obey him in every just and rightful wish,—to defend his actions,—to guard his home in peace and good report,—and to surround him with such tenderness as shall not fail! I swear my faith; and may God forsake me if I break my vow!"

There followed a deep and almost breathless silence. Then Aubrey spoke once more, standing before the throng with Sylvie by his side and her hand clasped in his.

"I thank you all, my friends! Strange and unlike all marriage ceremonies as ours is to-day, I feel that it is a sacred and a binding one! Your thousands of eyes and ears have heard and seen us swear our marriage vows—your thousands of hearts and minds have understood the spirit in which we accept this solemn sacrament! I will ask you before we go, to kneel down with us and repeat 'The Prayer of Heart-searching' which I have said with you so often, and to then quietly disperse."

In one moment the vast crowd was kneeling, and Cardinal Bonpré's aged eyes filled with tears of emotion as he saw all these human beings, moved by one great wave of sympathy, prostrate themselves before the simple Cross where the wedded lovers knelt also, and where Manuel alone stood, like one who is too sure of God to need the help of prayer.

And Aubrey, thrilled to the heart by the consciousness that all the members of that huge congregation were with him in his ideal dream of Christian Union, offered up this supplication—

"All-powerful God! Most loving and beneficent Creator of the Universe! We Thy creatures, who partake with Thee the endowment of immortality, now beseech Thee to look upon us here, kneeling in adoration before Thee! Search our hearts and souls with the light of Thy revealing Holy Spirit, and see if in any of us there is concealed an unworthy thought, or doubt, or distrust, or scorn of Thy unfailing goodness! We ask Thee to discover our sins and imperfections to ourselves, and so instruct us as to what is displeasing to Thee, that we may remedy these wilful blots upon Thy fair intention. Give us the force and fervour, the wisdom and truth, to find

and follow the way Thou wouldst have us go,—and if
our strength should fail, constrain us, oh God, to come
to Thee, whether we learn by sorrow or joy, by punishment or pity;—constrain us, so that we may find Thee,
whatever else we lose! Let the great searchlight of Thy
truth be turned upon the secret motives of our hearts and
minds, and if there be one of us in whom such motives
be found false, impure, cruel or cowardly, then let Thy
just wrath fall upon the misguided creature of Thy love,
and teach him or her, obedience and repentance! We
pray that Thou wilt punish us, oh God, when we have
sinned, that we may know wherein we have offended our
dear Father;—and equally, when we have sought to serve
Thee faithfully, may we receive Thy blessing! Make us
one with Thee in Thy perfect plan of good; teach us how
to work Thy will in the fulfilment of peace and joy; make
our lives of use to this world, and our deaths gain to the
next, and let the glory of Thy love encompass us, guide
us, and defend us now and forever, through Christ our
Lord, Amen."

After he had ceased, there was a deep silence for many
minutes, then all the people as if moved by one impulse,
rose from their knees, and standing, sang the following
stanzas, which Aubrey had taught them when he first began to preach among them his ideals of love and labour.

> * If thou'rt a Christian in deed and thought,
> Loving thy neighbour as Jesus taught,—
> Living all days in the sight of Heaven,
> And not *one* only out of seven,—
> Sharing thy wealth with the suffering poor,
> Helping all sorrow that Hope can cure,—
> Making religion a truth in the heart,
> And not a cloak to be worn in the mart,
> Or in high cathedrals and chapels and fanes,
> Where priests are traders and count the gains,—
> All God's angels will say, " Well done !"
> Whenever thy mortal race is run.
> White and forgiven,
> Thou'lt enter heaven,
> And pass, unchallenged, the Golden Gate,
> Where welcoming spirits watch and wait
> To hail thy coming with sweet accord
> To the Holy City of God the Lord !

* By the late Charles Mackay, LL. D., F. S. A.

If Peace is thy prompter, and Love is thy guide,
And white-robed Charity walks by thy side,—
If thou tellest the truth without oath to bind,
Doing thy duty to all mankind,—
Raising the lowly, cheering the sad,
Finding some goodness e'en in the bad,
And owning with sadness if badness there be,
There might have been badness in thine and in thee,
If Conscience the warder that keeps thee whole
Had uttered no voice to thy slumbering soul,—
    All God's angels will say, " Well done ! "
    Whenever thy mortal race is run.
            White and forgiven,
            Thou'lt enter heaven,
    And pass, unchallenged, the Golden Gate,
    Where welcoming spirits watch and wait
    To hail thy coming with sweet accord
    To the Holy City of God the Lord !

If thou art humble, and wilt not scorn,
However wretched, a brother forlorn,—
If thy purse is open to misery's call,
And the God thou lovest is God of all,
Whatever their colour, clime or creed,
Blood of thy blood, in their sorest need,—
If every cause that is good and true,
And needs assistance to dare and do,
Thou helpest on through good and ill,
With trust in Heaven, and God's good will,—
    All God's angels will say, " Well done ! "
    Whenever thy mortal race is run.
            White and forgiven,
            Thou'lt enter heaven,
    And pass, unchallenged, the Golden Gate,
    Where welcoming spirits watch and wait
    To hail thy coming with sweet accord
    To the Holy City of God the Lord !

The effect of the last eight-line chorus sung by thousands of voices, was marvellous.   Such a spirit of exaltation pervaded the music that the common wooden shed-
like building in which these followers of one earnest man
asserted their faith in God rather than in a Church,
seemed to take upon itself all the architectural beauty of a
temple costing millions of money.   When the singing
ceased, Aubrey raised his hand, and while his audience
yet remained standing, pronounced the blessing.

" God be with you all, my friends !—in your hearts and
lives and daily conduct !   May none of you here present
shadow His brightness by one dark deed or thought of
evil !   I will ask you to pray that God may be with me
too, and with my beloved wife, the future partner of all

my work, my joys and sorrows, that we may in our union make our lives useful to you and to all others who seek our help or care. God's blessing be upon us all in the name of Christ our Saviour!"

And with one accord the people answered "Amen!"

Then this brief service over, they began to disperse. Without any scramble or rush, but in perfect order and with quiet and reverent demeanour, they left their seats and began to make their way out. None of them were seen gossiping together, or smiling or nodding over each other's shoulders as is very often the case when a congregation disperses from a fashionable church. For these people in their worship of the Creator, found something reverent, something earnest, something true, valuable and necessary to daily living,—and though there were two peaceful-looking constables stationed at the door of egress, their services were not required to either keep order or compel any of those thousands of poor to "move on." They kept order for themselves, and were too busy with practical life and thought, to hang about or gossip on the way to their various homes. Several members of the congregation on hearing that their friend Leigh was going to take his marriage vows before them all, had provided themselves with flowers, and these managed to pass in front of the platform where, simply and without ostentation, they handed up their little bouquets and clusters of such blossoms as they had been able to obtain and afford in winter,—violets especially, and white chrysanthemums, and one or two rare roses. These floral offerings meant much sacrifice on the part of those who gave them,—and the tears filled Sylvie's eyes as she noted the eagerness with which poor women with worn sad faces, and hands wrinkled and brown with toil, handed up their little posies for her to take from them, or laid them with a touching humility at her feet. What a wonderful wedding hers was, she thought!—far removed from all the world of fashion, without any of the hypocritical congratulations of "society" friends,—without the sickening, foolish waste, expense and artificiality, which nowadays makes a marriage a mere millinery parade. She had spoken her vows before thousands whom her husband had helped and rescued from heathenism and misery, and all their good wishes and prayers for her happiness were wedding gifts such as no money could purchase. With a heart full of emotion and gratitude she watched the crowd break up and disappear, till when the last few were passing out of the building, she said to her husband—

"Let us leave the flowers they have given me here, Aubrey,—here, just at the foot of the Cross where you have so often spoken to them. I shall feel they will bring me a blessing!"

"It shall be as you wish, sweetheart!" he answered tenderly,—"and I must thank you for having entered so readily into the spirit of this strange marriage before my poor friends, Sylvie,—for it must have seemed very strange to you!—and yet believe me,—no more binding one was ever consummated!" He took her hand and kissed it,—then turned to Cardinal Bonpré, who had risen and was gazing round the bare common building with dreamy eyes of wistful wonderment.

"I thank you too, my dear friend! You have learned something of my work since we came to London, and I think you understand thoroughly the true sanctity and force of my marriage?"

"I—do!—I do understand it!" said the Cardinal slowly. "And I wish with all my heart that all marriage vows could be so solemnly and truly taken! But my heart aches——my heart aches for the world! These thousands you have helped and taught are but a few,— and they were as you have told me, little better than heathen when you came amongst them to tell them the true meaning of Christ's message—what of the millions more waiting to know what the Church is failing to teach? What have the priests of the Lord been doing for nearly two thousand years, that there should still be doubters of God!"

Over his face swept a shadow of deep pain, and at that moment Manuel left the Cross where he had been leaning and came up and stood beside him. The Cardinal looked at his waif wistfully.

"What did you think of this service, my child?"

"I thought that the Master of all these His servants could not be very far away!" answered Manuel softly, —"And that if He came suddenly, He would find none sleeping!"

" May it prove so ! " said Aubrey fervently. " But we own ourselves to be unprofitable servants at best,—we can only try to fulfil our Lord's commands as nearly to the letter as possible,—and we often fail ;—but we do honestly make the effort. Shall we go now, my lord Cardinal ? You look fatigued."

Bonpré sighed heavily. " My spirit is broken, my son ! " he answered. " I dare not think of what will happen—what is beginning to happen for the Christian world ! I shall not live to see it; but I have sinned, in passing my days in too much peace. Dwelling for many years away in my far-off diocese, I have forgotten the hurrying rush of life. I should have been more active long ago,—and I fear I shall have but a poor account to give of my stewardship when I am called to render it up. This is what troubles both my heart and my conscience ! "

" Dear friend, you have no cause for trouble ! " said Sylvie earnestly. " Among all the servants of our Master surely you are one of the most faithful ! "

" One of the most faithful, and therefore considered one of the most faithless ! " said Manuel. " Come, let us go now,—and leave these bridal flowers where the bride wishes them to be,—at the foot of the Cross, as a symbol of her husband's service ! Let us go,—the Cardinal has need of rest."

They returned to their respective homes,—Aubrey and his wife to a little tenement house they had taken for a few weeks in the district in order that Sylvie might be able to see and to study for herself the sad and bitter lives of those who from birth to death are deprived of all the natural joys of happy and wholesome existence,—whose children are born and bred up in crime,—where girls are depraved and ruined before they are in their teens,—and where nothing of God is ever taught beyond that He is a Being who punishes the wicked and rewards the good,— and where in the general apathy of utter wretchedness, people decide that unless there is something given them in this world to be good for, they would rather be bad like the rest of the folks they see about them. The Cardinal and Manuel dwelt in rooms not very far away, and every day and every hour almost was occupied by them in going among these poor, helpless, hopeless ones of the world, bringing them comfort and aid and sympathy.

Wherever Manuel went, there brightness followed; the sick were healed, the starving were fed, the lonely and desolate were strengthened and encouraged, and the people who knew no more of the Cardinal than that " he was a priest of some sort or other," began to watch eagerly for the appearance of the Cardinal's foundling, " the child that seemed to love them," as they described him,— and to long for even a passing glimpse of the fair face, the steadfast blue eyes the tender smile, of one before whom all rough words were silenced—all weeping stilled.

But on this night of all—the night of Sylvie's " religious " marriage, the Cardinal was stricken by a heavy blow. He had expected some misfortune, but had not realized that it would be quite so heavy as it proved. The sum and substance of his trouble was contained in a " confidential " letter from Monsignor Moretti, and was worded as follows—

" MY LORD CARDINAL,—It has come to the knowledge of the Holy Father that you have not only left Rome without signifying the intention of your departure to the Vatican as custom and courtesy should have compelled you to do, but that instead of returning to your rightful diocese, you have travelled to London, and are there engaged in working with the socialist and heretic Aubrey Leigh, who is spreading pernicious doctrine among the already distracted and discordant of the poorer classes. This fact has to be coupled with the grave offence committed against the Holy Father by the street-foundling to whom you accord your favour and protection, and whose origin you are unable to account for; and the two things taken together, constitute a serious breach of conduct on the part of so eminent a dignitary of the Church as yourself, and compel the Holy Father most unwillingly and sorrowfully to enquire whether he is justified in retaining among his servants of the Holy See one who so openly betrays its counsels and commands. It is also a matter of the deepest distress to the Holy Father, that a picture painted by your niece Donna Angela Sovrani and entitled ' The Coming of Christ,' in which the Church itself is depicted as under the displeasure of our Lord, should be permitted to contaminate the minds of the nations by public exhibition. Through the Vatican press, the supreme Pontiff has placed his ban against this most infamous picture, and all that the true servants of the Church can do to check its pernicious influence, will be done. But it cannot be forgotten that Your Eminence is closely connected with all these regrettable events, and as we have no actual proof of the authenticity of the miracle you are alleged to have performed at Rouen, the Holy Father is reluctantly compelled to leave that open to doubt. The Archbishop of Rouen very strenuously denies the honesty of the mother of the child supposed to be healed by you, and states that she has not attended Mass or availed herself of any of the Sacraments for many years. We are willing to admit that Your Eminence may personally have been unsuspectingly made party to a fraud,—but this does not free you from the other charges, (notably that of exonerating the late Abbé Vergniaud,) of which you stand arraigned. Remembering, however, the high repute enjoyed by Your Eminence throughout your career, and taking into kindly consideration your increasing age and failing health, the Holy Father commissions me to say that all these grievous backslidings on your part shall be freely pardoned if you will,—Firstly,—repudiate all connection with your niece, Angela Sovrani, and hold no further communication with her or her father Prince Sovrani,—Secondly,—that you will break off your acquaintance with the socialist Aubrey Leigh and his companion Sylvie Hermenstein, the renegade from the Church of her fathers,—and Thirdly,—that you will sever yourself at once and forever from the boy you have taken under your protection. This last clause is the most important in the opinion of His Holiness. These three things being done, you will be permitted to return to your diocese, and pursue the usual round of your duties there to the end. Failing to fulfil the Holy Father's commands, the alternative is that you be deprived of your Cardinal's hat and your diocese together.

"It is with considerable pain that I undertake the transcribing of the commands of the Holy Father, and I much desired Monsignor Gherardi to follow you to London and lay these matters before you privately, with all the personal kindness which his friendship for you makes possible, but I regret to say, and you will no doubt regret to learn, that he has been smitten with dangerous illness and fever, which for the time being prevents his attention to duty. Trusting to hear from you with all possible speed that Your Eminence is in readiness to obey the Holy Father's paternal wish and high command, I am,

Your Eminence's obedient servant in Christ,

LORENZO MORETTI."

The Cardinal read this letter through once—twice—then the paper dropped from his hands.

"My God, my God! why hast Thou forsaken me!" he murmured. "What have I done in these few months! What must I do!"

A light touch on his arm roused him. Manuel confronted him.

"Why are you sorrowful, dear friend? Have you sad news?"

"Yes, my child! Sad news indeed! I am commanded by the Pope to give up all I have in the world! If it were to give to my Master Christ I would give it gladly,—but to the Church—I cannot!"

"What does the Pope ask you to resign?" said Manuel.

"My niece Angela and all her love for me!—my friendship with this brave man Aubrey Leigh who works among the outcast and the poor,——but more than all this,—he asks me to give You up—you! My child, I cannot!"

He stretched his thin withered hands out to the slight boyish figure in front of him.

"I cannot! I am an old man, near—very near—to the grave—and I love you! I need you!—without you the world is dark! I found you all alone—I have cared for you and guarded you and served you—I cannot let you go!" The tears filled his eyes and rolled down his worn cheeks. "I cannot lose my last comfort!" he repeated feebly. "I cannot let You go!"

Silently the boy gave his hands into the old man's fervent clasp, and as Bonpré bent his head upon them a sense of peace stole over him,—a great and solemn calm. Looking up he saw Manuel earnestly regarding him with eyes full of tenderness and light, and a smile upon his lips.

"Be of good courage, dear friend!" he said. "The time of trial is hard, but it will soon be over. You must

needs part from Angela!—but remember she has great
work still to do, and she is not left without love! You
must also part from Aubrey and his wife—but they too
are given high tasks to fulfil for God's glory—and,—
they have each other! Yes!—you must part with all
these things, dear friend—they are not yours to retain;—
and if you would keep your place in this world you must
part with Me!"

"Never!" cried Bonpré, moved to sudden passion.
"I cannot! To me the world without you would be
empty!"

As he spoke these words a sudden memory rang in his
brain like a chime from some far-distant tower echoing
over a width of barren land. "For me the world is
empty!" had been the words spoken by Manuel when he
had first found him leaning against the locked Cathedral
door in Rouen. And with this memory came another, the
vision he had seen of the end of the world, and the words
he had heard spoken by some mysterious voice in his
sleep,—"The light shineth in darkness and the darkness
comprehendeth it not!" And still he looked pleadingly,
earnestly, almost fearingly, into the face of his foundling.

"We must speak of this again," said Manuel then,
gently. "But to-night, for at least some hours, you must
rest! Have patience with your own thoughts, dear
friend! To part with earthly loves is a sorrow that must
always be;—Angela is young and you are old!—she has
her task to do, and yours is nearly finished! You must
part with Aubrey Leigh,—you cannot help him,—his
work is planned,—his ways ordained. Thus, you have
no one to command your life save the Church,—and it
seems that you must choose between the Church and me!
To keep Me, you must forego the Church. To keep the
Church you must say farewell to Me! But think no more
of it just now——sleep and rest——leave all to God!"

The Cardinal still looked at him earnestly.

"You will not leave me? You will not, for a thought
of saving me from my difficulties, go from me? If I
sleep I shall find you when I wake?"

"I will never leave you till you bid me go!" answered
Manuel. "And if I am taken far from hence you shall
go with me! Rest, dear friend—rest, true servant of God!
Rest without thought—without care—till I call you!"

XXXIX.

THE night darkened steadily down over London,—a chill dreary night of heavy fog, half-melting into rain. Cardinal Bonpré, though left to himself, did not rest at once as Manuel had so tenderly bidden him to do, but moved by an impulse stronger than any worldly discretion or consideration, sat down and wrote a letter to the Supreme Pontiff,—a letter every word of which came straight from his honest heart, and which he addressed to the Head of his Church directly and personally, without seeking the interposition of Lorenzo Moretti. And thus he wrote, in obedience to the dictate of his own soul—

"MOST HOLY FATHER!—I have this day received through Monsignor Moretti the text of certain commands laid by Your Holiness upon me to fulfil if I would still serve the Church, as I have in all truth and devotion served it for so many years. These commands are difficult to realise, and still more difficult to obey,—I would rather believe that Your Holiness has issued them in brief anger, than that they are the result of a reasonable conviction, or condition of your own heart and intellect. In no way can I admit that my conduct has been of a nature to give offence to you or to the Holy See, for I have only in all things sought to obey the teaching of our Lord Jesus Christ, upon whose memory our faith is founded. Your Holiness desires me, first, to cease every communication with the only relatives left to me on earth, —my brother-in-law Pietro Sovrani and his daughter, the daughter of my dead sister, my niece Angela. You demand the severance of these bonds of nature, because my niece has produced a work of art, for which she alone is responsible. I venture most humbly to submit to Your Holiness that this can scarcely be called true Christian justice to me,—for, whereas on the one side I cannot be made answerable for the thoughts or the work of a separately responsible individual, on the other hand I should surely not be prohibited from exercising my influence, if necessary, on the future career of those related to me by blood as well as endeared to me by duty and affection. My niece has suffered more cruelly than most women; and it is entirely owing to her refusal to speak, that the memory of Florian Varillo, her late affianced husband, is not openly branded as that of a criminal, instead of being as now, merely under the shadow of suspicion. For we know that he was her assassin,—all Rome feels the truth, —and yet being dead, his name is left open to the benefit of a doubt because she who was so nearly slain by him she loved, forgives and is silent. I submit to Your Holiness that this forgiveness and silence symbolise true Christianity, on the part of the poor child who has fallen under your displeasure,—and that as the Christian Creed goes, your pity and consideration for her should somewhat soften the ban you have set against her on account of the work she has given to the world. As a servant of Holy Church I deeply deplore the subject of that work, while fully admitting its merit as a great conception of art,—but even on this point I would most humbly point out to Your Holiness that genius is not always under the control of its possessor. For being a fire of most searching and persuasive quality it does so command the soul, and through the soul the brain and hand, that oftentimes it would appear as if the actual creator of a great work is the last unit to be considered in the scheme, and that it has been carried out by some force altogether beyond and above humanity. Therefore, speaking with all humility and sorrow, it may chance that Angela Sovrani's picture ' The Coming of Christ ' may contain a required lesson to us of the Church as well as to certain sections of certain people, and that as all genius comes from God, it would be well to enquire earnestly whether we do not perhaps in these days need some hint or warning of the kind to recall us from ways of error, ere we wander too far. But, having laid this matter straightly before Your Holiness, I am nevertheless willing to accede to your desire, and see my young niece and her father no more. For truly there is very little chance of my so doing, as my age and health will scarcely permit me to travel far from my diocese again, if indeed I ever return to it. The same statement will apply with greater force to the friendship I have lately formed with him whom you call 'heretic,'—Aubrey Leigh. Your Holiness is mistaken in thinking that I have assisted him in his work among the poor and desolate of London—though I would it had been possible for me to do so! For I have seen such misery, such godlessness, such despair, such self-destruction in this great English city, the admitted centre of civilization, that I would give my whole life twice, ay, three times over again to be able to relieve it in ever so small a degree. The priests of our Church and of all Churches are here,—they preach, but do very little in the way of practice, and few like Aubrey Leigh sacrifice their personal entity, their daily life, their sleep, their very thoughts, to help the suffering of their fellow-men. Holy Father, the people whom Aubrey Leigh works for, never believed in a God at all till this man came among them. Yet there are religious centres here, and teachers—Sunday after Sunday, the message of the Gospel is pronounced to inattentive ears and callous souls, and yet all have remained in darkest atheism, in hopeless misery, till their earnest, patient, sympathising, tender brother, the so-called 'atheist,' came to persuade them out of darkness into light, and made the burdens of their living lighter to bear. And will you not admit him as a Christian? Surely he must be; for as our Lord Himself declares, ' Not every man that shall say unto Me Lord, Lord, shall enter into the kingdom of heaven, but he that doeth the will of My Father which is in heaven.' And of a certainty, the will of the Father is that the lost should be found, the perishing saved, the despairing comforted,—and all these things Aubrey Leigh has done, and is yet doing. But I do not work with him—I am here to look on—and looking on, to regret my lost youth!

"Touching the miracle attributed to me at Rouen, I have gone over this ground so often with Your Holiness, both by letter and personally while in Rome, that it seems but foolish to repeat the story of my complete innocence in the matter. I prayed for the crippled child, and laid my hands upon him in blessing. From that day I never saw him—never have seen him again. I can bear no witness to his recovery,—your news came from persons at Rouen, and not from me. I am as unconscious of having healed the child as I am innocent of having any part in

the disappearance of the man Claude Cazeau. The whole
thing is as complete a mystery to me as it is to Your Holiness or to any of those who have heard the story. I fully
and freely admit, as I have always fully and freely admitted, that I condoned and forgave the sin of the Abbé
Vergniaud, and this, not only because the man was dying,
but because we are strictly commanded to forgive those
who truly repent. And on this point, I cannot even to
you, Most Holy Father, admit that I have been wrong.

"And now coming to the last part of Your Holiness'
expressed desire, wherein you ask me to part from the
boy I rescued,—the child Manuel, who is all alone in the
world,—I cannot acknowledge it to be a Christian act to
desert anyone whom we have once befriended. The boy
is young, and far too gentle to fight the world or to meet
with such love and consideration as his youth and simplicity deserve. I will not disguise, however, from Your
Holiness that I have been often much troubled in mind
regarding his companionship with me,—for foolish as
you may judge my words, I feel that there is something
in him not altogether of earth,—that he speaks at times as
a wise prophet might speak,—or as an Angel sent to warn
the world of swiftly-coming disaster! Of the strangely
daring spirit in which he addressed himself to Your Holiness at the Vatican it is not for me to discourse—I cannot
explain it or condone it, for I was overcome with amazement and fear, and realized the position no more than did
Your Holiness at the time, or than did those of your con-
fidants immediately around us. It was indeed a matter
that went beyond us all.

" But the chief end of this letter is arrived at—Your
Holiness asks me to part with this boy. With the deepest
regret at the rupture you threaten to cause between myself and Holy Church if I disobey this command, I must
still utterly refuse to do so. So long as the child looks
upon me as a friend, so long will I be one to him. So
long as he will accept the shelter of my roof, so long shall
he receive it. I would rather break with a dozen
Churches, a dozen forms of creed, than be untrue to a
child who trusts me! That is my answer to Your Holiness, and in giving it I add the sincere expression of my
sorrow to cause you displeasure or pain. But I venture
to pray you, Holy Father, to pause and consider deeply

before you eject me from the Church for so simple and plain a matter. Let me as one who is nearing the grave in company with yourself—as one who with yourself must soon stand on that dark brink of the Eternal from which we see the Light beyond—let me most humbly yet most earnestly point out to you the far more serious things than my offence, which are threatening Rome to-day. The people of all lands are wandering away from faith, and wars and terrors are encompassing the land. The lust of gold and pride of life are now the chief objects of man's existence and desire, and there was hardly ever a time in history when utter indifference to the laws of God was more openly exhibited than it is just now. The sin of unbelief and all the evils attendant on that sin are steadily increasing, and the Church seems powerless to stop the approaching disaster. Is it, that knowing herself to be weak, she does not make the attempt to be strong? If this is so, she must fall, and not all the getting-in of gold will help her! But you, Holy Father—you might arrest all this trouble if you would! If you would change the doctrines of Superstition for those of Science —if you would purify our beautiful creed from pagan observances and incredible idolatries—if you would raise the Church of Rome like a pure white Cross above the blackening strife, you might save the sinking ship of faith even now! So little is needed!—simplicity instead of ostentation—voluntary poverty instead of countless riches, spiritual power instead of the perpetual cry for temporal power,—the doctrine of Christ instead of the doctrine of Church Councils—and the glad welcoming and incorporation of every true, beautiful, wise and wonderful discovery of the age into the symbolic teaching of our Creed. Holy Father, if this is not done, then things old must disappear to make room for things new,—and a new Church of Christ must rise from the ashes of Rome! We cannot but call to mind the words of St. John, ' *Repent and do the first works,* or else I will come quickly and remove thy candlestick from its place.' ' *Do the first works.*' Holy Father, those first works, as exemplified in Christ Himself, were love, charity, pity and pardon for all men! With all my heart I beseech Your Holiness to let these virtues simplify and sustain our Church,—and so raise it a burning and shining light of loving-kindness and

universal tolerance,—so shall it be the true city set on a
hill which shall draw all men to its shelter! But if unjust judgment, intolerance, cruelty and fanaticism,
should again be allowed, as once before in history,
to blot its fairness and blight its reputation, then
there is not much time left to it,—inasmuch as
there is a force in the world to-day likely to prove
too strong for many of us,—a mighty combat for
Truth, in which conflicting creeds will fight their
questions out together with terrible passion and insistence, bringing many souls to grief and pitiful disaster.
You, Holy Father, can arrest all this by making
the Church of Rome, Christian rather than Pagan—by
removing every touch of idolatry, every recollection of
paid prayers, and by teaching a lofty, pure and practical
faith such as our Redeemer desired for us, so that it may
be a refuge in the storm, a haven wherein all the world
shall find peace. This is for you and for those who come
after you to do,—I, Felix Bonpré, shall not be here to see
the change so wrought, for I shall have gone from hence
to answer for my poor stewardship,—God grant I may
not be found altogether wanting in intention, though I
may have been inadequate in deed! And so with my
earnest prayer for your health and long continuance of
life I bid you farewell, asking you nothing for myself at
all but a reasonable judgment,—unprejudiced and calm
and Christlike,—which will in good time persuade you
that it would be but a cruelty to carry out your indignation against me by depriving me of that diocese where all
my people know and love me,—simply because I have
befriended a child, and because having once befriended
him I refuse to desert him. But if your mind should remain absolutely fixed to carry out your intentions I can
only bow my head to your will and submit to the stroke of
destiny, feeling it to be my Master's wish that I should
suffer something for His sake, and knowing from His
words that if I 'offend one of these little ones,' such as
this friendless boy, 'it were better for me that a millstone
were hung about my neck and I myself drowned in the
depths of the sea!' Between the Church doctrine and
Christ's own gospel, I choose the gospel; between Rome's
discipline and Christ's command I choose Christ's command,—and shall be content to be glad or sorrowful, for-

tunate or poor, as equally to live or die as my Master, and *your* Master, shall bid. For we all are nothing but His creatures, bound to serve Him, and where we serve Him not there must be evil worse than death.

"So in all humbleness still awaiting a more reasonable decision at your hands, I am, Most Holy Father,

Your faithful servant and brother in Christ,

FELIX BONPRÉ."

This letter finished, signed and sealed, the Cardinal addressed it and enclosed it under cover to one of the secretaries at the Vatican who he knew might be trusted to deliver it personally into the Supreme Pontiff's own hands. Then stretching out his arms wearily he closed his eyes for a moment with a sigh of mingled relief and fatigue. The night was very cold, and though there had been a fire in the room all day, it had died down in the grate, and there were only a few little dull embers now glowing at the last bar. The chill of the air was deepening, and a shiver ran through the spare, fragile form of the venerable prelate as he rose at last from his chair and prepared to take his rest. His sleeping room was a very small one, adjoining that in which he now stood, and as he glanced at his watch and saw that time had gone on so rapidly that it was nearly eleven o'clock, he decided that he would only lie down for two or three hours.

"For there is much to do yet," he mused. "This one letter to the Pope will not suffice. I must write to Angela,—to say farewell to her, poor child!—and give her once more my blessing——and then I must prepare the way at home—for myself, and also for Manuel." He sighed again as the vision of his own house in the peaceful old-world French town far away, floated before his mental sight,—almost he heard the sweet chiming of the bells in his own Cathedral tower; which like a pyramid of delicate lace-work, always seemed held up in the air by some invisible agency to let the shafts of sunlight glimmer through,—once more he saw the great roses in his garden, pink and white and cream and yellow, clambering over the walls and up to the very roof of his picturesque and peaceful home—the white doves nesting in the warm sun—the ripe apples hanging on the gnarled boughs, the simple peasantry walking up his garden paths, coming

to him with their little histories of pain and disappointment and sorrow; which were as great to them as any of
the wider miseries of sufferers more beset with anguish
than themselves. He thought of it all sorrowfully and
tenderly,—his habit was ever to think of others rather
than himself,—and he wondered sadly, as he considered
all the bitterness and hardships of the poor human creatures who are forced into life on this planet,—why life
should be made so cruel and hard for them,—why sudden
and unprepared death should snap the ties of tenderest
love—why cruelty and treachery should blight the hopes
of the faithful and the trusting—why human beings
should always be more ready to destroy each other than
to help each other—why, to sum all up, so merciful and
divine a Being as Christ came at all into this world if it
were not to make the world happier and bring it nearer
to heaven!

"The ways of the Infinite Ordainment are dark and
difficult to understand," he said. "And I deserve punishment for daring to enquire into wisely-hidden mysteries! But, God knows it is not for myself that I would
pierce the veil! Nothing that concerns myself at all
matters,—I am a straw on the wind,—a leaf on the storm
—and whatever God's law provides for me, that I accept
and understand to be best. But for many millions of sad
souls it is not so—and their way is hard! If they could
fully understand the purpose of existence they would be
happier—but they cannot—and we of the Church are too
blind ourselves to help them, for if a little chink of light
be opened to us, we obstinately refuse to see!"

He went to his sleeping room and threw himself down
on his bed dressed as he was, too fatigued in body and
mind to do more than utter his brief usual prayer, "If
this should be the sleep of death, Lord Jesus receive my
soul!" And as he closed his eyes he heard the rain drop
on the roof in heavy slow drops that sounded like the dull
ticking of a monstrous clock piecing away the time;—
and then he slept, deeply and dreamlessly,—the calm and
unconscious and refreshing slumber of a child.

How long he slept he did not know, but he was wakened suddenly by a touch and a voice he knew and loved,
calling him. He sprang up with almost the alacrity of
youth, and saw Manuel standing beside him.

"Did you call me, my child?"

"Yes, dear friend!" And Manuel smiled upon him with a look that conveyed the brightness of perfect love straight from the glance into the soul. "I need you for myself alone to-night! Come out with me!"

The Cardinal gazed at him in wonder that was half a fear.

"Come out with me!"

Those had been the words the boy had used to the Pope, the Head of the Church, when he had dared to speak his thoughts openly before that chiefest man of all in Rome!

"Come out with me!"

"Now, in the darkness and the rain?" asked the Cardinal wonderingly. "You wish it? Then I will come!"

Manuel said nothing further, but simply turned and led the way. They passed out of the little tenement house they inhabited into the dark cold street,—and the door closed with a loud bang behind them, shut to by the angry wind. The rain began to fall more heavily, and the small slight figure of the waif and stray he had befriended seemed to the Cardinal to look more lonely and piteous than ever in the driving fog and darkness.

"Whither would you go, my child?" he asked gently. "You will suffer from the cold and storm——"

"And you?" said Manuel. "Will you not also suffer? But you never think of yourself at all!—and it is because you do not think of yourself that I know you will come with me to-night!—even through a thousand storms!—through all danger and darkness and pain and trouble,— you will come with me! You have been my friend for many days—you will not leave me now?"

"Neither now nor at any time," answered Bonpré firmly and tenderly. "I will go with you where you will! Is it to some sad home you are taking me?—some stricken soul to whom we may give comfort?"

Manuel answered not,—but merely waved his small hand beckoningly, and passed along up the street through the drifting rain, lightly and aerially as though he were a spirit,—and the Cardinal possessed by some strange emotion that gave swiftness to his movements and strength to his will, followed. They met scarcely a soul. One or two forlorn wayfarers crossed their path—a girl in rags,

—then a man half-drunk and reeling foolishly from side to side. Manuel paused, looking at them.

"Poor sad souls!" he said. "If we could see all the history of their lives we should pity them and not condemn!"

"Who is it that condemns?" murmured Bonpré gently.

"No one save Man!" responded Manuel. "God condemns nothing—because in everything there is a portion of Himself. And when man presumes to condemn and persecute his fellow-men, he is guilty of likewise condemning and persecuting his Maker, and outraging that Maker in his own perverted soul!"

The boy's voice rang out solemn and clear,—and the heavy fog drifting densely through the street, seemed to the Cardinal's keenly awakened and perturbed senses as though it brightened into a golden vapour round that childish figure, and illumined it with a radiation of concealed light. But having thus spoken, Manuel turned and went on once more,—and faithfully, in a mental ravishment which to himself was inexplicable, the venerable Felix followed. And presently they came to the plain and uncomely wooden edifice where Aubrey Leigh and his bride had plighted their vows that morning. The door was open—Aubrey would always have it so, lest any poor suffering creature might need a moment's rest, and resting thankfully, might see the Cross and perchance find help in prayer.

"Do you remember," said Manuel then, "when you found me outside the great Cathedral, how the doors were barred against me? This door is always open!"

He entered the building, and the Cardinal followed, wondering and deeply agitated. It should have been dark within, but instead of darkness, a soft light pervaded it from end to end, a warm and delicate radiance, coloured with a rose glory as of sunset—and Bonpré seeing this stopped, seized with a sudden fear. He looked about him—on either side the huge unadorned barn-like place was empty,—he and Manuel stood alone together as it were in the cold vast void. Before them towered the Cross on its raised platform, and below that Cross was the sloping footway leading to it, where lay many of the buds and leaves and blossoms of Sylvie's bridal flowers given to her by the poor, and yet—in this empty desolate shed there was a sense of warmth and consolation, and the light that illumined it was as the light of Heaven! Trembling in every limb, the Cardinal turned to his companion—words were on his lips, but they faltered and refused to be spoken aloud. And Manuel gently touching him said—

" Follow me ! "

Straight up through the centre of this place hallowed by the prayers of the poor and the broken-hearted, the light child-figure moved, the old man following,—till at the footway leading to the Cross he paused.

" Here will we pray together ! " he said,—and as he spoke a smile lighted his eyes and rested on his lips—a smile which gave his fair face the aspect of a rapt angel of wisdom and beauty. " Here will we ask the Father which is in Heaven—the Father of all worlds—whether we shall part now one from the other, or still remain— together ! "

As he spoke a rush of music filled the air,—and the Cardinal sank feebly on his knees, overcome by a great wave of awe and terror which engulfed his soul—for it was the same divine, far-reaching, penetrative music which had once before enthralled his ears in the Cathedral at Rouen. Kneeling he clasped his worn hands, and in all the dizziness and confusion of his brain, raised his eyes for help to the great Cross, bare of all beauty, save for the flowers of Sylvie's strange bridal that lay at its foot. And as he looked he saw a marvellous Vision !—a Dream of Angels standing on either side of that symbol of salvation !—of angels tall and white and beautiful, whose towering pinions glowed with the radiant light of a thousand mornings ! Amazed and awe-stricken at this great sight, he uttered a faint cry and turned to his child companion.

" Manuel ! "

" I am here," answered the clear young voice. " Be not afraid ! "

And now the music of the unseen choir of sound seemed to grow deeper and fuller and grander,—and Felix Bonpré, caught up, as it were, out of all earthly surroundings, and only made conscious of the growing ascendency of Spirit over Matter, saw the bare building around him beginning to wondrously change its aspect. Slowly, as though a wind should bend straight trees into an arching round, the plain walls took on themselves a form of perfect architectural beauty,—like swaying stems of flowers or intertwisted branches, the lines formed symmetrically, and through the shadowy sculptured semblance came the gleam of "a light that never was on sea or land,"—the dazzling light of thousands of shining wings! —of thousands of lustrous watchful eyes!—of thousands of dazzling faces, that shone like stars or were fair as flowers! The Vision grew more and more beautiful—more and more full of light—and through veils of golden vapour, great branching lilies seemed to grow and blossom out, filling the air with perfume, and in their flowering beauty perfected the airy semblance of this wondrous Place of Prayer built by spiritual hands—and like a far-off echo of sweetness falling from unseen heights there came a musical whisper of the chorus sung by the poor—

> " All God's angels will say, ' Well done ! '
> Whenever thy mortal race is run.
> White and forgiven,
> Thou'lt enter heaven,
> And pass, unchallenged, the Golden Gate,
> Where welcoming spirits watch and wait
> To hail thy coming with sweet accord
> To the Holy City of God the Lord ! "

A convulsive trembling seized the Cardinal's mortal frame—but the soul within him was strong and invincible. With hands outstretched he turned to Manuel,—and lo! —the boy was moving away from him—moving slowly but resolutely up towards the Cross! Breathless, speechless, the aged Felix watched him with straining uplifted eyes,—and as he watched, saw his garments grow white and glistening, and a great light began to shine about him—till reaching the foot of the Cross He turned,— and then—He was no more a child! All the glory of the "Vision Beautiful" shone full upon the dying body and escaping soul of Christ's faithful servant!—the Divine Head crowned with thorns!—the Divine arms stretched out against the beams of the great Cross!—the Divine look of love and welcome!—and with a loud cry of ecstasy Felix Bonpré extended his trembling hands.

"Master! Master!" he murmured. "Did not my heart burn within me when Thou didst talk with me by the way!"

Yearning towards that Mystic Glory he clasped his hands, and in the splendour of the dream, and through the pulsations of the solemn music he heard a Voice—the Voice of his child companion Manuel, but a Voice grown full of Divine authority while yet possessing all human tenderness.

"Well done, thou good and faithful servant! Because thou hast been faithful over a few things, I will make thee ruler over many things! Enter thou into the joy of thy Lord!"

And at that Voice—and in the inexplicable beauty of that Look of Love, Felix Bonpré, "Prince of the Roman Church," whose faithfulness Rome called in question, gave up his mortal life,—and with a trembling sigh of death and delight intermingled, fell face forward at the foot of the Cross, where the radiance of his Master's Presence shone like the sun in heaven! And as he passed from death to life, the Vision faded—the light grew dim, —the arches of the heavenly temple not made with hands melted away and rolled up like clouds of the night dispersing into space—the last dazzling Angel face, the last branch of Heavenly flowers—vanished——and the music of the spheres died into silence. And when the morning sun shone through the narrow windows of that Place of Prayer dedicated only to the poor, its wintry beams encircled the peaceful form of the Dead Cardinal with a pale halo of gold,—and when they came and found him there and turned his face to the light—it was as the face of a glorified saint, whom God had greatly loved!

.   .   .   .

And of the "Cardinal's foundling"—what of Him? Many wondered and sought to trace Him, but no one ever heard where He had gone. Now,—when the Cardinal himself has been laid to rest in the shadow of his own Cathedral spires—and the roses which he loved so well are growing into a crimson and white canopy over his quiet grave, there are those who wonder who that lonely child wanderer was,—and whether He ever will return? Some say He has never disappeared,—but that in some form or manifestation of wisdom, He is ever with

us, watching to see whether His work is well or ill done,
—whether His flocks are fed, or led astray to be devoured
by wolves—whether His straight and simple commands
are fulfilled or disobeyed. And the days grow dark and
threatening—and life is more and more beset with difficulty and disaster—and the world is moving more and
more swiftly on to its predestined end—and the Churches
are as stagnant pools, from whence Death is far more
often born than Life.

And may we not ask ourselves often in these days the
question,—

" When the Son of Man cometh, think ye He shall find
faith on earth ? "